RITUALS IN SACRED STONE

Yeshua and Mariam
King and Queen
Priest and Priestess

A HISTORICAL NOVEL BY

WENCKE JOHANNE BRAATHEN

BALBOA
PRESS

A DIVISION OF HAY HOUSE

ISBN: 978-1-4525-6133-2 (sc)
ISBN: 978-1-4525-6125-7 (hc)
ISBN: 978-1-4525-6134-9 (e)

Library of Congress Control Number: 2012919613

Balboa Press books may be ordered through booksellers or by contacting:

Balboa Press
A Division of Hay House
1663 Liberty Drive
Bloomington, IN 47403
www.balboapress.com
1-(877) 407-4847

Because of the dynamic nature of the Internet, any web addresses or links contained in this book may have changed since publication and may no longer be valid. The views expressed in this work are solely those of the author and do not necessarily reflect the views of the publisher, and the publisher hereby disclaims any responsibility for them.

The author of this book does not dispense medical advice or prescribe the use of any technique as a form of treatment for physical, emotional, or medical problems without the advice of a physician, either directly or indirectly. The intent of the author is only to offer information of a general nature to help you in your quest for emotional and spiritual well-being. In the event you use any of the information in this book for yourself, which is your constitutional right, the author and the publisher assume no responsibility for your actions.

Any people depicted in stock imagery provided by Thinkstock are models, and such images are being used for illustrative purposes only.
Certain stock imagery © Thinkstock.

Printed in the United States of America

Balboa Press rev. date: 2/11/2013

Dedicated to my daughter
who carries her name

TABLE OF CONTENTS

EXERPT
From "Memories In Sacred Stone"

The Third Book In
The Trilogy Of "Sacred Stones"

2007 PARIS, FRANCE.

She noticed the large, upright display case as she rounded a pillar on her way out of the church of Saint-Sulpice in Paris. It was a backlit slide image, life sized, of an almost naked man. He looked like he was sleeping peacefully, unaffected by the disturbing marks on his body. The image was so vivid, she had to sit down and catch her breath. Surprised by the sudden emotional response, she found herself crying.

Ellen was a skeptic. She was interested in relics for their historic value and the cultural importance the item had played. To find herself physically affected by this image shook her to the core.

Overwhelmed by sudden and unexpected emotion, her skin felt what the body in the image had experienced. The details showed where whips with small, sharp spoons had dug into the body and scooped out pieces of flesh. There were holes in his wrists and feet from the big nails. As she felt his pain, a peace descended upon her and she joined the powerful man in his meditation. He was absolutely not dead in the image. Instead it showed him in profound meditation transcending the intense pain of his body. He was at peace with God and mankind.

As she sat there, allowing this beautiful person's aura to fill her own, the image changed. Through her tears, she saw the face on the cloth lift off the flat surface and become three dimensional. She sensed the incredibly sophisticated technique that had caused this image. The image was preserved, not just as a photographic imprint, but as a holographic memory. Her wet face couldn't help but smile at his beauty. If this truly was Jesus Christ imprinted on his burial cloth, he sure was a handsome man.

Overwhelmed by what she had seen, she gathered her hands and bowed in deep respect. Lifting her head, she saw the flat image of his ribcage become a rounded chest that breathed. She blinked and steadied herself, as this tortured historically dead man showed himself as a handsome athlete with a mature body.

Joining him in his meditation, she transcended with him into another realm beyond time and space. All pain was gone. She felt him taking her with him floating up into the open space. They existed for a blessed moment together in love and tranquility between the dignified stone arches of the cathedral of St. Sulpice. Making sure she had felt his sublime essence, he gently delivered Ellen back to her stone bench. She was given some time to reunite with her body before he softly reminded her that it was time to get ready for her train.

He stayed with her through out her travels in France. She felt as if she had an invisible traveling companion next to her in the seat behind her on the train, in her rental car, always at a polite distance, but always there. After a while she understood why he stayed with her.

He had longed for his beloved for two thousand years. Ellen provided the perfect vehicle to find her. She had taken in his holographic form and allowed him to vibrate with her. And she was looking for the same woman.

Now at the basilica in St.-Maximin-la-Ste.-Baume, Ellen felt more than a little apprehensive. She reminded herself that she was only here because of her research. Spending a lot of time in the basilica admiring paintings and gaudy sculptures, she finally had to admit she was afraid to go down into the crypt. Her recent powerful meeting with a relic made her scared that the next encounter might be more than she could handle.

Again she felt the peaceful presence of the meditating Jesus. He reminded her that it was time. Meeting the Shroud of Turin in Paris was a surprise. The object in this cathedral, she had traveled far to find. Ascending the white marble stairs, she let her eyes admire the sarcophagi from the Roman period. Taking a deep breath, she turned and faced the relic she had wanted to see since she had started this research many years ago.

The skull was small, even for being of a woman. Some skin was still attached to it, and some hair was still apparent on the top. Ellen shivered. The bone was visible and the whole thing was browned with age and yellowed with centuries of reverence. Every twenty-second of July, it was the center of a parade through town in a golden case that looked like the smiling face of a young, beautiful woman.

It was claimed to be the skull of Mary Magdalene. The legend told that Lazarus, her brother, had become bishop of Marseille. The head had been put in his care and he had built a proper container to protect it. It had stayed in this cathedral since the thirteenth century.

Ellen sat down on the mosaic floor in front of the display case. She looked at the golden platform it sat on and the golden case protecting the back of the head. The lid with the face was shown behind it. Next to her, she felt the image from the shroud of Turin breathing. She closed her eyes. All was quiet inside her, as she tuned into the presence of the skull through the thick glass.

At first she just sensed awareness. She could feel another being resonating with her own, recognizing the frequency vibrating next to her. She felt their longing, the profound longing of eons of painful separation. Soft chanting emanated from the skull and filled the small crypt. The presence that had joined her like a ghostly hitch-hiker for weeks, joined in with his own sound. Ellen felt herself melting into the floor as she was calibrated by these two spiritual adepts. A question was respectfully put forth to her. It was a formal request for permission to enter her body. Ellen could only nod in agreement. How could you refuse lovers who had been waiting for two millennia to reunite? She had no idea what she had agreed to, but felt no fear, only deep compassion for their dilemma.

She sat for a while waiting for something to happen. As she sensed each of them assemble themselves on either side of her, Ellen had a sense that they were slightly more solid than a thought. Something in their fields had changed. She had resonated with their frequencies, their DNA material. His was vibrating in the hologram emanating from the Shroud. Hers was present right in front of her in the preserved head. Ellen was the one consciously resonating with them both and traveling between these two objects which after two thousand years still held their frequencies. Through her, they could now communicate. The tension, between their polite controlled action to protect her and their own joyful anticipation, held a taught string in the air.

Ellen sank into an even deeper calm. She felt each of her companions stretch out an arm and extend it into her body through the sides of her ribcage. These powerful streams of consciousness formed the shape of two hands reaching into her body. She took in air in awe and disbelief. The hands found each other and clasped a handshake inside Ellen's heart. The image Ellen saw was the Claddagh symbol in gold complete with the crown above the heart. Sitting on the cold stone floor, she was surrounded with a white light that seemed brighter than a summer day. Tears were streaming down her cheeks, as she felt the profound gratitude from the newly united couple. She felt the hands retreat, and was left in profound meditation. Ellen felt herself expand and unite with everything. In her inner vision she saw the face of the Shroud smile, and could hear the giggle of a woman.

"This must be the true meaning of Hieros Gamos," Ellen thought as she left the cathedral. Then she heard the voices of her new friends; "Get something to eat. It's important." She noticed that she was indeed extremely hungry. Ellen went looking for a restaurant and marveled at their practical sense. It would indeed be wise to eat before she headed back to her hotel in Aix-en-Provence.

EXERPT
From "Secrets In Sacred Stone"

The Second Book In
The Trilogy Of "Sacred Stones"

975 AD CARCASSONNE, FRANCE.

Carcassonne, in the area of Languedoc, was the center of the Cathar territory. The high culture of the Cathar religious group was evident in the prosperity of the region and the peace enjoyed among their people. The many castles were famous for their music and poetry enjoyed during festive banquets between walls adorned with tapestries and guests in silks and brocades.

The Cathars were known for their excellent education. Students at a Cathar castle were expected to know several languages beyond the local Languedoc, the language of Yes. French and Spanish were taught to all, but the students also learned German, English, Italian, Latin and the language of the Moors of Northern Africa. The Cathars studied the scriptures and traveled to the Holy Land. Their scholars were fluent in Hebrew and Aramaic. The students were well versed in mathematics, astronomy, geography and history. Their knowledge of the healing arts was legendary.

Aquitania, now the area of Languedoc, was a separate country with a coastline to the Atlantic and the Mediterranean and borders to France and Spain. The location made it ideal for commerce connecting merchants by sea and land. Aquitania was a respected country in its own right, situated between two powerful neighbors, neither of which enjoyed the same peace and prosperity within their own borders.

France and Spain were both Catholic and their bishops and kings were under the jurisdiction of the Pope. Aquitania, the region of Languedoc, did not recognize the Pope as an authority and were not Catholic. They were devout Christians and they claimed that they had been taught by Christ and Mary Magdalene almost a thousand years ago.

This irked the Pope. He found the obvious prosperity and high culture of the Cathar people insulting. Their religious practices were different than the Catholic liturgies and dogmas. For one thing, they ordained women. Women! The pope was outraged. What was the secret behind their peaceful, highly educated and annoyingly sophisticated behavior? The Pope concluded that since it wasn't of the Church, it must be of the devil.

The Cathar people knew that they irritated the Pope. They also knew that they didn't want the Pope or his minions to ever know the secrets they were still practicing the way they had been taught so long ago. They made sure that very few, even among their own, took part in their most private practices.

Young Chretien Trencavel was fourteen years old and the third son in a line of five. Contrary to his brothers, Chretien wasn't sure which direction his education would take. Bertrand, the oldest, would take over as Count of Carcassonne. Aton would become a priest in the castle church, a job Chretien did not want to have. He felt it involved too much politics. The younger Roger was in military training and little Orlando was the poet among them. They were all good at their studies, their mother, the countess, would have it no other way, and their respective tutors were proud of them.

So, when his father took him aside one day and wanted him to come with him, Chretien was surprised.

They left the big hall of the castle, passed the church where their people worshipped, descended some stairs and walked through a long corridor. Chretien knew most of the castle by heart, but when they went down another staircase and found another corridor behind a door which his father had a key to, Chretien was in unfamiliar territory.

"I've taken you here to show you something, and to present you for your further lessons. You have proven that you have certain abilities we watch for in this family. We would like to teach you further to protect you from harm and from these abilities to be misused."

Chretien knew of the special abilities that were praised in whispered tones among elders in the family. He had seen the nods in his direction and the shared glances among his aunts and uncles. He tried to remember what had occurred among the children at the time.

Chretien nodded. He started to understand what his father was referring to.

"You will be under the tutelage of Hiram from now on. He will guide you further in your studies. We have been watching you, and among all my sons, we think you will be able to protect the knowledge carried by our family. You will live among the perfected ones from now on. Learn their ways. I wish you well and I will see you at the next ceremony. I'm so proud of you, my son," Bertram Aton concluded as he put his arms around Chretien's shoulders.

A soft knock in the door to the small study broke the moment between them. The elder Trencavel announced "Enter", in his gentler, but still commanding voice, and Hiram, the high priest came in. He nodded and smiled to Chretien, and said, with deep respect to the lord of the city of Carcassonne and protector of all Cathars in the region, "Count Trencavel.You wanted to see me, Sir."

SEVEN YEARS LATER.

Chretien stood in the robes of an initiate in the circular temple room deep inside the castle. This was the tower his father had shown him seven years ago. He had been told to feel the sound in the room and asked if he wanted to take part in the secret ceremonies taking place here. His father had seen that he could work with unseen forces.

Now he was barefooted on the stone floor standing in line with other adepts of the deeper mysteries. His mind was silent. He had learned to control his inner life with the same dexterity his brother Roger wielded his weapons. The mystic teachings from many cultures were now familiar to him. He had been sent to the court of the Jewish Prince of Narbonne and studied with the Rabbis. He had been to the Kalif in Morocco to learn from the Sufis. The groups of Druids still practicing in their own region had accepted him. He had also learned how to hide what he knew and become a silent observer nobody would suspect was a student in mysticism.

All the novices lifted their heads, feeling the clue as a silent call in the tall, circular stone temple. The chanting started. The line of initiates walked in an ever tighter circle forming a spiral that undulated in and out from the center. Chretien felt the energy of the space change. These stones had been tuned over a long period of time and could sing the tones with them. The chanting went from one tone to a choir of many voices as men and women found their level of harmony. The music had substance in the room. Chretien could see the stone walls vibrate.

The high priest and his wife, the high priestess, stood in the center of the tower. Facing each other, they each held a platter with a round object. It was cloaked in linen with golden threads reflecting the candles in the room. The chanting among the group ended and the priest and priestess took over the tone. Chretien heard the eerie sounds of overtones resonating in the walls as if there were multiples of singers. The two adepts presented the round objects, as if introducing them to each other, like old friends who had been separated for a long time and needed a gentle reminder of who they really were.

Chretien and his fellow students had been told that they had a visitor. A man from the Cathars in Provence had arrived. He brought with him a precious relic which didn't travel very often. "One of these ritual objects must be it," Chretien thought. He had felt the excitement from their higher priests and priestesses about this important artifact now in their midst. People had tears in their eyes just mentioning this meeting, as if it was both holy and romantic. Words were used that usually described young lovers, puzzling the young novices among them.

Chretien heard the priest and priestess sing to them describing this holy moment, this sacred symbolic marriage. His mind surrendered to the shared conscious field of the honorable adepts. His body felt the waves of energy created as the spiral wave had grown into a force field filling the round tower. Invisible waves came up from the earth and stretched towards the sky. Another wave was coming down from the stars to join with the moving spiral towards the center of the earth. As they used their intention to create these interwoven fields of energy, Chretien felt the resonating movement in his body. Two opposite spirals were circling up his spine ending in his head like two fountain spouts. He knew that as this process built, two small drops of liquid would eventually fall out of the fountain heads. They would drop liquid life force into the glands in his brain forming the seat of honor where all wisdom comes from.

Chretien felt a swooning sensation. There was an unmistaken sensual pleasure to this. He was participating in an interactive ritual between the unseen forces of the Universe and the people of flesh and blood.

Holy names were called out. He heard male and female names of Gods and Goddesses that had been worshipped for millennia in many cultures. A line of ancestry was chanted; the family of Jesus and Mary Magdalene, or Yeshua and Mariam as they preferred to call their teachers. There were two verses to this chant. One was giving the line of ancestors of these two holy people. The next verse named the three branches of their descendants. Chretien recognized some prominent family names of his region, and some sounding curiously different even to his trained linguistic ear.

The chanting divided again into a chorus of harmonizing voices before it merged back into single tones. The high priest and priestess were facing each other with their veiled platters. The cloth was lifted off and a collective intake of breath was heard across the participants. On each platter was a human head.

Chretien held his breath in awe and amazement. The heads were of a man and a woman. Her head was small, and some hair surrounded the yellowed skin that still seemed supple. His head was larger, also with hair, but with a peaceful countenance exuding tranquility. Their faces had refined features and even though the heads were obviously from two people who were now dead, they seemed to just be in deep sleep or in a meditation lasting for centuries. Incense was burned and some new sounds were sung in a language he was not familiar with. He noticed that the high priest and priestess were wearing a garment covering their chests with precious stones woven into the fabric. The stones were now glowing. A loud crescendo ended the chanting.

The sudden silence filled the room. A soft sound was heard from the high priest, a single tone, an invitation. At that moment, the severed heads opened their eyes. There was a collective intake of breath in the room. A novice next to Chretien fainted and sunk towards him. He caught his friend, steadied him, and continued to watch as the spectacle unfolded.

The man's head picked up the tone from the priest and started singing. The high priestess made a sound like the morning song of a bird, and the woman's head continued the tune, moving her mouth. The two heads took over the sounds and created over tones and harmonies beyond anything Chretien thought a human could produce. He felt his own energy field change. All the participants in the room felt like one body, one frequency. Everything in the room became synchronized with the sound produced by the heads.

Chretien was filled with profound respect and gratitude for the privilege of participating in this moment. Now he understood who the heads were. They were their own teachers of ancient times. This was Yeshua and Mariam again creating enlightenment among their followers. They were showing them the unification of the male and female principles in Cosmos, the Hieros Gamos, the holy union between man and woman, between God and Goddess, and between the Gods and their people. A bright light ignited inside Chretien's head. The room flooded with white light brighter than the sun, and he heard voices speaking sounding like they came from both inside him and from the surrounding walls. The oracles had been brought to life and were again teaching from the ancient knowledge.

RITUALS IN SACRED STONE

Yeshua and Mariam
King and Queen
Priest and Priestess

PART ONE
ALEXANDRIA

A HISTORICAL NOVEL BY

WENCKE JOHANNE BRAATHEN

CONTENTS

CHAPTER 1

AT THE TEMPLE IN JERUSALEM

H ER EYES HELD ONTO HIM AS SHE watched him leave, his slender body evident in white linen as he hurried towards the gate of the Temple. The stolen moment they had spent together made this second farewell even more demanding. She had reconciled herself to the distance and time between them. Now, there was a new ache in her body she could not define.

Mariam was standing on the stone floor of the first courtyard. Only her eyes moved as they followed his movements through the crowd. His white, long shirt was still visible between people and against the yellow stone wall surrounding the Temple.

Yeshua turned at the open gate and their eyes met. She felt a rush of air as the contact between them found anchor in her body. A warm glow spread in her chest. She took a deep breath as she smiled at him across the noise and between the faces of other people. In the distance she saw him put his hand on his heart and bow his head towards her. She bowed her head in return and received the blessing he sent her. *My heart is with you, as well*, she thought. His rabbinic studies would take him back to the temple of Onais in the desert north of Heliopolis. It would be years before she'd see him again. She closed her eyes, and, when she opened them again, he was gone.

Her mother waited a moment, then called softly for her. She had been standing a little aside. *We give birth to innocent children*, she thought as she watched them. *Do they choose their destiny?*

Their mothers had wanted their betrothed son and daughter to have a memory of each other to hold on to. Their heritage pointed to difficult paths, separately and together. They needed to share each other's strength.

Mariam turned slowly to answer her mother. Eurochia had noticed the tear on her cheek and the shiver that went through her body as Yeshua disappeared; but, by the time she reached her mother, Mariam's back was straight, her face was dry and she answered politely to her mother's call.

Eurochia didn't say anything, but offered her arm in support and admiration for the strength already apparent in her young daughter. She patted the hand that rested in her elbow and looked away.

Hiram, Mariam's father, was waiting near the gate. He saw the two women he loved come towards him. Usually, the two were chattering lively with each other, but, now, both were silent as they approached. He squinted against the powerful sun reflected in the surrounding white stone. Herod the Great had almost outdone Salomon when he rebuilt the Temple of Jerusalem. The glittering gold ornamentation was too ostentatious for Hiram's taste. He admired his daughter's simple beauty, so much like her mother when she was young. But she had his dark eyes, which he was reminded of every time the serious little girl had looked up at him. She had grown into a graceful young woman. Walking towards him he saw her free hand pull the black shawl closer around her head and slim shoulders. *Why are they expected to carry so much?* Hiram wondered.

Eurochia lifted her head and looked around to find him. Her graceful dignity guided her movements. His face lit as he smiled towards his lovely wife. The connection between them was steady and strong. The feverish line between his daughter and future son-in-law might grow into that someday.

Hiram had approved of the meeting of the betrothed the day before with the parents present. That they had found each other again today was unexpected. Yeshua had left his parents and come searching for Mariam. She was at the Temple with her mother when he had come running to see her one more time. Hiram knew he should have scolded him for inappropriate behavior, but, as a father, he was proud of his beautiful daughter. If this young man was so spellbound – well, then, he would leave that speech to his own father. He had been young himself and stolen away to see Eurochia in Alexandria. But he had been smarter, and none of the parents had found out. So had the boy been more honest meeting her in public in front of her parents? Hiram decided to look at it that way.

Mariam saw her father's smile. She knew he admired Yeshua's courage and secretly enjoyed seeing the young couple together. The parents had arranged this future marriage, and she knew she was fortunate. The image of Yeshua's peaceful eyes stayed with her and blended with the blue sky.

CHAPTER 2

THROUGH THE CITY OF ALEXANDRIA

ALEXANDRIA WAS A THRIVING METROPOLIS IN THE Roman Empire. The port with the Faro lighthouse was a marvel of engineering and essential for the merchant ships sailing the Mediterranean Sea. Exciting markets offered enticing goods from as far away as India in the east and Ireland in the north. A lively and colorful culture developed as the population grew in diversity. The silhouette of the famous library could be seen long before your ship turned in for the harbor. The huge buildings forming a campus, much like a university of modern times, held hundreds of thousands of documents from every corner of the known world. Adjacent to the impressive building was the Serapium, a large temple complex dedicated to Serapis. Alexandria was recognized as a seat of knowledge just as much as it was a center for commerce and a destination for adventurers.

Mariam grew up in the city as the oldest daughter of Hiram and Eurochia Y Benjamin. The family owned a shipping industry and was well respected in the city. Their ships sailed many routes across the Mediterranean and beyond. Hiram's sons were well known as both captains and merchants. It was an honor to have Eurochia Y Benjamin and her daughters visit a shop at the markets. They knew quality merchandize and had the money to pay for it.

"Mariam," Eurochia called.

"Yes, Mother," said Mariam and left her younger sister Martha with a tender smile. *She looks older after the trip to Jerusalem*, Eurochia thought.

"Please get ready and come with me," she said. "We need to go to the market."

Walking next to her mother carrying their baskets, Mariam was listening to Eurochia name the food items they needed for the special family meal to celebrate her betrothal. As they prepared to leave through the gate to their home, Mariam's youngest sister, Sarah, came running, catching up with them.

"Father said to buy some extra blankets for Mariam for the winter. It can be cold inside the stone halls of the Temple." Sarah caught her breath. "And he said I could come with and pick them out. Can I, Mother? Please?"

Shopping was Sarah's favorite activity, and Mariam was her favorite sister. Nothing pleased her more than going to market. Eurochia thought Hiram was a little too indulgent with his daughters, especially with this youngest one. She laughed inside at their little scheme and her smile said yes.

"Mariam, what do you know about him?" asked Sarah as she was hanging on her sister's arm wanting to know more about Mariam's exciting trip to Jerusalem.

"Only that he is sixteen and very quiet," said Mariam, careful not to give out too much information. She wanted to protect her memories.

"Is he handsome? What does he look like now?" Sarah remembered him vaguely from the time when his family lived near by.

She had often met Yeshua's uncle, his mother's brother. Joseph of Aramathea often used their ships when attending his businesses in Jerusalem and Britain and was a welcome guest of their household. She wondered if Yeshua looked like him.

Mariam couldn't help but smile as she thought of him. "Yes, like his uncle, he was lighter than them," she answered. "Remember where his family comes from." Her sister's dreamy eyes told Sarah that Yeshua was indeed a handsome young man.

"How long were you together? What did you talk about?" Sarah was incorrigible.

Mariam honestly couldn't remember what they had talked about. The first day they had just stood between their respective parents and stared at each other. Her mother had told her that after his family had left Alexandria for Jerusalem, he was admitted to the temple school there. Now he had graduated and was ready to study at the less known temple school of Onais north of Heliopolis. His parents felt that he should learn the older form of their traditions. This much she could tell Sarah. The moment together alone in the temple courtyard she didn't want to share with anyone.

"Mariam, when will you get married? Wherever you go, I want to go with you!"

"I don't know, Sarah. And I'm going to study at the Temple first. You'll have to be used to being without me."

"But you'll still be in Alexandria. Tell me I'll see you often."

Eurochia turned and looked for her daughters. She wanted to make sure they didn't dawdle too far behind. Their two faces encircled with the blue and pink scarves sparkled in the sun. She admired them, both beautiful, and not totally aware of their own beauty yet. They were leaning into each other, matching their steps as in a dance. *I'll still have them for a little more time*, she thought to herself. *But Mariam will start her education soon. Sarah will miss her. And so will I.*

They were passing the Temple of Serapis. Eurochia slowed her steps enough to give the girls time to catch up and to give herself a moment to admire the looming structure. The steps up to the Temple were as wide as the full length of her own generous home. She studied the colonnade holding up the heavy roof inspired by the Greek temples. Serapis was a composite god. He was created to satisfy the many cultures coexisting in this largest metropolis of the Roman Empire. The wisdom of Sophia, the strength of the Apis bull, the stories of Isis and Osiris, and the mythology of Hera and Zeus were all honored at this temple. Large statues of each of the deities were on display along the sides. In the middle was an enormous statue of the god Serapis who represented all of them. He was very popular since people of many different traditions could find a familiar aspect in him. The statue was covered in ground gemstones making it sparkle in the sunlight.

Mariam looked up and followed her mother's gaze, bending her neck to take in the familiar sight. The massive sculpture shimmered towards her in purples and gold.

"Yes, it is rather impressive," she heard her mother say. "Do you feel ready to start your studies here? You know it's coming up soon." Eurochia took a deep breath, trying to ignore the cringe in her chest.

Mariam's twelve year old heart leaped. She couldn't hide her excitement. This is what she wanted, but was she ready? Having been accepted as a student at the temple school was an honor and a privilege. It meant that her tutors had given their recommendation. The Serapium offered studies in astronomy, mathematics and the healing arts. The Temple counted the time of the year and kept the relationship between the people and the gods in balance. Next to the Temple was the Library with more scrolls than she could count. Mariam was speechless. It would take a hundred lifetimes to absorb all the information and wisdom this place contained!

Eurochia looked at her two daughters staring up at the enormous shimmering sculpture visible behind the columns at the top of the stairs. She smiled enigmatically as she admired all it contained. Eurochia knew that her oldest daughter, always eager to learn something new, had found the place to satisfy her unquenchable thirst for knowledge.

CHAPTER 3

ENTERING THE SERAPIUM

THE SERAPIUM TEMPLE CAMPUS WAS A CENTRAL architectural feature of Alexandria. Mariam had grown up with it as a landmark. Its looming presence had always induced awe, but now, standing there next to her mother preparing to enter the rooms hidden behind the majestic columns, her chest tightened. The enormous sculpture of Serapis looked impressive from the plaza, but after climbing the steps of the Temple and standing next to it, she was overwhelmed by its sheer size. She had to move her head to follow it from its marble base, up the muscular figure to the large bearded head with long flowing hair and the container on top of its head.

"It looks like a flowerpot," she whispered to her mother.

"Yes," Eurochia agreed, "that's where the teachings of Isis and Osiris, Apis and Sophia are stored."

Mariam looked at the statue. She had been taught to honor the wisdom it represented. Was she ready to be introduced to what that bucket contained? One of the bundles she was carrying moved. She quickly pulled it closer to her body and took a step towards her mother.

The night before Eurochia had taken her aside and invited her into her own private rooms. The parents had a bedroom that they shared, but they also had their own personal spaces. Mariam had visited her mother's alcove many times, usually when her mother had something more serious to discuss.

"Come, Mariam, I want to share something with you." They walked through the parent's bedroom and through a door opening where a thick rug separated the rooms. This was where Eurochia came to rejuvenate. The floor was covered in several layers of colorful rugs. Each wall had a thick tapestry with woven patterns of birds and fish. There were big pillows on the floor, each with a woven pattern. Low shelves with objects and artwork stood along one wall. A small writing desk with a seat was opposite. In the corner was her mother's altar with her personal collection of objects. This was where she came to honor the relationship between the family and the Gods.

Mariam recalled the ceremony her mother had done for her when she started her moon cycles. Her mother had lit the incense and the candles in the red glass containers. She had chosen rose that time, the most powerful of the feminine scents. Together they thanked the Gods for this milestone in Mariam's life.

"You're leaving being a girl, and entering your time as a woman. From now on you will have the power of the universal mother within. You will collect wisdom while giving blood to the earth for many years. The blood is sacred. It contains memories. When the bleedings stop, you will have entered the time of the wise woman, the one who stores her blood inside and holds the wisdom of her ancestors for the next generations.

"Always know where you are in your cycle," Eurochia had said. "You should count out when you are most likely to conceive and when you will bleed again. I will give you cloth to collect the blood in. Soak them in water, and after the blood has left the fabric, give the water to your plants. It has life giving properties."

Mariam had remembered. Her plants grew. She also remembered her mother's altar and the symbols of the Gods invited to strengthen her household. There were some other items, round objects on stands, a little hidden, which her mother had not explained.

Last night her mother's space was again lit by the candles. The incense was lavender this time, the herb that counts time. They sat down next to each other in the small space. Eurochia took a deep breath.

"Mariam, you are going to leave our household now, and I know you will only be back for short visits. You have a big journey ahead of you. We have taught you as far as we can. You had Ezekiel to help you with the herbs and the women here to help you find the wisdom of your body. Your tutors introduced you to numbers and languages, and your father taught you our history and gave you self confidence. I have taught you our family traditions and to never forget who you are. It is time for you to start learning on your own."

Mariam listened. Her mother's wisdom became apparent to her. Eurochia had observed her growing up and knew of her desire for knowledge. She was now willing to give up her daughter to her further education because it was the next step, not because she wanted to.

A moment of panic flew through Mariam's body. Would she be able to live up to this new responsibility? Was she really all mother claimed? Eurochia took her hand, and to her relief, Mariam realized that mother only wanted to help her find the well. It would be her decision to drink.

"Mother!" she bent over to hug her. Eurochia took her daughter in her arms and they rocked back and forth, allowing their tears to run. Then she lifted her daughter's face and smiled. "Enough of this. We've got work to do."

Mother took out a handkerchief from her sleeve and wiped her eyes and blew her nose. *Her own nose this time,* Mariam noted. She remembered being wiped clean with her mother's handkerchief when she was little. Now she had her own, and needed her nose blown, too.

Mariam noticed that this time the candles lit up the round objects on the sides of the table. They looked like small doll faces. "I've wanted to show you this," Eurochia said. "These are heads of your ancestors from Ethiopia. They have been preserved with a special technique and shrunk down to this size. I honor them to have the blessings of our ancestors and to ask for their protection.

"Mariam, this is old wisdom. I don't know how old the heads are. Few people know how to prepare heads anymore, and even fewer know how to work with them. This is usually done to trap enemies, but these two were made to honor women who had lived great lives and to pass on their wisdom. Never fear death or the dead. It's just another transition, and the dead are communicating just as easily as you and I."

Mariam studied the heads. One was a little more yellowed than the other. They had some wrinkles, but mostly the skin was surprisingly smooth. The eyes were closed and their lips expressed an old woman's reserve and determination. They were remarkably well preserved. How were these created? She was curious about the techniques used. But as she looked at them, she was even more mesmerized by their beauty.

"They are from Magdola in Ethiopia, where our family comes from. I've been told they are link number twenty-three and twenty-six in the female line of Benjamin. You, my dear, are link number forty."

She had heard about the expectations of link number forty. Mariam only knew that she was a princess in a long line of royal ancestors, not that she was The One.

"So I have to marry number forty in the line of Joseph, the dream interpreter," she said. "That is the prophecy for the unification of the tribes after the Diaspora."

Eurochia nodded softly.

Yeshua. Mariam felt warmer inside. Eurochia noticed her inner glow. She was grateful that the betrothed couple had affection for each other. It would have been awful to marry an unwilling daughter. *Their passion has already been awakened. That will give them strength,* Eurochia thought.

"Keep this to yourself," said her mother. "You will know when the time is right to share it."

Mariam felt an open hole inside. What did this entail?

"That is why we are here tonight," Eurochia answered her thoughts.

"You need some help. Here. This is Bashra. She is yours. I want you to take her with you to the Temple."

Eurochia took one of the heads off its stand and placed it in Mariam's hands. The skin of the head felt like leather. It only weighed as much as the sand it was filled with. The head seemed fragile, and Mariam wanted to protect her ancestor. Her hands lifted the head to her chest, and allowed it to rest near her heart. Mariam closed her eyes as swirls of images created a whirlwind of light around her.

She saw crisp blue skies and large plains of land with little vegetation. Feet were stomping on the ground to the beat of big drums. A singular majestic tree was giving shade to people preparing food with tools of wood and stone. She entered a large square, stone building. A tall dark man with a red cape draped from his handsome shoulders and a golden headdress was standing watchful at the doorway. Bashra, dressed in shimmering translucent fabrics, was admiring him from the interior room. Mariam could feel the man's skin against her own creating the most sublime feeling in her body. She saw Bashra raising their daughter teaching her how to prepare animal skins for a ritual. An enemy was beheaded and Bashra and the daughter made a shrunken head to trap the enemy's spirit. Bashra was dying, and her daughter decided to shrink her mother's head to preserve her wisdom and keep her spirit close. Mariam watched the daughter opening the head and removing the skull. She could see the plants and barks collected for the process and tried to identify them. She watched the daughter crushing some of them, boiling another, and heating some in oil. The head was now an empty skin being dried out with hot stones. She watched the daughter anointing the skin with the mixture she had created, filling it with sand and arranging the features in her mother's expression. In her grief, by blessing and honoring the head, she was preparing to meet her mother again. Mariam observed how the head was placed on a pedestal like on her own mother's altar, incense was burned in front of it and incantations were sung. She saw the daughter pouring oil over the head and ordering it to speak. The head in Mariam's hands opened its eyes, looked directly at her, and said, "Welcome, daughter of mine." Mariam's eyes rolled back in her head and she collapsed on her pillow. The head of Bashra fell out of her hands and rolled down her body before landing on the rug on the floor.

"Dear Isis, forgive me!" The whole vision had lasted only a moment. Eurochia was shocked. She blamed herself for having let the situation get out of hand. She picked up the head and put it back on the stand. *Was there a smirk on it,* she wondered. Her daughter had simply fainted and was breathing normally. She took Mariam in her arms. "Daughter of mine," she mumbled, as she brought water to her lips.

Mariam opened her eyes and looked at her warm and loving, worried mother. She smiled, and in a flash the images she had seen became a single memory stored in the cells of her body.

Standing in the Temple of Serapis waiting for a priestess to greet them, Mariam was still a little shaken from the previous night. Somewhere in her bundle of personal belongings there was a lidded basket from Ethiopia.

"Here is the priestess. Remember your manners," her mother gently reminded her. Mariam smiled and loved her mother for treating her like a child one last time.

The priestess had come out of a side door, almost invisible in the wall. She was dressed in white flowing garments with a simple necklace signifying her rank.

"Welcome to the Serapium, may you be well in health and spirits," greeted the priestess as she approached them. "My name is Suri. I am Priestess of the fifth degree of Bast and responsible for the new students. Welcome, Eurochia Y Benjamin. The Temple thanks you for your generous gift. You must be Mariam. Your teachers speak highly of you. May you feel welcome and thrive here. Would you both please come with me?"

They were led through the door to a terrace with golden stone walls, glazed ceramic floor tiles and a group of low sofas. On a lower level there was a garden with ferns in huge pots, tall palms and pleasant walkways between low stone walls. Mariam exhaled as she took in the beauty of the place and felt a growing anticipation for the studies and work she was soon to start. The priestess extended her arm towards the sofas and signaled a young attendant to offer them tea. Mariam accepted a cup, and the aromatic fragrance challenged her fine nose to identify the herbs. Chamomile for calmness was obvious, a little fennel and maybe a dash of pepper for courage.

"Yes, the fennel is used also to make people feel comfortable and find their own strength," the priestess said. "I am glad you are already familiar with the herbs. Ezekiel has taught you well.

"We want to thank you, Eurochia, for presenting your daughter to the Temple. You are aware of the serious studies she will be undertaking. We have agreed upon the responsibilities it entails for her as a student and for you and your husband. Have you discussed this with your daughter? "

Eurochia explained to the priestess how they had prepared her. Mariam was overwhelmed with impressions. While the other women spoke, her vision took her to the Temple. She saw herself standing inside the columns staring at the sculpture of Serapis.

The statue was gigantic, a true vision of a God. Mariam saw herself climbing on it, nestling in the crease of an elbow. The statue felt alive. His skin was blue, but soft and warm. She nestled into him, leaning against his arm muscles. The giant God stroked her with his big fingers, grateful to have a little devotee crawling on him. She saw the jewels sparkle in his eyes and on his round cheeks. His curly beard was wonderful to climb into and hide in, listening to the giant God's rumbling belly laugh. He gently lifted her with his fingers and let her sit in his enormous open hand, then he bent over and drenched her in water from the vessel on top of his head. She stretched her arms up and allowed the water to wash over her, drinking it through her skin. Putting her face into the flowing stream, she opened her mouth and took in the wisdom of Sophia.

"Mariam?" Her mother pulled her back from her vision. "Do you understand what is being asked of you?"

"Yes, mother," she replied in a clear voice. "I understand." The statue was laughing as the container overflowed with water and she lifted her face, breathing it all in.

"So, Mariam, I understand you are interested in the healing arts," continued the priestess. "You will learn how to heal the human body, how to prepare it for life and how to prepare it for death. Our knowledge is ancient and comes directly from Thoth. Now, I need to hear this in your own voice. Do you want to live here and study with us?"

Mariam was at the bursting point with excitement. She was sitting next to the first entry of the mysteries. There were many doors and many layers ahead of her. She had to make the first step, and it started right now with the answer she would give the priestess. Mariam straightened her back.

"Yes, I want to attend the Temple school at the Serapium."

"Then we're glad to accept you here. Eurochia, is all this in agreement with what we talked about when you and your husband were here this spring?"

"Yes," Eurochia replied quietly, knowing that with her answer she would lose her daughter as a member of her household. Mariam would return many times, she knew, but never again as a young daughter under her influence, never again as a young girl needing guidance. Mariam would return with titles and responsibilities different than Eurochia herself had ever experienced.

"Your family is making a serious commitment. We thank you for your willingness to serve the Gods."

Mariam could only nod. The sincerity of the priestess's voice was a little frightening. What was she committing herself to? She felt much less prepared than she had in the morning.

The priestess gave another signal to the young woman who brought them tea. Her hair was blond and her eyes blue. Mariam thought she was strikingly tall and beautiful. She was wearing the same white linen garments expertly draped around her hips and over her shoulders. She smiled and approached the group.

"This is Sibyl. She is also studying herbology, and you will share living quarters with her. She will show you the dormitory and introduce you to the other novices. It is time to say goodbye to your mother."

Mariam stood facing her mother. Her feelings were a mixture of elation, fear and sadness. Eurochia's tears didn't make it any easier. They hugged for a long time, whispering reassurances. Then Mariam picked up her bundles and followed Sibyl. Eurochia stood behind, feeling her hands turn cold while watching her daughter leave. Mariam turned and waved to her mother. She hoped her brave smile looked convincing.

Then Suri closed the door behind them. The wooden door made a heavy sound as it closed against the stone. She had made the first step. She was inside the door of the Temple school and protected by an ancestor from Ethiopia.

CHAPTER 4

THE WINTER SOLSTICE

THE WINTER SOLSTICE WAS APPROACHING. THE SERAPIUM was getting the Temple ready for the ritual. Young novices brought in branches of evergreens filling the space with fresh scent while priests and priestesses were preparing for the ceremony.

Mariam's astronomy class had reviewed the orbits of the planets and she found the pattern of Venus fascinating. Venus draws a pentagram in the sky over a period of eight years as she shifts between being a morning or an evening star. Over an even longer time, the lines in the sky become the outline of a rose with layers of soft, rounded petals. Every eighth year the orbit of Venus coincides with the movements of the earth. For thousands of years she has followed the same pattern and given a reliable checkpoint for calendars at eight year intervals. Venus is the time keeper for this planet.

Miriam thought of how people measured out a week, a month, a season and how important it was to mark the quarters of the year and honor the solstices and equinoxes. The annual flooding of the Nile was predicted so the farmers could plan ahead. Her father anticipated the weather conditions for the journeys of his ships and would load a cargo accordingly. Knowing the time of the year gave the society power. Seeing the earth in relationship to a star creates an awareness of where we belong in the cosmos. The Temple was responsible for keeping record and to celebrate the festivals of the year at the correct time. The relationship between the earth and Venus was a marriage. And like all relationships, it needed to be nurtured.

The Serapium was architecturally planned according to the movements of Venus. There were small windows in the walls of the temple where the sun and the star would shoot through as thin beams, only once a year. Every eight years the planet would rise as a morning star together with the sun at the winter solstice. The Temple of Serapis was preparing for an important event.

Venus alternate irregularly between being a morning or an evening star. This makes up an eight year cycle creating a syncopated rhythm in her relationship to earth. Over the centuries of honoring the planet, the Temple had developed a song created by the intervals. Mariam had a good alto voice, and she hummed the song of Venus together with the others as they worked with flowers and greenery preparing for the ritual. She thought of Venus as a free spirited planet, a woman traveling across the sky drawing pentagrams in her wake.

Before dawn the morning of the solstice, everyone assembled in the dark in anticipation of the event. Students, priests and priestesses stood in two rows along the center aisle of the temple. Standing according to rank, they were all wearing the simple white draperies of the temple of Serapis. The youngest novices were placed by the entrance. New students had arrived over the years, so Miriam and Sibyl stood a little further up towards the altar.

In the middle of the floor, there was a platform covered with a white sheet. The outline of a body was visible beneath. The sheet was decorated with a golden circle around a pentagram, the symbols for the two heavenly bodies to be honored.

The high priestess was standing by the altar. She wore a head dress with the red sun disc and the golden horns if Isis, the earthly representative of Venus. A shimmer of translucent fabric in graceful pleats silhouetted her well trained figure. Her eyes were outlined in coal and turquoise. Isis faced the aisle looking down the lines of her people. The white clothing of the temple attendants reflected the light from the torches. Against the darkness, they appeared like the many stars dotting the night sky.

Mariam straightened her back and admired the elegance and beauty of Isis. The horns on the head dress represented the equinoxes. Between the solstice and the equinox, the path of Venus in relation to the sun would look like a horn tilting right. The sequel would be the counter part, the left horn. A full solar year was laid out in the graceful golden lines flanking the red circle on top of the head of the priestess.

The priestess started singing and they all joined her. The melody was well rehearsed and created a dramatic crescendo of sound which ended in a sudden silence as the torches were put out, leaving the temple attendants in complete darkness. Several hundred people stood silently ready to salute the morning star. The silent darkness created a void inside the Temple. The quiet anticipation of hundreds of people waiting for the first rays of Venus created its own presence.

As a thin light beam crept through the slit in the temple wall above the entrance, the priestess sang out a single note. They all held their breath as the stream of light hit the red sun disc between the horns on her head. She was prepared, and stood still, statuesque and elegant.

As the light moved, Isis came down the stairs with the graceful movements of a cat. The light of the star stayed in the center of her red sun disc as she moved in calculated steps. She came down the aisle and stopped at the platform. At that moment, the sun came through another opening higher up in the Temple wall. Its circle of light fell on the white linen and illuminated the golden lines of the symbols. Two priests stepped forward and pulled away the white linen revealing

17

the high priest lying on his back as if dead. A collective gasp went through the audience. His muscular body was covered only by a short skirt. On his head was a golden helmet reflecting the light of the sun. The sun disc widened and he opened his eyes. Isis put a foot by his side and took the hand he offered her. The two priests came forward again and took hold of his shoulders. In one smooth movement, they helped him rise as the sun crept slowly closer..

The first light of the sun and the beam from the star danced between their head dresses as they moved, enveloping them in a sharp bluish light. Mirroring each other's tense, elongated movements, they slowly circled each other, before they stopped and elaborately stretched out their limbs. Their bodies touched at the forehead, their palms and their feet, forming a double star with their bodies.

The light from the star had lowered and turned red. He put a strong hand behind her back, and she held onto his shoulder, as he gently put her down on the platform. His risen member was lifting the edge of his skirt and, as he lowered himself down towards her, she lifted her legs along his body and allowed him to enter her. The Temple breathed with them as the attendants sang their crescendo. The priest arched his back, lifting his head towards the ceiling as the golden dawn gradually lit up the temple. The priest and priestess yelled out as the red light of the star united with the sun in a flash of bright light.

Miriam felt sweaty. Her body had responded to the display. Wide-eyed, she had followed the grace of their movements. The elegance of the ancient ritual had stimulated all her senses until she thought she would expand beyond her skin. The physical beauty of the priest and priestess suggested Gods at play. The sun and the star had combined in morning light and united with the earth.

CHAPTER 5

TWO NOVICES

SURI TOOK MARIAM ASIDE A LITTLE LATER in the afternoon. They sat down on the terrace with the view over the garden where Mariam and her mother had entered the first day.

"You have been with us for a while now, Mariam. We have been very pleased with your progress, and I'm glad you have decided to continue your learning here." Mariam nodded, trying to curb her anticipation.

"Of course, you will continue your studies in astronomy, anatomy and herbology, but you are ready for deeper studies in the healing arts."

Yes, said Mariam triumphantly to herself, clenching her fists.

"All healing has to do with the flow of energy in your body. So, for you to learn about that, we first have to make sure you are familiar with your own body. You were present at the ritual earlier today, yes?"

"It was so beautiful!" said Mariam, placing her hands on her heart.

"I m glad you enjoyed it. Having seen it enacted many times, I still get warm inside seeing the sun and the star unite.

"Mariam, you know we do rituals like this for many purposes, including healing. You need to know how these energies work inside yourself. I'd like to arrange for that initiation for you. I think you are ready."

She had known that this would come. Her mother had told her, and the other young novices had talked about it. Still, the excitement in her body was hard to hide. She was ready to make the next step into womanhood.

"The priest you saw today is the one who has made himself available for initiations this quarter. His name is Gyasi. By seeing them at the equinox or solstice, maidens can choose if they would like to do the initiation with that particular priest or rather wait a quarter for another one to be available."

Mariam was still in a swoon over the handsome man she had seen, his graceful movements, the gentleness in his hands and his masculine beauty. He seemed to be the true embodiment of the God he had represented in the early hour of dawn.

"He is gentle and sweet and quite knowledgeable. He will teach you about yourself. I have been with him. He's a good choice for the initiation of the virgin," said Suri. Mariam felt dizzy.

"We want to coordinate this with your monthly cycle. You will be most ready two weeks after your moon time starts. And remember to take the herbs. This is not the time for conception; this is a time for learning. We will assign a time from dinner in the evening to the following morning. You can decide what you want to have served and it will be brought to you. It will be in the ritual rooms downstairs beneath the temple."

The handsome priest from the ritual that morning was going to initiate her into womanhood. Mariam's head was spinning She knew he taught medicinal herbology and self defense, but right then his titles and position at the temple meant little. He was a grown man and knowledgeable in the arts of bodily love. Mariam glowed. She skipped over the stone floor as she ran along the corridors.

"What's that silly smile for?" asked Sibyl. "I think I know. You were impressed this morning, weren't you? And now you've signed up with him."

Sibyl was organizing her belongings, folding clothes and putting them in shelves. Mariam could only nod.

"Well, let me tell you. Tulari was miserable after she had been through that initiation. I don't know what you're smiling about," she said as she briskly shook out a skirt before putting it away.

"But Sibyl, aren't you excited and curious about it? He looks so gentle and elegant. I can't imagine it being anything but wonderful!" Mariam danced a step or two before picking up a shawl from her bed and draping it around herself.

"Suit yourself. I can't imagine it being wonderful at all, not even with a handsome priest. You go ahead and do it, you go and get yourself ready to make some babies." She grabbed a blanket and shook it so it snapped in the air.

"But Sibyl, it is done to honor the Gods! It is done to find the deep connection between man and woman! There are mysteries connected with all this. Don't you want to know about it?"

"Not really. I have no desire to have a heavy man crawl all over me. To me it does not hold the route to a conversation with God. You're welcome to your fantasy, Mariam, but I'm not sharing it."

"It is also done for healing, don't you believe in that either?" Mariam was stunned.

"I believe in my herbs. They have no judgment, no anger, no burning desire to be satisfied. Without even an opinion, they just do their work. The sun and the stars are in orbit even without the display we witnessed this morning. It was dripping, Mariam, didn't you see? I get shivers of disgust just thinking about it."

"I thought it was beautiful," said Mariam quietly as she sat down on her bed.

"What? Do you know what men think about throughout the day? They're

looking for a way to ... If they can find a way to corner you, they'll.... My father...
Well, he is not like yours – "

Mariam looked down on her hands in her lap. She thought of how her father
had come to visit her bringing fruits and sweets from home. How he had spent time
listening to her and hugged her affectionately when he left. She recalled the feeling
of safety she had when near him and she knew how proud he was of her and her
studies.

"I'll tell you something, Mariam. Your parents might have been gentle and
caring towards each other. Mine were not. I saw my father force himself on my
mother, and I watched her helplessly letting him do it so she could survive. There
was no dance between them. It was an animal force that needed to be released. My
mother had fourteen children, Mariam. I didn't come to the temple to learn about
how lovely it might be. I came here to not have to do it. I will join the renunciates
among the priestesses and keep their vows."

At a loss for words, Mariam looked at her hands again, wondering what had
happened to the exuberance she had felt earlier. She was shocked. This was something
she had looked forward to. She had watched the relationship between her parents and
admired the strong bond between them. She loved her father. She loved her brothers.
She looked forward to love Yeshua. Men were not scary to her. They were the other
half of the partnership in a marriage. Nature needed male and female to reproduce,
whether you were a plant, an animal or a human. God was male and female, and the
partnerships were constantly shown to them: the Sun and Venus in their intimate
dance across the sky; Isis and Osiris and their beautiful story of devotion; the beauty
of the priestesses and priests honoring the Gods in this manner.

Besides, Mariam found men fascinating. She looked forward to getting to know
Yeshua better, to feel that every cell in his body carried a message a little different
than hers.

"Sibyl, I'm so sorry," she said, feeling a deep sadness. For Mariam, it took on
the same emotional response as if Sibyl had announced that somebody close to her
had died. Mariam felt they needed to prepare a ceremony; a funeral for Sibyl's lost
experiences, a healing to repair what her family life had ruined for her. Her friend
would never feel the excitement Mariam had been floating in just minutes before. If
Sibyl went through with her plan, she wouldn't have that conversation with the Gods
and, possibly, never mother children. Just the thought made a shrieking sound inside
Mariam's body. She wanted to hug her friend, sit by her, comfort her.

"It's not that important," said Sibyl. "I just don't want to." Her voice revealed no
emotion. To her it was not a loss; it was a relief. She was glad to have found a place
where she could live her life in a meaningful way, the way she wanted to. She did not
need to be comforted. Not right now.

On the day Sibyl told her family she was leaving for the Temple to study herbs, she had her few belongings packed and her hand on the door prepared for a quick getaway.

"That's where they train whores like you," her father had yelled, and slapped her cheek. "I know what they do at that Temple. For all the public to see!"

"That's where I'll go to get away from brutes like you!" she had yelled back. Her mother had shrunk down in the corner by the fireplace. She tried to make herself as small as possible. Her father had turned like a tiger.

"And don't you go socializing with her either," he screamed at his wife and lifted a hand to strike. "We don't associate with harlots like that."

"You're the one who has made us all into your whores! May the Gods give you what you deserve!" Sibyl had screamed.

Then she realized that she never had to see these people again. She felt a new strength coming up from deep inside and she spoke with a resonance of dark power. The quality of her new voice made her father feel cold inside and he froze in motion, hand ready to strike. Her mother held her breath as she heard her daughter utter the curse.

"I swear, as soon as I know how, I'll make a potion that will make your member shrivel up and become a deadly poison killing you slowly as you rot from the inside."

Sibyl stood for a moment staring at these people who had somehow brought her into life. She left her curse hanging like a string of icicles, as she grabbed her bundle and ran away.

Mariam looked up at her friend with deep pain. Sibyl's eyes met hers. She hadn't said anything; she felt no need to share her story in words. Her images carried quite well in the open space between them. Her eyes didn't show anger or regret. They expressed absolutely nothing. Sibyl didn't understand why Mariam was so disturbed. Should she comfort Mariam, perhaps? That seemed absurd. She said she was going to the drying barn and left the room.

Mariam sat for a while with a tangle of contrasting emotions. It struck her that Sibyl's decision to come here was very powerful, perhaps more powerful than her own. Mariam was following the program of the Temple School with her parents blessing. Sibyl had gone against her parents, and she was deviating from the normal path in the Temple. Not that they weren't welcoming renunciates, but it was a less well trodden path. The temple would honor her decision and be grateful for her contributions. If she changed her mind later, they would help her through that transition.

Mariam realized the powerful foundation of her upbringing. Her parents had demonstrated what a marriage could be. Her brothers had taught her how to have male friends. She had never had any reason to fear any man. And she was betrothed to a man she adored. She felt a deep gratitude to her family, and a sudden pain in her chest told her how much she missed them. Sibyl had no one to miss.

After allowing her mind to settle, she decided it was time to set up her own altar the way she had learned from her mother. Privacy had been difficult in the other dormitory, but now that she had the status of an older student, she and Sibyl had been given more space. Mariam decided on a shelf to the right of the door where it was hidden from first view. She had been collecting items for some time in the lidded basket from Ethiopia.

Mariam lifted the lid off the finely woven basket and found the little piece of linen she had saved from her Temple dress. It was not bigger than a napkin, but would do very well as a table cloth for her small space. She put a stone from the beach on the altar and filled the seashell with water. A beeswax candle from the temple was lit in a blue glass. An incense stick gave swirls of smoke changing the atmosphere of the room. She arranged the items according to the compass directions and spoke to each as she assigned the elements to their corresponding force in nature.

"North, the tip of the arrow along the axis of the earth, the point showing us the noble way, I give you this stone to ground us.

"West, as the earth circles you become the yesterdays, teaching us to leave the dead behind. I give you this shell with water for cleansing.

"South, the force behind the arrow giving it motion, generously giving us energy and light, I give you this candle for fire.

"East, where the sun always rises, the earth circles into you as we welcome everything anew. I give you the incense for air.

"Together, these forces, the straight line and the circular motion, give us the spiral movement of the earth."

She stood with each item in her hand addressing the direction, turning her body in a circle as she shifted. The earth continued its movements and Mariam felt it move underneath her feet.

Her hands returned to the basket and she found a small soft leather bag closed with a drawstring. Carefully she took out the bundle wrapped in white linen, and unbound the cloth. The head of Bashra lay cradled in her hand. Again she studied it and admired how meticulously the features were preserved. Her feelings for her ancestor carried both a deep respect and an equally deep fear of the power it could unleash. It had been hidden in its covers. Mariam felt it was time to get over her fears. She needed to consult her multiple times great-grandmother. She found a small stand for it and placed it behind the items already present on the altar. She put a pillow on the floor and sat down in front of it.

"Bashra, I want this to be a conversation with God. I never want to fear any man. I want this ritual of union to always be done to honor the Gods, to be the union of the morning star and the rising sun, to be honoring every time a seed finds its way to the fertile soil left behind by the receding Nile."

"Oh, child, stop philosophizing. Admit it, you've felt the urge. You've become aware that you have an open space and now you want the experience of having it filled. And you've seen the one with ample equipment to do it. Daughter, you are ready, and your body is purring like a black temple cat."

Mariam laughed. She had to admit that Bashra was right. Now, she felt validated and could allow herself to look forward to the event. Her daydreaming for the next two weeks was filled with the image of the handsome priest and her sense of her own waiting wet and silky insides.

CHAPTER 6

Mariam's First Initiation

They met at the statue of Serapis in the main temple. She noticed again his well trained body, and, also, that he wasn't as tall as she remembered. Admiring his thick dark hair, she smiled in a shy greeting. Gyasi took her hand, and they bowed to the great statue and dedicated their ritual to Isis and Osiris. After stating their intentions to the Gods, Mariam was invited to follow him through the doors to the inside of the temple and down stairs to the inner rooms.

Their room had been warmed by a brazier burning. As she had requested, a light meal had been provided with fruits, bread and cheese. Wine was poured into pretty green glasses. There was a thick, colorful silk rug on the floor surrounded by several blankets and pillows of different colors. A vase of tall papyrus leaves stood in a corner and flowers in small vases were placed in niches in the walls. After closing the door behind them, Gyasi lit the candles and soon everything absorbed and reflected a soft, golden glow.

Mariam, still standing by the door, studied his confidence. This was familiar ground to him and though his efforts to make her feel comfortable were reassuring, she was still only one in a history of nervous young girls. Part of her wanted this to be a singular incident for him and part of her was grateful for the anonymity.

Gyasi turned and smiled at her. He understood her hesitation, and took her hand leading her to the rug. They lay down on either side of the food and she chose some grapes and her favorite cheese.

"So Mariam," he said, "I hear you like herbology the best." Mariam nodded as she reached for a piece of bread. "What about plants do you find most fascinating?" he said to start a conversation.

He managed to get her to talk about the scents, the oils and the new combinations of her experiments. He poured her wine and made her laugh. After a while he removed the tray and returned to her on the rug.

Gyasi sat down cross legged in front of her and encouraged her to do the same. They were mirroring each other, human beings in male and female form. Mariam again admired his physique, his athletic build, and his strong muscles which still gave him the grace of a dancer. His skin was darker than hers, and his shiny black hair was organized in small braids compared to her lose, dark brown waves. Bracelets adorned both his upper arms, gold with turquoise and lapis inlays. His wrap was white and fastened in such a way that it was tightly fitting across his buttocks and draping in the front. She wondered how he folded the fabric around himself to make it do that. It occurred to her that he must have spent some time preparing himself to meet with her.

He waited patiently for her mind to quiet. Gyasi had been with many young virgins and knew he needed to allow them their fantasies about him and his body. They all seemed to have their own hurdles to get through before he could secure their attention. He needed their mind quiet and ready to learn, not their admiration or fear of him.

Gyasi put his hand on top of her head and drew a circle.

"This is the lotus flower on top of the column in the temple," he said. "This is where the gods of the sky enter your body to speak with the gods of the earth. This is where the star shines through and makes your inner temple luminescent."

He moved his hand and placed a finger on her brow between her eyes.

"This is the cave in the mountain where you have the vision of the hawk when the sky has left the black of night. This is where you find your inner golden crown with the indigo pearl." Gyasi smiled.

Mariam wasn't quite sure what it all meant. Her inquisitive mind wanted more explanation. She memorized the imagery and hoped more understanding would be revealed to her.

His hands moved again, this time making a circle on the base of her throat.

"This is where you speak your truth and the gods hear every word you utter. The dawn illuminates the mountain path and the sky is bright blue."

He placed his palm flat with his fingers pointing up between her breasts, feeling her young body vibrating beneath, and listened for that little gasp of breath each emitted. His reassuring smile calmed her, and she returned a quiver of a smile.

"This is the palace on the green meadow. This is where the gods from above and the gods from below meet. This is where love has the strength of a thousand Apis bulls. The morning sun tells you that today anything is possible."

He turned his hand sideways and placed it flat over her navel.

"This is the city market at noon in bright yellow sunshine. This is where Mariam presents herself to the world. This is the relationship of many. "

Slowly, he turned his hand again now with fingers pointing down and placed it above her pubic bone. Her slight uneasiness returned.

"This is the beach house with the big fireplace. This is where Mariam goes to be in partnership. This is the relationship of two. This is where new children of heart, mind and body are created. You will become a powerful healer. Remember to find your glowing power here in the orange sun of the afternoon."

Slowly and deliberately so she could see every move he made, he changed the position of his hand again. With palm up and fingers pointing towards her, he reached between her crossed legs and put his hand beneath her. Mariam was startled, but allowed him to do it.

"This is the base of the column in the temple. This is where your ancestors brought you wrapped in a red blanket to the temple for your first blessing, the celebration of one. This is where the gods of the earth enter your body to speak with the gods of the sky. The sun is setting and bathing your body in glowing red."

Gyasi left his hand there for a moment before he withdrew it. Mariam swallowed.

He got up, but motioned for her to stay seated. Mariam watched him bring back two glasses of wine and offer one to her, while he took a sip himself. She dutifully drank and gave the glass back to him grateful for the refreshment. He replaced the glasses on a tray and came back. This time he positioned himself on his knees behind her. His hands were gently placed on her back. Holding onto her left shoulder he traced her spine with his right hand from her head to her seat and up again.

"This is the River Nile. It flows through the column in the temple from north to south *and* from south to north at the same time. This river has two tributaries. They have the names of Isis and Osiris and they flow in a spiral like the movement of a snake, mirroring each other on opposite sides of the Nile."

He used his two forefingers and started at her tailbone. Then he made a loop to either side and crossed at the small of her back. His hands made new loops and came back where her spine met her waist. She felt new loops being drawn crossing behind her heart. The next loops brought him to the base of her skull. His fingers made a slanted line above her ears and come to the front of her head where they crossed in the middle of her forehead and came to rest on the side of each nostril.

A shiver went through her body. These energy lines had apparently been active for years, and she was not aware of them. Her body became a road map of cities and connection points, each holding a strange sensation.

Gyasi said, "Let me repeat the route of the King and Queen. This is Osiris", he poked her back lightly with his right finger. "And this is Isis," she felt his left finger on her left side. He started at the bottom of her spine again.

"Feel Isis on the left side, Osiris on the right, and the Nile in the middle. You're the baby in the red blanket carried by your grandmother. Now they spread out." His fingers made the loops on her skin.

"The King and Queen meet again and make love in the orange glow at the beach house, loving their fertile land." He put his fingers together the small of her back.

"Now they cross over, Isis goes right Osiris left, and they meet again on the trail to the palace in the bright yellow sunshine." His fingers came together at her waist.

"Now, Isis goes left and Osiris right before they meet at the palace on the green meadow in the hills. This is where they love their people and rule their country. Now they cross over again. Osiris left and Isis right, before they meet enjoying the crisp blue sky over the mountain trail. The tributaries don't follow the Nile to the lotus flower. They relate to your breath, so they meet in the cave in the mountains and watch the evening star come out against the dark blue midnight sky. This is where the King and Queen find the wisdom to rule their country and earn their crowns. Then the lines cross over and meet again on either side of your nose."

Mariam followed the route of Isis and Osiris. She could see the beach house, a pavilion by the water. The trail leading up to the palace followed the undulating hills through the meadows where cows and sheep graze. The palace was positioned in the hillside, with a magnificent view of the water and the valley. She saw the King and Queen enjoy a cold drink by the columns on the terrace. They traveled on through a more rocky terrain on their way to the cave in the mountain. The trail was steep and went through a magnificent pass between blue mountains before they reached the temple where the crown with the indigo pearl was waiting.

"Breathe," commanded Gyasi, bringing her back. She dutifully took a deep breath. He had come around and was again sitting cross legged in front of her. "Breathe with me. Tongue to the roof of your mouth, breath in through your nose. Relax your jaw. Now breathe out through your mouth. This is breathing for the Nile. You breathe in, the river goes south, you breathe out, the river flows north. Try it."

Mariam followed him and learned how it felt to allow breath to become a flow over her head and down her back. As she exhaled, it returned up her front and met again at the roof of her mouth. They breathed together for ten concentrated breaths. The flow of air became a loud sound and the movement of her chest the only thing happening in the room. His dark eyes were her focal points and they turned into two dark tunnels leading into black velvet rooms. She felt the smooth softness envelope her.

"Now, try this," Gyasi said. "Let's breathe for the Nile towards eachother."

He put his face close to hers and breathed in, then motioned to her to inhale as he exhaled. She took in the air that had been inside him, and let it fill her, before releasing it back to him. He breathed in her air and smiled at her, his eyes twinkling in the candle light. As they developed a rhythm back and forth, the air they shared took on its own substance. It became a unit which had visited the insides of each of them and had a warm sweetness to it. When it returned to Mariam, she felt she knew him better. Her cells noticed something his cells had wanted to share. Gyasi was full of laughter. He was sharing with her the joy of being alive. She giggled, and he joined her.

Laughing, he pushed her shoulder and tipped her over on the rug. They were lying on their sides facing each other and turned quiet as he put his hand on her shoulder. It was crystal clear to both of them that he was a man, and she was a breathtakingly beautiful young woman. His hand followed her side and down her hip. He found the edge of her tunic and followed her thigh underneath it. Noticing a little uneasiness, he took her hand and placed it on his own shoulder encouraging her to familiarize herself with him. She looked at the big shoulder beneath her hand and his arm showing ample muscles under beautiful dark skin. Her hand followed his shoulder and down his chest. Finding his nipple she caressed around it and found that he responded with an intake of breath. Enjoying a glorious moment, he stopped himself. He had to be careful. This was her time, not his.

His hand was back at her shoulder. He followed her collar bone, noticed her lovely neck and very lightly let his hand come down her front. His fingertips brushed across the fabric covering her breast and let the young breast rest in his full hand allowing her to feel how perfectly round and immensely soft it was. She purred and curled up closer to him. He pulled her towards him for a full body embrace.

"Remember, the star in the temple cave at midnight," he said as his forehead touched hers.

"Tea at the palace in the morning," she said feeling her breasts against his chest.

"And making love at the beach house in the afternoon," he whispered as he let her feel his hardened member through their clothes against her abdomen.

He rolled back and lay down on his back to let her explore him. She needed to touch this body, look at him and be allowed to overcome any fear of the male form she might have.

She saw the softness of her own arm, the gentle curvatures of her own muscles. All his lines were more angular, sharper. His skin was rougher and firmer. He loosened his wrap, but left it to her to lift it off. She felt there aught to be some music at this revealing moment as she pulled the white fabric away. There it was. Now she could look

He let her touch him. She took note of its size and wondered how the next step was going to work. His pouch was lifted and his two stones held gently in her hand. Then she touched his shaft, held around it, and was surprised when some drops appeared on top. When she touched it, it was slippery and allowed her finger to slide easily on the head. He sighed, and meeting her eyes he rose on an elbow, and got up on his knees in front of her. Swiftly he pulled her tunic over her head and then gently laid her down among the pillows.

He kissed her lips, her neck, licked her collarbone and found those incredibly soft young breasts so eager to be caressed. Gently, he teased them with his tongue. Her chest would rise towards him when he did something she liked. He loved her unabashed response, and silently thanked her father and brothers for teaching her to trust. His hand worked its way down her abdomen, played about her pubic hair before going further down between her legs. Hesitantly, she opened up a little for him, and he stroked her thighs a bit before finding her crevice. He let the side of his finger move along its full length before parting its lips.

Her whole being followed every move he made. Through his hands she experienced herself as silky, wet and tantalizing. He found her rose and her rosebud, and she found the black velvet room his eyes had promised her.

His hard member was awaiting its turn. She could feel it against her leg asking permission. She moved her legs a little wider and he placed himself between them. He had promised the Gods to be gentle, but it required some self control to hold back for her sake.

He entered her slowly, and pulled back again after covering just a short distance. She gasped, and he wasn't quite sure if that was pleasure, surprise or pain. He entered again, knowing that soon he would meet the barrier that signified the virgin. He knew he had to break through, but it pained him to see her pain. He made this a night of wonder and delight, and didn't want to ruin the magic. At the third entry he felt it, the membrane blocking his way. She winced, and gripped his shoulder digging her nails in, but she didn't move away. He pulled out, waited a moment, and then entered again. This time he went through it and found more open space. He kept a measure, that was as far in as he would go. His full length could not always be accommodated, and he certainly did not want to hurt her. He pulled out and entered again, this time giving himself permission to enjoy.

Mariam felt the ripping of her hymen like a short sharp pain, which made her want to pull back and push him away. She knew this would happen, and didn't move. Appreciating every effort he had made to make it easier for her, she accepted him again. Her open space had been waiting for this, and she allowed him to fill her up. As he moved, she felt electrified. The river Nile was moving inside her. It was going north and the King and Queen were running along the paths of their kingdom.

He came inside her as they both cried out. The sun rays penetrated with shots of orange light flooding the interior of the beach house.

CHAPTER 7

WAKING YOCHANAN

GROWING HERBS AT THE SERAPIUM WAS VERY different from working in Ezekiel's secure walled garden. A few beloved plants were grown with love and care, from which he and Mariam extracted the most aromatic oils. It was their secret world, away from the busy life of others.

The Serapium produced large fields of herbs that needed the same kind of attention. After a successful harvest, the preparation of huge quantities of plant material began. Whether an herb was to be dried, boiled, distilled, or extracted, or hurried to the kitchen for immediate us, it was a lot of work. The priests and priestesses hired local help, but still were overwhelmed administrating the replenishing of the Temple's impressive pharmacopoeia. People arrived for healing from as far away as the width of the Mediterranean Sea. Physicians came to Alexandria to buy expertly grown medicinal plants. Local people came and bought herbs for the needs of their households.

Mariam looked up from the field of blue lobelia. Her job this morning had been to check on the status of the plants. She had counted them, calculated their harvest, the number of workers necessary and designated where the plants would be hung to dry. She estimated a substantial yield and looked forward to see the dried flowers ready for use.

She told the head gardener of her findings and was sent back to the Temple for lunch in the dining halls. They served grains from the fertile fields along the Nile boiled in sweetened milk and there were spinach leaves and goat cheese from their own farms. The food was welcome, so was the calming tea.

"Mariam," she heard Suri call. "Can you come with me? I could use your help."

Sibyl was already at her side, and Mariam quickly dropped her finished palm leaves into the compost basket. They followed Suri through the garden to the building where the herbs and balms were kept. There was a workroom there for mixing the products. Last time they were here they had made a soothing ointment for burns.

"Let's get started. Sibyl, would you crush the herbs I have laid out on that

31

table, and tell us what they are and their properties. Mariam, you can prepare the combination of extracts for the mixture. Here is a bowl to start with."

"What is this liniment for, Suri?" asked Sibyl.

"Let's see what you can figure out as you work," was her answer. "You know the properties of the plants. Tell me what you think it will do for a human body when applied."

She didn't really want to explain the purpose of this product. It was too early in their studies for them to work with this material, but they needed this salve now, and these two were the only novices available to help. She had to trust that they were ready.

Sibyl picked up an herb. "This one is easy. This is the geranium I picked some months ago which is now dried and ready to for use."

"Very good," said Suri. "Now tell me what it is used for."

Sibyl thought for a moment. "The herb will be good for the blood, and the color will strengthen the root center of the body."

"Yes, you've got the strongest factors; go on with the next ones."

On the table there were rose petals, sandal wood, fresh jasmine flowers, dried pineapple flowers and same stalks of Bella Donna. Sibyl identified them all easily, and concluded that they were to strengthen the blood circulation, create warmth in the body and provide stimulation. The Bella Donna puzzled her.

"Suri, this one is a deadly poison, why are we using it?"

"Used in the correct amounts it is a heart stimulant, given in large doses it can kill," was the answer from Suri. "We need an extra heart stimulant for this specific purpose," she continued.

On Mariam's bench there were three glass bottles. She sniffed the first one and announced that it was camphor. The next one was easy. It was her own personal favorite, rose extract, the finest distillation of the rose oil. The last was another favorite, one of the more exotic fragrances: Patchouli.

"These are all blood and heart stimulants. If we make it strong enough we could wake the dead."

Suri said nothing. She had no intention of telling these girls exactly what this product was going to be used for, but she realized she didn't have a choice. She needed their help and eventually they would have to know why.

"Sibyl and Mariam, I need your help to empower this unguent to give it the strength it needs. We will crush the herbs and mix the oils here, and then we will take them to the Temple for some more ingredients. This is a strong stimulant. We need it for a very important purpose."

Mariam and Sibyl had both stopped what they were doing. They looked at Suri and were silent. Both understood what this meant. They were going to be allowed into the inner rooms of the Temple. Wide eyed and eager, they awaited Suri to tell them what they were making.

She didn't. She told them to stay focused and follow her. The girls quickly finished and each carried a bowl as they left the herbarium. Suri led them across a courtyard, along a row of columns and through a door leading into the Temple. They appeared before the statue of Serapis.

"We ask for blessings for this medicine," Suri intoned in her clear voice. The girls sang the repeating chorus.

"We ask for the wisdom of Sophia to come through this ointment and into the body we want to heal.

"We ask for the strength of the Apis bull to come through this ointment and into the body we want to heal.

"We ask for Isis and Osiris to find their paths in the body we want to heal.

"We ask for your wisdom to guide our hands on the body we want to heal."

They separated into a three part harmony with Sibyl's birdlike high notes reaching the blue star-studded ceiling above and Mariam's deeper tones grounding them to the marble floor while Suri kept the main melody floating between the statues. People in the plaza saw the three priestesses at work and felt reassured that the relationship between the humans and their Gods was in balance.

Suri led them through a door behind the statue of Serapis. They came into a corridor before they descended a set of stairs. Below was another corridor lit by torches.

They descended another staircase, and Suri led them into a work room with a rug on the back wall and a little store room on the side. There was a low table in the middle where the girls placed their bowls. "Good, I see Lucia has been here with the other things we need." Suri took two small glass vials containing two liquids from a shelf; one white and foamy; the other very dark red and place them on the table.

"First, we need to prepare the room," said Suri. In the store room, she found a large red piece of silk fabric and four red stones. Suri gave them instructions for hanging the silk from hooks in the ceiling. The candles on the tables at the four walls of the room were lit together with the incense in front of them. The stones, a large ruby, a garnet, a red spinel and a fire opal, were placed in front of each altar and they filled the water bowls.

"Anu should be here soon, I asked her to come with the harp. We need to give this medicine the right sound. From this point on I want there to be no spoken words. I will communicate with you silently. When we go further into the temple you will follow my lead. Trust that I will guide you."

Around the low table there were pillows on the floor. Anu joined them and sat down with her harp and played a single note. Suri and the girls sang the familiar incantations for the directions and the elements in front of each altar. Then they sat down at the table and Anu started variations on specific intervals from her note.

Suri started singing again, repeating Anu's tones. She motioned to the girls to continue stirring their bowls while encouraging them to sing, too. Suri took the two small glass vials and kept turning them in her hands, moving them in a circle, one clockwise the other counter-clockwise.

Mariam and Sibyl had been instructed to stir their bowls steadily in the same manner. The blossoming scent, the light from the candles reflecting in the red silk, the rhythmical movements and chanting put the four women in a collective meditative trance.

Suri reached for Mariam's bowl and poured the contents of the vials into it humming the song of Isis and Osiris from the solstice ritual. She then took Sibyl's bowl and emptied the ground herbs into the mixed liquids and stirred it with a circular motion. The girls watched the compound turn into a salve.

Suri signaled to them to come with her as she pulled aside the rug on the back wall. Anu continued the music on the harp as they walked trough to an empty torch lit hallway leading to another staircase. They were several floors beneath the temple now. Suri led them to a door opening covered by a similar rug. It had a symbol woven into the pattern that Mariam had never seen before.

Pulling aside the rug, Suri guided them into a small anteroom where an old monk was waiting. They bowed respectfully to each other. Mariam admired the older man's face under his white turban, his wrinkles telling of a long life in devotion, studies and prayers. His long burlap jacket over his white tunic showed that the desert winds were familiar to him. The man looked at her and met her eyes. He pleaded her to take good care of his student. She promised she would do her part to the best of her ability. He smiled back at her in gratitude and lifted his hand making a small movement with his fingers.

Mariam got a vision of his monastery in the desert. A young man with his head wrapped in layers of linen protecting him from sand and wind was tending a camel. He looked up for a moment, and Mariam saw his face. She recognized Yeshua and took a quick breath. He sensed her presence and his face brightened. The old man smiled at her. He had delivered his message.

Suri sang a line, carrying a question to the monk. He responded in a beautiful baritone that his student was ready. The priestesses bowed, and the monk pulled the rug behind him aside and let the women pass. This was their domain; he respectfully stayed behind.

The room they entered had black walls, and black ceiling and floor. Mariam wondered if her eyes deceived her, if she was seeing an optical illusion. It was hard to find where the surfaces met. She looked again and noticed that every line in the room was of equal length. She was standing inside a perfect cube. A stone table stood in the middle covered with a white sheet. There were altars and candles burning along each wall. Suri went to each altar and sang the incantations. She touched the four elements present and encouraged the girls to do the same.

Beneath an altar there was a small door which opened to a storage space. Inside there was a headdress of a black panther. Suri put it on and was now representing

Isis. She stood there looking at them, and as they watched, her eyes changed and became elongated. Her pupils became vertical lines. The other three women bowed to Isis who had now appeared among them.

As she got used to the dimmer light, Mariam noticed that the walls were covered with pictures and symbols. She realized they contained a description of the process of initiation. It started with the preparation of the student: the foods he was supposed to eat, the mental preparation he needed to make and the prerequisite knowledge for such a journey. The vibration of color and sounds for his surroundings where specified. It listed the herbs for the anointment of his body to induce the proper trance, and showed him being covered by a large linen sheet. The hieroglyphs explained that his breathing and heartbeat would stop. Then he should be left alone for three days. The next pictures depicted the inner journey the student would take while in this state.

Mariam read about his meeting with Isis and Osiris, who welcomed him to the other side. They showed him a mirror, a profound and honest meeting with himself. Then Isis monitored his body with an ankh. She identified where he needed to be healed, or, more correctly; upgraded, before he was ready to visit the world of the dead. Mariam had to correct her interpretation. The other world was considered the world of the truly living.

Suri called for her attention. No sound was uttered, but Mariam could feel that she was needed, and turned her head towards the stone table. Now she noticed that the large white sheet doubled over a male body. The long fabric folded creating both the sheet he lay on and the cover over him. His head was protected in the crease of the linen. The side of the stone he was lying on was covered in beautiful renderings of Isis dressed in the wings of the underworld.

He is well cared for on his journey, Mariam thought. *I wonder who he is.*

The scent around him carried all the herbs that had been applied to his body. The composition of herbs was unfamiliar and heavy. Mariam read the hieroglyph again and tried to identify them.

Suri gathered them around him on four sides. Anu kept a single tone waiting for her to start a new melody. Suri started to hum and made sure they all shared the same sound. When she felt that the room was vibrating a safe note for him, she slowly and gently lifted the sheet and gathered it on the stone above his head

Mariam stared as the linen was removed. His face was revealed last, and she was both disappointed and relieved that it was not Yeshua. This was another beautiful young man about the same age. His fine features were framed with thick, dark, wavy hair. Lying on his back, his hands were placed modestly over his genitals. His eyes were closed as for sleep, but he seemed gone from this world and in no hurry to return. The yellow pale skin had lost its pigment and the gray of the grave had taken hold of him. Mariam hoped they had used enough Bella Donna to bring him back. There was something familiar about his features. Who was he?

Suri showed them how to encourage him to find his breath. She bent over his head and exhaled softly over his nostrils. After waiting three counts of the music, she did it again. She motioned to Sibyl to take over giving him the softest breath in measured intervals.

Suri began with his left foot. The balm they had made was rolled and warmed in her hands before she started. Mariam admired her systematic approach. All her movements were rhythmic and steady. She encouraged Mariam to start on his right. The soft tone of the harp soothed between the black walls and the scent from the sheet spread a pungent note. *Would they save the aromatic sheets he had been wrapped in*, Mariam wondered. *Could it be used by anyone else after he had traveled through the fibers?*

Suri answered her question silently. *It belongs to him now. Part of him lives between the linen threads.*

They continued giving him breath and gently massaging his body. He was still not breathing on his own. Sibyl looked with sadness on the beautiful young body thinking the student was lost to his wise old mentor. His skin was pale and yellow under her fingers, and he appeared thinner than he should for his age. His limbs were stiffer than they expected. They would indeed have pronounced him dead if they had found him in a bed in the hospital wing. *Patience*, Suri lectured them in their thoughts.

By now Suri had finished working on his leg. Her hands followed his body along his side and continued to his shoulder. She wanted to work on his chest before she lifted his hands. The girls were not unfamiliar with the male body, but they couldn't deny their curiosity about what would eventually be revealed from beneath those protective pale hands. Suri decided to wait. Keep them curious. A little tension in the air might help pull him through.

Slowly, carefully, tenderly they worked on his torso. Sibyl noticed that although thin, he was a sturdier built man than first assumed. He seemed very young for undertaking this initiation.

Mariam studied his features. He still looked gray and lifeless. He was not breathing, although Sibyl had rhythmically shared breath across his nose for quite some time. She recognized him now, had felt it for a while. Of course it was not Yeshua. The message from the monk told her that he was at his monastery in the desert. This was his relative, his cousin. They had played together when their families lived in Alexandria. This was Yochanan, the older boy. Their mothers had been close friends, and the children played together often. She smiled as fond memories made pictures in her mind.

Suri could see the pictures of Mariam's memory like a ribbon floating in front of her. *The stars must look at him favorably. He'll need her strength and fondness for him for his return.*

Suri encouraged the young women to be more vigorous. They rhythmically massaged the whole body. Sibyl got to do his head with her sensitive fingers. The herbs and oils were applied and gently massaged across his forehead and carefully into all the small muscles across his face. Sibyl still sent her breath across his nose, each time hoping that he would draw breath himself. He still seemed without life, and she wondered how long it usually took to revive people after this initiation.

Patience, came Suri's gentle reassurance one more time, although she had hoped that he would have come to by now. She motioned to Sibyl and encouraged her to be intuitive. She applied more salve right beneath his nostrils so he could smell it, and continued massaging around his nose.

Suri decided it was time to try something else. She lifted his hands away from their protective position and the young man was now totally exposed to the four women. She took a good amount of oil in her hands and gently massaged it into the soft skin exposed. The young women looked at her hands and took in every nuance of her movements. They wanted to learn, to know how to do that without hurting him. How do you move your hands to heal, when you are working in such a sensitive area? How do you keep your mind on healing, instead of wanting to pleasure him?

Suri answered their questions silently:

Admiration of his beauty is healing. Appreciation for the most intimate parts of him is healing. Pleasure is healing. Lovemaking is healing. Love is healing. The love we embedded in this ointment is healing.

Love him like a mother loves her child. Love him like a woman loves her lover. Love him like you've been married to him for a long time.

Awaken his love of life. Awaken his love of his ability to give life to more life. Awaken his masculine need to enliven a woman. Awaken his desire to find the divine in joining with a Goddess and being a God.

Sibyl understood what Suri meant. Mariam also understood, but felt overwhelmed by her own feelings for this good looking youth, her old playmate, now a man, as she herself had grown into a woman.

Suri motioned to Mariam to come closer. She massaged along his sides and across his abdomen finding his line of hair pointing down from his navel. Suri stepped aside and moved her hands closer to his heart. Mariam was encouraged to follow her intuition and inspire him to live.

They now were focused on an essential part of him each. Mariam remembered what she had learned from Gyasi about the different homes of the King and Queen. Sibyl was welcoming him to his mountain temple. Suri was getting the castle on the hillside ready, and Mariam was at the beach house listening to the waves of the water. She picked up more fragrant oil for her hands and came to wipe her finger underneath her own nose. The fragrance was potent, and made her a bit dizzy, but also tuned her to how it worked on him. Mariam exhaled and filled her lungs anew. They all watched his nose and listened for breath. Sibyl smiled and looked up at them. There had been a stream of air across her fingers.

Suri motioned Mariam to be extra gentle. There was no need to shock him. Mariam cupped her hands protectively over his resting genitals, letting them feel the soft warmth of her hands. His whole body was in a suspended state. He was waiting for the completion of the ritual; the return after the journey. The vision he was given needed to complete its message. A deeper breath was drawn.

Mariam allowed her emotions to flow, showing her love for his male body. Her heart opened in appreciation of what this part of him was capable of. She sent thanks to the good woman who had initiated him into the world of love and to the future young woman whose vulva he would plow for her first time. She blessed the lucky woman who would be his wife and enjoy the masculine power he could stream into her. The oil and herbs went into his sensitive skin together with her blessing as Mariam's hands gently caressed him.

His breathing was better. A little color came to his face lifting the shadow of death. Suri signaled them to stop moving and just hold him. Her hands rested across his heart, Sibyl was holding his head, and Mariam created a protective lid over his most sensitive parts. He was now left alone to discover himself. Slowly they withdrew from direct touch to his body to a stance several inches above him, still holding their good intentions. His fingers started to stir.

With each breath, his color changed. His blood was starting to move. The herbs included a pain barrier to ease the blood flow; otherwise it would hurt too much when the heart started to pump. *He seems to be easing into it*, Suri thought. *The gods be praised for his youth and health.*

Inside Yochanan's mind a gradual appearance of color was slowly bringing him back to his body. He was one with The All, one with the field where a single thought, a suggestion of a concept, felt like a drop of water falling in a still lake. Feeling omnipresent in the love and acceptance of The All had been an experience of fulfillment. He was in unity with everything, merged with the Creator. Life beyond life felt so much more alive. He still experienced himself as a unit, the same size and shape as his body, but the limitations of the human body were lifted. Suri would call this his Ba, his awareness of himself as something unchangeable, unaffected by earthly life. His Ba was free floating and he could travel with it when it was free from his body. The human body carried both its limitations and its sublime experiences. The reality of The All existed in the free flowing space between the minutest substances inside him. He had experienced eternity within every cell of his holy body, and heard every genetic code sing the name of Yahweh.

Yochanan knew that existence exists. He was aware of awareness. A warm, reddish field introduced human vision behind his eyelids. His awareness of everything expanded to the awareness of himself and the realization that he existed within a defined field. He could feel blood streaming in his ears and heard it, like a trickle of water close by. He could feel the protective field around him created by good women who were holding him in their love and between their capable hands. The scent of the room inundated his senses with a fragrance he registered as pure beauty. His fingers and toes were tingling. He moved them ever so slowly. The rest of his body seemed paralyzed, but, as he breathed more, blood streamed into it all. He was not afraid. He knew in due time, his body would come to full function again.

Who were these women caring for him? He wanted so much to see them, but where was the mechanism to open his eyes?

The women were holding their own breath as they watched his become steadier and a soft smile of well-being appear on his face. They looked at each other in triumph. They had helped him choose to come back. In the back of their minds they knew he could have chosen otherwise. The other world is very tempting.

Suri warmed a blanket before covering him with it. They moved the braziers closer to keep him warm. She found another mix of herbs on a shelf, filled a cup with water and set it to heat for tea. Soon he would be ready for a nourishing drink.

Mariam just watched his process with awe. *This must be how it feels to be born,* she thought.

Suri decided it was time to introduce him to his identity. She knew he was still in a state where such concepts were foreign and insignificant, but, for his awakening, it was important.

"Yochanan," she said softly. He turned his head slightly in her direction. *Yochanan,* she directed her two young helpers to repeat with her. He pulled one hip up a little, stretching his sides, as he found his muscles and brought blood and nourishment to them. One knee bent and his foot wiggled a bit.

Suri knew he was beyond danger. This young man would soon be back at the monastery and his studies with his mentor. She also knew that he would be changed forever. His thoughts and concepts would include this experience. He would always know that he carried The All within him. He would know that all human bodies hold the wisdom of Sophia, the strength of Apis, and the journeys of Isis and Osiris. He would always hear the name of God pronounced in every cell of every human being he would meet.

He has seen the love of Isis and Osiris and knows that their physical union transcends life and death, thought Mariam. *Will he remember that forever, as well?*

Yochanan opened his eyes and stared right at Mariam. He had noticed her question and answered her thoughts with a very simple *yes.* He would remember. And he would remember her in particular, the first face he saw when he came back. A beautiful face, belonging to a little girl who had loved being held by him, who had learned to feel safe in his arms, and at this moment his whole being wanted her to touch him.

Mariam extended her hand, took his and held it between both of hers. Suri brought a chair over for her. She continued to hold his hand and stroke his arm. He just looked at her and glowed in the golden light.

Suri adjusted the red silk so the light in the room was filtered. His eyes would need time to adjust, and the red would encourage his blood flow. She motioned for Sibyl to make sure that the braziers were fed and would burn for a while. The tea was prepared, and she also poured a cup for Mariam. She observed them as she carried the drinks over. They hadn't broken eye contact. Suri was pleased and relieved. She observed his vital signs improve as the two young people shared life energy simply through human eye contact and loving intention. She decided to leave them alone, but let Anu stay and continue her soft music..

Sibyl and Suri left the room to tell the monk that his student had returned safely. She let him know that she had left him with another priestess who would take care of him in his gentle state and, as soon as she left, he could visit with him. The monk praised the priestesses for their work, obviously relieved that his young novice had come back from his journey. Suri sent Mariam a mental message that she would return in a while, but right now Yochanan was her charge. Mariam sent a grateful reply. *I'll take good care of him.*

They smiled at each other for the longest time. Mariam felt that he shared his experience with her, and she traveled with him through his memories. The other side carried so much beauty. Having seen that beauty, the beauty of this world became more apparent. With the knowledge of the omniscient presence of The All came a profound appreciation for life in its infinite expression. How could anything disharmonious ever disturb all this beauty? With this knowledge within, how could one ever harm anything?

Mariam thought of how protected and loved she had lived most of her life in contrast to her friend Sibyl's unsettling story. She saw how Sibyl had bypassed all of her disturbing experiences and given generously from her heart to a young man she didn't even know. For Mariam it had not been a challenge. There was nothing in her that questioned giving freely to a friend she had learned to trust. Sibyl, on the other hand, had done her own immense inner work to be able to do this. Her relationship with men was limited and circumscribed by her refusal to be intimate with them. Mariam felt that this had been a very intimate experience. It felt more intimate then a physical union, and, suddenly, she understood Sibyl even better. *This* she could do. And she was wonderfully good at it. Mariam grew a new appreciation for her strong and wise friend.

Yochanan was gaining strength, lying still on his stone. In the golden light of the room she noticed that the stone had golden flecks in it. They seemed to radiate glimmers of sparks, little small meteors encouraging him to fully find the life force of his body. She wondered about the relationship between the stone and the initiate.

He heard her questioning mind. This was a topic he knew. At the temple of Onais, they had taught him about the power of metal. Precious metals could hold life energy if you charged it with the right intentions and high enough frequencies. The different frequencies humans could work with registered primarily as emotions. If you evaluated them through different criteria, they would take on color and specific levels of frequency. With this knowledge in mind, you could use chosen emotions for specific effects. You learned to never allow an emotion to be left unchecked. The fact that it would transfer to everything and everyone gave a new responsibility for how the environment was affected. Only when the student was willing to take full responsibility for his daily life would he be allowed to work with enhancing metal. *First you must prove yourself harmless; then you can take on power.*

The stone had been enhanced by priests who had gone through the required levels of training. It was composed of specially chosen wet ground stones and molded to the shape they wanted before it dried and hardened back to stone. The golden specks had been tuned to work with the frequency of love and life. Yochanan was lying on a stone that had been used for this ritual for centuries.

Mariam accepted the teaching he conveyed and felt its truth deep inside her body. Knowing the history of the initiation made her step into the timelessness of tradition. Taking part in something practiced for generations was both humbling and expanding. Gratefully, she thanked him for sharing this information. He simply smiled back to her enjoying the fact that now they both knew.

She monitored his energy level and noticed that he seemed cold. The tea cup from Suri was next to her and she offered it to him assisting him to drink. He took a sip and leaned back into his blanket. Mariam stepped away from her chair and sat down on the stone next to him. He quickly understood her intentions. With her help he rolled on his side making room for her next to him. She lay down behind his back stretching out, matching his body, curving with him. He sighed contently, enjoying her body warmth and the physical closeness after being merged in spirit. She noticed the gold sparks beneath them creating a tingle on her skin.

Yochanan soaked up the healing herbs and the healing intentions vibrating in the room. He felt the protection of his teacher in the adjacent room and of the guides that had helped him travel. His appreciation for the beautiful women next to him sharing her health and love with him knew no bounds. He patted the hand she had placed on his chest and felt his heart warm.

CHAPTER 8

THE FESTIVAL OF BAST
IN LEONTOPOLIS

A DELEGATION FROM THE TEMPLE WAS PREPARING TO travel to Leontopolis for the annual festival of Bast. The city was a little more than halfway from Alexandria to Heliopolis and the priests and priestesses from the Temple of Serapis were natural and honored guests. The Temple of Bast in Leontopolis was responsible for the festival and they welcomed the contribution from the Serapium. Mariam had seen her parents prepare and go to the festival. It was their own vacation away from business and household duties. They had a romantic eye to eachother before they left and came back having participated in a big celebration.

The festival of Bast in Leontopolis was known for its lavish parades, plenty of luscious food and generous supplies of good wine. It was a festival of the arts with entertainment in the streets, music from all over the known world being performed, and exotic guests from unknown places offering their products or their talent. This was also a festival of love and pleasure and people came far and near to refresh their appreciation for life. The rules of propriety were lifted and gave participants freedom to indulge. People would wear more colorful draperies and stronger perfumes than usual. Couples whose love life had suffered would find new enjoyment and people who needed encouragement would find it. Those who were ready to enter the wonderful world of earthly love would find gentle hands and loving bodies. Judgments were low and the spirits were high. It was a time for rejuvenation.

One of the highlights every year was the enactment of the story of Inanna and Tammuz, the ritual theatrical performance of the wedding of the goddess and the king. In olden times the actual King would ritually marry the Goddess, represented by the high Priestess. This was done to secure the fertility and continued wealth of the land. These days, the ritual was still done for continued prosperity, but the King was played by a man chosen by the temple. The Goddess would still be a priestess from the Temple of Bast. Egypt was ruled in a triumvirate with Rome and Greece which changed members quite often. The work by the temples shifted in importance with the influence of new rulers. Culturally, the legend of Inanna and Tammuz was much older than the Roman Empire and a story the people knew and loved. They cheered seeing the holy royal marriage ceremony and recognized the sequence of stages for the inner development of the king. The story originated in Mesopotamia and had taken root in different forms in the expanded region between the Mediterranean Sea and the Persian Gulf. The story of Isis and Osiris was equally old and came from the land around the Nile. This tale of love and devotion would be told by the delegation from the Serapium. The temples continued their traditions, relating the gods to their people, defying the rational hero worship of their occupants.

Sibyl and Mariam found their way to the dining hall where everyone was meeting before they left. There was a wagon that would take them and their luggage to the pier where a barge was ready to sail to the temple of Bast. They would follow the shore of the Mediterranean Sea east for a short distance before heading down a tributary of the Nile taking them straight to their destination.

People waved, recognizing the colorful priests and priestesses and where they were headed. It was springtime, time to think of planting and sowing seeds in fertile land.

The barge had been used many times, but every year it received a new layer of decorations. The people from the Temple would attach new flower wreaths, garlands and fabric buntings. Every year they used the same theme, but found new interpretations. An Apis bull in a brass cutout was attached on either side to the front of the barge. The flower pot of Serapis holding the wisdom of Sophia became the throne for Osiris and Isis. This year they were enacted by Darwishi, one of their priests, and Suri, their usual representative of Isis. They both looked magnificent with the white linen draped expertly around them and golden sashes down their front. The makeup was exaggerated with the black coal lines and the turquoise eye shadow giving a dramatic effect and their jewelry as magnificent as the kings. Darwishi was tall and muscular with a regal bearing, and Suri looked stately and elegant next to him. They were treated like royalty and would stay in character for the duration of the weeklong festival.

Mariam was trying to stay calm with all the excitement. This was a welcome break from their regular work, and her first time to a big, citywide celebration. Her bag with her chosen finery was stored on the larger boat that held their supplies and pulled the barge. Mariam loved festivities and looked forward to wearing her own colorful draperies when they were not representing the temple. She watched as Isis and Osiris found their way to the seat prepared for them, high up so they could be seen from afar. They were situated on top of the pavilion in the middle of the barge which housed necessary facilities for the participants and had lovely draperies in black and white in the windows.

The younger novices were dressed like people of the court of Isis and Osiris wearing simple white linen and colorful capes. They all had been pared in couples and were supposed to sit together and wave as the barge passed the villages. They were told to remember that they were a symbol, a representation for these people, not just a flock of youngsters going to a festival.

"There you are." Ausar, who had been chosen to be her partner, was happy to find her. They found their seats along the side of the barge ready to wave for several hours.

"Don't they look lovely," said Mariam, pointing at Isis and Osiris on their perch higher up.

"I agree, but would you want to have their responsibility for the whole week? We at least get to go off on our own for some time," Ausar noted.

"I look forward to it. Have you been to the festival before?" asked Mariam.

Ausar had attended the festival several times, and entertained her with tales of tigers at the arena, elephants that could do tricks, music she had never heard and food she had would never have tasted before. She had a lot to look forward to.

They arrived in the middle of the afternoon the following day after having been smiling and waving to the gathered crowds who had been awaiting the barge from the Serapium. Mariam joined in the excitement. She felt proud of the group she belonged to and sensed the awe and admiration these people felt for them. Ausar's hand on her back felt reassuring. She sensed the muscles of his chest when she was leaning against him and the strength of his leg next to hers. Her female curves had been duly noted by him and he was truly enjoying himself being so close to a lovely woman in the sunshine floating down a peaceful river.

The barge made berth at the pier in Leontopolis where the priests and priestesses of the temple of Bast were waiting. They were also dressed like a court, and the Goddess and King were in their finery, both wearing head dresses of catheads. The two courts greeted each other, and the court from the Serapium were ceremoniously welcomed. They left the barge gracefully and walked in the procession through town. Trumpets announced their arrival, and athletes dressed as cats prowled between the rows of priests and priestesses. Banners announced the glory of Bast praising the time for planting and the return of fertility to the people and their land.

The streets were lined with people in colorful garments waving palm leaves and flags. There were shouts and laughter and encouragements in many languages. This festival was famous, and the world was out to celebrate.

The procession followed the main street along the markets which had been cleared for the day, but wasted no time in setting up again as soon as the temple parade had passed. They turned and proceeded along the promenade between the smaller sphinxes with true lion heads. Here the space was wider and they spread out giving more space for their acrobats who moved like elongated cats weaving between the procession and the audience. Children in cat suits joined in after them. Soon they had a meowing trail of kittens.

Ascending the steps to the temple, the King and Queen turned and addressed their people who heralded them with a roar. Isis and Osiris walked up besides them, and the courts arranged themselves in a fan shape according to their rank. The tableau was complete. The four main characters were present in the temple. The Goddess of the spirit world and the King of the land were together between Isis and Osiris, the queen of heaven and the king of the underworld. All was well. The people felt that the cosmos was again in balance. Let the revelries begin!

After a long salutation from the people and a blessing bestowed upon them, the courts adjourned inside the temple for refreshing drinks. Mariam felt elevated by the attention from all these celebratory people. The sparkling drink was most welcome and added to her already overwhelmed senses. The master of ceremonies at Bast welcomed them and complemented them on the quality of their procession this year. He talked about the importance of the festival and how wonderful it was to have this occasion to unify the forces of the two temples. They were expecting guests from other temples, as well, but the Serapis delegation was the largest and the only one that would stand next to the Bast people in the ceremonies. He then gave the podium over to a priestess who explained practicalities about meals and sleeping arrangements. They now had some free time before dinner and the evening festivities. Lighter refreshments were presented on trays and there would be bowls of fruit waiting in their rooms.

Mariam grabbed a small thing from a tray as it passed by, pretty as a sculpture, colored like a piece of art. It had a piece of bread to stand on, a piece of cheese and was draped in red and orange vegetables with a flourish of green spiraling around it. It tasted heavenly and she looked for another one. All the trays had different creations that looked equally enticing. She indulged herself in one more before looking for Sybil.

A nap was most welcome in the dormitory space provided for them. Sybil and Mariam shared a sleeping space like they did back in Alexandria, and the girls fell asleep spooning their bodies together for warmth and comfort. The other girls found equally comfortable positions and soon the dormitory had a quiet hum of sleeping, breathing nymphs.

The festival would save the enactment of Inanna and Tammuz for the last night. For the following two evenings the Serapis temple would show the story of Isis and Osiris. The temple steps would be the stage and the whole delegation had different parts to play. Mariam and Sybil were both in the choir that would sing the story. Sybil had a solo where she was going to be the voice of a bird giving Isis a message.

They dressed in their choir dresses in turquoise with golden sashes. Mariam helped Sibyl drape it correctly. It was composed of two lengths of fabric that each fell over a shoulder and down in the front and back. On each shoulder the fabric was cinched with a golden ring which treaded in on the fabric from its end. Then the fabrics cover each breast down the front and spread out in the back. The belt held the four pieces in place. It would show a length of leg in the breeze, which was both cooling and intriguing. It was easy to assemble, but did well with Mariam's expert hand at arranging the folds.

After dinner, they gathered in the courtyard to warm up before the show. Palm trees and flower arrangements were placed on various steps to signify different places where Isis and Osiris would meet. Tonight, the first part of the story would be shown, which contained their courtship and wedding and subsequent tragedy. There was a romantic overtone to everything, but also darker spaces for the evil broodings of Seth, the brother of Osiris.

The audience had been gathering for hours, securing a good spot while eating exotic food from the many vendors offering samples from cultures far away. They made themselves comfortable on folding chairs or benches, on blankets and pillows they had brought with. As it grew darker, torches were lit and big urns were started with their sparkling fires. The musicians came in on the right side of the stairs with their trumpets, drums and rattles. The choir was gathering on the left side.

The show started with trumpets and drums. The voices joined in for a crescendo of sound. The torches stood along the stairs on both sides, and the big urns had tall sparkling flames reaching violently upward. Isis and Osiris were presented before the music exploded in sound. Then it was quiet for a moment before starting with a soft flute tune announcing Osiris coming looking for his Isis. Her sound was a gentle harp melody following her graceful footsteps as she was searching for her Osiris in the gardens.

Mariam knew the tale by heart. The story of the courtship, the marriage, the jealous brother and the devoted wife had been told at many an evening fire and she had seen it enacted in Alexandria. Tonight they would show the trick murder by Seth and the spreading of the body parts of Osiris to the ends of the world. Tomorrow they would follow Isis to many countries as she found all the parts of him and assembles him back together.

So far, Mariam had thought of the story as a tale about the meanderings of the gods. After her experience with bringing Yochanan back to life, her curiosity had been spurred. How far could people go into death and still be called back? The story of Isis was a little extreme, but, if taken literally, she did assemble him back from pieces that had been buried. Had that been possible at some point in time?

Her focus went back to the stage and her part in the choir. She watched their romantic encounters and the preparations for their lovely wedding. The love of this famous couple was shown in tender attention and in the pink and golden setting surrounding them. His brother, Seth, was hidden in dark spaces, spying on their love, growing in jealousy. For their wedding he brought a curious gift; a casket, built to his specifications. He introduced a competition; who can fit inside it? Various people tried, but only Osiris fit correctly. With a slam, Seth closed the lid of the casket killing his brother. The wedding party screamed and dispersed with Isis. Seth remained on stage. To make sure he was indeed dead, Seth took his brothers body out of the casket and cut it triumphantly into several parts showing the audience each piece. The decorations on the steps represented different countries, and Seth traveled around the world burying the body parts far away from each other. Upon his return, he expected to find Isis ready to marry him according to their tradition. An unmarried brother of a dead man was supposed to marry his widow.

Isis was struck with grief and hate towards Seth. She had no intention of marrying him. She vowed to find every single part of her beloved Osiris, regardless of how long it would take, and set out alone with a humble scarf on her head to travel the world.

The choir sang a song of lament as Isis left the stage. The audience praised their portrayal and was looking forward to the continuation of the story the following evening.

Exhausted from a big day, Sibyl and Mariam returned to the temple for an evening meal before the dormitory again hummed with the sound of sleeping nymphs.

CHAPTER 9

Isis And Osiris

THE FOLLOWING DAY WAS FILLED WITH LECTURES by the combined temples. The sharing of knowledge among both scholars and novices was a treasured tradition. After learning more about the healing properties of herbs, a refreshing nap and a nourishing meal, Sibyl and Mariam were again ready to sing in the choir.

In the second part of the enactment, Isis goes looking for all her husband's body parts. Several geographical places were mentioned in the story and on the steps to the temple all the different cultures were presented while Isis searched for Seth's hiding places.

Assyrian musicians performing in the city for the festival were invited to play as Isis visited their country and found a leg behind a rock. She went to the island of Rhodes, and a Greek dance group gave a performance while she found an arm in a cave. Isis went to Gaul and found his head while a romantic song was presented in a beautiful language which intrigued Mariam. A dance group from Spain performed with much drama and enthusiasm while she found his torso. From India the group brought their famous Bengal tiger on stage together with their dancers and musicians while Isis picked up another leg. Isis went to Ethiopia to find his other arm and some part of Mariam resonated with the powerful drums. Finally, an Egyptian group played and after some frantic searching, Isis found Osiris' genitals under the sphinx.

When all of Osiris' parts had been found, Isis brought them all together to reassemble her husband's body. A space had been made ready for her at the bottom left of the stairs resembling a room deep inside the temple. Mariam was reminded of their work with Yochanan, how they had prepared the room, the herbs, the incense and the sounds. Isis did a similar ritual to inspire Osiris' return. She stitched the whole body together and worked for a long time with incantations and prayers to bring him back to life. But even with her devoted effort, Osiris didn't wake up. Exhausted, she crumbled over her husband's still dead body and surrendered to her tears. A little bird came to Isis and announced another option. Sibyl's lovely voice made the bird thrill awaken hope. Isis stood up and waited. The bird issued a warning. Changing the rules of life and death has its price.

The music changed from the soothing tones of Isis trying to gently wake him up, to a powerful clamor announcing the arrival of a powerful being. The big torches were blown out and only the big urns gave their mysterious inner glow. A red light came on inside the temple, and a different cat figure leaped out among the columns. She stopped on the top of the stairs for everyone to see her and greet her with the expected hushed sound of awe.

This priestess was also wearing the hood of a feline, but she was not a charming Bast temple cat. Her hood was black and more elongated. She was draped in shimmering black and wore a necklace of big animal teeth. She turned to show her profile, and Mariam realized that she was neither a cat, nor a lion. This was a black panther. She stood for a moment in a pose that showed her as a powerful predator. Then, with the fast movements of a panther, she came down the temple steps and entered the space where Isis was waiting. She circled around the byre of Osiris in a slow, cunning dance, raising and lowering her hands over the dead body. Light came up from underneath creating shadows on her face. The stealth and power in the priestess' body brought a shiver down Mariam's spine and she forgot to breathe.

The panther cried out an incantation. The words sounded like menacing lashes of a whip and Isis curled her back in response. The cry cut through the air again, and Isis arched her back before falling to the floor. For the third time the blood curling incantation was heard from the black panther, and this time Isis rose to meet the challenge. In a shrilling voice she confronted the panther. The powerful animal stopped her dance. She changed her movements to a lower pose, moved on her hunches, and offered her deal to Isis.

Osiris would have to stay in the underworld. "He is dead," the panther announced. Isis screamed. She wanted a child with him. The panther changed the conditions. Isis will have to spend half the year in the underworld with her husband and the other half here with her child. Isis screamed again. The Panther stood up and declared her final offer. Isis can have a son, if she is willing to go between the world of the dead and the world of the living. Isis accepted with a heart wrenching cry, and collapsed on the floor. The Panther left her shimmering black cape over Isis before she disappeared in light and smoke.

The audience finally breathed. Isis got up. She was now wearing the black shimmer of the panther and was standing by her husband's byre. With a powerful voice she called to Osiris. She called again as she stepped up to where he was lying and stood over his body. The audience watched as the erection of Osiris lifted up from the dead body. At the last call, she placed herself over him and sat down starting a rhythmic motion. The choir joined her as she chanted invocations for the conception. The audience picked up the tone and sang with them, watching the movement of Isis and rocking with her. A dove flew up from between the two bodies, as Isis arched her

49

back, faced the night sky made a guttural scream. The audience shouted in triumph as they followed the flight of the bird. Horus was successfully conceived.

Isis kissed Osiris, crying in grief and elation, before she left him in his chamber. She walked up the steps of the temple, growing heavier as she ascended. On the top step, she lay down and gave birth to her son. Then she stood up, holding him triumphantly for the audience to admire.

The crowd cheered and then cried for Osiris to wake up. He heard the cries of his people and the dead king rose from his table. He left his byre and walked up the stairs to find his family and take his place as king, this time of a different world. At the top steps, he was greeted by his wife and stands holding a protective arm around his Isis admiring his newborn son. The royal family is together again as rulers of their kingdom, the underworld, the place that is more alive than the land of the living.

The audience stood up and roared. The musicians and the choir created a new crescendo as the torches along the avenue of the sphinxes were relit. The people were ecstatic. This was an electrifying performance. Loud approving comments were heard as the audience got ready to go on to their parties and continue the celebration. Breathless, the choirgirls rushed back to their sleeping quarters to change.

"Think about it, she visited seven countries to find all of him. That's devotion."

"Wasn't Suri great as Isis? Who played the black panther? I've never seen that figure before."

"She doesn't come out very often, and the one you saw tonight was an actor. The real black panther high priestess is hardly ever seen in public."

"How could she do it with him? He was dead! Disgusting!"

"I guess if you want it badly enough…"

The discussion went on as they fixed their hair and found new outfits. The choir dresses were hung up and their colorful skirts, tops and shawls came out. A giggling flock of lovely young women fluttered out the gate of the campus behind the temple. The celebration of a whole town was waiting for them.

Mariam and Sibyl walked into a field of sounds and smells that were overwhelming. At first they held onto eachother, bombarded with impressions, all different than what surrounded them at the Temple back in Alexandria. They were familiar with the markets, and they could certainly be noisy enough, but this was different. The evening was lit by torches giving faces a golden glow. Combined with ample food and wine, it gave people a different expression than what you saw in daylight. The effect was kaleidoscopic, faces coming in and out of focus, fabric in black and white patterns, draped shawls in jewel tones, skin tones and hairdos resembling all the different populations of the known world. They passed people talking in languages they couldn't identify. Vendors were selling food with names they couldn't pronounce. Some looked quite delicious; others had strange sea creatures crawling out of wraps which made the girls stop and stare. They finally found something they wanted to try. Soon they were licking their fingers, scooping a spicy yellow stew out of a palm leaf with a piece of bread as they watched street performers prance about. The musicians were everywhere trying to outdo each other, and the dance groups were proudly showing the traditions of their cultures. Mariam and Sibyl had become numb to everything but the horses and acrobats performing in front of them. Wide eyed and mesmerized, their hands continued to move food to their mouths.

"Mariam!" Someone called her name. She turned to see who it was and almost dropped her palm leaf in surprise. She hadn't expected to see him again until their parents arranged for another gathering of their families.

Mariam was speechless. He took her hand and they stood there looking at each other for a while. Then they realized their parents weren't with them, nor were they inside a temple with many rules of conduct. They giggled, dropped their hands and embraced shyly. Pulling apart they looked at each other again and laughed some more. Sibyl had been standing to the side. Then she made a sound to remind Mariam that she was there.

Mariam looked at her friend. These two people belonged to different aspects of her life. She needed to explain. "Sibyl, this is Yeshua. We have been betrothed since we were children. He is studying at the Jewish temple of Onais north of Heliopolis, not far from here. Yeshua, this is my roommate, friend and fellow student Sibyl." The two people so important to her greeted each other.

"I saw the enactment of Isis and Osiris by your temple. The panther made it very dramatic. I've never seen it performed that way before," he said as he licked his fingers from another exotic piece of food they were sampling.

"We hardly ever see the panthers either," said Mariam.

"I've heard they live hidden lives in the secret rooms deep inside the temple," said Sibyl.

Mariam and Sibyl remembered well their own experience in the inner rooms in the depth of the Temple. Had they brought a man back from the land of the dead? Had Yochanan visited the land of Osiris? Yeshua sensed that they knew more than they could talk about right then.

"I'm glad you liked the performance. We're both in the choir. Sibyl has the most amazing voice. She sang the voice of the bird," said Mariam, wanting to keep the conversation in a lighter tone.

Sibyl relished the praise. It hadn't been abundant in her life. She liked this young man who so obviously adored her friend, and wondered why Mariam hadn't said much about him. Most girls who were promised in marriage could hardly speak of anything else. Yeshua seemed kind and cultured and was young and handsome. Mariam had more to brag about than most of the young brides-to-be Sibyl had listened to. Why wasn't she sharing this?

Mariam felt elated having Yeshua so near. She had reconciled herself to being separated until they finished their education, except for the few meetings the parents arranged for. Meeting him here felt like a stolen moment, a gift of time, an anonymous group of hours where it didn't matter who they were or what their destinies held. They were just two young people at a romantic festival bathed in golden lights.

Yeshua was part of a group of students that had been allowed this rare holiday away from the temple of Onais. His days were filled with academic studies of scriptures, both Judaic and old Egyptian works. Rigorous self discipline and adherence to the daily routine was expected. Still, the rabbis had a tradition of taking some of them to the festival in Leontopolis. It wasn't more than a days travel away and usually the students had fresher ideas in their heads when they came back. Yeshua was grateful for the wisdom of his teachers.

Mariam and Yeshua were sharing another leaf with some spiced fish and tempura fried vegetables as they watched a preview of a show that would be at the big arena the following day. Two strong girls seemed to be defying gravity with their somersaults and back flips over the backs of young men impersonating bulls. The announcers proclaimed that in the arena they would be jumping over real animals. Sibyl and Mariam thought it sounded awfully dangerous. Yeshua said that it wasn't as hard as it looked. You had to tune into the animal, feel its movements, and also take in the environment around you. Once you were connected to the whole, your body would intuit your motion in relation to everything else. "If you are well enough connected to the whole, then all the parties involved will move together to support your intention."

"Is this what they are they teaching you at the hidden temple? I thought you were studying old manuscripts covered in desert sand," said Mariam and laughed.

"Yes, I do blow old dust off of manuscripts that haven't been looked at for a while," he replied, laughing with her. "But a lot of those old writings tell you secrets about how to use your body. I've learned a lot about what the human body holds and what it is capable of. I'll share it with you someday." Mariam said she would like that.

They watched the acrobats for a while and agreed that they would like to see the performance at the big arena the following day before attending the enactment by the temple of Bast. They were going to present another strong story in their culture; the legend of Inanna and Tammuz.

Walking along the pier by the river, the three young students were admiring the different boats, relishing this time together, away from strict studies and daily tasks. They bought an interesting fruit drink served in a pineapple and sat down swinging their feet above the water. The golden lights of the festival twinkled in the surface of the Nile as they found their way back to the temple and their separate sleeping quarters.

The following day they went to the arena in the early afternoon. The three of them found seats on the steps for the large audience.

The event started with a group of soldiers entering the arena to announce the entertainments for the day. The movements of the Roman patrol were rough compared to the elegance of the athletes they had seen earlier. Whereas the bullfighters blended with their surroundings and merged with the movements of the bulls, the soldiers seemed to claim their presence by force.

Sibyl felt safer with the Roman soldiers walking the streets contributing to an orderly society. Her family was Greek and Egyptian with some Saxon blood accounting for her blond hair. She was a Roman citizen, however simple her upbringing had been. Mariam and Yeshua were Jewish and Egyptian with ancient royal blood they didn't want to mention. Their families were not Roman citizens and the Roman occupation had a very different meaning to them.

As the performers came running into the arena, people roared to welcome them. It was announced that the techniques these athletes were going to use came from old Babylonia.

Mariam watched them jump and tumble and do their athletic stunts, but her thoughts were elsewhere. She noticed that Yeshua was quiet too, and wondered what he was thinking. Seeing the Romans march across the arena, she was again reminded that they belonged to an occupied country. Even though her family did very well in Alexandria, they would always feel that they lived in exile. The longing for the land of the tribes would always sing in their bodies. Yeshua's parents lived in Judea, but could they walk safely in Jerusalem? Could they claim their ancestral rights? Could they teach the old knowledge? She remembered visiting the city. The Temple had been rebuilt. But who did it honor? Whom was it built for? With the magnificent palace of Herod the Great, the Roman installed King, built right behind it a little further up the hill, which building was outshining the other? Somewhere she could feel Herod acclaim that the Jewish people should be grateful. Contrary to Roman tradition, he had built the temple according to the original instructions by Salomon. He knew it would be futile to attempt to change the Jewish traditions, or to absorb them, like they did everywhere else. *Or had he just been more shrewd about it*, Mariam wondered.

Yeshua felt that Mariam was sharing her thoughts with him. He took her hand, and sent her an image of the golden rounded bluffs and hills surrounding the Temple of Jerusalem. Then he shared with her scenes from the inside of the temple. They walked through the gate to the courtyard where they had met. He motioned for her to stay and watch, then he opened the gate to the area for the men. The space was centered on the steps up to the inner temple where only the priests were allowed. Elevated, the tall square with large impressive doors was only entered once a year. She could see the tall golden portal to the holiest of holies opening slowly. A red light was emanating from the room, flowing out like a smoke as the doors opened wide. In the middle of the tiled floor was the Ark of the Covenant. The golden wings of the angels on top sparkled in the red light. Suddenly Yeshua appeared on top of the ark and stood there with his arms stretched to the sides, bathed in warm, red light, welcoming her.

Mariam turned and looked at him. He closed his eyes and nodded softly to her. She could only stare at him and hold the image for a moment before storing it in her own internal library.

What was Yeshua showing her? It seemed like he was breaking all sorts of rules with this vision. She thought of how old her own culture was, and how different from what the soldiers in the arena believed. Yeshua and Mariam had both been told how important their union was. She was certain that wherever it led them, the Romans would not approve. But how would the rabbis of the Temple respond?

Yeshua held the vision between them for a while. The imagery had surprised him, as well. What was it trying to tell him? He was studying the scriptures preparing to become a rabbi, but there was so much more beckoning for his attention. Studying prophesies of old had its merit, but he wanted to experience God. He had listened to Yochanan when he came back from his initiation at the Serapium. Yeshua wanted the same experience. But he wanted more than that. He wanted to live it every day. Live with the gates between the other world and this world wide open. Live praising God in everything you did. Live with love and equality between people. Live in serenity, simplicity and community.

Yeshua had heard of a place where they lived like that. Every day they were singing. In large choirs including the whole community, singing their praise of God while doing daily tasks, singing in gratitude for the beauty of creation. .

Mariam saw the soft smile which spread a glow on his face. Her eyes showed him that she understood.

"It is called Therapautae," he said. "It is located not far from Alexandria, near the beautiful lake Maryot. I would like to visit there with you. We need to study the community and understand how they live."

"I've heard about them. They practice very advanced forms of healing besides living very devout lives. We send people to learn from them," Mariam answered back, sharing his enthusiasm.

"Good. Maybe we can study there together." They held eye contact for some time, until Sybil broke in.

"Oh, look. The gymnasts are finished. It is time for the bull dancers."

Mariam thought of studying next to Yeshua and blushed in shear excitement. Having just experienced how easily they shared thoughts, she knew that learning together with him would mean shared knowledge. She grabbed his arm and held onto him as the bull dancers were presented. A moment later, the gates for the bulls were opened and the show captured her full attention. As the excitement grew, both girls clung to his arms and Yeshua smiled to himself.

They watched as the well trained athletes planned their steps and ran towards the charging bull. Then, at a measured distance before the bull reached them they would flip and land on their hands on top of the bull's back and then flip over again and come down safely behind the bull. The whole thing happened at lightening speed, and the audience would respond reflecting the build up and the excitement. The bulls would continue running, never catching their fleeting targets. The life-threatening danger made the audience share the performer's intense concentration. Yeshua had mentioned planning your steps intuitively, but one misstep out of alliance could mean instant death.

Sibyl watched the incredibly athletic women do their tricks. She followed one in a minimal green outfit with ribbons flowing behind her as she flew across the bulls. She was especially graceful and the audience followed her every movement. The musicians enhanced the effect. But wait, she got off a little cockeyed towards the bull. Sibyl watched as the young woman had calculated that this bull usually took a little dip to the left, so she had already anticipated its movement. Her hands landed easily on its back, having tricked the bull by knowing its habits, and the audience held their breath in admiration as she landed running behind it.

The show ended with spell binding acts beyond human capacity. People roared in approval as the arena was cleared for bulls and the next show was announced. This time they promised them athletes from India and Bengali tigers. Admiring the colorful silks of the athletes and commenting on the beautiful cat animals, the three friends found their way through the crowd. They had seen their act the night before and now they were hungry and wanted to look for some exotic food.

They found their spot at the pier again after buying something else served in a big leaf. Munching on spicy morsels, they discussed what they would have done to help the performer who had been taken aside with an injury.

"We have people who know how to align the bones," said Mariam.

"And then there are those who know how to regrow an organ," added Sibyl.

"Only the panthers know how to do that," Mariam said in admiration for these peoples extraordinary knowledge.

"And we would supply the herbs to strengthen her system," said Sibyl, proud of her own learning knowing it would still expand.

"You can also heal by raising her frequency. The injury will have caused her to function at a lower speed, and she needs to be ehh…upgraded." Yeshua was looking for the right words.

The girls found his suggestion interesting.

"You have to make sure you exist at a higher level yourself. Then on contact, the lower vibration will want to align with the higher."

The girls liked talking to him. Everything he said sounded so simple, even though many of the concepts he presented were unfamiliar to them.

The afternoon light was changing. It was time to go back to the temple complex and have dinner before the big event of the evening.

CHAPTER 10

INANNA AND TAMMUZ

MARIAM, YESHUA AND SIBYL WALKED THROUGH THE city back towards the temple. They passed the food vendors and the sellers of everything else imaginable. The streets were packed with festival participants and performers. Some were quite entertaining copying people on the street to the delight of others, while the originals walked by without noticing. The exaggeration of walking styles and attitudes were expertly done by actors prancing about to the merriment of their impromptu audience.

Sibyl's head was filled with imagery and sounds. She clung to Yeshua's arm and let his taller head find their way. Mariam was also dazed by the events of the day and held onto his other arm. Yeshua felt responsible for getting the two young women safely back to the temple complex.

They arrived within the gates and went to the dining area where a refreshing fruit drink was offered to them. They agreed to meet later in time for the evening performance before they returned to their own quarters.

"Mariam, you are a lucky girl," Sibyl complimented her friend.

"Yes," Mariam said absentmindedly.

"You haven't told me much about him. How long have you been betrothed?"

"I thought I'd said something." Mariam was not in the mood to justify her earlier silence.

"He knows so much. Where did you say he was studying?"

"He's at the Jewish temple of Onais, north of Heliopolis. His family wanted him to get a solid background in the oldest scriptures."

"You know them?" said Sibyl with a muffled voice as she was pulling her tunic over her head.

"Our parents are friends."

"Oh, so you are marrying the neighbor."

"No, not really."

"Why are you so evasive? Aren't you happy about it all?"

Mariam didn't know how to answer her friend. Was she happy about it? Her vision at the arena came back to her. She didn't really know what the future held. What did it all mean?

Sibyl went for water to wash off the dust of the city. She didn't really understand her roommate. According to her own vow, intimacy held no interest for her. On the other hand, she had never met a charming, learned and gentle man like Yeshua. Mariam should be starry eyed and ready to fly. Sibyl had seen young girls promised to older men that were rough and scary. This story was romantic and beautiful.

Mariam also took off her outer clothes and was supposed to think of what she wanted to wear for the evening. This was the night she had been looking forward to dress for, this was the highlight of the festival, and she had brought colorful and festive clothing to wear. She laid her tunic down on a chair and sat down on her bed. What was with her? Sibyl was right. She should be behaving like a butterfly, not a moth.

Carrying a jar of water for their wash basin, Sibyl came back filled with practical concerns. She poured the water in as she talked excitedly about whom she had met on her way to the water source.

"She asked me if I would help them out. They heard my voice the other night and need a soloist for the part, so they asked me if I would sing it for them. Mariam, are you listening? This is important!"

Mariam brought her attention to Sibyl. She didn't want to insult her friend and from the little she had absorbed from Sibyl's waterfall of words, she would agree, yes, this was important. "What a great opportunity. Tell me more," she said.

"Finally. You're here. They want me to sing the wake up call for Tammuz. I know the song. And they want me to come and practice with them. I can wear the choir dress we use. Oh, Mariam, this is so exciting! Will you help me put it on?"

Mariam helped Sibyl arrange her hair, she made sure her dress draped nicely around her body, and lent her a necklace. Thankful for a distraction she was also delighted for the recognition Sibyl was receiving.

"Thank you, Mariam, you're a true friend," said Sibyl as she kissed Mariam before she ran off, skimming the air like a butterfly.

"The way I should be feeling," Mariam said to herself. She waved after Sibyl, before taking her tired body and brooding head and putting them both down for a nap.

She fell asleep and dreamt about Roman soldiers, eagle standards and shiny swords making clanking sounds. Then her dream changed and she heard Yeshua's soothing voice near her and felt the warmth of his hand in her own.

She woke up feeling much better. Inspired, she found the clothes she had brought with and put together a lovely ensemble in turquoise, red and pink. Delighted to wear something else than the white temple outfits she was looking forward to spend the evening with the handsome man she had been betrothed to for as long as she could remember. The history and expectations had no weight on her young shoulders tonight.

There was a spring in her step and sparkle in her blood as she walked along the hallways feeling the approving hum as she passed people by. She saw him waiting for her in the dining hall. He had also changed into different clothes, but true to his station as a rabbi in training, it was all tasteful layers of natural linen. He lit up as he saw her.

"Mariam, you are beautiful," he said as he pulled her closer and whispered in her ear his delight that they had found each other here. She smiled up at him and just beamed her return of the sentiment.

"Where is Sibyl, I thought she would be joining us?"

"We will see her later. The Bast singers asked her to do a solo at the performance tonight, so she is practicing with their choir."

"What an honor, I'm so happy for her." Yeshua had been totally prepared for having both girls with him, but he couldn't hide his delight to have Mariam to himself.

"Yes, I know it is a rare moment." Mariam had heard his thoughts.

As they left the temple and entered the streets of the city, a silence fell over them. They noted all the details of eachother with heightened sensory perception; the scent, the sight, the sense of his hand on her back, the feeling of her curve in his palm.

She remembered playing together as children and felt the same warm personality, recognized the gentle grace of his body and the innocence of his movements. She wondered and saw how he pulled away from her a little and looked away.

"Look," she said, grateful for the distraction. There were hundreds of white birds in cages assembled close to the stage.

"Doves," he said, "for the performance. The bird of Isis."

Hundreds of white doves, they symbol of love, of Isis and of Venus, were present at their feet. Mariam smiled up at him. She had always loved him, but now she was falling in love with him, one more time. It had happened at the temple, and also at the betrothal signing. He smiled shyly at her, a little overwhelmed by her beauty and the romantic theme of the festival. He took her hand, and guided her silently through the crowd looking for a good place to view the performance from. They had entered their own sphere where peace and quiet reigned, impenetrable by all the sounds of the festival.

The temple steps were again made ready for performance. The props had been rearranged and the choir and musicians had found their places. Mariam thought she saw Sibyl among the choir members. Yeshua found a spot for them on top of one of the hundreds of sphinxes that lined the wide open space leading up to the temple. She sat quite comfortable along its back holding onto its head, and gave him room on its tail end. He placed his arm around her, just as much to steady them both as for the joy of holding her. Mariam relaxed her body towards him and found an eternal moment of perfection.

The performance started with the loud music of drums and horns announcing the characters. Enki, the wise man, was presented in his rich robes and turban. Inanna, the queen, was shown in all their finery. Tammuz was the Shepard king, the young man that marries the queen. Ninshubur was the priestess, and wore a whole palm branch painted gold pointing up above her head. The steps were all lit up and the temple with the columns and roofs was the backdrop. There were more large crocks with fire inside, and torches were being held by men standing as guards along the back of the staged area. Mariam noticed that this night there were also some Roman soldiers among the audience. They seemed to enjoy the festival, and do their job watching for order in the crowds. She didn't see them bother anybody unnecessarily. *I hope they'll enjoy the play,* she thought. *Maybe they will learn some about the cultures of the countries they occupy, even if they consider it only amusing entertainment.*

It suddenly struck her how old this story was. Mariam knew it came from Babylon and had gone through several developments through time before it had become part of their own folklore. The temples honoring the goddesses were still strong in Ephesus, in Baia, in many places in Syria and all over Egypt. These were the places where initiations were offered, where they knew how to lift the veils between the worlds. The Egyptians had known how to visit the world of Osiris and come back for thousands of years. They lived with this in mind every day. Their ancestors and their unborn children were living right next to them in parallel worlds that could be contacted at any time. The spirits weren't hindered by the needs of a human body and could move more freely. The humans needed to be on good terms with them so they could help each other.

Yeshua could feel her meanderings and had his own thoughts about it. It seemed sometimes that the spirit world could be demanding. He was reminded that if you are born royal, then certain obligations follow. Yeshua sighed, and pushed the thought aside.

Tammuz was proposing to Queen Inanna. He presented her with huge amounts of food items, the gifts of a prosperous harvest. She was sitting at the gate of a store house for all this wealth. It had an elaborate double door with carvings and decorations from the many stages of sowing, growing and harvesting. People were carrying huge pots with fruits hanging over the edges, big amphorae with wine and heavy sacks of grain. There was a parade of carriers bringing Tammuz' offer to the queen.

Mariam looked at the pots and recognized the similarity with the pot on top of the head of Serapis. Was that also a reference to the bounty of harvest, a reminder that seeds are the germination and the end product of the fertile fields? Mariam liked how the concepts overlapped and could be understood on so many levels. To her the pot also meant the seeds from the man germinating in the woman to create offspring. It represented the relationship between Isis and Osiris, between the queen of the world and the king of the world beyond. The pot would hold the mixture of their liquids which eventually grew into Horus, showing that humans lived in both worlds, being both spirit and matter. The connections back and forth were endless, and it all served to make people comfortable with the coexistence of parallel worlds.

As Inanna accepted the gifts, she agreed to marry the shepherd king. The shepherd had many connotations. In Egypt it referred to the Hyksos, the shepherd kings who had occupied Upper Egypt. By marrying the queen of the Lower Egypt the kingdom was again united, and the Hyksos was accepted into their people and culture. In Babylon the shepherd king was the Canaanites who also by this marriage got accepted and included. The same was true for the Israelites and the Canaanites. Mariam thought the populations in her known world were a mixture of many strong cultures. Still, her people had insisted on keeping the ancestral lines clean. It was important to know who your ancestors were and which tribe you belonged to. Mariam sighed. Maybe it was easier being like Sibyl, carrying a little from many different cultures?

The wedding was being prepared for with all the finery befitting a queen. This time it was the new king who got the gifts. She presented him with all the ritual objects of a king. He was anointed by the queen's priestess, Ninshubur, who poured oil over his head. He was undressed and covered in new clothes. A majestic robe was put around his shoulders by Enki, the queen's advisor. The king was given a scepter and an orb. Enki entrusted him with the wisdom of how to rule a kingdom. Tammuz was given scrolls on statesmanship, containing instructions on how to bring civilization to their people. Finally, the crown representing the unification of the two kingdoms was placed on his head by the queen herself. The making of the king was complete.

Enki officiated the wedding in front of the gates of the storehouse. The king and queen looked magnificent in their robes and crowns. They exuded serenity and love for their people. Mariam had a sense of being presented with real royalty, not just an enactment.

Yeshua also felt moved by the beauty of it all. The music added to the scenes and the lights accentuated the different vignettes. He knew this was a ritual enacted every year in the full knowledge of its profound meaning. It was a parable for regular people to learn by stories. It was a vehicle for the temple to interact with the people in their care and to strengthen their own work with the multiplied power of human attention. This was the unification of the people with their gods through the work and initiations done at the temple.

While the bride and groom were preparing for their wedding bed, the old poetry of Inanna was being recited. The explicit wording built the excitement of the moment. Mariam listened to the queen asking who would meet her at the gate while the king promised to be there. The queen asked who would plow her vulva, and Tammuz promised to be the man to do so. The priestess and Enki helped them take off the crowns and robes and put them all in designated places so the audience could see them displayed. The gates were again opened, and the storerooms had now become the bridal suite of the king and queen. A bed decorated with flowers and draperies was ready for them. Their last shifts were removed as they walked naked through the gate and stood on either side of the bed. The poetry went on claiming that her vulva, her horn was full of eagerness like the young moon, her untilled land had been lying fallow. The music announced that the king and queen were ready, and they took the step up to the bed and lay down and embraced. The audience saw them from their side and could follow their actions closely. They kissed sweetly before Tammuz positioned himself between her legs. He nuzzled his face in her breasts, and kissed each nipple. Inanna faced the audience and showed her pleasure. The poetry pronounced that Tammuz had sprouted, had burgeoned and was ready. The music was building and waiting for Tammuz to enter her. He met her eyes and smiled at her before finding her vulva and plowing it as the poetry suggested.

"My honey man sweetens me always" announced the voice of the queen. Her fallow land had been plowed and fertilized. Her lover had pleased her.

Mariam noticed an extra squeeze from Yeshua, and she pulled closer to him.

The marriage had been consummated. The young moon was visible above the temple accompanied by a multitude of stars. The king and queen put on their robes again assisted by the priestess and Enki. The store rooms were pronounced full, the harvest was finished. It was time for the land to go into winter. The priestess came and gave the king, the symbol of the fertile time of spring, a potion which he dutifully drank. He lay back down on the bed and appeared lifeless. Inanna woke up and wailed that her king was dead. The gates closed as she wept by the bedside, and the choir takes over as the voice of the people grieving loudly over the death of their king. Nothing will grow while their beloved Tammuz is gone.

Next the king's spirit appeared in a cloud of smoke outside of the doors to the bridal chamber. Ninshubur dressed him as a king one more time. He was ready for his journey to the underworld. Enki came with him to give advice. Seven arches made of young palms had been placed on the temple stairs forming a diagonal line down the steps.

Tammuz was reassured with Enki's presence. They walked across the top step by the gates together. On the next step down they encountered the first gate. Enki sang in a beautiful baritone that it was time for Tammuz to give up his crown. It had to be left outside the gate before he entered. Tammuz took it off his head, looked at it, looked at Enki who nodded back, and dutifully placed it by the entrance. Enki showed with his hand that Tammuz was allowed to enter. He walked through, and seemed lighter as he arrived on the other side. Enki walked around it and met him beyond the gate. Together they walked along the step before they stepped down and turned to face another challenge. At this gate Enki demanded that Tammuz gave up the scrolls about the wise ruling of a kingdom. He wouldn't need them here. Tammuz left them by the foot of the gate, and walked through. The music changed into something more sinister. They walked to the end of the step before turning around on the next step down. At this arch Tammuz had to give up the other scrolls on creating a civilization. Reluctantly they were left before the gate. They walked along the steps to the next arch below. Enki announces that he has to give up his scepter and orb, the symbols of his right to reign over his land. They were heavy to carry anyway, Tammuz could leave them behind. At the next gate he was asked to give up his robes, then his jewelry. At the last gate he has to give back the oil that anointed him. Enki produced a jar and cleared the oil off his head with the edge of his hand and made it flow back into the container. Tammuz looked like a stripped bird.

Now he had lost all the accoutrements of kingship. There was nothing left of any of his status as a king or his relationship to the queen. He was standing there in a thin linen shift, bare footed. The only music was the beating of a soft drum. His shoulders had slumped. The athletic young king chosen for his virility was gone. Tammuz seemed haggard and old. Enki looked at him with compassion. He knew that the trials of Tammuz were not over yet.

The eyes of the king looked vacant. The exuberant glory he experienced as a newlywed king was replaced with a vacant stare. He remembered the queen he loved and knew that since they were in different worlds, she was dead to him, just as he was dead to her.

Enki said something gently to Tammuz. The last sacrifice was near. The drums picked up a serious even beat. Tammuz let Enki lead him to the edge of the steps. In front of them was a gnarled tree. Enki lifted Tammuz off the ground and hung him up on a branch. He tied Tammuz' feet at the trunk and stretched out his arms to the side where he tied them to the branches at his wrists. Enki looked at the dead king, took one step back and bowed in respect before he turned and left.

Tammuz was hanging on the tree like a dead corps. Women dancers appeared dressed like birds. The birds came up to him, pecked at him, eating pieces of his flesh. The musicians made sounds of wind and the choir made the wailing noises of bats. The queen's lament was heard from behind the gates at the top steps. More poetry was recited describing her mourning over the king, her lover. The land was grieving the loss of the virility of the king and their fields. Tammuz had made the last sacrifice. He had gone as far from the world of the living as he could. His eyes closed and a loud sigh was heard. The wailers made a final exasperated cry of despair. Then all is quiet. Even the festival audience went into total silence joining Tammuz in this solemn moment.

A single sound charged through the silence. Sibyl's clear voice started with a sweet single note becoming a tentative aria.

Enki reentered the stage. He walked over to Tammuz and painted an eye on his forehead.

Tammuz slowly opened his eyes and looked around. Enki untied him and helped him down from the tree. Tammuz touched his new eye and showed the audience that he could see the world with singular vision, his head had been opened. He had experienced life and death. He had completed the initiation and had traveled between the worlds.

Tammuz took Enki's hands. He thanked his advisor for having seen him through this ordeal. Enki sent his student off to find his way through the arches again. As Tammuz walked through he picked up all the items he had left behind. At the first gate he was again anointed by the priestess who poured the oil over his head one more time. The audience roared at him. He was again the king. He put on his robes and sandals, picked up his scepter and orb and put on his jewelry. His scrolls went in the pockets of his robe and finally Enki puts the crown on his head. Now, he is ready to meet his queen again.

He stood outside the gate for a moment facing the audience lifting his hands and letting them greet him with shouts of honor and encouragement. Then he disappears in a cloud of smoke.

The doors of the bridal chamber opened and Inanna was still weeping at the bedside. She was sitting there in a shift crying over the loss of the king and the fertility of the land. As the gates opened she looked up, before throwing herself on the dead body of Tammuz with another wail. Suddenly the scene was blocked with white flapping wings. The hundred doves were released. Inanna watched their flight as Tammuz started to stir on the bed. He sighed deeply and she turned to him and screamed in delight. Her king was back, her lover had returned from the dead. The choir sang as Tammuz embraces his queen. Inanna hugged him and they danced around the bed. She called for Ninshubur to help the queen put on her regal attire.

Inanna and Tammuz returned to the majestic appearances of their wedding and together they greeted their people, again united as king and queen. The choir sang a large choral arrangement and the whole orchestra joined in with flutes, strings and drums. Enki and the priestess reappeared and stood to the right and left of the king and queen. The audience roared in approval. The king and queen were together ensuring the fertility of the land for the next spring. The king had been initiated into knowledge of life and death. All is well with the world. The people praised the Temple for doing excellent work.

Mariam and Yeshua both clapped enthusiastically. This was a particularly riveting performance. They were both familiar with the story, and had also seen somewhat different renditions.

"In the last one I saw Inanna went to the underworld and Tammuz stayed ruling the country," said Mariam.

"I guess it can be told that way too," said Yeshua thoughtfully. "The seven levels of initiations were nicely shown. I liked the palm tree gates."

"Wasn't Sibyl great? I'm so proud of her. Maybe now she will get other engagements."

"That would be great. She really is quite talented."

They found that they were both hungry and agreed to go back to the temple and have some of the delicious creations the dining hall had been serving. They left the festival people behind and found one of the many gates to the temple complex.

CHAPTER 11

LAST NIGHT IN LEONTOPOLIS

A T THE TEMPLE DINING AREA THEY WERE serving locally grown vegetables made into small works of art. Twirls of bread, celery, tomato and spinach were served together with pieces of fish spiced to perfection. A glass of papaya and lemon juice completed the meal.

Sibyl emerged among them, all excited.

"How did it sound? Please, please tell me!"

"My dear, you were perfect," Yeshua said. "A newborn baby couldn't have asked for a sweeter tone to awaken into a new world."

"Oh, you are too kind."

"Sibyl, it was beautiful. Did you notice how everything became quiet? Only you could silence a whole festival," Mariam said proudly to her friend.

Sibyl beamed.

"They said nice things in the choir too, but I needed to hear it from you. I've been invited to spend the evening with them. I need to go. I'm sure you two can have an enjoyable evening without me."

She smiled at them, and left before they could protest.

Yeshua and Mariam turned towards each other. A new silence descended over them. He offered her his arm, and they walked into the festival protected by their innocence and devotion to each other.

They went down to the pier again and sat down to look at the boats and the bustling life of celebrating people. The Nile was calm as always. Yeshua threw in a pebble to see a ripple in the still surface and they admired the reflections in the rings it created. She leaned into his shoulder and stared up into space. The stars were abundant and she relaxed into the warmth of his body.

"See the constellations? The Greeks call that one Hercules. But Aquarius over there was named by the Babylonians. Even though people have attached different stories to the stars to identify them, the planets still have their impact on the earth."

Mariam liked to listen to his voice. She had no need to say anything, she just wanted him to continue talking and hold his arm around her.

"The pole star is right there. Right now we are in the constellation of Libra, and Mars and Venus are both in the same water sign. The moon is in Aquarius, and…"

"…we are here together," finished Mariam.

"And we are here together," he agreed as he turned and looked at her. She moved her face towards him and he kissed her softly. Mariam returned the kiss and smiled up at him. Their telepathic minds created a sphere around them, a world which was understood through intuition and insight. This was the language of the stars and the dark night, the language of love and young bodies.

They stood up and embraced. He kissed her again, and offered her his arm as they left the pier and walked back into the city. The noise of the street vendors was irrelevant and the sounds of various animals had no impact. People seemed to move in slow motion and all the lights had soft halos. Their stable point was where their arms united, where they kept a dance between the weight of her arm shifting as she walked and his support of her changing according to her need. They walked with no particular goal in mind, but their feet took them away from all the people who were enjoying the last night of this festival celebrating love and romance.

The young couple sensed a simpler urge between the festival attendants which was different than what they felt between each other. Their profound education made them operate with more refinement. Too much wine didn't appeal to them because it would cloud their exchange of nonverbal information. Among telepaths there could be no secrets. Intentions behind words were felt physically and the spark of God within vibrated between them.

Their feet had taken them through throngs of people, along shouting vendors and endless animals and performers. Now they found they had entered a quieter place. They found themselves back at the steps of the temple with the long colonnade of sphinxes leading down to the water. Since the performance was over, the place was deserted. No food or drinks were offered for sale within the temple grounds so regular festival attendants only came here for the enactments. Both Yeshua and Mariam belonged to groups of invited guests to the temple and were encouraged to explore the vast grounds of the campus.

The din of the festival could be heard in the distance. The sounds here were the warm breeze blowing through the colonnades and the silence of the river. The torches were blown out and the fire in the crocks was extinguished. The gate was still standing on top of the steps, closed, allowing them to study the beautiful carvings on the arched doors.

"Do you think they use this every year? The artwork seems to be too fine for something made just for this evening performance." Yeshua was letting his finger follow the wood carving.

"Probably," Mariam guessed. "The tradition of doing this play at the fall equinox is very old. I'm sure it has a storage space for the rest of the year. Or maybe it's used for other ritual enactments." Mariam was reminded of the one she had seen at the summer solstice. Yeshua could see the image she produced in her mind. She didn't realize that she continued her inner imagery to include her initiation with Gyasi. Yeshua did a sharp inhale of breath and turned and looked at her. His eyes were serious, but without reproach.

"It was my initiation," she explained. "It is supposed to happen with an older, more experienced man. He taught me a lot about the energy ways of the body."

Yeshua's training had been much more academic. He understood that most of what she had learned was taught through personal experience. He appreciated his years of absorbing the old scriptures, but wanted to know how to anchor that knowledge in his body.

He had not been offered this initiation. Yeshua had learned verbally about all the same things, and since he already had a betrothed wife, he was considered lucky. After his wedding, he would be a rabbi. Rabbis were expected to marry. They would be considered half men if they weren't. There were so many responsibilities that belonged to the woman of the household. She didn't just light the candles for the Sabbath; she *was* the light of the family. She prepared the meals, but she was also responsible for the general health of every family member and would have learned from her maternal ancestors how to cure simple ailments. He had learned to respect the balance and the dance within a couple. His teachers had covered a lot of this with their students. But there was no talk of an initiation. That was left up to them and their betrothed wives.

Mariam had had an Egyptian based training. Her continued learning about the health and function of the human body required her own experience of how her body worked and responded. Yeshua understood that, but there was another layer of him that felt something else.

Mariam wasn't quite sure how to respond to this. She could feel his mind working on this issue and could intuit what his inner voices said. Within her education, this was part of her training. She needed that experience to understand human bodies better, but could see that his more traditional schooling would make him see the situation quite differently.

"I needed that initiation to work with your cousin, Yochanan, to bring him back."

"Did you do it with him, too?" His eyes widened.

"No, but I needed to direct the flow of life through his body. I wouldn't have been able to if I didn't know how."

They sat down on the temple steps. This was a lot to take in for both of them. A little distance had been created between them, and they were not touching as they sat down.

"So tell me," he said after some silence. "How does the flow of life work through your body?"

Mariam started to tell him the story of the King and Queen meeting at their different houses. She expanded it a bit, and started with the red forge where the life force is created. Here the King and Queen were created as flames dancing around each other creating two intertwining spirals around the central core, the spinal cord. To cool down they would enter the water and swim to the beach. There the beach house was waiting for them and they were treated to a charming breakfast before they were shown the platform bed in the shaded room nearby.

Yeshua smiled. Being taught in parables was so different than discussing scriptures. The concepts came alive and the imagery gave so much more information.

The King and Queen united, Mariam continued, and, after a refreshing drink, they continued on their journey. Now, they had to walk across the sunny midday meadow with the gazebo where they stopped. They sat down and discussed their roles as royalty. They stood at the entrance and proclaimed to their country what they wanted to do for their people. The people listened and agreed that these two would make a great partnership as rulers. Now, they were invited to come to their beautiful castle further up on the hill. They followed the path through the green meadow to their main residence. It was a magnificently detailed building with all the rooms needed for them. After resting in the green royal bed chamber, they came to a gilded hall where they sat down to a beautiful dinner. The hall had tall windows and opened out to a balcony. They finished their meal and as they walked out hand in hand, they could hear the roar of approval from their people.

As Mariam had been telling her story, Yeshua, had relaxed next to her. He laid down on the temple step and put his head in her lap. She continued her story while stroking his hair. He closed his eyes to take in the fragrance of her flowery perfume. While Mariam had been talking, he had followed her story in his own body. He understood that the King and Queen had now occupied the heart inducing a new balance in their land, the land being the wholeness of the human body. To him, the story was also about himself and Mariam, and he relished the thought of visiting the gazebo, running through the meadow and eventually finding their way to the beach house.

Mariam trusted that he was following her story, and knew that all the places described would make sense to him. She continued with the King and Queen, it was time for them to visit the higher realms of their land. The path went from the castle along the hill and up the mountainside. They found another pavilion with columns for the court of justice. The royal couple was asked to bring their wisdom to the case in process. The King and Queen were united in balance and made a wise ruling. The people liked the decision and the royal couple was encouraged to continue. The path became steeper and rockier. It was colder as they followed the mountainside and the light was waning towards evening. Now they were on their way to the mountain cave.

"Come," said Yeshua. "Let's move a little further up. It is getting chilly."

They walked inside the temple and passed through the impressive colonnades. A couple of torches were lit by the statue of Bast, the black cat, and they sat down on the steps leading up to the black, smooth stone feline. Mariam continued her story as Yeshua held around her to keep her warm.

It was night by the time the King and Queen reached the cave. The guardians outside told them that they had to be silent, no words were allowed between them. It was dark inside, and they were supposed to find their way without the help of a torch. The King and Queen entered, holding onto each other and stumbling along the rocky floor. They realized that their royal finery and privileges would not help them now. They could only rely on themselves and what they had learned as they traveled through their beautiful country. Silently, they expressed their appreciation for each other and their gratitude for having been guided on this incredible journey. Further into the cave they saw a shimmer of light. Proceeding carefully along the uneven ground, they found that the cave had a hole in the ceiling, and the light was from a star.

"I'd like to think it was Venus," said Mariam. "But they taught me that it is supposed to be the North Star."

"I'd like it to be Venus as well", said Yeshua. "You're Venus to me," he whispered into her ear. Mariam pushed him away, he was distracting her story. She had no idea how distracted he was.

Where the light from the star landed, there were two cups filled with a liquid. The king and queen each drank. The drink made them sleepy, and, to their relief, they saw that there was another platform bed for them to rest on just beyond where the cone of light hit the stone floor. They lie down and fell asleep. Their dreams were filled with prophetic visions.

After they had rested for a bit, they were called for the last leg of the trip. They needed to climb to the mountain top and await the dawn. By now the King and Queen were tired. Their clothes looked worn and they felt as if they had aged. Still, they scrambled up the last part of the path along boulders and rocks. Panting, they reached the top and were greeted by attendants awaiting them. Hanging from their arms were new gowns for the King and Queen. They were helped out of their tattered old clothing and the new gowns were slipped over their head. The Queen looked down at her new attire. It was white with an iridescent sheen to it, shaped like a long gown which covered her completely. She admired it and saw that the King was wearing the same. Gone was any distinction between their genders and all the accoutrements that distinguished them as royal. They smiled a little hesitantly to each other and held hands as they walked to the lookout place at the edge of the mountain top. The dawn was about to break and the golden light was visible over the horizon. They stood in silence and allowed the sunrays to reach them one by one. Closing their eyes, they allowed the blending white light with all its iridescent colors to envelop them as they raised their arms upwards, and dived.

"They dived? Where to?" The logic was lost to Yeshua.

"Well, they have to get back to the water," said Mariam matter-of-factly.

"But that would be an impossibly long fall," Yeshua protested. So far, the story had made sense.

"Maybe there is a pool on top of the mountain with an underground tunnel that would take them all the way through back to the ocean surrounding their island." To Mariam this was a perfectly reasonable solution.

Yeshua laughed. As far as metaphors go, yes, that would be totally reasonable. He stood up and took her hands. While he had been listening he had also looked around and taken in the details of the space.

"Where are we going?" she said.

"Come with me, I'll show you."

Mariam had been engaged in her own story. Now she saw that right in front of them, behind the gates they had admired a little bit ago, was the platform bed of Tammuz and Inanna. The gate and the big bed must have been too heavy to move tonight. They were still standing on the top of the temple steps.

They both giggled as they approached it. The pillows and blankets were of the finest of Egyptian silks in deep jewel tones with golden ribbons and tassels. Wide eyed they silently admired it for a moment. Sharing a stolen glance, they laughed out loud together.

Yeshua turned serious and took her hands. "If anyone finds any fault with your education, let it also be mine," said Yeshua. "Let's share this. We'll be separated for many years yet. We need the strength of this memory for the work ahead." She looked into his eyes and shared the solid devotion between them.

Yeshua turned to Mariam, and in one strong swoop he lifted his bride in his arms. She put her arms around his neck and let him hold her for a precious moment, before kissing him and enjoying being gently put down among the royal fabrics.

"Fit for a King and Queen?" He asked as he lay down next to her and pulled the thick cover over them.

Mariam was giggling. There was a bubbling fountain sparkling inside her. She moved closer to him and felt the warmth of the full length of his body. She also felt his hardness against her thigh and needed an extra breath. Yeshua leaned his head in his hand and freed the other to look at her and touch her face. She locked eyes with him and let his hand explore her body. Very gently he followed the line of her neck and shoulder and let his hand rest over her breast. The unbelievable softness, the rounded mound of woman, the delight his whole body felt by having this heavenly honey cup in his hand. He kissed her eyes, her lips, her neck, and pulled her blouse a little aside to reach it with his lips. Mariam sighed. She was a woman doing this with the man she loved. She was the Queen doing it with her King. She was mother earth welcoming father sky.

He lifted her skirt and his own tunic and watched her pull her legs aside for him. Here in the darkness he was invited to dine with the queen in the beach house. Yeshua turned into a fish which found its watery pool. Like the King, he dived and it didn't matter how impossible the fall was. He was with his Queen, he was going to fertilize her fields and they were going to climb that mountain together. He knew that.

"Together," said Mariam as the stars of the night turned into wildflowers in a green meadow.

CHAPTER 12

THE COMMUNITY OF THERAPAUTAE

"HEY, WAIT FOR ME!" MARTHA'S CAMEL WAS a little slower than the others. Lazarus, always the big brother, looked back and slowed his animal.

"Don't let it be lazy, show it that you're in control", he explained to her. He took her camels rope and pulled to bring it up to the others.

They were quite a flock on this outing. The more Yeshua had explained about what he wanted to study at this place, the more the other young people wanted to go with him. His cousin Yochanan was in town on break from his temple studies, and Mariam's brother and sister also wanted to come. Yeshua had the directions for the road, so he was leading the little caravan which the parents had happily supplied. Joseph had also decided to come with to provide an adult among all these excited youngsters.

"Don't worry, Lazarus", Joseph said. "I'll be the last one and I'll make sure no one is left behind. You're doing a fine job with your camel, Martha. Don't let anyone tell you otherwise."

Joseph looked over the young people in front of him. He had watched them all grow up and attended most of their births. Yeshua was the natural leader of the expedition, mostly because it was his idea. But next to him was Yochanan, more broad shouldered and equally studious and educated. They had been study mates at the temple, but Yochanan was further along. Yeshua had been traveling in between as he insisted on learning from other places too. Joseph had already traveled to Hibernia with him, his mother had taken him to Ephesus, and he had traveled many places on his own. Lazarus had been at the Library of Alexandria for some years, and young Martha, also at the library, showed a gift towards poetry.

Mariam on the other hand was the one he found most interesting. She knew so much of the healing arts, just like him. He would like to take her to Hibernia and let her learn from the Druids. But he had heard from Mary that Mariam wanted to go to Ephesus. She was also interested in the secret teachings of Hermes Trismegistus. Mariam didn't just want to learn about it. She wanted to experience it, and, then, learn how it was done so she could teach it to others. Joseph admired her thirst for knowledge and felt she was a fine match for his equally unquenchable son. He acknowledged their fine pedigree, but these two were already a good working couple on their own. He hoped the others would find equally compatible mates. He had heard that Elizabeth and Zachary were considering young Anya for Yochanan. Joseph, always interested in the young, had noticed the young woman and knew she was now studying here at Therapautae. Oh, yes, there was a reason why his parents had wanted an adult to come with. But Joseph also knew that he was the one parent they all felt comfortable traveling with. He was beaming with pride of being the chosen one, and couldn't be more pleased with the plan and the company.

This was a fine flock to be with on this lovely, blue skied day. They all had years of learning behind them and all, except Martha, were considered adults in their society. Still, today, they behaved with the excitement and abandon of children.

The beautiful Lake Maryot was visible as a blue mirror in front of them. The green Mediterranean was on their right and they had just passed another tributary of the Nile on its way to the sea. The landscape was breathtaking in its beauty. Cypresses lined the road and the camels happily trudged along. They passed vineyards and fields of grain. Some Roman soldiers on horses passed them, and they all exchanged pleasant greetings in Greek.

"I've heard they sing a lot," said Yochanan to his cousin.

"All the time. They consider vocal music to be a way of honoring God while doing all their daily tasks. Also, creating these harmonies in your body has an added healing effect."

"I've heard that women and men are treated with equal respect," chimed in Mariam from her camel. "We do that of course at the temple, but these people have more of a Hebrew background, and, with them, men and women are quite separated in their daily lives."

"Anya has written me about her days there, and I get the same impression," Yochanan was warmer inside thinking about the lovely young woman he would soon see again.

"That means you'll have a hard time controlling your wife, cousin," laughed Yeshua. "She has never learned to be subordinate."

"As if you will have it any easier?" Yochanan shot back blinking at Mariam. She wondered how her husband would respond to that.

"As if either of us would want it any other way," said Yeshua thoughtfully. "I am surrounded with strong, wise women. All I can do is bow down and learn." Yeshua made a big sweep with his arm towards her holding onto his saddle with the other.

Mariam laughed. She felt honored and knew that these two good kinsmen had both learned from the partnerships of their parents. She also knew that not every one felt this way.

"Not in Jerusalem," said Lazarus. Growing up with Eurochia and Hiram, he also admired his parent's gentle closeness, but he had seen people live differently.

"Women are not allowed further into the temple than the women's court."

"They don't educate them," complained Martha. "If they don't know anything, how can they take part in any decisions?"

How can you have a fully functional temple without women doing some of the temple duties? thought Mariam. *The mother of creation will not be honored. What do they do in that temple anyway?* She had heard about all the sacrificial animals and thought of it as needless slaughter. She heard about the candles and the worship service, but still wondered what *work* they do. Her familiar temple to Serapis was a workshop. The purpose for all their work was to bring people physically in contact with God. Whether that meant to bring them back to health and balance in their bodies, to honor the seasonal rituals and celebrations, or the more secret work of administrating the initiations to experience traveling between the worlds. The veils were thinner at the temple, there was communication and travels between different realities constantly. *Wasn't that the purpose of the temple, to make sure that the cooperation between the Gods and people was tended to and kept in balance and flowing freely at all times?* In her young mind, Mariam felt that all temples should work the way hers did. The temple in Jerusalem seemed to follow a different track. Unbeknownst to her, she would soon get to know that temple very well.

These summer months, they wanted to learn about this society. They were called Therapautae because of their extensive healing work. People came from far and near with various ailments and were miraculously well when they returned to their families. Mariam had heard about use of small devices to amplify the human effect. She knew how they constantly made sure that they were functioning at optimal health and balance.

Yeshua kept thinking about their daily routines of greeting the sun. They would stand at the shore of the lake and watch the sunrise with raised arms honoring the God of Ra as he rose over the water. They would sing songs in marvelous harmonies, all calculated to carry the frequencies of the light they were bathed in. He was fascinated with the thought of using the quality of sound to live in health and balance.

To bring people into harmony with God, Mariam finished his thought. They had talked about this phenomenon and discussed it in fine details between themselves. They both felt honored and excited to finally be able to see this in action. What techniques did they use? How did their society function?

Yochanan was also interested. He had heard of their rituals with water, and he wanted to know how they empowered the water to have this effect on people. He had heard that since all illness is caused by imbalance in the body, by introducing a powerful element that is in complete balance, the frequency of the body will simply realign and find its own balance. The end result is healing of what was bothering the person, but the treatment is the same for everyone. He had to know more about this, and had asked Anya to arrange for him to study this with the appropriate people.

Lazarus was thinking about the music. How could they compose music for all the different times of the day, different seasons and different purposes, all coordinating with the frequency of the light, the season, the time of day? He was fascinated, and wanted to know more.

Martha had grown up a little more protected in Alexandria. She didn't have the same interest in complicated studies like the others. Her quiet nature made her study people and relationships. She had seen many different ways of living together, relating together, being married or being in partnerships together. She wanted to study how this community functioned. They were famous for having men and women serve equally at their gatherings and in their ways of worship. She needed to know how they accomplished that. It sounded so intriguing, and especially for a young woman growing up knowing that she would be given in marriage at some point. She hoped for a good man, similar to the three handsome men in front of her. Mariam and Anya were lucky.

Joseph could feel their inquisitive minds working. He had his own reasons to be curious about this place. He had heard about a stone that they used to enhance the human body, and about their extremely accurate astronomical predictions. Joseph was also interested in seeing what information would interest each of his young companions, what would they find out. What mystery would be discussed on the camels as they were heading back home?

Anya was waiting for them at a big fig tree at the beginning of the encampment together with one of their monks. They were all greeted warmly and shown to the simple houses which would be their guest quarters for the time they were there. The dining hall was pointed out and they were told when the meal times would be called out. They were encouraged to take part in the activities going on and were told they could ask questions of anybody, except the ones who were in silence. They would wear a scarf in front of their face, and not answer if you approached them. The monk explained that several people would devote their day to silence. Also, singing was encouraged, feel free to join in, and wait with a question until there was a pause in the music.

The monk asked what they were interested in. He had heard from Anya, but he wanted to hear it from each of them. The young friends stole a glance to each other across the flock, and they settled on Yeshua as their spokes person. He explained that Joseph, Mariam and he were interest in the healing arts, Yochanan wanted to know about how they empowered water, Lazarus was the musician and Martha wanted to know about the community. The monk was amused and quickly sent the healers off to the hospital with a name of a person to ask for further instructions. He was the choir director and took Lazarus with him to his own quarters. Martha was left with Anya and with instructions to ask Mirella for more information. The monk was totally pleased with this group who had come to study. He was tired of the tourists who just came to look. The sick came for healing in a steady stream and few of them asked how they were healed. This group of people wanted to learn. He put an arm around Lazarus' shoulder and walked off towards his own sparse hut.

Martha noticed the green land around the lake. The small houses they lived in were simple, but comfortable. And there seemed to be many different ways to live here. Anya explained about the dormitories, the bigger sleeping houses where the unmarried ones were housed, and the smaller buildings which were for families and couples.

"So, if Yochanan moves in here, we would have a house like that," she said pointing at a charming little house with a tree and some plants growing near it. "The fields are over on that side. Most of the things we eat are grown right here. The only things we need to go to the market for are spices, but we could actually live without that, too. No animals are slaughtered here; we eat only vegetarian food."

"I look forward to learn," said Martha.

"Come with me. I have kitchen duty this afternoon for the evening meal. You can learn the songs. We'll practice while we work." Anya took Martha's hand and they ran towards the big building where all the food was made. On the way there they passed the workshop for spinning and weaving. Martha looked through the door to the open hall and saw looms at work with both men and women operating them. There was hand spinning of linen going on, and she saw a woman teaching a young man how to do it.

"The linen field is on that side, and the sheep are with the shepherds up in the hills." Anya whispered to her since all the people in the hall were singing gently back and forth in an answering song. It gave rhythm to the movement of the weavers and the spinning wheel full of wool on the bottom of the string seemed to also take its rhythm from the song.

In the kitchen, Anya presented her friend as her fiancés cousin's fiancés sister. The cook raised her eyebrows and was relieved when the girl was called Martha. Could she chop vegetables? Martha ensured Mirella that she was quite good with a sharp knife. Mirella smiled and resumed her singing while guiding them to cutting boards, carrots and spinach.

Martha was happy to be put to work. From here she could observe and, maybe, ask a question or two if there was a pause in the singing. The melody was simple and the words thanked God for the fruits of the earth and the trees and hoped that the kitchen workers could give this food the blessings and love that would enhance the food for the people who would eat it. Martha already was a fan. The idea that food would take on the moods of the people who prepared it and affect people accordingly was not new to her. But to consciously imbue the food with good intentions was a new concept. And to keep everybody singing, creating this gentle vibration of well-being between themselves while they made nourishing meals for the rest of the group, was soothing to her. She had seen her share of kitchen help not getting along over the smallest things. Here they didn't really have a chance to argue. The singing made you communicate differently, and the potential cruelty of words was gone. Martha picked up the melody, a knife and a carrot and smiled at Anya who had done the same. Their thought patterns melted with the others in the kitchen and it simply hummed *soup*.

Lazarus went with the monk who called himself Sutek. They walked to another mud house with wooden thin trunks on the roof covered with big leaves from the palm trees. It had a wooden door and shutters on the inside of the window openings to shield from the bad weather that sometimes would come. Otherwise the temperatures around here were almost the same year round, and they could keep a continuous growing season.

Sutek was also one of the farmers and spent every morning working in the field. "While singing," he added to his eager young student.

The afternoon was devoted to his study of music. At his advanced age, working in the field became too hot after the noon meal, and the community had asked him to spend more time on their expanding music program. Inside there were drums and flutes, lyres and other stringed instruments Lazarus had never seen before. In the middle of the room there was a big table and pieces of papyrus was stacked in piles on shelves and chairs everywhere. Sutek cleared his throat and welcomed Lazarus to sit down. Lazarus realized he would have to move something before he could do so, but he gently lifted some sheets of papyrus and a long stick instrument with a string on it over to the table. Sutek found his favorite chair on the other side, and asked Lazarus if he could read musical connotations. Yes, but maybe not exactly the ones Sutek had on his papers. Sutek gave him the one stringed stick and a papyrus notation and said; "Play this."

He tried not to be nervous. He tried to figure it out without appearing ignorant. Sutek was in no hurry and let his young student take his time. In fact, once Lazarus could quiet his mind and actually focus, it was not complicated. The one stringed instrument had lines on it. For each segment there was a symbol. On the papyrus he found the same symbols. Above the symbols on the written material there was either one, two or three short upright lines. That had to be the beat. One line meant one length of beat, two lines made double that time, and three made it triple. To make the sounds you had to push down on the string with a small flat piece of wood to shorten the string. He tried for a little bit, and soon had a short sweet little melody, sounding somewhat like a lullaby for a child. "Or a way to put sheep to sleep", said Sutek. This song was for the shepherds when they gathered around their fires at night. Lazarus would totally agree that this sounded like a good song for tired sheep. "But how do you make a song for the morning?" he asked. "How do you make it sound the way morning feels?" Sutek loved the question and waited a bit with the answer.

"Each part of the day has its own tone", he explained. "Each part of the day has its own favorite interval between the first tone and the next. Each part of the day has its own rhythm. So, everyone here knows which part of the day it is according to how we sing it." Abasi, another monk, helped him with words. The kitchen people needed words about the ingredients they were working with. The farmers needed lyrics about the earth and the fruitfulness of the harvest. The shepherds needed melodies and lyrics about sheep and goats that would inspire the shepherds to take care of the animals, and the animals to behave like ideal forms of themselves.

"Plato, have you read him, young Lazarus?"

Lazarus had indeed read Plato, the philosopher, and a delightful discussion about Plato's ideal forms kept them engaged until Sutek remembered that they were also supposed to be singing. As an exercise, he encouraged Lazarus to sing his arguments back to him, and Sutek would sing his answers while trying to keep in mind the proper song and rhythm for late afternoon. They laughed as they stumbled with the song, but continued anyway, being immensely amused.

Yochanan had walked with the others to the hospital, but when he stated his interest in water he was redirected towards the woods further away from the village. There was a small stream there; it probably came from the Nile at some point, but here it traveled over the stones and rocks in a crystal clear stream. He noticed the children had been sent to get water and were standing at the platform where it was easy to fill their buckets. There was also a system of reeds bringing water to the main kitchen, but if you wanted water for your own use, you'd better carry it on your own. He assumed that the children were instructed to clean something. Further up he found a waterfall and next to it on a flat grassy spot, there was another interesting house. He had seen where the mud bricks were fabricated down by the lake, and all the houses were made with the same materials, sturdy bricks and reed roofs with palm leaves on top. Not the fanciest of building materials, but actually quite sturdy, and easy to replace as needed. Yochanan admired the ingenuity of using these old techniques that had proven themselves reliable over thousands of years. They could so easily be made into any shape of building you wanted. The one he was approaching had a tower on one side that was three stories high. This seemed strange to him, but he was soon to find out why.

Yochanan found himself alone by the waterfall, and sat down to gather his thoughts for a minute. The sound of the water coming down had its own melody and rhythm, and he created a hum to accompany. He tuned into the water in front of him and allowed it to flow through his mind as it flowed in the landscape. The sounds of the water resonated with him and created a little melody with a beat. He gave voice to it and felt the trees making small movements towards him.

After a while he heard a door creak and an older monk came out of the strange house with the tower. He had a gray beard and his long shirt showed the wear of the desert. As he came closer Yochanan noticed that the monk was singing the same tune that he himself had been humming. The older man walked over to Yochanan and sat down besides him, still singing the little melody that resonated with the sounds of the water.

"I didn't think others could hear the song of the water fall", he said to Yochanan after a while. "You must really appreciate water or you wouldn't have heard it."

Yochanan had to admit he hadn't given much thought to it; the tune just seemed to fit the moment.

"But that's it! The way is to find the song that belongs to the moment. You found the song of the waterfall and you did it all by yourself. Good work, young man, excellent. What can I help you with?"

Yochanan was pleased with the compliment. He had never considered himself particularly musical, but apparently, intuiting melodies from water was easy for him.

"I want to learn what you do to the water you use for cleansing people's bodies. What do you do to it that makes it so effective? Why do people feel that their spirits are lifted, their bodies feel better and they have peace inside after they have been dipped in your waters?"

"A noble pursuit I'm sure, young student, but I can't teach you that in one sweetly sunny afternoon. This takes preparation and time, both of you and the water."

"I can stay. I want to learn." Yochanan was direct and adamant. He hoped he wasn't too pushy.

The monk seemed to like his approach, but repeated that it would take time. Yochanan didn't care how long it would take. He needed to learn this.

"I need you to commit to staying until you have mastered this. There is nothing more dangerous than someone with a little knowledge." The monk shuttered with the thought of Yochanan thinking he could do this and dipping people in water that hadn't been properly prepared.

"Remember, don't confuse the ignorant. And never teach something you haven't yet mastered yourself." Yochanan promised.

The monk invited Yochanan to follow him up to the building. Yochanan noticed the beauty of the stream and the meadow they were passing through, and the blue water of the lake blinking behind the cypresses forming a line between fields. The tranquility of the setting was extraordinary. As he came closer to the building he turned and looked at it all one more time before following the monk through. He knew that after he entered that door his life would never be the same again.

Yochanan wasn't quite sure what he expected. A blessing he could say over the water? A new incantation that carried the vibration of water in a more exalted state? A meditation that was required of him before he touched the water? Any of these things would have made sense to him. Maybe they needed to prepare him with prayers and fasting before he could bless the water source, and that was what would take time? He had heard about the 40 day fast and that there was some special bread to eat. His head was full of earlier impressions, all the scriptures he had studied, all he had heard from the scholarly rabbis at the temple. What he did not expect was what met him inside the door.

What first struck him was the sound. He had gotten used to the idyllic sound of the waterfall outside. Inside this building there was water being directed to go in pipes, ditches and trays in every which way. Water was dripping, rippling, pouring, running, being pumped, being carried, being directed in a complicated system of guiding it through various processes before it was delivered in a huge receiving tub.

After his eyes had gotten used to the dimmer light and he could take in what was going on. He was staring at a huge contraption designed to guide water in specific ways. At the end receptacle tank it still looked like water. Did it have a different light to it?

"Over here," said the monk, who had introduced himself as Enoch. If he had said Noah, Yochanan would have thought it more fitting, but he knew Enoch to be a respectable priest of antiquity and left it at that.

"First of all, don't touch the water as it is running through. Your own vibration will change this process." Yochanan nodded.

Enoch was standing in the staircase that surrounded the water system. He motioned to Yochanan to come with him. Yochanan took in the height of the staircase, the sizable contraption next to him, took a deep breath and stepped onto the bottom step.

"I will explain how this works, and next I will expect you to set up your own water enhancement system. When you can reproduce what I have here, I'll say you have mastered it." Yochanan took one overlook of the wooden trays, the reeds, the bamboo pipes dripping water everywhere, and thought, *yes, this will take some time.*

"First the water is guided in from the creek above the water fall." Enoch pointed to a wider pipe taking water in at the top of the tower. At the top of the staircase he could observe clean water coming out of a reed and starting its route along various gutters through different trays on its way down.

"First it goes through this tray with manna in it."

Manna? Yochanan hadn't heard of that substance other than in the scriptures about the Exodus of the Israelites. He thought it had something to do with dew drops, or maybe something God just let fall to the earth to feed his people. Both sounded somewhat fairytale like, when he thought about it. He looked into the round, shallow tray. The water swirled around in a counterclockwise fashion before exiting through another gutter and was guided downwards. In the bottom of the tray there was some white sand.

"Is that the manna? What is it?" Yochanan asked.

"Gold."

"Gold?"

"Gold. In it's white powdered form."

Yochanan understood that it would behoove him to be quiet.

"After the water has been in the manna, it goes down and visits the crystals."

He followed the water stream as it splashed along its gutter and saw it enter another tray. This one was more like a tub, deeper and cylindrical. In the center of the tub, suspended between its sides was a spiral. It was made of some glass like material that shone with many colors. Yochanan wondered what it was. Was he expected to make all these devices? He would need some help.

The water swirled around the spiral and he could feel that something powerful was taking place. He noticed there was an extra item hanging outside of the tub where the spiral was attached.

"See the batteries on the sides? Elektrikus!" said Enoch proud. "Got them from the temple at Serabit."

Yochanan had heard about Serabit el Khedan. The temple of Onais north of Heliopolis where he had studied was in close communication with them. Serabit was located in Sinai and was the biggest workshop temple in the world. They were mining too, refining all the metals and materials you needed for the work at the temples. Yochanan could feel in his body that he was touching very secret information.

"Yes, that's right," Enoch communicated back to him, having picked up his thoughts. "And I would never have invited you in here to see if you were just curious. But you understood the water. You picked up its song. And you asked sincerely to be taught."

Yochanan felt honored and humbled at the same time. He would do whatever was asked of him to be allowed to continue.

The last tub for the water to go through had another glass like device in it also connected to the famous Elektricus! Yochanan understood that the two devices on the sides made an energy current go through the glass like spiral which somehow changed the quality of the water. His work with healing people had taught him about currents and how you can heal someone by bringing the currents in their body to balance. The theories behind this seemed to be following the same lines of thought, just amplified. Yochanan was not just fascinated, he was mesmerized.

"Now if you're going to work with this, you'll have to first work on yourself."

"I'll do anything!" blasted Yochanan in his thoughts with the enthusiasm of youth who do not generally know what they get themselves into. Enoch sighed.

They had come to the bottom of the staircase and were following the water along the one story part of the house to where it was collected in a larger tub. Some younger monks were busy filling amphorae, labeling them and storing them along the walls. They looked up when they saw Yochanan and nodded at him not interrupting their work nor the soft melody they hummed. He recognized it again as being the simple little tune he had started outside, but the monks were improvising along the theme.

"Give our guest a cup of our good water. This is Yochanan and he will be working with us for a while."

The monks smiled at him, and one of them found a cup, poured some water from an amphora and handed it to him. Yochanan made the sign of gratitude to the young monk and to Enoch before he tasted this special water which was going to mean so much to him and many others.

How did it taste? It had an oilier substance than he expected, and it tasted faintly sweet, like honey. Otherwise it was water. He looked at it. In the dim light inside, it seemed to have a little glow to it. He drank it up and returned the cup to the monk and thanked him. The monk looked at him with a friendly inquisitive smile, but Yochanan wasn't quite sure what the question was, so, he just smiled enigmatically back.

CHAPTER 13

ASPIRATIONS

Three months had gone by before Joseph led the camels and his young charge back to Alexandria. He had been looking forward to listening to them discuss their adventure, but the flock was surprisingly quiet. They didn't really want to leave. Living with these good people had made a great impression on them. They were familiar with the similar groups near Bethany where Joseph and Mary lived, but it wasn't the same. There was something about the lake, the setting, the remote location containing everything a community would need to sustain itself. It was its own little paradise.

"*They didn't seem to age either,*" Joseph added to their shared thought field and made them all laugh.

"Oh, Sutek seemed old enough," said Lazarus. "Although for his advanced age he was surprisingly agile."

"Enoch could have stepped out of the scriptures. I have no idea how old he was, but he seemed ancient," chimed in Yochanan.

"He certainly gave us enough to work with. I know all about bamboo pipes at this point." Yeshua had been helping Yochanan build his project. Together with Joseph they had made a miniature of the system inside the building.

"Thanks, cousin. Will you help me build a bigger one at Bethany?"

"Another one? Are you serious?"

"Yeshua, this is what I want to work with. This is what people need. Think of how many people we can heal, how easy it would be. We can raise the vibration of all of Judea!" Yochanan was pure enthusiasm.

"But, Yochanan, this is very secret knowledge. I don't think the elders would like it if you present it to the public without some preparation." Mariam was cautious.

"Oh, we won't let them know how it works. All I want to do is to raise the vibration of their hearts. What harm can there be in that?"

"It is a noble ambition, Yochanan, but Mariam is right. We have to be careful." Joseph felt that they needed an older perspective, although he didn't want to curb Yochanan's enthusiasm. "What do you have in mind?"

"Well, you see… I've thought about this for a while, and I figured if we built it like this." Yochanan was unstoppable.

He had been refining his idea as they had been working on the model. Here they had built the water ways with bamboo and numerous trays and pipes to guide the water through all the different refinements. Water had been siphoned off after each process for different purposes. Only the very last water was used for the most secret rituals. He didn't plan to go that far.

Joseph's willingness to help had been of immeasurable value to Yochanan. He could never thank this man enough. Joseph was thirty years younger than his revered father Zacharia and obviously more fit to make this journey with them. As they worked together, he had learned to admire Joseph's practical sense and his subtle leadership. Yochanan took Joseph's advice seriously, and he wanted him to approve of his idea.

The river Jordan had a tributary flowing freely towards Jerusalem close to Bethany. Yochanan was familiar with it; he had played there as a child and had carried water from its pools many times for his mother. He knew how this tributary twisted and turned creating small pools and eddies one after another as the brook bubbled and splashed down the hillside. All he wanted to do was to put the effects he had learned about in the water as it passed along its already established path. No building needed. And, then, he could make his baptismal station at the larger pool at the bottom. To the people who came to be baptized it would just be water. It wouldn't look any different, and if they walked up the brook to check, they would only notice some different colored stones here and there if they were observant.

People would be baptized with water that had had its vibration altered which would affect each of them in a healthy way. The water would improve the balance in their bodies and make them feel better. Whatever ailed them would be improved. The simplicity of this plan overwhelmed even Yochanan himself.

Joseph had listened to his explanation together with the others. This might actually work, he thought. The elders might not even find out. The idea was ingenious.

"But Yochanan," protested Mariam. "We aren't supposed to treat people without their permission."

"If they come to me and ask to be baptized, that is giving me permission to heal them," Yochanan insisted.

Joseph had to agree that he had a point.

"But do you really want to bring this to just about anybody?" Yeshua was still not convinced.

"It cannot harm anyone. It can only heal. It can only bring people into better harmony with each other and the world at large." *Yes, the world at large.* Yochanan was getting inspired by his own words. "Lazarus, help me out here. You know about harmonies."

"Eh, yes." Lazarus was usually the quieter one among them. "I got to learn about the importance of harmonizing with each other when you share a task, with the time of the day, with the season of the sun. All this has its own vibration."

"And in the heart there is a small part that works independently from the rest of the body. It resonates with harmony and realigns itself, creating a new rhythm." Martha had spoken. They all turned and looked at her.

"What?" She said and looked at them. "They showed it to me on the heart of a sheep they had to kill. Humans have the same feature. We want to raise our vibration. We want to live from love all the time, and we have an internal device that helps us with that. It's when we forget and feed the wrong raven that we lower our tone."

They had all heard the story about the two ravens while they were sitting around the fire in the evening. The people of Therapautae were great story tellers, and this one was told many times to the delight of their children and their guests. The story tells of an old man and his grandson discussing the two ravens battling inside all humans. One thinks good thoughts and one who thinks bad ones. The child asks which raven will win the battle. The wise man answers; the one you feed.

They all got the concept that your thought patterns are powerful and will control you, unless you observe your own thoughts and make choices. Martha made it clear that the physical body responded to the quality of thoughts.

This was what Joseph had been looking forward to. This was what he wanted to hear on their way home.

Mariam was quiet. Joseph had noticed, but didn't want to disturb her. She had her right to her own thoughts.

Mariam felt that they had visited a Utopia. Was this a form of paradise? Life isn't that simple. Or is it? Mariam was struggling with conflicting feelings. She was not attracted to overt simplicity. Her teachings at the temple were complex. There was always another level of understanding. Life had so many fascinating intricacies. The constant singing at Therapautae made her brain soft. It bothered her that the others accepted everything without discernment. She admired Yochanan's enthusiasm and was glad he had found something that really excited him, but she sensed something ominous about his project. She wasn't quite sure if he showed the proper respect for the teachings that had been shared with them. Had he spoken to Enoch about his plans? Mariam was quite concerned, but she didn't want to be the one who ruined it for him, so she kept it to herself.

Yeshua had also learned something he wanted to test out. Just as he had helped Yochanan figure out the water alteration system, Yochanan had helped him build a small device he could hold in his hand. It had some of the same principles as the water system, and could enhance the effect of his healing. They had made a coiled spiral of quartz crystal with a ruby inside that fitted nicely in his palm. The effect could be extended with a rod to reach further. The principle of it was simple. It would enhance the charge you sent through it. You would use the electrical charge present in the human body and amplify it. A highly evolved human being would send his intention through the device, direct it to someone who was ailing and it would immediately affect the patient's condition. It would only do one thing; it would raise the vibration of the body, which was usually the only thing needed. Healing was more a question of realigning a frequency pattern that had gone astray back into the powerful frequency of life itself. This was the way Yeshua wanted to heal. This is the only way you ultimately could heal. All other techniques were eventually trying to do the same thing; realign the body to life. Yeshua wanted to be more efficient. He wanted to heal larger groups of people.

Mariam was riding close by him, and she could hear his thoughts loud and clear. How could he keep himself from becoming enamored with the admiration he would receive? How could he remain humble and without glamour if he worked in this way? If he healed crowds, he would have crowds following him. He would have crowds thinking he could save them from anything, from the trials, tribulations and the learning of life itself. Mariam was worried. One thing was having the noble desire to heal people. Another was spreading knowledge among the common people that usually was privileged students of the mysteries. Nothing scared her more than an excited crowd looking for a leader. Any loud suggestion would be followed with no thought of the usually regrettable consequences.

Joseph had his own revelations on the trip. He had learned more about the bread that was served. The daily bread baked at the common kitchen served with every meal was delicious. It seemed to embody the blessings the grain received in the field, the singing of the field hands as it was harvested, threshed and ground, the blessings of the people in the kitchen and the blessing of the food as it appeared on the table in the evening. Their daily nourishment had been like eating solid hymns. But that was not the bread he had been studying, even though he had enjoyed it like medicine for life.

He was talking about the bread that was served every forty days in a ceremony led by the elder healers. They had the same tradition among the Nazareeans and the Essenes. Both groups worked with the miners in Qumran. Joseph wanted to know more about it. His nephew through his wife was considered the new hopeful among them. Consequently Yochanan's family was given the knowledge. Joseph was a little further removed and not included in the most secret things. Here at Therapautae they welcomed his questions and were happy to share as soon as they saw his sincerity. Joseph knew that this was going to be important in the near future. He also sensed what Mariam saw. They both felt that the activities of these young enthusiastic men would cause unexpected changes.

Young Martha had also visited the colony in Bethany. What scared her was the group of young men with weapons among them. The helmets with eagles on them were also walking those streets. Why did they have to leave this wonderful colony?

Lazarus saw both his sisters turn melancholy. He understood that they were worried about further development which they both intuited. He also heard Yochanan and Yeshua become filled with confidence and excitement. All he wanted to do was sing the song that spoke of this sunny afternoon and his trusty camel. And he wanted to learn more. He wanted to be initiated into the mysteries just as Yeshua and Yochanan had been. He knew Mariam knew how.

"Yes, I do," Mariam shot back at her brother. "But in the safe confines of the Temple and under the strict guidance of Suri. What are you thinking about?"

"You know the cave close to Mary and Joseph's house in Bethany. That's what I thought would be a good place."

"You don't know what you're asking for. If it is not done right, it could kill you."

Mariam didn't like how all this was developing. Her young friends were playing with ancient knowledge which had been hidden for a long time for good reasons. She didn't want to go to Bethany. She wanted to go to Ephesus and learn more. She wasn't ready to work with Yeshua and Yochanan and their overly courageous schemes, and she didn't think they were ready either.

Joseph heard her. He reassured her that he wasn't going to let them do anything dangerous. He trusted the intuition of his daughter-in-law. Mariam was grateful. She felt a bit better and joined in with her brother's camel song.

Deep inside, she knew that the time was coming closer where she would have to be continuously at high alert. Her whiskers needed training.

CHAPTER 14

MARY SPEAKS:

THEY WERE SITTING ON THE DECK OF the boat taking them to Ephesus, when Mary touched her arm. "And so Mariam, as your husband's mother, and also becoming yours, I think you need to know my story."

Mariam sat down to listen.

Hibernia is very green. The hills are gentle, the meadows abundant. Animals thrive there, cows, sheep and goats. The cragged coast line makes good defense and are dramatic to watch. The ocean comes in and splashes noisily against the land sending tall geyser like frothing spears of water. The wind sweeps across the land never leaving any scent for long, except for the salt green sea.

My parents never tired of telling me the story of our ancestors. They felt it was important for my education, and they wanted it to be as natural for me as the thick goat milk you serve the little ones to make them grow strong.

I learned of Scota and her husband Gaythelos and their journey from Heliopolis to Hibernia. The Egyptian princess had to escape to avoid death and she decided to look for new land for her entourage to settle. They tried on several coasts, but were treated as invaders, so they continued north until they reached a green beautiful island where people were more welcoming. Here they settled and found the landscape inviting, albeit quite different from their Mediterranean shores.

Scota was the daughter of Akhenaten, who later became Moses. He was the son of the pharaoh and his wife, the daughter of Joseph, Pharaoh's trusted advisor, the dream interpreter. Young Scota had to leave Egypt when her father was overthrown for teaching the religion of his mother's ancestors. She and her Greek husband brought with them the worship of Aten, the one God, and his symbol, the sun Ra. Among the people they brought with them were priests and scholars who established temples in stone and great schools of learning. The natives found that their ways were peaceful and not too difficult to bridge, and they learned from each other.

Eventually other people came, as well, and expanded the population with new ideas and customs. Still, the original flock had set the tone for the unfolding of this civilization.

The priests and scholars had left their mark. The druids of Hibernia accepted students from all over the known world who came inquiring with open minds. They taught astronomy and mathematics, anatomy and the healing arts, as well as the mysteries of their religion.

Miriam, I am a direct descendent of Scota. Her grandfather was Tutmose III, the first pharaoh of the eighteenth dynasty. Her mother was Tiye, daughter of Joseph, the pharaoh's adviser, one of the twelve tribes. I am a legitimate princess of both Egypt and Israel.

My mother Anna made sure I always knew that. We lived in modest ways, but, still, people knew who we were and treated us with respect. Being on an island meant we had to travel by sea to engage with the world, and our people became expert seafarers with good ships. There was always an influx of people, goods and ideas, almost like your familiar Alexandria, but on a much smaller scale.

I was fifteen years old when I had a vision. You know that place you go between wake and sleep, where the Gods have an easier time speaking to you. While in this state of mind, I was told I needed to go to Heliopolis and conceive a child and give birth to him in Jerusalem and name him Yeshua. I should not be afraid, I would be protected.

The message didn't make any sense to me. It did not give the name of the man I was supposed to meet in Heliopolis. It did not tell me how to get there. And what would I do in Jerusalem?

My father Joachim was not happy about this. He respected visions, but the implications of mine were disturbing. Yes, I was a princess of both the countries mentioned, but he was much more comfortable letting that be a small factor in our life on Hibernia. One thing was having a child in Hibernia by a good man of my parents' choice. A wedding first would be in order. Any child of mine would be carrying my bloodlines, and while it was a small matter on an island far north, it would mean a lot more in the countries of Egypt and Judea. He didn't like the way the Gods made the fact that I was a princess justification for giving me instructions to produce a child.

Being a practicing druid himself, he asked the druidic priests for advice. They consulted at length and asked me for details about my experience. Then they asked my parents if I was a pious daughter or if I was prone to hallucinations. After meditating on the issue they called us back. Imagine what my mother felt, taking her young daughter to a discussion about childbearing with someone totally unknown, or possibly with God himself? She knew me as a serious student and obedient daughter. It would be against my nature to have made up something like this. My mother Anna didn't know what to think.

The druids advised that I should make the journey to Heliopolis and present myself at the temple there. They would know what the vision meant. My brother Joseph had traveled the route many times. He owned ships that carried tin from mines in England to Egypt and Judea besides other merchandize that also needed shipping back and forth. I could safely travel with him. They advised against sending me with too many companions. That would just cause unnecessary attraction and might actually complicate traveling. Besides, hadn't the vision said I would be protected? To help me and my future child, they would send one of their own ranks. A respected Druid named Joseph would accompany me. He knew the scriptures and had earned a degree at their university, and he was young enough that the adventure appealed to him. I liked him right away.

My mother also said that we could visit with her relatives, her cousin Elisabeth who lived in Alexandria at the time. And my brother had recently purchased a house in Jerusalem. All this planning made my father more at ease. He also made me promise to come back and show him the child at some point. I promised to do so. The druids were pleased. They had brought a practical solution to a difficult matter.

Preparations were made and letters were written to all the people involved. My mother and I packed clothes and personal items, the druid Joseph and my father made plans with my brother Joseph.

The druids asked us to wait until the winter solstice. They wanted us all to attend the ceremonies at the temple and see the morning star and the sun unite in the early dawn. The blessings of these powerful heavenly bodies would be good for our journey. This was the last time the queen of heaven would appear as a morning star before she completed her pentagram path. The following year she would be an evening star on this auspicious night making the last line connecting back to her beginnings. And on that night she would also complete a forty year cycle and appear very big in the sky.

We arrived at the temple after traveling through the cold night in the darkest of winter. The druids met us at the old temple by the Boyne River where we all had come to see this rare phenomenon. It would take eight years before it would appear again.

This temple was older than the druids. It had existed for longer than anyone could remember. When the Egyptian priests had arrived they were so impressed with the building and precision of its positioning that they had wanted to learn from the natives and then incorporate both schools of thought into later rituals.

We arrived in the middle of the night in a flood of moonlight. There was some snow in the ground, but a lot was still bare. When we came to a turn in the river, we knew we were close. Like an apparition, as if a sister of the moon had fallen to earth, we saw this round structure, a mound in the landscape reflecting white in the moonlight. The stones were white and shiny, a mound made with many smaller round ones piled on top of each other. At the entrance there were larger stones reflecting the light from our torches making tongues of fire play on the white surface. The many spirals decorating the stones seemed to swirl in the combined light of the moon and the flames. We were all too stunned and frightened to speak.

There was a long tunnel into the small chamber inside. We all had brought torches and were told to leave them standing outside. They continued their flaming dance on the walls on the outside, while we followed the high druid who held the only torch. The tunnel was also lined with the stones enhanced with crystals. The light of the single torch danced in all the reflections which played from side to side. The tunnel had a small curvature, a *little swing to the right and then back to the left. After the curve we walked another longer pace and came to a small opening on either side, creating a space shaped like a cross making the end of the tunnel. The space was small and barely enough for all of us. They placed me in the middle with one Joseph on either side. My parents and the high druid were in one of the side spaces and the three other druids in the other. The high druid extinguished his torch and we waited in darkness for this miracle of light to take place. Venus, the queen of heaven was about to unite with the sun, the king of creation.*

Silence takes on its own tone, and darkness will quiet your mind to hear it. When the first tentative light beams arrived through the opening above the lintel the tone intensified. The light from the star created a white sharpness, not like the colors of any phases of the journey of the sun. It became a sharp beam of red light. I felt its red dot on my forehead and watched as it slowly followed the length of my body all the way to the floor. It could have cut me in half. Then the light changed to bright white light filling the room in a blinding flash before the sun came up. The people looked like skulls and we all gasped. We were bathed in the combined light of the peach of dawn and the brightness of the light from the star. A moment later the sun took over. It was soothing and familiar and we all could breathe again.

I stood in the golden sunlight, closed my eyes and lifted my head towards the light beam. I could feel the reverence from the druids and my family. The star and the sun had united on me. My body had been truly blessed by God.

After leaving the druids with quiet greetings, we went home in total silence through the winter landscape.

As the time drew near for our departure, I decided to learn as much as I could before we left. The druids welcomed my questions and I learned about the movements of the stars and the measuring of time. They taught me the relationship of numbers and some basic phrases in Greek and Aramaic.

My parents had seen Joseph leave and watched him return many times, so they weren't worried about the travel. But my plans were so open, they weren't sure when they would see me again. They looked forlorn as they waved at me from the pier.

The journey by boat was exhilarating. I simply loved watching the sea. Joseph, the scholar, continued to teach me while we were on the boat. We practiced the languages and studied the movements of the stars at night. He said the temple in Heliopolis was most famous for their ability to heal. Serious injuries were something they handled easily. They had techniques to regrow tissues and bones. He had heard of someone even grow back an arm. This was something he wanted to study further, and I was glad he would benefit from the trip, as well.

We became quite close while we watched the sea and admired the coastline of Gaul, and the gate that made the entrance into this narrower sea, the Mediterranean, which we would follow almost to its end. He was more than twice my age, but he enjoyed my curiosity and respected my decision to act on the message I had received.

Arriving in Alexandria took my breath away. I had never seen so many people. The variety of skin tones and clothing, the different languages spoken, the smells of strange food was quite overwhelming. I hung onto my brother as we found our way to our relative's house.

Elisabeth and Zachary had gotten our letter shortly before we arrived and welcomed us warmly. They had their own joy to share, they were expecting their first child. They giggled a bit and blinked at each other as they told us, since Zachary's hair was gray and Elizabeth was considered beyond childbearing age. We rejoiced with them, but withheld our main purpose for coming all this way. We would tell them later when we knew more from the temple.

After some relaxing days with them in Alexandria, Joseph was ready to sail on and we said our farewells. I promised to come back and help Elisabeth before the summer solstice when the baby was due.

Joseph's ship was too big to go down the Nile, but he arranged for us to travel with a smaller boat south to Heliopolis. The Nile was quiet and beautiful, not a wave on it as it flowed lazily north towards the sea. Again, we had time to study and think.

Heliopolis was almost as busy as Alexandria, but we found our way to the temple and Joseph introduced himself as the druid scholar from Hibernia. They had indeed received his letter and were anticipating his arrival. It seemed like the priests were looking forward to have someone to exchange knowledge with. We were given sleeping quarters within the temple grounds, Joseph among the priests and I among the young priestesses. Finally I could relax. I had reached my destination so far, now I had to be guided further for my mission to be accomplished.

I hardly saw Joseph while we were at the temple. The work with the priests took up his time. After familiarizing myself with the place and being introduced to a myriad of different people, I finally had the courage to speak to one of the priestesses about my reason for being there. She told me that many people came to the temple in the same errand, but that was usually because they had not been successful conceiving a child and needed help. I, on the other hand, was still a maid and stepping into my most fertile years. My story puzzled her, but she felt that the message I had received was important and should be taken seriously, especially since the druids had sent me to them. She would talk to another priestess and arrange for a meeting.

The next priestess I talked to invited me to a chamber beneath the temple. She was wearing a headdress of a black panther, and introduced herself as representing Isis. I was reminded of my earlier meeting with the star and knew that Isis was considered the earthly version of Venus, and they both were called the queen of heaven. I told her about the blessing I had received at the temple in Hibernia, and I could tell that even her panther ears perked up. She had heard about the unusual temple, but didn't know where it was. I suggested that she could pay my family a visit. Isis just smiled.

I could tell that she hesitated a bit. There was apparently some information she wasn't sure if she should share. I reminded her that I had arrived here with Joseph and had been studying with the druids for years. She admitted that what she wanted to tell me was best shared between women. I just seemed so young to take part in such advanced knowledge. I felt honored, and tried to look older than I was.

She asked if I had heard of the successes they had had in rejuvenation. I said Joseph had mentioned it, and that was what he wanted to study while he was here. Isis told me that they had also been successful at starting pregnancies in fertile women without a man being involved. She couldn't go into details of how, but they had developed a method to achieve creating a child involving only the mother. This time my ears bent to hear every word. The only problem was that it only produced female offspring. I thought back to my message and remembered the voice saying distinctly that I would give birth to him *in Jerusalem. I would love to have a daughter. And skipping the involvement of a man altogether was fine with me, but that was not the message. It had said that first I would receive a holy blessing, and, then,* the most high would overshadow me.

Isis stopped for a moment. "Well, you have already had the holy blessing. The king and queen of heaven have shined on you with their combined light. Now, we have to let the Most High overshadow you." She smiled enigmatically.

Next time I met with Isis, she told me that she had discussed my situation with the other priests and priestesses and they had an invitation for me. Would I like to take part in the enactment ritual the next time the king and the queen would meet? That would be on the spring equinox which was coming up in a couple of days. I thought of my mystical, but beautiful experience at the winter solstice and said it would be an honor.

They took me to the temple of Isis in the dark hours of the morning and dressed me up as the queen of heaven. I kept myself in quiet meditation and prayer as the priests and priestesses filed into the temple. I was again overwhelmed with the size and beauty of the space. The enormous columns with their painted hieroglyphs gave it all a dazzling display of shifting colors in the light of the few lit torches.

They had instructed me in the motions I was supposed to perform in the enactment, and, having been to the temple in Hibernia, I had an idea of what to expect. But whereas the experience in Hibernia was full of awe and wonder, this one became one of terrifying pain.

I stood still by the altar when they extinguished the torches and filled the silence with prayer while waiting for the single line of light from the star. She didn't disappoint. Soon I saw it hitting the sun disc of Ra on my head dress and then I felt her fine beam on my face. I took the steps down to the byre in the aisle, took a grip on the sheet and pulled it aside in a dramatic swoop. I heard a collective gasp from the people in attendance along with my own expression of surprise. The king this time was wearing the head dress of a black panther underneath the symbol for the sun king Ra. The powerful animal was portrayed covering most of the priests face and coming down over his shoulder. The headpiece of Ra rested around his cat ears. The contrast created with the gold against the black was dramatic. The reaction from the other participants told me that this was all most unusual.

I extended my hand as instructed, and as the now almost forgotten beam of the star fell on our bodies, two other priests supported his body to an upright position. He opened his eyes as he stood upright, and I stared into two almond cat eyes, with slits for pupils. His movements were sleek, and elegant, but without warmth. We did the embrace. Then he guided me expertly and with authority, turning us around and laying me back down on the byre. Now I saw what the next step was going to be. His erect member was ready and presenting itself from underneath the minimal linen wrapped around him. I had been raised an obedient daughter, and I had no intention to not comply with this ritual attended by the entire temple. But I was unprepared for this. My maiden inexperience took over and I was petrified. He knelt down by me and I had to allow him access. He entered me with a force worthy of the powerful animal he represented. My body was not welcoming this, and I felt ripped and burned. He came inside me as the light of the sun and the star fell where we were united. The temple people made a loud shout as they welcomed the light. The colors in the temple started spinning as I felt my tears running into my ears. I disappeared in a whirlwind of small stars and flying jewels.

I came to in the arms of Joseph. He had attended the ritual together with the other priests and watched it all unfold. His tenderness for me and his outrage for how this had been handled merged into a devotion to me and for my protection. He told me later how he had raged against the priests and been told simply that I had requested to be overshadowed by the most high and they had complied. The black panthers were the highest priest and priestess of the temple. They were hardly ever seen by the public. I should feel honored. Besides, they couldn't do the regular initiation of virgins first since the panthers didn't do those and the conception was supposed to be with the highest ranked authority of the temple. They felt they had found a unique solution to my unusual mission and wished me the best for the pregnancy. With the earlier blessing of my body and this powerful conception, this child would be precious to the gods. The priests would keep track of his birth. My pedigree was familiar to them. The stars already told them that this child had an unusual mission ahead of him. He would be born when the star was at her most auspicious point. And he would be a prince of two kingdoms.

Joseph couldn't argue with their reasoning. He guessed that the gods had their ways of doing things and focused instead on me. The whole experience had been harrowing. We stayed at the temple for a couple of days for me to gain strength and find my balance again while Joseph arranged for transportation back to Alexandria. We had promised Elizabeth and Zachary that we would return in time for the birth of their child.

Elizabeth was well advanced in her pregnancy and happy to have my assistance. Her delight in my pregnancy made me feel a little better. For a while we left it as Joseph's child and said we were betrothed and would get married in Jerusalem. In a moment of closeness with Elizabeth I told her what had happened. She then confided in me that she had also gone to the temple to be helped for her barrenness. They had blessed her body and given her herbs and then sent her back to Zachary.

"A little simpler than your story, but I guess the gods were involved here too," she said.

Their son, Yochanan, was born at the summer solstice. I was assisting at the birth to become more prepared for my own lying in, which unbeknownst to me was going to be a very different experience. The baby was a robust child who welcomed the world with a healthy voice. His father, who had been somewhat speechless in surprise since the onset of the pregnancy, was gifted with prophecy. He couldn't stop praising his newly born son's greatness. Joseph and I admired the child and learned how to care for an infant.

We stayed in Alexandria until my brother came back on a ship. He could take us to Joppa and arrange for transportation to Jerusalem where he had a house we could stay in. I had to fulfill my mission, however much I had grown tired of the whole thing by now. Joseph became my anchor and my strength. He promised we would get married in Jerusalem after the baby was born. And then he whispered to me that we would do the initiation of the virgin afterwards. Being an honorable man he had hardly touched me other than in sweet affection. Understanding how important this would be for our marriage, he wanted to give me time to get over the experience in the temple. Then he wanted to create a new bond between us in quiet serenity.

We arrived in Joppa later than we had expected because of storms at sea. From there we were part of a caravan towards Jerusalem. But the caravan also got delayed because of weather. The child started to announce his imminent arrival, and I knew we would never reach Jerusalem in time. We were close enough that we let the caravan go and took a side road into a town called Bethlehem. On the way we found a cave where cows and sheep were kept. As soon as the camel was stabled, my water broke and there was no time to do anything else than try to be comfortable in the straw. Joseph, again the pillar of strength and endurance, used his knowledge in the healing arts, and quoted scriptures to me like a bard when I needed distraction. The Gods be praised, the birth was normal, and the babe that had such an auspicious beginning was delivered to the sounds of congratulating animals.

Thankful for the foresight of mothers, we wrapped him in linens Elizabeth had sent with us, and I rested with my son at my breast. He was an unusually beautiful child and in spite of how angry I was at the gods for the turmoil they had sent me through, I fell in love with him, like all mothers do with their newborns. Joseph, always right next to me, was also enchanted with the child, and cooed to the baby who looked back at him in total trust and admiration.

We rested in our own trinity of peace and perfection. The night sky went from midnight blue to purple to black making the backdrop for the appearance of our old friend Venus. She had now started a new cycle and appeared as the evening star. The queen of heaven was alone in greeting us, which seemed fitting for the night of a birth.

Speaking to the star, we admired her brightness and thanked her for the safe delivery of the child we were going to raise. The night of the winter solstice had a black velvet texture to it and the star became brighter and for a moment shone with the brightness of the sun itself.

To the sound of bleating lambs, some shepherds nearby came to greet us. They had *seen the unusual light from the star and felt it was pointing to this cave. We showed them the newborn child, and they agreed, he must be special indeed.*

Our quiet time of reflection was interrupted with more visitors. We heard bells of camels, and three richly decorated camels appeared carrying travelers in jewel tone robes with distinctly different turbans and head gear. I thought they were too fine guests for the humble place we were in, but they enquired about the newborn child, and we had to admit, our son had just arrived.

Joseph went about making me comfortable and presentable. He welcomed our auspicious guests and made space for them. They started to explain who they were and in what errand they had come, and I wondered what fairytale I had fallen into.

They were astronomers from Persia, Assyria and Egypt. The astronomer in Heliopolis had written to his colleagues about the unprecedented conception that had taken place, and the others had concurred that the stars showed an unusual alignment. There were also several planets that were appearing in strange relationships to each other, all pointing to a priest king about to be born. So they had all met in Jerusalem earlier and waited for this night. The star light seemed to fall outside of the city walls so they had traveled the short distance towards Bethlehem to find out exactly where it pointed to. The cave was brightly lit from the star, and here we were holding a newborn child. We certainly fulfilled their story.

They brought strange gifts to the child, which they told us he would understand later in his life if we let him study at the universities at the temples. We agreed to support him in his learning and looked at the beautiful containers they brought.

Caspar from Assyria came forth and brought a decorated alabaster jar with oil perfumed with frankincense. He said it was for the anointing of the king. It smelled lovely, but he told us to not open up its seal. Only a priestess of the highest rank could administer it to him. The prince would know when the time was right.

Melchior from Egypt brought a gilded box with an ornate lid. He carefully opened it and showed us that it was full of a white powder that shimmered in the light. This was for the priest side of him, he said. It was pure gold. All I could do was stare at its beauty and hope that my son sometime would understand what to do with it. I had never seen gold in that form. He said it was for the Shining One, the substance that would make him know God inside. We nodded in acknowledgement and respect with no understanding of what it entailed.

Balthazar from Persia brought another jar decorated differently, and said it was myrrh, for the embalmment of his head. I thought, he had just been born, let him live a life first before we start thinking about his death. But Balthazar smiled, and said that this child would gain so much knowledge in his lifetime, his people would want to be able to access it even if he was no longer with them. Joseph understood and said some appropriate words, while I still just stared dumbfounded.

They stayed with us for a bit and we shared our bread and wine with them. Then they mounted their camels and left us. They said they were going to visit the temple in

Heliopolis and headed straight into the desert. We never heard of them again. But the mysterious gifts were at our feet reminding us that this strange visit had occurred.

The following morning we gathered up our few things and loaded them on one of our two camels, the other one would carry me and the child. Joseph felt safer walking the short distance to Jerusalem leading the two camels. We found the house of my brother were servants were anxiously awaiting our arrival. They had expected us with the caravan the previous day, and were relieved that we finally showed up. The women cooed over the child and made sure everything possible was done to assure our comfort. The special gifts from the astronomers were put in a hidden closet in our bedroom. I finally felt that I had arrived.

Joseph and I settled into our place in Jerusalem. The servants my brother had hired were wonderful. He had explained who we were and given instructions to treat us like masters of the house. We could never thank him enough for his kind support.

When Yeshua was three weeks old we took him to the temple for his circumcision. Joseph had been there already and familiarized himself with the place. The rabbis respected him as the druid from Hibernia, and felt honored that he wanted to do this Jewish tradition with his son. Joseph and I had discussed it, and decided that since he was a prince of Judea, he should have this mark on his body which was so important to them. The tradition had fallen out of practice in Hibernia. We brought a sacrificial lamb and listened to the singing. I stayed back in the women's court while Joseph took the child to the rabbis. I heard the cry of my son, but by the time he was brought back to me, little Yeshua was calm.

We had a quiet wedding at the temple some weeks later. My brother Joseph was expected back to Jerusalem and we wanted him to be present. The ceremony was quite beautiful and more meaningful with the baby among us. Joseph acknowledged the child as his, even though he had never been near me, but Yeshua himself seemed to bring an extra blessing to the day, which we all noticed. The rabbis felt that our marriage had already been blessed with a child and wished us many more. I couldn't help but blush, as the thought of being with Joseph actually excited me. He had been my pillar of strength for a year by then, always at my side, always ready with a wise word or a supporting hand. I was looking forward to sharing a marriage bed with him.

As my brother got ready to leave back to Alexandria, we decided to go with him. My mission was accomplished in Jerusalem, and I longed to be with family again. We joined Joseph's boat and went back to Elizabeth and Zachary. We established ourselves in a house in their neighborhood, and spent several years in the cultural excitement of the city.

I had promised my parents to come back and show them the child. They had received my letters, but were longing to see me again. By the time we got to travel to Hibernia I was pregnant with James. Joseph stood proudly at the prow of the boat as it landed holding our first born on his arm and having his other arm around his pregnant wife.

We stayed in Hibernia until James was born. Then we headed back to Alexandria, to prepare for our sons education, and for Joseph to start working at the Serapium in the healing program there. He both wanted to use his skills and to learn more. As little Johanna were born we got to know your family, and all the children became playmates. It was a wonderful time. Your mother, Eurochia, Elizabeth and I became good friends and supported each other through these intense child bearing years.

After Johanna was weaned I felt a need to continue my own education. I asked Elizabeth to look after my children together with our trusted servants and my husband while I traveled and spent time in Ephesus. I had heard about their work with song and sounds, and I needed to learn about the work of the oracle to understand my oldest son and his mission. He was old enough, so I took him with me. We spent three months there before returning to Alexandria.

When we came back my dear Joseph suggested another change in our lives. He wanted to learn more about the preparation and the use of manna, the holy bread served by the righteous. I agreed with him and we moved again, this time to the community of Qumran and the work of the Essenes. There were many groups there focused on different aspects of the teachings of the ancients. We joined the group of the Nazareeans and lived a very active community life in their village a little north of Jerusalem. So you didn't see Yeshua again until we arranged for the meeting at the temple. By that time the two of you weren't children anymore. You were adults and you both knew who you were.

I'm so glad you want to learn about the work done in Ephesus. You will become a priestess of high rank. I'm honored to take you there, my future daughter-in- law, so you can continue your studies. I look forward to see the temple again, and Tallia knows that we are coming. She has welcomed us and I will introduce you proudly as my daughter, my son's wife.

CHAPTER 15

RETURNING FROM EPHESUS

THEIR SHIP ARRIVED IN EPHESUS AND JOSEPH arranged for transportation for
them to the Temple of Artemis. They were sitting comfortably on a donkey
cart which gave them a tour of the city before they reached the temple up on the
hill. Ephesus was an old temple where the ancient teachings were kept alive. There
were other, smaller local temples, where the traditions were starting to water down.
The Roman influence affected the work. The change from small towns to large cities
shifted the focus. Fewer people were attracted to work in a temple setting and the
rigorous training required.

Mariam had come to this ancient center of knowledge to learn and continue
the traditions. With her high status from the Serapium and the recommendation
from the High Priestess, she knew she would be respected here and included in the
work of the temple. With Mary at her side, whom the priestesses here knew from
before, Mariam was looking forward to a time of forming new friendships, and of
revelations.

Mary knew she was doing the right thing. All her instincts said that her daughter-
in-law needed this step in her education and she was happy to be of assistance. It was
also a long time since she had been here and she was looking forward to see some of
the people that had become her friends when she was here, many years ago.

"How the city has grown," said Mary, noticing the busy streets, the abundance
of booths and tables with items for sale everywhere. They passed an arena, a theatre
and a large public bath. The columns and triangular pediments adorned every
building. People were walking up and down the steps of the official buildings for
the administration of the city. It had become just as metropolitan as Alexandria and
almost as big. Patrols of Roman soldiers walked the streets and kept law and order.

"They always make me nervous," said Mariam. "My world is so different then
theirs, even though we live in the same cities."

"I know what you mean, but think of all the good things the Romans have
brought." Mary could always find something pleasant to say. "We can travel safely
in the whole known world."

"That's true. And within the Empire, there is peace. We can admire their engineering and incredible building projects. I appreciate the aqueducts and the sanitary system. What I miss is the profound connection with nature, the knowledge of the unseen forces so familiar to you and me. People slowly forget that there is so much more to experience than what you find with your senses. I am worried about the future of the temples. There aren't enough young people learning the arts anymore. And the older generation is in danger. Mary, I fear for the loss of the knowledge." Mariam was concerned.

"I wonder if the old teachings scare people. It requires people to take responsibility for their own inner life. Would they rather go to the circus? I don't know anymore. Don't they want to know how the universe works and how it relates to their own bodies? Is there no desire to evolve into wiser, more self sufficient, more powerful humans?" Mary was still puzzled over the human race.

"I don't know anymore. Among people of the cities I see more concerns for the size of their homes, how well they will marry and what's the latest entertainment."

"With that they all become Roman. If you want to marry well, marry a Roman. If you want a big home, build like the Romans. If you want to be part of high society, get invited to Roman parties. This is the life that's in fashion now. I've noticed it too, Mariam. But living in Bethany has shielded us from a lot of that. Among our own people we can still live the old ways."

"Tell me, how did you join the Nazareeans? How did you get involved in Qumran?" Mariam wanted to change the topic, and this was something she had been wondering about since her mother-in-law had told her own story.

Their wagon rattled over the uneven road. Perched on seats behind the driver, they had to bend with the movement of the wagon. Mariam was glad they weren't traveling with anything grander. There was no need to draw attention. Two powerful priestesses arriving for more profound learning at the temple would maybe stir some commotion, whereas two women on a donkey cart on their way through town went unnoticed.

Mary was happy Mariam asked. She liked to tell about the friendly group they found in Bethany. Joseph worked his healing arts with them and learned more. In addition he became involved in the mining work in Qumran. Many of their products were used in their healing work. He quickly earned respect in the gold mines. Mary gave birth to more children and had to take care of their education. Knowing Yeshua's path they made sure he was trained by Joseph at an early age and by the elder Nazareeans before he started his travels between the temples. He knew the techniques of healing from the Essenes in Qumran and was considered gifted in their craft. At the colony in Bethany both boys and girls were educated, so young Mary and Johanna had as much education as Mariam before she started the Serapium. Mary was now engaged to Jacob and was in priestess training among the Nazareeans. Her mother was very proud of her, and Mariam found both the young women interesting and looked forward to know them better. She didn't know then how much she would later depend on Johanna.

The Temple could be seen from far away being situated above the city. The city was expanding, but the temple complex was still separated from the throng of city life. The buildings had dignity and glimmered of ancient authority. The temple was built long before the Romans and displayed a different building style. There were columns, but the rooflines were straight, and the stones used for the walls were larger.

On the road they met a patrol of Romans soldiers walking the streets.

"Ladies," they greeted them and pointed their hands to their helmets.

The two women greeted them back respectfully, and even though Mariam felt a chill down her spine seeing the eagle on their helmets, she couldn't complain about their politeness. The powerful emblem never failed to tell her how wide and far the arm of Rome could reach, but they also stood for a high level of civilization.

"Be glad they can't read your thoughts, Mariam." Mary knew exactly how she felt.

"I wish I couldn't read theirs," said Mariam wondering how they could feel so invincible and immortal. As far as she knew they would bleed and die if injured just like other people.

"And they don't trust the temple healers," Mary sent back in her mind.

"They are scared of our healers since they don't understand how it works. They call it dark magic and would rather see it gone."

"There is nothing more dangerous than an ignorant man with power. Smile Mariam, there is another group of them."

Mariam smiled a sheepish smile, and the Roman soldiers didn't just tip their helmets, they smiled back acknowledging with their eyes that she was a woman. Mariam sneered through her teeth. This was an insult to her status. Her body felt attacked with their thoughts. She controlled her urge to send an unseen attack back. They are ignorant, she told herself. They didn't know that she could feel their thoughts like clawing fingers on her skin. Could she blame them if they'd never been taught?

They were getting closer to the Temple and could admire the grand impression as they came closer to the gates. The colors were astonishing and the gold used on the structure had not been spared. The huge statue in the front could be seen for miles. It represented Artemis with her welcoming hands and her generous offering of food from her body, the food that would make your body glow; the holy bread served only to initiates.

They came to the public entrance of the temple and asked the donkey driver to stop for a moment so they could study the temple complex.

"The first court is for the common people," Mary explained. "There is a court for the initiates, and then the court for the priests and priestesses. Underneath are the halls where the secret rituals are done. The hospital is over on the right side and the temple school is on the left. Then you have the campus with living quarters in the back. There is a new wing to the hospital which wasn't there when I was here. We have to ask Tallia about that."

Mariam admired the fountain in the courtyard, the protective wall around the complex and the beauty of it all. She noticed the simplicity of the design and the harmonious proportions. It all contributed to a sense of peace and serenity. This was an island where hundreds of year's old traditions were practiced surrounded by a world where everything was changing rapidly.

The two women turned and looked at the city below. They were standing at the gate between these two worlds. As soon as they entered, a familiar approach to life would surround them. Right here, they could feel the rumbling of the expanding city underneath their feet.

"Mary, what will happen to this place? I see the knowledge I represent dwindle."

"People will become head blind, and the wisdom of the goddess will be forgotten."

"But it will return, please tell me, it will rise again?"

"We will return. Wisdom will return," Mary said with quiet conviction.

Mariam stood at the deck of the ship recalling this conversation with Mary at the time when they arrived at the temple of Artemis. Mary's powerful serene words had stayed with her, and, now that her training was complete and she was returning to Alexandria, it seemed even more potent.

After several years at Ephesus, she was aware of how few they were at her level of education. The temples, which hadn't changed in thousands of years, were now changing rapidly in her lifetime. The people who had the deepest knowledge were getting old. There were few young people in training to replace them. Mariam was aware of her rare position.

She sat down for a minute to enjoy the breeze and the ocean air while she absentmindedly stroked the head of the animal next to her. She hoped Mary was visiting in Alexandria, but find that somewhat unlikely. Where was Yeshua now? Last she heard he was in Bethany. He had finished at Therapautae and at the hidden temple in the desert. His rabbinic training was over a long time ago. He had been to Hibernia with his father. Thinking of Joseph made her smile. She really liked her father-in-law, his warm affection, his interest and pride in all the young people surrounding him. Maybe someday she could also visit his green island.

How was her own family? She had been gone for a long time. To learn the deepest mysteries of Ephesus required many years of uninterrupted training. There had been letters. Martha had followed Lazarus to the colony at Bethany. Sarah was still waiting for her beloved big sister to come home. Mariam smiled again. Sarah's devotion was unshakeable. She had stayed in the family home with the parents as they aged. They were both in good health, happy to watch their grown children raise their own and to leave more responsibilities to a younger generation. She thought of them fondly. Her father's constant support, her mother's subtle training. Bashra was still with her.

Bashra was kept in a leather pouch in a lidded basket among Mariam's belongings. They still had their conversations. Now she understood how important it was that the ancestral head from Ethiopia was given to her at an early age. She was used to the idea of a severed head before she came to Ephesus. The training included how to work with the oracle and how to prepare a new oracle. She had learned about the preparation and use of ancestral heads. If they were prepared correctly, they could be preserved indefinitely. With the proper work they could be an incredible support for future generations.

She had made friends, strong friendships she hoped to nourish. Her partner, Herodias, had become as close as Sibyl. She wasn't sure if she would see her again. Herodias had been called to Rome to get married. The man's name was Philip, he was a Roman procure and they would be stationed in Syria. He was the son of Herod the Great and this was an important political match. Mariam sighed. How could her family send her to important priestess training and then order her to leave to join in a marriage she had no desire for? Apparently her family's position in Rome made this important. Mariam remembered that she herself had been betrothed since she was a young child. But between her and Yeshua, their education came first. They needed all this knowledge for the work they were going to do.

They didn't know about her ancestral lineage at the temple. She had wanted it that way. The fact that she was a priestess from the Serapium was enough for them. Mariam had proven her learning with them many times over. Her hand followed the black fur on the back of the animal next to her. It looked up at her in recognition with big green eyes.

The crew had wondered when she brought it on board. She had leashed it at the time, which was unnecessary, but to calm everybody she figured it was best. Her hand rested between its round ears, and she felt how much she resonated with it. She shared its alertness, the way it was taking in information from the environment at every breath, living with its paw to the pulse of creation in one eternal now.

Her training made her function in a similar way. She was always alert, always reading people, always adjusting her move to the movement of others. The hardest of all, she found, was protecting the balance of her body from harm. She had learned self defense, if someone physically attacked her, she could defend herself effectively. She didn't consider that difficult. What was hard was to interact with people who were untrained; people who unconsciously were sending harmful intentions from their bodies. She needed to create a protective layer around herself to be able to interact with the world at large. Inside the temples she was surrounded with people who had learned to be responsible for their own thoughts. Going through the city to get to the ship she walked through crowds of people and found it a challenge. She found herself becoming more isolated as a result of what she knew, and however painful it was, she could never go back. She was both grateful for the privilege of her studies and pained at seeing how much it set her aside in society.

Mariam looked forward to share her new knowledge with her fellow priests and priestesses at the Serapium. This was reserved for people who had been in training for a long time and had been through several initiations. Only the inner circles would have background enough to be allowed to partake. This was powerful information, and if given to people who hadn't already gone through the required levels it could create dangerous individuals. The question wasn't if you had been in training long enough, the question was if your body was strong enough to hold this knowledge. This wasn't about fasting and exercises. This was about the amount of light you could hold in your body. It was crucial that you had worked through all your own issues and were familiar with everything stored in your genealogy from generations back.

Mariam had learned to respect that everybody contained the history of their ancestors in their body and also resonated with their future relatives. She liked the metaphor of seven generations back in time and seven generations in the future, all lined up, locking arms and dancing. The long line of people would move in a circular fashion, like the diameter of a circle, moving around the center, the person of now. The people of the past would move backwards and the people of the future would move forwards, creating a powerful motion of shared consciousness filling the circle. Mariam smiled to herself trying to visualize herself dancing with her mother next to her, but as she continued the image, she realized that Bashra was part of her line as well. Her future people included her siblings and all their possible children. She realized her immense responsibility of choosing her thoughts and actions well. Everything she did would affect many people, located in both directions of linear time.

The waves splashed along the side of the boat. She rose and walked over to the railing and held onto the ropes. Her hair flowed in the wind, and the long, black cape she was wearing bellowed out behind her. Herodias had given it to her before she left. It had a purple ribbon which lined the front edges and around her neck and made a stripe down her back. She needed the warmth for the sea ride, and Herodias was always concerned with peoples well being. She was going to miss her friend. She hoped to see her again. Mariam found that unlikely. She knew the time for the work she and Yeshua were destined to do together was coming near.

She was looking forward to be back in Bethany for the annual communal meal, to again taste the food that would illuminate. Yochanan would officiate now that he was fully trained and holding the office of the Messiah. He would lead them in their further growth. With his extensive knowledge he would know how to advise them wherever they were on their path. She had heard he had taken it upon himself to baptize people in the holy water. How did that sit with the elders? The holy water was privileged for the first or second initiates, not to be distributed among the common people. But she had heard that he would pour his special water over anybody who came and asked for baptism and watch the transformation as their heart became tuned to the vibration of light. They didn't know why they felt so much better. They just knew they liked the effect and went and told their friends. Mariam wasn't sure how she felt about this. Baptism wasn't something you just distributed like a cup of tea. She would have to talk to Yochanan about his practices. She knew they were preparing for changing times, but this was also a time to be very, very careful.

Later in the evening she went back to the deck and watched darkness descend. The light would play on the water as the sun went down, and she enjoyed every color change as it shifted through a whole spectrum. Just before the sun set below the horizon line the first star could be seen. Mariam had been waiting for it. Venus was an evening star at this time. She wanted to welcome the star that had become a profound friend as she understood more about its mysterious ways.

Mariam had learned about her movements in the sky in the shape of a pentagram every eight years. If you waited fifty-two years she would describe a whole rose in the night sky. The astrologers had lists of her expected behavior. At Ephesus Mariam had been taught that Venus also would relate to certain spots in the landscape that had five high tops around a valley. The star would recreate the same pentagram pattern in lines between the mountain tops as energy lines that you could tap into. Mariam found this absolutely fascinating. She had learned how to recognize the pattern and how to use it. The astrologers had told her that the most powerful one known to man was above Jerusalem, the city dedicated to Venus a long, long time ago.

She bit her lip. There was so much information, so much to take in. She was grateful for this sea journey across the Mediterranean. Holding onto the rope at the railing and the collar of her black furry friend she allowed the wind to blow her hair and felt her brain being refreshed.

The sailors noticed the beautiful woman traveling alone. She was obviously well off, and her "companion" made her somewhat unapproachable. It was kept on a leash and next to her at all times. She picked up after it and fed it herself, so it was no bother. But it wasn't everyday that they had passengers with such an unusual pet. The boss could remember someone bringing a bear at some point, but that one was kept in a cage the whole way and did not look happy. A big hawk had been brought another time, and that one squawked from Alexandria to Rome. They were glad when it reached its destination. This lady and her big cat seemed like good friends. In fact, the animal had almost a human presence which made them all jump when it was near. The feline and its owner gave an appearance of being a team of working companions. "Twins," suggested the young deck boy and they all turned and looked again.

It was morning. Mariam had risen early. She wanted to watch the sunrise and do the greetings of the dawn she had learned at Therapautae. The simple ways of those beautiful people to show their respect to nature every day would always stay with her.

She could see Alexandria now. The silhouette of the library was visible. She could see the roof of the Serapium behind it. *Home.* Yes, wherever she went, however many places she visited, this was home.

Her letters to the temple and her family had arrived and they knew when to expect her. She didn't want to be a total surprise and enjoyed the shared expectations of her arrival.

The stately boat made a good figure in the morning sun as it sailed slowly in towards the pier through the glittering waves. There seemed to be some commotion there. Mariam guessed that it was the harbor crews ready to unload the cargo. Maybe her brothers would be there, maybe her father. She hoped so.

Sarah was running back and forth between her parents and her brothers. They had positioned themselves at either end of the pier, so all she could do was to cart back and forth. The parents wanted to be out of the crowd and stayed by the buildings, her brothers said they wanted to check the condition of the cargo right away and were ready where the ship came in.

"Such a fuss, as if we don't have boats making birth here everyday," said the man who lived on the pier. "Must be someone important coming in. Isn't a Roman, though, I don't see any soldiers. There is a group from the temple over there, must be a visitor from Rome."

Sarah knew who was coming, but she didn't stop to answer him as she hurried by to greet the people from the temple.

"Sarah!" Sibyl opened her arms wide and hugged the young girl. "This is the one, don't you think?" she said pointing to the boat coming in. "We got word yesterday from a ship that left Ephesus the day before them."

"Yes, this should be the one," Sarah answered out of breath as she grabbed Sibyls hands.

The two women held hands so tight they almost broke fingers. They were both expecting someone who was very important to them.

Mariam was standing at the bow shading her face with her hand to see. Her black simple gown shifted in the wind underneath her flowing cape. The purple stripe on the cape was her only other color besides a purple ribbon tying her thick dark hair. She had gold bracelets and a necklace identifying her rank as a high priestess. Her black companion was sitting down next to her.

They reached the inner harbor and the captain maneuvered the ship expertly up to the pier. The sailors were pulling on ropes and giving orders about tightening knots. The gangplank was laid out and the few passengers milled out with their packages and luggage. Mariam waited a little. She didn't want to startle anybody.

Sibyl and Sarah could hardly stand still. "Is it her at the bow? Would she soon come down to meet them?" The temple delegation behind Sibyl shuffled and shifted. She had picked out six handsome novice priests carrying standards to escort them back to the temple. They had been instructed to form two open rows of three and give the priestesses ample space between. The little parade would use the full width of the road all the way through town.

"There she is!" Shouted Sarah and pointed.

The other passengers had found their families and spread out from the pier. The sailors were waiting for Mariam to leave so they could start to unload. A gasp went through the crowd.

Mariam, the high priestess, all in black with the sun shining in her gold jewelry, came walking down the footway, tall and elegant with a keen alertness. Next to her, sharing her gait and green eyes walked her animal twin, a stately black panther.

RITUALS IN SACRED STONE

Yeshua and Mariam
King and Queen
Priest and Priestess

PART TWO
JERUSALEM

A HISTORICAL NOVEL BY

WENCKE JOHANNE BRAATHEN

CONTENTS

CHAPTER 1

ON THEIR OWN

MARY HAD BEEN ANTICIPATING THIS DAY SINCE her sons fifth birthday. He was now an adult, well respected for his wisdom and knowledge. He was ready for marriage.

She remembered when the betrothal between Mariam and Yeshua had taken place. The parents had found each other in Alexandria after searching for the other half of this historically significant couple. They knew how important their own offspring was and needed to find the other one with the matching pedigree. Mary's relatives, Elizabeth and Zachary knew who they were looking for. They were active in the synagogue and their rabbi had told them that these families would meet in the beautiful city of Alexandria. Upon further analysis, they found that these two youngsters fitted the prophecy. The fortieth link of the tribe of Joseph after the Diaspora would find the fortieth link of the tribe of Benjamin. Together they would anchor the Star of David in the city of Jerusalem and prepare for their people to come home.

That was the only details they had. They trusted that the children would understand what to do at the right time. Mary sighed. It was easier when they were playmates as children. The parents could look at them playing together and surround them with a golden glow of love, protection and lofty expectations. Living close to Jerusalem and having seen the brutality of the Roman occupation there, so different than in other parts of the Empire, she didn't even want to think about what lay ahead of them.

"Eurochia, what do you think? Should we serve the roasted lamb before or after the goat meat?" The two mothers were working together planning the details of the wedding feast. Mary wanted to include Eurochia. Giving her attention to practical concerns was a relief.

Joseph and Hiram were walking together outside. The canopy was being set up and they decided where the people would gather around it. The blessings and poems to be read were already selected.

"So do you think they are ready for this now?" Hiram asked. He had been waiting for this day for some years. Mariam seemed almost a little old now. Thank God she had been betrothed early in life. Most girls are married at fifteen. Mariam was many years over twenty! He wondered if she would bring the panther. Hiram shook his head. He hoped not. He wasn't quite sure how it would be received. Her animal companion wasn't a regular house cat.

Joseph sympathized with Hiram, but he knew why his daughter-in-law had taken her time, and he was grateful. They needed all her learning for the destiny that lay ahead of them. She didn't need to bring her furry companion. Mariam herself was a black panther.

Yeshua had spent many years studying as well. Joseph knew he had traveled east to places he didn't tell them much about. He remembered fondly the trip they had taken together to Hibernia. For a whole year they had stayed and studied with the druids. Nostalgia overtook him thinking about the green island he was born on. Looking out over the landscape around him he saw olive trees and palms. He shook his head. This had been his home for the last three decades and he had learned to love it, too.

"Yes, Hiram, that's a good idea." Joseph wasn't quite sure what he had agreed upon, but he wanted Mariam's father to feel at home.

"But where are they? It is hard to have a wedding without a bride and groom." Hiram was always practical, and in this case Joseph had to agree, this was a concern.

"When is she coming, Eurochia?" asked Mary. "I thought she would want to be part of the planning."

"She'll be here. But she trusts that we will make all the proper arrangements," Eurochia answered evasively. Mary decided to leave the subject alone and go on with the work at hand.

Eurochia thought about her strong willed daughter. When she was younger she wouldn't have missed this for the world. She would have been in everywhere, making decisions on everything, making sure every detail was done to her liking. At the age of fifteen she had excellent aesthetic sense. It would indeed have been beautiful. She could see how Mariam would have arranged for flowers to hang from baskets and silks to be draped expertly. Martha and Sarah were doing this now, together with Johanna, Mary and Salome. It was pretty, but it didn't have Mariam's artistic flair.

Her daughter had changed. The biggest shift was after the years she spent at Ephesus. Eurochia had expected the changes that happened while she was at the Serapium. That was normal coming of age and learning from social interaction. But her later learning made her more serious, more sensitive and more secretive. Eurochia watched her daughter change from a bubbling fountain of energy and joy to a serene water pool with gleaming stones on the bottom.

Where was she now? Eurochia honestly didn't know. The wedding was three days away and the bride and groom were nowhere to be found. Together with Sarah,

Hiram and Eurochia had left Alexandria a month ago without their oldest daughter. She had been summoned at the Serapium and promised to meet them in Bethany later.

Mary avoided the question too. Yeshua had left to go to Galilee with some of his followers and had promised to be back in time for the wedding. That was two months ago. Mary sighed.

They knew how important this wedding was. They had known and been told since they could understand language. They knew who they were going to marry. They knew what their responsibilities were. They also knew that they would have no time by themselves after the wedding.

So they stole away. The wedding date had been set years ago according to favorable formations in the sky. There was no question about the timing. And there was no question about what they wanted to do.

The big ship had taken them from Alexandria after her parents had left. He had arrived from Joppa the day before and found her at the Serapium. This was a journey they had wanted to do for some time, and they didn't want to tell anybody.

Mariam stood at the bow of the ship allowing the wind to blow in her thick dark hair. Yeshua looked at her and admired the strength of her body, the beauty of her dark silhouette against the light. The quiet time they could share right now was precious to them both. They knew that as soon as they arrived in Joppa they would spend a day on a caravan before they reached Bethany. And from then on they would never be alone.

Mariam turned and looked at her husband. As far as she was concerned they had been married forever. She could not remember not thinking of him as the man who would stand next to her. Still, they had been separated more than together. The stolen moments they'd had were almost chance meetings when their paths had crossed. They had developed into two strong individuals used to making their own decisions on their own terms. She wasn't quite sure if she was marriageable material anymore. What did he expect? What did the parents expect?

Yeshua came up behind her and put his arms around her waist leaning his chin on her shoulder. They were staring at the horizon allowing the line between the water and the sky to blur. She turned and kissed his cheek.

"Do you think they'll understand?" she whispered to him.

"We don't have to tell them," he answered back.

They stood there like two strong trees growing close together with their limbs intertwined. Their canopies had woven together above their heads.

Baia was located near Naples at the southern tip of Italy. It was a monastery some distance from the Roman town, and known among initiates for its secret temple. Yeshua had heard about it and wanted to go there. Mariam had heard it mentioned in Ephesus in relation to sacred waters. He wanted to go there with his wife. She wanted to have one learning experience together with the man she loved. And they wanted to be there without anybody knowing about it.

Mariam thought he was too bold when he suggested it. Then she made the plan for how they could get there. The only one they told was his uncle Joseph. They needed his help with the transportation. He promised to keep their secret and to be at the wedding.

She had felt that they were two bad children when they arrived at the pier. He had felt that they were skirting all the rules about the time of separation before the wedding. They both knew how much was asked of them afterwards. They justified claiming this time for themselves. This was their wedding. This was their way of tying a stronger bond between each other.

The ship made a special stop for them and put out a dinghy to get them to land. There was no port at Baia because of the rocky shore there. Subsequently they rarely had visitors. When the dinghy left with the sailor Mariam wondered what they had let themselves out on however much the sailor promised to be back in three days. All she could see was a sandy beach beneath cliffs and a steep mountain in front of them. Yeshua had found a path among the rocks and was following it into the woods further in. Mariam picked up her bundle and followed him.

The path led through the woods to a clearing where the monastery was situated. Some small stone buildings in need of repair were surrounded with trees. A few monks still lived there, but Mariam and Yeshua quickly got the impression that the place was in decline. They were invited to the evening meal after they introduced themselves and stated where they had been taught. The monks were honored to have guests of learning among them and wondered what their mission was. All they could offer here was the experience of the caves of water. Yeshua stated that that was why they had come. The monks guided them to sleeping quarters and promised to show them the caves the following day.

After a simple breakfast the older monk led them through the mountain pass to the waterfall.

"From here you're on your own," he said. "This is the site of the oracle of the dead. We do not operate the oracle anymore. People come here to visit the healing water, not to talk to the other side. The last monk who knew how to work with the oracle died years ago. Enjoy the waters. Come back and tell us what the oracle said, if it decides to speak to you."

Yeshua and Mariam listened to what the monk said. They stood there next to each other watching him leave between the trees. Soon he was gone between the tree trunks, and they had to make a decision on how to proceed. They could see the sculpted entrance beyond the trees a little further down the path.

"I didn't know that the monastery didn't operate the oracle anymore," said Mariam shivering in the cold morning air. "At Ephesus this place was admired because they upheld the traditions."

Yeshua looked at the entrance to the caves. For a moment he wondered what had prompted them to take this journey. What had started this growing, gnawing desire to travel to an almost unknown place to partake in an adventure they had little foreknowledge about? He recalled years of desert air being warm and dry. This was the exact opposite, cold and damp. It made his skin crawl.

"I didn't know either. But let's not think about that. We came here because something inside us said we needed this experience. Besides, I haven't been able to spend this much time with you before, ever. And I don't know if we'll get to do that again."

"Well, this is not exactly the most romantic place I could think of. Remember Leontopolis when we were very young?"

"I lived on that through all my travels in the east."

"I sang in that reenactment several times after that, but it was never as intense as when I saw it with you."

"We didn't just see it, we lived it. Celebrating!."

"Remember their robes? That is the finest silks I've ever seen."

His fingertips felt the texture of the red silk. He remembered her wearing it, and how beautiful she was when he carefully pulled it off her. His eyes met hers. She felt the familiar spark between them as they embraced.

After a while he loosened his arms around her and they stood facing each other with only a hands breath between their bodies. They continued breathing together, sharing breath and air as they alternated breathing in and out. An energy flow was created between them. Mariam drew from the stones underneath them. Yeshua pulled in from the air above them. Together they created an energy flow that went simultaneously up and down between their bodies. They took each others hands and created a bigger circle for the growing column of energy they had created. The column used their spines as guides and went through their bodies as well as through the air between them.

"This will be our strength for this journey," he said.

"Let's take it with us," said Mariam practically.

Holding hands they walked into the cave opening at the entrance. The carved opening had stone structures in arches with stone relief depicting Inanna in the underworld. The steps leading down had short walls of bricks and stones. Flowering plants had grown here in a long overgrown impressive landscaping design. This temple had once been frequently visited and carefully maintained. Now they wondered what spirits had decided to take up residence here.

They prayed to Inanna and Tammuz to protect them. They invoked Isis and Osiris to walk with them and the God of their ancestors to bless their journey. The column they had created floated with them as they entered the first cave.

The temperature dropped as they stepped in. The passage was narrow and they had to walk single file. Yeshua had the oil lamp which he could light with the device he always carried in his hand. As soon as he sent his powerful intention through it, the device would magnify it and produce a flame to light the wick. There was some light where they were going, so he decided to save on the oil until they really needed it. Mariam carried a leather pouch with water across her back and her usual herb bag in her belt. She held onto the hand he offered behind him. The column of strength floated between them.

There was water dripping along the walls and green vines grew in the semi darkness. Some light came in from some openings way above, giving the large leafed foliage enough to grow on. The first arch they passed through was obviously hand carved in the stone. Otherwise what they saw was created by the passage of water though eons of time. From then on they had to maneuver through the narrow stone opening between by two mountain walls where the water had dug a thin opening over many hundreds of years. It was barely enough to walk through, and several places they had to place their body sideways. Mariam was glad she had a small frame.

Finally they came to an opening formed by two stone pillars that looked like petrified pine trees. There was enough space for Mariam and Yeshua to walk between them. By now their hair was wet from the dripping water and their clothing had black stains from rubbing against the stone. Neither of them seemed to notice.

Yeshua stepped through between the stone trees, and looked around. There was a step down before a new opening into the mountain. A light shaft high above gave this small entrance area a spotlight where they could stand for a minute together.

He looked at her. His own face was wet with dew and his eyes showed his excitement for the exploration they had undertaken. He checked for fear in her eyes, but she just looked up at him with the mischievous smile of a child being in an unknown territory on a secret expedition. He laughed and kissed her. She giggled back, answered his kiss, and then turned and looked into the next opening.

"I think we need the oil lamp."

He lit it and held it into the opening and they found that it was a long narrow tunnel with no light and no plants. They stepped down into it.

In the light from the oil lamp the walls of this part looked golden. Here the walls were perfectly flat. Yeshua investigated a part that was pealing and found that it was shaped similar to the plaster they put outside their houses built with bricks. *So this part was man made*, he concluded.

The tunnel was long. Mariam behind him couldn't see the end, but the floor was flat and even so she trusted they would be led somewhere. Was it leading downwards, further into the mountain?

There was a formed arch at the end. How far was this going? Did she hear water?

At the arch at the end of the seemingly endless tunnel he turned in the narrow space and faced her.

"We could return at this point. I could find our way back."

"Did Tammuz turn when Enki led him through the gates?"

"No, but he was eventually hung up on a tree."

"Yes, and then, after he was willing to give up his life and stay on the other side for a while he was given his earthly life back, even beautiful Inanna."

"Yes, he was." Yeshua beamed at the thought.

Never had he seen Mariam this beautiful. Her strength shone through her eyes and every part of her body. All he could do was admire this incredible woman he had called his wife since he was a child. There was always light around her. He took one step closer to her and let it envelope him too. The energy column they had built was moving around them. Little sparks of blue lines were forming above their heads.

Between their hearts there was a large purple sphere. Their eyes were shining and no word would form in their brains. It didn't have to. Words were too poor metaphors for what they were experiencing. They sensed that they had become the embodiment of a live symbol, something that contained many multifaceted concepts which it would take an eternity of time to decipher and put in words, but could be intuited in an instant.

They stepped through the arched opening and found themselves on some rounded rocks with a river running by in an underground stream. Again, there was some light from above, enough to see the section they were at. The sound of the water echoed in the tunnel it was going through. The path ended on the rocks, pointing down towards the water. There wasn't any place to walk along the side of the stream. The water filled the bottom half of the round tunnel. The rounded ceiling gave plenty of air above the water level.

They walked carefully down towards the edge of the water. Mariam put her hand in the water and brought up a sample of it. She tasted it.

"Fresh, lots of minerals," she said. " Must be coming from a spring inside the mountains."

"And probably heading for the sea," he replied as he searched around the rocks looking for their next clue.

"Aha, a boat. Look at this."

Yeshua started to have a sense of what this journey entailed. If it was an initiation in water, of course it would involve a boat floating in a tunnel with an underground river.

There was indeed a small row boat, with two seats, but no sails and no oars. Mariam looked at it and wasn't sure what to make of it. Yeshua noticed that it was tied in an interesting way. There was a rope attached at either end. After some further investigation they found that the rope was attached to the front of the boat and went down the stream floating in the water. It apparently came back through metal rings attached to the side of the tunnel and was attached to the back end of the boat.

"There must be another rock with a metal ring somewhere down there," he said.

119

"So that you can pull in the boat regardless of which end you are at," Mariam said. She had figured it out and felt reassured that this journey had some plan behind it.

"Where do you think it goes?" She asked as she watched him find a long staff leaning against a rock.

"Would you like to find out?" He said as he stepped into the boat and offered her his hand to help her get in.

This is insane, Mariam thought to herself. *The stream leads into a tunnel and we have no idea where it goes. This complex hasn't been used for years. What if the water level is taller now, then when all this was planned?*

Let's trust Enki's guidance, he echoed back into her head.

She sat down on the front seat formed by a board across and he stood behind her maneuvering the staff to push them away from the sides. The stream seemed mellow as it started off into the narrow tunnel. The rope tied to the boat slid nicely through the metal rings and anchored them at the rock they left behind and at their unknown destination.

The water picked up speed as the passage way got narrower. Mariam could feel her hair rising on her head. She held onto the oil lamp which gave a weak glow in the tunnel, just enough for them to see around themselves, but not enough to see behind them or farther than a couple of feet in front of the boat. Yeshua had to steady the boat pushing to the sides of the tunnel with his staff. Mariam protected the small flame from the splashing water. She watched the rope at the front disappear in the water, and the rope going back following through the metal rings on the wall next to them move in the opposite direction. They existed in a small ball of light which moved with them, but didn't let them see where they were going or where they came from.

"Watch out!" She warned him. The ceiling in the tunnel was lowering. Yeshua was tall enough to hit his head if he wasn't careful.

Was it the ceilings that was lower or did the water get higher? Soon he had to sit down and pull the staff in. The water went downwards it seemed, and at a faster pace. Mariam's eyes were as round as the tunnel as the boat was thrown in the rougher water. Her knuckles turned white as her hands held onto either side of her seat.

The ceiling continued to lower. Soon they had to bend down in the boat to not get hit. The rope from the front of the boat was still there. It kept the boat somewhat steady on either end. The movement of the boat in the current kept pulling the rope in the back. It both slowed the boat down a bit, and steadied it. There had to be a beginning and an end to this ride.

Soon the space between the water and the ceiling was only enough to let the boat through. They had to lie down in the bottom of the small rowboat. Mariam lifted the seat away and carefully lay down next to Yeshua. The oil lamp had gone out. The boat sailed on in utter darkness.

There seemed to still be air for them. Holding around each other in the bottom of this simple little boat inside a mysterious mountain, they closed their eyes and tried not to think. The column of strength shaped itself into a cloud and settled in the boat over them like a blanket.

Between their bodies a golden light was forming. It gave them warmth and enough light to see the love emanating from them. Enki told them not to fear the water. Inanna told them to be patient. Tammuz told them to go on. And the boat sailed quietly along an underground stream inside a mountain.

The tip of the bow of the boat scraped against the stone above them. Some light was streaming in on either side. They pressed against the bottom of the boat as it passed through this last narrow passage way before it was let free in a larger space. The boat slowed down and they looked up into a large cavernous room. There was an opening far above them accounting for the light that had welcomed them.

The boat found a pebbled shore and stopped. They turned their heads and leaned on their elbows in the boat. The room was as big as a temple. The shape reminded her of the upper half of an egg. The sandy shore made the ground along the cutting line of the egg, and part of it was under water. Yeshua found his staff and steadied the boat as they found safe footing on land. Mariam didn't even have time to sigh in relief. The beauty of the cavern made her gasp. She looked up and there were crystals hanging down from above. The gleam of sunlight came through the opening made them blink at her. Round stones on the walls were creating a surface of a repeated pattern several feet up all the way around.

Turning their heads around they tried to take it all in. Further in on the shore there were some other structures silhouetted against the straight stone wall behind it. It looked like chairs to sit on with a table in front. Curiosity led their tentative steps towards it.

Thrones? Asked Mariam in her head. *And an altar?*

Made of human bones, Yeshua echoed back trying not to sound alarmed.

As they got closer she saw that he was right. A quick look around told her that all the round bumps on the walls were skulls.

Mariam had never been afraid of death. They worked with the land of the dead in the Temples all the time. After her initial help with Yochanan, she had helped others make the transition to the other side and back. Sibyl and Mariam had become an expert team on awakening students who had come that far in their studies. In Ephesus she had learned to prepare oracular heads with her other partner, Herodias. They knew how to wake them to share their knowledge. Besides, Bashra had been a close friend of hers for years. Death had no edge to her.

She was sure of all this. In the temples they honored life on both sides of the divide. Death was not really a concept for them. Being surrounded with thousands of skulls staring empty eyed at her, gave a different feeling.

Yeshua had also worked with death in his healing practice. In the east he studied dead bodies to learn more about how they worked on the inside when they were alive. This unabashed display of skulls was unfamiliar to him and seemed surprisingly primitive. Was it supposed to be frightening?

As they looked around wondering what it all meant they came closer to the thrones standing on the rock platform a step up from the pebbled beach. The bones appeared gray in the dim light, almost blending in with the background of gray stone. The skulls eyes could just as well be darker patterns in the mountain crevices.

Yeshua looked back at the boat they had left and saw the large metal ring the rope went through and the leading rings along the wall. He wondered how hard it would be to pull them selves back up where they came from.

"That will not be necessary," said a booming voice close by. "You have entered my Temple. Now you are mine."

They both were startled and fell into the two thrones standing next to them which were indeed constructed of human thigh bones and other longer internal structural elements.

Sitting on the thrones made them stare straight on the wall above the small tunnel hole they had just appeared through. The wall had skulls attached further up covering a larger area of the wall and there was a ribbon of skulls following a circle of the space. . As they studied it they found that the skulls in front of her formed a pattern. Mariam tilted her head a bit to make out what it was.

The booming voice laughed at them. Suddenly they could see perfectly well what the pattern became by the placement of the skulls. The skulls had been placed with calculated distances between them creating an image hanging on the wall. They formed the contours of a large face. The face was now laughing at them, with a grinning mouth and menacing eyes.

Death laughing? Mariam wasn't really afraid. Death didn't have a persona like that. This was a spirit that had taken possession of this cave and got fed through the lives of all the dead people it was decorating its space with.

"Oh, let me talk to it!" said a familiar voice only Mariam could hear. "It's just a confused spirit who's picked up strength from stupid adventurers who ended their lives here."

Yeshua was just getting annoyed. He expected something profound to happen. Not this tale you could scare small children with. He watched as Mariam looked into the herb bag she carried hanging from her belt.

"I had to take her with. I couldn't leave her with the monks."

"Who? What?"

Mariam didn't want to explain. She unfolded Bashra and set her standing on the table facing the skulls on the wall. Then she quickly said the incantation to wake up her ancestor.

Yeshua looked from Mariam to the small shrunken head on the altar. What more did she have hidden in her bag that he didn't know about?

Mariam spoke in a loud voice. Yeshua echoed her strength in the intentions she put out.

"We are here on pilgrimage. We are here in the name of Isis and Osiris. With the strength of our ancestors and our future generations, we came to meet the oracle."

"You are not afraid, young Mariam?" Boomed the voice as the skulls rattled about depicting the changing features of the face as it spoke.

"*We* are not afraid," corrected Yeshua. He wasn't going to let this imposter divide their united front.

"I see," said the face and rearranged his features. "Not even of this?"

A long tail of bones which had been forming a line along the wall came lose. It flailed a little in the air before it moved across the water and they saw a skeletal hand on its end. It touched the side of their heads with its bony fingers.

They both squirmed away from it, but fear did not enter their minds.

"Oh, stop it, you big blabbermouth!" shouted Bashra. "You're nothing but a pile of empty bones."

Yeshua jumped in his seat, and Mariam smiled to herself. Never underestimate an ancestor from Ethiopia.

The skeletal face shivered in all its many skull incarnations. It made some new rumbling sounds, and suddenly the skulls in the entire room lit up inside. Bright light was shooting out of the orifices of every round bump on the walls. The face on the wall made a roar, and another light came on showing all the eye sockets having acquired blue shimmering stone eyeballs.

"I am the God of this space! Bow down to me!" boomed the spirit followed by a drum roll of rattling skulls.

"Go home to the underworld where you belong!" said Bashra loudly, as if she was scolding a misbehaving child, who didn't know his manners. Their pillar of strength had joined with her.

"We're here to meet Isis and Osiris. You're a dead spirit. You need to find your way home," Mariam stated clearly.

"Your hunger for power has trapped you in matter. If you leave, you will have more freedom in the land of the dead. Osiris is waiting for you," added Yeshua.

The face roared again, more like a whimper this time.

Attachment to matter weakens you, thought Yeshua. *I see it proven again and again.* He watched Bashra focus the power of their pillar of strength and send a light beam directly to the middle of the face. The light broke the web the spirit had created holding it's imagery in place. Now it was free and could leave. A whirlwind blew up from the water surface. It roared as it circled the walls of the room and blew drops of water splashing the walls. They watched it disappeared in a swirl through the opening in the ceiling.

With the spirit gone, the face on the wall fell apart. All the skulls lost their hold and started rolling down, bumping into each other creating a racket of noise as they fell into the water in an avalanche of broken bones. As the face disappeared, they noticed a new golden light in the room.

The chairs they were sitting on had changed. The bones were gone and the thrones appeared made of fine wood painted black with golden inlays.

"That's better," said Bashra satisfied.

With the light in the room came a new sound, like singing voices. New precious colors were lit up in the ceiling in amethyst, aquamarine and tourmaline. The golden light filled the stone cathedral, and they could only stare in awe at the beauty of the display of crystals and light.

Bashra spoke again. "The spirit posing as the oracle is gone. Isis and Osiris, I know you are present here. You have been in this cave for a long time. Please come forward and show yourselves. We are ready."

The light concentrated itself in an orb suspended in the middle of the space. The orb lowered down and divided in two. The two golden spheres took shape and formed two golden rings. They played with each other. They showed themselves overlapping, forming an upright eye in the middle which blinked at them. One ring flew through the other. Then they positioned one inside the other, creating a three dimensional globe. Lines were formed across the diagonals crossing inside with all three lines meeting in the middle. A flow of silver along the lines showed how it multiplied its strength.

Yeshua and Mariam were mesmerized watching the display of the golden figure. The silver enhancing it gave them energy too. They could feel it flow through their own bodies just as easily as it flowed in the symbol in front of them.

Yeshua and Mariam saw themselves as bodies of consciousness. Their physical bodies were their anchor points to the earth, but their unseen spirit was how they identified themselves. While watching the golden circles play, their consciousness had grown. They both felt as big as the cave they were sitting in and equally golden in color.

As fields of spirit they united with the golden symbol floating in the space above them. This was the way Isis and Osiris wanted to teach them, here in this beautiful cave lit by gem stones. There was no separation between them. Mariam and Yeshua were one in the big golden sphere and Isis and Osiris were one with them. The four of them had become one big golden consciousness playing in a big open space decorated with semiprecious stones. In one endless moment all life in all eternity was kept in a golden balance of beauty. Male and female had merged. God and Goddess had merged. Spirit and matter where the same thing. The golden light encompassed them all.

The subtle colors of the stones let them create cryptograms which they beamed in light coded ribbons out through the opening in the roof of the cave. Yeshua watched messages of unity and love fly into the open skies like the fireworks he had seen in China. He saw the symbols form ribbons flying as messages of colored light landing in a time far into the future. This was his message of light. This was his first installment of new light connecting heaven and earth which would be read in a future time he couldn't see.

Bashra turned her head to the side and looked at the staff Yeshua had used to steady the boat. She sent it up in the air and held it hanging vertically suspended in the middle of the open space. Yeshua and Mariam made themselves into silver and golden spirals and wound themselves around the staff. Isis connected them on the top and created wings, and where they met on the bottom of the staff Osiris made a solid round ball. When the symbol was completed it split into two snakes which flew into their bodies and settled at the bottom of their spines. Mariam and Yeshua had anchored this power forever inherent in the human body.

Turning around in the open space, they saw their bodies sitting in the chairs with their eyes closed. They appeared as shining gold with a crystal inside each head beaming out white light. The light beams from their heads united in Bashra, the small head on the altar table, which focused the beam into one powerful spot of light. Bashra lifted her gaze and shot the concentrated light beam straight into the wall in front of her.

The beam cut a hole in the wall to the left of where the stream had come in. It was a little higher up on the wall than the water level, and led out of the cave and onto a promontory in the open air.

Yeshua and Mariam felt new fresh cold air stream into the space. Sensing the cold air on their skin pulled them back to their bodies. Gently they centered their awareness and found their hands and feet. They opened their eyes and saw blue skies through the opening.

"Hurry, before it closes again," said Bashra.

Mariam quickly scooped up the head and put it in the bag hanging from her belt. Yeshua was already out of his chair ready with his feet in the water holding out his hand for her. She gave him hers and they ran across the shallow water. Using the broken skulls as stepping stones they climbed up to the round hole in the wall. Outside was a shelf they could stand on while the hole closed behind them.

The view over the Mediterranean Sea was breathtaking with the scraggly shoreline and the archipelago of small islands. They stood on the narrow shelf and filled their lungs with fresh sea air. Never had she been so grateful for the simple gift of breath.

The shelf led onto a path, and they walked along the mountainside until they came to the edge of the forest. There was another path there that went back to the monastery. They walked in silence smiling to each other beaming golden light back and forth.

The monks welcomed them to their evening meal and asked how they had spent the previous night. Yeshua remembered lying in a small boat with his arms around his beloved and assured them that they had been quite comfortable. The healing waters were wonderful. Mariam thanked them for their hospitality and said that they would be ready to leave in the morning. The monks just nodded and smiled.

CHAPTER 2

HOMECOMING

THE CARAVAN CAME INTO JERUSALEM AND YESHUA and Mariam went to the Temple. Lazarus and Martha were there with some of the followers.

"Where have you been? The wedding is tomorrow! We've all been worried about you." Lazarus wasn't quite sure what to feel, anger or relief.

"Your parents are in Bethany and they have been everything from worried sick to furious. You were supposed to be here a week ago." Martha knew exactly what she felt. People should be more responsible.

Yeshua and Mariam knew where they had been. They knew how important this experience had been for them. Their calm spread to the others, and the mood changed to joy and anticipation of the great celebration that would soon take place.

"We almost cancelled, but the astrologers say that the time is right. We needed to do the wedding before the Passover and your families have made time to be here. It was now or never."

"We've been preparing for several days. We hoped you would be with us, Mariam, to choose flowers and help with the food. Mother said we should have the party anyway, and call it a funeral."

"And Joseph said he would have a word or two with both of you. If you were children you would be whipped!"

Lazarus would never have submitted himself to such humiliation, of misbehaving and be talked about this way. *Was this a suitable husband for his sister?*

She chose to go wherever they went, brother. And have you ever seen Mariam do anything she didn't want to do? Martha shot back in his head.

Mariam understood their concern, and wanted to help them.

"I'm glad to be here now, and it's so good to see you," she said. "Let's stop by the market. You'll know what we need."

"That would be good. Joseph mentioned we could use some more rugs for the area outside," said Lazarus relieved to have something practical to think about.

Mariam let Martha dominate the conversation with plans and preparations and left Yeshua and Lazarus to find the items for Joseph. She wanted to be with her sister this last day before the wedding, and it would be good if she and Yeshua arrived in Bethany separately.

The donkey cart took them to the market while Martha described all the things they had made ready. It seemed like all the food items were taken care of. All they needed was some flowers for the corners of the canopy. Martha knew what would look nice.

"What are you going to wear, I mean right now? They will be all over you when we arrive, you won't be given time to wash or change," stated Martha thoughtfully. Mariam had her head in a memory of a golden light and wasn't listening.

"Wear?"

"Yes, have on, you know, a dress! You can't wear that." Martha pointed to her sisters travel stained tunic covered in dust. "It would be dishonoring the work everybody else has done. You look like you've been dragged through dirt. Sister, what have you been doing?"

Mariam looked at herself. Oh, life was so much simpler at the Temple. She only needed one temple gown which got washed by the attendants. What was she supposed to do?

"Let me tell you," said Martha. "Let's find something suitable at the market and wash you off at the well. Luckily, the outfits for tomorrow have been planned a long time ago. Sarah is also here, and we will be your attendants. She's been missing you, sister. And by the way where have you two been? Have you been together all this time? The elders will have something to say about that."

Mariam didn't answer right away. She let Martha talk about her concerns and was willing to do whatever her sister suggested. For explanation, she said they needed her at the temple and that they had traveled together from the Serapium. She wasn't lying. She was telling a truth that would be easier to accept. Her tunic was indeed dirty and stained, and there was hardened salt from the ocean on the bottom. She agreed that she needed something to wear.

"How is Mother?" Mariam asked.

"She sure is not happy the way you're behaving. But the outfits for tomorrow are lovely. You remember how much thought we put into it? Mother knows how you've always enjoyed dressing up for festive occasions. So the last details are still up to you."

Mariam looked forward to just walk right into something already lying on a bed that was the perfectly respectable outfit, and that it was loose enough to fit her and could be tightened with a belt. She would have agreed to anything, but she was grateful for the lovely dress that was waiting for her. It had been planned since she reached her adult height. Mother had hired the best seamstress in town. They had chosen natural linen and red silk thread for the stitching. It had taken her a year to finish.

This date had been decided by the astrologers at Qumran for its auspicious positions of the stars and planets. It boded well for the prince and princess and for a country redefining its identity.

"The dress is of course in the traditional style for the bride. I'm not quite sure how much they're going to focus on your royal status."

Oh Isis, help me, thought Mariam. All she wanted was to marry the man. All she *really* wanted was to turn around and run away with him again. Run away from all these expectations, the destinies in front of them, all these obligations which had been waiting for this time to be carried out. She wanted to scream; *Let us do the rituals and be done with them, and then leave us in peace!*

But she knew it wasn't that simple. She had been preparing for this for a long time. So had he. And their relationship was somewhat secondary in importance to what they represented. She knew they were living symbols with many layers of meaning. A lot of people believed strongly in their cause. Some had put their lives on the line, and many more would continue to do so.

This would be the first time in forty generations that these two royal lines would be united. To a lot of people this meant that the people of Israel would claim their country. They would again unite in the Holy Land that was theirs. The temple had been rebuilt. All they needed was a King and Queen in Jerusalem to symbolize that the people and their relationship to God was restored and anchored in the land of their ancestors.

It was also the time to be very cautious. The country was under Roman occupation. This was a political issue which could have dire consequences.

All this was very beautiful, and also very powerful. Mariam could only think about it with burning patriotism. She would support this with all her training, with all the powers she had built in her body over years of studying at the temples. And she knew Yeshua felt the same. His learning was a little different than hers. They reflected what they symbolized. She represented the people and the land. He represented the relationship with God which his people had developed for thousands of years. She held her responsibilities with a strong back and the expression of a black panther. He held his with the strength and beauty of ancient wisdom and the spirit of young courage. She smiled thinking about him. Yeshua always brought blessings wherever he went.

Mariam felt romantic about her cause, but she shook her head and tried to consider how the Romans would respond. Judea was an occupied country now. This would be in total defiance of their foreign government. To the Romans they were just a small population with identity problems. The importance of this wedding, and the ceremonies that would follow, would be meaningless to them. They would much rather see this unruly group properly integrated as good Roman citizens who allowed their culture to be absorbed and then dissipate. But the twelve tribes had lived in foreign countries for thousands of years and their people had maintained their culture and their devotion. The knowledge about inner light was intact. It was their responsibility to again anchor it among their people.

What were the elders trying to do? Was the whole thing going to be held very secret? Was it all going to be presented as a religious ceremony for their people, which the logical Roman generals wouldn't put any meaning to? Or were they actually going to proclaim that Israel now had a new King and Queen? If so, were they safe? Is that why some of the followers were sicarii, the sword fighters, they were needed for security? Mariam wasn't sure how to interpret it all. They had indeed run away when they went to Baia, for a stolen time to be together on their own. It had been wonderful, absolutely wonderful. Had it been real? Right now Mariam wasn't sure what was real anymore.

The cart reached the market and they looked at flowers. Tuberoses were in season. Mariam loved their scent and wanted some of them. Pink sprig roses were also available and beautiful blue iris.

"Look at this," said Martha excited, making Mariam lift her face from the bouquet she was holding. Martha held an Egyptian hand woven shawl in pink, blue and white, just like the flowers. Mariam allowed her appreciation for pure beauty to fill her up and took a deep breath.

"Isn't it beautiful? Look, I found one in darker tones for Yeshua. You know we need prayer shawls for both of you." Mariam didn't know that, but she definitely liked what Martha was suggesting.

"And here, I found a white dress, similar to his shirt, and a peach colored tunic to have over it. What do you think?"

"That looks lovely, Martha. What about the blue sash I see hanging up above there, that will complete the outfit, don't you think?"

Of course, Mariam always knew how to accessorize. Martha was glad to hear her take part in this. She had been worried about her sister's earlier lack of interest.

"And the blue ribbon for your hair. This is lovely. Let's change you right here in the back room and then go to the well and wash your face. You'll be quite presentable."

They arrived in Bethany later in the day. Mariam was sitting in the front of the cart in her new clothes holding the flowers they had chosen. Martha was so pleased with her own work. She knew she had softened a situation that could have been rather unpleasant. The mothers welcomed them with excitement when they arrived and Sarah was jumping up and down as usual even though she was now considered an adult. Yeshua and Lazarus had walked the short distance from Jerusalem, and had arrived there before them. Yeshua looked like he had taken time to clean up, as well.

He was beaming, as always, and helped his wife out of the cart.

"What lovely flowers," Yeshua said lifting them out of Mariam's hand and handing them to Sarah.

"But nothing can compare to your beauty, my flower, my Mariam," he said for all the people around to hear. To her he said, "I love you, Queen of Heaven."

Mariam smiled at him and let him hold around her waist as she jumped down. It was again just him and her, and all they had experienced together. As soon as her feet were on the ground, the families shouted their welcome and the moment was over. They were enveloped in hugs and well wishes. Mariam noticed visible relief on many faces, and a scorn here and there.

They have the right to feel that way, she thought to herself. *We were indeed irresponsible. We claimed our time, but we also stole it from other people.*

The meal that evening felt more important than the meal of the wedding. Their little community had prepared well. Big pots were waiting for them. The mothers agreed that they needed to celebrate this evening as well, and they decided to serve the goat stew that was actually intended for the following day. They would have a new pot started tomorrow morning. Lovely bread was also served, and Joseph offered wine from his own private collection. His son was home and had brought Joseph's favorite daughter-in-law. He couldn't scold them. He could simply not stop hugging them.

Eurochia took Mariam aside when she had a chance.

"And where were you, daughter of mine? You were supposed to come with the next boat from Alexandria. What were you doing? "

"There was another initiation I needed to attend," Mariam answered and hoped her mother would be satisfied. Eurochia knew Mariam was often involved in the initiations at the temple. Mariam and Sibyl were the foremost authorities on herbs, balms and oils.

"Hm. When did you join up with Yeshua?" Eurochia did not approve of the bride and groom apparently having had the honey moon before the wedding.

"He found me at the Serapium, and then we came on the same boat." Mariam avoided the word "together".

Eurochia felt that something was missing from the story, but her daughter was an adult now, she couldn't treat her like a child. She also knew that If Mariam didn't want to tell, there was no way to get it out of her.

It wasn't that Mariam didn't want to say anything. It was more that she honestly couldn't. How could you explain where they had been or what they had experienced?

She didn't want to share this experience with any one. She could hardly put it into words herself. How could she possibly explain this profound experience so anyone would understand? The big golden ball she held inside would change if she limited it with words.

She agreed that the wedding was important, but to her they had been married for a long time already. She had been promised to him since she was three. They had married under the stars with Inanna and Tammuz as witnesses. This wedding was to honor the traditions they both came from, to honor the God of Abraham and Isaac, for their parents, for their ancestors and for their people. She knew that and accepted the situation. The experience of Baia would always be a secret memory in her heart, a memory of when they were united in love by Isis and Osiris.

Sarah came running. "Mother, Mariam, come. We have laid out your outfits for tomorrow. You have to come and see."

Martha and Sarah had assembled it all on the bed the way it would be on Mariam the following day. There was the blouse and skirt in natural linen. The red silk thread was shimmering in the light of the sunset outside. Eurochia stroked the sleeve, touching the row of cross stitching going down its length. She remembered discussing with the seamstress exactly where the embroideries would go according to the tradition in her family. They made sure the embroidered panels down the sides of the skirt followed the contour of her daughter's shapely figure. The shawl for her head was in the same light material, but the pattern was richer and spread out over the entire panel.

Eurochia had shown Mariam how the pattern told the story of their tribe, where they had traveled and where they had settled. She had pointed out to her where Bashra's homeland of Ethiopia was mentioned, and what signified Jerusalem and the land around the city. Eurochia looked at the lovely outfit and remembered her own wedding day. Her own dress had been darker, and she had been betrothed to Hiram at an older age. They had just been expected to marry and multiply, both in offspring and in commerce. She looked at her own wise and beautiful daughter. Honor belonged to her new status, but also responsibilities beyond what she could name. Eurochia was grateful for her own marriage. However complicated, she knew that this daughter would handle her own situation with grace and dignity.

Martha held up the headpiece that would go on top of Mariam's hair on top of the shawl. It had a circular thicker piece of cloth and then the heavy piece with coins attached.

"I guess you are a queen," she said thoughtfully.

"There are coins here from many of the cities our family has lived in," said Eurochia. "Your ancestors traveled."

Mariam looked at the blouse, noticing the heavily stitched front piece. It had a pattern forming a triangle pointing downwards, the symbol of the feminine in the Star of David. As a bride she would embody that part of the ancient symbol. According to their tradition, Yeshua would have the opposite triangle embroidered in white on his white tunic. Standing there with her mother and sisters Mariam was reminded of the powerful tradition she was part of. Her many years at the temples had made her forget.

"And look, we all got Atlas silk belts. Would you believe it?" Sarah wanted everybody's attention. "Father got them from the silk merchant in Aswan."

She showed them the burgundy and yellow tight stripes in thick silk that would go around her waist. Father had wanted his women to appear in style.

"Come. Look what we got for Mother." Sarah's usual enthusiasm made everybody smile. Her dark curls were bouncing on her head, and Mariam noticed what an exceptionally beautiful young woman she had become. She cherished these days with her knowing that her younger sister would return to Alexandria with her parents after the wedding.

Sarah led them over to Mother's bed. The blouse and skirt were in black linen. The embroideries were all in reds and oranges. Mariam remembered the patterns from before. It had been decorating her mother's finest garment for years. She recognized that the patterns were similar to the ones chosen for her own dress. The family patterns had started here, but changed as well. The blouse had the same triangle in the front with flowers as well as geometric parts. The panels on either side of the skirt were placed wider apart to complement her mother's fuller figure. What Sarah was all enthused about was the new shawl. It was in a much finer silk than the courser Egyptian material, and in a dark burgundy, almost black background. The astonishing embroideries with large red poppies and light green foliage covered the whole piece and were enough to take your breath away. .

"I needed something new," said Eurochia and blushed. Hiram had insisted on buying it for her, even though it cost three times as much as Eurochia was prepared to pay.

"It's from India, but I think it originated in China. Look at how the fringes are knotted. And poppies are a more typical Chinese motif."

Her hand touched the fine stitches, which were not the tight cross stitch typical for their traditions, but long threads in a flat stitch that covered the background completely. Eurochia always appreciated fine handywork, and this told of high quality craftsmanship as well as artistry.

"We have new things too." Mariam had to admire the lighter gold dresses of the sisters, the atlas silk belts which were the same as hers, and the gorgeous shawls that were different for them all.

"Mariam, look here. We have something else for you." Martha was holding a bundle in her arm and presented it to her sister. "We have been collecting for you for a while. Whenever we went to the market we would find one more thing."

Eurochia watched her daughters and felt the shift of the generations. Her oldest daughter was getting married. Eurochia would now have to take on the role of an elder. She stood back and watched, allowing some tears to flow hoping that the young women in front of her wouldn't notice. It wasn't that she was sad. This was the way families evolved. This was the way it should be. The young women had taken on their roles and stepped into a lively young adulthood. It was time for herself to retire into a quieter chapter of her life. The responsibility of carrying wisdom was different. At the wedding tomorrow she would don her black outfit and wear it with dignity.

Mariam was sitting on the bed with a sister on either side as she admired the things they had assembled for her.

"These are kitchen towels, we thought we would start there," said Martha. "They have the same red stitches on one edge."

"But then we found these and couldn't help ourselves." Sarah would always go for beauty. Mariam unrolled lovely window valances with long fringes in blues and turquoise, her own favorite colors.

"Here are more towels, and then some sheets and pillowcases. Mother said you needed those for sure. But we chose this blanket." Sarah unrolled a light wool blanket with crocheted silk edges.

"Mother said we shouldn't get too carried away, but really, you need warm bedcovers, and this has alpaca wool blended in with the sheep wool. I hope you like it."

Mariam lifted the blanket up to her face. It was lightweight, but thick. The sheep wool made it strong and durable while the alpaca added the luxurious feel and extra warmth. She was so moved thinking of all the work her sisters had taken on for her sake. These were duties that she herself should have taken care of, and quite frankly, she hadn't even thought about it. These were items needed for a good household, and she was getting married, that meant she was going to live somewhere. A good home had items in every room, on every body, that bore witness to the craft and creativity of women. The family was surrounded with textiles that had been imbued with love and care. Women would make their love take on physical form with all the items that they labored over and made. In most families the women would have made all these items themselves. Mariam's family was wealthy enough to pay for others to do the labor, but it was still their choices that entered the household. Mariam admired the traditions of family life and felt how far removed she had been from all this for so long. It all reminded her more of the way children played setting up "house" somewhere and inviting each other in for imaginary tea. She smiled, and knew she would indeed have her sisters over for tea and serve it on the lovely table cloth included in the dowry they had put together for her.

Eurochia allowed her daughters to sweep her away in their enthusiasm. Soon she was laughing with them and agreed that it was all lovely and Mariam's household would be colorful and comfortable. Mariam was so glad her mother was over her anger. She kissed her younger sisters in gratitude many times before the evening was over.

Outside by the evening fire, the men were sharing stories. Yeshua had apparently told them enough about boats and sea to satisfy. His eyes told her that their own adventure remained theirs.

He got up from the fire and came towards her. She took his hands and they stood there sharing eye contact. It grew silent around them. Their families had needed time to calm down after fervent worries about this young couple whom they all had built their hopes on. This quiet evening they could let their shoulders drop, sink their voices to more normal levels, allow their stomachs to rest and digest food properly, maybe even have a good nights sleep. They all just stopped and stared, and allowed the light emanating from these two radiant beings, whom they all loved so much, illuminate their own bodies. For a long quiet moment the light from the fire seemed dim and insignificant compared to the golden glow they all could sense around Mariam and Yeshua. The collective exhale was audible and the smile that formed on everybody's face was soft and easy. The older people thought about the people they loved in their lives. The younger ones hoped that at some time they could experience the same. But most of them didn't think of anything. They allowed this golden light to settle in their hearts and bring peace to their bodies.

Joseph finally broke the silence. "Welcome home!" he said, placing his big arms around their shoulders.

"I thank God that you are safe. I thank Him for this splendid night, His sparkling stars and I ask His blessings on the ceremony tomorrow. Let's all celebrate the unity of these two strong families."

Mariam turned towards Joseph, took his face in her hands and kissed him. She loved this good man who always knew how to say the right thing.

CHAPTER 3

PREPARING FOR THE WEDDING

MARIAM WOKE UP EARLY. THIS WAS A sunrise she needed to experience. Behind the colony there was a hill, and she found the path leading to the top. She passed some cedar trees and sycamores, a fig tree and some blooming bushes. It was spring time and the bougainvillea was already putting on flowers. It was light enough to see but the sun wasn't up yet. Her friend, Venus, was still visible.

It didn't take her long to get to the top. Johanna had showed her the way last time she was here. She had been in Bethany several times, but it was always short stays. It had been up to Lazarus and Martha to establish the household for their family while she was still studying. Was she going to stay here now, at least for a while? It depended on where her husband wanted to go, where his work took him. He didn't work the way Yochanan did. Yochanan and Anya had set up their household closer to the river so he could continue teaching and baptizing people. They had a little boy by now.

Was Yeshua going to do some of the same? He had been teaching all over Galilee and had attracted quite a following. Mariam had only traveled with him once along the countryside. She had helped him in his healing work and listened to his speeches. He was quite inspiring, telling people to go within, find the strength within them selves and remember that love was the strongest force in the universe. Mariam observed how he taught the parables and stories to the large flocks, the multitudes that came to hear. To smaller groups he would be more specific, it was as if he knew what each group wanted and needed. This population had been occupied for many years. The people were hungry for inspiration. He encouraged people to find power within themselves, to build self confidence, to find strength and develop individual abilities. People were fascinated. Mariam could understand why.

Since the time of Moses, the knowledge of how to build physical strength from the fortified bread and purified water had been taught only to a very select few. Yeshua felt that they needed more people who had the ability to carry the power of light within their bodies. Mariam agreed, but knew that his approach went contrary to old teachings intended to protect both the practitioners and the knowledge. She had learned to look at knowledge as an entity that should be respected. Protecting the knowledge from dilution was just as important as teaching it correctly.

She sat down on a rock on the top of the hill and looked over the landscape in front of her. In the distance she could see some of the tallest features of Jerusalem. Close by were vineyards and the colonies of Qumran and Bethany. She saw roof tops, storage houses and familiar homes for families. The Roman garrisons were easy to recognize with their adherence to straight lines which looked out of place among the local villages. Gatherings of people generally formed in a more organic way, and the Roman's did everything with mathematical precision. She could smile at their ignorance in areas that were so important and natural to her, but at the same time she had to respect the way they worked. Through force and fortitude they established themselves and brought every culture they put their foot into towards a higher level of order and civilization. *Except for this stubborn corner of their vast empire,* she thought.

It was easier in Alexandria. The city was already so metropolitan, such a mix of so many different cultures and philosophies, they had developed systems for learning from each other instead of fighting. The price had been national identity. It was easier to think of themselves as Roman citizens than to figure out where they all came from and where their loyalties lie. The result was that they were left alone to continue what they already were busy with, being citizens of lovely Alexandria.

Judea was a different story. Here there were fewer cultural entities, but the loyalties went deeper and the national hearts were beating loudly. They weren't satisfied with working quietly under the Roman canopy. They wanted to get rid of the Romans all together. Mariam knew this would be difficult. In her travels she had seen how far the Roman claw could reach, and she had seen the cruelty exhibited to people who opposed it. You didn't have to love the great Eagle, but you had to be aware of its power.

She tried to focus her thoughts about the ceremony which would take place later this day and say the incantations to bring blessings to this new union. Part of her was genuinely excited about it all. She longed to be together with Yeshua as his wife, and to do so with the blessings of their families. She longed to help him more in his work, to join forces with him in his healing and teaching. She also knew that after this day there would be other rituals that would be expected of her. She was willing to do them, willing to be part of this powerful building of momentum for the cause of their people, but she was also very aware of the dangers they were facing.

Her prayers went out for the safety of them all. She asked for blessings for everybody involved and for God to be with them in the work they were going to do.

The sun was showing its sharp rays over the horizon. Mariam had been watching the star all through the morning. As the sunrise crossed the path of the star, she sang the song they had learned at Therapautae dedicated to the meeting of these two powerful heavenly bodies. It was comforting to honor them again. She needed the strength they gave her. She needed to remember the power of the male and female forces. She lifted her arms towards the sun, and as she sang the next lines the melody was matched with other voices. Up the path came Yeshua with Lazarus and Martha. Behind them were Yochanan and Anya. They were all singing the song, and apparently this group was used to doing the morning ritual together. They smiled at her as they all joined on the top of the hill. Together they formed a long line of men and women all facing the sun and singing in unison. As they lifted their arms to honor the new day their voices divided into harmonies creating new frequencies strengthening the bond between each other.

They continued singing all the way down the mountain path. Lazarus kept the beat and had them sing about trees and grass and beautiful vineyards, beautiful people and the great breakfast they were soon going to share. Mariam's heart was filled with love for this community which had embraced the teachings from one of her favorite places. The summer at Therapautae was remembered with fondness.

The simple houses of their colony surrounded a small courtyard which also functioned as a meeting place. This was where they had their fires at night and where they met to talk. The hard dirt was their floor and the mighty sky the roof over their meeting hall.

Martha and Lazarus shared a small house and another house further back had been built recently for Mariam and Yeshua. The other homes had been there for years and housed the many other members of their colony. Another colony met the outskirts of their own which housed Yochanan and Anya and their extended families.

The houses were made of local materials, which meant the rocks and stones of the ground around them. In the old tradition, anything made with stone got a layer of mud on the outside. Each place used their own proportions of sand, water, ground limestone and some organic material. It dried quickly, held up pretty well and was easy to replace.

Most groups of houses were arranged in a circle to create a courtyard between them for the communities to meet. Usually people were closely related in addition to sharing the same traditions. They considered all their members family and took care of each other.

Breakfast in the community was held at the fire in the gathering place in front of Joseph and Mary's home. Food had been prepared and they all sat down around the fire to enjoy bread and couscous with cheese and milk. Tea was warmed for them and green herbs were shared.

Mariam sat down between her sisters knowing this was probably the last morning she could take that for granted. Later she would be expected to be next to Yeshua. She held around them and savored the bond she felt with these two beautiful women.

Gratitude filled her body thinking of the support that had always been there. Young Mary, Salome and Johanna joined them, and their sisterhood was expanded.

Yeshua stole a glance at her across the circle. Lazarus and Yeshua's own brothers James, Jude and Joses were teasing him, calling him a lucky man. Fayed and Ezra also fell in with ease among them. The four parents had joined in a group together. They admired the young flock they had around them, and Eurochia thought it was definitely time to marry them off. Too many young ones unattached would lead to parties and idle talk. Joseph agreed with her with great humor. He had seen these studious minds at work. He knew they needed their time to be young for a day. There was not a worry in his mind that they would be led astray. He reassured Eurochia that she had nothing to worry about.

Hiram stood up and wanted to say something. He tapped his tall walking staff on the ground to get their attention. Mariam noticed the over coat he was wearing, the two long pieces of woven wool sewn together in the back, but split at his neck. The colors belonged to her family which he would always wear on his body. But this particular coat was the one she had woven for him at an early age. It was the one where she had made a mistake in the loom and later embroidered over it in the shape of a llama. Her father loved this one. He was wearing it because of her.

"Family," Hiram announced. "Family and extended family. I am proud to speak to you, and I think I speak for everybody, when I say I'm looking forward to the ceremony which will commence later on this auspicious day. And I am inviting you all to Alexandria, not just as honored guests, but as members of my own family. The group of people gathered here has shown me and my wife and children the utmost in hospitality and welcome. I am proud to be a member here, and I am proud to say that all of you are members of my closest tribe."

"Hear, hear," went through the group.

"With this wine I ask for this first blessing of the day to be for our new couple, who finally arrived so that we can spend a whole day celebrating their union. So blessed be in the morning light, Mariam and Yeshua."

People lifted their glasses with him and drank to their honor. Lazarus thought it was good that their late arrival had been alluded to. With that acknowledgement they could now laugh about it.

"Mariam come, we have to get you dressed," Sarah called.

"Please join us," said Mariam, inviting her three sisters-in-law to come as well.

Six young women were in the bedroom Mariam and her sisters shared. Mariam breathed in the sweet odor of excited young women. Her life at the temples had been so focused on learning rituals, doing rituals, using herbs and other substances to enhance the inner experience of communicating with the Gods. There was little time for the intricacies of daily family life. The community of sisterhood with beautiful women dressed in colorful clothing and thinking about handsome men had only been experienced in small increments. She had fond memories of time with Sibyl at the festivals and with her sisters when she visited her parent's home in Alexandria. But here, in this small colony, where you had the closeness of families who knew each other well, the experience was very different.

"This is gorgeous," exclaimed Johanna. "Did your family do all the embroideries?" Martha and Sarah had to admit that they had paid a seamstress to oversee the work.

"It is outstanding. Look at this shawl!"

Mariam explained what the different parts meant. The pattern was telling the story of their family. "See, here is where they lived in Ethiopia, after coming across Sinai."

"And this is where we live now, in Alexandria," added Sarah.

Mariam admired Johanna and Mary and young Salome, her new sisters. Mary and Johanna both had the lighter skin tone of their mother, and Johanna even had Joseph's reddish hair. But the young girl Salome was dark like her own father and looked more like Sarah. Mariam and her sisters were much darker skinned and their hair was so dark brown it was almost black. Mary had blue eyes, whereas Mariam's family all had brown eyes with bigger dark eyelashes. Sarah had the curls, her ringlets were unruly at any given time. Martha's hair was totally straight, and Mariam's was somewhere in between. Thinking of women, she gave Sibyl a thought, her best friend and partner at the Serapium. Sibyl was blond, blue eyed and fair. She never got to know where she got that look from. And then there was Herodias, her partner at Ephesus. She was probably the prettiest of all the women Mariam had ever known with her golden skin, finely shaped dark features and jet black thick wavy hair. She was also the feistiest. Remembering Herodias' quick dark eyes and quick temper, she wondered how she was doing in Rome. She was supposed to be stationed somewhere in Syria. Maybe their paths would cross. Sibyl was easy to find. She would stay at the Serapium with her herbs, at least that's what she'd said last time they talked.

"Mariam, you're not listening!" Sarah brought her back to the flock. "This is the first thing we need to do. We'll take you down to the river to wash. You need to be cleansed. It is part of the ritual for the ceremony later today."

They walked together towards the river carrying various items needed for the task. Mariam was amused, and relieved that all the others seemed to know what to do.

All this belonged to the tradition of their ancestors. The wedding had to be in the land of Canaan, between the two tribes to be united. The importance of all this was obvious to anybody who claimed membership of the tribes. *That's a lot of people,* Mariam thought to herself. *This is important to all the twelve tribes of Israel.* She pushed the thought aside. All she wanted to do right now was to go to the river with five lively women and feel water on her body.

They ran into Yochanan on his way to his part of the river Jordan. He was carrying a bucket of good water from his baptismal pond.

"I was hoping to find you," he said. "Here, take this. Use it for Mariam. It will be good for her." He handed the bucket over to young Mary and wished them all well before he was on his way in a different direction.

"That was nice of him. We will use it to rinse your hair," Mary announced.

The women had already established a spot where they used to go and wash. It was somewhat hidden behind an outcrop of rock and a handy bush had grown to give them more privacy. Still, they had brought a large sheet to hold up for Mariam to hide behind. Mariam thought of the pools at the Serapium and the elaborate Roman baths in Ephesus. This reminded her again of the simplicity of Therapautae and the close contact with nature. The sun made her eyes squint, and she was aware of that some of the dust on her body had come all the way from Baia.

Mary efficiently tied the sheet to a protruding branch. Johanna held onto the other end and walked a little out in the water. Their own space was secured. Mariam stood with her arms outstretched and her sisters pulled her tunic and under dress over her head. She was encouraged to walk into the water and given a piece of cloth and a bar of soap which she recognized as one of the gifts she had sent from the Serapium at some point. It was Sibyl's favorite blend with lavender and rose.

Martha pulled her dress up around her waist and fastened it in her belt. She took two steps out in the water and offered the fortified water for her hair. Mariam ducked her whole body under the water. To everyone's surprise she swam underwater for a bit before surfacing. She went further out and swam a couple of strokes before turning over and looking back at her astonished company.

"What? I learned to swim in the pools at the Serapium. They wanted us to be safe in water. I'll teach you," she laughed back at them.

She swam dutifully back to shore and let them wash her hair. The water from Yochanan felt like liquid sunshine flowing down her face. It cleared her thoughts and calmed her head. Sibyl's soap was familiar and smelled lovely. It resonated with her femininity and together with the laughing women around her she could leave her role as a priestess and just be a beautiful bride for a day.

They came giggling back home with Mariam smelling wonderful and her hair dripping. A lose clean tunic had been provided for her to come home in, but now it was time to get her into her bridal attire.

Their moods were more serious as they approached the embroidered gown again. The history of her family was present. As soon as she stepped into the clothing she would be a link in a long tradition. Her attendants were hesitating. She was still just their Mariam, sister, friend and playmate. Wearing the bridal outfit she would become something else.

They helped her in silence. First she got a light shift of fine cotton next to her skin. Then they pulled the blouse over her head and held the skirt so she could step into it. It was pulled up and Martha fastened it at her waist. Sarah pulled on the blouse to make it comfortable and look balanced around her body. Johanna looked at the Atlas silk of the belt. She had seen the same colors on Eurochia. The burgundy with the yellow stripes were hanging ready for Sarah and Martha to use as well. Their own colors were red and black. Joseph had talked to their uncle Joseph and made sure that his daughters had just as fine belts to wear.

Sarah got the honor to put on the headpieces and the shawl. They decided to wait until her hair was dry, so instead the other women put on their own outfits. There was much squealing and laughter from the bedroom which caused both the mothers to come in and check on them.

Eurochia was a little perturbed about her daughter's loud behavior. Mary was used to her unruly bunch and knew how much they would enjoy this process. In her own quiet way she calmed them all without saying much. They both admired how Mariam looked in the embroidered dress, and Mary also got the story of their family as told in fine cross stitching on a shawl.

Yeshua had also been to the river with the young men who had made a lot of splashing sounds as well. Now he looked somber standing in the courtyard in his fine white shirt with white embroideries on from his family. Black wide pants and a belt with silver coins on it completed his outfit. He was done playing bachelor with his brothers. He was waiting for his bride.

"Mariam, I want us to do something before the ceremony."

"Yes, husband," she replied.

"You experienced the water from Yochanan this morning. I want to be baptized by him."

"Yes. There is time."

"Let's go to the river, wife."

They felt awkward. It felt so foreign to speak to each other like that. It felt formal and stiff, but somehow correct for the day.

Before they were finished with the sentence, all the women came from one side of the courtyard, and all the young men came from the other pulling them apart and telling them loud and clear that they weren't supposed to see each other before the ceremony. With lots of laughter they were escorted to two different ends of the colony. Mariam was taken for a walk in the orchard, whereas the young men went with Yeshua to the river to find Yochanan.

The orchard was blooming. The women walked underneath the branches with white flowers knowing that soon there would be fruit on the trees ready for picking. This was a peach grove, and the trees themselves gave the sent of the fruit they were promising later. Mariam took a branch, bent it towards herself and buried her face in white petals. They allowed the orchard to mesmerize and hypnotize, allowed nature herself to create a shower of white fluffy petals around the young women who for a day could live in a dream.

Yeshua and the men arrived at Yochanan's baptismal place in the river.

"Cousin," called Yeshua. "I want to be ready for my wedding. Purify me with the same waters you gave my wife."

"Yeshua, you know just as much as I do about purified water. We drank the same amount at Therapautae. You can have some any day you want. You don't need any baptism, and certainly not from me."

Yeshua wasn't going to listen to any argumentation from his lifelong playmate and friend, his partner through years of studies, even if he was the elected Messiah among the Nazareeans at this point. He would accept the fortified bread from his hands later on, bur first he wanted to feel the water.

"Brother, you blessed my wife, bless me the same way."

Yochanan smiled. The water kept flowing down the river through all the little steps he had set up, and he did have some water on the side which had gone through an even finer process. *I will give you a blessing, brother, this is your day,* he thought. *Thank you,* his cousin sent back to him.

Yochanan invited Yeshua to step into the river. He said the incantations that awakened the vibration in the water that was already latent there because of the devises in higher up in the river. Having watched the effect it had on multiples of people, Yochanan was proud of his system. He knew it worked, and he knew how and why. Bringing peoples genetic material back to their original perfect blueprint was simple. The effect was instantaneous and accumulative. Over time they would look younger and feel stronger. This was Yochanan's observations with regular people. He was not sure how it would work on Yeshua.

Well, it couldn't possibly hurt anything, said his playmate back in his head.

Yochanan smiled in agreement.

Yeshua pulled his white shirt over his head and handed his clothes to his brother James. Then he stepped into the water and immersed himself in it. The water had a sweeter smell, and felt slightly slippery between his fingers. As soon as his whole body was under, he could feel the water working its effect on him. His frequency was matched with that of the water. He could feel his inner sound going up three tones. And then he could feel that he resonated back to the water, making the water sing those notes too. As he stood up from the water to the sound of Yochanan's song, he could see the surrounding stones having changed their inner vibration. Their color was clearer. The tree next to the water looked a little straighter. The sky looked a little bluer. The birds flew out of the trees and made a couple of swift circles over him before flying off.

"Doves," said young Joses. "No hawks or eagles for you, brother. Doves."

"Love birds," the others laughed.

"The birds of Isis," corrected Yochanan, as he poured the further purified water over Yeshua's head.

Yeshua closed his eyes and let the water cover his head and flow down his hair and face in small rivulets. The top of his head was always ready to receive from above.

It had felt like an open field too sensitive for touch, almost too sensitive for water. He had wondered what to do with this part of his body. The channel had to stay ready at all time, but he didn't want to be too vulnerable. As the water gathered on his head, the grid work on top turned from loose organic threads to a lattice of open squares being filled in with a golden substance, flowing like honey. It filled the openings on top of his head protecting him, but still keeping him open for input from above. He felt fortified. A deep intake of breath solidified the experience. He stood for a while taking it all in. Then he opened his eyes and looked at his companions, again spreading calm and compassion. Now he could get married. Now he was ready. He thanked his cousin for providing this experience for him.

The young men attending him were not joking anymore. They had seen the birds and they had seen the blue sky change. As the stones around them had taken on a cleaner frequency, their own bodies had done the same just from standing near as witnesses. Yeshua looked up and saw six young men staring at him. He stretched out a hand for his shirt and smiled. This was not the day for explanations.

The elders had arrived when they came back. There were representatives from Qumran, from the Nazareean community and from the Essenes. These were all people held in high esteem in all the communities and who had been teachers of Yeshua at some point. He greeted them all respectfully according to their own traditions and thanked them for coming. It was time to start the ceremony.

CHAPTER 4

THE CEREMONY

THE YOUNG MEN WERE HOLDING UP THE canopy. The young women had decorated it with flower garlands along the fabric and bouquets in the corners where the poles were holding it up. The elders were all gathered for the ceremony. The bride and groom had arrived. The wedding could take place.

With much laughter and much serenity the families had also gathered, standing witness to this important event.

The rabbi had brought the scroll with the marriage vows. The elders knew the prayers by heart from many years of having this responsibility at weddings.

The sun was bright and the air was crisp and clear against the intense blue sky. Mariam thought she heard the birds singing an extra verse for her, which completed her image of a perfect wedding day. Yeshua just smiled.

They had stayed inside Joseph and Mary's house until the ceremony was going to start. The family had kept them apart earlier, but now they were allowed to be together. Some fruit had been made ready for them, but they were occupied standing still, facing each other studying each others faces which they thought were familiar, but today somehow looked different. With all the care of their attendants they had each been prepared according to their tradition. Sweet smelling lotions had been applied to their skin and aromatic scents surrounded them.

"Mariam, my beautiful wife," he said and took her hands.

"You look lovely," she beamed up at him.

"I love you," he said touching her cheek. "Are you ready for this?"

"I'm ready to be married to you. I've always been married to you."

"I know," he said softly, and kissed her hands.

James pushed the door aside. "They're expecting you," he announced.

Mariam and Yeshua didn't move their eyes from each other.

"I guess it's time," he said and offered her his arm.

"Yes," she said as she exhaled and gave him her hand.

They turned and faced the door. Lazarus held it open for them, and they stepped out in the bright light. Their families greeted them with applause. The rabbis and officials bowed respectfully. The bride and groom stood for a moment and allowed themselves to be admired before they proceeded between their families towards the canopy.

Mariam had attended weddings in Alexandria and remembered visiting wealthy homes with guests in bright silks and sparkling jewelry. The simplicity she was experiencing here made the whole event more powerful. There wasn't any room for pretence or emotions that didn't belong. All there was room for was the creation of a bond between two families who had wanted to be united for centuries, a bond tied with love and care between two families and a bride and a groom who truly loved each other. Mariam thought about her friend Herodias who had been told by her family to leave Ephesus and come to Rome to marry a man she didn't know. Mariam squeezed Yeshua's hand as they walked slowly between family and well wishers and knew how fortunate she was.

Eurochia looked at her daughter and son-in-law. They sure were a handsome couple. That outfit looked wonderful on her. The seamstress had done an expert job and the choice of colors suited Mariam beautifully. Eurochia was quite pleased. Sarah and Martha looked smart too in their dresses. It would be their day soon. *Did she still listen to an ancestor from Ethiopia?*

Hiram looked at his daughter, the studious one, the strong minded one. Would this man be a match for her active brain? He certainly had been studying hard, but would all this learning help them in their marriage? Hiram surely hoped so, and sent them his best wishes.

Mary saw her son come towards her with his lovely bride and at the same time she saw a powerful young priestess being married to the man she loved. She saw what came next in the vision and knew that she would be part of the story as the other priestess with knowledge. Sighing, she tried to lift the heavy cloak it represented. Today was a lovely day and she wanted to celebrate with everyone. Mary beamed a smile at them and ignored the tears streaming down her face.

Joseph just beamed. He had no space for tears. Of all the people there he was the strongest admirer of his-daughter-in law. He was bursting with pride that his son was getting married to this incredible woman, with so much knowledge, such wisdom beyond her young years. There was a refinement in the air that happened every time Mariam entered a space.

Joseph admired his son, as well. His dedication to self development was remarkable. Joseph had never seen anyone take new teachings to heart and immediately apply them to himself like his own son. Yeshua had traveled to the Far East and studied with wise people there, and at the most esteemed learning centers in their culture. Every time he came back he had something new to share with his father, a new technique, a new approach, a new way of thinking. And the goal was always to embody more of the divine and live from that source.

The fullness of his inner life made Yeshua appear luminescent. Other people applied it to him living closer to God and being gentle and wise. Joseph knew better. Yeshua had learned the laws of physics governing how the divine worked. He healed the sick, and people called him a miracle worker. Joseph knew that Yeshua left it at that. It was easier than trying to explain how he worked with light and love as powerful forces he wielded with the precision of trained master. Joseph still swore by the effectiveness of the gold products he was an expert on. He knew part of Yeshua's secret was that he had been exposed to it at an early age.

The rabbi welcomed them all to the ceremony and acknowledged the people who had traveled all the way from Alexandria. He mentioned that this was a big day for Canaan and for the people of the twelve tribes. This would also be a personal day of atonement for the bride and groom as they cleared their previous lives of being in two bodies and entered their new form as one. From now on they would be as one soul in two bodies.

"The bride and groom are like Adam and Eve," the rabbi continued. "They represent the perfect beings God created to live perfect lives on our earth. And like all new couples, their life together will be dedicated to restoring Jerusalem for all the people that came from the twelve tribes of Abraham, Isaac and Yacov."

"Let all who have ears hear," said James.

"Hear hear," joined his other brothers Joses and Jude together with Lazarus, Fayed and Ezra.

Mariam listened to their enthusiasm and thought of the powerful patriotism that lay behind it. She knew how much they relied on this couple to fulfill their destiny. And she knew how ready they were to support it with their lives if necessary. Were they also ready to take on the teachings and live it, like Yeshua always did? She wasn't so sure about that. She knew the self discipline required.

Joseph listened to the rabbis blessing. He admired the wise and graceful choice of words. This blessing was part of every wedding following their tradition. No outsider would notice that this was a very special wedding indeed.

At this point Mary and Eurochia left their places in the circle and came towards the wedding couple. They took Mariam's hands and guided her in a circle around Yeshua. Then they instructed her to walk around his body seven times. Mariam complied while listening to quiet incantations from the two women whishing her abundance, happiness and many children. She had left Bashra inside the house, but in her mind she could hear her blessing joining up with the mothers with an additional; *You know you're always protected.*

Mary carried a ceramic plate which had been specially made for this day. She invited the other two women to hold onto it with her. Together they threw it to the ground in the middle of the circle where it broke in many pieces to the shouts and encouragement of their guests.

The rabbi declared that Miriam now had joined in the household of Yeshua and the two families would eat many meals together. He then proceeded to tie their wrists together with a red ribbon.

Yeshua and Mariam stood in front of the rabbi under the canopy as he poured wine over their hands. "This is to sanctify this new bond, this spiritual bonding between two souls. We now see the fulfillment of the divine, the joining of the male and female as husband and wife. Blessed be," he sang before he poured some wine on the ground, then lifted the glass of wine and drank from it.

Mariam and Yeshua were instructed to turn around and face the audience. They turned their bodies showing the red ribbon with Mariam's skirt as a backdrop.

The seven blessings were going to be said. The elders had been given a glass of wine to use in the ceremony.

The rabbi from Qumran stepped forward and declared; "You are blessed, Lord our God, the sovereign of the world, who created everything in glory." He poured a little bit of the wine on the ground, and lifted his glass to the couple before he drank from it.

The rabbi from the Essenes stepped forward and said in his quiet voice; "You are blessed, Lord our God, the sovereign of this Creation, Lord the creator of human beings, of men and women." He also poured wine on the ground and toasted the couple. They nodded politely back.

The rabbi within their own small group took a step into the circle and said; "You are blessed, Lord our God, the sovereign of this creation, who created human beings in his image, in the pattern of his own likeness, and provided for the perpetuation of his kind. You are blessed, Lord, the creator of man." Then he also toasted the earth and the couple.

The rabbi from the Nazareeans stepped into the circle and said; "Let the barren land be jubilantly happy and joyful at her joyous reunion with her children. You are blessed, Lord, who makes Zion rejoice with her children." His offering to the earth was generous and his drink to the couple emptied his cup.

Hiram had also been given a glass of wine. He stepped in to the circle, cleared his throat and said in a loud voice; "Let the loving couple be very happy, just as you made your creation happy in the Garden of Eden. You are blessed, Lord, who makes the groom and bride happy." Hiram ended with taking a big gulp from the wineglass. The circle smiled and Hiram smiled with them.

Joseph knew it was his turn. His voice was steady and strong, and he turned as he spoke to reach everybody.

"You are blessed, Lord our God, the sovereign of the world, who created joy and celebration, bridegroom and bride, rejoicing, jubilation, pleasure and delight, love and brotherhood, peace and friendship. May there soon be heard, Lord our God, in the cities of Judea and in the streets of Jerusalem, the sound of joy and the sound of celebration, the voice of bridegroom and the voice of bride, the happy shouting of bridegrooms from their weddings and of young men from their feasts of song. You are blessed, Lord, who makes the bridegroom and the bride rejoice together."

His toast to the earth was deliberate and his greeting to the couple heartfelt.

The last one to speak was Yeshua's oldest brother, James, a big supporter of the cause who had gone through some of the same training as Yeshua.

"You are blessed, Lord our God, the sovereign of the world, creator of the fruit of the vine." He poured the wine on the ground and lifted his glass. "To Miriam and Yeshua, may you be fruitful and multiply! And brother, you have the most beautiful bride in Judea! Let's celebrate!!"

Everybody rejoiced and drank their toast. Yeshua and Miriam had to use their lose hands, which was a little awkward, but they managed. They both smiled to their families, taking in all the well wishing from so many.

The evening proceeded with the big meal which had been prepared for days. The pots were taken out, more wine was offered. Soon everyone was sitting on the ground, on the rugs they had recently bought in Jerusalem, with a plate of food. Music was played and Lazarus lent his good tenor to the traditional songs. Mariam and Yeshua were still tied at their wrists and fed each other to the great amusement of their guests.

Mary came over and whispered something in Yeshua's ear. He raised his head and looked over to his parent's house. Soon his brothers were bringing out more amphorae with wine. Hiram held out his glass to be filled as James offered more to the guests. He lifted the glass and drank, and lifted the glass again, toasting Joseph as a great host.

Sarah got up to dance together with Yeshua's sister Salome. They had practiced a little together and were now showing a dance where they used two shawls to make themselves concealed and revealed in surprising poses. The night turned dark, the fire was lit and the stars came out. In the courtyard there was a warm celebration between two families who were now united forever.

The young men insisted on singing, and they started a lewd drinking song. Joseph joined in with them to show them it was acceptable for tonight. Hiram held around his wife and rocked back and forth to the song. Eurochia knew she would have to help him to bed later, but not yet, she was still enjoying herself too much. Soon there were shouts for the bride and groom to dance. They pulled each other up and straightened out their clothing, much to people's amusement. Yong Jude came with a comment, which Miriam didn't hear, but she could tell from their looks that it had something to do with how lovely she was and how lucky Yeshua was going to be. She smiled at them and sent them a message to their heads saying that she looked forward to it as well. That silenced them very quickly and their faces turned red. She swung her skirt in front of them as she went out to the center to dance with her husband.

CHAPTER 5

THE WEDDING NIGHT

T HE GUESTS HAD LEFT, THE MUSICIANS HAD gone home. Good people were cleaning up food items and wine glasses. Sarah and Salome had taken their shawls and gone to bed. The young men were still sitting around the fire, but the singing had died down to a soft hum.

It was a while since their families ceremoniously and with lots of laughter had taken Yeshua and Mariam to their bedroom. Their little one room house had been ready for them for some time. Yeshua and his brothers had built it with help from other men in the village. All the women in the family had contributed something while they were waiting for Mariam and Yeshua. They needed this distraction while worrying about their whereabouts. The result was lovely, and Mariam had admired the simple furniture and the practical placements of blankets and bed linens, pots and dishes. Sarah had even insisted on hanging up the window valances yesterday. Mariam was grateful for all their efforts. They had a place to be alone.

They listened to the boisterous noise as their young relatives left to continue their revelries in the courtyard. Now they could return to their own quiet way of communicating.

"Is there any water in here do you think? I'd like to wash my face," Yeshua said.

"I would like some water to drink. Let me see what I can find."

Mariam went to the table where some dishes and cups were gathered and indeed, there was a water jug there which had been filled for them. She poured water into a bowl and a glass, which she immediately drank up before carrying the basin to her husband.

He had sat down on the bed, waiting for her, but got up and readied a stool to receive the bowl. She produced a piece of soft fabric and dipped it in the water. He lay down on the bed, and she sat down next to him and washed his face. Then she dipped the cloth again to refresh it.

"The ceremony was beautiful," she said thoughtfully. "Now we have everybody's blessings."

The traditional prayers are so meaningful, he signaled to her head as he closed his eyes and let her clean his forehead.

"I feel as if I'm included in a chain of connections," she said. "I feel as if I've been entered into a system I've long been part of, but not active in. I've lived so many years apart from this."

"Many years in preparation, and now you're ready."

"And you too, husband."

They were silent for a moment, acknowledging what had been said. She washed her own face and put the bowl away. When she came back, he had crawled under the blankets so she climbed into bed and lay down next to him.

"And now we have their blessing for what we are going to do tonight. They're even expecting us to," he said turning towards her.

"I'll feel your brothers peeking over your shoulder all night."

He laughed. "We'll block their attention from that. I can create an invisible egg around us which they can't see through."

"Then they'll wonder tomorrow if anything happened," she laughed back at him.

"Hmm, that's a problem. They'll tease me forever if they think it didn't. Maybe we should allow them in anyway," he joked. *That's the problem with a telepathic society. Privacy is hard to find.*

"We'll let them have a peak," she murmured back at him curling up to his shoulder.

"At least this far," he said as he pulled her closer to him and kissed her passionately.

Their embroidered clothing and headpieces had been carefully removed by their giggling attendants. They were both in their cotton undergarments. The sheets on the bed were the fine Egyptian cotton Sarah had picked out and the blanket on top was the wool and alpaca blend. The linens had been scented with rose and lavender.

"Now you can create that egg around us," she said.

"It is about time," he said as he stroked his hand along her shoulder while he visualized the two of them inside a golden cave with amethyst and emerald crystals in the ceiling.

Outside the stars were showing all the constellations of the season. The moon was new and the young men were saying goodnight to each other. The celebration was over, the families were united and the young couple was bedded. They yawned as they waived each other off and promised not to stir anybody too early the following morning. James still thought his brother was a lucky man and saw a sweet kiss between them.

He smiled to himself, as he looked for a glass of water hoping his head wouldn't hurt tomorrow morning.

Inside a golden egg, the bright light made the crystals in the ceiling sparkle as two golden circles were creating new geometric formations. He was a tetrahedron pointing up. She was a tetrahedron pointing down. Together they formed a Merkaba, the three dimensional version of the Star of David.

CHAPTER 6

THE DUNGEON

SHORTLY AFTER THE WEDDING, MARIAM GOT NEWS about her friend from Ephesus. Her parents and Sarah had left for Alexandria and the colony was back to normal. Only a few flowers remained from the wedding, but even those were wilting at this point. Mariam was holding one of the last tuberoses to her nose when someone came running up the path from Jerusalem. The whole city was talking about the latest drama and the story found its way to Bethany as well.

"You were studying together at Ephesus, weren't you?" Asked Lazarus when they were gathered in his and Martha's house later. Yeshua was in Galilee with his brothers.

"We were partners learning as a team," Mariam said trying to clarify, but making it more cryptic. "Herodias got called to Rome shortly before I left," she said stirring a pot trying not to show how much she missed her strong friend.

"And she married Herod Phillip, right, the procurator in Syria?" Martha wanted to get her facts straight.

"His funeral will be at the palace in Jerusalem," Johanna filled in. "After all, his father built it, they want to do it in style."

"The funeral will be immediately followed by the wedding of his widow and his brother," Lazarus lifted his eyebrows. He wondered how his headstrong independent sisters would respond to a woman being treated like that.

Martha, Johanna and young Salome all started talking at once, to the great amusement of Lazarus. Kings or not, women had to at least be consulted before they were married off.

Mariam tried to listen as the story shifted back and forth between her relatives.

"You mean, Herodias has lost Philip and will have to marry Antipas, all in the course of a week?"

"Yes, she's here in Jerusalem."

Mariam had to sit down. Her head was buzzing. How could she get to see her? She was sure Herodias would appreciate a good friend right now. Could she show up at the palace and say she was an old acquaintance of the Queen? In fact, Mariam was the true Queen of this country. *She would like to have a word with the one appointed by Rome.* Her thoughts became ridiculous. Herodias would have liked that. The more ludicrous, the more it would have appealed to her sense of humor. In spite of the situation, Mariam laughed inside and wished Herodias could have laughed with her.

At the fire that evening the whole colony was discussing what they'd heard. Yochanan came up from his place by the river with Anya and little Yahya to discuss it with Joseph and Yeshua.

"He can't do this and think he can get away with it," he said loudly.

"Well, Herod Antipas is the king proclaimed from Rome. He can pretty much do what he wants," added Joseph with the same grain of salt he reserved for all Romans.

"According to his tradition, he's supposed to marry his brother's widow," said Yeshua who had studied many cultures.

"But he's been trying to become a Jew!" Yochanan protested loudly." If that's what he desires, he'd better follow our laws. He was already married!"

"I heard he simply sent the poor princess back to the country she came from," said Anya sympathizing with the young queen who was sent back to her father with a decree of divorce.

"Divorce is not permitted according to our law," declared Yochanan. "If he wants to be one of us, he has to respect our scriptures!"

"What's with the man?" wondered Yeshua. "Why does he desire to become Jewish?"

"He's been hanging around at the Temple and wants to be on the council," said Joseph. "I've heard your uncle talk about it. The members of the Sanhedrin aren't quite sure what to make of it either."

"It's a disgrace!" said Yochanan loudly. "If he's let in at the council after making this spectacle of himself, it will be a blatant disrespect to our people. The fact that he thinks he can carry on like this and still have a chance with the Sanhedrin, shows that he has no true desire to become like us at all. It's all a political move from his side. I have to speak about this at the Temple tomorrow. This is too disturbing."

"Be careful, son," said Joseph. "If you criticize him openly it will be seen as an attack on Rome. Don't put yourself in danger."

"How did his brother die?" asked Miriam.

"Under rather shady circumstances," continued Lazarus. "Somebody said poison."

"So Herod Philip was murdered? Why?"

"His brother, Herod Antipas, apparently fell in love with his brothers wife. She's is supposed to be lovely."

"And smart too. Antipas doesn't know what he's getting himself involved with," added Martha who'd heard stories.

"He sure doesn't," concluded Mariam thinking of the gorgeous, brilliant and headstrong woman she'd been fortunate to learn to know in Ephesus.

As the appointed Messiah of the Nazareeans, Yochanan felt that he had a responsibility to speak. If the rabbis wouldn't call Antipas on his actions, he would. The others continued the discussion the following days. They both admired his courage and thought he was too outspoken. The response came from the palace very quickly. Yochanan and his followers received a warning. Any more statements like this from him, and there would be consequences.

An unexpected guest came to their little community. A woman wearing plain clothes and a black shawl came with Lazarus up from the city one day. She had asked for Mariam, married to Yeshua, and her brother was glad to show the visitor the way.

Mariam saw her from a distance. She recognized her regal bearing immediately. She wanted to shout her name, drop the basket she was carrying and run to embrace her. But Mariam and Herodias were both temple trained. Herodias had already heard her welcoming shout and asked Mariam to not reveal her identity.

Calmly the two women met in the middle of the community space, and calmly Mariam invited her for a cup of tea in her own kitchen.

Inside her home their embrace was long and warm. They both cried of joy to find each other and in grief over the difficult circumstances.

"Mariam, you have to get him to shut up," said Herodias as soon as she was seated with a cup of tea in her hand. "It won't change my situation, even if he's right."

"Yochanan feels that it's his duty to be the voice of righteousness," said Mariam.

"I admire his courage."

"A courage that will cost him dearly. He has been warned. Even I can't do much for him if he gets arrested."

"He wouldn't expect you to. Yochanan will face it with strength and dignity, whatever they would do to him."

"Mariam, the Romans don't play fair. Dignity counts very little if you're being executed."

"Why would they execute a peaceful man who baptizes people in the river Jordan?"

"Because he is a blabbermouth who shouts accusations against Rome from the steps of the Temple! Mariam, Rome doesn't want rebels. There have been enough of them in this country trying to be heroic only to get themselves brutally killed, poor souls."

"Contrary to other countries the Roman Empire has absorbed, Judea has never accepted occupation."

"I admire their patriotism, but at what cost, Mariam? When is the price too high?"

Again Mariam saw the troublesome vision of the burning temple. She tried to shake it out of her head, but as usual Herodias picked it up in a flash.

"So it's true, then. When?"

"I don't know. I just know that it will happen."

The two women were sitting at a simple kitchen table sharing a cup of tea while they both felt the shifting of history shake the ground.

Some days later Yochanan was arrested while speaking on the temple steps. The rabbis did nothing to interfere. He was placed in the prison cells at the palace under the Kings personal guard. His followers tried to communicate with him through prison air holes. The rough guards moved their prisoner further down in the dungeons.

Mariam was discretely summoned to the palace. She was asked to come and administer to her relative. She should bring her herb bag. Grabbing her medicines and wrapping a shawl around her she hurried towards Jerusalem.

The prison underneath the palace was a cold and unwelcoming place. She was escalating her concern as she followed the servant and his lonely torch deeper down stairs and through corridors cut into stones. This was designed by Herod the great, Antipas' ruthless father, when he built the new temple and his own palace. She heard anguished sighs and whimpers from prisoners they passed and she tried to not look at them. There was nothing she could do to help them. Yochanan was her concern.

She was met by Herod Antipas, the king himself, at the crossing of two long dark hallways. He sent the servant away and told her to follow him. Mariam had only seen Antipas from a distance before. In the darkness of the underground tunnels it was hard to get a clear picture of him. Her body shivered as she followed the cold and cunning man in front of her. He had let his hair grow longer, but wore the draped toga of roman officials. His desire to be closer to the Jewish people was a farce. There was something very manipulative and calculated going into this, and her cat ears were on full alert.

"This way," he said curtly and led her further down the lower corridor and finally through a small gate to a cell. As soon as Mariam put her feet inside Herodias fell upon her in loud sobs. She gasped as she saw Yochanan chained at his wrists to rings in the wall looking like a haggard wild man.

Mariam had to use all her willpower to stay calm.

What is going on? she questioned Yochanan in his head. But he was boiling inside with hatred and fury and couldn't give her a coherent answer. He turned his head away from her. Herodias heard it too, and she tried to formulate a sentence through her violent crying. This woman always kept her dignity. Mariam could never remember having seen Herodias look anything but regal and under full control. Now she was close to hysteria. Mariam sensed that she was being pulled into a sinister plan.

"You have all you need. Now get to work," barked Antipas, as he pointed to the table in the middle of the room.

Then he left the cell and locked the gate from the outside.

"I'll be sitting right here watching you, and you know the consequences if you don't comply."

"He'll kill my daughter Salome and send a cohort of soldiers to wipe out the colony in Bethany. Qumran will be pulverized and we will be left here to die together with Yochanan," hissed Herodias.

"What does he wants us to do?" whispered Mariam with growing suspicion. Why would the Roman king of Judea request two priestesses to appear with a prisoner in one of his deepest dungeons, two priestesses trained in Ephesus and a prisoner known as The Prophet?

Mariam was starting to see the shape of the monstrous plan Antipas was putting into action. Her hair started to rise on her head and her skin felt cold as she took in the impact and significance of what was being proposed. Antipas must have studied the temple better than anybody had anticipated. He must have found things very few people were supposed to know about.

"He wants my head prepared as an oracle," snarled Yochanan pulling on his chains.

"How does *he* know anything about oracles?" Mariam wondered how this very secret knowledge had leaked to ignorant fools like Antipas.

"He has studied the mystic traditions from the outside. He thinks he knows how it works." His words came in angry spurts.

"A little knowledge in a power hungry man is disastrous!" said Herodias.

"Oracular heads build power," Yochanan couldn't contain his contempt. "There is nothing that can stop him from achieving this, and, then, nothing can stop him at all."

"But we can't let him!" protested Mariam. "We simply won't do it! Do you realize how dangerous he would become?"

"That's exactly what he wants. The man has become despotic." Herodias shared Yochanan's contemptuous sneer.

Mariam looked at her two friends. Yochanan's face was contorted in hate, pain and fear. His tunic was ripped and soiled and his long hair hung in dirty clumps. She remembered him as a peaceful young man with the softest skin. Through his profound spiritual work Yochanan had developed into a powerful scholar. The man in front of her was a desperate dungeon dweller.

Herodias was so furious her mouth was frothing. Every word she said was shot with spit. She would have sacrificed her daughter, if that was the king's only demand.

But she couldn't bring down the whole colony. Who would carry on the knowledge? They were few enough as it was. That would end Yeshua's work right then and there. So far he had worked on healing people in Galilee and had taught the common people in beautiful parables. He had established himself among many groups and his colony was well respected. She knew all his work so far was only preparations for something bigger. His most important work was still ahead of him.

Mariam went from confusion and bewilderment to a cold realization of what this actually meant. They could either make Herod Antipas the most powerful man in the Roman Empire, or they could risk that everything their group had been struggling to uphold for generations would be eliminated from the collective knowledge of the earth. The work Yeshua had been prepared for through forty hereditary links would be left undone. Or, Yochanan's wisdom and heritage as well as The Prophets strength and willpower, would be made available to Antipas and his demonic ambitions.

She calculated a little further, inviting the others into telepathic discussion while she opened her herb bag to check what she had, appearing occupied.

If Antipas becomes the most powerful man in Rome, he will kill us off anyway. We will be a threat to him, and he will use his power to eliminate us, she started.

He can't do that. He knows he needs us to make the oracle speak. That is priestess work, and he is scared to death about it. He would have to keep me alive. Herodias could snort even telepathically.

If he is that stupid then you two can outsmart him, said Yochanan pragmatically.

We can't trick him now, there is too much at risk.

Mariam saw no way to create an illusion to the man outside the dungeon. How can you fake a severed head and a headless body?

Maybe we can accomplish that later, but you're forgetting that we will have to kill you first! Herodias had to make sure that he understood the obvious.

"You can't risk Yeshua's work for me," Yochanan said with a new clear voice.

"And I don't want to put the colonies in danger. My wife and son are there, so is your family, Mariam. Countless others would be in danger as well. I am not afraid of death. I am more afraid of the knowledge being lost."

Herodias and Mariam turned and looked at Yochanan. They wiped their teary, angry faces and felt a new clarity descend. The wailing had ended, now it was time to decide on an action.

"What did you say?" Herodias asked.

"I am willing to die." His beaten up face had a new glow about it.

I trust that you will find a way to retrieve my head.

"Being the next oracle in the line of the ancients would be an honor to me. I am ready to relinquish my body and make my permanent home with God." *And in doing that, I know I'll become the link for our people between the worlds.*

"Yochanan, you can't mean that, we have to find a solution!"

"This *is* the solution, Mariam." *You are Yeshua's wife and high priestess. You'll need my head for him and his mission. I am the blood relative who will represent him in the other world. My head will speak through him after my death. He will take on the knowledge and power I had. He will speak with my voice, he will heal with my healing powers in addition to his own. I hereby give over my title as the Messiah of Israel to my cousin Yeshua in the presence of two priestesses and God above.*

Mariam remembered every word he had spoken for the rest of her life. His understanding of his role as a link in a long succession of important people was crystal clear. His unafraid acceptance of death was unwavering. His willing sacrifice of his own life to the good of the many was done with the benevolence of a Messiah. He would always be remembered as the most noble of men, and be immortalized because of his courage. In this beautiful, but gruesome moment, Mariam wept for the man in front of her. She would for ever honor Yochanan and his dedication to preservation of the knowledge.

With this resolution the three friends had a new goal. Mariam tried to quiet her thoughts so she could focus. Her anguish had settled in her guts and was knotting her intestines into tight balls. How could she kill a man she loved? A man she had once brought back from the dead? How could she work on the preparation of a head she knew every feature of, whom she had grown into adulthood next to? How could she watch the lifelessness of the dead eyes of a man who had been a live teacher and friend a minute before? Who of them was going to kill him, and how? Her tears were burning her cheeks. And what new dangers were they facing? If Antipas could do this now, how would he respond when Yeshua's work became public? Maybe satisfying him would make Antipas go back on his promises, and Yochanan would die in vain. How could she come back to Anya and tell her that she had killed her husband? Mariam had no answers. Her questions came in fast succession and seemed to have ribbons tied to them that wove themselves into a strangling web.

Herodias didn't fare any better. The inside of her body felt like a big open hall with brick arches and tall ceilings. Between the walls lose bricks were flying back and forth at high speed crashing into the walls and each other. The bricks were ricocheting as they hit other things, and her whole body felt bruised on the inside. She had no words, just this sense of that nothing made sense, and her body was under severe internal attack.

Yochanan was at peace. A quiet pool surrounded him. He trusted that these two intelligent women would handle Herod Antipas. He sent all his love to his wife and son. He sent a cloud of knowledge to his students. To the people waiting around his baptismal pond in the Jordan River he sent healing. His back was straight, his eyes were tranquil. He calmed the women and knew he would continue doing so as they worked after he had left his body.

Herodias and Mariam had learned to do this as a surgical team. Ephesus was the only place that still taught this technique and few were interested in learning. These two powerful priestesses were the only ones properly trained in several years. The old priestesses were dying off or replaced with Roman dyads as the temples became rededicated to Roman gods. There weren't many new novices, and very few knew how deeply into the mysteries Herodias and Mariam had gone.

With the coming of the Roman Empire, and their hero worship, the new fear of death made people shy away from this knowledge. The priestesses who knew how petrified them. Death was seen as a final end of life, whereas people of old had seen life, death and rebirth as a circular continuum. Birth and death were transition points to be honored and respected, not to be feared and despised.

Herodias felt that the deifying of male war heroes had made people negate the circle of life. Heroes existed in a measure of linear time, whereas so many aspects of life developed in an ongoing circular fashion. In their focus on the male powers, the other half of creation was negated. She could only roll her eyes thinking about the ignorance this view represented.

Herodias felt that they were naïve, ignorant and arrogant. Right now, the biggest example of a Roman grasping for power with the movements of an infant, was outside the cell staring at them. She smiled with glee as a new plan was presenting itself. He had no idea whom he was dealing with. Getting Yochanan's head back would be like taking a toy from a baby. Herodias relished the idea.

The two priestesses in the dungeon looked over the items Antipas had collected for them. They had the herb collections from both of them, and they had Herodias' surgical tool bag. They needed fire, a brazier and water, and they needed some very fine unguents that neither of them usually had among their healing herbs. Looking around they found that fire and water had been provided.

"Yochanan, I wish I could have prepared better for this," said Mariam. "Herodias, do you have any myrrh incense or bark? I have here a lavender salve we could use as a base if we could get some myrrh in it."

"Let me see," Herodias opened her bag and rummaged around.

Yochanan was mildly amused, unaffected, as if he was watching them cook something in the kitchen.

"Here!" Herodias was pleased. She did indeed have some myrrh incense. She almost wished they were missing some main ingredient, so they could tell Antipas that it was physically impossible. But she knew they wouldn't get very far with that.

They prepared the unguent they needed, looked over their knives and other tools, sterilized them in the fire and laid their equipment out in the order they needed them.

Putting together surgical tools had brought back thoughts of student days in Ephesus. It had all been so exciting. They knew that hidden knowledge was passed onto them. They also knew that when they left they would be different from anybody they would ever meet.

Right then Mariam would have given up all her education not to be in this position. It was because of her knowledge that she was in this prison cell preparing to behead her childhood playmate.

The table was ready. The tools were in order. The unguent was mixed. Herod Antipas had been following them with interest. As long as they were working he didn't disturb them.

"Here," he said and threw the key to the chains to them.

Herodias retrieved it and opened up his cuffs. Yochanan rubbed his wrists.

Yochanan had also been observing them. He walked over to the table and looked at their tools and wondered which one they would use to kill him.

The priestesses looked at each other. Getting this far was one thing. What was next was unthinkable.

"I can't!" cried Herodias and fell on the floor. She quickly got up and ran to the locked cell door. "You can't make us do this!" She screamed as she rattled the metal bars.

Antipas laughed back at her and pulled out his dagger. "This one is for Salome!" He saluted her. Herodias banged her head against the wall and sunk to the floor.

Mariam and Yochanan watched the display. They didn't feel any better than Herodias, but this wasn't solving anything. Yochanan sighed, and silently climbed up on the table. He lay down on his back and stroked out his long hair behind him. Mariam reassured him telepathically that she would wash it as soon as the head was in her possession.

Herodias finished her sobbing and came over to them. She realized the futility of her outburst, but she needed to get some anger out of her system and sneering at Antipas was accomplishing that.

Are you done? Mariam asked sternly, the way you ask a child if they're finished protesting against something inevitable like going to bed. Herodias felt somewhat sheepish, but the rumbling noises inside her had subsided and she could look at the situation a little more clearly.

Mariam was ready to start. She lit the flame on the brazier to prepare for the ritual of condensing his spirit into his head. They wanted to preserve as much of his essence as possible. She burned some of the incense and spoke quietly to the others.

"Yochanan, first we have to do the ritual where you willingly release yourself to this process. You need to state that you understand that you will be summoned to descend into your head after your death. I will also give you a potion that will put you to sleep."

"But Mariam, you can't do that! He has to be alive all the way up to..."

"Alive but not awake!" Mariam's voice changed to a high pitched scream. "If you think I can put the... use the kn... while he is looking at me... " She turned her face away.

Herodias was done crying. She had turned practical. Her voice could cut through stone as she declared; "I'll do it."

Mariam turned and looked at her in disbelief.

"But you have to cut the head off," Herodias shot back.

All Mariam could do was nod.

Yochanan declared, in the most eloquent of words, his dedication of his body and in particular his head, for this purpose. He restated his love for his family and asked Mariam and Herodias to take care of them. They promised to do so.

"Now cut the sentimentality and get to work! He is still alive!" Antipas wanted results.

"The ritual has to be done right or the oracle won't work. Do you want it to lead you astray when you ask for advice?" Herodias was not going to take any more orders from him. Ever.

"I'm ready," said Yochanan. "Do it quickly. God bless you." And with that he closed his eyes.

Mariam stood there holding his warm hand. Herodias grabbed the longest thin knife, found a place between his ribs, and ran it straight through his heart. He coughed and sputtered, opened his eyes and stared straight ahead, and was gone. The two priestesses joined telepathically with him in his passage and gently handed him over to Isis and Osiris. They blessed the blood that started pooling on the table and dripping down on the floor. They blessed the man, they blessed the tradition, they blessed the long line of ancestors he would join. In their singing they also wove in a spell that would prevent Antipas from having much benefit of this oracle.

They continued singing to anchor Yochanan in his head, to calm themselves and to change this dismal dungeon into an honored preparation room in the secret chambers of Ephesus.

To separate the head from the body required certain cuts in the skin and a cut through the spine at the fifth vertebrae. Mariam was quick. She cut a longer piece of skin from his chest, almost down to the incision Herodias had made, then cut over the shoulders and lifted the skin flap and folded it over his face. She cut through his trachea and aorta and exposed the spine. Herodias quickly sealed the major blood arteries in both the body and the head with some stitches and singed them with fire. With a larger knife Mariam found the fifth vertebrae from the skull and started cutting. Even though the knife was sharp, she had to use her weight on it to break through. Herodias kept murmuring the incantations to make his essence find its way to the head. She watched her friends work with admiration.

There was blood floating on the table, but they had quickly stopped the main arteries from squirting. He had done a good job himself preparing his body for the ritual. Mariam had cut the skin along his back to have another piece to work with. The head was now away from the body. They pushed the body aside and focused on the head. The two pieces of skin were folded over at the neck and stitched up to finish it off and to give it something to stand on. Mariam poured some water over her hands and wiped them off before she looked at his face again. Carefully she pulled his features a little to make the face look more like him when he was alive. Then they massaged the unguent with myrrh into his skin. It would preserve him for centuries.

Mariam looked at his face, this good man she had loved and worked next to for many years. Big tears streamed down her face and fell on his still warm cheek. Her whole body ached and she couldn't formulate any words inside.

Herodias allowed her body to grieve, but her mind was already spinning her own plans to turn the tides Antipas had set in motion. The strangling web he had tried to establish wasn't around them anymore. It was thrown high in the air and Herodias knew when to release it and who was going to feel the strength of its sinister fibers.

CHAPTER 7

THE PALACE

THE PALACE IN JERUSALEM WAS BUSY WITH preparations this morning. Decorations were hung, musicians were practicing and the stage was readied. The kitchens had been cooking for days and the wine cellars had been replenished. Rooms were readied for royal guests and the stables were cleaned to house visiting horses and carriages. Today was the king's birthday and a three day celebration had been planned.

King Herod Antipas was walking back and forth answering questions from his stewards and house servants. His gardeners and brick layers also came asking about the latest out door designs. He was a particular master and wanted everything done correctly. Herod Antipas was educated in Rome and had a developed aesthetic sense.

Antipas turned around and admired the magnificent palace surrounding him. His father, King Herod the Great, had rebuilt the temple in Jerusalem to the Israelites boundless gratitude. He and had also built the palace for himself, now the home of his son. It was built it in a style almost as lavish as the holy site. Located a little further up the hill, the magnificent temple could be seen from above. The structure was truly impressive. Old Salomon knew how to plan on a grand scale, and Herod the Great had followed the scriptures to the minutest detail. He had found a way to lay down his own signature as well. The amount of gold that had been used surpassed even the descriptions of Salomon's own landmark. Herod the Great had hired master craftsmen from many countries and been generous in his allowances for decorations. He became quite popular with the people he ruled.

The same was not to be said for his sons. Herod Antipas and Herod Phillip shared the country of their father, and the two brothers could never quite agree on how to rule. As an added complication, there was another country between their two sections belonging to the Samarians.

If ruling an occupied divided country between two very different bothers wasn't difficult enough, the biggest contention between them was their chosen wives. Phillip had married a beautiful woman who was also intelligent and cultured. He had chosen her himself because of her knowledge and heritage. Herodias was a citizen of Rome, educated at the universities and temples, and had a grandmother of the tribes. She was the perfect queen for his court.

Antipas, on the other hand had been forced by his father to marry a princess of a neighboring country. It was a brilliant political match. From now on they could be sure that King Aretas of Nabatea would never wage war on them from the south. The princess was beautiful, but she spoke a different language, was young and uneducated in anything but being beautiful, her skin was darker than his and the music from her culture did not appeal to him. He longed for the life of Rome, the life of high society, and an evening with a lively conversation that could sharpen his wits. Herod Philip seemed to have brought Rome to his own court. Herod Antipas felt left in the backwaters to rule an unruly country he had little affection for.

But today was his birthday. Everything had changed over this last year and he had multiple reasons to celebrate. Antipas had made new political moves that changed his status forever. Antipas had discovered how to build invisible power.

It was really quite simple, he thought. *You acquire a precious object with certain capabilities, and then you get the person who can make the object perform. You set it all in motion and then you wait.*

Antipas had done all that. Tonight he was just going to sit back, have a good time and watch his powers grow.

His wife came into his audience chamber. "Your Royal Highness, may I speak with you," she inquired.

He would appreciate it if she would drop her formalities. After all they were married, he visited her bed regularly, and she was legally his.

How could you possibly call this marriage legal? She shot back at him having heard his thoughts.

How did she do that? Antipas couldn't hear a thing from other people and knew no technique for how to send his thoughts anywhere. He was always shocked when he heard her voice inside his head. *She was temple trained, how could I forget*, he chided himself, again forgetting that she could hear his thoughts.

How could you possibly forget? You wanted me because of my abilities.

Antipas didn't know how to handle this. He wanted what his brother had. And he was smitten with her. Her beauty, her charm, her Roman ways, as far as Antipas was concerned, he loved her. Why couldn't she love him?

She didn't send anything back in his mind, and he was grateful. Instead he heard her speaking voice suggesting something that was totally to his liking.

"My daughter, your niece, would like to entertain your guests tonight. She has been practicing her dancing and would like to dedicate this performance to you. Salome will never forget the generous present you gave her for her birthday."

Herod Antipas had been in a splendid mood that day and wanted to cheer up both the women. Young Salome had received her own Arabian mare. Included with the gift was her own stable boy, the master who would teach her to ride it, all the accoutrements that belong to a horse, an outfit for herself and jewelry and decorations for both her and the horse for festival days. Salome had been speechless. To his delight, the girl had allowed herself to be taught by the master. She had practiced riding until she had become quite good at it. Antipas knew that he at least had one person who appreciated him. To allow her to entertain his guests tonight would be an honor and maybe that would also soften the mother.

Never!, thought Herodias. No gift giving would ever change her deep rooted loathing for this man. But this time she kept her thoughts to herself. No sense alienating him further. Tonight she needed him in on his good side.

How could he expect her to feel anything but hate after what he had put her through? She had grown to appreciate her marriage to Philip. His sudden, not to mention suspicious, death, had shocked her. Being forced to marry this oaf shortly after the funeral had made her ice cold. The events that followed had made her cunning.

Herod Antipas gave his delighted response to Herodias, and the servants waiting for his attention took it as a good sign. Maybe the household would settle down again after all the turmoil of the last year. The death of his brother must have been hard on the man. But to marry his widow so soon after, was that a good idea? And the poor young Queen! The lovely girl had been sent back to her father with a letter of divorce! King Aretas was furious. He now had a daughter on his hands unsuitable for marriage, practically used goods, and totally useless for another political alliance. As for a political friendship with Judea, Herod Antipas could kiss his royal rump.

Herodias held her head high and told him the girl would be ready. She turned with a swirl of her robes and left the room quickly.

The servants might have been wishing for everybody to just get along and for happy songs again to be sung among the pillars of the palace, but there were many opinions about the goings on in the court over the last year. The Jewish people were still grateful for the temple, and left it to the kings appointed by Rome to live their own lives. Whatever the dispute between the two brothers was their concern. If they wanted to fight over women, let them to it. It gave the common people things to talk about for weeks.

The new problem was that king Herod Antipas wanted to go further than his father. Herod the Great had reinstated the Temple and the center of faith for the Jewish people. He welcomed the Israelites back to their holy site. Then he left them to themselves. His son wanted more than that. He wanted to become one of them.

Antipas wanted to join the Temple council and become a voice in Temple matters. He did have some tribal blood, but it was a weak link and certainly not enough for him to get the welcome he wanted. He did not want to undergo circumcision, the thought made him squirm underneath his royal tunic, and he had no intention of going into rabbinic studies. So he had figured out another way to make himself more to their liking. Herodias had a Jewish grandmother which made her free to go between the worlds of Rome and the world of the Jewish people. Besides, she was temple trained at Ephesus. With her at his side, they would allow him into their midst, he thought. But a fully trained priestess was something to be reckoned with, which Antipas would learn only after his well planned scheme had come to its desperate completion.

"Yes, the azaleas should be planted according to plan. And have Ahmed and his men fix the brick wall by the stables, a horse kicked into it yesterday. The goat meat? No, follow the recipe we usually use, this is no time for experimentation. And Sharim, would you go and ask Princess Salome what she needs for her performance tonight. She will be entertaining the guests after dinner. She should be the last act, after the musicians and the other performers."

Antipas had a party to prepare for. He did not have time to deal with haughty women.

Herodias went back to her quarters. She couldn't do it for him again. Never. The whole thing disgusted her. Herod had forced her to wake up the oracle. To force a man she respected to show reverence to a man she despised was an emotional challenge for her well disciplined character. Her stomach churned just thinking about it. To put her mind on something else, she looked for her daughter to see if she needed any assistance.

"Mother, look, what do you think?" Salome was all veils and gold and excitement. "I spoke with Sharim and we agreed on how to make my entrance dramatic. Casparam will be there with me, and you know how handsome he looks in all his finery."

Herodias agreed, it all sounded like a fine plan. She knew her daughter's capabilities, and trusted fully that her performance would be remarkable. She had tried to stay out of the rehearsals as much as possible to allow Casparam, the Persian, to add his exotic flavor to the tableau. Her own plans she kept to herself.

When the prophet in Bethany had spoken loud and clear against Antipas, she knew he was in danger. John the Baptist, Yochanan among his own, had expressed what everybody else had kept quiet about. According to Jewish law, divorce was forbidden, and there were strict rules about marrying your brother's widow. If Antipas wanted to be a Jew, which he had stated several times, he would have to follow a minimum of protocol. The actions of Antipas were done in self service and in blatant disregard to the culture he was trying to ingratiate. Yochanan had even suggested that the death of his brother Philip was suspiciously convenient for Antipas. Nobody had enough courage to speak up, not even the priests at the Temple who were plenty loud enough about temple taxes and sacrifices. His statements were not just a criticism of Herod Antipas; they were a voice against Rome. Herodias had been quite concerned, not only for Yochanan, but also for his followers and friends.

There weren't many temple trained priestesses any more. The heavy footprint of Rome was seen everywhere, and nowhere more prominent than in the religious centers of the known world. The temples training priest and priestesses in the old tradition were being replaced with Roman priests and the temples became rededicated to Roman deities. The shift seemed smooth and easy, you just give the goddess a new name and otherwise let people worship as they pleased. All this was fine and well for the regular population who simply wanted to bring their offerings and get the services the various temples provided. What worried Herodias was the shift away from actual services to places where people could deliver their offerings and be reassured that their lives would be blessed. What was happening to the actual work that was done at the temples in earlier years?

Where were the astronomers, who kept track of the stars and planets? Who knew where they were in the cycles of Venus and when she shifted from a morning star to an evening star? Who observed the reunion of the star and the sun at the next solstice?

Where were the real healers these days? Who knew how to grow a new foot after a bad injury? Who knew how to do surgical work anymore, or change the vibration of the body of the ill? The salves and potions for minor cuts and bruises didn't count as more than work of novices.

Who traveled between the worlds? Who spoke directly with the Gods? Who knew how to do initiations? The Serapium seemed to be one of the last strongholds that still kept up the good work. And the only oracle in function was at Ephesus. The one in Delphi was a fraud as far as Herodias was concerned. And few women dedicated their lives to the long schooling a fully trained priestess required. As of now, she only knew of one besides herself.

She assured Salome that her outfit was lovely and encouraged her to continue practicing her dance and stay limber all through out the day. That seemed like the right thing to say before her mind went to a completely different issues.

Herodias put on some darker plain robes and hung a black shawl over her head. This was not the time to look regal, this was a time to be inconspicuous. She left the palace through the servant's quarters unnoticed and found her way through the city.

She arrived at the Gethsemane gardens looking for familiar faces. There was usually someone from his flock there, especially after The Prophet had been taken away from them. She wanted to find someone who wouldn't recognize her, but whom she could trust to put a message forth. Some if his men were standing around his military friends. The zealots will not be satisfied until they have their King installed and accepted by Rome, thought Herodias. She wished them good luck, but knowing the power of Rome, she couldn't see how they possibly could succeed. And quite frankly, any groups with a military agenda were usually a band of unruly hot heads in her opinion. Still, this flock would suit her purpose today.

She touched the shoulder of a young man in the outskirts of the group.

"I am a follower of Him, the Fisherman," she said quietly as she showed the hand signal familiar between them.

"You are among friends, Lady, how can I help you?"

"Is Lazarus among the flock here? I need to talk to him."

"He is standing right over there. Let me get him for you."

Lazarus was notified and as soon as he turned his head he recognized Herodias' figure and came quickly over to her.

"Can you take a message to your sister? It is urgent." Herodias had no time for small talk.

"Tell her to come to the palace tonight, dressed as a poor woman and stand in the line of the poor outside the kitchen back door waiting for scraps from the Kings tables. There will be a crowd of them after the big celebration. Tell her to wear a red shawl and to accept what is given to her and leave quickly. This is important, Lazarus. Extremely important. If you would wait for her yourself outside the gate with a few men, that would be good. Take her somewhere safe. Very safe."

"Can you tell me what this is all about?"

"She will understand. I will contact her later through your people."

Lazarus nodded. He was used to cryptic messages among them. He gave a respectful greeting to Herodias before she turned and left.

Herodias returned to the palace to get ready for the party. Guests had been arriving already. The queen better be in her finery soon.

Would she ever see Mariam again after tonight?

CHAPTER 8

THE CELEBRATION OF HEROD ANTIPAS

THE SERVANTS WERE TRYING TO LOOK DIGNIFIED and walk slowly, but that was hard with so much that needed attention. Horses and carriages were arriving with people in colorful clothing from many traditions. The King and Queen were greeting them at the grand entrance. The dining hall was set with their finest silver, and the kitchens were making final adjustments to ensure the most exquisite flavors. Young pages were sent on errands and the musicians were already setting the mood.

The dignified king and queen was the picture of a happy marriage. They smiled at their guests and each other. The congeniality could convince even the stoutest disbeliever. Herod Antipas was beaming. His beautiful wife showed herself from her loveliest side. She was the perfect hostess and diplomat. All guests were greeted by name and title, and she had a charming comment relating to the relationship they had with the royals, their family or the lovely life they all lived in Jerusalem. There were Roman dignitaries and representatives from Egypt and Assyria. The Jewish high priest was there with a flock of Rabbis and of course Herodias managed to remember who were Sadducees or Pharisees, and who of them were members of the Sanhedrin council. Herod knew he had married the right woman. She would be his entry into every group. She would help him to finally become powerful, rich and respected.

Herodias smiled to another guest, said the right words, all the while observing with keen attention. She took in the different nuances in relationships between the men in power, knew who had good relationships with their wives, who sided with whom, and most importantly how each felt about Antipas and his brazen exchange of wives. By the time they all left for the dining hall, she knew who to watch out for, who might become an ally and who was of no importance. She also watched Antipas and how he related to people. He picked up clues too, but without her training in reading people, he could only see the most obvious. His field of vision was narrowed by his own selfish ambitions as well. She smiled disarmingly to another guest and recognized her own immense power.

After all the guests were seated, the king and queen were announced and made their entrance. Herodias had put on another robe and looked splendid in her dark blue long dress with a bright orange veil coming down from her shoulders and falling on the floor behind her. Her gold tiara in her dark, almost black, curly hair had a blue and an orange stone. Lapis and coral. She needed the wisdom of her intuition and the power of her center. Herodias was ready.

Antipas couldn't have been happier. He entered the room holding his wife's hand high, showing off the beauty of his chosen queen. He cut a handsome figure himself in his white long toga showing off his royal jewelry circling his neck. His cape had the colors of the tribes. He had tried to dress to satisfy all the factors he was working with and there was a discussion among his guests about what it all signified. No one was totally sure that he was on their side. They were all puzzled. He liked that. Keep them wondering. By the end of the evening he would have them buzzing like a happy flock of bees all singing his praise.

Each sat down in an appointed place, and the food was carried in on large platters. Herodias noticed the care the kitchens had put into the presentation of the dishes. She would make sure to notify the cooks of her appreciation later. Even the waiters had been checked to make sure they all looked right. She had made sure that the more dignified guests had been given the most experienced servers.

Herod Antipas stood up to make the welcoming toast.

"Welcome guests from near and far. I am delighted to have you all here in celebration of my birthday. Today I am also celebrating my marriage of this year to the beautiful Herodias. Please drink her toast with me to welcome her here."

The guests lifted their glasses and drank with Antipas, smiling to Herodias who received the greeting with benevolent grace and dignity. Antipas continued.

"I am honored to have you as my esteemed guests here at my father's palace in this beautiful city blessed by Venus, the city of Jerusalem. I wish that you may leave this celebration with inspiration to build tolerance for all our different views. Let's be ready to start a new wave of cooperation between all nationalities and religions we represent here tonight. Take a look at people around the table, and get to know where they all are from. Please enjoy your cultural differences as we will enjoy many diverse artistic performances this evening."

Antipas lifted his glass as he observed that his guests were indeed taking inventory of how many countries and languages were represented. They all drank with him thinking it was a splendid speech and feeling the love for their neighbors and fellow men grow across old grievances. The room was aglow with goodwill and cultural understanding. The popularity of Herod Antipas seemed secured.

"Sharim, what do you have to entertain us with tonight," the King said with a flourish as he gave the floor over to his master of ceremonies before he sat down next to Herodias. He exhaled deeply and patted her knee in recognition. She smiled convincingly back at him. All the guests noticed.

Sharim was prepared for the evening. He started off with musicians from

Jerusalem. Flutes, drums and stringed instruments were brought forth to the stage, which was a square platform with three steps up in the middle of the room. The music was soft and it encouraged people to go on with their meal and continue with sweets and warm drinks. Herod was delighted and could finally relax.

Then, there were the Assyrian jugglers, dancers from Phoenicia, snakes and their trainers from India. From Egypt came more musicians and magicians who could do fascinating things with flames and disappearing objects. The guests applauded and asked for more wine. Pages were sent running, and the master of the wine cellar started serving from his less expensive shelves. Lamps were replaced with new ones filled with aromatic oil. Large flower arrangements were moved to the side to give a better view of the performers. Couples were holding each other in loving embraces and exchanging stolen kisses in the sheer joy of a lovely party. People who weren't couples would also do the same things under the excuse of forming cross cultural diplomatic ties. The king beamed to his lovely queen and they kissed to the loud encouragement of their guests. Herod Antipas couldn't remember a more splendid day in his entire life. Did her eyelashes flutter at him?

Sharim came forward on the stage again and announced the last performance of the evening. Princess Salome was going to dance for them. There was a hush among the guests as some of the lamps were removed and the musicians played a melody announcing a royal entry.

Salome made a spectacular entrance standing on her horse. She was attired in all the detailed splendor Antipas had given her. Caspara, her trainer, held the reigns. He wore opulent silks from Persia. His eyes were on the lovely princess balancing on the back of the Arabian. She had the same dark curls as her mother and from her tiara stood an arrangement of tall peacock feathers. She was a vision of youth and beauty.

As the young mare trotted along, Salome did graceful movements from the back of the horse as Caspara led it circling the hall. Then the horse went into a gallop and she did a handstand before jumping off over its tail and landing on her feet. The guests applauded and Caspara and the horse took a bow before they left. Now it was up to the young princess alone. The stage was hers.

Striking a graceful pose on the platform, she nodded to the musicians. They started a complicated rhythm as she moved around a circle in an intricate pattern. People recognized it as the ritual dance of the hours. The pattern was familiar as a print on fabrics and in mosaics, but to dance it meant that your feet would have to describe every curve and curlicue without having it painted on the floor as a guide.

Salome looked lovely. Her long pants had many pleats around her waist and were gathered at her ankles. The dark blue pattern on the turquoise silk resembled the pattern her feet were following. The blouse had a solid fabric on her body and the sleeves were a transparent shimmer. She had ringlets on her ankles and bracelets on her arms with bells that rang at measured intervals. While her feet had a specific pattern to follow, her arms and body also had a prescribed series of poses to complete. Everything had meaning and many in the distinguished audience knew what every position of her fingers signified. She had studied, she was focused and she was breathtaking. The audience was mesmerized.

She finished in the center of the pattern she had defined on the floor circling around on one toe while her costume plumed out around her. Her small figure became a three dimensional swirling figure eight in mixed blues. With her hands up in a point over her head and standing on one toe with one knee pulled up and to the side, she swirled for longer that what seemed humanly possible. The guests were getting dizzy by the time she put her foot down and stopped her movement. Her face showed the exertion of her body and the lights were reflected on her glowing skin. She flashed them a brilliant smile before she bent down to receive the applause.

The guests were standing and clapping. They had never seen a more engaging performance. And at her young age? Herodias was praised for having raised a lovely daughter and Antipas received comments for having a new outstanding princess in his household. Young Salome turned and bowed again in all directions from the platform. The applause went on and on.

Herod Antipas had tears in his eyes. His lovely niece and stepdaughter had not only enchanted his guests and honored his party, she had touched him profoundly. He was familiar with the dance of the hours and how complicated it was. Seeing it performed with so much grace and innocence transcended the experience of art and revealed the ritual it represented. The concept of honoring of the day in its different aspects as the Sun transverses the sky interweaving its path with the pentagram described by the planet Venus was made clear to him now. The essence of the relationship between these two celestial bodies had come to him in an epiphany of glowing lights and a flurry of blues and greens. He would understand this culture now. What had until now been foreign to him had sunken into his skin and left its print on his body because of Salome's dance. He had opened himself to allow this new culture to reveal itself to him. His ambitious goals took on a religious meaning. How could he ever thank her?

Salome stood up as Antipas wiped a tear from his face. He waived at her to come down to him. Taking some steps towards her as she tiptoed down the steps to meet him, he embraced her young shoulders and accepted her kiss as she whispered; "Happy Birthday, Father," softening his heart further. He almost crushed her in a bear hug around her small body.

As they loosened up and the king one more time wiped his face with his sleeve, his guests' misty eyes watched their shared family love. He raised his hand to get their attention as he prepared to speak again.

"Again I speak to you, distinguished guests. I know you have enjoyed this performance as much as I have. My princess has honored us all making the meaning of this dance come alive. I now understand the profound respect this culture holds for the Sun and the star of the city of Jerusalem, the city of Venus!" Herod held Salome's hand high as the hero of the evening.

"And now, my dear Salome, what can I give you for your reward? You have honored my guests, my celebration and me. Name anything you want, and if it is within my power, I will give it to you."

Salome looked speechless and once more out of breath. She stood for a moment while her captivated audience waited for her answer. What would such a beautiful, well educated and obviously intelligent young woman ask for?

Salome looked bewildered. She lifted her head and met the eyes of her mother, and instantly heard her voice inside. *Come to me!*

The young princess was brought up to be polite. She whispered to Herod that she would like to ask her mother first. Antipas stretched out his generous arm pointing to his lovely queen and sent the girl towards her mother. He was looking forward to satisfy their request. What could the two most important women in his life possibly ask for? Maybe a beach house along the coast? A shopping trip to Rome for fabrics and jewelry? A trip to Egypt to visit the pyramids? How could he make these two wonderful women in his life even happier than they already seemed to be? He was ready for anything, he thought, and would only be too happy to fulfill any wish.

Salome stood on the opposite side of her mothers table. She leaned closer. The queen pulled Salome towards her as she said something to the princess. The girl pulled back and looked aghast. The audience raised their eyebrows. The face of the Queen had changed. She was no longer disarming, benevolent and kind. Her eyes had narrowed and the arm that held her daughters clothing showed tensed, well trained muscles. The hand that held Salome by the neck seemed to have awfully sharp nails. Her face had the stealth and cunning of a black panther. The powerful command of the Queen was repeated and the Princess had to obey.

The graceful dancer stumbled as she turned and faced her stepfather. Her face which had been flushed with excitement was cold and pale. Antipas was puzzled. He wanted to delight the girl, not scare her. She took two steps towards him and declared.

"I want the head of the prophet Yochanan, John the Baptist."

Herod's face contorted. Had he heard her right? Salome struggled to stand upright as she repeated her request, this time louder for all the guests to hear.

The guests turned around and looked at each other. What was this? The prophet was imprisoned as far as they knew. Yong Salome wanted him executed? Herodias, the Queen, did she want him dead? What an extraordinary request. The buoyancy of the evening was gone. Something dark and sinister was spreading like smoke between the guests. Had they misunderstood the friendly Queen? All eyes were on Herodias who smiled the triumphant smile of a predator who held her prey. Their attention went to her husband who looked like he had just received a well placed kick from his horse. A servant brought him an armchair and he sank down grasping an armrest and holding his head. Utter confusion broke out among the guests and whispering conversations were shared between small groups. The unity they had felt earlier had scattered, and they were forming new groups and alliances.

Herod Antipas was a crushed man. He had been humiliated publicly. All he had tried to accomplish this evening had gone up in green, bitter smoke. He couldn't go back on his promise and risk further embarrassment. But bringing the head out for all of them to see would not rectify the situation; it would make everything worse. And he knew it. Still, he gave his command to Sharim to bring what the princess had asked for. He instructed him to talk to his own personal man servant who would understand. Sharim came back with the servant who wanted to hear the order from the King himself. He left the hall with a puzzled look on his face to act out the King's command.

While they waited Herod was slumped in his chair. The table servers encouraged people to return to their seats and offered them more wine, the best quality this time. The King refused the glass offered to him with a wave of his arm.

Herodias had left her chair and was standing next to her daughter on the stage. She signaled Salome to keep her head high and her back straight. The young princess did her best, but tears were streaming down her cheeks. She was mortified. Her mother had ruined her performance, and she had dishonored the king with whom Salome was building a friendship. Antipas had been good to her and she was looking forward to being his daughter. In her young heart the man's desperate humiliation felt like the deep cut of a claw. As a favored princess of his household she could have continued her dancing and probably have asked for a handsome husband. Her mother had condensed her golden life into a dangerous moment. The draped pillars surrounding her dance floor suddenly had hidden blades. Her future seemed to hang in a blue silk thread over the pattern she had painted with her feet.

The servant was announced. He came through the door in the back of the hall carrying a huge platter. On top of it was a severed head. A gasp went through the audience. After all the lovely food they had been served, a dead head presented in the same manner was bizarre and appalling. Some of the women turned around and buried their heads on their husbands' chests. This was too gruesome. The men braved the sight, expecting the blood and gore they had seen before at beheadings.

But wait, this was not the head of newly executed man! There was no blood or gore. The face did not display the horrors of a doomed man, the fear of death drawn out in every feature, the silent scream of dread still hanging on his lips. The eyes were closed as if in sleep, and the features were arranged to look as lifelike as possible. It did not display the horrors of an expedient execution. It showed the serenity of a wise man prepared to be woken up when summoned. This head had been carefully separated from its body and the skin at the neck was expertly stitched together so it could stand upright. The skin was leathery and had entered into a permanent texture it would keep for centuries. This was a head prepared for ritual.

173

What had Herod Antipas done? This man had been dead for a while, you could tell on the quality of the skin! Why did he have the head prepared in this way? Few people knew how to do it, and the few that did were quiet about their knowledge. It was a procedure done to honor people of historic significance. Or to prepare an oracle.

Ancestral heads were kept in the most secret vaults of the temple, added the Rabbis as an icy fact to the buzz of thoughts going through the room. *How did Antipas know about that?*

Had Antipas stolen it from the temple? His palace was situated awfully close. Did it come from Ephesus or Delphi? Had the king prepared it for his own rituals? Either way, it had been done right under the noses of the respected Rabbis who were standing here as his honored guests. The group of several hundred people was holding their collective breath.

Herodias greeted the head with an almost unnoticeable bow of recognition. This head had seen her face in many other expressions than the composed control of tonight. She had raged in front of it, she had screamed in front of it. She had tried to escape from an intolerable situation while its eyes were still alive and followed her every move. And she had put her colleague in danger by being forced to ask for her assistance as the only other Ephesus trained priestess in Jerusalem. She couldn't let the sweetness of revenge flow yet. This was only one step in what was needed to be done, and the dangers ahead had just been multiplied by her actions.

The servant looked to the king for further instructions of what to do with his thought provoking treasure. Herod Antipas didn't even look at him. He waived his hand in the direction of the stage where Herodias and Salome stood ready to receive it. The bewildered servant looked back at his master taking in the man's profound misery but followed orders and walked towards the stage. He ascended the steps with two hundred pairs of eyes following him. Finally, he presented the queen with the platter as he bowed respectfully. The queen nodded back and took it from him. Salome glanced at the platter and took in the condition of the dead head in front of her. Quietly she lost consciousness and sank softly to the floor in a blue heap of silks. The queen stepped over her daughter's body, came down the three steps with her royal robes flowing behind her and quickly exited the room through a door in the back carrying the platter in front of her.

The web had been released.

CHAPTER 9

REVELATION

MARIAM HURRIED THROUGH THE FAMILIAR STREETS OF Jerusalem. The route from the temple to the palace wasn't far, but she took the hidden roads where the poor people went. Lazarus had told her to wear a red scarf on her head. She made sure it was one of the older ones that had a faded worn out look to fit with the rest of her neutral clothes.

She knew she was not being summoned to receive food from the kitchen. This was something else. Herodias had something specific in mind. Mariam had great respect for her friend's status and the dangers they were both exposed to. Being temple trained, disguises and disappearing in a crowd was easy. This ability had been a lifesaver many times. They both had enemies in high circles. A word from these people would mean certain death for either of the two women, especially if they had known what they had done in the depths underneath the palace. Mariam would rather not think about it.

Walking through the courtyard, looking for the back of the kitchens, Mariam wished she had Herodias' clear focus tonight. Her head was filled with concerns for the aftermath of what they had set in motion. Only Yeshua knew what had happened. She couldn't hide her distress from him and he could see the images in her mind. They had agreed to not say anything to the others. At least until there had been another move from the palace.

She tried to lighten up knowing that she was coming as requested and trusted that Herodias had her reasons to summon her like this. *The rest will be apparent as the evening goes on*, she thought. She couldn't have imagined everything that would be revealed this night before she would be allowed to find a place to sleep.

How could they have done what they did? How do you prepare to murder a friend? How do you prepare him to lie still and be willingly murdered? Mariam felt like vomiting as she stood next to a flock of beggars and tried to blend in.

Herodias was right. There was a large crowd at the palace. Mariam hoped to not be recognized, and did her best to not make eye contact with anyone. The palace showed all the signs that there was a royal celebration going on.

Are you satisfied now? Your power is growing and noble guests are at your birthday celebration. Rome is pleased. What more could you ask for? Mariam thought.

In her head she heard Herod's voice say; "I want the oracle to make my wife love me."

She would rather make you rot slowly and watch your flesh fall away from your bones smelling like dung from a thousand camels. Her laughter would reverberate in your miserable afterlife for all eternity, Mariam sent back to him.

There were torches lighting up the building and banners exclaiming Herod's greatness. Music was heard and people were coming and going everywhere.

I can't believe this, thought Mariam. *They're celebrating this horrid man as if he was a Roman emperor! In the city of Jerusalem on the land of my ancestors!* Her heart cringed. Whatever she was picking up tonight had better be worth the anguish of being within the palace grounds again. She headed for the back of the palace where the poor went to receive generous scraps from the kitchen.

The cypresses in the courtyard smelled a lively green. She breathed deeply to remind herself that she was no longer in that dismal dungeon being forced to do despicable deeds. The green scent of the evergreen trees reminded her of Yochanan's dedication to life, his courage and his sacrifice.

There were many poor people patiently waiting for the kitchen help to bring food out. Some of them had brought bowls to receive food handed over from big pots with ladles. Assessing the crowd she found she was the only one with a red scarf.

One potential problem avoided, Mariam exhaled.

The kitchen servants came out with big pots and huge ladles. Normally the smell of aromatic soups would make her mouth water. But this time the thought of food was repugnant. The poor didn't know that the smell gave away that this was exceptionally well spiced and that the ingredients had been the best of quality for the King's party. To them it was simply something to put in their mouth to hold them over to the next day. Mariam tried to not to draw breath through her nose. The thought of food preparation and kitchen utensils made her see the knives between her own fingers and remember what her hands had done.

A little commotion at the kitchen door got her attention. A larger woman, dressed different than the kitchen help, came out carrying an infant. *She must be one of the house servants,* Mariam thought. The woman looked over the line of beggars, and her eyes stopped at the red scarf. Mariam recognized Herodias' own chamber maid, Danutia. What was she doing out here?

Danutia walked briskly along the motley crowd, cooing to the large baby in her arms. She stopped at Mariam, their eyes met in a moment's recognition.

"He is much better now, dear. It is time for him to go home," she said as she handled the bundle over to Mariam.

She expected a warm, snuggly child in her arms, and was surprised to find that what she was holding was cold, and didn't bend with her at all. Danutia looked at her sternly.

"Be safe, child," she said to Mariam as she quickly turned and went back to the palace.

Mariam looked down at her "baby", hugged it closer to her and cooed something soothing. Apparently it was working; the child didn't make a sound. She lifted the blanket a little to see its face and found a sturdy gourd. The rest of his body was made of something else. Not wanting anybody to ask to "see" the pretty baby, she wrapped her cloak tighter as she quickly exited the courtyard.

Lazarus was waiting for her at their appointed place. He sighed in relief to see his sister and lifted an eyebrow at the child in her arms. *Don't worry,* she voiced in his head. He knew his sister well enough to know that this was not the time to ask questions, and instead he put his arm protectively over her shoulder, wrapping his cloak around them both. They looked like a beautiful young family. Two men of their flock walked behind them with their heads covered in black. Mariam felt protected, but wondered where Lazarus had planned to go. She knew Herodias had said to be safe, but where could they go where they wouldn't be found?

Their own place in Bethany was well known. They couldn't put the whole colony in danger. The monastery at Qumran was out of the question. Yochanan's widow, Anya, also lived in Bethany, but their place had been searched many times after Yochanan had been taken prisoner. Mariam thought of all the wonderful women who had opened their homes for them and been so supportive of them for so long. She didn't want to put any of them in danger either.

Mariam was starting to get a grip of what she was carrying. Herodias didn't just want *her* to be safe. She wanted to hide away the most powerful tool in the Kings possession, and hide it well.

Her feet walked on next to her strong brother. Her arms were getting tired from her heavy bundle, which looked less and less like a baby as its pronounced roundness became more apparent. She wrapped the blanket tighter around it, and steadied the baby's head. The illusion still worked.

Lazarus was fast and had apparently already planned the route they were taking. He felt it was important not to be seen on the street for too long, so he took a shorter way to his destination all the while choosing less known darker streets. They ended by a gate in a wall around the backyard of a house in the richer part of the city. Lazarus said a password and the gate was opened. They quickly filed in and it was locked after them.

Mariam looked up and recognized Joseph of Aramathea's house.

"But Lazarus," she said, "we don't want to put any attention to him. He is one of the trustees at the Temple."

"And how much safer could you possibly be," she heard a reassuring voice say nearby. Uncle Joseph, the man that lent his strength to them again and again was there, and so was Joseph, Yeshua's father. She was alarmed that she had brought more people in danger. Then she realized they were all in this together. All these beautiful people worked for the same cause in different ways.

They walked across the shaded yard and were well hidden underneath the trees. Joseph opened a door on the ground level and they were in the food cellar of the kitchen. "Come with me," he said.

The servants had gone to their quarters for the night. The group could walk freely around the house. The two men who had walked with them, Judas and his fellow sicarii were told to wait downstairs. *It has come to this,* thought Mariam. *We need well trained assassins to protect us.*

Uncle Joseph led the way upstairs. They headed for the guest bedroom. Mariam wondered what they had in mind. She was not going to relinquishing her bundle until she was satisfied that it would have a safe hiding place.

As they entered the luxurious bedroom, Mariam was greeted with another familiar voice. Her mother-in-law was sitting on the bed waiting for them.

"Good to see you, Mariam. I am glad you made it here safely. Thank you, Lazarus."

"How did you know?" Mariam felt that suddenly the world knew more than her, even though in this event, she was one of the main players.

"A message from Herodias, you receiving something secret that needs to be hidden? Child, I know what Herod Antipas made you and Herodias do. I know how hard it has been for her to satisfy the king while planning how to thwart his plans. And I know how hard it's been for you to keep all this to yourself."

"Oh, Mother," said Mariam as she collapsed next to Mary after dumping her load unceremoniously on the bed. The gourd rolled out of the blanket and showed itself to not be anything like a baby head. The blanket fell a little to the side, and the heavy round object she had been carrying rolled along the edge of the bed before it fell to the floor with a clunk. Five sets of big eyes followed its movement with a gasp of breath until it found its resting place by Mary's feet. Then the eyes of the head opened and stared at them. A yelp was heard and everybody took a step backwards and grabbed onto the person next to them. There was a moment of silence before Mary simply picked up the head, gracefully closed the eyes with her fingers and said, "Now Yochanan. There is no need to scare your family and friends."

The situation loosened up in smiles, and what could have been a grieving session over a lost friend became a welcome back for him in their midst. They all remembered his sense of humor and agreed that this was exactly what he would have done had he been there alive; make a joke so they all laughed.

"So," Mary changed the topic to practicalities. "Now that he is here among us, I'd like to suggest that we put him in the safest place I can think of. Mariam, this is something I wanted you to know about. You are the one who will know how to use all these precious objects at their appointed time."

With this she nodded to her brother Joseph who walked over to a corner in the room with a niche where some pretty tiles were inlaid in the wall. He pushed on the bottom one of the tiles and the whole back wall of the little alcove opened up. He caught it and set it to the side. It looked like it hadn't been opened for many years and lots of dust fell on the floor. Lazarus came forward to help him, and when the dust settled Mariam saw that there was a shelf inside where some items were stored. She looked around at the others for an explanation.

Mary volunteered. "Remember on the boat to Ephesus, the story I told you, Mariam?"

"You told me about Hibernia and Yeshua's beginning. How helpful Joseph had been on your journey and at the birth." Joseph bent his head in acknowledgment as he received Mariam's love and admiration.

"And do you remember the auspicious guests we had that night?" Mary continued.

"The astrologers who brought gifts," Mariam almost whispered.

"Mariam, these are the mysterious gifts they gave us. We didn't understand their significance then. But we kept them safe knowing that at some point the one who would understand would be among us. Mariam, that one is you.

"You know what these precious items mean, and you know how to use them. You also know why it is important that we now have the oracular head of a family member who is also a prophet.

"Mariam. We have always known that your work here with my son would be profound beyond measure. We didn't know before in what way. Maybe you can tell us when the time is right."

They were all looking at her. Mariam rose from the bed and walked over to the opening in the wall. There were three containers on the shelf. They were covered with dust but underneath they showed remarkable craftsmanship in wood and design. The men moved aside to give her room.

One container was square and had a lid that came up to a point with a jewel on top. It reminded her of a bejeweled tent, what you would imagine a King would have if he was traveling. She put a hand on either side of it and lifted it carefully out of the shelf. There was a small table in the room which was brought to her to place the royal gift on. Her hands were tingling as she handled it. She understood that whatever it contained had an effect on her and demanded respect. It could be quite dangerous if not dealt with correctly. She placed it most gingerly on the table, unclasped the lock and opened the lid. Being careful to not place her head directly above the content she peered at what was inside. All the other four heads were bending forward in anticipation.

At first it simply looked like white powder. Untrained eyes would have taken it for finely ground and sifted flour. Mariam had seen it before, but only once, at the great pyramid in Giza at her own initiation. She knew how rare it was and how few people knew how to work with it.

"Gold," she said. "For the initiation of internal illumination. Only the King can serve this."

The others felt the solemnity of the moment and didn't ask any further. Only Father Joseph knew the process for refining gold. He didn't say anything. This was not the time for technical explanations.

She closed the container and brought it back to its hidden shelf and picked up the jar. It had a seal on the top which she broke carefully when it was placed on the table. The jar was filled with rare oil and had the aroma of a fine perfume.

"Spiced with frankincense," she said. "For his anointment as king."

His mother nodded.

The jar was resealed before returned to the shelf. The last gift was a crock with another sealed lid. When opened it contained a fine salve with another beautiful scent.

"Balm of Myrrh. The same kind we used for Yochanan. To ensure Yeshua's place among his ancestors," she whispered as she took in air realizing what that meant.

Mary was pleased at what she heard. Mariam knew what these precious things were, which had been enigmas to her for many years. All she knew was that they were all profoundly essential for her son's life. Her intuition told her that it was important that Mariam knew where they were kept and that she had taken inventory of what they were intended for. She trusted that her wise daughter in law would know when to make use of them. And she felt they would be needed soon.

They wrapped up Yochanan's head in the blanket it had arrived in and placed it on the shelf with the other items. Joseph replaced the wall in the niche with the tiles and Lazarus had found a small broom to sweep up the dust. The room returned to being a beautiful bedroom, and nobody would have been the wiser of what was hidden there.

Mariam was exhausted. This night had brought more emotional upheavals than she could possibly have been prepared for. Nevertheless she felt calm through it all, and a new reassurance fell over her. Missing pieces of her internal puzzle fell into place and she started to see the magnitude of the plan for Yeshua and herself.

The others were also overwhelmed with the serenity and power of the last hour. Silently they went downstairs and met with the two sicarii who had been watching for them. Everybody was hungry, and Judas had been kind enough to put out some bread and cheese for them from the kitchen. Mariam ate without tasting what it was. She just knew she needed nourishment.

Dawn was starting its early stripes of light over the city before a small group left Joseph's house. Joseph and Mary decided to stay there as his guests. The others were heading back to Bethany to join with Yeshua who had spent the day preaching in Galilee. He deserved to hear every detail of what had transpired that night. And he did get to hear it as Mariam crawled up to him in the early morning hours.

CHAPTER 10

THE RITUAL

IT WAS ANOTHER DARK NIGHT. THIS WAS the night when the following day would be of equal length; the spring equinox. Their flock was walking the short distance into Jerusalem. There weren't many with them this time. This was an expedition that had to be done in secret.

Mariam was aware of the danger they were exposed to. She also knew the importance of the ritual they were going to do. The wedding in Canaan was done for the world to see and bless. Now they had to do the ritual wedding according to the ancient scriptures. It was time to anchor a new connection between the people of the earth and the Gods of the sky.

She knew what this entailed. She was trained in the old ways, which made her the priestess queen, just as Yeshua was the priest king. The importance of this ritual was clear. But how many would understand?

Don't worry about that, her father in law sent back to her. *The important thing is that the ritual is done. Venus will know our intentions. The star will connect from above and the earth will connect from below. All we need is to set up the initial conditions, and then all these connections will happen by themselves. God will recognize things done in His honor.*

It sounds so simple when you say it, Mariam answered him.

Yeshua had his own thoughts which he shielded from the others. Why were they doing this if the temple was going to be destroyed? He knew it would happen in their lifetime. He had seen it; the flames, the blood, the dead bodies on the steps. The visions had been detailed and real. He had spoken to the elders about it, but they just saw it as a stronger reason to get behind their cause. Why was this particular ritual so important?

Son, because of what will happen tonight, the tribes of Israel will forever be rooted to the stones of the foundations of the Temple of Jerusalem, his father reassured him.

Herodias was going to meet them at the palace. They had been instructed to come to the back and go to the kitchen entrance and just stand there. There were always beggars there asking for scraps and alms, they could blend in if their outfits didn't look too grand. She came out of the kitchen door with the hood of her plain black cape over her head. "Let's go," she said.

She took them through the garden of the palace. No lanterns were lit. They relied on the faint light of the night, and did not want to be seen. The garden had been landscaped to perfection with lovely paths through groomed flower gardens. Mariam allowed the scents to inspire her and was reminded of her days with Sibyl at the Serapium, days filled with sunshine and manual work dealing with plant material in various forms. She remembered scents and textures and golden light from the friendly climate in Alexandria. Her toe got caught on a stone and she was quickly drawn back to the dark night in the garden of the palace of Herod the Great.

They arrived at a stone structure with a door in the garden behind a large fountain. Herodias produced a substantial key and opened the door. The first thing they saw was the pumping mechanisms for the fountain. Next to that was another door. Another key came out, and the door was opened. Now the lanterns were lit and they all filed through the door before Herodias locked it again behind them. She put the keys in her pockets and passed them all to lead the way.

Do you think this is wise? asked Mary, Yeshua's mother, quietly. Mariam sighed. *Wise? Probably not.* The rational for doing this ritual was beyond physical concerns. In the same way the wedding had been important for the families of the tribes to unite, this was important on a larger scale. They were going to unite Jerusalem with her star Venus. As humans doing the ritual on earth, it might not seem significant. For forces working on much larger spheres of influence; this was of paramount importance.

Judas, the sicarii was leading the back, always ready with his knives. Yeshua was right behind Herodias with the lantern and Mariam followed him holding Mary's hand. Joseph was also with them as a senior member. Lazarus was the last male member and also the representative of Mariam's family. He was needed for his knowledge of how to work with sounds and vibration.

Mariam steadied herself in the narrow passageway they were following. Some steps in front of her told her to pay attention. They were going further down in the terrain.

"This passage way was created at the time the Temple and the palace were built. Herod the great, twice my father-in-law, wanted this secret entry for his own purposes." Herodias informed them.

"The new Temple will be remembered as the most generous gesture of all times," said Yeshua speaking for all the people of the tribes. The rebuilding of the Temple was an incredible gift. He wanted to think of its grandeur and pushed aside the disturbing visions of its destruction.

Herodias could appreciate her late father-in-laws ingenuity. The ruthless Herod the Great probably used this secret entry to investigate the temple on his own.

They continued in silence for quite some time. At one point the tunnel turned towards the left, and the whole time it kept going downwards. Mariam guessed it made sense since the palace was placed higher up in the hills then the temple.

Mary's hand squeezed her harder. Her mother-in-law was not quite sure how much she liked this, but she knew what they had to do and understood its importance. Mariam always admired Mary's peace and calm. Her grounded strength was needed tonight.

They finally arrived at a room that seemed bigger and gave them all space enough to stand inside at the same time. There were many doors which all had locks on them.

"We need number three counting from the right," Herodias said as she was digging for another key.

Inside the room there were shelves with ornate stone boxes covered in dust.

"Ossuaries," said Mariam. "For your family tomb?"

"My dear, this *is* the family tomb. The entrance from the outside is sealed until it needs to be opened again. Philip is in room number five, decomposing before his bones get moved to his own box."

They walked through the room with the ossuaries. Mariam saw nothing indicating an opening and wondered if they were expected to walk straight through the walls. Herodias stopped in front of the wall and looked up.

"It is here, I know it. Give me a hand, will you?"

Lazarus stepped forward and found a rock to scrape away some mud. Soon they found the outline of a door hidden behind dust and mud. Was it hid intentionally, or had time just grown its grime on it? The lock gave reluctantly, and Lazarus and Judas pulled aside a bigger door opening up to a tunnel shaped through rough hewn rock. It was short and led into another bigger room. This was not the family tomb of the Herod's. This was inside the foundations of the Temple of Jerusalem.

Mariam looked up and tried to get a sense of where they were underneath the temple. They would have to be in the back parts, towards the palace, and they couldn't have gone far enough to be underneath the holiest of holies yet.

"I think it is this way," Herodias said.

"I'll lead the way," said Joseph. "I've been here before." They all looked at him.

"I was invited by the high priest to a specific area to see things related to gold," he explained. "I remember this room. We need to take a right."

"Actually, Joseph, it is a left," said a voice, and they all froze.

"Thank God, you're here," said Joseph, and stretched out his arm preventing Judas in his silent approach as the voice became a body coming out of the shadows.

Joseph turned to the others and explained. "I invited Joseph of Aramathea to join us. We weren't sure if he could get away, so I didn't' say anything to you. But here he is. Please welcome your uncle. He is on the board of rabbis at the temple and has been supporting the cause from the beginning, as you all know. He particularly wanted to be part of this ritual, and frankly, we need his help."

The rest of the flock nodded in stunned acceptance. Mary silently hugged her brother and the others gave him respectful short greetings. They all knew about this powerful man, but usually as someone who helped behind the scenes. Given his high position, they respected his need for secrecy. They rarely saw him in person, but here he was, in flesh and blood.

"I'll lead you from here," he said with authority.

There were many openings, many corridors leading in different directions. Mariam had a sense of entering a mace and tried to keep track of their meandering so she could find the way back.

The corridors changed. There was tile on the floor, and the shape of the spaces more defined. Mariam tried to give a reassuring hand to Mary.

Joseph of Aramathea led them through an opening to the left and they were standing in a room that didn't open into further corridors. They all filed in through the low opening and admired the ceiling height and the roundness of the space. This was not tiled, but had dirt floor and stone walls that seemed to be carved directly out of the firmament. Mariam looked up again and got a sense of that there was a tiled floor with a large star in the center above them. She had never been there, but she knew exactly what room they were standing under. As a woman, she would never be allowed to enter there.

She studied the room they were in. There was a rectangular stone in the middle coming up two feet or so from the floor. In a circle around the edge of the room were more stones. They formed a wide circle, twelve of them around the larger square rock in the middle.

Joseph instructed Judas, the Sicarii, to stand guard outside. Mariam wasn't quite sure what he could do to help them if they were discovered, but it felt reassuring nevertheless. She knew they were in a space forbidden to anybody but the high priests, and however much Uncle Joseph could defend their presence there, she knew they would all be killed as traitors if found.

The high priests of the temple didn't allow women inside the temple. Well trained priestesses doing rituals of the old traditions would be a direct threat to their establishment. How could you tell them that these priestesses knew the old traditions better than the ordained priests? How could you tell them that *working* with the Gods was different than *worshiping* the Gods?

We don't intend to tell them anything. We just need to do what needs to be done. Joseph's strong words were heard by everyone.

Yeshua felt as if blood was dripping from his body. The visions wouldn't leave. What if they would blame the destruction of the Temple on them and their illicit presence here?

His father again reassured him. *The destruction of the Temple will happen anyway. It has happened many times, it will happen again. But the Temple is just a gilded building. The anchor is here, in these sacred vaults. This is what we are here to strengthen. This is the connection we need to reestablish.*

Mariam looked again at the room they were in. This felt old. She knew the foundation was original. It had not been changed, even when the temple had been torn down or rebuilt. The platform for the temple in Jerusalem consisted of three enormous stone slabs stacked on top of each other. People kept wondering how they had been put in place. *I have a theory,* answered Joseph back in her head. *This is gold technology. Powdered gold, gold refined to its finest particles, has different properties than the metal. It levitates. Moving large heavy stones is not a problem. Think of the pyramids.*

Mariam remembered the pyramids, and wondered if the Serapium and Ephesus had been built the same way.

She suddenly realized what this meant. They were standing in a hall built and used by King Salomon! This was the foundations built for the original temple that stood her fifteen hundred years ago. The implications were staggering, and Mariam was now holding onto Mary's hand.

Joseph of Aramathea stood by the stone in the middle and faced them.

"You're right, Mariam, these are the vaults of Salomon, and that's why we are here tonight making history, significant history in the long saga of our people. Listen."

In the most efficient of communication, shared vision, he sent each of them a strip of images, a timeline of the history of their people and the importance of the Temple. It only took a moment of time, but covered thousands of years of human evolution.

They were shown Abraham and his son Isaac who was almost sacrificed to God. They saw the twelve brothers who started the tribes and Joseph with his magnificent coat who ended up in Egypt as a dream interpreter. He became the trusted vizier and married the pharaoh's daughter, and their daughter in turn married the pharaoh's son, and they had Akhenaten, who was trained in the mysteries of the Egyptian temples. Because his mother was of the tribes, he spent many years with them and was influenced by Joseph. When he became pharaoh, he decided to change the religion of Egypt. He wanted them to believe in one God, like his mothers family. The high priests of Egypt didn't like this and dethroned him. He had to flee to his mothers people. His daughter escaped on a ship and went north. *My ancestor,* added Mary. The tribes hid Akhenaten and sent him into the desert. On the mountain of Sinai, at the temple of Serabit he learned about gold technology. He came back as Moses, and led his people out of Egypt and brought them to Sinai. The Ark of the Covenant was made there under the instructions of the temple and the people were taught how to use it. They collected their gold and made the powdered gold to have inside the Ark which gave it electrical currency and enormous power.

The people used the Ark as a weapon and fought their way all the way to

Jerusalem. Here they chose their king, David, and his son, Salomon, built the Temple to house this Ark securely. Their priests of Aaron knew how to work with the Ark and how to safely use its technology. After some generations the knowledge wasn't taught in the same strict manner anymore. Other people came and fought for the land. Some priests with the old knowledge were killed. The Ark was stolen and carried away, but after the thieving people found it too dangerous to work with, they returned it to the temple. The priests decided to take it out of the holiest of holies and place it even more securely down here in the basements, in the foundations, underneath three thick slabs of stone where it couldn't be stolen or do damage anymore. The knowledge of how to handle it dwindled until the priests themselves wouldn't dare to handle the powerful Ark and its mysterious content.

The flock of people gathered in the hall understood. The magnetic pull of the Temple of Jerusalem on all the people of the tribes, regardless of where they spread out over the surface of the earth, originated here, in these foundations, in these vaults created by Salomon. The Diaspora had separated a beautiful people, who managed to keep their culture intact over hundreds of years, waiting to return.

They all stood there silent for a moment taking in the magnitude of their expedition. Joseph of Aramathea brought them back to practical matters.

"First we need to prepare the room," said Joseph efficiently. "Lazarus and Yeshua come with me and give me a hand."

The three of them went to the side of the room and Mariam saw a small anteroom she hadn't noticed before. They brought back a chest with carvings on it. It looked like the ossuaries they had seen before, a simple box of lime stone, but something told her these were not ordinary burial boxes. Joseph took the men with him again, and they came back with one more of these boxes before he told them to gather around him.

"I need the priestesses of Ephesus," said Joseph. The three women gathered around him.

"I brought the missing one. It is time for him to join his ancestors."

He handed Mariam a bundle, which she recognized. She held it close to her heart, and silent tears flew down her cheeks as she remembered her friend. Herodias held around her waist to steady her. Mary turned pale, but understood its importance.

Yeshua and Lazarus had started to work on the box they had brought out. They carefully brushed off old dust and pried open the lid on Joseph's suggestion. Inside were two round bundles wrapped carefully in old pieces of linen. "I thought there would be three," said Joseph sounding perturbed.

There were some markings on the ossuary, but it was in such old script, Mariam had never seen the letters before. Yeshua looked at them and recognized the old language. "Abraham and Isaac," he declared.

"Good, we need them. Now open up the other one. Be careful. These have not been out in a long time."

Mariam brought up the images Joseph had shared with them and studied how the temple had worked in earlier days. They had used the same techniques as they did at the Serapium. They had known how to communicate with the Gods, how to travel between the worlds, how to work with the gold substances. Now it seemed the temple had been reduced. The Ark of the Covenant was not present in the holy of holies anymore. The blood was running in streams from the sacrificial blocks in the courtyard and animals were killed unnecessarily. The focus seemed to be more on rules and regulations for good people's everyday lives, than to teach them how to empower themselves. Mariam shook her head. She remembered all she had learned at Ephesus. Herodias met her eyes, and between them they knew who they were. Herodias snapped her fingers. Mariam was brought out of her reveries. They had work to do. It was time to workshop with the Gods.

Joseph of Aramathea instructed them to prepare the room. They worked quickly and silently. Oil and wicks had been brought and Joseph and Mary lit small lanterns by each stone in the circle. Yeshua and Mariam lit candles and burned incense at the altar in the center. "Water, did anyone bring water?" Lazarus had a water skin and they filled a dish and found a suitable small rock to mark the four directions at its base.

Herodias and Uncle Joseph carefully uncovered the bundles from the ossuaries. The leathery skin, the life like features made Herodias hold her breath staring into the face of Abraham as if he was just asleep. Isaac's face, so much like his father, had some of his facial hair intact. Their eyes were closed, and the wrinkles around them gave the impression that they were pinching their eyes closed to not be tempted to look until they were invited to do so. Joseph found the stands for them in the box and carried them over to the circle.

In the other box the bundles were smaller, and it was three of them. They called for Yeshua to read the letters on the side. They were in a different script than the first, but he deciphered it with ease. "Miriam, Rachel and Batsheba," he announced. Mariam joined them in the unwrapping while Yeshua went to help his parents. *Could it really be the sister of Moses?* Miriam was well known as a powerful woman among the tribes. Mariam held her tenderly and studied the exceptionally beautiful face. The eyes expressed so much authority even when closed. She had the unmistakable jaw lines of women who knew their own value. Mariam handed it to Joseph as he was ready to place her in the circle. The next one was Bathsheba, the wife of Salomon. Mariam almost dropped it when she realized who she had in her hand. The head felt light as she carefully lifted off the ancient linen wrapping. She blew away some dust from the crinkles around her eyes, and saw it pull some muscle to shake it off. *I've done this before,* Mariam heard in her head the same way Bashra would talk to her. *Please join us,* she heard the head in her hand communicate with the head in her herb bag. *I'd love to,* was Bashra's reply. Mariam wondered how she was going to handle a possible conflict between honorable severed heads.

Uncle Joseph and Lazarus were figuring out where in the circle people should be placed. They were apparently struggling to lay out the proper order of people and ancestors to be placed at each of the twelve stones.

How beautiful you are, said Mariam, as she held the head of Salomon's wife in her hand. She still had the fine features praised in the old scriptures. It had shrunk smaller than the male heads, but not as small as Bashra who were preserved according to a different technique. *Travel sized,* Mariam heard from her own herb bag.

Herodias was uncovering the last one and Mariam turned to see Uncle Joseph scratching his head as he was pointing to the different stones. She called for him.

"I brought my ancestor too," she said shyly. "Can she have a place in the circle?"

"Just in time," said Joseph as he exhaled in relief.

Mariam showed him the head as she unfolded it from her pouch.

"What a perfect specimen," he exclaimed. He was sweating from his temples as he instructed her to place it on one of the stones.

They were now twelve. Twelve people tied through time and history, hereditary lineage, marriage and friendship. Uncle Joseph had placed them in order to build strength, to honor family lines, and he had nearly lost his bearings when he was one short. There were no more ossuaries in the anteroom and he didn't want to use the sicarii. He was needed as guard and didn't have the education or bodily preparation. But miraculously, there was another ancestor in Mariam's herb bag. He could hear an old woman's giggle in his head.

Herodias and Mariam sang the incantation to wake up the ancestral heads. As the last note was intoned, seven heads, who had all been dead for a very long time, opened their eyes and the little flame in front of each of them shone on their faces. The light in the room changed and they were illumined from another source.

Mariam and Herodiasf walked around the circle and stopped at each stone. One by one they welcomed them all by name and tribe. Each member of the circle was asked to give their support to the anchoring of this intention. Herodias had a deeper voice than Mariam and together they sang the incantations. The answers came, in the musical soprano of Bathseba, the resounding alto of Miriam. Abraham and the Joseph's were all basses and the young men were tenors. They walked the whole circle, establishing the route of the line of strength they all shared.

Mary had understood what was going to happen, but she had to admit that the effect was startling. Seeing Abraham look around the room and take them all in. Miriam, Moses' sister, look like she wished she had hands to rub her eyes a bit and Batshebah seemed to be looking for a mirror. It all made the hair on her head rise, and brought on a smile she couldn't deny.

Joseph, Yeshua's father, had been expecting this effect. He had visualized what it all would look like. He had discussed it with his namesake brother-in-law. They had planned the position of the different entities, and he had visulized the disembodied heads standing at the marking stones. But he hadn't seen them with eyes open. It looked like their bodies continued down into the ground underneath them, and that one or two thousand years of time didn't make any difference. His skin was crawling, but he was totally ready to do whatever the two priestesses would suggest.

Lazarus could only stare. He caught a glare from Abraham, and the message; *What are you looking at, boy? What did you expect?* Lazarus had no clue what he had expected. He was invited as the musician.

Joseph of Aramathea took a deep breath. It looked so easy when the priestesses of Ephesus awakened the ancestors. This was what the high priests did not know how to do. The younger priests didn't even know that the heads were hidden here. These women were working with forgotten materials, using knowledge that was lost in the vaults were only a handful of venerated priests were allowed to go. This night could never be mentioned outside of this grotto, this hidden chamber underneath the holiest of holies of the Temple of Jerusalem.

Herodias found her place in the circle and Mariam sang the questions to her as well before she returned to Yeshua standing at the altar. He welcomed her, taking her hand and kissing her. They stood at the north side of the center stone block and faced Joseph of Aramathea with the heads of Miriam on one side and Bashra on the other. They both bowed deeply honoring their esteemed relatives. Miriam blessed their undertaking and Bashra assured them that she would keep everything in order. They knew she would.

They turned east and faced Herodias flanked by the heads of Isaac and Yochanan. Mariam and Yeshua bowed deeply. Mariam acknowledged their supportive friend and squeezed Yeshua's hand. They bowed to the left to honor their historic relative and received a bow and a blink back, Mariam held onto Yeshua's arm. Turning and facing Yochanan, Yeshua fell on his knees and wept. Mariam knelt down next to him and looked into the face of their dear friend, playmate and cousin. Yochanan expressed only peace. "I love you two," he whispered to them. "I'll always be with you now. Take care of my wife and son."

They had to get up and continue. Facing south they found the reassuring face of Joseph, their father and father-in-law. He smiled deeply to them and wished them the best on their journey. To his right was the head of Batsheba, who smiled at them and gave them the blessing of the house of David while she showed them the vision of herself and Salomon taking part in the same ritual fifteen hundred years ago. Mariam blushed. The head of Rachel on Joseph's left gave them her blessings from her line.

Turning west they faced his mother Mary, who looked the image of calm, although they both picked up her unease at this venue. The head of Abraham at her right thanked them for taking on the continuation of their traditions. Lazarus, her dear brother, too young and inexperienced to partake in this, wished them well from Mariam's family and the tribe of Benjamin.

Everybody was waiting for the next part of the ritual. All the members of the circle were alert and ready. If you added up all their ages you would get a five digit number.

Mariam and Yeshua untied their robes and let them fall to the ground. Dressed in their white cotton shifts they sat down on the altar. Joseph of Aramathea nodded to Lazarus. He was supposed to guide the singing and the overtones. The young man nodded back. He was ready.

In his resonant tenor voice, Lazarus started with an A and one by one they all fell in toning with him. Abraham held the base note together with the Josephs, the brothers-in-law. Lazarus and Yochanan held the tenor voices. Bashra and Herodias had the altos and Miriam, Rachel and Batsheba were all sopranos. Mary intoned the highest notes, nobody could match her coloratura. Lazarus began making resonating overtones in his nasal chambers and his own skull. It seemed as if the sound was coming from the surrounding walls. The heads of Abraham and Isaac knew how to do that too, and the resonating voices ricocheted among the walls in ever more complicated overtones holding the arpeggios.

Yeshua and Mariam were on the altar. They knew what was expected of them. They had never done this with an audience before, and even though they both had seen others perform this as an enactment or a ritual before, being part of it yourself was all together a different matter. They fell into the tonalities sounding between the walls and started humming a deep note that resonated with their bodies. Focusing on each other and remembering the yellow egg that had surrounded them on their wedding night and their experience in Baia, they surrounded themselves once more with golden light. Remembering the golden light within, and all the enlightened filaments of their bodies they surrendered to their own desire to vibrate with this powerful frequency that was generated around them. Remembering that they were the embodiments of earth and sky, the land and the spirit, the Gods and their relationship to mankind, they once again became the two triangles of the Star of David.

Yeshua sat cross legged on the altar. Mariam found her position facing him, sitting on his lap. Her legs were enveloping him around his back. They embraced each other. He lifted her body slightly, she helped with her legs, and he entered her. They sat there for a minute just feeling how they became one body, one organism, being as surrounded by each others bodies as physically possible.

Lazarus introduced the triads. The other voices fell in and created resonating sounds through nose, throat and cranium. The twelve voices surrounding them sounded like a large choir. The grotto became a resonating chamber and the sound reverberated through the entire Temple Mound. The mountain took on the frequency of the sound created and vibrated down into the center of the earth and out towards the stars. Venus felt the frequency of the reverence from the city dedicated to her.

Mariam and Yeshua moved on the altar to build the internal energy inside their bodies. He felt his entire life force going down in uniting with her. She felt his energy building going up inside her body along her spine. She acknowledged his energy in her and created a counter flow going down in her body and into him. He was somewhat surprised to feel energy flowing up along his spine at the same time as feeling the powerful urge going down inside himself. They created simultaneous circles of energy going down his body and up in hers, and also going down in her and up along his spine. The two energy circles met at their heads and switched over, going down their spines and again finding their uniting point where their bodies were physically connected. He held around her back with his hands and felt his love go from his heart through her body and meet his own hands. She sent her love for him from her heart and let it follow her arms enveloping him in her love. They kissed, meeting and uniting in as many ways as possible creating a human gyroscope of energy lines. The Merkaba they assumed with their bodies was generating golden light.

Lazarus watched his sister and brother-in-law, and all he saw was a golden ball. The light they were emanating was pulsating with the sound he and his choir was creating as it reverberated in the room.

Joseph of Aramathea took in the magnificence of how the ritual unfolded. "*This is for the balance of all creation, from the atom to the cosmos,*" he thought, "*for the entire population of humankind from time immemorial to the end of time.*"

Mariam and Yeshua exploded in a starburst starting at the stone of the altar and flowing out of their heads like a fountain squirting stars twenty feet above them. The stars they had generated made wide arches, descended down, and fell on the twelve entities that had been encircling them and supporting them throughout the ritual. They lifted their arms towards a sunrise. The ancestral heads levitated six feet above the ground. The sounds continued in a crescendo of overtones reaching two thousand years back in time and two thousand years into the future. The golden ball became bigger until it generated so much light it shone like the sun itself and extended beyond the room. There was nothing but light and sound in the hall. Lazarus watched the golden ball touch him with small flames on the end of light beams. He looked at the stone in the center and there was nobody there but an opalescent ball hovering over the stone spinning in every direction. With all his willpower he kept the tones, kept allowing this enormous sound to vibrate with his body. Opening his lungs to their maximum capacity he brought them to a volume of sound way beyond what was possible for twelve voices. After the crescendo, he brought in the overtones one by one until they had all reached the single A he started with.

Mariam and Yeshua were again visible on the altar, hanging onto each other with their heads resting on each others shoulders. Their limbs were soft and no muscle tone was visible. Slowly they lifted their sweaty heads and smiled through a golden film. Mariam lifted her hand and moved a lock of his hair away from his face.

The collective deep breath from the twelve in the circle was audible. There was a respectful moment of tangible silence. Then they all burst out laughing in sheer relief.

Venus continued along her pentagonal path enriched by the shower of light from the earth that night.

CHAPTER 11

THE ANOINTMENT

THERE WAS A GATHERING IN THE COLONY of the Nazareeans, near Bethany. They were both mourning the loss of Yochanan and it was time to honor somebody else to take his place as the chosen Messiah.

This was a traditional title given to a chosen man of high standing, both in learning and character, who also had the right lineage. His responsibility was to inspire the spiritual development of their group and to serve the holy meal once a year. The Nazareeans had long experience with the fortified bread. It had been made in Bethlehem, the city of bread, for centuries. There were gold mines in the nearby mountains and men trained at Serabit in Sinai to refine it. Yochanan's work of bringing enlightenment to people with water and bread was following the expectations of his title. That he offered it to people outside their community was another matter. The elders didn't totally approve of his practice, but nobody wanted the man dead.

After the celebration at the palace the gossip ran like wildfire about the Baptists head on a platter. What was the young princess thinking?

In Bethany they knew more details. His body was finally given to his followers who burned the mutilated corpse in the desert. The work was obviously done by experts. Since the queen had requested the head, she must have been involved. And hadn't she been to Ephesus? The story told around the campfire had to be straightened out.

Yeshua and Mariam had told them what had happened. They also said that the head was secured. Their group was in shock for days. The elders let the story calm down before they called for the anointment of a new Messiah. They all knew who was next in line for the title. Reluctantly, the colony gathered. This was supposed to be a ceremony filled with pride and joy. Instead the evening carried many different justified emotions too difficult to handle.

Yochanan's mother Elizabeth was there together with his widow, Anya and his son, young Yahya. Anya now knew how Yochanan had died. She had not reconciled herself with the story she was told. Why would two grown women kill a man whom they all loved? She didn't care that they were priestesses and might have had their reasons. The fact was that they were there, they did it, and in her opinion they could have done more to prevent the event. They simply did as they were told. Anya would never have let anything like that happen. She knew she had to be present tonight, but she did not like the idea of being together with Mariam. And who was Herodias anyway? If she was the wife of the procurator she could have turned the whole thing around. Anya was fuming with anger and grief. Her little son clung to her, having lost his father too young.

Elizabeth sided with her daughter-in-law. There was no good reason why anybody could kill her wise and gentle son. There was no justification in any of this. Her grief was bottomless. Why couldn't they at least have a proper funeral for him? Why?

Mariam didn't have any answers to give the women. She grieved with them, with a different bitterness. She had played an important part in the process of a friend losing his life. She knew there was nothing good she could say, other than show them that she was grieving too. Yeshua showed them respect and they allowed him to comfort them. He hadn't had anything to do with the grizzly event, and was grieving the same way they were. He understood his wife's part, but he couldn't carry it for her. So Mariam carried her own grief silently inside, knowing that just the sight of her solicited hateful comments behind her back and caused good people who had been her friends to turn their heads away when they saw her. She bent her head.

The sicarii were there, the blademen who wanted their country back. They had lost many of their people to the Romans, and their hate grew for every day their country remained occupied. If this man was the new King, they were willing to stand by him as their new leader, the one who would sit at the high seat in Jerusalem and represent their people. The usurper installed by the invaders had to be removed. They were ready. And they were training more people. Passover was right around the corner.

The elders of the Essenes were there. The meeting tonight was important to them as well. This was their new King. He had been married recently and his wife was going to anoint him according to the older tradition. They had respected Yeshua for a long time as one of their learned men.

The Nazareeans were hosting the event. To them this was the night of honoring the new Messiah, a bittersweet celebration. They had been so pleased with Yochanan. His family was of the right lines, his father was greatly respected. Yochanan was known to live a simple quiet life, and do his duties with grace and dignity, until he came back from his summer traveling with Yeshua with new ideas in his head. Refining the water to bring about more powerful healing was all well and good. But their quiet community didn't appreciate all the trafficking it developed. They were becoming a destination developing unnecessary attraction. All they wanted was to live in peace and continue their traditions. Yeshua was becoming too politically involved, and Yochanan didn't know when to keep his mouth shut. Criticizing the procurator, how could he possibly think he would get away with that? And he didn't just say it once, he kept insulting the Roman until his statements were an attack on the whole establishment of the Roman Empire. Of course Herod Antipas had to respond. Otherwise he would have been the laughing stock among his own people.

They remembered when the Roman soldiers took him at the Temple. He went without protesting. They guessed he thought he could talk himself out of it, the way he had used his tongue before. His followers were upset. They heard about the prison dungeons he was kept in and tried to bring him food or consolation, but to no avail. So when Mariam was called to come and visit, they all had their hopes up. The gruesome story she told was almost too fanciful to be true. Then they heard about the party at the palace and understood that there was truth to it. Well, Antipas was in disgrace. Rome didn't like that he had ruined all the diplomatic lines which had taken decades to establish. A new procurator had just arrived, not liked any better, but at least the man seemed intelligent. Antipas had never been convincing. They wondered what happened to the wife and the young dancer.

The Nazareean elders were getting ready. The new choice had been agreed upon. They didn't like it, but they didn't have any choice. Yeshua had the same pedigree as Yochanan and even had a line from Aaron, the priest of Moses. His father was also respected in the community and his mother was much loved, just like Elizabeth. The only thing was that Yeshua seemed to be the center of a lot of political gossip. If it was something the elders despised, it was gossip. Respected people weren't talked about in whispers, rumors spread behind hands held near the talker's mouth, loud sayings among servants at the wells. Respected people were never talked about unless they were honored in a setting with many people where things were said loud and clear. It was hard to talk about Yeshua with clarity. There were too many things about him that weren't that easy to explain. Why there were so many different groups present at this gathering, for example? Who were those ruffians with knives protruding out of their shabby clothing? And what were those simple fishermen from Galilee doing here? What did they know? They didn't have the education needed to understand the implication of what they were going to do here tonight. The elders were quite perturbed and were shuffling their feet. The situation was quite uncomfortable.

The group was gathered, all the elders were there. Yeshua was invited to come forward and sit between the two elder men. It was announced that he was the new Messiah who was going to have the same responsibilities as Yochanan. Yeshua tried to not remember his cousin the way he had seen him just a couple of nights ago. But he couldn't. He cried when Yochanan's name was mentioned.

Yeshua's parents were also present, Joseph as one of the elders of their circle. Mary turned pale and hid inside her shawl. Joseph bent his head in respect for his son's grief while Anya let out a loud cry and ran to him to comfort and be comforted. Little Yahya, a brave boy of about six now, grabbed the closest relative, who happened to be Mariam, and hid in her skirts. When he realized whom he was seeking comfort with, he looked at her with the angry eyes of a child who hates. He walked backwards and was scooped up by Elizabeth, who sent Mariam the same look. These were angry eyes with a question; Why? Mary leaned against Mariam and was also given the same treatment. *Oh Lord,* thought Mariam. *I have caused all this hatred. What can I do?*

The elders saw this emotional display and were even less sure that this was a good decision. If there was something they disliked more than gossip, it was rifts between their women. Usually they felt helpless to remedy the situation, and this one was even worse. In this case they could understand all sides. Mariam had done what she did to save the communities. And she had done it after Yochanan himself had made the choice. To go against Rome would have been futile. They secretly admired the procurators wife, the way she managed to ruin his career at the festivities at the palace. Where was his head now? They were told it was safe, but where? His followers had been given a mutilated corpse which they burned, so that no one would ever find the body that had been so grievously dishonored. They could understand the painful anger of the wife and mother. The elders tried to comfort where they could without talking too much. The issues were too complicated.

Mariam stood there watching the angry child move away from her. She felt the angry eyes of Elizabeth towards herself, but it was even more painful to feel what Mary was going through. Elizabeth and Mary had been closer than sisters, closer than mother and daughter. They had shared pregnancies and sons with great destinies. They had shared raising precocious children who liked studying better than playing and had supported each other while their sons were traveling in search of more knowledge. Could their relationship ever be healed?

Remembering what they had seen and been part of in Salomon's vaults made Mary stagger. She couldn't share what she had seen with Elizabeth, and even if she could have, she didn't think it would make anything any easier. Just thinking about her son's favorite cousin and his new function made her feel green and queasy. She couldn't imagine Elizabeth feeling any better if she knew the truth. She tried to remember that she was here to honor her own son, but her emotions were too entangled to appreciate anything.

Sitting in the circle of the elders made Joseph straighten his back as he rose to bring Anya away from Yeshua and guide her back to Elizabeth and her husbands followers. It was time to get this ordeal over and allow everyone to be alone with their own emotional turmoil. He told Yeshua telepathically to pull himself together, he wasn't the only one grieving a friend, and this evening had a different purpose. Yeshua nodded back to him and stood up to speak.

"We all remember Yochanan and his sad end under the Roman procurator. Let his memory be praised and let us all give our love to his family. I have been asked to take over his responsibilities as the chosen Messiah, and I humbly accept this honor. I will prepare the holy bread the way our people have done since Moses and Aaron and preside over the holy meal during the Passover. Again I thank you for trusting me with this auspicious title."

One of the elders came forward and stood next to him. He waived at Mariam, who came forward carrying a stone jar.

"The anointment will now take place by his wife according to the tradition. Please come on this side Mariam."

Mariam positioned herself behind Yeshua so all could see what she was doing. She sang an incantation as she opened the alabaster jar. The scent of its content sifted slowly out of the jar, almost as an invisible smoke. It spread out among the people present who took a deep breath to smell the lovely perfume. Mariam continued her song as she poured it out and let it flow over Yeshua's head. The song was soothing to listen to, and the aromatic scent calmed people down. In all their grief and sorrow, this was at least pleasant and had an element of beauty to it.

As the jar emptied and the anointing oil flowed over his head and down his hair, the air became saturated with the heavy scent. Some people noticed that this was a more expensive oil than what was usually used. Anya, who was more experienced with herbs was alerted; spikenard. That was it. It was mixed with the frankincense. Not just the regular oil. It had to be better, more luxurious than the one that had been used when Yochanan had been anointed. Would the insults never end?

Mary recognized the jar. It had been hidden inside a wall in the mansion of her brother Joseph for many years.

Joseph recognized the jar, as well. They had given her the responsibility to use those items when the time was right. For a little respite they had needed other things to think about. Mary had felt the blessed release of stirring a big pot of soup to ease her mind, and Joseph had walked the fields. Mariam had remembered.

Yeshua looked like a statue. He sat perfectly still allowing the oil to flow wherever gravity took it. The mixed emotions going on around him were coming to him like prickly needles. The domed part on the top of his head was always ready to take in new things from above. This was his opening for receiving energy from God, or messages from above. It opened to a tunnel going through him along his spine creating an open cylinder for the connection between the skies above and the earth below. With this part of his body open, he became a vehicle for bigger purposes than he could explain. Some vibration from the earth needed to connect with the matching vibration from above, and it needed a human nervous system to go through to accomplish that. His body had been refined through many processes through out his life, and as a result, his nervous system could do the job. This high voltage energy field could go through him without burning him up or harming him in any way. He had worked with his own inner demons and refinined his own body's functions. Having gone through many initiations in many different cultures, he was considered a master of the craft. He had eaten his manna and his gold. Now he was being anointed as the Messiah, and he knew he was the right man.

He closed his eyes and prayed. As his left brain formed the words and his right brain shaped the concepts, a new pathway between the two functions was formed. Other organs in his brain were awakened. Inspired by the oil, new chemicals were created inside his head. New serums were secreted from glands that had always been there but been dormant until now.

He was reminded of the soma of the sages of India. He was reminded of the effects described in the hieroglyphs. He was reminded of the conversations he had with the druids of the green island of Hibernia.

The golden light of Baia wasn't just the golden dome of a cave with gemstones inside. The golden dome was the inside of his own skull. The gemstones were the color of these new refined substances that were flowing oiling the pathways of his thoughts. Inside his head he saw a new light being created. A golden light with ribbons of soft greens and purples was pulsating with the flow of energy streaming through his body.

A gasp went through the crowd around him. The light emanating from him was visible for everyone to see. They saw the streams of golden light coming out of him as if the sun itself was inside his head. As the light reached them, their pain eased like oil being poured upon their sore and tender skin. The places that had been burning with anguish were being kissed as if from a loving mother. They exhaled, as peace spread like a smooth river among them and a gentle sweet taste, like the lightest of honey, formed in their mouths.

Mariam stood behind him and just watched the effect. She had joined energetically with her husband's body and let the energies flow through her as well in the way that was so familiar to them. As the oil had flowed over his head, she had named each of the small glands in his brain that needed to wake up. She had called their name, their sound, and heard their response. When the new pathways hooked up she had listened to a different sound from him like a faint high tone growing stronger as the new routes of thought were established. She knew the symbol from the hieroglyphs. She knew the song they would sing. Silently she called in the tone from the depths of the earth. Silently she established the link with the skies. The new song from him was the connection between the two. She let it reverberate through her own system. Then silently she took her alabaster jar and left.

CHAPTER 12

THE INITIATION OF LAZARUS

"**B**UT, SISTER, WE TALKED ABOUT THIS."
"Lazarus, we are not at the Serapium! This is not safe."
"You've done it before and you promised!"

Lazarus changed his tone. He did not want to be whiny, definitely not to his younger sister, especially not since he needed her so desperately. He knew whom he was working with, and he had great respect for her. But this was very important to him, and he spoke with a sense of urgency.

She knew he deserved it. Lazarus had been as astute in his studies as anybody. He was mentally and spiritually ready. To be given the status in the group which his responsibilities merited, he needed this experience. He needed to be able to say he had been to the other side. And since Yochanan was gone, they needed him as one of the inner circle. She would have to find a way.

How could she explain this? People changed after that experience. Mariam had seen it many times. When you could communicate with the other side, your vision became wider. You could take in more information from your surroundings. You merged your consciousness easily with the group you were with and with the landscape around you. It was so much easier to communicate with someone who was initiated. The pretences were gone. You couldn't play games anymore since your intentions and inner thoughts became so much more transparent to other initiates. Yeshua was very particular about who were in his inner circle and who were in the next sphere. It had nothing to do with status of importance, and then again it did.

It was easy to understand the status of people with wealth or a position of responsibility. It was harder to explain the status of someone who could work better with unseen forces. Generally people understood that the disciples who had gone through this initiation were allowed closer to Yeshua. But then that became a status too. Mariam tried to get around it all. How do you explain that it is easier to work with people who have a cleaner energy flow through their bodies? Telepathic messaging worked so much easier without murky overtones. Healing power didn't work at all, if it wasn't coupled with clean lines of love and compassion. And issues of inflated egos made it difficult to even have regular conversations about bread and milk.

Mariam sighed. It was easier to live among the temple trained. And it was more important to learn how to work with the force inside your own body, than to discuss the intricacies of scriptures.

"Mariam, please? Martha could help you."

If it was one thing Mariam was sure of, it was that Martha could *not* help. She had experience from Therapautae, but she was not temple trained. If Yeshua had time, he could help her. He had at least gone through the experience himself. She couldn't really ask the recently dethroned queen to help her placate a begging brother.

Mariam corrected herself. Lazarus was not begging. This was indeed something they had discussed before and she had promised to guide him through this experience when the time was right. Apparently he felt it was. She was not so sure.

"Mariam, there is a cave just behind the colony. I've been there with Martha. And you always have herbs in your bag. Don't you have the right ones?"

Mariam made a mental inventory of what she had. She was indeed missing some important ones. And she liked to harvest her own, prepare them correctly and endow them with the right intentions. Just picking them and hanging them to dry wasn't good enough for her collection. Oh, Lazarus, she really wanted to help, but she wanted to do it right. Not to mention safely.

"You know there is a risk involved. Not everybody comes back."

"But none of your candidates were lost, were they?" Lazarus had infinite trust in his sister's abilities.

That's true, thought Mariam, *but I can't work miracles. It takes knowledge and technique, not just faith that it all will work out. Oh, beloved brother, if I lost you...*

She couldn't even finish the thought.

"What would they have at the temple which we don't have here?" Lazarus asked practically.

"Well for one thing an extensive support system with people who would know what to do if something did not work out right. A space dedicated to this kind of work where even the walls remember what needs to be done, and an extensive herb collection that has been prepared the right way. Sibyl takes such personal pride in making sure the shelves are full, all labeled carefully and ready for use. Lazarus, I miss the Temple."

Mariam slumped down on a chair. She felt so alone here in this dry land where hardly anything grew and where she was so misunderstood. Everything she did which would have been everyday fare at the Temple was seen here as if she was a magician. Or a witch. Or a freak of some sort, who had been hit by lightening and thereby had magic powers. If she tried to explain, they looked at her strange. The explanation almost proved that she was a witch, especially if she tried to simplify. *You see,* she said to herself, explaining to an imaginary audience. Her inner voice was full of irony.

Our bodies have electric currents and if I magnify them with my intentions you can feel them in your body. Since my current is vibrating at a higher frequency than yours, your lower vibration will simply tune itself to mine and you will feel better. Then your tummy ache will go away. See?

They didn't see. All they saw was that she was scary because she could affect their bodies with apparently very little effort on her part. She hoped they would never see the device Yeshua had along his arm which magnified him manifold. He had a powerful field to begin with, and when magnified he was more protected within his own aura, but he could also heal in a wide circle of people just standing around him. His words were magnified and they carried his healing frequency also. She had seen how it worked and admired how successfully he used the technique.

But now her own brother wanted to be closer to the small group who understood all this. He knew it all theoretically, but to plug into it all he needed this initiation. *A trip on the boat of Isis and Osiris would be good for him,* Mariam smiled to her self.

"Let me see what I can figure out," she said. No sense committing herself if it couldn't happen.

Lazarus went dancing out the door to look after the animals. She knew they would enjoy his singing as he filled their cribs. Maybe the goats and sheep would understand his desire to sail through portholes between the worlds.

Mariam put her cape on and went into town. She told Martha she would be back before the evening meal.

The short walk to Jerusalem gave her time to think. Even though she didn't favor the dry landscape, she enjoyed this particular walk along the cypresses and sycamores. A fig tree was in bloom and a donkey was nibbling at some tufts of grass behind a simple fence. She smiled at some neighbors who waived at her and sent some loving thought to their children playing. They were used to the friendly woman on her walks. She had helped with an injury caused by a cow stepping on a young man's foot. He was healed and they liked the idea of having healers in the neighborhood.

Mariam smiled again. She did remember the broken foot. His ankle was broken in many small pieces. It had taken both hers and Yeshua's healing abilities, and Yochanan's water, to make it heal. The ankle grew nicely together while they kept the patient with them. His family would be their allies forever. Without their help they would have had a cripple on their hands. Now they had a handsome young man with a strong back.

She allowed herself to smell the fig blossoms as she passed by, and to feel the sunshine as warmth, not heat. It took some adjustment.

In the city she went to the nicer part of town. The stately home she was looking for had a brick wall around it with a gate. She had to identify herself to gain access. The servants all knew her and welcomed her in. She was offered water to drink inside while they fetched Joseph of Aramathea.

"Mariam, what a pleasant surprise," he beamed at her. "How are things in Bethany?"

"Everything is well, uncle, I bring greetings from both my husband's family and my own."

"What is my busy nephew up to these days?" asked Joseph to make small talk.

"He is out walking the roads of Galilee," answered Mariam, trying not to sound worried.

"In preparation, I see."

"Yes," uncle.

"And you are not with him this time?"

"I… needed to spend some time with my brother."

"I see."

"Uncle, can we speak privately, there is a favor I need to ask you."

Joseph asked her to follow him as he walked up the stairs to the upper floor. He opened the door to the bedroom she had visited before. He pointed to the bed and pulled up a chair for himself in front of her.

"What's on your mind, daughter?" Joseph of Aramathea shared her father-in-laws admiration for this powerful woman, who was also charming and lovely. Yeshua was indeed a lucky man.

"My brother Lazarus wants to go through the same initiation Yochanan and Yeshua did. He wants to be one of the ones that know. He is asking me to make it happen."

"Your brother is a wise young man. He wouldn't ask if it wasn't important to him. And he has been an incredible help so far. We couldn't have done what we did at the equinox without him being with us."

"I know he deserves it. But this is something usually done in the safety of the temples. I don't have the same resources here. I'm afraid for his safety."

"I see what you mean."

"Uncle Joseph, I cannot risk my brother's life, however much we need him among the inner circles, now that Yochanan is only with us in spirit."

"But what a spirit. He's always near, you know." Joseph lifted his head and looked at the wall with the secret space behind. She knew her friend again was safe after the incredible night they had shared not long ago.

Mariam understood his message and bent her head in deep respect for Yochanan's memory. Then she looked up. She met Joseph's deeply concerned eyes and formed a question in her mind.

Of course, my dear, came the answer. *I'll see what I can do.*

Mariam left Joseph's house feeling much better. Joseph of Aramathea had a way of making everybody at ease. Somehow things just worked out if you presented your situation for him.

Yeshua came back the following day. Mariam had helped Martha cook a large meal for all the followers. They were crowding the courtyard, sitting everywhere, hardly letting Yeshua have any rest. Serving the meal gave her a good vantage point to observe them all. Nobody noticed a woman with a pot of stew or carrying used dishes back to the kitchen. Why couldn't they use palm leaves like they did so much in Alexandria? It would make things so much simpler. Yeshua caught her thinking and said; *Remember Leontopolis?* She smiled back at him across many heads and wondered when she last had some time alone with him.

As she brought in a basket with bread she gave herself time to pay even closer attention to the people flocking everywhere. She saw some that needed immediate attention. A man walked with a cane, she wanted to find out what was his problem. A young man had a greenish tone to his skin and she knew he had an infection somewhere. A woman had a more grayish appearance. She simply needed someone to tell her how beautiful she was, and that the child she carried would be taken good care of regardless of her circumstances.

Those were easy. She would take care of them shortly. But first she wanted to simply observe. There was a group of men that seemed to always find their way to be next to Yeshua wherever he was. Mariam walked slowly around the outer periphery of their tight group. The one called Simon Peter was right at Yeshua's feet on the floor. Simon was a large man, and even as he was sitting lower, his head was almost at Yeshua's eye level. He was so eager, he wanted so much to understand. He soaked up every word Yeshua said as if it was water, and he became almost drunk as he absorbed them. *We need to watch him,* thought Mariam. *He is simply getting overloaded. The sound from Yeshua is powerful. Simon Peter needs to give himself some time to digest it all. Besides, he has not had any of the early initiations yet. It might be a little too much for his system to be that close.*

There were others too, equally eager, but they were less forthright and more humble in their approach. *How many of the Zealots from Galilee do we have here?*, she wondered. *Did they all bring weapons?*

"Mariam," Martha called from the kitchen. "Can you give me a hand?"

"Coming," Mariam hurried back to her sister.

"Johanna is here to help, besides young Mary is here, don't worry, and young Salome is always willing to fetch and carry," Martha reassured her sister. "The other kitchens are busy too. You have a visitor. I didn't want to create too much attention. She is waiting for you by the back door."

Mariam hurried out and looked around. She would recognize that profile anywhere. The thick brown curly hair, the straight proud back, you can't hide that you're a queen however humbly you dress, at least not from your temple sister at Ephesus.

"Joseph told me you needed my help. Here I am. But what's with all these people? Has somebody died?"

"I am so glad to see you, no, there is no tragedy. Yeshua is simply back, and all these people came with him."

"Are they expecting you to keep them for the night? There must be close to a hundred here!"

"They are humble people with simple needs, Herodias. Not all people have your taste. We're getting used to it. Martha uses bigger pots. The whole colony helps."

"I guess it is for the cause. But this is crowded. How can we work here?"

"The conditions are far from ideal. How long can you stay?"

"Only for the evening. We are leaving for Rome tomorrow morning. Antipas has been called to Caesar."

"What do you think will happen? Are you and your daughter safe?"

"Oh, Mariam, it's been awful. For a while I feared for our lives."

"Well, you ruined his career. He has a right to be angry."

"We are safe within the palace as long as there are other people around. I'm a born citizen of Rome. If he harmed me he would be prosecuted. But I have to be very careful."

"So being here is not safe for you."

"Not really, but here I am. I should be back tonight."

"Herodias, I want you to be safe. Not just for tonight. You can't run around like this, hiding out of fear in your own home."

"Well, my days as queen are over, that's for sure. Salome is angry with me too. She liked being a princess."

"There has to be a solution."

"Yes, but first we've got work to do. Where is that brother of yours?"

Herodias didn't put people at ease, she put people to work. Mariam sent a friend of Lazarus to fetch him. Then she called for Salome to get Herodias whatever she asked for, while she went and found her own herb bag. They needed linens and blankets, healing water, oil lamps and wicks. They tried to not make too much commotion, but with a hundred people or so visiting there was a coming and going everywhere anyway. Nobody seemed to notice three women being busy. Women were busy running to and fro in the whole colony.

They met again at the edge of the courtyard.

"I have been fasting for two days," said Lazarus. "I spent the morning praying on top of the hill. Yesterday I cleaned out the cave."

Mariam didn't doubt that he was ready. Was she?

Herodias simply picked up baskets and bundles and asked him to guide the way. Nobody thought of sending Salome away, even though she had never attended anything like this before.

"I helped a woman give birth, just last week," she said.

"That will do," was Herodias' reply. Mariam rolled her eyes.

They walked around the hill and found the cave on the other side. There was

203

a bush in front of the entrance, and a tree close by. *Picturesque,* thought Herodias. Some flat stones were nearby. They could make a makeshift cover for the opening that would at least keep animals away. Everything seemed makeshift to Mariam.

Inside the cave had been swept and cleared. Lazarus really had prepared for the event. The cave was not big, but had an outcrop of rock forming a bench of sorts. The walls were simply rough stone. There was just enough space for all of them to be inside and for the women to move about.

"Start the brazier, Salome, would you?" Asked Mariam.

"And here is the scent we need for the oil." Herodias brought a jar out of her basket.

Lazarus didn't say anything, but quietly sat down on the bench.

Mariam looked at her brother. She took in his fine features and his thick mane of reddish brown hair. He looked more like Yeshua's mother than like their family. May the Gods protect them. Nothing could happen to this favorite brother of hers.

He looked at her with his big brown eyes. Always gentle, always sweet, so different from the older brothers who were happily attending the shipping business in Alexandria.

"Sing, Lazarus, please. You'll know the tone we need."

He looked at her again. Sure he could find the tone. The cave, the purpose of them being there, the smell of the fragrant herbs being prepared all gave him the notes and the melody. The rhythm was given by the women moving at a steady, calm pace. He started with a low note and built a lovely melody from that. The women fell in and repeated the simple song.

The lamps were placed in four places creating a protected space within. The three women invoked the four directions and the spirits from the four elements to protect them. The incense gave a pungent heavy smell in the room.

The priestesses looked over the herbs they needed. Herodias had brought the unusual ones Mariam had asked for. A tea was brewed for him to drink and they instructed Salome to mix a salve they were going to apply to his head and feet. Wide eyed and with big movements she stirred a wooden spoon in a bowl taking in everything. She was used to watching her brother Yeshua work. Helping the priestesses was very different.

Well, for once she is speechless, Herodias shot to Mariam, and the two women shared a smile.

Lazarus was in prayers while waiting for his potion.

Mother Isis, protector of all life, I beseech you and your husband Osiris to meet me on the other side and guide the steps of my journey. Let me feel the strength of life force permeating creation, bridging dimensions, creating pathways and portholes. Make an opening for me here, in this safe cave, for me to be with you.

Herodias and Mariam brought themselves in line with the hum of the space and their shared intentions. They faced each other and held the cup between them while singing the incantations for the herbs to do their work. Then they turned and gave Lazarus the cup. He looked at each of them and thanked them with his eyes before he drank. No words were necessary anymore.

The blankets had been readied on the bench. They had brought several for him, since the surface was rough. A thick wool camel blanket was closest to the stone, then a thick tapestry before a sturdy cotton blanket. On top was a large white sheet in two layers.

The women rolled the white linen over so the top layer was above his head, then they instructed him to lie down. Lazarus lifted his shirt over his head and stood there with a piece of linen wrapped around his hips. Mariam looked at his thin body, and wondered if he ever would fill out. *He is handsome enough. Don't worry so much,* Herodias sent to her mind. He smiled at them as he sat down on top of the linen. Then he lay down and positioned himself on his back. They smiled at him again, and wished him a good journey. He closed his eyes, and they watched as the herbs did their work. . Mariam noticed that he stopped emitting signals very quickly. His life force simply turned inwards.

Herodias motioned to Salome, and she brought the unguent she had been mixing. Some of it was spooned out for his feet, and then the bowl was passed on towards his head. Herodias and Salome took a foot each and massaged the fragrant thick oil into his foot soles. Mariam used the rest to work on the top of his head. As their hands moved in circular motion she monitored how well his channel was opened. After a while she could sense a gentle wind blowing across her hand, and she knew that the energies were moving the full length of his body. The three women let their hands do some caressing strokes and then left his body to its process.

Mariam stayed next to him monitoring his progress while Herodias and Salome refilled the lamps. When she felt that he was on his way and protected, she said some welcoming words to Isis and Osiris before she pulled the white linen over him.

Herodias started another song while they picked up their things and filled the baskets. Mariam checked the herb content in the lamps and how safely they stood on the stone surface. Everything seemed to be good for a safe journey. In her mind she saw him crossing a river on a raft he needed to punt with a long staff. The golden light reflected in the ripples of the blue Nile water. Two figures stood on the other side ready to receive him. Mariam knew that his journey had started.

They left the cave quietly. The lamps would burn until the oil was gone. On the outside they turned and looked back into the cave to take in the sight. The white linen sheet covered a grown man's body underneath and the lamps gave warmth and a golden glow.

The three women struggled some with the flat stones, but soon they had them lifted so they covered most of the entrance. There was a little opening on the top where some of the light shone through. That little glimmer was the only proof that there was a powerful process going on inside the space. Lazarus had entered the porthole to visit with the gods.

They walked silently back to the colony. As they came closer Salome couldn't keep her silence anymore.

"But Mariam, he is breathing, isn't he?"

"No Salome, he will not be breathing for three days."

"But, Mariam, he could die!"

"No, Salome. He will appear dead, but he will not die."

That was all the explanation young Salome got, besides being told not to talk about it. She had to be satisfied with that, because back at the houses people were still milling about looking for food and places to spend the night.

Herodias returned to the palace. Mariam sent Judas with her for protection and for once she didn't protests. Martha was calling and Mariam returned to the kitchen wondering if Yeshua ever got to rest. She had just started an initiation between kitchen duties. If she took it all in, she would faint with worry.

Sibyl, where are you? Mariam called out in the dark night.

CHAPTER 13

THE RETURN OF LAZARUS

THE FOLLOWING DAY YESHUA WANTED TO CONTINUE his teaching rounds. These walks in the country sides were also to recruit more people for the cause. He had many reasons to circulate among them.

He wanted to spread well being among these simple people who only asked to be left to live in peace and tend their small farms. The Romans focused their attention in the city of Jerusalem and in the port cities they had built themselves. In Galilee there were fewer of them, and Yeshua could work more at ease.

Healers didn't frequent there often and people ailed from simple imbalances that caused illness in their bodies. He worked on bringing people back to balance. Then he taught them to empower themselves by staying connected to a larger consciousness and allow it to work through them. For people who understood, he would offer empowering bread or the healing waters. For the closest he would mention the first initiations. These were introductions into further learning which he administered himself. In this way he gradually built his fellowship. Mariam had great respect for how he worked and was genuinely impressed with the amount of people he counted as his flocks.

At the same time she wondered if he always screened carefully enough who were given the first initiations. She also wondered if he was aware of how the elders at the Temple in Jerusalem talked about him. They felt that he was betraying their secrets. Many at the temple worked well with the Romans, and didn't want to see that relationship disturbed. They were not happy with what was developing in Galilee.

Mariam tried to understand his motivations. Did all these people around him know him as their King? Did they see him as only a spiritual teacher or did they understand the magnitude of his mission? He was the Priest King, the one talked about in the old scriptures. He was the only one in many generations who had prepared for this job to the extent he had, and who had accepted the role gracefully. His marriage to her completed the prophecy.

His followers had great respect for her, but she didn't think they truly understood what she was either. She was acknowledged as a master, and called Mara by many.

They saw her as the Magdalene, the tower, the one who knew. They saw her as the one who could bring light inside their bodies with her magical medicine.

Mariam wasn't quite sure what to make of it all. She was the Priestess Queen. She and her husband were the couple needed for this enormous task. Still she felt that she often healed minor injuries to infinite gratitude, but very little understanding. *Yeshua, why are we doing this?* She asked one day.

Because we love them, he answered her warmly back. He was not tired. He was not exasperated with their ignorance. He was tending to his people.

The following day they were gathered at the top of a hill, and as far as Mariam could see, there were people everywhere. She heard that they had come from Jerusalem and Judea to hear him as well as the cities along the coast.

What are we going to do with so many?, she wondered.

Yeshua looked at her. They stood there in the middle of their closest people with several feet between them and shared eye contact. They were both strengthened by each other.

Wife, give me strength. Connect me with the earth and the sky, he sent to her. Mariam gently opened up his channels from the top of his head to the soles of his feet. He stretched out his hands, palms first towards her, and she enlivened all the power points on his body until they all shone gold, beaming out from him.

"You are the shining one," she said, and smiled at him.

You are the illuminator, he smiled back.

He walked to the top where he could be visible in all directions. His disciples sat down around him giving him space to move about, and all the people covering the whole hillside quietly sat down too.

Mariam listened to him speak. The things he said were simple and they carried so much comfort for the people who had been suppressed by foreign armies for a very long time. She saw them calm down and feel better. Then he spoke in parables telling stories that had multi layered meanings. The simple people could understand the first layers, and the people who were looking for more would find it.

She saw some priests and rabbis among them and she heard Yeshua's words be received different by them. They heard quotes from the scriptures showing them that Yeshua was a very learned man. Then they heard new interpretations of familiar scriptures, new ways of seeing the wisdom in light of the situation of their time. They didn't like what they heard, but Yeshua worded himself so well that his arguments were irrefutable. They liked that even less, and felt that he didn't respect their status as elders. *Oh, Yeshua, sometime you should forgo a challenge however tempting it is,* Mariam thought.

He had been speaking for a while and she sensed that all these people were getting hungry. Some of them had brought some food, but many had traveled a long distance to be here, and didn't have anything with them.

Mariam turned around and questioned their men.

Did they have any fish from their catch earlier today? Could they please bring it here now?

Simon and Andrew looked at her. They didn't like a women initiating action.

Oh, get over it, Mariam thought to herself. *There is a need to be filled here.*

The men brought what they had, and some women brought bread. Mariam set some to fry fish and somebody else to carry the basket around. She kept her eyes on the baskets and made sure they kept replenishing themselves. As the fish was being fried over a simple fire, there seemed to always be more in the net as they flayed them and got them ready for the next round. Mariam's eyes were focused on the net on the ground. Making something duplicate itself is not as hard as it may sound. You need the first sample to copy.

She kept them so busy they didn't really notice that the fish never ended and the baskets never emptied. The people were staying quiet and calm. Yeshua's voice was soothing and also gave them food for thought. There were some Roman soldiers around checking for anything that might brew into a rebellion. After all, a crowd can be teased into doing dangerous things, and they were ready to squelch anything before it even began.

Johanna turned to Mariam.

"What do you think they are looking for? I really don't like them being so suspicious. The flock of people here is so peaceful, what could they possibly have to be suspicious about?"

"Johanna, don't be naïve," said Mariam.

"We have the Sicarii with us. Do you see the shimmer in the blades underneath their capes? The Nazareeans are also ready with swords hidden on them. A nod from Judas and they would know exactly what to do. Even the fisher men from Galilee aren't as simple as you might think. Some of them are leaders of groups of Zealots and have followers among themselves, and it is not spiritual illumination they are looking for. They want a new country."

Johanna looked at her with big eyes. She hadn't seen all this before. What was her brother doing? Everybody liked the mild mannered rabbi who spoke of inner enlightenment. People liked the healing that was taking place among them. The Priest King was gathering his people in peace and brotherhood. What did Mariam mean, they had weapons?

Mariam was silent. She wanted Johanna do find out for herself. Besides, she loved her strong sister-in-law too much. She didn't' want to break her trust, her belief in the cause and the promise they had made to the tribes to make Jerusalem their own again. The promise was already fulfilled. History would show how it manifested.

It was late in the day before the people started to leave. Many had been healed from various ailments, and they all marveled at the wisdom of this man. As she listened in on peoples conversations she realized that they all left with a different inspiration. Some people had heard comfort in their hardship; it would soon end.

Others had heard new ways of building their own confidence. One man felt that he had gotten an answer to a life long question about his relationship with God. Several said that they were coming back to hear more.

Yeshua held her arm as they walked along the dusty road on their way back to Bethany. This time he was indeed tired. She gave him strength and tried to talk him into resting when they reached their home.

"Mariam. The work. There is always work to do."

She couldn't help but agree, at the same time he wasn't going to be good for much unless he got some rest.

"You're always concerned with me, Mariam. What about you? I haven't seen you lying down all day either."

"True, but I didn't have five thousand pairs of eyes on me for a whole day, each expecting their own miracles," she answered.

As they entered into Bethany, several women came running towards them. They were extremely concerned and told Yeshua and Mariam to hurry up. Martha came running towards them wailing.

"Oh thank God, you're here. It's Lazarus. He is dead! Mariam, he is dead. We found him in the cave. What happened?"

Mariam had hoped she didn't have to explain all this. She had hoped that Martha would assume that Lazarus was with them and not look for him. Salome had come with them to help, so she wasn't there to explain. Mariam would have him back among them tonight. She hoped. Yeshua also looked concerned. What had happened here that he had not been informed about?

"Yeshua, can you do something? This is too much to bear!" Martha was hysterical. Her last hope was her brother-in-law.

"Come," said Mariam. She had her herb bag with her, and she knew what to do.

At the cave they insisted that all the people stayed at a distance. Only Yeshua and Mariam went inside. Martha came running.

"Can I help? Please? He is my brother, too." Mariam insisted on calm. She instructed them to sit down and pray for his soul's safe return. Then she let Martha and Yeshua come with into the cave.

Martha was instructed to light the lamps and invoke the protection of the gods. The fragrance of the specially chosen herbs started to fill the room. The brazier created some warmth and soon light filled the cave which had seemed cold, damp and without life a moment earlier.

When Martha found him like this, Mariam understood her reaction. With the linen sheet over him, he did indeed look like a corpse. When she lifted the sheet, she would have seen that his skin was gray and cold and his breath had left him a long time ago.

Martha swallowed a yelp as she observed her brother being revealed. To her, he appeared totally without life. She had seen Yeshua perform miracles before. She knew he could do it. It was different watching someone she didn't know be healed.

She stared at her brother's dead body. Her own limbs were turning stiff and cold as she held her hands up to her heart. Holding her breath, she prayed to Isis and Osiris to deliver him back safely from his journey. She knew the gods would love him too, just like they all did, but please, send him back to her.

Yeshua had not seen someone come out of the initiation. He had done it himself, but had not helped from the priestess' side. He could also understand that the others took Lazarus for dead. But in his fine tuned discernment, he could sense that there was life somewhere inside. He looked at Mariam.

Mariam turned ashen as she wondered if she had to make her brother into another oracle.

If Mariam had looked confident, Yeshua would have felt a lot better. But she didn't. She seemed scared and flustered, two attributes that were out of character for her. He stopped everything with a simple gesture of his hand. Then he took her two hands in his and stood facing her the way they had done so many times building strength together.

Remember Baia, he sent to her, and together they created the pillar of invisible strength one more time.

Martha stood next to them and stared at the beam of light being formed between them. Then she watched them transfer that strength to her brother's body.

"Martha, mix these ingredients, please," said Mariam, as she found the oil and the herbs she needed. She looked over the ingredients and felt that something was missing, but she couldn't tell what it was. *Oh, Isis, oh Gods of our ancestors, I need to do this right to bring my brother back.* She had a hollow feeling in her chest as she looked over the herbs one more time.

Remember Bella Donna, she heard Sibyl's voice in her head. The master herbologist would always have a link to her partner priestess. Mariam exhaled, and looked for a sample in her bag. She found a small twig of the plant which was about the right dosage. They wanted to stimulate his heart, not overexcite it.

While she waited for Martha to finish mixing the unguent, she instructed Yeshua to breathe across Lazarus' nose in rhythmical motions. She found the notes to sing, and encouraged Yeshua to do the overtones. He had learned how to create beautiful tones in his throat, nose and skull simultaneously on his travels to the Far East. Martha found the soprano thrills while Mariam took the deeper sounds. When the fragrant massage oil was ready, they all worked on the body in soothing motions while they continued the eerie tones.

Mariam instructed Yeshua and Martha to work from his feet whereas she herself took position at his head. She took over the breathing across his nose in regular intervals as she monitored the state of the body.

Yeshua understood that they were drawing energy through his body awakening the tunnel that goes through the middle along the spine. One of the ways to diagnose people was to find the strength of this passage way, how much energy they had passing through, how much new energy could the person handle passing through their own system. It was an easy way to find where there was a problem, and an efficient tool to monitor how much energy to give to people.

He checked the body of his dear friend and found that only the thinnest of threads of energy was going through. If this had been a sick person he would have said that he was close to death. But since this was a healthy person who had sent himself to death, Yeshua took it as a good sign of life.

Mariam noticed it as well. There was indeed a thin line of life force going through him. She felt better and smiled at Yeshua. Martha saw the communication between them and felt better too. Their singing got a stronger tone, and their movements became more vigorous.

They massaged the fragrant oil into his body from his feet up and from his head down. Soon the whole cave was filled with the aroma from the healing herbs and from the incense in the braziers. Their toning of sounds made the particles in the air dance and invited the spirit of Lazarus to return to his body. Isis and Osiris were impressed with the efforts of his relatives and decided to encourage him to go back, even though it would be hard to part with him. Just as Martha had been afraid of, they had indeed fallen in love with this beautiful soul, this gentle young man who carried so much wisdom. They marveled over the frequencies around him. Isis could hardly get enough of the music emanating from his spirit.

Lazarus heard his family calling him. The genes in his body resonated with his sisters. His brother-in-laws seeds flowed in his sister's body. It wasn't hard to recognize his presence. He caught the sounds they were creating for him, and he realized he needed to train them better. It was indeed time to go back.

The boat shaped loophole was made ready for him one more time. As soon as his desire to return was formed in even the faintest of intentions, the journey back started. He thanked Isis and Osiris for all he had learned and promised to stay in touch. They smiled at him acknowledging his time with them and their further contact. They all knew that he would return a different man than when he left. The contact with the other side would never leave his conscious mind. He would forever have a foot in both worlds.

Lazarus was sucked through the tunnel at high speed. The tunnel ended and he felt himself filling the cells of organic material like honey being poured onto the hexagonal cells of bees. As he felt the limitations of his physical body, he took a deep breath. Mariam sighed in relief and watched his color come back. Yeshua looked up and met her eyes. Martha had big tears rolling down her cheeks.

They continued massaging his body to encourage his blood flow. Otherwise it would be painful for him to move. As soon as they could spare her, they sent Martha out of the cave to announce to the others that Lazarus was back. They were all relieved and were told to go and make soup for him. Johanna and young Mary immediately got up and headed for the kitchen. Salome refused to leave. Mariam invited her inside the cave. She had a right to see for herself.

Inside the cave the golden glow had intensified. Isis and Osiris were saying goodbye and thanking Mariam for having sent her brother to them. Mariam and

Yeshua heard them and smiled back in recognition. They were now focused on Lazarus' body and bringing back awareness to every part of him. He had opened his eyes by now and was looking at them observing what they did, but his body would not move yet. They continued their intense massaging of his limbs and soon he could move fingers and toes. No words were said. When you just come out of such a state, words are harsh and uncomfortable. They are too specific when you exist in a euphoria of loving emotions. The concepts of love and life, the strength of family ties, become big warm spheres of knowledge that you exist within. Words are like pinpointing a position somewhere in the sphere with mathematical precision. The sphere would get lost and someone would say that another number would describe it better. They all wanted to stay within the bigger sphere were so much was felt as loving intention.

Lazarus moved his head towards them and looked like he had just woken up from a long sleep. Martha rushed to him, but stopped herself so she wouldn't come onto him too strongly. Her relief felt like a heavy rain cloud dropping to the floor making a puddle by her feet before it disappeared between the rocks. She sat down next to him and just held his hand showering him with love.

Mariam and Yeshua took a step back and stood by the wall giving Martha a moment with her brother. They held around each other and realized that they hadn't had time to do that for days. Yeshua turned and kissed her. He was so proud. The true miracle in his life was that he had a marvel like her. She looked at him and kissed him back.

You're pretty awesome yourself, she sent back to him. Martha noticed and put the vision to memory.

Soon they had him sitting up and with some help he was on his feet supported by Yeshua. Mariam gathered up her things and Salome helped carrying. Lazarus had his shirt on again and a blanket over his shoulders. Martha hoped Johanna's soup was ready for him.

Salome ran ahead to prepare the others. They didn't want to create too much commotion around him. Ideally Lazarus should be in his own bed with just his sisters around him. Salome had her instructions and knew what to do.

Of course people wanted to see Lazarus, but they also understood that he needed time to recover. There was no need to explain any further. Yeshua had apparently brought people back from the dead before. This was another miracle that proved his powers. They left it at that. There is no reason to confuse well intended people.

Leaning on his sisters shoulders, Lazarus hobbled slowly towards his home. Yeshua walked in front to make sure the people gave them a wide berth and that they didn't try to touch Lazarus' body. Seeing him would have to be proof enough. The flock was silent. They stared at the young man who, as expected, looked very much like someone just back from the dead, but his smile towards them told them that he was very much alive. It was a triumph that was celebrated all through the night and talked about for a very long time. But Yeshua never mentioned it. Mariam didn't refer to this in her writings and Martha kept the whole story to her self.

213

CHAPTER 14

ENTERING JERUSALEM

THEY ALL KNEW WHAT THIS DAY MEANT. They all knew what this day was supposed to contain. It had been prophesied for hundreds of years.

In his own quiet way Yeshua had given instructions for a couple of events during the day. A few key people knew what to do.

Mariam was more concerned with the Passover meal she was preparing with Martha and her sisters-in-law for the evening than the events of the day. But she figured she should be there and offer support. The women were glad she had helped as far as she did, but said that all the three Mary's should be where they were needed.

Mariam, Mary, his mother, and young Mary, his sister, went to Jerusalem together. Their status gave them their own protection. They were three priestesses honoring the Passover.

The spring weather was lovely as they found their way towards Jerusalem passing familiar neighbors. The Essenes sent a delegation of people, and the Nazareeans came with their whole families. From the monastery at Qumran the monks had already picked palm branches and were ready to honor their Messiah. They all knew. And they all knew that they were taking a risk this seemingly innocent day of spring.

Mariam wasn't sure if the other women sensed the tension already building in the people that were coming to attend the event. If this many were coming from Bethany, how many were coming from other places?

She got her answer as they came closer to town. It seemed that all the people he had spoken to on the hill top in Galilee were there. Passover was the busiest time of the year in Jerusalem. But this wasn't just the regular crowd of good people coming to honor their traditions.

Mariam passed a group of men standing near a brick staircase leading to the top of a house. They quietly saluted her and bent their heads in respect. She greeted them back with an almost unnoticeable dignified bow of her head all the while checking with her probing vision for weapons.

"Did you see that?" said young Mary, trying to not let her mother hear her. "There were blades in every fold of their garments. Who are they? What do they want?"

"They are ready," said Mariam trying to sound reassuring. "And they're on our side."

People had gathered many layers thick along the road towards the temple. The three women found a place near a tree for shade, and somewhat hidden among a flock of Nazareean friends.

They shared Passover greetings and Mariam scanned the situation to get her bearings. She felt responsible for the other two Mary's and wanted to be able to respond to anything that might transpire. The men by the stairs weren't the only ones bringing weapons today, she had noticed. And as far as she could tell, the Romans seemed to have multiplied, as well.

"I have been here for the Passover for many years," said Mary. "But I've never seen crowds like this, with this many palm branches."

"The people are filling the street. Do you think they will get through?" Young Mary was concerned.

Peter led the way down the road separating the people who had crowded into the street. His broad shoulders were not to be argued with and people gave him way. To them it was reassuring to see his solid frame. Mariam noticed that he kept a keen eye on who were lining the streets. He knew where all the Roman soldiers were, and he received the silent signals from his own men situated strategically along the way.

Behind Peter were more of the men of Yeshua's closest circle. They were carrying palm branches too. They were encouraging people to wave with them as they shouted Hosanna in honor of the Messiah. Mariam wondered if the prophets of old had intended all this to happen spontaneously, or if they had given the description as a signal for people to know him by. She knew who Yeshua was. This was the way to let everybody else know.

The space around Yeshua was wide open as he approached riding on a white donkey like the scriptures dictated. Lazarus had been sent out to find such an animal, and Mariam noticed her brother walk right behind her husband. They needed him to keep the donkey calm with all the fuss around its arrival.

There was a sphere of calm in a wide circle around him. Mariam felt reassured as she took in the air he surrounded himself with. She heard the deep breath going through the crowd as he passed through them, and knew they all felt new hope. The prophecies would come true. The Messiah was here.

Yes, the Messiah is here, Mariam thought. And immediately around him there was a calm message of peace. Wherever Yeshua went, he created a sphere around him that proclaimed a golden moment. It was such a contrast to what was going on around him. Immediately after the donkey had passed, the street filled in with soldiers, the zealots and the sicarii, all carrying hidden weapons they were ready to brandish at a moments notice.

The crowds filled into the streets behind Yeshua's entourage and followed him to the Temple, waiving their palm branches and singing the Passover songs. Mariam and her companions were shuffled into the crowd, but the Nazareeans made sure they were surrounding them. Mariam knew that would be of little help if a riot broke out, but she appreciated their effort. She noticed Judas, the head sicarii close by, and understood he had been appointed specifically for her safety.

Did Yeshua know how many of his own supporters were bringing swords instead of palms? Did he know that his own message of peace and acceptance existed mostly as a golden ball around him and his donkey?

The crowd was moving towards the temple. The women were pushed between bodies that were moving like one big entity towards the temple. Mariam could see Yeshua's back on the donkey, and how Lazarus seemed to be singing to the animal to calm it down in the mayhem around it.

Some groups of people kept themselves out of the moving stream of human bodies. They stood in the shade of the trees and managed to not be dragged in.

Their black robes will also make them unapproachable, Mariam thought as she watched the rabbis from the Temple called the Pharisees. Her body was swept passed them and she heard a couple of phrases of their conversations.

"…and he teaches people things that the temple hasn't taught for centuries."

"He is sharing information with people with no temple training,…"

"…who shouldn't know these things in the first place."

"Where did he learn all this?"

"Who gave him the right to distribute initiations left and right…"

"They say he's of the line of Joseph, the dream interpreter."

"We know. We had him in the temple schools as a youth."

"He still can't go on the way he does. He is undermining the authority of the Temple!"

"He has powerful supporters."

"I don't like this."

"You know what the prophesy says…"

"Yes, and so does the crowd. They seem very pleased".

The crowd moved quicker and Mariam and the other women with it.

"I heard them too," said Mary. "Don't let it disconcert you. They don't like change of any sort, forgetting that the temple itself has been rebuilt several times. Each time some knowledge was lost. Some tradition shifted. They can be as stubborn as they want, but we all know that change will happen."

Yes, but at what prize? Mariam worded back to her.

They continued with the snakelike movement of the crowd. As she was being turned around, she heard another conversation over the milling shouts of the people. These people are wearing a different head gear than the first group, and their robes are brown. She still knew them as a different group of rabbis from the temple.

"They think they are bringing in the new change by cooperating with the Romans. As if our people would ever succumb to that!" snorted Mary.

Mariam had never before heard her mother-in-law express herself like that. She was astonished at the force of contempt in her voice. The tribes of Israel were a proud people. Nothing would ever make them cooperate with the Romans. They were ready for the liberation the Messiah was promising.

It is a big promise, thought Mariam. She had made the same promise on her wedding day. She knew the wows they had said were of ancient wording. Every couple married in their tradition had said them before and would say them again, continuing to make the same commitment.

"To the rebuilding of Jerusalem. With all their heart and soul, and with the partnership inherent in a marriage."

Mariam gasped at the magnitude of the words. The partnership with Yeshua contained so much. The sphere of light encompassing that concept was enormous. And it was all dedicated to the rebuilding of Jerusalem. Their Jerusalem.

"Stay alert!" hissed the centurion. "We've had enough trouble from this guy."

"He seems peaceful enough," said the soldier from Britannia.

"Posing as the Messiah, the one to save them from *us*," whispered another in a shower of spit.

"I thought they liked us, bringing civilization and all…"

"Oh, don't be daft, we're the occupation. Nobody likes to have their country taken away. Besides, I've seen the guy do miracles…Heal people, you know."

"Watch out, I said," snapped the centurion. "They've got weapons hidden, mark my words. If I see the glimmer of one blade underneath those nightshirts, I'll give the alarm."

"There might be a lot of them, sir."

"We'll need a larger force to take them. Today we're just observing."

A larger force? Yeshua, are we expecting bloodshed? Mariam sent her thoughts to her husband and got an instant reply. *Mariam, find a house to get on top of so you can get out of the crowd. I don't want any of you to get hurt. The scene at the temple will be chaotic.*

She appreciated the warning and started looking for a suitable place. The Nazareean brothers were ahead of her. They had already found a staircase to a rooftop close to the temple ground. Mariam felt herself pulled by strong, polite arms.

The three women came to the top and stood there at the railing trying to see. The crowd was still boiling in the street. The gate at the temple became a needle point for the crowd to squeeze through. They had to become more orderly before they entered the temple ground. Most of the women stayed behind at this point, and the crowd thinned out some.

It was hard to make out exactly what followed. There was some exchange where some of the brown robed rabbis gave Yeshua a small item and asked a question. A coin? He looked at it for a while and then said something which seemed to give different responses to the different groups in the crowds. Mariam hoped to ask Lazarus later what that was about, but both he and the donkey had disappeared.

The crowd stood still. They were expecting Yeshua to start speaking to them, the way they had heard him speak from the steps of temple many times. Instead he stood up and shouted something and started tearing down the tables of the money changers and the people selling sacrificial animals. Coins were rolling down steps and along the yellow stones. Young goats and sheep were suddenly running freely, and a new mayhem was created. The people of the crowd were launching after coins for their pockets and live meat to bring home to their pots. The money changers with tables intact created impromptu sacks out of the bottom of their robes and scooped their money into it. As quickly as they could they slithered away along the back walls in an attempt to get away.

Yeshua and his disciples were a force of righteousness as they approached. Their shouts were serious, and they egged on the whole crowd. The money changers who couldn't escape fast enough were attacked by the crowd and lightened from their load. The men selling sacrificial animals were soon outwitted, and many were exposed working for the temple. The most lucrative income for the temple was scattered as bleating lambs and clinking coins were running and rolling away down the temple stairs.

The rabbis were standing on a higher ground observing the debacle. Their dignity was gone at this point. They were shouting among themselves as they pointed in different directions and pulled at their hats and robes. Mariam could almost find it humorous if she wasn't so keenly aware of the danger present.

"Oh, Mariam, make him stop it. You can tell him, can't you?" Young Mary couldn't take the suspense anymore and wanted it all to end.

"I don't want to disturb him, Mary. He started this whole thing and he seems to know where he is going with it."

"Where is he? Can any of you see him down there?" His mother was concerned.

They all looked. Yeshua was nowhere to be seen. The disciples were gone with him, and the zealots and sicarii had blended back into the crowd. The only ones keeping up the mayhem inside the Temple mound were the rabbis, the Roman soldiers and the people who had their peaceful Passover celebration end in a cleansing of the Holy place of Salomon. Change never comes quietly.

CHAPTER 15

THE EUCHARIST

"M ARIAM, WE HAVE TO PREPARE THEM. THEY have worked hard for this."
"But they will then become the shining ones. They will prove that you
have been giving initiations unauthorized by the Temple."

"I know the rabbis will not approve. But our people need this experience, and
I am dedicated to them."

"Yeshua, I don't think they all understand what you're trying to do. They each
see the meaning of this in a different way. It can be dangerous to give ignorant people
too much power."

"Wife, stay with me on this."

"Of course, I will always stay with you. I just want us to be careful."

"The time is now. I'm ready."

"I understand."

"Tomorrow then. In Jerusalem."

"Yes. In Jerusalem."

Mariam was worried. She knew this was coming. They had talked about it
before. She had just hoped that by now she would feel more confident that they all
could handle what he was proposing.

When Yeshua and his father came back after 40 days in the desert, they arrived
in Bethany looking changed. Something very powerful had happened to them. The
desert winds had torn their clothes and their hair was ragged. They could both use a
bath and some oil on their skin. That was expected after their long journey. Through
their ragged appearance there was a light emanating from their bodies. Their own
people didn't know what to make of it. Could they touch them? Were they still
human? The time they spent on top of Mount Sinai had left its mark on the inside
of their bodies. The outer sign was unmistakable. If you knew what you saw.

She watched the change continue. They had both turned into "Shining Ones"
forty days after they had been inside the holiest of holies at the Serabit Temple on
the top of Mount Sinai.

She knew what they had done. She had experienced the same effect in her own body after her initiation when she was very young. Her teachers at the Serapium had felt she was ready and sent her to Giza to undergo the same traditions that were done by the Pharaohs of old. She had traveled the journey explained in the hieroglyphs preparing for the initiation at the pyramid. The initiation chamber itself had no decorations, no carvings and no furniture. Its purpose was to be a black space of nothing.

She started to understand how learned her father-in-law was. He knew a lot of the scriptures of their culture and he brought the druidic healing techniques to them. He knew a more about then anybody else about metals. Joseph had the title of master. He was a master of how to refine gold. Joseph and Yeshua had been initiated the same way the old pharaohs were. They were illuminated from the inside.

Mariam remembered her own powerful experience. Inside the big pyramid in Giza, after she climbed the steep, angled ramp inside, she arrived in a black room. It was like being inside a cube, with black granite surrounding you on all six equal sides. She was led up there by the high priest who would guide her through the initiation.

Wearing only a thin shift over her body, the priest guided her to the only object present in the space, a black sarcophagus.

She had prepared herself the way she had been instructed. For a whole month she had only eaten certain prescribed fruits and vegetables. For the last three days she had had nothing to eat or drink, and had spent her days doing the herbal baths and oil massages that would give the right messages to her glands and nervous system. Her time in silence had prepared her to receive non verbal communication. She had also practiced telepathic messaging with the priest so that he could continue his instructions to her while she was on her journey.

Mariam felt the power of the black room with no impressions, and the matching state of her own insides, a black void, black as the outer space she was going to visit. She noticed the small sparkles in the stone around her. Little sparks shooting at her, welcoming her to the night sky she was heading for.

Jerusalem was dedicated to Venus and also aligned with the most powerful point on the earth resonating with the star. The pyramids in Giza were aligned with the constellation Orion, and the three pyramids formed Orion's belt. There were four other pyramids placed far into the desert that marked the four corner stars. This was the mark this powerful constellation printed on the earth. This was where the Orion communicated with the people on earth and this was their gateway to the stars.

She stepped into the sarcophagus. The priest gave her a hand as she lay down. There was no blanket to soften the stone against her skin. There were no candles to create a golden glow in the room. This was a journey into darkness.

The priest made eye contact with her and she felt that he had been doing the same preparations she had. They enveloped the same black empty space inside echoing the space they were surrounded by inside the pyramid. He was her earthly counterpart.

He would be her navigator, and to do so effectively they needed to share the same brain wavelength. Her hand received a gentle squeeze before he let her go.

She watched as the lid was pushed over the sarcophagus sealing her off to the outer world. To quiet down the functions of her body she started the mantras she had been taught. As she sank into the natural meditation, her breathing quieted, and her heart rate slowed down. Soon her body had entered a form of hibernation where she safely could leave it protected in the stone.

Gravity pulled her into the granite. Her body merged with it. She was stone, black, hard, dense and cold, vibrating at a low, powerful frequency. Vibrating on the level of stone, she was pulled into the center of the earth, and also pulled out into space. She felt the vibration of a tone, a musical note that found a resonance inside her. This elongated line between the center of the earth and the galactic core was the frequency she existed on.

The power of the center of the earth pushed her out along the line, further out into the universe. She saw stars fly by, dots of stars everywhere and marveled at the vastness of it all.

She recognized the Orion constellation and knew where she was heading. The power line she was traveling on changed from being a force pushing her forward to being a force pulling her in. At lightning speed she was pulled towards the biggest star in Orion's belt.

At the speed she was traveling, she thought she would crash with the star. There was no way to control this traveling mode, she could only trust the process.

The biggest star in the belt of Orion is connected to the Center of our Galaxy. As she crashed with the star, she realized that it didn't have a dense surface. It had a membrane which she was pushed through. On the other side she was sucked with even greater force into the space called the Core.

It had a much more organic texture than what she expected. After she left the membrane, she found herself slithering through a slimy substance. Her senses took in the information and registered it as golden in color, sweet tasting and smooth. Her brain said honey or nectar, even though all of these faculties were still lying in the sarcophagus. She smiled to herself, and enjoyed this unexpected physical experience.

As she continued to explore this place she had a sense of not being alone. There were other people like her around. They seemed to know where they were, and that they were visiting on their way somewhere else. She found that in this substance they were floating in, she had assumed her physical shape again. Her body was still safe in its sarcophagus. She could feel it as she resonated through the stone. But the unit she was when she traveled through the black blinking night sky had now changed from being a unit of light into something denser then air with the shape of her body. Her senses could register certain things, but she couldn't really see. She was reminded of the tactile way newborns respond to their environment through taste and texture.

The other beings had taste and texture. As she floated among them she could register their frequencies through these two screening facilities. She found that it gave a lot of information. By tuning into taste and texture and finding their frequency, she could tell where they came from, where they were going, and how long they had been in circulation on earth or other planets. It seemed that the ones that were used to earth life stayed with earth life, whereas other beings would visit many other systems.

This puzzled her. As soon as she had framed the question she got answers. The one closest to her explained that they had specialized, and the earth experience required certain skills that not everybody wanted to develop. Besides, you either loved it or you didn't. Earth being the densest of the planets, you had the heaviest body and the slowest development. In fact, the other planets were wondering why they created earth in the first place. Their extraordinarily slow evolution was keeping everybody else behind.

Another unit, whom had been in circulation for a long time, added, that many of the other planets, had used earth. They had used humans for their own experimentation and development. The human nervous system lent itself to certain experiences other entities enjoyed. For the humans to be useful, the more evolved units had adjusted the earthling's DNA structures. Consequently, humans had been stripped of some of their abilities. Their genetic material had been simplified making them more cooperative for other planets who wanted to use their nervous system and emotions. If humans were too evolved they wouldn't allow the other beings to manipulate them the way they did.

This information did not sit well with Mariam. What had happened to her beloved humans on planet earth? Was this the darkness she sensed so strongly among the people she observed?

"It happened a long, long time ago," the ancient unit replied. "We deeply regret the incident. We were ignorant about its profound effect. It has slowed everybody down, including the rest of the galaxy. They're all blaming us. To remedy the situation we are offering techniques to bring more light to the human body. Use the golden metals. Use it wisely."

Mariam was taking in what it all meant. She felt like a mirror and a lens where she could see the history they were presenting to her, the immense problems they had caused and the solution they were attempting to introduce to earth. She also saw how instrumental she was in implementing it.

Towards her came a light that was spinning. The light had shape. There was a ball shape on the bottom and a rod up from its center and it had wings on the top. The spinning motion had the form of a spiral. She recognized it now as the same figure she and Yeshua had created together with Isis and Osiris at Baia. How old was this symbol? Did it speak to her from a point in the future or a time in the past? It was all golden light and it spoke to her using the same frequency resonating technique she had experienced with the tone in the stone. It was a pleasant vibration, sending love and reassurance. It had a new important message to her.

At first the sounds it emitted came in beeps, and they reminded her more of the cooing of a pigeon. It was pleasant to listen to and reassuring the way you would speak to an infant to calm her down. The message was of gratitude for her willingness to help and a reassurance that she would be assisted. She allowed it to harmonize with her and imitated its state of mind, the way you follow a small child into sleep. She purred back to it and sensed a blanket being gently draped around her, and something safe and warm rocking her into a golden slumber.

Mariam shook her head to wake up from the powerful memory. Now she understood more of what the message contained. She had needed to be reminded of these experiences in her youth to understand what she was working with now.

Her own initiation had been so dramatic, but also so beautiful. It was done in the pyramid, in the initiation room used by the priests for thousands of years. She had been so protected. She had been surrounded with powerful stones that remembered thousands of years of initiations that had taken place. Her first experience with gold had been at the table with the high priests. They draped a red cape around her and silently invited her to join them and eat the holy bread. As she sat down at the table, she looked up and was met with twelve wise pairs of eyes shielded by red hoods. She nodded her head in deep respect for the tradition they represented. As she turned her head, she noticed the wall behind them. The hieroglyphs were fifteen feet tall and showing Osiris serving the conical holy bread to his priests.

Mariam was again walking the distance into the city. She had to speak to Joseph of Aramathea. Her route went along the fence marking the neighbors, and the trees lining the road were now in full bloom creating clouds of blossoms against the blue sky. She had fresh goat milk to drink before she left and the flavor in her mouth matched the feeling of the day. She was in such a good mood she even smiled to the Roman soldiers as she passed them by. They saluted her politely and walked on.

The weather was indeed lovely, but her mission required more serious thinking. She had spoken with Joseph and Lazarus. They all needed to work together to make sure these events would run smoothly.

Oh God, oh my dear Isis - if she only could trust that this would all work out the way it had to be. To think of the dangers she had exposed her dear brother to. In a cave which had never had an initiation before.

Mariam shivered at the thought.

And now Yeshua was asking her to do another initiation outside of protected parameters. He was right that they needed more people with this experience. They needed more people who radiated light from inside, but they didn't have time to prepare them properly. Would they be able to handle the new vibration in their body? She was responsible for this initiation. She was the priestess. Could she keep everything under control?

She arrived at Uncle Joseph's house and was let in by the servants. In his study she explained what Yeshua had planned, why he had deliberately created a riot at the temple and why they needed his help.

Joseph listened to her attentively.

"Mariam, your husband has discussed these events with me, as well. I am aware of what he's planning. Is Yeshua really willing to go through this for his people?"

"He wants to fulfill what's expected of him according to the tradition."

"I know the sacrifice that is expected of the priest king. I thought we were going to do it more symbolically. He wants to make it into a public event? What about the Romans? This is a powerful initiation."

Mariam explained what Yeshua had told her to be prepared for.

Uncle Joseph turned pale.

"Mariam, this can all become very dangerous."

"I'm aware of that, Uncle."

She also told him of the more immediate plans and that they asked if he knew of a suitable hall.

"I understand he wants to spread the light, but I question using the Nazareean holy meal to empower his own flock. I don't know. Is all this wise?"

"I'm glad you understand my concern. Uncle, we have so many factors here. Within our own flock we have people from many groups with their own expectations. I don't know if any of them understand how profound Yeshua's work is. We kept the Hieros Gamos ritual in the Temple secret from them. The anchoring of our people with the true temple of Jerusalem is secured. But does anyone know? Does anyone need to know? Yochanan has made sure our generation is represented in the line of ancestors. Does anyone understand what that means?"

"It was a great sacrifice he made."

"Anya is still not forgiving me."

"I can understand her. How could she possibly comprehend?"

"I know."

"She was supposed to be the Queen, you know."

"I'd be willing to trade. But everything is different now. I am the Queen and Yeshua is the King, but in the situation at hand with the Roman occupation, I don't see how we can hope to be recognized as that."

"It will have to be secret for a while more."

"Maybe it will never be fully known. Our people will be anchored to this land for all eternity. The light we have established here will spread from these sandy rocks to cover the entire earth. Enlightenment will come. Love will prevail."

"We might not see it in our lifetime."

"Maybe not. But I knew what I signed up for when I married Yeshua. I have a responsibility as his wife and priestess. We might be asking history to change, but history has asked us to fulfill certain roles, and we've been well prepared to do so. It's time to step into the story laid out for us." Mariam spoke with conviction.

Joseph of Aramathea could only admire her strength. He looked at her and saw the truth she carried continuing from a point in history long before them and point to a future he couldn't fathom.

She held the moment with him for longer than she intended. Looking down at her hands, her immediate concerns came back to her. Again, they couldn't deny the vision of destruction they both had seen.

"But Uncle, don't you see where this is heading? The zealots are building strength. They think they can overthrow the Romans. Uncle Joseph, you have traveled the whole Roman Empire. You know you can't argue with the power of Rome. These people only know the road between Jerusalem and Galilee. They see a handful of Roman soldiers here and there. They don't know that the centurions can summon thousands more if the need to."

Joseph of Aramathea was looking out the window. He knew she was right. He had also seen the visions of the fate of this country which he called his own. He loved his life here. He loved his family.Yeshua and Mariam represented what his family had worked towards for centuries. How could the situation ahead of them, which contained so much profound truth, also represent so much danger?

"Uncle, who is on our side? Even the rabbis question his right to be the Messiah. They question the validity of my ancestry. They even question Mary's lineage and do not accept Joseph with all his knowledge and wisdom. It frightens me, Uncle. There are many people in Judea who would rather see Yeshua and his family dead."

"…and his people did not recognize him." That is also part of the prophecy," said Joseph quietly.

His head was filled with pictures of the Temple burning and the smell of burned flesh filling the city of Venus. He saw his people again spread to the corners of the world. It would happen soon, he knew.

What do you see?, worded Mariam silently back to him. He replaced the pictures of horrific images with a plan that carried a lit candle for the future.

CHAPTER 16

GETHSEMANE GARDEN

JOSEPH, THE DRUID LOOKED AT THE GILDED box Mariam gave him. She had carried it with her from Jerusalem, and he recognized it.

"Now? Mariam, are you sure?"

"Yes, Joseph. Yeshua requested it to take place on Thursday."

"I will speak with the Nazareeans and we will have the bread ready for him. You will have to gather the selected people. In Jerusalem you said? Is that safe? The holy meal has always taken place in their village."

"This is what he wanted. I'm sure he has a reason for it," Mariam tried to reassure her father-in-law.

She had carried the ornate box carefully. This was one thing she didn't know much about. She had felt the effect of it, and she had seen it described in the initiation rooms deep inside the temples. But her training had not taken her to the preparation of the metal.

Joseph, on the other hand, had experience from Hibernia and had worked with the Nazareeans refining the techniques for years. He was greatly respected in their community. With his son being the Messiah, he had partaken in the holy meal on their invitation. And after he had spent time at the temple of Serabit on Mount Sinai, his esteem among them grew. He was now considered the foremost authority among them on its use.

Mariam knew they started down in the mine finding the gold. The mountains around Galilee contained minerals. Gold mines had existed here for thousands of years.

Gold was used for all the ornamentations on the important temples and palaces and for numerous items of high value in the temple. The big menorah lighting up the courtyard of the priests was famous for its enormous size and considerable weight. Gold was of course used for coins and jewelry, all these items that seemed so important in everyday life. Through several levels of refinement, it was used for a very special initiation creating light inside human bodies. Forty days later, it became visible flames the size of a candle on top of their heads.

She knew the metal had to be refined through a process involving high heat and a much more powerful apparatus producing electrikus! than she had ever seen. It was all done in the workshop at the temple of Serabit and the product, the white powdered gold was only given out to initiate people. This was considered secret work, done by only the highest of priests, and then only the ones trained for this specific purpose. Usually they required that the priests were a descendent of Moses or Aaron. Their genealogy was used to working with the white powder and somewhat immune to its side effects.

In the first temple of Salomon, this work was done in the temple of Jerusalem. At the first destruction of the temple, most of the priests were killed, but some escaped and established the temple of Onais in Egypt. In Jerusalem, it was difficult to replace their priests with equally qualified people. The knowledge of how to refine the metals and how to work with them dwindled. The current priests of were afraid of their powers, and rightfully so. It could kill just as easily as give life, if not handled right. Mariam understood that it was out of deep respect as well as profound fear that the Ark of the Covenant had been placed in the most secure vault in the foundation underneath the temple.

The richly decorated box she had handed to Joseph contained a very fine specimen of this auspicious powder. She could tell from its fine quality and from its history that it probably had been prepared at the temple of Jerusalem during the time of Salomon. It had been saved for this special occasion by learned astronomers for nearly fifteen hundred years.

Exactly 1440 years, said Mariam to herself. *Venus takes 8 years to create her pentagonal pattern and the light of the Shekina only occurs every 960 years. So the right time is now.*

Mariam was on her way the following day to find her father-in-law and see if he needed any help. She found him at the Nazareeans discussing how to have the holy bread ready at the right time.

"But, Joseph," said the Nazareean rabbi, "the ceremony is always done here with our people."

"I actually do agree with you, but my son wants to have it in Jerusalem."

"Our people will not go to Jerusalem. We will not condone this."

"We will do it with your people later."

"The Messiah does it with our people once a year. This is not something that can be shared with ignorant folk."

"I understand. I will speak with him." Joseph bent his head in respect and left. How could he make Yeshua understand? Joseph agreed with the Nazareeans, but Yeshua apparently had a plan of his own. Mariam agreed, as well. She knew what was at stake.

They decided to only involve family members in the preparation, so Mary and their daughters were going to come with and help Joseph. Mariam had her own duties that day, and would be occupied.

How can I do this? Mariam thought. *I will again be preparing a man I love for something I can't control in a situation I consider highly unstable. Suri would not have approved. Neither would Sibyl. And Herodias is on trial in Rome. I pray to Isis and Osiris that the priests in Egypt never find out what I'm doing.*

Mariam had to stop her downward spiral. She felt the need to drink some goat milk and went looking for a bowl in Mary's kitchen.

Mary found her daughter-in-law sitting in her kitchen sipping fresh goat milk.

"My dear, you're in tears, how are you?"

"I'm scared, Mother," Mariam said letting her fear show.

"You have all reason to be. There is a lot resting on you right now. A lot of people are relying on you. Not to mention the new light you're carrying."

Leave it to mothers-in-law to figure it out. Mariam hadn't really noticed that she was two weeks late. She had been too busy to keep count.

"You've had a lot on your mind," said Mary empathically.

She looked at her otherwise radiant and powerful daughter-in-law whom she loved as one of her own. Right now her face was tear streaked, her hair in tangles and her otherwise glowing complexion had turned dull. Mary knew all the signs.

Mariam was both elated and troubled. This was not the right time.

"They never are, dear," Mary said. "But now you know why you're finding things overwhelming that you normally are confident about. I'll prepare some of the lavender and chamomile. That should help." Mary made herself busy making tea.

Mariam slumped down on her seat. It was wonderful to be mothered and taken care of. She allowed herself to push everything else aside and be glad for the seed she had growing inside.

She really wanted to tell Yeshua, but it was hard to find him alone. He was always surrounded by his followers. And today he was preparing his closest circle for the holy meal tomorrow. Mariam sighed. Even in this he was defying somebody.

The Nazareeans wanted him to do it at their tables, with their flock, honoring their annual holy meal. Yeshua was taking the ceremony to Jerusalem, using his own holy ingredients and inviting only a handful of Nazareeans to the event. The Galileans were going to be present as well. She knew they were stout supporters, but what preparation did they have for this very special soul food? Would they understand what was happening to them afterwards? Enlightenment is not a question of faith and deeds. It is a question of how much light you can hold inside. This material would change your capacity for holding light. It would change the frequency of your body. Everything inside that wasn't vibrating at the right speed would come to the surface and made to comply. The effect could be brutal if you hadn't prepared your body to receive it.

She had seen it, and the results were magical. Light would start shining from the inside of your body. It would be visible for people to see. Should she tell them that it took forty days for it to take effect? She left the teaching to Yeshua. There was something else she needed to prepare.

Uncle Joseph had arranged for them to use the home of Simeon, another prominent man among their supporters. Joseph himself had some other important things to attend to.

Mariam arrived together with Yeshua. Their brown robes and hoods made them blend into the crowds. They had walked quickly from Bethany. They had a lot to discuss, and they managed to keep the followers at a distance behind them. She chose to believe that they showed respect for her as his wife and priestess, but she couldn't help but notice the cold eyes she got from some of them. *How can there be cultures with no priestesses?* Mariam wondered, knowing that those men came from different traditions. All forces of nature and all the gods she had ever known operated in couples. Who would speak for the female part of God if no women were involved?

Yeshua opened the door for her, and held his hand protectively around her waist. They shared a stolen smile before they were through the door and were greeted by his parents. Joseph beamed at her, and simply opened his wide arms and enveloped her in a big hug. There was no time to say anything more.

Mary guided Yeshua to the dining room which had been made ready for them. He would sit at the end so he could see everybody. The table was long with benches on either side, and another table had also been made ready to accommodate everybody.

Yeshua found his place at the end of the table. People started to fill in. They all arrived quietly and serene. His closest friends sat down at the big table with him, and others found seats at the extra tables in the room. She recognized many of them, especially among the women. His message appealed to them. Empowerment from within was such a different concept than the power by force they experienced around them. The contemplative approach was easier for them as well. The women could find strength in Yeshua's gentle ways. Many of the men identified with the strength of standing strong instead of the strength of flexibility. The cutting edge of logic appealed to them more than the soft side of intuition. She sympathized with them, but didn't have a solution for them.

Mariam stood quietly next to her husband. She felt better and her back was straight. Her hair was clean and had been arranged in a lose gather on her head. Her blue silk robes gave her dignity, and the red shawl over her head gave her the unmistaken identity of the High Priestess. She was ready.

Yeshua looked around and met each person's eyes. This was his way to greet them all individually, but also his way of monitoring them. He needed to know their strength and if they could stomach what would transpire soon. Who could he count on?

Yeshua greeted them all formally and welcomed them to this holy meal he wanted to share with them. Mary and Joseph had sat down among his people. Johanna and young Mary were carrying in the trays with bread and wine.

"We have shared bread and wine together many times," said Yeshua. "But tonight I want to share a meal that is blessed especially for you. Remember me as you eat this, and as you feel the effect of this special bread through your body, remember the energy I have sent through you many times. I want you to know that you have this inside yourself always. Remember, you and your own body are the most powerful tools you have. Through developing your body, your abilities, your mind, soul and spirit you will find The Way. I have shown you, and you will do even more than I have done."

He took a pointed bread loaf, broke off a piece for himself and passed the bread to the person next to him.

"Eat this in remembrance of me."

He poured the wine in a cup and drank from it, then passed it on to be circulated around the room.

"Drink this in remembrance of me."

Is he leaving us? Mariam heard what Salome was thinking. She tried to reassure her with a wordless, soothing sound. How many of them knew how to hear thoughts? She wasn't sure, but she didn't want to startle anybody by sounding too loud in their heads.

Mariam had been standing next to Yeshua. As the bread and wine was passed around the room she opened her alabaster jar and a sweet fragrance was noticed. She faced him and poured out the fine oil over his head and massaged it into his scalp. Then she bent down and removed his sandals and massaged the oil into his feet. This way she opened the channel through his body for the soul food to take immediate effect.

The guests were watching what she was doing as they chewed on the unusual bread they had been given, feeling somewhat intoxicated from the strong fragrance. The candles in the room cast a golden glow in the evening light, and they all wondered what made everything seem so magical.

The gold is starting to work inside them, Mariam thought to herself. *I am forever grateful to the Gods of old. These people all need this strength.*

Yeshua looked at Judas, found his eyes and nodded. Judas quickly left the room, and didn't look back.

Not Judas! Mariam worded in alarm to her husband. This was the man among his followers she held in high esteem. Were all the men she loved… *Not him! Couldn't you have asked somebody else!*

Only somebody with his devotion to me could do what we have agreed upon.

Her anguish formed a silent, gut wrenching cry.

Yeshua told his people that he was going to go to Gethsemane garden to meet his extended groups of followers. He encouraged people to go home unless they felt they needed to be there. Then he retired to a back room with Mariam.

Mariam silenced her insides and worked quickly. She had to cover his entire body with the salve she had prepared. Silently she massaged the skin on his back, layering it thick and making sure it all sank into his body. He stood there with his arms stretched out and let her work around him. As she turned to his front and worked down his abdomen, she looked up and caught his mischievous face. His member lifted up and tickled her chin. She turned and gave it a quick kiss before she covered that part too with her expert fingers.

Oh, husband, when will we get to do this again? He stroked her head, and worded back to her; *You already have me inside.*

His body was slippery from the oil, and it smelled strongly around him. Mariam hoped she had made it strong enough. According to her calculation, he shouldn't feel much sensation in his skin for the next forty eight hours.

They went to Gethsemane together with the closest companions. Silently, they walked through the garden towards the hill were they saw people gathered.

"We're all here, and we're ready," Peter greeted them in his booming voice and presented his zealots with pride.

Mariam opened her eyes wider as she saw the large group behind him. The moonlight flickered in shining blades, and the faces she saw underneath the turbans and shawls had not been present at the magical moment an hour earlier. These good men were dedicated and there were hundreds of them. They were dedicated to a cause their great grandfathers had been burning for. This was a group of strong, well trained men proud to be here tonight. The fire of their ancestors was a glowing ember in their eyes.

They have their own inner gold, thought Mariam. *The refiner's fire doesn't take the same form in everybody.* She silently admired them, and wished them success with all her heart. Her mind struggled to push away the visions of a different fire, consuming, eating.

Yeshua stood with the leaders and spoke quietly. Mariam kept a distance and stayed with Lazarus between the trees when she felt the earth trembling. She knew this was not an earthquake.

She saw them coming through the gates of the garden, marching in formation. Mariam gasped at the sheer number and held onto her brother.

"How many do they need to send? Are they expecting a battle?"

"It seems so. How many hundreds of men can you count? I hope Judas has done what he was asked. Otherwise there will be massive bloodshed."

"Are the sicarii here too?"

"As many as they could gather."

"May the Gods protect us all."

A lonely man in blue robes walked in front of the high priests and the centurion leading his cohort. The Roman official only needed to wave his hand, and his hundreds of men would have fallen upon their people. But he followed Judas. All he wanted was the leader. Then he trusted that these ruffians would all disperse and disappear.

Never underestimate people who have been burning inside for more generations than you can count, Mariam thought.

Centurion, do you know who your great grandfather was? You're probably a Roman mutt with a blood relative from every country of the Roman Empire. You don't know anything about these people. Their hatred for you has been burning for all the three hundred years of the rule of the Eagle. It has followed the same blood, the same cinnamon skin, the identical arrangement of the turban above dark brown eyes with the same ember glowing. They'll be back. And the same burning ember will be born again and again, burning with a patriotism for their country you know nothing about.

Mariam watched the centurion shift his feet uneasily as his cells received the message she sent him. He nervously waited for Judas to show him who was their leader. Judas met the eyes of Yeshua and they shared an understanding. He walked up to his friend and kissed his master farewell. Then Judas turned around and announced, "This is the man you want."

The centurion lifted his arm, signaling that no action was necessary. His soldiers followed their orders and stood still in readiness. The centurion apprehended Yeshua himself.

God bless Roman discipline, thought Mariam. *Good dogs.*

The tension was held like an arrow pulled back on the string of a bow until a sound pierced the air.

"Nooo!" screamed Peter, as he watched his beloved master being led away by the centurion. He lifted his sword and brought it down near the head of one of the high priests! Everybody took one step forward and clenched their fingers around the handle of their weapons, soldier and Zealot alike. Mariam felt every hair on her body stand up as she put her hand to her mouth and froze.

Yeshua was immediately at Peter's side and put his hand on the arm brandishing the sword. He said a couple of words, and Peter sheathed his sword and stood still looking at his feet in shame. Yeshua looked around and without a word he commanded his people to be still. They obeyed.

In slow motion, Yeshua bent down and picked up something from the ground. He lifted it up and asked the high priest to remove his hand which had been covering the side of his head since Peter's outburst. Quietly he reattached the ear, and apologized for his own man's behavior. The high priest thanked him and checked if the ear worked.

The centurion watched the whole spectacle, still holding his men at a standstill.

If anybody had as much as heaved a breath, there would have been casualties on both sides.

Yeshua calmly took the few steps over to the high priests and made it clear that he would come with them freely. The high priests turned and they marched between the roman soldiers who had positioned themselves on either side of the road. As the centurion followed they filed in behind him. The noise of feet moving in unison was deafening for a while. None of their people moved until the last soldier had left the garden. Then Mariam watched as the zealots disappeared among the trees without a sound.

CHAPTER 17

THE CRUCIFIXION

MARIAM AND LAZARUS FOLLOWED THE SOLDIERS. THEY stayed in the shadows and hoped the torches of the soldiers didn't shine on them. She had to know where they took him. She had to stay close by.

They were heading towards the home of the high priest. A crowd had gathered around. The household was woken up in the middle of the night with the crowd shouting and banging on their gate with clubs and spears. The neighborhood came to life, and more people joined in with torches. Jerusalem was full of people for the Passover. If Yeshua had wanted this to be well known, he had picked the right time to make a spectacle of himself.

Mariam knew he had chosen his timing. She kept in close contact with him telepathically as he was led like a criminal through the streets.

Inside the courtyard there wasn't room for all the soldiers, so most of them stayed outside. Mariam looked around and noticed their own people in trees and among the spectators. They might disappear in the blink of an eye, but they could also reappear as if materializing out of the shadows. Mariam admired their skill. Did she feel safer with them around? She wasn't sure.

The priests came out in the courtyard and started questioning him. Their main complaint was that he had taught the secrets of the temple without their permission, and to lay people with no preparation. Mariam thought of all the people she had seen who had experienced the light inside their bodies, good people who wanted to feel their own power and what they were capable of. These were people who felt powerless in an occupied nation who now found their own strength and felt the wisdom of their ancestors flowing in their veins. The experience would never leave them, and the thought of Yeshua and all he had brought to them would renew their strength for years to come.

She heard shouts from the courtyard. Apparently Yeshua weren't giving them satisfactory answers. He was so well versed in the scriptures; he probably outwitted them in their own field. Mariam didn't think this was the time to humiliate them further, but she knew he wanted to make his point clear. There was no reason to limit the knowledge to the tight circles inside the temples. Look what happened when all the priests were killed at the last destruction of the temple! Their knowledge was lost. It was time to spread the knowledge out. Let as many as possible participate. Enliven anyone who presented themselves for baptism. Empower anyone who asked the right questions. Enlighten our people.

The priests didn't like his answers at all. It was important to keep it all pure. Next he would bring their knowledge to gentiles. Yeshua answered that he already had. This brought further outrage among the priests. Their wisdom should stay within their people. He was diluting it all. Yeshua pointed out that what they called the wisdom of the temple came from many different cultural traditions. Did any of them know how to work with the Ark of the Covenant? Why wasn't that powerful ancient weapon used against the Romans?

"He sure knows how to rile them up, sister. Is this what he wanted to do?"

"I've never seen him like this. I've never seen the high priests like this."

"I'm glad his parents went home after the holy meal. They shouldn't be here."

"I asked Martha to look after them. I saw her leave with Mary."

The arguments in the courtyard intensified. The soldiers had tied Yeshua's hands in front of him, and the high priest slapped his cheek. Yeshua didn't move. He quietly reminded him about his ear that had been dislocated earlier that night, but now seemed to have returned to normal function. The high priest held his ear, and his tongue. Could Yeshua reverse a healing he had recently done? The priest's fear of the powers of this miracle man was evident.

Some new shouts were heard and apparently a decision was made. The high priests had condemned him as a blasphemous individual who was poisoning people's minds. They prepared to leave the courtyard and head for higher authorities.

Mariam and Lazarus pulled back as far as they could. The street was narrow between two solid walls surrounding private courtyards. They stood with their backs against the wall and were scraped from the movement of the crowd milling by.

"Where are they going now?"

"I guess the next authority up is Herod Antipas."

"I thought he'd left for Rome."

"His wife and daughter did. This is the last case he'll hear before the other Roman takes over."

"But the high priests don't like Antipas after the debacle with Yochanan. Why would they expect him to help them out?"

"He is the functioning king. They need him to give a sentence."

Mariam didn't think they would get any further with this. What was the high priest thinking?

They followed the crowd and listened to the shouts. Some people threw stones at Yeshua which he dodged. A rope was tied to his hands and he was pulled through the streets. The people of the night were having their sport with him. She asked a man if he knew who the prisoner was. He didn't. She asked if he had heard of Yeshua, the Nazareean, the preacher. "Who?" He asked in accented Aramaic. She switched to Greek, but that only confused him more.

Where are the followers? Where are our own people? Mariam wondered as her dislike for the situation grew.

Stay strong, she heard Yeshua in her mind. *I need you.*

She understood that she needed to change her view of the situation. Instead of seeing blame and wrongdoing, she chose to see that everything was in process.

Oh, Yeshua, is it? Is this what you wanted?

He couldn't answer her right then. She heard the sharp sound of a heavy hand hitting human skin. If they had been in direct contact, she would have felt as if it hit her.

Sweet Isis, have mercy on us. Mariam looked up and saw a zealot in the tree above her. Was he guarding her? She wasn't sure. *Remember Osiris. Remember Tammuz,* she heard in her head.

They reached the palace of Herod Antipas. The soldiers filed into the courtyard and presented their prisoner. The high priests stood as a group of black robed strange birds ready to deliver their pecking message. Mariam felt that reality had shifted out of focus.

She heard them speak to Antipas in the sounds of crows and ducks. She heard Antipas answer with a guffaw of laughter. To her he sounded like a goat. He directed some questions towards Yeshua, who didn't answer. Apparently this was below him to deal with. Mariam tuned into him and found him withdrawn deep inside his body. Antipas bleated some more and the centurion barked some orders. The cawing black crows grouped together with the ducks and led the way out of the courtyard, soldiers and prisoner following. The people were disappointed. Not enough had happened here to entertain them. Mariam disagreed. She felt like singing a children's song about barnyard animals.

Lazarus kept watch over his sister. He could see that she was fading and that this whole experience was overwhelming. As soon as they reached a source of water he made sure she drank some. Mariam splashed more water in her face after drinking two good cups and felt refreshed. Did she know any songs about water? She remembered one about a small boat and the sunshine playing with the waves. Lazarus heard her humming as they continued on their way.

The mansion of Pontius Pilate was not far from the palace of Antipas. Pilate had recently been appointed and was going to replace Antipas. Pilate was an all time Roman, not like Antipas who had desperately wanted to be included in the Jewish mysteries. Antipas' twisted ambitions had backfired on him with a vengeance. How could he have anything to say in this case?

Mariam felt a new fear creep into her body. Did Herod Antipas want revenge on *her*? Was this his way of getting back at her and her people? Herodias was protected by

Roman law. Who protected Yeshua? This was the third figure of authority they were seeing this morning. No one spoke up defending him. Not even his own people, his own teachers or his own supporters. Not one voice. She realized their vulnerability. Lazarus lent his slim shoulder in support. Were they all in danger? Their whole community? All the colonies?

They arrived at the porch of Pontius Pilate. Mariam could see that Yeshua was fading. It was almost day break and he was close to exhaustion. Could she get anybody to give him some water?

This was home turf for the soldiers and they filed inside in an orderly fashion and lined up on either side of the courtyard. The centurion took his place in front of the porch and the prisoner was placed in the middle. The flock of black crows grouped themselves to the side. People were hanging over the fence, pushing at the guards at the gate, hanging from tree branches, everybody wanted to see how this was developing.

Pilate was a reasonable man in a good mood this early morning. He had had a good evening the night before, had been welcomed in all ways fashionable after his arrival. His night had been spent among three lightly clad lovely ladies, who had been well trained in their arts. He was looking forward to a splendid breakfast which his cook from Rome was preparing this very minute. He could spare half an hour to listen to the locals. So, what was the problem here?

The crows all cawed, Antipas bleated, the centurion barked something and all the people hanging from various vantage points joined in squawking like birds. The cacophony was deafening. Pilate had been told that these people were quite civilized, downright formal. What was all this noise this early morning? He would have to separate the wheat from the shaft and see what would surface.

Pilate started with the priests and let them tell their story. He could understand that they didn't like their secrets to be given out indiscriminately. How come this man knew so much in the first place? After some more quacking and cawing, at least these people could speak Greek, he found that they had taught him themselves. Hm. And what was Antipas' grief with this man? He claimed to be King of the Jews. Well, that was a problem. Antipas was the king now. Didn't the people understand that? The centurion kept on about disturbance of peace and his many weapon carrying followers.

This got Pilate's attention. Now he started to see a picture. This man claimed to be their king. He indulged secrets to his people which they otherwise would not have had access to. In addition to these charges, he had organized an army of knife wielding rebels who made this experienced centurion bring a whole cohort of soldiers to apprehend him. Hm. Pilate wrinkled his brow.

How long had this man been a problem? Why hadn't they gotten rid of him before? Antipas! Come to think of it, hadn't he actually heard about this troublesome rabbi in Rome?

Mariam leaned heavily on her brother. She heard every word. She knew where this would lead. Rome didn't like disturbances. They didn't like anybody troublesome and rebellious and certainly not somebody with a following the size of Yeshua's. She knew exactly what would happen next. Yeshua had been counting on it.

After more noise from everybody, Pilate finally pronounced his verdict. A servant had just announced that his breakfast was ready. Death by crucifixion after a good flogging. That would teach them. Rome didn't take disturbances in the provinces lightly. Never.

Mariam again saw fire and smoke. She could smell the burned flesh of hundreds of people who succumbed to the flames. He was right. Rome didn't take disturbances in the provinces lightly. Damn their golden temple. Damn the zealots. Give them their martyr.

He received his verdict with dignity. The courtyard was cleared and Yeshua was tied to a pole. His shirt was ripped and pulled down leaving his back exposed. Two sturdy executioners each equipped with a whip presented themselves for duty. Forty nine lashes. That should do. Few people survived more.

Mariam turned her head away, but she could hear every time the whips hit his body. The whips had small cups with sharp edges at their ends that dug into his skin. He would have ninety eight indentations where skin would be missing before they were done.

Lazarus tried to watch the procedure. He was turning pale and felt nauseous before the tenth count. Yeshua didn't make a sound the whole time.

The executioners looked disappointed when they were finished. People had been counting with them. They couldn't put in any extra whiplashes for good measure. They bowed to the centurion who had been standing by, before they returned to wherever they came from. He acknowledged them, they had done their job.

The centurion received a paper with a written order. He opened up the scroll and read. Then he scratched his head and adjusted his helmet. The sun was getting higher in the sky. He hadn't had a chance for food himself since yesterday because of all this commotion. It seemed to be coming to an end. He was glad.

The prisoner was untied from his pole. He was bleeding from numerous places on his body. Small red trickles were running down his sides. He made no attempt at wiping himself but simply pulled his shirt to cover his body. The soldiers wanted to mock him further. They had made him a wreath of thorns and placed it on his head. The centurion couldn't deny his soldiers some fun. There certainly wasn't much to do in this godforsaken place. Why couldn't he be stationed somewhere exciting, like Caesarea or Alexandria?

Mariam's sympathy pains were excruciating. Did they know how vulnerable the top of his head was? Did they think they could prevent him from pulling in strength from above, or disconnect him from his inner power? Was this something Antipas had conjured, to make sure Yeshua couldn't do any of his magic?

The soldiers gathered around the prisoner. The crossbeam was placed across his shoulders. His hands were tied along it so he would hold it straight. There was no need to tie a rope on the prisoner. He had nowhere to go. He was surrounded by soldiers, and the crowd couldn't open space for him with his wooden wingspan.

It was time to move again. The Romans knew how to march. But this was slow moving and had nothing to do with the rhythmical trot of a good flock of soldiers. This was a funeral procession led by the deceased while still alive.

Mariam felt sick. Really sick. Lazarus bought some bread from a vendor. They had showed up this early morning ready to make a profit. Some goat milk was offered from a bucket. He made sure his sister got some. They stood in the shade of a tree and watched the group in the courtyard get ready.

Mariam gathered her strength. She dutifully ate the bread and drank the milk she was offered. Her gratitude went out to her brother. As she looked up to find his face, she saw that two other familiar faces had joined them. Her mother-in-law was there with her daughter Mary. Mariam collapsed in their open arms.

Lazarus looked ashen. Mary gave him strict orders to go back to Bethany and take care of Joseph. He did not take this very well and needed help. The two Mary's would take care of Mariam. Lazarus had had enough of this event. He couldn't take his brother-in-law being hurt and humiliated any further. He knew what would come next, and he didn't think he would be of very much help. Mariam seemed to be in good hands with the women. Relieved, he left to do as Mary told him.

The three women watched as Yeshua passed them on his path, surrounded by soldiers, and burdened with the tool that was intended to kill him. He swayed underneath its weight, but kept on walking. They all pulled in their breath and felt their anguish spread from their throats and hearts and close their airways.

The women followed him as close as they could. At the steps by the Temple Mariam saw a familiar face. It was Simon of Cyrene, a man she had seen among the followers before. He was easy to spot with his height and wide body. She grabbed his arm and told him to follow with them close by. Soon they would need his strength.

They passed Veronica who was ready to give Yeshua water and wipe his face. Susanna was there, offering her tears and prayers. Salome and Johanna stood along the path, showing their love for him with their golden glow.

The people of the night had vanished back into the shadows they came from. The people along the path were their own followers. They offered what they could as the procession found its way among them.

Soon Yeshua fell, and the centurion was looking for someone to carry the beam for him. Simon was ready. He took the large piece of wood and handled it like a twig. Yeshua got on his feet slowly. He slurped some mouthfuls from Veronica's ladle and let her wipe his face. A new sound was heard among the crowd. The yells for his crucifixion had stayed behind in Pilate's courtyard. The sound heard now was a quiet murmur of encouragement. The people who loved him had arrived. They lined the road for him. They showed him the way, just like he had shown them the way to themselves. The words were condolences for his gruesome ending. The words were gratitude for what he had taught them. The words were love for a man who had healed bodies and souls.

Mariam was moved. She walked silently with the other two women. And where they came, people made room for them.

"There is his mother," they said.

"I see his sister."

"That is his wife."

The people showed them their sorrow. They showed them their tears. Other men and women carried their pain and grief with them. The three women walked straighter, sharing strength with multitudes.

When they arrived at the hill where the poles were erected, Mariam noticed that this was not the usual place for executions. This was on a hill, and could be seen from far away, the hill of the skull, the hollow hill of Golgotha. Mariam felt the cold water run down her spine. Then she corrected herself. There were reasons for this, however morbid.

A warm hand found hers. She turned and saw the lovely eyes of a good friend. Young John had found her in the crowd. He stood with the women representing the disciples of the man who had taught so many so much.

The soldiers lifted the pole out of its holder in the ground. They laid it down on the sand. Simon was told to place the cross beam in the cut out indentation where it fitted so they could tie them together. Yeshua was told to relinquish his shirt and lay down on the cross. The centurion produced three nails and pointed to the hammer waiting in its holder next to where the pole belonged.

Mariam watched her husband stretch out his arms and lie still while the soldier hammered the nail through his wrists. They knew not to hit his main arteries. Then he would die too quickly. She listened to the clangs of the hammer as it hit the nails and watched his face for his response. He didn't cry out, he didn't protest, he silently allowed it all to happen.

His feet were placed on top of each other and the third nail was sent through them. A soldier produced a plaque which got hammered to the top of the cross.

Then they lifted it up, and carried it over to where it needed to go into the receptacle in the ground. It was pushed upright and it sank into its hole with a clank.

His body slumped down and was hanging from his wrists. He lifted his head to breathe better, pushing a little up from his feet. The pain was convulsing through his body and he was forced to allow gravity to win.

The three women rushed up to the cross as soon as the soldiers left him alone. They touched his feet, they cried with him. Mariam touched his leg and reached for him. She felt how exhausted he was. The excruciating pain was numbing and at the same time it kept him alert. Using all she knew, she tried to fuse with him, merge with him a little, take on some of the pain he felt. He didn't let her. He had closed his field. His life force was being concentrated in the center of his body. She knew he was dying.

Remember the sponge, Mariam heard from somewhere. Bashra was talking to her from her herb bag. She had prepared a sponge with some special herbs for this occasion. Now was the time to use it. *Thanks.*

She turned away from the others and found it quickly in her bag. Looking for one of the soldiers, she found the centurion standing there looking at the inscription on top of the cross. He was again scratching his head and adjusting his helmet trying to give the words meaning.

"Please. Dip this in water and give it to him. He is thirsty."

"He is dying, madam. It won't help."

"Please. Let me comfort him, even for a moment."

The centurion had instructions to allow the women to administer to the prisoner. He didn't see any harm in offering a dying man a drop of water. The centurion called one of the soldiers and gave the order. Mariam watched as he dipped the sponge in a water bucket and attached it to a long reed to be able to reach him. Yeshua was hardly conscious, but he noticed the wet thing touching his lips and managed to suck some drops off it.

That will do, Mariam thought to herself.

She finally gave herself time to look at the plaque that had puzzled the centurion. There was an inscription on it in both Greek and Aramaic, and it said Yeshua, the Nazareean, King of Judea. She stiffened as she read it. What was Pilate thinking? Would the insults never end? Or was it an insult? After all, this was what Yeshua claimed. Did Pilate in his lack of understanding, actually proclaim what they had been trying to say all these years? Pilate was a follower of Mithras, the Roman god of warriors. What did he know of priest kings?

Mariam watched the blood streaked, flogged body of her husband give up its last flickers of life. The flame went out. His color turned gray and soon there were no more movements in his body. He looked contorted where he was hanging. The hill was called the Skull, and over the hilltop the sky turned dark.

The soldiers were making their rounds to see that the prisoners were indeed dying. If they felt that the process was going too slow they would break the crucified man's legs. Then he wouldn't be able to push his body up to breathe and would suffocate. The soldiers were tired of their games, they wanted to go home.

"Hey, this one is dead already. That went fast."

"Open his side. See if he bleeds."

The soldier went over to Yeshua and stuck his lance in his side. Some blood came out.

"He's bleeding a bit."

"That's fine. He's dead. Let's go home."

Mariam was grateful that the soldiers were ignorant of the process of death. And that the position they pointed from made it hard to stick the lance any further in.

Mary had been very quiet and standing over to the side. Now she touched Mariam's arm.

"Dear, it is late in the day. The Sabbath is approaching. We have to take him down before sundown, or he will hang there for a whole other day. The animals..."

"Yes, Mother."

As they spoke, Joseph of Aramathea approached the soldiers who were picking up the things they had brought with them for the watch.

"I have spoken to Pilate, and as a relative I have claimed the body of the prisoner."

"He is all yours. Help yourself. We're leaving."

Mariam looked at Joseph and they shared a moment. It was quiet on the hill now. Most people had gone home. Only a few followers had decided to stay to the end. Simon was one of them, and they asked him again for his help. Young John supported it on the other side as they managed to lift the cross from its foundation and maneuver it down to the ground.

He was almost cold by now. Mariam touched his arm and followed it to his hand where the massive nail went through his wrist. How could they get him off of this torturous device? Simon found the hammer the soldiers had used and gave the nail a good whack on its side. It moved enough in the wood that Simon could pull it with his hand. He tried to be careful, but still the hole in the wrist got widened.

"Let's be quick," said Mariam to Simon to speed up the process.

Joseph had brought a linen sheet and they transferred him to it so they could carry him between them. Simon took the heaviest load, and young John proved stronger than he looked, and took the other end next to Joseph. The women hurried around them as they left on the path down the hill.

"This way. The tomb is to the left," Joseph instructed them as they entered the fragrant garden behind the hill. He had said they could use the tomb he had purchased for his own use when his time would come.

The tomb was an open cave in the mountain wall. A large stone could be rolled in front to seal it off. Inside there was a bench to lay the body on. They all came inside and Yeshua was placed on the stone.

He was even colder now. Young Mary was crying and her mother was comforting her. They all needed to say their last goodbyes. After some time, Mariam asked if she could have some time alone with her dead husband. She needed to do her duty as a wife, wash the body and lay it out the traditional way.

"John, would you take young Mary and his mother Mary and walk them back home to Bethany? I will just stay with Uncle Joseph in Jerusalem tonight."

"As you wish, Mara. Make sure you get some rest as well."

"I'll take care of her," said Joseph.

The women hugged each other goodbye for the night and Mariam watched them leave through the garden. John knew the way and would see them safely home. Simon left with them and was invited to stay with them in Bethany.

As soon as the others had left, Mariam started administering to Yeshua's wounds. She washed the body, and did her best to heal the many scrapes his skin had taken. The cut from the soldiers lance wasn't very deep and was stitched together quickly. The ointment she had applied the previous day had worked well. The whips had not dug into his body as badly as they were built for. With enough white camphor and lavender, besides some pure oils she had and some cactus plants, they would heal very well. He also had eaten the holy bread recently. His whole body was tuned into life, even though he now appeared absolutely dead. The little belladonna and opium he had gotten from the sponge had done its job.

"Here are your herbs, Mariam. How can I help you further?"

"I need water, Uncle. And a brazier."

"It has already been brought in, daughter."

"Thank you, Uncle."

"Nicodemus and I brought aloe vera to heal his skin. Lots of it. Be generous, Miriam. There is a lot of regrowth that needs to happen."

Mariam looked over her supplies and saw that Joseph had brought aloe vera in abundance. She could reapply it all through out the night. It would prevent infection and encourage new skin to be generated.

They worked together creating a new herbal balm for Yeshua's body. When it was ready it was applied while the lion goddess Sekhmet was invoked with incantations. Mariam sang a note and uncle Joseph picked up the lower tone. They created harmonies with deep frequency which resonated in the stone surrounding them. When Yeshua had been prepared with the balm, they laid him out straight on the linen. The piece was long enough that it also covered his body on top when folded over from above his head. Before they covered him, Mariam looked at her husband. She admired his strong physique and his fine features. His hands were modestly crossed by his hips. As her eyes viewed where his fingers overlapped she laid her hand over her own abdomen, remembering.

I'll always be with you, he'd said.

CHAPTER 18

THE SABBATH

JOSEPH OF ARAMATHEA LEFT IN TIME TO celebrate the Sabbath at his own house. He had planned the meal with his usual companions for the Passover Sabbath, and told them that his sister's daughter-in-law was resting upstairs. They all understood that she had had a trying couple of days. Joseph was part of the council to the temple, and had to play his political alliances very carefully. The friends he had in his house for the meal were sympathetic with his dilemma.

"It is really sad to hear about your nephew, Joseph. But what did he expect, carrying on the way he did?"

"He was a good man. I met him and heard him preach. Very knowledgeable."

"Too knowledgeable. He knew more than most of us, and wasn't shy about showing it."

"I heard he was educated in Egypt."

"His father seems to be high among the Nazareeans."

"But they're foreigners! I can't even pronounce the country they come from. No offence, Joseph, I know you travel that route, too."

"Still, they claim tribal blood. Like you, Joseph. His mother is your sister. You have the same ancestry."

Joseph tried to observe more than to engage in conversation. He agreed where he could, and clarified when needed, but what he really wanted was for them to reveal what they knew.

"I wonder what the Nazareeans will do? They have lost their second Messiah this year."

"Oh, they'll choose another one. The only job of the Messiah is to serve their meal once a year. They still want that done by someone with the right heritage. Traditionalists."

"But what about the zealots? They put all their hopes on this man."

"He sure disappointed them. They wanted a military leader, not one who spends most of his time in prayers."

"And with women. It was quite an entourage he gathered around himself."

244

"I've heard they helped him financially too. Rich old widows, if you know what I mean."

"Maybe they were good cooks. I've heard he ate well."

"You never see women among the zealots though. Serious warriors, those men."

"Don't worry about them. They'll make a martyr of him and rally around his memory even better than they supported him alive."

It was hard to listen to all this without commenting. But Joseph needed to hear all this so he poured more wine. Then he introduced a new topic.

"How do you think the Romans feel about all this?"

"They've gotten rid of another rebel at another outpost. I don't think they'll remember him tomorrow."

"The zealots will not forget, though. And they are just going back into the hills waiting for a better time to strike. Don't underestimate the combination of highly skilled warriors fighting for a fanatic cause. They want their land back. And I can't blame them."

"Having a man who claimed to be the rightful King certainly helped."

"Well, he's gone. They'll have to think of something else."

"Did he leave any children behind? If so, they're next in line."

"I would hide any offspring form his loins really well. There are too many factions here who would rather see him and his cause be dead and stay dead. If a child of his were known, it would be in constant danger. His son would be the next in line for kingship. His daughter would continue the royal line."

"He had a wife, didn't he? The priestess from Ephesus?"

"I heard she was good friends with the wife of Antipas. What was her name?"

"Isn't she in Rome? Or were they both banished to their estates in Gaul?"

"Were you at the party where that pretty daughter of hers danced? What a show!"

"Which one? The dancing or the drama afterwards?"

"How could they? And who has that head now?"

"Who cares. The time of oracles is over. Who believes in that in our time?"

"And who knows how to work an Oracle anymore?" Added Joseph slowly, taking a sip from his wineglass.

The walls were cold inside the tomb. The brazier gave off some light, and did it's best to heat up the place, but the massive stone won. She could really feel that she was inside a mountain, and when Joseph rolled the stone in front of the entrance, she was shut off from the outside world. She wasn't quite sure what time it was anymore, but could guess it was night time since it was colder by the opening. Otherwise, the stone kept a constant temperature inside, making it a perfect place for a tomb, or an initiation chamber, like in the pyramids.

245

He was far gone now in the other world. She couldn't reach him, nor did she want to. He was supposed to take this journey on his own, like she had done in Giza many years earlier.

His color hadn't changed since the others left. He was still gray and lifeless. He was supposed to be. His journey back hadn't started yet. He was still on an outward line of motion.

She had monitored his life signs. Deep inside him he had collected his life force into a small sphere. For her it was easy to find. His heart was very familiar to her.

He had started moving inward while they were in the courtyard of Antipas. She knew it was the right timing for him and he had begun shrinking his aura already then. He had stopped talking, and the golden glow around him which people found so inspiring had diminished. Within a couple of hours he had stopped relating to anything external, but could still walk and follow orders.

At the court of Pilate he had nothing more to say and nothing external to relate to. He stopped giving any energy out. His generous sharing of his own endless energy stopped.

Mariam had observed this, monitoring him all the way. She noticed an unexpected change occurring. When he stopped giving so generously of himself, people started giving back to him. His followers, his people, remembered. On the walk towards the hill of the skull his people had come to him and poured their love towards him. She had seen the lines of blue and gold find their way from their hearts to him. As they wept for his fate, they also released their profound love for this man who had taught them so much. With his own life he had shown them the power of love, generosity and inner wisdom. They had built their own inner strength with what he gave them. These good people wanted to show their gratitude and devotion by giving love back to him. Hundreds, maybe thousands, of loving souls had followed him on his march to his death.

Because of his self induced inner state, he was in a position to receive it. He was vulnerable and humiliated, and they showered him with affection. The whole hill of the skull had been bathed in the golden light of love from thousands of people following their prophet, and he had taken it all in. The hollow inside of the hill called Golgotha had been a receptacle for all the collective golden light his loving people had sent him. And she had channeled it all into another skull. It was sitting right next to her now. It was glowing.

Joseph had been thoughtful. There was a thick blanket made of camel hair among the things he had brought to the tomb before they got there. She made herself some tea and sat down for a long night.

CHAPTER 19

THE RESURRECTION

IN THE DEEPEST OF MIDNIGHT MARIAM STARTED her work. The brazier provided a golden glow in the tomb, and gave her a little heat. It was time.

Yeshua had appeared dead since Friday afternoon. It was now almost Sunday morning. The Sabbath was over. She had tended his wounds throughout the night. Now she could start her work of bringing him back. Again, she found the right herbs for the end of the journey. Again, she found the right notes to sing.

The head of Yochanan had been glowing, keeping the life force of Yeshua present. It was time to wake up Bashra. Mariam needed her help.

Bashra was taken out of the herb bag, and her incantations were sung. Mariam lit more candles in the space, and refreshed the brazier. Soon the air was filled with the scents of herbs warmed in oil, incense burning and essential oils from fragrant plants. The sounds she created established the right frequencies in the room. Yochanan and Bashra joined in. Soon she had the reverberating overtones she wanted.

She silently intoned her own mantras and changed her consciousness to take in the environment of the tomb. For Yeshua's sake, she needed to vibrate with the stone surrounding them. She needed help from the mountain itself to send her own life force inside him to find his fine stream of life. Matter contains an immense force. She could utilize that force, when she had established a strong rapport.

The life within him had already found the stone underneath. The stone held him, kept his life in place so it would stay near his body. The gravity of the stone called his spirit back stronger than his body was able to do alone. Mariam needed to talk to the stone and she needed Bashra to help her. There was no need for words between them. Their ancestral connection spoke through their shared cell memory.

Mariam continued the tonal sounds. She loved Yochanan's deeper tone and the sounds he could resonate in his scull. He was always the best at inner overtones, and that skill had not diminished. Verbal communication with him was also redundant. They communicated through the body of their relative. Yeshua's essence was already growing in her. The two cousins had the same genetic material. She carried Yochanan's ancestral knowledge with her as well.

The new balm was ready. A thick salve had been formed as she had stirred together the ingredients. The sedatives she had given him yesterday would have worn off by now. She was more concerned with the strong ointment she had applied on Thursday night to desensitize him. Hopefully that had lost its effect, as well. The strong tincture she used this time should penetrate that shield.

When the space felt properly prepared, she started applying the oily substance to his head. She had to open the portals of his body where the energies of sky and earth could nourish him. Invoking Sekhmet, and remembering Suri wearing the headgear honoring the lioness, she envisioned her animal companion in Ephesus, the black panther. She realized she needed his steady strength this time. Yeshua had gone very far away.

Entering his body with her mind, she looked for the sphere of condensed life force inside him. She borrowed a strain of golden light from Yochanan's reservoir of loving emotions, and went searching more thoroughly. Usually she could find him without much effort, and strengthening his life force was just a matter of transferring energy.

She could feel that he was still here. He had not left his body for good. But where was he hidden? Earlier she had found him near his heart region. Searching in that area brought no result.

Mariam called for Bashra. She needed her ancestral strength. She counted on Yochanan to keep the golden energy flowing. She blessed all the beautiful people who had poured so freely of their love. She could feel that their continued prayers kept feeding the light emanating from the head next to her.

Like twin light beams, Mariam and Bashra went inside Yeshua's body. Mariam's fingers kept working on the top of his head and down towards his neck. The sensitive section on the top of his skull got most attention. She needed to awaken the small glands in the middle of his brain. Together they secreted a fine chemical which would start his brain activity and encourage his heart to find its rhythm.

The light beams found the two points in the brain and gave them each an impulse. They continued down his body in search for his sphere of concentrated light. At his neck they spread into two lines coming down his chest, being extra diligent around his heart. Everything seemed silent. The tissues had the color of rain clouds.

Mariam was alarmed. Healthy tissues had a pink, reddish tone and glowed according to her patient's force of life. Gray was usually a sign of lack of life, of death creeping in stealing away the colors.

She didn't like his appearance. Feeling a glimmer of lifeforce beneath him, she knew he was there, somewhere. But the signal was weak, and this gray mass had to be removed before she could continue.

Clouds. Clouds move. Rain drips. Clouds forms raindrops, they drip down, they follow gravity, the form rivers. Following her own imagery, she could hear the sound of twinkling rivulets of water sloshing down crevices in a mountain side.

She kept encouraging the gray mass to think of itself as water and be willing to behave like liquid. She made it move as a cloud of rain that needed to settle, needed to find lower ground. Gradually it left his body, like a substance in water settling to the bottom. It followed the gravity underneath him and sank into the mass of the stone.

Mariam could see it now. It was visible on his skin. Not like color returning. More like color leaving, following gravity. She could see the upper part of him get lighter, whereas the part he was lying on had a denser, grayer look.

The stone liked this substance, and the gray color liked to unite with the stone. Suddenly, all the grayness was pulled into the stone in one sweeping motion. Then it was gone.

"Bashra, what was that? I've never seen anything like it," Mariam asked her relative.

"Remember all the people he has healed. However pure he is, there will be some residue of the negativity he clears from them. Even though he was very successful at sending it through him and into the ground, there was a gradual build up in his body he wasn't aware of."

"He healed thousands. The sheer number of people's essence he allowed through his body would do that, I guess"

"And don't forget, he is in timelessness now. He will continue his work."

"You mean; the gray cloud we're clearing now contains residue from the future?"

"Timelessness, dear. You sent him there."

Mariam shook her head over the conundrum of time, and returned to the search for his essence. It had not been located yet.

Continuing as two search lights, Mariam and Bashra systematically looked through his entire body. They needed his own life force to start his return. His spirit had to be called back to itself.

Mariam noticed that his body felt cold. It was not surprising. He had appeared dead for close to three days. She felt alarmed.

Borrowing heat from Yochanan, they induced his body with soft warmth in the form of light. They were gentle not to shock his system. Mariam asked Bashra to warm him like a blanket covering him, while she continued looking inside.

Her spirit roamed down his legs and up his spine. She searched his arms with the marked wrists, his inner organs and his lymphatic system. By now she was going through her anatomy lessons, making sure she had covered everything.

Behind a shoulder blade, underneath a kidney, tucked away in the corner where his urethra led away from the kidney towards his bladder, there was a glimmer. She found a small star, a spark that felt familiar.

"Isis and Osiris, help me! He is weak! Send him strength. Send me strength."

As soon as he had been identified, everybody congregated to help. Bashra and Yochanan strengthened Mariam, letting her inspire him out of his hiding place.

Yeshua, husband, come to me. Love is here, warmth is here.

She sensed his fear. Fear of the enormous power he had been fighting against. Fear of the powerful process he had volunteered for. Fear that his body wouldn't be able to go through it all. Fear that the gray mass he had been surprised to find in his body would prevent him from returning. Fear of being lost. His fear made his spirit identify with being cold.

This was not good. Mariam knew that he was not afraid of death. What was death other than a further journey into where he had been? To him, death was a journey into the land on the other side where welcoming spirits were waiting for you. Death was a journey home to a space with an overview of God's creation, where you would be given a different job. He feared not being able to return and finish the work he had signed up for here. He feared not being allowed to return to the woman he loved and their growing seed.

His spirit felt like a shivering, naked child left outside in a rainstorm. Cold to the bone, racked with fear, clattering his teeth, she took him in her arms and warmed him with her body. She sang soothing sounds to him and felt him rest his head by her breasts and find calm. She sat there, rocking back and forth, holding him for a long time.

The child loosened himself from her arms. He was warm now. He was convinced that he was loved. He knew where he belonged. She let him go and allowed him to find his own heart and know that it also contained love, just love.

Mariam could breathe again herself. She allowed Yochanan's golden light to stream through her to Yeshua, and watched a glow settle in his heart. Then she started the rhythmical breathing across his nose. He was present.

They needed to get his heart to begin beating and his breathing to start. That seemed easy now. His essence had been found and acknowledged. His body had identified the spirit it belonged to. His spirit had found the body it lived in on earth. There was a new joy in the room.

Mariam put more of the unguent in her palms and continued massaging his body. She covered his head, his face, his nose, his neck, his chest. All the while she continued suggesting for him to breath on his own as she sent a breath across his nose. It became a dance with her body as she found a repetitive pattern for her movements.

She gently suggested for his heart to beat by giving a soft pressure over it alternating with her breathing. His body responded to her hands. He was occupying his heart again.

As his body was infused with energy and strength, the pull for his spirit to come back was stronger. She could feel that force building as she worked on him until a stream of golden sparkles arrived at high speed flying through the cave. They swirled over him a moment before entering his body in a line, being pulled in from one point. As a port of entry they chose his navel. His body made a sudden heave, and he gasped for air.

The sense of relief overwhelmed her. Mariam cried as she watched him find his breath and color return to his skin. She slumped down in her seat and allowed her own fear to flow out of her. She hadn't realized how scared she had been.

After a moment, she felt Yochanan's and Bashra's energies like fine hands on her shoulder. It was time to continue. He wasn't anchored yet.

The energy from her two disembodied companions felt like the gentle touch of friends, the sweet stroke over your back offering sympathy. They understood that she needed to be touched with the most delicate of hands.

You are so vulnerable, you have given so much. The little energy that is left in you needs to be honored and strengthened. Your thin line of strength needs to be widened.

She needed them now. He needed their gift first, now it was her turn. She breathed in their offered strength and felt it nourish her.

His breathing was very soft, but steady. His heart had found its rhythm. She moved her hands to his feet and worked on grounding him in his body. The stone helped again with its gravity pull. But now she needed him to stay within the boundaries of his body and recognize it as his home, not identify with the stone he was laying on and by extension the mountain. Her job was to remind him that his body was a great place to be and the human body was capable of sublime states. He needed to remember that the limitations were really opportunities.

She had started with his feet and worked up the leg. The gray color was disappearing now and being replaced with his familiar golden glow. It was still weak, but she could see it being present and getting stronger. She reached his knees and his thighs. His muscles were well developed after all the walking he had done in Galilee. His circulation was usually good and it didn't take long for the body to reestablish a healthy blood flow.

She remembered how carefully they had awakened Yochanan years ago, and the great companionship she'd had with the women at the Serapium. Her brother had been awakened with another good group of workers. Through her time she had initiated quite a few people who had requested this particular experience. They all needed her to send them in and bring them back, and each experience had been very different. This was the first time she was alone with the task. She realized how tired she was. When was the last time she had eaten anything? When was the last time she had slept?

Her hands had worked their way up his body and she removed the linen that covered his hips. Protectively, she placed her fingers as a lid over his genitals near his own hands. She didn't necessarily want to encourage him, she wanted him to become aware of this part of himself. If his body could remember the ecstasy and joy they'd had together, he would want to experience this magnificent gift of creation again. She felt the new life inside her resonate with the reservoir its original seed had come from. The star of life, the size of a mustard seed, sent a signal to its father, and she felt him ignite a spark in response. This was just what she wanted to accomplish. She watched a smile form with his lips and he shifted a little where he lay.

The last of her worries vanished. He was here. She relaxed a little, and looked for a glass of water for herself.

It was time to heat water for some refreshing tea for him. She stirred the brazier and got a new flame going. The metal cup got heated one more time, and new herbs added. The first birds had started to sing outside announcing the dawn.

As she turned to offer him tea, he hadn't improved as much as she expected while she had turned away from him. He was very much alive, although still unconscious, but his strength had not returned as quickly as she wanted. His wounds were healing, but he still showed the rough handling he had received. Even though the familiar golden glow was there, he had a pale complexion she didn't like.

She applied another ointment underneath his nose to wake him up. It was time. They needed to leave.

His eyes opened slowly and he looked into the loving face of his wife. She kissed him and he tried to respond. He tried to put his arms around her, but didn't have the strength to lift them. She wanted to lift his upper body up from the bench, but he was too limp and heavy.

"Give him time," she heard Yochanan say.

"He needs to gather strength. If you handle him before he is ready, it will take longer still," Bashra warned.

Mariam knew that they were right. Time was running short.

She had to have him ready to move any moment now. But right now she treasured her time resting her head on his chest listening to his heart. They were given another moment to share strength. Mariam just wanted it to last, for all three of them.

She heard some rustling outside and knew their time alone was over. The stone in front of the opening was slid to the side, and the two men she had expected arrived. Yochanan had closed his eyes by now, and Mariam wrapped him up. Bashra was already packed in her herb bag.

"Good morning," said Uncle Joseph. "How is our patient doing?"

Yeshua looked at his uncle, but didn't seem to register totally who it was or what the situation at hand was.

"Yeshua, husband, it is time to go. Do you think you can walk?"

Joseph's friend Nicodemus had come with. He also had been temple trained and Mariam trusted him completely.

"I would have loved to give him time to recover more here, but we can't do that."

"He will have more time where we'll bring him. He can rest there for several days before he needs to be seen again."

"Where are you taking him, uncle? Your house cannot be safe right now."

"Dear daughter, we don't want you to have an answer to give if you are questioned, or if someone could peak into your mind. So we are not going to tell you. Trust me that he will be safe."

"When can I see him?"

"We will contact you and arrange for that when it is safe for you to do so. Now he needs to be prepared for the next part of his work."

Mariam had to accept that. She knew what her next part was, and she trusted that she would see her husband again soon. In her herb bag Bashra blinked and sighed.

Yeshua quickened with the other men present. He still looked pale, almost bluish thought Mariam. She wished she could stay with him, but knew that the plan they had made called for them to be separated now.

I love you, she worded to his head. *Stay strong till I see you again.*

Joseph pulled Yeshua's legs around on the bench and made him sit up with a lot of support while Mariam packed up the things in the tomb. He was still not speaking, but his eyes spoke volumes of his gratitude towards them all. Mariam found a clean shirt for him which they pulled over his head before standing him up. Joseph had brought a thicker brown robe for him, both to keep him warm, and to hide him from sight on route to their destination.

They left the tomb as quickly as they could move. Mariam watched as the men hobbled along the path out of the garden. There was a gardener there tending the plants. She didn't want him to notice the group of men shuffling off behind the trees, so she walked over and started a conversation with him about the flowers he cultivated along the paths. Soon the others had disappeared and she saw them as shadows in the twilight leave through the gate towards the city.

Mariam hurried down the path in the opposite direction. First she needed to reach Josephs house to drop off the bundle she was carrying. Then she had some announcements to make. And then, maybe she could have some food to eat.

CHAPTER 20

THE ANNOUNCEMENT

MARIAM QUICKLY DEPOSITED HER PRECIOUS BUNDLE IN the safe hiding place in Joseph's house. Then she ran off to find Peter and the disciples.

Would they all be joined together? Probably. They were grieving their Master's death and would most likely support each other. After all, they had been traveling and working together for several years.

They usually surrounded Yeshua wherever he was. Yeshua had spent his time between their home in Bethany, preaching at the Temple and traveling the country side.

Now that he was not there as their focal point, where would they go?

She remembered their fear when the soldiers took Yeshua away. They had scattered quickly, even Peter and his famous zealots. Most likely they would try to avoid contact with the Roman soldiers, and they would avoid the places the soldiers would search for them.

Mariam went back to the house of Simeon in Jerusalem where they had celebrated the holy meal. That place was not so well known, and had a hall that could accompany all of them. There were several homes in Jerusalem where they were welcomed, and she had to start looking somewhere.

Her logic had sent her on the right track. She found some of them at Simeon's. The others were spread out over the city. They wouldn't leave, and yet they all knew that they couldn't stay. Now that Yeshua had been killed by the Romans, his followers were also seen as threats to the Roman Empire. The priests of the temple didn't like them any better. The Pharisees didn't like that they didn't follow tradition, and the Sadducees had chosen to cooperate with the Romans and didn't like anybody who opposed the occupying forces. The Nazareeans were exasperated that they had lost their second Messiah, and decided they didn't want to have anything to do with any family member of Yochanan or Yeshua, so Joseph was banished from their colony. The Essenes were sad about losing a great healing rabbi, but didn't want to get politically involved.

This left Yeshua's flock without leadership and without a network. They relied totally on their few powerful friends in the city, and they couldn't count on their continued support. The despair was heavy in the room as Mariam entered.

She could feel that they needed someone to say something that reminded them of the powerful charismatic man they had lost. It was hard stepping into their heart wrenching grief when she herself felt so elated. She was still concerned. Yeshua was in good hands, but when she left him he wasn't as recovered as she had expected. But that concern was not what she wanted to show them. They simply needed to know that he was not in the tomb anymore. He had indeed risen from the dead.

"Peter, Philip, Andrew! I have great news!" She announced enthusiastically.

They slowly turned their heads and she saw their ashen faces devoid of hope. Her optimistic cry hurt on their skin. They had accepted their despair. It would lift when they had allowed their grief its expression. Her loud happiness had the effect of a bucket of cold water dumped on a sleeping body. She sensed the annoyance from them all.

"What is it, woman?" growled Peter. Didn't she know how to behave the day after the burial of their leader?

Mariam was a little taken aback with his response. Peter had never gotten used to the respect the other men gave her. The fact that she was a high priestess of several temples didn't seem to register with him. She tried again.

"I have been to the garden. I have seen the tomb. It is empty! Our lord is not there!"

"Somebody has stolen his body!"

"No, I saw him in the garden. He is alive. He told me to go and tell you."

"How can we know that you are speaking truth? You were always near him. What were your motives?"

"Peter, hold your temper. If the master bestowed love upon her, she must have been worthy. Tell us, Mariam. Tell us what you've seen."

Philip was always supportive. Mariam thanked him for his kind remarks. She started to tell them that they had taken him down before the Sabbath and put him in the tomb that Joseph of Aramathea had provided. They had heard this from John already, but they liked hearing how she told it. She spoke about putting him on the shelf and laying his body out according to tradition.

This morning she had come to administer to him with her herbs. The stone had been removed by strong hands, and then she saw, the tomb was empty. He was not there. The linens were left there, but his body was gone.

She had gone to the garden and talked to a gardener. Then she had seen him, alive and well. He had told her to find them and tell them the good news.

Their attention had grown as she told her story. Their eyes had grown bigger as she spoke. At the end, she even had Peter on his toes. He wanted to go to the garden and check for himself. The three disciples went to Gethsemane together while she went to look for others.

She ran through the streets to Lydia's house and found two of them there. They promised to spread the word to more of their own. They knew where they were hiding.

Mariam liked being the bringer of good news. She felt buoyant as she walked hastily through the street. At the same time her sense of imminent danger was also present. Were the flames she had seen in her vision going to come now? Already? She was prepared for that event to happen much further into the future. And she hoped she wouldn't be there when it happened.

The warning she sensed was not for the battle at the Temple. She knew that would come. She knew the zealots would start it, and she knew the Romans would win. It would be a long siege, a bloody battle and the Romans would win a brutal and regrettable victory. And she also felt sure she wouldn't be in Jerusalem to see the destruction of the beautiful Temple.

The uneasiness she felt was immediate. She knew Yeshua had many enemies. And she knew anybody who had been his follower would be open prey.

Their marriage had been kept hidden. Announcing the existence of a King and Queen would ask for opposition, so her true status had been unknown to most of their surroundings. Would this event change that? Now that he had fulfilled the role of Tammuz, of Osiris, having defied death and had the experience of the underworld, was he now worthy of being their King? A while ago she would have assumed so. Time in Jerusalem had made her wiser.

There were so many different people here. This was not Alexandria where people tolerated each other and lived in relative peace with the Roman presence. In Judea, the Romans were always seen as an occupying force, something to be despised and opposed at any opportunity. To complicate it further, the various groups were all feverish about their own cause and difficult to unite.

She was on her way back to Bethany. There was no reason to go back to the tomb. The disciples had Peter as their new leader. They also had James, Yeshua's brother. They certainly didn't need her.

On her way she was met with wailing women and received tearful condolences. Why was she alone on a day like this? She should be with her sisters and mother-in-law. Mariam agreed and said that was indeed where she was heading. She had something good to tell them. He wasn't dead, he had risen! People looked at her as she left them. Poor girl, she had totally lost it. Who could blame her. What a shock. She came from a fine family in Alexandria they had heard. And she was temple trained. Hm. Really?

As she came closer to the colony the wailing became a choir. She started running. What she could tell them would change their tones, she was sure of that.

"Martha," she called. "Lazarus!"

She found them in their house, slumped together on the floor, crying. The wailing women were gathered in the courtyard between the houses. She hoped her news would be seen as sunshine emerging on a rainy day and not cold water thrown on their faces. A softer approach seemed to be called for and all she could do was whisper: "He lives!"

Martha and Lazarus pulled her into their embrace. She was surrounded with family. It was wonderful to feel their support, and suddenly she felt how tired she was. The euphoria of the good news, her own exhaustion and the fact that she was now home, safe and sound, was too much for her. Mariam fainted and collapsed in her brothers arms.

"Mariam!" Martha cried hysterically.

"She has only fainted. Help me put her on the bed."

They arranged their sister in the bedroom and left her to rest.

There was knocking on the door. An authoritative voice yelled outside for them to open up. Martha and Lazarus looked at each other.

They had to open the door or it would be torn down. The Roman soldiers marched in.

"Yeshua, the crucified rabbi, he lived in your village?"

Martha nodded. She had never before been addressed by a Roman centurion.

"What seems to be the problem?" Lazarus took the role of the oldest male in the household and wanted to protect his sister.

"We are looking for people connected with him. Did you know him?"

'We knew *of* him," said Lazarus evasively.

"He was married, wasn't he? All rabbis are married. Any children?"

"Not that we know of," Lazarus continued his approach.

"We will have to search your house for other people to question."

With a large arm he shoved Lazarus and Martha aside and made room for his soldiers to look around. They were respectful, they didn't break anything. All they wanted was to find people.

In the bedroom Mariam was on the bed, still unconscious. The soldiers tried to wake her, but she remained unable to respond.

"Who is she? Why didn't you mention that you had more people in the house?"

"You didn't ask, officer," said Lazarus.

"This is our sister, Sarah, who is visiting from..."

"Leontopolis," finished Lazarus.

"She is..."

"... under some drug we gave her to sleep better. Martha here knows quite a bit about herbs." Lazarus held proudly around his sisters shoulders.

The Romans didn't totally believe them, but they didn't find them suspicious enough to warrant further harassing. They left and politely wished them a good day.

Martha could scream with concern. Lazarus felt like covering her mouth with his hand, but he saw that she controlled herself.

"What in the name of all the Gods was that? What are they after?" Lazarus was in shock.

"We're in danger! We're all in so much danger!" Martha was on her toes turning in circles in sheer fear.

"We need to warn Joseph and Mary. We need to get Mariam out of here."

"We all need to leave Bethany."

Martha ran out the back door to get to Mary and Joseph's house. She came in the kitchen door as quietly as she could. There already was some commotion at the front. She tried to stay out of sight, but couldn't help hear what was going on.

"Yes, he was our son. Have you come to apologize?"

"He is not in the tomb. We are searching for his body. We don't want a cult to grow because they now have a martyr to worship."

"He is not in the tomb? But I saw him there myself. I was with the party who put him there. The stone was rolled in front." Mary knew what she had seen.

"Did you see that yourself?"

"Yes, we carried him to the tomb and laid him out on the bench. Then we left back for Bethany because of the Sabbath."

"Did everyone go with you?"

"Mariam stayed behind to say goodbye to him. They were very close."

"Where is she now? We need to question her."

"I don't know. She hasn't been here all night."

The centurion walked about lifting things, looking underneath.

"Do you think we could have hidden a corpse in here? Do I look strong enough to carry an adult body all the way from Jerusalem?" Joseph didn't like the situation.

"Somebody did. And we know that you have knowledge of building effortlessly with huge stones. Carrying a body would be easy for a wizard like you, druid."

Joseph hadn't been called a druid for close to forty years. He would have loved to take it as a compliment, but he knew it wasn't intended that way. How did they know where he came from? What else did they know?

The centurion didn't like anything about this situation. He thought the crucifixion went too quickly. Usually criminals were thrown to the animals after they died, but this man was treated like a hero. The colony at Bethany, which seemed to be his headquarter, was full of suspicious people. And they were all suspicious in weird ways. Did they have contacts in high places? What clandestine activities were going on? If the dead prisoner had an army built up, where were they?

There was something here that made his skin crawl. He felt watched by unseen eyes wherever he went. It even felt as if these people could peak into his mind and see what he was thinking.

The centurion knew about good weapons and strong men. He attended masses to honor Mithras, the Roman patron of soldiers. If someone had asked him how he *felt*, he would simply have scowled.

There were too many lose ends here. Obviously, this woman had to be found, wherever she was. He had learned how these people felt about dead bodies on the Sabbath. It was very unlikely that they had wanted to handle it. So it would all have happened this morning. Somebody had simply taken it away. Why? Martyrs weren't hard to come by. People died all the time. People were crucified on a regular basis. What was so different with this one?

His orders had been to first of all identify any children of his. His superiors had wanted to make sure there wouldn't be any continuation of his family, any grooming of new rebels. They grew up very quickly, vermin like that. Children of martyrs often took on their parents cause and continued the rebellion. If Rome could prevent that from happening, Rome would.

Mariam woke up with her brother and sister standing around her shaking her and shouting her name.

"Mariam, there is much to be done."

They were interrupted by another knock on the door, softer this time. They heard the door open and someone come in. The gentle efficiency of the movement told them it was one of their own.

"Joseph," said Mariam rubbing her eyes.

Martha and Lazarus rushed to greet him. He hushed their concerns with a lifted arm.

"We have no time to lose," he announced. "Mariam needs to leave Bethany and go far away. Her child must not be born here and must never be known to the Romans, or the priests and Rabbis of Jerusalem."

"Child?" Lazarus was shocked. He turned as Mariam joined them. Martha's face lit up and she hugged her sister.

"I will go with you to Alexandria to your parents. They can help us find a boat to take us to Gaul. We will find our people in the colonies there."

"But Joseph," Mariam protested. "There is a desert between here and Alexandria."

"We can't risk any delay, and the ports will be swarming with soldiers. I have a strong donkey and have traveled the desert before. Please, Mariam, pack some things and we'll leave immediately."

"Yeshua! Will I ever see him again?"

"We will give him word where you are in Gaul. He will find you."

Mariam stood in the middle of the floor with her arms stretched out wanting to ask many more questions as she watched Joseph leave. Lazarus and Martha shared her frozen pose for a moment before Martha spoke.

"We'll have to pack up the colony."

"None of us are safe here anymore."

"We'll come after you."

"We'll be there, Mariam. Together we'll continue his work."

"I've never been to Gaul."

"May all the Gods protect you."

Mariam went back to her room and started to pack a bag. Her practical side was glad her child was still a small plant inside her. Packing for a baby on an unsafe journey was a task she was glad to be spared for.

Some clothes for her self was simple. But she had other items in her care she couldn't leave behind. Her herb bag was obvious. Her tools. And the bundle she had hidden before she rushed off to tell the disciples earlier. It could not be found or seen by anyone, so few would understand. They would have to visit Uncle Joseph's house before they left Jerusalem. Could they? Was it safe?

Joseph was already at the door with the donkey. Mariam realized she couldn't say goodbye to her-mother-in-law. Would she ever see her again? She had to leave the village without talking to anybody.

Silently she hugged her beloved sister and reached up and kissed her tall brother. Not a word was shared. In a few quick, graceful movements Mariam was down the steps and at her father-in-law's side. A backward glance from the donkey's back gave her a picture she would always remember. Martha and Lazarus were standing by the house in the village that had also been her home, watching her disappear between the cypresses.

Nothing was said. They didn't know who could be listening. Joseph led the donkey along less familiar paths towards Jerusalem. Mariam felt the movements of the donkey underneath her. She pulled the dark cloak around herself as the chill of the night came upon them.

Through the city they followed the usual crowds of people. There were many donkeys with a woman on its back led by a man. There were many Mary's being led by a Joseph, their names being common among their people. But there was only one temple trained priestess on a donkey led by a druid on their way to Egypt.

The city of Jerusalem had the usual evening noise of people hurrying home, soldiers looking over the city, youth scurrying between people looking for adventure, poor people hoping for one more scrap of food before they found places to rest for the night. Some carried lanterns or torches, other torches were attached to house corners. People's movements created shadows between light and dark.

But the city had a heavy atmosphere tonight. The people were aggravated by the recent crucifixions which seemed unnecessary and unusually cruel. A new resolve started forming in peoples minds. An unwritten resolution against the oppressors found words and willing bodies.

The blood in the streets. The fire. The beautiful temple being torn apart. Mariam saw it all one more time. She saw it in their eyes as she passed defiant faces. She saw it in the soldiers as they felt justified in showing these people who were the true masters.

Was it all hopeless? Had it all been in vain? The peaceful message of her husband was nowhere to be seen or felt.

Never in vain, said her father in law's voice in her head. *Think of all you've done!*

Mariam could only see that she had helped strengthen a rebellion that would end in massive bloodshed.

Joseph received her imagery. *When?* He asked her.

In our lifetime, she answered silently back.

They couldn't go to uncles Joseph's house. That would be too unsafe for everybody involved. Joseph had sent a message to him which he hoped he had received.

They continued through the city and followed the road towards Bethlehem. Mariam was struggling to stay awake. Joseph promised her that they would soon rest.

They passed the little town and went on. Joseph had a goal in mind. The big rock was still on the side of the road as he remembered. He left the road and turned in towards some nearby cliffs. The donkey followed willingly behind. It could smell sweet hay nearby.

There was a fire and some shepherds sitting around it. One of them stood up as he saw them approach. Joseph followed him into the cave behind them and Mariam could see several animals being sheltered there for the night. Joseph helped her down from the donkey. The animal found the hay he had been hungering for. The cave was warm and the other animals looked curiously at the unfamiliar people. Did the sheep smile at her? She felt exhausted and starved. The hay looked tempting for a rest.

"Mariam?" A familiar voice called softly for her.

Could it be? Where? She saw Joseph conversing with two other men whom she thought she recognized. Beyond them was a light, gently beaming in the golden hay.

She moved towards the voice, all bodily discomfort forgotten. Was he here?

"I wasn't sure," said Joseph quietly. "But I hoped." He stood by his son one more time in this cave as the pillar of support.

"We've done the best we could," said Nicodemus. "Aloe Vera is the answer. He will recover."

"Thanks to your work immediately after," Uncle Joseph assured her. "He wouldn't have been able to return without your knowledge."

Mariam simply nodded to them as she passed them. He was here! Her husband, the man she loved, the one she wondered if she'd ever see again, was here.

"Yeshua insisted on seeing you before you again will be separated."

Mariam didn't hear him. She sat down next to Yeshua on the blanket he was lying on. His chest was exposed and she could see from his wounds that he was healing, although weak. But he was alive! He had come a long way. All he needed was more of the excellent care he had received, and he would soon be back walking in Galilee again. Silently she thanked God for all the people that had helped along the way, including the three brave men standing next to her.

Tears were rolling down her cheeks as she reached for his hand, but realized she couldn't hold him there either. His hands and wrists were heavily bandaged and would always have scars from the gruesome events he had just completed. Her whole body longed to touch him, to unite with him again the way they loved to. She put her hand towards his cheek and stroked him with her fingers. Her wet eyes conveyed all her emotions. All he had strength for was to repeat her name.

The three men gave them time alone while they prepared some food to be shared before Joseph and Mariam continued on their journey.

How are you feeling? She asked silently.

Weak, but happy, was his instant reply, accompanied with a smile.

You will be well, yes?

With time. Traveling is the worst. They don't want to keep me for too long in the same place. I've been moved three times already since we left the tomb. I don't even know where we've been. And I know we'll have to move again.

If only I could stay with you.

I'll find you in Gaul. It's safer there.

I do understand, but I don't want to leave you.

My father will take care of you. Then your brothers will get you across the sea.

Martha and Lazarus are coming too.

And my mother. We'll all be together again. John is taking care of her.

They kept reassuring each other knowing perfectly well that all these plans could so easily change. There was no guarantee that they would find each other in Gaul, or that all these people would be able to start over again together in another country. They didn't even know that they would all make it to the shores of this new land which was unfamiliar to most of them. The Roman arm was long and hard. If you had first made enemies with them, they wouldn't let it rest.

But they think I'm dead, he sent her.

But they know that I'm not, she replied. *And they know you're not in the tomb.*

Thank God they don't know about the child, he said, as he lifted his bandaged hand and laid it in her lap.

There were three spheres of light making the straw glow golden that night.

His breathing was heavier and she told him to rest. She walked over to where the other men had prepared a meal and took a bowl of soup with her back. Sitting down next to him, she was feeding him slowly, carefully she also took some spoonfuls in between.

"It's mother's, isn't it," he asked her.

Mariam also recognized Mary's well known chicken soup and was grateful to everybody involved providing this meal for them, including the chicken.

Joseph loaded up the donkey again with the help of Nicodemus. Uncle Joseph came over to them and stood next to her.

"He's doing remarkably well. He'll be back to full health very quickly. I'll be traveling your way soon. Listen, Mariam. In Gaul, find the Egyptian Temple dedicated to Ra. It is on an island with a fort called Oppidum Priscum Ra, not far from Massilia where your brothers are familiar. They will welcome you. You can also leave messages for me there. I'll find you. He'll find you. But now you must leave."

Mariam turned and saw that the donkey was ready. There were extra bundles attached to it, and water skins. She thanked the animal for its services before she turned towards Yeshua one more time.

"I love you," she said. *We love you.*

"I'll meet you in Arcadia," he said.

She turned and left together with his father. Looking back, there was still a golden light emanating from inside the cave.

CHAPTER 21

LEAVING THE LAND OF CANAAN

S HE KNEW SHE WOULD NEVER RETURN.
    The friendly donkey carried her along the road in the twilight between late night and early morning. She watched her father-in-law's sturdy frame as he walked steadily ahead of her. Right now she couldn't be worried about his age. She couldn't be worried about her husband's health and safety. She left the concerns about the colony in Bethany in the hands of her sister and brother. Her beloved mother-in-law was in the good care of a trusted man, and on her way to Ephesus.

Would she ever see any of them again? She wasn't really convinced, however much they had been trying to reassure each other. All she knew now was that she needed to get to anonymous safety with the child she was carrying. She was feeling fine. Her herb bag held all the remedies she could wish for. It didn't show yet, but she was aware of a shift in her body.

Would she and the child be safe? If Rome wanted to get hold of her they would have a hard time after the desert sand closed behind her. They hardly knew of her existence. Her marriage had been kept secret. The land of Canaan hardly knew that they had a Queen.

After a while she was less comfortable on top of the donkey and she signaled to Joseph that she wanted to get down. For a while they walked together sharing the fine morning light.

"She's a morning star now," he said as he pointed to a light in the sky.

"Yes, the switch was last month," she said remembering that she had wondered which month it would happen. At the temples they kept good track of the movements of the star. It was harder when she was on her own. Still, she could look up and know what she saw.

She loved this star. Venus had been with her through her entire life. It would be a welcome companion on this journey.

They passed some smaller settlements before the landscape to their left became an endlessness of sand. Joseph kept them on the path with the coast line on their right.

"I've been this route before, you know."

"When?"

"Remember when Yeshua and I went away into the wilderness? That's what these parts are called. We went to the temple of Serabit el Khadim on Mt. Sinai. He needed to learn from the elders there. It was also time for him to visit the Field of the Blessed."

"Tell me about that, Father." Mariam remembered her own initiations at the pyramids, but wanted to hear what Joseph had experienced. She knew they had been to Serabit, she didn't know she was now treading the same route.

"There is so much to learn, which I'm sure you've found in all your travels too."

"Yes, Father."

"I was welcomed there because of my background with metals in Hibernia and all I had learned in Alexandria and in Heliopolis. We had stayed with them for a while on our way from Jerusalem to Alexandria when Yeshua was little. I spent some time there alone while Mary was in Ephesus as well. So they know me well."

"Are we going there on this journey?"

"It would be a safe place to disappear for a while. But it is far. There is a lot of sand to cover between here and there."

"I can do it. I'll walk and you can rest some times."

"Yes, my daughter, I know you are brave and strong. If we can join a caravan, we will be safer."

"Tell me about the Field of the Blessed."

"It is only done with forty days of fasting and in a safe setting. It is considered one in a series of many initiations which are all strictly monitored by elders. Yeshua was at the right age and had reached the appropriate level. I could safely take him there for the experience."

"So you walked all the way across the desert?"

"...for a while. We did join a caravan, and some friendly Bedouins took us in for a night and showed us where to find water."

"People told me about it at Bethany. How changed you both were when you returned."

"Yes, it changes you. You become illuminated from the inside. That's what the bread of gold will do. At Serabit, they use the gold to fertilize their field, as well. Their water is enhanced as well as the food. Once ingested, it will change how your body works."

"What does it feel like?"

"First, the inside of your body feels clean. Your thoughts change. There are sounds inside your head as if your body is singing a song of praise. And if you get injured you heal easily. Mariam, do you know how old I am?

"To me you are ageless, Father."

"I know, and to you I will always be that. But I'm further up in years than you might think. After all, I was a grown man when I accompanied Mary from Hibernia, and she was just a young maiden. The Field of the Blessed has worked generously with me for many years. I am grateful for the traditions I've been allowed to take part in."

"Would you like to stay at the temple?"

"The brothers there are wise and have dedicated their lives to this knowledge. I would like to give something in return."

"We'd miss you, Father."

"I know, daughter of mine, I know. I'd miss you too."

The donkey trudged through sand. They traded off riding.

They were lucky. A caravan was heading their way and offered them to ride on the camels while the donkey walked behind.

Later they did meet Bedouins who showed them water. They even met another monk on his way to Serabit.

After many days of sand, Mariam saw the monastery on the top of the mountain through eyes full of dust. The monk cheerfully announced that they had arrived, but all she could see was that there was another mountain to climb before they would reach people.

As they got closer, a delegation from the temple came to meet them. At the Temple they had heard Mariam's group coming through the desert. Returning brothers sounded to them like clanging bells through the sand.

Joseph and Mariam collapsed inside the courtyard as water was poured over them. Mariam didn't realize how exhausted she was until she was laid down on a bench and fed something refreshing. Did they grow fruits here? The answer was *yes*, coming silently from the monk attending her.

Joseph wasn't well. The trip had taken its toll on him, however young he might seem. His internal supply of the Field of the Blessed could use some reinforcement. He needed a long rest and proper care from experienced brothers. She had watched him be carried inside by three strong monks and noticed how his body had thinned out from the time in the sand. Had he given her all the water?

After a full week of rest, water and nutritious food they found themselves sitting in the courtyard wrapped in blankets, sipping tea and listening to the monks practicing singing. Mariam felt that she could think clearly again as she felt a fresh wind sweep across her cheek. The sounds of harmonies from the monk's full baritones and clear tenors changed the tones in the landscape. Then the sounds changed. They tried a different technique. Suddenly they sounded like twice as many and the overtones reverberated in the surrounding stone walls. She turned to see them better. Their number hadn't changed, but she saw that a couple of them looked like they were concentrating differently.

"It is so healing," said Joseph. "Those overtones can change the vibration of your body. Right now they are doing tones that are especially invigorating, just for us."

Mariam was grateful. The hospitality shown them was more generous than she had expected. The care they were given had saved their lives. Had she been participating in the Field of the Blessed? She wasn't sure. The days had been blurry.

A little in your water. I asked them to consider your condition in their dosage. They rarely have women here. And a pregnant one is just a privilege for them.

Mariam laughed a little, as she heard Joseph's thoughts. She caught the eye of one of the singing monks who bowed to her in a respectful greeting and realized that they could hear everything she was thinking. She didn't even have to send her thoughts out. They were picked up like loud messages bouncing between the walls. With this in mind, she created thoughts of gratitude and allowed them to dance between the singing brothers. They laughed at her and smiled to the beautiful woman among them.

Her beloved father-in-law wanted her attention. She could feel it across the air between them.

"Yes, Father, I'm listening."

"Mariam, it is time for you to go on."

"You want me to leave without you?"

"Yes, Mariam. It is better that way. Alexandria is still a long ways away. You are well enough to travel soon, but I'm not. Brother Emmanuel will go with you. He knows the way."

"You will stay here, then."

"I want to give back some years of my life to these good brothers and their important work. I can contribute here. There are young people to teach. There is knowledge to protect."

"I know you inspire young people, Father. I was one of them." Mariam smiled at him in gratitude.

"I enjoyed every minute of it. Remember the time at Therapautae, with all you youngsters so eager to learn? You were like thirsty camels. All I needed did was accompany you safely to the water."

"We were so eager. And we all found something there. Something we continued to build on."

"Those were delightful months, Mariam, a time of learning, days of building a body of internal knowledge."

"Then came the days of using what we'd learned."

"...which you did beautifully. I wish we weren't surrounded with such conflict."

"We should maybe have stayed more hidden."

"I thought Yeshua was too willing to take risks many times."

"He wanted to expose himself. He always trusted that he was protected."

"...which he was. Both seen and unseen forces were on his side."

"Will he be able to continue his work?"

"Nothing can keep him from teaching. He is born with that gift. It is driving him forth."

Mariam turned quiet.

"Father, will I see him again?"

"I think you will, my dear. But your child will be born first."

"Father, will I see *you* again?"

"In Arcadia, my dear daughter. In Arcadia."

The following days were used preparing Mariam and Emmanuel for the next part of her travel. The donkey was loaded carrying its own food and the two bundles Mariam had seen on it from the cave near Bethlehem. She hadn't asked what they contained, but she could guess, and was glad that someone had thought further than her at the time. A small caravan was preparing to go to Alexandria to deliver some of the products from the temple of Serabit to the temple of Serapium. Each temple had their specialties, and there were often caravans going between them. This time the monks timed the next delivery to accommodate the delightful guest they had enjoyed. The donkey was tied to the last camel and was happy walking with a lighter load through the desert this time.

Brother Emmanuel felt honored to travel with the high priestess. He promised Joseph and all the monks that he would protect her with his life all the way to her parent's home. Emmanuel was well traveled, and knew his scriptures as well as how to handle a sword.

Joseph felt relieved and trusted that she would be taken well care of. He didn't tell her how sick he actually felt. Watching his beloved son put himself in danger and be brutally tortured before publicly humiliated, was harder on his emotions than he expected. He knew he would live, but he also knew that his daring son would probably put himself in the public eye again, and was worried about him. His own lovely wife was on her way to Ephesus with young John, a trusted follower. His other children were going to be scattered, he knew that. And some would perish in the big battle Mariam had seen. Joseph could do more useful work here than to be running around trying to protect his family. They were all facing their own destinies independent of any help he could offer.

Losing Mariam was going to be harder than letting go of any of the others. She had always been close to him. They had a rare understanding between them. Was it because they both felt like strangers working on foreign soil? He had seen her Alexandria. Would she ever see his Hibernia?

CHAPTER 22

THROUGH THE DESERT
TO ALEXANDRIA

THE CARAVAN KNEW ITS WAY AND MARIAM felt safe on her camel with Emmanuel at her side. Leaving Father Joseph behind had been hard. She had a sense that she would find her husband, but she wasn't sure that she would see her father-in-law again.

Allowing her tears to flow, she let the camel swing her from side to side in its gait. She felt Emmanuel's concerned eyes, but didn't try to stop her grief. Thinking of the new life she carried, she tried to remember stories she would tell this little one about her wonderful grandfather.

The monotony of the desert and the wave of the camel's backs will roll your thoughts. A melancholy came over her. What had she actually done in Jerusalem? Had it all been in vain? Had they accomplished anything at all? Yes, she had healed some people and attended some initiations, but had she really done what she was destined for?

Will you shut up! A powerful voice chimed in.

Mariam would recognize that one anywhere, and had to admit that she hadn't talked with Bashra for a while. She patted her herb bag.

Do you know how many people now believe in a new way of living? Who consider love a force to be reckoned with? Who see hatred as a weakness and do not feel threatened by the strong arm of Rome? Bashra reminded her.

Well, he tried. He gave a lot of inspiring speeches. And some of his followers got to experience more of his knowledge, Mariam continued her desert thinking.

Don't underestimate your husband's work. How many did Yochanan baptize with Blessed water? Bashra asked.

Was it effective, though? I felt it myself, but I was never so sure about everybody else. Mariam couldn't get out of her melancholy that easily.

That was the beauty of it all. People didn't really know. They only knew that they felt better. You couldn't explain to them that they were being upgraded as humans. They became a better model. He created a whole force field of powerful people.

I guess so. Why was his work cut so short? Mariam would never forget the handsome man baptizing by the river.

It wasn't, she heard in her head. It must have come from one of the bags on the donkey.

My work was not cut short. My work ended when others could continue what I'd started. I am more useful in this format.

But, Yochanan, how much more wouldn't I've preferred to have you alive here with me! What happened to you was awful. We tried to find a solution in an impossible situation. Mariam had to make sure he understood how she felt.

And you got back at him too, didn't you. Mariam was sure she heard him chuckle.

Herodias was brave and clever, she answered back in admiration.

What a show! She got her revenge on the man in style. Yochanan enjoyed knowing how thoroughly Herodias had ruined her husband's career.

..which he deserved. I wonder where she's now.

You know, you'll see her again.

Do you really think so?

Ask in Alexandria. Someone there will know.

Mariam was being entertained by her lifelong companion and her old friend. They comforted her on the long trip and reassured her when her thoughts turned dark. Young Emmanuel listened to the exchange, but couldn't really figure out where it all came from. He told himself that she could talk to her ancestors through the ethers and was satisfied with that.

The sand didn't seem as bothersome or dangerous this time. In three days time they left the desert behind and could see the green delta of the Nile. Mariam was grateful for the change of color. She knew it was safer to travel across green land with the river close by. As far as she was concerned, she had no need to travel across a desert ever again.

The caravan went through a small town and they bought a warm meal and settled for the night. Mariam almost missed the sand which could be formed into any comfortable shape she needed. The place on the ground she found herself didn't offer the support she needed for her growing belly. Where would her child be born? There were still many months until it was due. She had now idea where she'd be by that time.

In the morning the caravan leader took them to a port and they booked fare on a ship to Alexandria. The camels were left in good care until the monks would return with the supplies they needed. The donkey came with them on the boat. This trusty companion would help them through the city with their packages. The animal didn't seem to mind being at sea. The camels wouldn't have been willing to walk on board. They loved their sandy world and created their own wavy movements which could resemble how a boat moved at sea. People were known to become seasick from a prolonged trip on a camel.

Mariam stood at the railing taking in the breeze from the water. This was her sea, her ocean which she had sailed many times. She knew the next trip would be longer and riskier. Now they traveled along the land and it was not far to Alexandria. She loved this immense body of clear blue water.

Hello, little one. Last time I traveled across this water I was with your father. We ran away from our wedding for a little time alone. We did come back. We did get married.

Remembering the wedding with all the family members present made her cry again. All these lovely supportive people she had lived with for too short a time. She remembered the group of women going to the water together on her wedding day, and handsome Yeshua with his brothers and brothers-in-law teasing each other as they returned from their water trip. The dress her mother had made for her carrying their family history. The lovely ceremony. Being together with Yeshua, again, with everybody's blessing. She hoped the life she carried could take in all her feelings as she took a deep breath of the salty air.

They arrived in Alexandria without anybody expecting them. There was no delegation from the temple ready to lead them in a parade through town. None of her relatives were waving at the pier.

It's just as well, she thought. *I would rather not draw attention.*

The little donkey went with Mariam and Emmanuel as they walked through the busy streets of the town. She recognized every turn they made. Every corner was familiar to her and carried a particular memory. It was exciting to be back. None of the Roman soldiers they passed even turned their helmets in her direction. Her time at Serabit was well spent. Maybe the whole ordeal was forgotten.

Emmanuel was duly impressed with Mariam's home. It was large and architecturally pleasing. At the gate the servants made a big fuss about her return. Oh, Mistress Mariam should have told them. They would have made a feast. Mariam tried to hush them down as she saw her mother come running from the inner courtyard. She made sure the gate was closed again before she fell into her mothers arms and allowed her feelings to show.

"Child, how wonderful to see you. We haven't had a word of you coming. And what's happened to you? Has your travel been too strenuous? Why didn't you send for your brothers? Is it true what we hear from Jerusalem? And who is this good man traveling with you?"

Mariam couldn't answer to anything. All she wanted to do was curl up in her mothers lap and cry. She let Emmanuel explain their travel route. That was at least a start.

"Is it true what I see? You are with child? What wonderful news, Mariam! Why haven't you told us?"

Eurochia called for servants to bring food and drinks for them and led them both into the courtyard to rest. The donkey was taken care of by able hands. Emmanuel accepted an offer of food, but said he needed to return to the monks and help them with their errand. They had a delivery to make to the temple and would be housed there while in town.

"And let him have the donkey," said Mariam. "He needs it to carry supplies. And don't let the servants open my bags." Then she collapsed in a soft chair.

Eurochia gave the servants instructions to take care of Emmanuel after thanking him profusely for his generous services. She wanted to give a donation to the monastery, which he accepted. Then she rushed off to be with her daughter who had been carried to her room.

"My dear child," she said trying to sound calm.

The servants brought water and food to the room. A sweet older woman who had been with the family for years washed Mariam's face. Mariam tried to stay conscious accepting all this activity around her.

"Mother," was all she managed to say. Then she smiled and fell asleep.

She slept for a day and a half. When she awoke the whole family was assembled for the evening meal. Mariam was carried down to the atrium and placed in the softest couch there. Her eyes met the people around her, her brothers, her father. Carefully, they hugged her one by one. They were all quiet, not wanting to disturb her too much in her fragile state. At the same time, they were eager to hear her stories.

Mariam looked for another face. Where was Sarah, her favorite little sister who was always full of enthusiasm?

Sarah was sitting in a chair a little distance from her. Why hadn't she come to hug her welcome? The brothers had been with her as soon as they saw her.

Mariam looked at her and tried to take in her expression. Sarah's body looked defiant. The crossed arms showed anger. The sharp, but shivering line of her mouth showed that she felt hurt and her eyes were accusative. In her exhaustion, Mariam couldn't read her sister any further.

"Welcome home," Sarah broke the silence. Icicles were hanging from the string of her voice.

All Mariam could muster was a puzzled look. Ezra went over to Sarah and stood by her side. "Now, now, little sister, this is not the time…"

Sarah pushed him aside roughly. All eyes were on her now.

"You've been gone for three years and you never sent for me."

"But Sarah, I…"

"Not a letter, not a note, not a greeting came my way." Sarah's tears were hopping out of her face. "And now you're pregnant, and you didn't even tell me. How do you think Mother feels about not being informed? How do you think your family feels about being left out of your life?"

"Sarah, things happened. It's hard to explain."

"I'm sure it is! You were the princess! You were the one getting married to the handsome prince! You became the "queen" of another country! And now here you are. Stealing in with no entourage, no husband, no servants, and no explanation, expecting a child we know nothing about. What did you do to it all? There's got to be a pretty good story behind all this."

"Sarah, if you only let me explain…"

"You wanted the education! With all your knowledge you should be able to magically produce a camel if you needed one! What do you mean disgracing us all like this?"

"I did have a camel. And in the colony we all worked together. Sarah, please…"

"You forgot me, *that's* what you did! Martha was with you, but you forgot me!"

"There was never a day I didn't think about you."

"You! The princess!! Where is your handsome prince now? You were wild about him, don't you remember? Has he deserted you for a prettier woman who looked more like him? Those blond locks are hard to come by in our family!!"

"Sarah, enough!!" Ezra tried to stop her. Mother Eurochia was speechless. Never had she seen her children behave like this.

"No, I'm not finished! And now, all this fuss over your return. I've been here all these years. I've taken care of mother. I've watched father when he was sick. I've even helped noble Ezra get out of a scrape he didn't want his parents to know about."

Ezra reddened from his hair to his sandals. "Sarah, please! You promised."

The parents attention where on him with questioning eyes, but they remained silent.

"Where were you? Where was your concern for the family that raised you? The family that was so proud of the high ranking priestess and the noble marriage in Judea. I've listened to bragging stories about that wedding until my stomach turned!! And it wasn't that impressive, really. I was there, remember?"

"Sarah…," Mariam tried. She was crying now.

"You promised that I could come with you! I made a little girls promise of never leaving you! Have you forgotten everything? Not a word, Mariam. Not a word." She had stood up from her chair and was shooting lightning bolts from her eyes.

"Sarah, behave yourself. That's enough. How easy do you think it was, being a new bride in another country? Do you think having all my education only gave me privileges? It gave me more responsibilities than I ever asked for."

"You asked for it, alright. There was no end to the temples you had to learn from. And you hardly even spent time here in between. All that was your own doing. You wanted the fame and attention that went with it."

"I learned things I would rather not have known, Sarah."

"Yeah, like how to please a man better? I know what goes on inside the temple."

"That's not fair!" Mariam was angry now. "Ezra, go and get the leather bag from my room with the red tassels on the bottom and the embroidery on the front."

Mariam was standing up now. All eyes were on her.

Ezra returned with the right bag while his family was still frozen in their positions.

"Open it!" Mariam commanded.

Her brother pulled at the strings and took out a large round object wrapped in cloth. As soon as he noticed the contours of what he was holding, he gasped loudly and dropped it on the floor. As it fell, the cloth got caught in a chair and it rolled across the floor and out of its cover. It turned over once more and stopped by Sarah's feet. She jumped high in the air and screamed.

"I knew it! You learned necromancy! You know how to work with the dead!"

"Yes, I do, Sarah. And it's a job I'd rather never do again. Pick it up!"

"I don't want to touch it, or you!!" Sarah covered her face with her arm.

"Pick it up! Look at it!" Mariam demanded.

Ezra walked carefully over and lifted the head from the floor. He almost dropped it again when he looked at the face. Finding courage and taking a deep breath he turned it so it faced the others. A collective gasp went through the crowd.

"It's Yochanan! screamed Sarah. "You killed him!"

"Yes, I did," said Mariam firmly.

"I hate you!" She heard her sister scream.

Eurochia fainted and was laid down in a chair. Fayed was fanning her. Sarah took two quick steps towards her sister, her hands shaped like claws ready to attack, but Hiram was faster. She was held in a firm grip from behind by her father. She could kick and scratch in the air, but she couldn't reach anybody.

"Everybody, sit down!" said Hiram in his most authoritative voice. "This has gone far enough. Sarah. Do I have to tie you up or are you going to control yourself?"

Sarah pulled on his hold, but his arms were stronger than hers. He quickly pulled his handkerchief out of his pocket and tied her wrists together. Before Sarah knew what happened, Hiram and Ezra had tied her to a post in the atrium.

"Now Mariam, maybe we can hear your story. Another word from you, Sarah, and I'll put your belt in your mouth." Hiram had never experienced his family this unruly. He should have taken control much earlier. Again, he chided himself for being too lenient with his daughters.

With all eyes on her, and everybody's full attention, Mariam began.

She told them how she had been forced to kill Yochanan and prepare his head. It was all part of a political coup for power. Now he had taken his place in the line of ancestral heads at the temple. She couldn't leave him there in the dark, but kept him with her.

Wanting to share about Lazarus and Martha, she told them that they would be coming soon. She didn't want to tell about how she had helped Lazarus visit the land of the dead, how risky it had been, how heavy the responsibility was on her for bringing him back and how she couldn't have done it without Yeshua's help. But, for Sarah's sake she told the story anyway.

Her husband? Her eyes turned dreamily to the ceiling. Where could she start telling anything about him, anything that they would understand?

She told about the followers, the numbers that grew out of proportion. How he led them all in learning more about the power of love. How he had given them experiences of enlightenment. How he had used what he had learned over the years to educate and give them back their self respect. How he gave a whole people new confidence. How he gave them all the experience of their own spiritual powers. And how he was hated for it. She described the different factors who didn't like what he did for their own good reasons. At the same time he was loved by a growing number of his own.

"There were thousands of people who would come from far away to hear him. He would speak at the steps of the temple and teach people things that had been held back from them for centuries."

Of course the temple priests were upset. Of course the Romans saw him as a rebel. He empowered the oppressed. He gave new hope of release from bondage, both the very physical oppression from the occupants, but also from the bondage held over people's minds by the temple.

They had tried to warn him, both his father and his wife. They could see where this was heading.

Then you had the armed forces of the Zealots and the Nazareeans who expected the new King to quickly overthrow the Romans and start a new kingdom of light and gold, and the Essenes who only wanted to quietly pursue their wisdom. These people relied on him. He was their icon. If he disappointed them, some of them would just as well have him dead.

The Romans themselves offered the solution. They decided to crucify him.

"We heard about what an uproar that crucifixion had stirred in Jerusalem. We didn't know it was him," Hiram spoke for the family.

"Nicodemus and Uncle Joseph helped us plan it. I knew what herbs to use. If only the Romans hadn't been so brutal!" Mariam sobbed.

"Dear daughter, can you tell us what happened? I know this is hard for you."

"They whipped him before they nailed him to the tree. He was bleeding from 98 places on his body where a piece of skin had been dug out by little cups with sharp edges attached to the end of the whips. I stood right by him trying to lift some of his pain.

"He hung there for three hours before it felt right to give him the final herbal brew. From then on he appeared dead. They took him down without breaking his legs, thank God. It all happened right before the Sabbath, and the Romans know how strictly the Jewish people adhere to the scriptures. They let us take him before the Sabbath hour so we could deal with the dead body before it would be forbidden. I stayed with him that night, tending his wounds. Nicodemus and Uncle Joseph had brought enough aloe vera to cover his entire body. On Sunday I took him out of the trance. Then they took him away from the tomb and I left him in their care.

"I ran back to the main followers to tell them that he lived! We couldn't tell them of our plan ahead of time. What if he had died! They didn't believe me and wanted to check for themselves. But back at the colony the Romans were investigating, and we all realized that we were in danger. I was smuggled out with Father Joseph in the middle of the night. Mary left with young John to go to Ephesus. The followers scattered. Martha and Lazarus were left to pack up the colony."

The silence in the room was loud. Nobody moved. Sarah had sunk down in a pile on the floor, sobbing, her cheeks wet with tears.

"Joseph took me on the donkey and we walked towards Bethlehem. He stopped in a cave he knew about from before, where the shepherds kept animals at night. Nicodemus and Uncle Joseph had taken Yeshua there to let me see him. He was weak. He couldn't even hug me goodbye. He said we'll meet in Arcadia. But that only exist as a meeting place outside of space and time. I can only reach him there with my thoughts. I don't know if I'll ever see him again."

Sarah was shaking now. Eurochia had woken up without anybody noticing and was listening quietly.

"Joseph took us to the temple of Serabit in the Sinai desert. They healed us from the trip through the desert and gave me Blessed Water to drink. Joseph remained there. He wanted to give some work back to this temple that has meant so much to him. He will probably never see his beloved Hibernia again.

"I'm only here for a short time. It's not safe for me and the child. The Romans considered Yeshua a state enemy, and by extension so am I. For the safety of the child I will travel to Gaul. I need safe passage across the ocean. I will again start anew in another country."

Eurochia and Hiram looked at their beautiful daughter. What more could befall her? Why was so much demanded of this one? What had prepared her for all this? Where did she take the strength from?

"Did you know?" Mariam directed the question to her parents.

"Did you know how hated we would be? Did you know that Judea was not the slightest bit ready for a King and Queen, however strongly it says in the scriptures? Did you know what we were facing when you promised me in marriage to a handsome youth? We were children, and our future was already laid out for us.

"Thanks for the education. It gave me enough knowledge to know how to kill a dear friend, how to send people to the world of the dead, how to make them look dead for three days and then be expected to bring them back at the right time. I was expected to perform miracles! I brought people back to health from impossible situations. I brought back the man I loved after he had lost more blood than any human can survive from, after his whole body was an open wound, feeling every pain of his as my own for every time I said "I love you". I brought him back from the world of the Gods to a wounded body in indescribable pain. He could have died again, right in front of me, right there.

"Yes, Sarah, I know many ways to make a man feel more pleasure. I joined with the man I loved. In the most physical sense, with our minds and hearts, with every piece of my skin next to his, with every emotion flowing through me, with every thought we shared. I joined with him as the land and its people while he was the God watching over them. I'm joined with him through hills and valleys and towns and villages. I'm joined with him in the stones of the Temple. I'm joined with him in the spirit we share as one in two bodies.

"I now have a new spirit inside started from that union. This will be a very special new being, and I need to protect her. Even if she'll never meet her father, I need to teach her about her heritage. And I'll teach her all I know. I wish I didn't have to. But I have a responsibility to the knowledge entrusted in me.

"I need your help, Sarah. Will you come with me to Gaul?"

RITUALS IN SACRED STONE

Yeshua and Mariam
King and Queen
Priest and Priestess

PART THREE
GAUL

A HISTORICAL NOVEL BY

WENCKE JOHANNE BRAATHEN

CONTENTS

CHAPTER 1

Oppidum priscum ra

THE TWO SISTERS WERE STANDING NEXT TO each other at the railing staring at the sea. The wind blew their dark hair from their faces and the afternoon sun gave them both haloes.

Sarah was happy. She was beyond happy. The days had been filled with preparations for the journey, and after she had stammered forth a *yes* and been released to hug her sister, her outburst had not been mentioned. She had thrown herself into the work ahead of her, to her family's relief and delight.

Eurochia had taken her younger daughter aside. She knew Mariam was too busy thinking of herbs and seeds to think the same practical thoughts she did herself.

"Sarah, dear, you know you'll be the one taking care of the baby. Mariam will have other responsibilities, and the little one will be left with you."

"Yes, mother. I understand. I'm ready to help in any way I can."

"I know you're willing, dear, but have you ever changed a baby's swaddling?"

Sarah had to admit that she hadn't. She had held a couple of Ezra and Fayed's young ones, but they all had wonderful nannies who didn't want any help. They knew their job description and had excellent references. Sarah couldn't claim experience.

"I thought so," said Eurochia matter-of-factly. "Well, you'll need this."

Eurochia and some of their older servant women had collected a small bundle of things for a newborn. Sarah was shown swaddling clothes, towels, and blankets.

"The best herb to wash the swaddling is crushed needles from a cedar tree. It gives it all a fresh smell. Find a good river to wash them in."

"I will, Mother."

"It is a lot of work, my child. You're taking on a big responsibility."

"I know, Mother. I wanted this. I've always wanted this."

"Yes, Sarah. I know you'll take this on, and I know you'll find your way. Trust your intuition. Don't be afraid to ask other mothers for advice. Every region has their own way of solving practical things, and it's usually a good solution based on what's readily available. You'll find the local mothers at the wells."

"Yes, Mother."

Sarah's head was filled with information about child care and the process of child birth. She knew there was still a while until the baby was due and she hoped they would come to a place where they could get help by that time.

At the moment she was enjoying her sister's presence next to her. Her own arm felt warm next to hers. Finally her wishes had come true. She was accompanying her sister instead of being left behind. Mariam couldn't have asked for a more devoted companion.

Ezra was with them on this trip, even though the ship had an excellent captain trusted by the family for years. Father Hiram had insisted.

"You deliver these two women at Oppidum Priscum Ra safely. I want to hear that they're under the care of the priests and priestesses there. Hopefully the child will be born at the Temple under the protection of the Sun God himself. Do come right back to Alexandria, even if you don't get a full load of cargo. I want to know that they are settled as soon as possible. And keep an eye on those two. They'll need to stay friends forever from now on."

Ezra wouldn't dream of doing anything else. Hiram appreciated his obedient son and wondered how he had gotten such unruly daughters.

The voyage took several days. They watched as the ship passed the islands of Cyprus and Sicilia. The beautiful islands had different vegetation than what they were used to near the deserts. The land turned greener as they came further north. The sisters stayed at the railing and marveled at the beauty of this new land as it appeared.

When they rounded Sardinia and followed its coast north, Ezra told them they were close. He wanted to prepare them, and told them of his observations of the ports he was familiar with.

"We will get you to the Temple of Ra on the island north west of Massilia. Then I'll go to Massilia and port there. You should visit the place if you have a chance. There are beautiful temples there, and a big forum. Just north of the island you're going to, inland, you'll get to Arelate, a magnificent city. They have both a theatre and an arena. A lot of Romans winter in Avenio. Glanum is a popular place. The Via Domitia goes through the area, all the way from Rome, and if you follow it to Narbo Martius you'll hook up with the Via Aquitania that takes you to the Atlantic Ocean. That's the road Joseph of Aramathea takes when he goes to Britannia for his tin trade. He usually ports in Ruscino, then goes over land to the Atlantic. He has boat contacts in Bordigate that will take him to Hibernia and Cornwall."

The sisters were listening with interest. They didn't know that their brother was so familiar with Gaul. They wanted to know everything he could tell them before he left.

"Ezra, promise, that, someday you'll take our parents to come and visit. I can't live thinking I'll never see them again."

"No problem, sister. We go this route quite often. Much more often then we go to Judea. But do be careful. If the Romans in Jerusalem didn't like you and Yeshua, word might have gotten to the garrisons here to watch out for you."

"I know, I know. I'll stay with the Egyptian Temples where I'm safe. As a priestess, I have protection."

"Didn't you have a Roman friend, Mariam? What was her name?" Sarah meant she had heard of a woman Mariam was close to at some point.

"Herodias? She is in Rome as far as I know."

"Lot's of Romans vacation here," Ezra chimed in. "You could ask around."

The possibility of meeting Herodias again brightened everything. It all depended on what the Romans had decided to do with Herod Antipas. The Romans were quite disappointed with his performance. They didn't want any dispute with the officials at the Temple in Jerusalem. The situation was tense enough as it was in Judea. The last thing they needed was one of their own creating troubles. Mariam still admired Herodias courage and clever revenge. Was there anything that woman couldn't do? Mariam realized that if Herodias wanted to be in Gaul, she would find a way to be here. She decided she would ask some questions when they arrived. The special bundles in her luggage also told her that it would be a good idea.

The ship was leaving the coast of Corsica and heading for Massilia. After some time in open sea they could see the southern part of Provence. Mariam admired mountains and forests. As they came closer she could identify tall trees which Ezra called pines. Sarah was pointing at the city of Massilia as they passed it. She definitely wanted to visit there.

"North of Massilia you'll find Aqua Sextiae. Prettiest city I ever saw. Dedicated to the arts. You'd love it."

Ezra felt like staying with them and showing them the country. But he had promised father to come right back. The girls would be safe at the temple, at least until the baby was born. Could he trust them that they would stay put? He wasn't sure about these two.

The island of Oppidum Priscum Ra appeared in front of them. The Temple could be seen from quite a distance, and the fort towards the ocean was apparent.

"Why the name Priscum? It means boat, or raft, doesn't it?" Sarah knew that Oppidum meant fort.

Ezra was, again, full of information. "It comes from the Celts, who came here first. They named it. The dedication to Ra came with Egyptians later. It is also dedicated to three Celtic goddesses of water."

Mariam liked that. She could relate to the honoring of water. It is the most important element we have, and she knew if that importance wasn't acknowledged, the water gods would revenge on the people. If it wasn't honored when it was present in a useful way, as in a well in the middle of the city, or as a holy well in a sacred place, it would dry up and then come back as a destructive force. The stories of old, of "bad" cities that had disappeared in a flood or a storm, were legends to learn from. She would be honored to pay her respect to the Celtic water goddesses.

Sarah was showing her usual excitement. She hugged Mariam for the fifteenth time today, and her feet got restless. Mariam just smiled, and admired her dark, curly hair in the light of the sunset.

The pier at the temple was too small to take in their big boat. The captain made anchor further out, and Ezra arranged for a smaller boat to be made ready for them. The sailors helped them with their bundles, and four sturdy rowers took them all to land. The people at the peer saw that they were getting visitors, and sent a message up to the temple. They could tell that these people were important, by the size of the boat they arrived in, and the transport that took them to land. By the time their boat reached the pier, a delegation from the temple was ready to meet them.

After introductions and hearing that she was temple trained in their own traditions, they were honored to have Mariam and her brother and sister visiting. They walked back to the temple conversing in their own language, which they were all grateful for. Most visitors would address them in Latin or Greek.

The sisters were given comfortable guestrooms and they were all invited to take part in the evening meal. Ezra stayed with them for the evening to talk to one of the priests about Mariam's situation. He needed to report back to his father that they were taken well care of. The priest understood, and even wrote a note for Hiram thanking him for sending his daughters to his care. Ezra left a substantial sum for the temple and promised more on a later return. The priest was more than happy to oblige.

The women were fed and happy. The journey had been pleasant enough, but they were both grateful to be back on land. Mariam appreciated being in someone's care after all the traveling she had done. She sent grateful greetings back to her parents, and wished that she indeed would see them again. Ezra hugged his little sister and promised to see to it someday. He couldn't say when.

They waved him away from the pier as he was rowed back to the ship. When they turned their backs to the ocean they were met with the silhouette of the temple against the sky. The many birds in the coastal area made their different calls.

"It is all welcoming us, don't you think?" Sarah asked.

"I think it is. I really think it is," said Mariam as she grabbed onto her sisters arm and squeezed it. She needed her support so intensely. The smile back told her that her sister would be at her side, in whatever form of support Mariam needed, for as long as Sarah drew breath.

Days went by with Mariam learning the ways of this temple. Being dedicated to Ra, she recognized the rituals. What fascinated her was that they kept the Celtic rituals as well. There was a mysterious underground space where the water goddesses were honored. Water went through there in its own channel and a there was a green light in the temple room coming through colored glass discs. Mariam was fascinated, but had only been there once, since the steps were slippery. She told them of her wise father in law, the druid, and how much she had learned from him. Some time in her life, she would love to visit his land of Hibernia.

"It is very different from the Camargue," the priestess told her. "Here they raise white horses and black bulls. The swamp lands have an incredible amount of wildlife of birds and animals that swim. Hibernia has animals bigger than cows, with huge antlers that live only on green food in the forest. They are big, but as long as you don't scare them, they won't hurt you."

"Not like the crocodiles of the Nile," laughed Mariam. "Watch out, or you'll be their meal."

There was so much to learn. Sarah secretly asked an older priestess to teach her more about childbirth. She wanted to be a little more prepared when the time came.

"Sweet child, as long as she is with us you have nothing to fear," said the old women. "We have welcomed numerous babies to earth here, and they all arrive a little differently."

Somehow that didn't reassure Sarah as much as she would have liked.

After a while Mariam felt familiar with the temple. She started to get restless for other scenery than the small island they had landed on. Thinking of her Roman friend, she realized that for her to travel more freely she would need some protection from a Roman official. The Temple couldn't keep them forever. And what would they do when Lazarus and Martha arrived?

Would they come? Would she see them here? Were they safe as they left Bethany? How would they get to the coast? Would they find passage? They were in the same danger as her. The Romans knew they belonged to Yeshua's inner circle. How large of a group could go safely with them? She sent her prayers for their safety.

As her thoughts formed questions, she felt answers coming. Her connection with Lazarus was profound after his initiation. She could feel his answers inside her. He told her it had been an adventure, but now they were safe and on their way. She got a vision of the people surrounding him, and they were quite a flock! *How are we going to provide for all these people?* Mariam suddenly saw new problems. Lazarus laughed back at her: *And how did we do that in Bethany, sister? We provided services and people paid us. We can do that again.*

Mariam looked at the country visible from the island. *We'll be in a new country with a new language where people don't know us or what we can do? It might not be as straight forward as you think,* she thought.

The temple needed supplies. Every week they went to the market in the city of The Mouth of the Rose, where the river Rhone met the sea. Mariam asked if she and her sister could join them. She wanted to set foot in this new country and felt it was time. The priests looked at each other. Was this safe enough for the Egyptian princesses in their care? Would their father approve? One of the younger priests offered to come with them, a well trained young man, both in scriptures and defense. The priests knew that he would be a friendly companion to the sisters, but that he also had his weapons and wouldn't hesitate to use them. They breathed a sigh of relief and told them when the boat would leave the following day.

It was great being at sea again, even if it was just the short trip into town. Felix was standing right behind them, watchful and ready in all his movements. Mariam sensed she was well guarded and was grateful for the priest's caution. She did her part, by making sure she and Sarah would wear simpler clothing to blend in better.

Sarah protested mildly. She liked to dress more colorful.

"We're princesses, aren't we?"

"Yes, but *we* know that. We don't need everybody else to know it today."

Mariam needed to go away from the island for a bit. She felt a little closed in, which she wasn't used to. She was curious about this new country they were going to live in and wanted to do her own investigations before more of her people arrived. The child was getting bigger, she had a harder time sleeping and got bored easily. Bashra had corrected her, and told her to be patient and remember whose child she was carrying. This wasn't just any little girl coming into the world.

She knew that. She knew it every day, every moment. She also knew nothing of his whereabouts, or how he was faring. While in Alexandria, she had been busy planning for a new beginning. The journey over had been filled with days reconnecting with Sarah. The time at the Temple of Ra had reconnected her with the powerful purpose of her life.

"Calm down," said Bashra. "Quit whimpering and get yourself in order. It doesn't help him that you're moping about. Take a day in town."

She decided to do as Bashra recommended. Sarah had asked who she was talking to, but this was not the time to tell her. Yochanan's head was securely packed away. She didn't know when she would communicate with him again.

All that could wait. Right now she was a young expectant mother at the market with her sister.

"Let's buy some fruit. I'm thirsty," said Sarah practically. "Remember, it's important for you to get enough fluids."

They looked at the displays of fruits, many were unfamiliar. After buying plums and apricots, they went to the herb tables. Mariam's nose was overwhelmed with the fresh scents. Such good quality, she was reminded of her years with Sibyl at the Serapium. Where was she now? Mariam had heard that she had left Alexandria.

"I need five bunches of this, my mistress only wants the best," she overheard a woman say next to her.

Mariam noticed that what she picked out was not the fragrant lavender, the rose extracts or the lilies, the most popular plants for perfumes. It was not anything you would use in cooking. The herb the woman wanted an unusual quantity of, had very few purposes. It was mostly used to create powerful unguents or scents used in rituals.

"Anything for the house of Herod," said the herb grower. "Is young Agrippa in town?"

"His step mother is visiting in Arelate. And between you and me, I'm glad she's alone. That Antipas was not a good man. Even the Romans didn't like him. She got rid of him, all right. I heard she made quite a scandal for him in Jerusalem. They can't return to the palace there ever again. The beautiful palace his father built. Fine with me. I thought the Judean's were difficult people. Stirring up riots here and there. Not understanding their place, if you ask me. Look at us here, we're from everywhere and we're getting along. Why couldn't they just make peace and go on with their lives? But no. Not the Judeans. Wanted to get rid of the Romans, they did. Not an easy task, I wanted to tell them. And look. We've got water running in aqueducts coming right into our houses. I tell you, the Romans know how to build, they do. We're better off, as far as I'm concerned."

The conversation went on, but Mariam had heard enough. After the woman had left, she picked up some herbs she wanted and decided to ask the herb grower further.

"Yes, they have a vacation place in Arelate, not far from here. We have young Agrippa here quite often. Nice young man. Sometimes we see his step mother with her beautiful daughter. But she never smiles, the young one. The mother is lively enough. Good customer. Knows her herbs, too."

Mariam could answer to that. The only one who knew more about herbs was Sibyl. She missed her two headstrong friends, so different from each other, and both so important in her life.

The thought of Herodias possibly close by made Mariam flutter inside. She wanted to go to Arelate and investigate. She patted her round belly and realized she wasn't going anywhere soon.

Back at the island, the temple was buzzing with activities. Another shipload of refugees had come ashore from the ocean. She heard questions from the servants as they were running back and forth. How many siblings do they have? How many more will come? Two princesses is one thing. A shipload of people is an entirely different situation.

Before she could think any further, she was swept up by big strong arms.

"Lazarus!" she said.

"Little sister, how big you've become," her big brother joked.

"We just arrived," said Martha. "How wonderful to see you well. You look radiant."

Mariam could testify that the temple took good care of her.

There were many guests in the dining hall tonight. Mariam was greeted by many familiar faces from the colony. She got the stories of how they had left and how they had ended here. Along with heroic stories, she also got sad news. Many had died in the process. The one she was most sad to hear about was Anya, Yochanan's wife. They had offered to take her with, but she didn't want anything to do with them. Little Yahya had come running to Martha while they were packing, looking like a small wild animal. His mother had been killed by the Romans when she couldn't answer their questions. They could see on the child that it had been brutal. He had hid in the desert until it was safer for him to run to them. They had buried her among their own, and little Yahya had been taken in by Martha. He was very quiet, but Mariam could sense that he was on the mend. The child avoided her though, and she wondered how much he knew.

The priests and priestesses were glad to have many guests, but they also inquired gently what their further plans were.

"We're planning to continue to Aquae Sextiae," Lazarus reassured them with a comforting smile. "One of our friends have settled there and invited us to stay with him until we found our own places. Our ship will take us to Massilia and we will arrange for transportation north from there. Ezra just insisted that we visited here with our sisters first. In her condition, it's best that she stays here until the child is born. We'll send for them when we are more established."

The priests were relieved. They welcomed guests, Egyptians were a treat to them, but they wanted everyone to be comfortable, and there was a limit to how many they could accommodate.

The banquet in the evening was a memory Mariam treasured the rest of her life. Most of her siblings were in the same room at the same time. There was a glow between the walls, and she told her little one inside to remember this night.

"Lazarus, tell me, how is he? What do you know?" Mariam asked her brother fervently when they had a moment alone.

"I've seen him," he said. "He is still recovering. This took more out of him than we thought. Nicodemus had him in his care for some time, but then Yeshua insisted on meeting with people again. You know how he loved his work."

She knew how much he loved his people. Tirelessly, continuously, insisting on meeting another flock, using the opportunity to heal another collection of hearts and minds. His coiled crystal device of course amplified his application, so he could be quite efficient, but he wore out his followers. He wore out her and he wore out himself. She wished he would understand the importance of rest and respect his own needs.

"He's traveling east, as far as I know. After meeting with several of the followers to make sure they knew he was alive, he gave instructions for spreading the knowledge and then he left," Lazarus continued.

"East, Lazarus? Where? Why?" Mariam tried to make sense of her husband's movements.

"The tension with the Romans had intensified. The priests at the Temple weren't any happier. The rumors of his empty tomb grew into a hero worship of the man who had defied death. We couldn't deny it. It was true. This new movement irritated the Romans and the priests even further. The Romans have a saying. *The only thing worse than a hero, is a dead hero.* This one wasn't just dead, he had *overcome* death. Yeshua's heroism was beyond martyrdom. His popularity was growing like a wildfire. For his own safety, he went underground."

"Will he come here?"

"...eventually, when all this has calmed down. But he needs to leave the Roman Empire entirely. You know how vast it is by now, it is hard to avoid. As far as I know, Uncle Joseph arranged for him to follow a caravan of spice traders who knew the route over the Zagyos Mountains."

"He is heading for India?" Mariam gasped.

"I think they mentioned Kashmir."

"That is very far away, Lazarus. There are many dangers on the way. Why would he undertake such a dangerous endeavor? He knows the child will be born soon. Doesn't that concern him?"

"Sister, that's what concerned him the most. The Romans aren't only after him. They are after his family. His mother got out with young John, the disciple, just in time. Father Joseph left with you, and is safe at the Temple of Serabit. Yeshua's brothers and sisters have all scattered, except for Johanna, who is with us. There are nobody left in Judea anymore. Some of them are with our group, some have already settled here in Gaul, and I intend to find them and connect everybody again. One brother of the flock is in Aquae Sextiae, and we want to start over there. I don't even know where they all are at this point."

"I didn't know how bad things had gotten."

"Mariam, he couldn't come to you, however much he wanted to. It would have put you and the child in danger. Yeshua is too well known. For a while he has to stay as far away from you as possible. India sounded like a good place. Nobody knows him there they way they do here, and the Romans are far away. He wanted to study their old traditions further. You know, he was there for a while when he was young. He's always been fascinated with the Hindus quiet, wise ways of living."

Mariam had to accept this, however much her whole being was screaming in protest. *I can only meet him in Arcadia,* she thought. *In Arcadia, then.*

She meandered through the halls of the temple looking for the quiet enclosed garden to sit down and collect her thoughts. There was laughter and people everywhere, she could hear them in other rooms. This had all happened so suddenly, so many changes so quickly. And her body was continuously changing. She figured she still had three weeks or so before the baby would be born, but she seemed to be getting bigger every day and she could feel the spirit of the child hovering around her. She needed to be alone.

Under the olive tree there was a stone bench. She slowly sat down supporting herself carefully and took in the scents of lavender and sage, rosemary and myrtle from the herb gardens close by.

Arcadia. How do we reach that place? She knew the concept of using it as a meeting place outside of time and space. *How do you access it?*

She needed to see him. She needed to talk to him. She needed to feel his familiar skin, feel the sensation of his gentle hand stroking her body.

She was stirred out of her thoughts by somebody entering the garden. It was Johanna, Yeshua's sister. Mariam smiled to her good friend and sister-in-law. It was a welcome interruption.

"Mariam, can I talk to you?" she asked gently.

"Of course, come, sit down." Mariam shifted a little on her bench to give her room.

"This is a lovely temple. I'm so grateful for their hospitality."

"They have been more than kind," said Mariam.

"I know Lazarus plans to take the people to Aquae Sextiae."

"That seems to be where he wants to settle. Bartholomew is there already."

"Yes." Johanna turned quiet.

"What's on your mind, dear, can you tell me?" Mariam took on the older woman's role.

"Mariam, I want to stay with you. You need extra help with the birth and the care of an infant. I know Sarah is at your side. She is so devoted to you. But she is young and inexperienced. I would love to help you."

"I'm honored. That would be wonderful, Johanna. Yes, do stay with us."

Johanna's decision came as an immense relief. Now she could do what she had wanted to take care of for a long time.

"Brother Niem, can I ask for your help?" She inquired one of the priests at the scriptorium the following day after Lazarus and his flock had left on the small boat that took them to shore. They felt that she would be safe staying comfortably at the temple of Ra while they met with Bartholomew and found the next step on their journey. They would send for her when they were more settled.

Ten days later a luxurious boat with a tent on top made berth at the temple. It had come down the river Rhone and had arrived to escort the revered Mariam of the temples of Serapium and Ephesus to the Roman villa in Arelate. A carriage with four horses would be waiting for them as soon as they reached the pier in Arelate which would take them to the estate of the house of Herod. The honorable Mariam and her two women in waiting said goodbye to the Temple of Oppidum Priscum Ra, and took the hands of handsome Roman soldiers, members of the personal guard of Herod Agrippa, who guided them into the luxurious boat and placed them on striped pillows in black and white with golden ribbons and tassels.

The three women were speechless, but Sarah smiled from ear to ear. Being treated like a princess suited her quite well.

CHAPTER 2

ARELATE

MARIAM HAD LIVED A RATHER QUIET LIFE most of her life, more in hiding than in the public eye. This reminded her of the trip to Leontopolis on the decorated barge from the Serapium. She wasn't totally comfortable being visible to such a degree. As they were floating up the river, people waived at them from the shore. The three women waived politely back hoping they were doing the right thing.

Food was served to them by beautiful servants, and when night time came they were offered comfortable places to lie down. The boat continued sailing noiselessly up the river while they all tried to sleep.

Mariam couldn't help wonder if she was taken prisoner or if this was done in her honor. With the Romans you could never know. She didn't know the current state of the house of Herod. The one thing she knew was that Antipas was no admirer of her. His son Agrippa, on the other hand, was known as a friendly youth, who adored his stepmother. Mariam felt safe. Everything was done for their comfort and there was no indication that this was a political move with an ulterior motive. She could sense an organizational talent of proportions. And she knew only one who could be behind it all.

After the boat had found its dock, they were escorted on land to a stately carriage pulled by well trained horses.

The carriage took them to the opulent mansion through the streets of Arelate. They passed the arena which announced the upcoming spectacles, the theatre where a new production was being readied, the baths, the forum and some temples. They could hear and smell the lively markets. The carriage followed the paved main roads, and people were waiving to the guests of the house of Herod.

The whole world knows that I'm here, thought Mariam. *Is that a good idea?*

They passed through a gate and into a courtyard. A carpet had been rolled out and a person in a white toga was standing there ready to welcome them. Mariam wished she was wearing something else than her black and purple capes, but Sarah made up for it with her colorful silks. Sarah had lent an orange shawl to Johanna which looked lovely against her auburn hair. What they lacked in style, they would have to make up for in dignity.

"The honorable Mariam of the Temples of Serapium and Ephesus, be welcomed here," announced the man on the steps. Mariam gathered it had to be young Herod Agrippa. She had never met him. He was away at university in Rome when she knew Herodias in Jerusalem. Now he was a handsome young man, and was actually welcoming them to his father's house, their summer home in the province.

The three women walked onto the soft carpet. Mariam led their procession with Sarah and Johanna right behind her. She bowed in acknowledgement of the warm welcome and followed Agrippa inside.

She had just put her feet inside the cool stone building when Herodias was around her neck.

"You're in Gaul! My best friend is in Gaul! Honestly, Mariam, I thought I'd never see you again. Did you have a pleasant journey? Johanna, how lovely to see you. I'm so glad you came. Mariam, you're with child! How immensely wonderful! Soon, it looks like. We'll take good care of you, won't we? And this must be Sarah, the favorite little sister. I can see you belong to the family."

Herodias was delighted beyond measure.

"And you all belong to my family now. There are women in the house! I have friends! I have new found sisters! This calls for celebration."

Herodias switched language. She'd been speaking Aramaic with them, but the servants spoke Latin and she gave some quick orders. In the lovely atrium with a fish pond in the middle, sitting groups were arranged underneath the portico. Green palms and refreshing herbs grew in pots, and flowering plants were hanging from the ceiling in tasteful placements. Servants brought drinks and culinary snacks to the table Herodias had pointed out, and the women were seated.

"Herodias, please tell the servants not to open my bags," said Mariam cautiously.

"Already taken care of. They don't touch anything belonging to a priestess."

Young Agrippa came and joined them. "I trust you had a pleasant trip? You are under my protection now. Please stay as long as you want."

Mariam couldn't thank him enough for his bold gesture.

"It was the best we could do. I would have loved to be on the boat myself, but we wanted it to look like you were Agrippa's guests, not mine," said Herodias. "So we did all we could to make it very clear that you're under the protection of Rome. I hope we didn't scare you."

No, they couldn't say they had been scared. Rather mesmerized with the display, they were all used to simpler ways of traveling. Mariam knew she would have to tell Herodias about her trek through the desert, about how the swinging movement of a camel felt to her pregnant body.

"See, it is now known that Agrippa has an honored guest, and your name will be famous as a welcomed person everywhere. If they ever figure out your connection with a Roman outlaw, you're still protected under our house and by extension the Roman Empire. Simple." Herodias finished with a flourish of her hand like a magician.

Mariam had to admit it was a brilliant move and quite beneficial for them, at least for a while. Somehow, she knew, this protection was temporary. Sarah wouldn't mind if it lasted, but her devotion told her that she would follow Mariam under much tougher conditions.

Finally, Mariam could relax. She allowed herself to luxuriate in the lovely bedroom allotted her, and relish her pregnant body. So far, her own safety and immediate concerns had been foremost on her mind. Even at the Temple to Ra, she knew it was a temporary situation. Here she was under powerful protection, in surroundings that overwhelmed with its beauty, and she was with women she loved. She stayed in her bed among silk sheets and embroidered blankets, enjoying her good fortune, much longer this morning than usual. Mariam found herself humming.

There was a knock on her door, which she answered with a smile, holding around a big soft pillow.

"How about some breakfast? Would you like to eat with me?" Herodias was asking.

"Please come in," Mariam answered with delight.

"I asked the kitchen to make my own favorites," said Herodias as she came in carrying a tray.

"Looks delicious. I'm really hungry."

Mariam rearranged herself in the bed, which required some work. Moving a pregnant belly has to be planned. Herodias laughed and helped her.

"You can laugh. You've been through this yourself."

"Yes, but that was many years ago, and I didn't have to travel across a desert on my own during the middle trimester. I was a whale in a palace surrounded by servants. You, my dear, have had quite a different experience. Enjoy this. Please."

"Thank you. What would I do without you?"

"Not much, but neither would I."

They laughed together, spilled some food in the bed, and behaved like silly school girls.

"Let's have an outing. Arelate has wonderful markets. My treat." Herodias was unstoppable.

The four women were given a carriage with two horses and two body guards. Sarah smiled like this was all normal to her, and Johanna giggled like she was in a dream.

Mariam was more concerned with getting all of herself included, and Herodias couldn't have been in a better mood.

She took them to the tailors with the best fabric collections, and they all were measured for new dresses. Mariam's old sense of style and fashion got rekindled, in a softer more subdued form rather than the flamboyant style of her youth. Sarah had taken over that role and advised everybody on colors and textures.

They went to a lovely restaurant for lunch and sat on the private back porch enjoying a couscous salad, samosas and tea. They all had stories to share.

Johanna, Martha and Lazarus had helped each other pack up their homes in the colony. The Romans had come several times looking for followers or family members of Yeshua. Johanna had said she was the servant. She couldn't believe that they actually wanted to eradicate them, annihilate them from the earth.

"It's not unusual for the family of a rebel to be treated that way," said Herodias. "I'm glad you were clever enough to divert them until you got out of there."

"Apparently we weren't interesting enough. We didn't have or do anything suspicious. I was happy to leave and find Ezra in Joppa. That boat trip to Alexandria was such a relief. We did get to see your parents, and visit your beautiful home."

"I'm glad," said Mariam.

"Did everybody make it out alright?" asked Herodias.

"We did lose some. Old Hannah got roughly handled and died from an internal injury. All the powerful healers were gone. I know some simple things, but this was beyond me. Most of the people they wanted left early without a trace. But Assan said some things he shouldn't to a Roman, and got a sword through him. We buried him there, in Bethany."

Herodias listened to the stories of everybody else, and even when probed she didn't want to say too much about her own experiences. But they did get out of her that Antipas had been sent as ambassador to a remote outpost in Africa. The Romans couldn't justify killing him, but they could give him a job he would hate. Young Agrippa took over his father's estates and they retired here, to her favorite place in Gallia. What she went lightly on was the harried days in Rome during the trial, when they were both in jail and treated like criminals. It had lasted for a year. She didn't know if she would have to accompany her husband to his fate, whatever it would be. There had been questions about the head of Yochanan. Where did it go after the drama at that fatal birthday party? She had expected something like that, and been prepared.

"What did you do?" Mariam knew her crafty friend would have thought of something.

"Shortly after I gave it to you, I created a substitute head."

"Really? Who?"

"An old servant died, and I simply used his. So now there is a useless oracle being touted as the real thing floating among the Romans. Even the best necromancers aren't going to make that one talk. I commanded it to silence. I am forever grateful to the old man. His head bought me freedom."

Only Herodias, thought Mariam to herself. *Only her. Besides, no prison could hold her for long.*

Sarah thought the talk had gotten too dark. She wanted to get back to the markets, or go back to the palace.

"I think I'm ready for a nap," said Mariam.

"You're entitled," the other three agreed.

Napping among silk sheets which had been refreshed since this morning, Mariam couldn't believe how fortunate they all had been. She thanked her stars and Venus in particular and understood how protected she was.

Some lovely days passed in the sweet fellowship of women. Johanna wanted to prepare for the birth, and brought needed supplies into Mariam's room. She insisted on doing some exercises with her that would ease the process. Sarah was in on every part of this, she wanted to learn. Her admiration for Johanna was endless, and she soaked up every word. *Good,* thought Mariam, and yawned. She felt another nap coming on.

Her early twinges started while she was sitting by the fish pond in the atrium admiring the movements of the fish. She had many voices talking to her now. Bashra had her opinions, the young life inside had a stronger sound, and every so often even Yochanan would give her some positive encouragement, even though she hadn't unraveled him for months. But right now, the only sound she heard was the fish waking in the pond, as she felt the first little pinch in her body. She had been warned about the first signals, which could come days and weeks before the right time, but somehow she knew that the process had started for real.

It didn't happen again in half an hour or so. She took a slow walk in the herb garden and taught the child the names and uses of the plants. After a while she found herself back at the fish pond, and Sarah came and asked how she was feeling.

"Fine dear, but the contractions have begun," Mariam said in her quiet way.

Sarah's heart leaped, but she stayed calm. She offered her shoulder for Mariam to lean on, and suggested they walked slowly around the atrium.

"Do you know all the symbolism connected to fish?" Mariam asked to have something else to focus on than the twinges that came every ten minutes.

"Tell me, sister," said Sarah, understanding Mariam's desire to think of something else.

"You know the hieroglyph for holy water? It looks like a fish hanging down. To create more of a code, they started putting it sideways. Then it looked more like a fish swimming. The ones with eyes to see would understand. To other people it would simply be a fish."

"I've seen that one. It is becoming a code between the followers too."

"Did you know that Yeshua was called the fisher of men? The hieroglyph for shepherd shows a man with a stick over his shoulder with that symbol on its end."

"Why a fisherman?"

"He had fished the mystical key, the key of Salomon out of the cosmic oceans. Yeshua enlightened people from within. He evolved them to another level of human functioning. They felt better. Things worked better for them. They felt more gratitude in their lives. They became mystical fish."

"How do you do that?"

"Have you ever seen somebody tune a stringed instrument?"

"Yes."

"It's the same technique. You tune the vibrations of the body to each other."

"How does that work?"

"In our body we have many glands that produce different chemicals. Each of them is responsible for an energy center. They also have a master controller in the middle of the brain. It is almond shaped, and the sign for it is the same as the fish without the tail."

"Yes?"

"This master controller is called the amygdala. If you can tune that one, it will tune the rest of the body. Yeshua knew how to find the frequency emanating from peoples brains, and improve it."

"Another fish symbol belonging to him."

"And to me," said Mariam. "That almond symbol also means light, the light shining from inside your body. It gets brighter the more in tune you are with yourself. It is also a gate. You can travel on that light. You see, within the human body, you'll find everything. Our bodies are capable of the most magnificent feats imaginable. And I am about to deliver another one."

Sarah understood that the time of the mystical discussions were over. She walked her sister back to her room and quietly ran off to tell the others.

Mariam was put to bed. She laid there feeling the work her body was doing preparing for the emergence of her child. Johanna had told her that first her body would work on shortening her vagina by pulling it up around the baby's head. She rounded her back and felt ripples follow her spine as her body did its own work, which she had no control over. She allowed the ripples to massage her energy centers and felt as if they were all checked over by the child. This little one wasn't going to leave without making sure her mother was in optimum health before she was on her own.

Herodias came in with extra blankets she insisted on putting underneath her on the bed. Mariam obliged all the while listening to Johanna tell her how far she was in the process. Sarah watched with wide open, serious eyes. Even Bashra was silent.

Mariam could feel the child move. Suddenly her water broke from all the pressure and warm liquid flushed out of her.

"Perfect!" Said Herodias. "Just what we needed."

She moved Mariam over a little bit and pulled out something from underneath her. "I used a sheep stomach to collect the water. It works remarkably well. I'll just put it aside."

The others stared at her for a moment, but then returned their attention to Mariam.

"I feel like standing up," she said and started getting out of bed. The help of gravity would bring the child down. Herodias supported her as she walked around the room. Mariam started to make powerful noises. Her attention was totally tuned with the child now. The center of her thinking rested below her heart. Sarah came and stood on her other side. Johanna came with more blankets and put them on the floor. Mariam put an arm around the shoulders of her sister and her best friend, widened her stance on the floor and squatted down in front of Johanna. It felt like a very large fish was squirming out of her body. *Welcome to the world, little fish*, thought Mariam as she made a loud guttural sound and felt the child freeing itself and landing in the capable arms of her aunt.

Soon mother and daughter were back in the bed, clean and fresh. The baby was nursing and Mariam was beaming.

"What's the name of the new little princess?" asked Sarah, with a tear, ready to give up her own title.

"Your name means Princess. You'll always be the little princess of our family."

"She is beautiful," said Johanna.

"How could she be anything else, look at her mother," said Herodias, admiring the glowing radiance emanating from Mariam.

"Her name is Sarah Tamera. She is the princess of the land of love and wisdom."

Sarah cried silent tears of joy. Her new little niece was named after her. She would love this child forever, she knew that.

Johanna smiled without words. *She named her after her own country*, she thought. *The new princess will have powerful protection.*

A deep sigh was heard through the room. All was well with the world.

CHAPTER 3

THE TEMPLE OF DIANA

"I HAVE A PLACE RIGHT HERE IN ARELATE that will be perfect. Let's plan it for the full moon. Venus is a morning star now, so she won't be visible."

Mariam had wanted to do this, and she knew she needed the help of Herodias. This was work for two priestesses.

At the night of the full moon, they let a much less ostentatious carriage take them through town. They were on an ox cart.

"How come you always find the right mode of transportation?" Mariam asked.

"You have to be good at telling convincing stories, and quick at making them up as you go."

They were dressed in simple clothing with gray shawls over their heads. Little princess Tamera was with, also wrapped in indistinct brown and gray blankets. They had a couple of bundles with them, and looked like any women from the countryside.

Mariam recognized the man in the front of the cart with the reins. It was Aiu, the caretaker of the herb garden.

He is very discreet, answered Herodias in her head. *He's helped me numerous times. After I healed his wife from a deadly infection, he doesn't question anything.*

They arrived at the small temple. It was open for anyone to use since there was no priestess on duty. People came there on their own to honor the goddess, one of the many versions of the great Mother.

It was smaller then Mariam had thought. A graceful roman arch was at the entrance. Inside, there were steps up to the platform where the statue of the goddess stood. Herodias hadn't said much about what she was planning. Mariam was wondering what she had agreed upon.

Mariam carried the baby and Herodias picked up their things. Aiu took the heavier items and carried for them. He walked with them inside the building and stopped by the sculpture of the Roman goddess Diana waiting for further orders.

"Isn't she pretty?" said Herodias after she formally greeted the goddess as an official priestess. Mariam mirrored her movements in respect. She recognized Diana as the Greek goddess Artemis, who had again been inspired by the Egyptian goddess Hathor.

"This is where we're going," said Herodias and headed down some stairs that went down on the left. The others followed.

At the bottom of the steps there was water. A well brought up fresh water from the ground. The basin was probably ten feet in a square, Mariam figured. There was a curious light coming through the water, a green, clear glow moving with the small ripples across its surface.

Herodias thanked Aiu for his services, and asked him to come and pick them up in a couple of hours. He politely bowed his head and left them.

"We want to use the underground temple on the other side of the water," said Herodias practically.

Mariam looked for an entrance that would seem to take them there, but didn't see any.

"Remember Ephesus? You visited the Celtic temple to the water goddesses on the island of Ra? Come on, Mariam, don't be dense. We have to go through the water."

"But we have the baby with, and our things, it will all get wet," Mariam protested. One thing was going through water wearing a thin shift and arrive at a temple in the protection of a row of priests and priestesses. That ritual had felt protected. This temple belonged to the wrong tradition, and they had a living little being to think of. Sometimes she didn't' understand her friend at all.

"I've brought oiled cloth bags for our things, they will survive. And babies actually swim. We will only be under for a moment. We'll put oiled cloth around her too."

Before Mariam could say anything more, their bundles were efficiently waterproofed, and a stiff cloth was handed to her to wrap Tamera in.

"Just blow on her face, she'll close her nose."

Mariam prayed to Venus to keep her sane, and to keep them all safe, as they walked slowly down towards the water. At the end of the stairs, she put her feet in the water, which was surprisingly warm, and watched as Herodias continued into the water as if there was no change of elements from the air.

"Look here," said Herodias turning back at Mariam with water up to her waist. "The wall ahead ends a couple of feet below the water. All we have to do is duck under it and come up on the other side. We'll only be under for a moment."

Mariam walked dutifully down the stairs in the water and felt it crawl up her skirt. She lifted the baby higher as she came closer to Herodias.

"Listen, I'll go under first and then you'll see how deep it is. You'll have to swim a little. Squirt some water on Tamera's face and face her down in the water. Then you come down yourself, get under the wall, come up and hand her over to me."

Mariam tried a few drops. Tamera didn't seem to mind too much. She watched as Herodias went underwater, swam a few strokes and disappeared under the wall. It really wasn't far. She didn't know how far it was on the other side. She went as far into the water as she could herself, then she put more water on the baby's face, blew on her to make her close her nose, and pointing her in front of her, she swam some strong strokes down, underneath the brick wall and up again. Herodias was ready and received Tamera as she was shooting out of the water. Mariam came panting after.

"This is the craziest thing you have ever done!" Mariam sputtered water and accused her friend. Then she looked beyond Herodias, and saw the mysterious space they had entered. Even Tamera quieted when she got interested in the beautiful light surrounding them.

Mesmerized with the green light, they found a new set of stairs underneath their feet and walked up and out of the water. They stepped out of the basin where the water was kept and continued down some wider, prettier steps on dry land. Mariam looked back and realized that the basin they had come through was quite small and insignificant compared to the magnificent space they had entered.

The light came through a green, round glass disc in the ceiling. The moon shone through and bathed it all in green light. The room was much larger than the small temple visible from the top. It was shaped like a small amphitheater with a stage area as the center. They were now walking down the steps towards the stage. Twenty eight steps Mariam counted.

The backdrop for the stage had a gabled front and pillars holding it up, all placed on a shelf higher than the stage floor. Herodias headed for the pillars and started opening up bundles. The space was surprisingly warm, and Mariam's wet clothes didn't feel too uncomfortable. She unwrapped little Tamera and sat down to nurse her and calm both herself and the child.

Herodias unwrapped their bundles. First she handed them both dry robes to wear. She had brought a brassier and herbs to burn, and a seashell for a water container. A thick blanket with a woven pattern in red and gold was laid on the floor. The brassier got placed in the middle and started. Soon they could smell the incense she had chosen. Mariam recognized the herb the servant woman had bought at the market. The sea shell was filled with another liquid and placed next to it. Mariam wondered what it was. *Remember what I collected in the stomach of a sheep?* Herodias sent to her. Mariam nodded. *An important ingredient for tonight.* She admired Herodias sense of placement as all the pieces got put on the blanket and she lit four oil lamps she found among the pillars and placed them in the corners of the fabric.

"Mariam, it's your turn. I'll hold Tamera for you."

Herodias had found and created the setting. It was Mariam's turn to bring the ritual together. First of all, she drew a circle with a stone around their space to protect them. Mariam liked natural settings better, then she didn't have to work with the culture already present in the place. The vibrations in this place felt friendly. She stopped fretting. This would work fine.

Mariam picked up the round bundle, and carefully allowed Yochanan to emerge. He seemed grateful to be allowed to participate. He was placed along one of the sides of the fabric. Out of her own herb bag she pulled the small head of Bashra and placed it on her stand along another side. Mariam created a pillow out of another length of fabric and placed it closer to the brassier. She motioned for Herodias to bring Tamera, and the baby was placed on the pillow where she could look straight at the green eye in the ceiling and watch the play of light by the moon. She stretched up her hands to touch the light beams.

Mariam and Herodias took the other two sides left of the space they had created. They started the intonations that would awaken their companions. Yochanan opened his eyes and took in the tableau in front of him. He sent his blessings to the new baby, and continued singing the tone they had established. His bass voice harmonized nicely with Herodia's soprano and Mariam's lower range. Bashra opened her eyes too, and blinked towards Tamera before she intoned with her deeper voice.

"Oh Isis and Osiris," sang Herodias.

"Oh Tammuz and Inanna," sang Mariam.

"See the holy water we have brought to you."

"It surrounded this child before she was born."

"Oh Venus"

"Oh Ursa Major"

"Oh Akasha"

"Oh Arcadia"

"We beseech you"

"Send the father of this child through the mists"

"Let this child know her father"

"Allow this mother to meet her husband"

"Through the mists"

"Through open space"

"Through open time"

Mariam used the silent sound Father Joseph had taught her to summon the mists.

The smoke from the brassier changed and became moist. The mists formed and surrounded them, but it stayed within the wide circle Mariam had drawn.

A red light appeared among the flames of the brassier. The orange flame shot up but gave no heat. Inside it they saw the tall shape of a body. Slowly it formed a face and features. Mariam felt his presence in her body. His energy flowed through her from the bottom of her spine, along every vertebra and through the top of her head. She gasped and exhaled.

The figure in the flame opened his eyes and looked at her. Mariam almost jumped into the flame, but he put an arm out and said silently: *No, sit still dear. You're holding the space. I'll disappear if you move.*

Herodias recognized Yeshua's features and bowed to him in respect and recognition. He bowed to her in gratitude for her help. Mariam blew more mists out of her mouth. Yeshua stepped a foot out of the flame and touched the water in the seashell.

Suddenly he became solid. His skin left the field of red flames and took on his normal tones and he fell out of his hold in the air and landed clumsily on the floor in a fetal position.

Mariam wanted with all her heart to come to him, but she was afraid the apparition would go away, and she couldn't bear that. Yochanan and Bashra had kept their tones and Herodias provided the overtones. Mariam did her best to fall back in with the chanting.

Slowly he moved, finding his limbs. He sat himself up on the floor and shook his head. "What a way to travel. I didn't know it would work this well. Mariam, wife, where are you?"

She was here. It was him. She could feel him. Carefully she stretched an arm out and met his hand. It was warm and soft, and gentle. He scooped her up in her arms and they rolled to a bundle on the floor laughing.

Herodias quietly went over to the baby and lifted her up. She sat down ready to offer the child to her father.

"Yeshua, she is here, our daughter. I named her Sarah Tamera, like we talked about," Mariam said gently after wiping her eyes.

Carefully Herodias placed the beautiful infant in her fathers arm. Again they all had a sense of that all was well with everything.

They heard about his travels in India and Kashmir. The beautiful people he had met, how open they were to his teachings. How wonderful it felt to be far away from the turbulent Roman Empire. "But I understand you've been living in luxury since you came here. Well fitting for the arrival of a Princess," he said and lifted the cooing infant high in the air. "Thank you, Herodias, for everything."

Mariam sat next to him holding around his arm. She looked at his skin and saw that he had healed beautifully. There were some scars, but they had all grown over nicely, thanks to Nicodemus and Uncle Joseph and a hundred pounds of aloe vera.

Herodias noticed the light emanating from his body. It lit up the whole space for them. *So it was true.* He taught people how to enlighten their bodies. Herodias didn't think she'd ever seen a more beautiful man. She sat quietly, taking in the beauty of the family in front of her, the perfection of the mother, father and child. It brought her to a peaceful, golden silence which she remembered in her heart for the rest of her life.

They didn't see the other helpers they had in this undertaking. Behind them there were angelic beings hidden in the shadows. Isis and Osiris were represented, so was Innana and Tammuz. There were endless circles of beings creating protective fields around them.

Yeshua got to hold his daughter, play with her, coo with her. The child made lively movements with her arms and legs, communicating her joy back to her father. Mariam stayed close by and held around them both.

After a while she noticed that her hand could reach into his body. He was leaving his solid state. It was time to send him back.

Mariam cried, but she knew what she had to do. She picked up Tamera from his hands before she floated to the floor, and handed her to Herodias. Then she made sure that everything was in place and stirred the brassier again.

Yeshua stood up and thanked them all for making this possible. To his cousin Yochanan he bowed in the greeting of Namaste, the most respectful gesture he had learned on his travels. "The God in me recognizes the God in you," he whispered as silver luminescent tears ran down his glowing cheeks.

As the tones were again vibrating the underground space, Yeshua stepped into the flames of the brassier before he turned totally into ether. The flames became red and tall before disappearing in a flash and Mariam fell on the floor and cried a flood of tears.

In silence they packed up their things and found their way back through the water. The bundles Herodias had left on the steps contained dry clothes for all of them. They walked through the temple of Diana and silently thanked her for making her space available for them on a moonlit night. Aiu was waiting for them with well fed oxen He did not ask why some of the oilcloth bags now seemed to be dripping.

Little Tamera fell asleep at her mother's breast and slept through the night dreaming of stars and galaxies.

CHAPTER 4

AQUAE SEXTIAE

"You really didn't have to do this," Mariam would never get used to traveling in style.

"My dear friend, I'm going to Massilia anyway, why shouldn't I give you a ride?" Herodias couldn't see any reason for Mariam to complain. She was enjoying herself tremendously. What was the sense of being rich if you couldn't enjoy it?

Sarah had helped them all into their new gowns. They were quite a colorful group in the open carriage, waving to the public.

We look like cackling hens, Mariam thought. *It doesn't matter if our chicken coop is gilded.*

Johanna was holding the baby. Little Tamera had left the stage of being an infant. Now she was a baby and was quite interested in her surroundings. She was wearing a colorful dress, as well, fit for a princess.

"Egyptian silk. Only the best for my niece," Herodias had said.

So the baby was parading in orange and pink matching with her favorite aunt Sarah. Aunt Johanna was in green and orange, and Aunt Herodias in yellow and light green. Mariam had finally given in to orange and purple. They were all in the latest styles from Rome. At least that's what the tailor in Arelate had said. Sarah had been delighted, Johanna mesmerized and Mariam had sighed. Herodias hadn't had this much fun in years. She didn't tell them that when the time in prison in Rome was over, she had needed a long time to recover. These women's company was an elixir of life to her.

They were on their way to Aquae Sextiae to visit with Lazarus and the family. They had sent a message that they were coming, and that they were eager to show them the new child.

In Aquae Sextiae, Lazarus and Martha has established a home for themselves and a small colony was growing with followers. They all worked in their own professions, but gathered for meals and inspiration. Knowledge of these peoples way of healing spread in the city, and people came to them for help.

"Weather it's a problem with their body, their relationship to their family or to

306

God, we treat it all pretty much the same way," said Lazarus. "We teach them about love, and how love creates harmony."

Most people seemed to think they were doing miracles. Those who understood more wanted to learn and Lazarus wanted to teach. Their group grew.

The news of expected guests excited everybody. Martha was preparing for their arrival. She wondered if Herodias would stay too, and worried about how to accommodate for her. After all, she was Roman, how was that going to be perceived? And how would their simple living sit with her fine ways?

The Romans hadn't found a problem with the new group in Aquae Sextiae. They were left alone, and if the Romans knew whom they had learned from, they didn't say anything. Yeshua seemed to be a forgotten case in Gallia, and Lazarus hoped that it would stay that way. He mentioned his teacher often, but new code words became established. He was called by all his attributes instead of his name. *Those with ears to hear will understand,* thought Lazarus.

The carriage and horses had some trouble getting into the narrow streets where their people had settled. The driver maneuvered gingerly, and people cleared way for the stately roman vehicle. The commotion outside made Martha run into the courtyard to see. She told young Joses, Yeshua's youngest brother, to help her open the gates. They pulled it open as wide as possible, and the carriage managed to get inside. People were standing around to see who these fine people were, who would arrive with such fanfare.

Martha hadn't expected all this, but she found solutions for care of horses, driver and guests. Sarah and Johanna stepped right in to help. Martha liked giving orders, and she had a whole colony of people who were willing to help, both because they wanted to help Martha, who was much loved, but also to gawk at the guests. Words went around about who they were, what they were wearing and who the fine Roman lady was. Herodias was much pleased. She wanted it to be known that this group of people was accepted by the Romans. She was running a political campaign more than offering a day's ride through the countryside.

The meal that evening was splendid. They used the courtyard of Bartholomew and Celia and set up tables everywhere. Young Yahya had moved in with them. They had more space and no child of their own. Martha had a lot to oversee, but welcomed the boy any time. The driver was invited too and had stories to tell when he returned to Arelate. "These people live with no distinction between them. The head priest and his priestess sat with everybody else. I got to talk to the blacksmith, and he said that was how they lived."

Herodias sat next to Lazarus and laughed. The light hearted atmosphere among her friends was heart warming. She also met other Roman ladies who had joined the group. They were invited for this evening. Martha had made sure that Herodias could stay with Juliana, and Lucilia was there as well. They both had welcomed these people into their homes and supported them among their own. Herodias saw that this group was well established. She started looking for other ways to help.

The following morning Herodias stopped by at Lazarus before continuing to Massilia. She found Mariam and Sarah with Johanna and Martha in the kitchen feeding the baby.

"Look, she likes this cereal Martha made," said Mariam proudly presenting the princess with a satisfied smile. Martha was holding a glass, drying it with a towel before putting it away. She didn't need to say anything. Her world was complete.

"That's lovely," said Herodias. "Good girl," she patted her favorite niece on the head.

After some pleasantries about the previous evening and how well they'd done getting established, Herodias said what was really on her mind.

"Mariam, would you like to come with me to Massilia? Leaving you all here right now is a little abrupt for me. I need to ease off having you around. Tamera comes with too, of course. We'll be back tomorrow, and then I'll return to Arelate."

Massilia was a shorter distance than to Arelate, it was located straight south of Aquae Sextiae. Herodias had to go through Aquae Sextiae on her way back, following the excellent Roman road system. Massilia was an older port and had the grime and dirt of an older city. Herodias was on an errand for Agrippa regarding shipping. She knew which office to go to and who to speak with.

The others thought it was a good idea and encouraged Mariam to enjoy the trip. Martha asked her to pick up some things she needed for the kitchen.

They left the following day, and after half a day of traveling, they reached Massilia. Inside the city, Mariam asked to be let off at the market while Herodias did her errands. She tied Tamera to her waist with a shawl and went looking for herbs. Herodias pointed her in the right direction. It wasn't hard, Mariam could follow her nose.

She passed the fish market, the meat stalls, and the fruit market where she bought peaches for herself and bananas for her daughter. The herbs and spices had a section to themselves. She passed the cheese mongers and entered the town square set aside for all things aromatic. The scent of roses and lavender, coriander and cinnamon tickled her nose. Servants were there looking for flowers to decorate their masters homes, spices for the kitchen and medicinal herbs for the household cornucopia. She saw well trained hands checking quality and freshness. Every herb needed to be harvested at the right time. Their quality depended on how well the grower understood the balance of ripeness of the plant and ideal time for harvesting. The phases of the moon had a strong influence on plants. Some you wanted at full moon to give them that flavor, some you wanted at dark moon to give them that strength. Only a well trained grower could stay on top of it all.

Mariam stopped at the fresh flowers and showed Tamera the colors. "I'll teach you everything I know," she told the child.

Herb bundles were laid out on a table as well as hanging from strings above. Mariam had passed several tables she didn't feel were up to her standards, and stopped at one that looked promising. She picked up a bundle of origen and saw that it had been harvested with a scythe, not picked by hand. The plant had grown in a meadow, not along the road where you could easily find them. Next to it was marjoram, the same plant but another variety which only grew in cultivated form. "The plant of Osiris," Mariam whispered to herself. "I'll buy some for Martha's bread. And here is myrtle, the plant of Venus."

She couldn't help herself, but lifted the herb to her face. "And harvested to perfection, at the full moon to give strength to new brides," she whispered as she closed her eyes to take in the full aroma.

She noticed a bundle of sage hanging above her and stretched a hand up to check the leaves, not brittle, not too dry, but still moist on the inside having been cut and hung at the right time for optimal juice retention.

Mariam turned her head to give her compliments to the grower. This was the same quality they produced at the Serapium.

She stared right into big blue eyes with a bundle of blond hair on top. Tears were running down the cheeks as the other woman took in the beautiful mother and child in front of her.

"Don't say my name," she whispered before Mariam could say anything.

Calmly, Mariam walked around the booth and was greeted with long arms that encompassed both her and her child. They both wanted to say everything at once, but couldn't. They knew that with time the stories would come, and they knew they did not want to be separated again. Mariam sensed that Sibyl had experienced a darker story since she had seen her last. There was pain and fear in her eyes, which she tried to cover up. Mariam knew she would have to be patient. It didn't matter. They were together now. Mariam invited Sibyl to join her among her people, and Sibyl was happy to accept.

Herodias was waiting for them at the water fountain when they returned. Sibyl had to tell the herb farm owner that she was leaving. He was sad to see her go. Sage was the best help he'd ever had.

"Trym will take over. I've been teaching him for a while. Thank you for hiring me, "said Sibyl.

"Not everybody has someone from the Serapium working for them," said her employer with pride. "And now I can say that Trym has been taught by a master from the Serapium." Suddenly the herb grower was quite pleased. "I'll have Trym send your things to your friends in Aquae Sextiae."

"Sage? That won't do. You're much too pretty to be named after a common herb. We'll just change your name to Cybelle and say you come from Gallia," said Herodias. "You look light enough to pass for a Visigoth." Herodias was looking forward to dress her in blues and help her with her long, blond hair.

Back in Aquae Sextiae, she was welcomed back. Mariam thought it was good to get the attention off herself and Tamera for a while, and enjoyed watching her friend be taken in so warmly. Several of them had met her in Alexandria many years ago. Martha noticed a nervous movement in Sibyl's eyes and wondered what she could possibly be afraid of.

Herodias was preparing to go back to Arelate, but her head was on something else. She decided to stay for another day.

The colony was getting bigger. *Too big,* thought Martha. It was time to spread out.

"Didn't the Lord tell them to preach everywhere? So why were they all together here," she'd like to know. Lazarus agreed, and they brought it up for discussion. There were many things to consider. Who would go, and where would they go, and where could they go safely.

"We know the people at the temple of Ra. There are also temples to Diana where we would be welcomed. Many of the oppidums still have Celtic priests who would welcome us to share information. Any of those would be a start. There are also settlements of the tribes west in Narbonensis. That's close to where Joseph of Aramathea usually ports to reach Via Aquitania which will take him to the Atlantic Ocean." Lazarus had good information and wanted his people to know many options.

"There are also places along via Domitia to the east that might be open for us." Joses was always a welcome voice among them. The young brother of Yeshua had grown up among them and had become a young man of few words, but deep wisdom.

"But that's towards Rome. We don't want to go there," Martha chimed in.

"We don't have to go very far. This province is large in many directions, and I find the landscape very inviting. The road is there and makes access easier. "

"Let's listen. He has been wandering the countryside," Lazarus encouraged his brother-in-law. "We've seen his well worn walking stick."

"I wanted to tell Mariam and Sibyl that there are lavender fields growing wild around here. I'm not well versed in herbs, but that one is easy to spot. I've walked through more naturally good smelling fields around here than I ever did in Judea. What I saw didn't even look cultivated. There must be some land around here where you could get a field started."

Herodias had also listened in on the discussions. She knew that without well grown herbs, Mariam could not do her work. She also knew that Sibyl had become the best herb grower outside the big temples. What was bothering her? Herodias had noticed that she went into hiding whenever she saw a Roman soldier. She'd been thinking about all of this, and the solution was starting to form.

"Mariam," she said at the end of the day. "I have a suggestion for you."

Mariam sat down with Herodias with baby Tamera on her lap.

"You know I can't come back to Arelate with you," she said.

"I know, dear, I have something totally different in mind. Listen. I have friends along Via Aurelia. It comes off Via Domitia, not too far east from here. Joses probably already knows where I mean. Suzanna and Gaius live in Villa Lata. It is a large farm, and they have olive and fruit groves. I have written a letter of recommendation for you to take to Suzanna. She'll remember me from all the times Herod Philip and I came this way on our way to the estate in Arelate before I was married to Antipas. Our children played together. Young Salome was quite popular with them. Ask about their son Markus. They were about the same age. I have recommended you two as expert herb growers. It seems that Joses wants to go with you too, so I included him as well. What do you think?" Herodias was waiving a big envelope with a Roman seal on the back in front of her.

"But Herodias,…"

"Don't protest. I need the herbs you two can produce, so does Suzanna. If you live on the estate of Villa Lata, I'll know where to find you."

Herodias went back to Arelate, and after some weeks of discussion, things were decided. Mary and Jacob from the colony of Bethany, would go towards Oppidum Priscum Ra and establish a new community in the town on land called The Mouth of the Rose. They wanted to spread out the family members of Yeshua, for their safety sake. If somebody were searching for them, they wouldn't find all of them in the same place. Salome, Yeshua's sister decided to go with Mary and Jacob.

Mariam and Sibyl were going to go east with Joses and present themselves at Villa Lata to start an herb farm. They needed to be able to make the essential balms and unguents from their own sources, and with Herodias' letter they hoped to be welcomed there.

"And you know I'll go with you," said Sarah. "Little Tamera needs me."

"And you need someone to take care of your household. I'm coming, too," said Johanna.

Sarah and Johanna had become inseparable friends. Sibyl was a hard worker. It seemed natural that Mariam and Joses would become the heads of the household. Mariam suddenly felt she had a lot of responsibilities. How would the Roman lady of Villa Lata feel with this whole flock arriving at her door?

As they were all preparing to go and two wagons were being packed in the courtyard, a man came asking if they had some work for him or if they knew where Sage had gone. He had some things for her. Mariam overheard him, and turned.

"My name is Trym," said the man. "I'm looking for the woman who taught me to take proper care of an herb garden. These are her tools."

Sibyl came out of the house and recognized him. She turned white, and immediately ran back inside. People saw her running through the house and hide in a garden shed.

Lazarus went out in the garden and called Martha and Mariam to him. After some coaxing they got Sibyl out of the shed.

"I think it's about time we hear your story, Sibyl. We don't have secrets from each other in our community. What are you running from?"

Sibyl was crying. She was scared of the authoritative tone Lazarus had taken, but she was even more scared of them sending her away. And she was deadly afraid of something else.

"I'm wanted by the Romans. I can never return to Alexandria."

"But why? Why would they want to arrest you? Is there trouble at the Temple?"

"Yes, I'm in trouble there, too. The Romans want to arrest me, and if they do, I'll be executed."

"What? Why? What have you done?"

"I killed my father."

Now they were all silent. The Romans were tough on murder, even of a less important person. And if it was done by a murderess, the case got even more attention.

"My dear, what did you do?" Lazarus used a very gentle voice now. He wanted her to tell her story and understood that this was a sensitive subject.

Mariam knew some of her story. It was told to her at a time when she couldn't listen.

Sibyl's young sister, Muir, had come to the Temple and asked her for help. The father was after her all the time. If he couldn't force himself on her, he beat her for being disobedient, or he threatened her with taking one of the even younger sisters instead. Once he had, and insisted that she watched. The mother had listened to the screams and continued her housework with the same vacant face. Muir promised to be pliable after that. She could bear him, more than watching the younger sister suffer.

She came to Sibyl because she was pregnant with her father's child, and he wanted her to get rid of it. He didn't like pregnant bellies, and there were enough children in the house. He wanted Muir to satisfy him in other ways instead, until she could get rid of that monstrosity inside.

So Muir and Sibyl made a plan. First Muir would get her father used to fancy oils and creams and Muir's well oiled fingers. They would keep the pregnancy so that he would find her repulsive, and say they were working with herbs that worked slowly. All the while Sibyl would create more exotic oils and creams.

The first ones were lovely. Smooth, silky and aromatic lubricating creams perfect for Muir's small hands to be creative with. The little sisters were spared.

Mariam felt faint when Sibyl described what she had used for the last oil. She had instructed Muir carefully on how to use it. First she needed to put another cream on her own hands to protect her from it, and afterwards she needed to use another strong liquid to wash it off her fingers.

"Otherwise it will eat your skin up," said Mariam.

"Not only your skin," said Sibyl triumphantly.

Muir had done what she'd been told. She covered as much of her fathers genitalia and the area around with the poisoned cream as she could while massaging him, and left him alone to sleep after he was done. Then she ran to wash it all off her hands. His screams when he woke up was worse than his daughters had been while he tortured them. It was all gone. As he rose to check, his testicles had fallen out of the holes in their pouch, and his member had shriveled up and fell off in pieces. Between his legs he now had a gaping hole and the cream was continuing its work inside his body. He fainted from the pain while the daughters stood around him watching in silence as he rolled around, screaming on the floor. His body continued to squirm until enough of his insides had burned away and he died from internal bleedings.

Muir had immediately taken her two little sisters and run to the Temple. They presented themselves as orphans and were taken in, but Sibyl had to flee. The neighbors had alerted the guards in the city. There was now a hunt for a powerful sorceress who had learned her craft at the temple. She could murder people, in the most despicable ways. What was the temple teaching these days?

"Oh, Mariam, it was awful. The Temple got accused of teaching horrible things, and it was all my fault. I hid in a ship at the pier and it brought me to Massilia. I was lucky. At the market I saw the herb grower, and he needed help. I've lived in the garden shed on his farm for three years. Trym knows I'm running from something, but he doesn't know what."

It was silent for a long time. Martha rose and started to make tea. Mariam put an arm around Sibyl's shoulder. Lazarus tried to comprehend the cruelty that exists in the world.

In the courtyard, Trym had fed and watered the horses, loaded all their luggage and gardening equipment, and spoken to Joses who definitely thought they could use another able hand as they established a new herb farm, especially one who had been well trained by a priestess from the Serapium. They sent a note to the herb grower about their decision and promised to supply him with high quality merchandize.

CHAPTER 5

VILLA LATA

JOSES HAD WALKED THESE HILLS. HE HAD seen where Via Aurelia went off towards the mountains, away from Via Domitia, which continued towards Rome. The road was well built and easy to follow with their wagon. The horses were relaxed and glad to be out in the pleasing landscape. They passed Roman Villas up on the hills, well tended olive groves and wild lavender fields with small creeks. After following the valley for a while, they caught sight of a taller mountain further east.

"That's Mount Aurelia," said Joses. "Via Aurelia will be visible when we have the mountain on our right."

Martha had packed some food for them, and they stopped and ate along the wayside. Johanna spread out the blanket and opened the basket from Martha. Sarah tended to Tamera. Trym tended to the horses and checked the wagon. Joses walked a little higher up the hill to get an overview of the road and Sibyl and Mariam went with him and checked the natural vegetation in the area. Then they all gathered around the blanket to eat.

Mariam looked at the flock gathered around her. She thought of the trust they all showed, the hopes they had for this plan to succeed. Her deep gratitude to them all gave her tears. She could see years of hard work ahead of them. She also saw no Roman soldiers on the road. The pleasing landscape was soothing. Mariam took a deep breath and felt the warm breeze blow through her hair.

Joses was right, it wasn't very far. They arrived at Villa Lata around dinnertime. Mariam asked a servant to guide her to Lady Suzanna. She had a letter for her from Herodias.

"Oh, do come in, dear. Your reputation precedes you."

Mariam wondered how this noble woman could know anything about her, but greeted her politely and was invited into a stately room.

"Sit down, oh, do sit down," said Suzanna in a cultured friendly way.

Mariam presented her letter from Herodias and sat down.

"Yes, we knew you were coming. She already told us to expect you."

Mariam's puzzlement grew.

"You see, the courier came a week ago with a letter. Gaius thought it was the most delightful idea. We've always wanted to have an herb garden on the property. Tended by two expert herbalists from the Serapium, it couldn't be in better hands. Your products will become popular among the villas in the area. I've already spoken with Juliana and Lucilia. We're all looking forward to buy from you."

• "Thank you," Mariam said quietly to Suzanna.

"And with the arrangement Herodias is proposing, Gaius and I have decided you can have the area on the hillside where so many herbs are growing already. There are some stone buildings there that you can use. Thaddeus will help you put them in order. I understand you're bringing more people with you?"

"Yes, we are a small group."

"Lovely, dear. I look forward to my first cup of tea grown by you. But first have dinner with us. I insist."

Mariam left in a daze. This was more than she had hoped for. She came back to the others and told them that food was waiting for them in the atrium.

"A child? How absolutely adorable. We haven't seen a small child here for a long time." Suzanna was delighted. "She's yours? Oh, then you must be the aunt, the likeness is striking," she said pointing to Sarah.

They were all presented by name, and the relationships were explained. Suzanna had heard about them and their mysterious teacher, but she was more interested in the benefits of having expert gardeners on her property.

"Of course the land you use will eventually be yours, just as Herodias proposed."

They stayed overnight at the manor before starting up towards their new herb farm the following morning. Thaddeus showed the way.

"This part hasn't been used for a while. We picked the herbs we needed from what grew wild around here or bought others at the market. There hasn't been any cultivated herb fields on the farm before. The buildings aren't much to speak of, but with some work they will do, if you don't mind living simple."

They climbed the hillside on foot to make it easier for the horses. It was pretty steep and there wasn't much of a road, more like an animal track. They had to leave the wagon by the manor and had loaded their things onto the animals.

Mariam again admired the beauty of the landscape. As they climbed higher, she could see wider, and the panorama that met her eyes was soothing in its soft lines and gentle colors. She breathed in the fresh air and recognized familiar scents. They passed tall trees which told her that there was enough water in the ground to sustain them. The many greens surrounding her went from the lightest shade of sage, to the bluer tones of the olive trees, to the dark greens of pines and the brighter greens of the deciduous trees. In between were bright red poppies, broom bushes with their surprising yellow orchid flowers on their stiff stems and the early light shades of the lavender. If she could bottle the beauty of what she saw, she would use it as healing waters.

When they reached the stone buildings they realized that Suzanna was right. They needed some work.

"We're going to live in that?" asked Sarah.

"It needs a stone here and there, and some roof timbers and tiles. I'm sure there are local craftsmen who know how to do it," offered Johanna.

Joses thought that two of the buildings could be living quarters and another one could be a work room with one part for the horses.

The men started discussing how to go about all the practical issues, what they could do themselves and what they needed help with. Sibyl went to look for good soil for fields. Johanna and Sarah checked the housing arrangements.

Mariam didn't say anything. She sat down and nursed Tamera, facing the view. She was totally confident that they all would come up with good solutions. Mariam had taken it all in and saw the potential it held. She smiled to herself. If they all needed to be out of the Roman focus, then this was a perfect solution. Little Tamera fell asleep in her lap with a bubble of milk between her lips.

The next months were filled with hard work. Mariam walked about with Tamera on her back and helped everybody. She realized that she was needed to help make decisions. They all came up with good ideas that needed her approval. She liked the job of overseer, and the others liked that she took in everything. Mariam became the weaver of the fabric of their community.

The walls were patched, the roofs installed and rooms started to form into bedrooms, common space and kitchen. Johanna took over the household and Sarah became her natural helper. Sibyl organized the workrooms and requested drying racks to be ready for their first harvest. It would be mostly naturally growing herbs, which were abundant and waiting for someone to harvest. Trym showed himself to be a man of many talents. He could build, just as well as grow herbs, and their animals were well taken care of. Mariam was growing in appreciation for the man's contributions. Joses had taken a role of leadership next to Mariam and was respected by the others for his calm wisdom. *"So like his father,"* thought Mariam, appreciating her young brother-in-law.

Little Tamera grew into a toddler and walked between them. Sarah got the job of herding the child. Johanna fed them all, and the small community found their tone.

With Tamera getting older, Mariam was freed up a little and could go exploring on her own. She went out with Sibyl to admire the humble beginnings of plants growing. She and Trym had big plans for expansion, but needed an ox and a plow to get any further. Mariam suggested they talked to Thaddeus; maybe they could borrow them from the farm at Villa Lata. Sibyl had come to the same conclusion.

"There is room here for several rows of plants, and the climate here will support the growth of most of the plants we used in Egypt. We are also growing some food that should help us over the colder months. We need seeds or starter plants. Some I can find around here and transplant, others I'll need to get at the market in Massilia."

"Why don't we plan a trip when you feel the time is right," said Mariam. Sibyl thought that was a good idea.

"But first let me show you something," she said with a secretive smile.

Sibyl took Mariam on a walk down the hillside. They talked about the plants they could grow, and the things they could make with them. The list grew, watered by their enthusiasm. Medicinal plants, herbs for oils, creams and unguents, spices for the kitchen, teas for Suzanna, vinegars for preservation of food, herbs for aromatic purposes, maybe even roses for fine perfumes. They already had customers ready to purchase from them. All they needed was a good crop.

After walking for a while, Sibyl sat Mariam down on a rock.

"Look, that's mount Aurelia. Do you see the dark spot in the mountain side? I think there is a cave there."

"A cave?"

"Yes, this landscape has caves in many places. The mountain is porous enough so caves will form as water digs in. The Celts were familiar with these natural phenomena. They made holy places close to water coming out of the mountains or water welling up in the earth itself. I think we're looking at a good one right there."

"Sibyl, how do I get there?"

A few days later Mariam arranged an expedition with Joses. He was the most experienced hiker among them, and she explained that she needed to climb a mountainside. They set off with ropes and sturdier foot wear and promised to be back the following day. "There are indeed a lot of caves in the area. We can ask some of the local people if they know of other ones."

"Let's start with this one and see if it suits our purpose."

"What exactly is your purpose with a cave, Mariam?"

"I need to be surrounded by stone."

Joses didn't ask any further.

They found the mountain side and saw the opening up on the wall. In the distance they saw a slim path along the mountain leading up to it. After some searching, they found it among the trees.

The path gave out some places and Joses tied the two of them together. There were treacherous parts that demanded strength and dexterity. Mariam blessed her health and resilience. Joses took his for granted as an obvious benefit of youth. He led their way and got them safely to a plateau at the opening of the cave.

"Here it is, Mariam. Now tell me what you want to do here?" Joses had been patient for a whole day. He sensed there was more to Mariam's request than an exploration of the geography.

As they walked into the cave, he checked for sturdy walls that wouldn't fall in and if there were tracks of animals which had already claimed it for a home. There were signs of human occupation, but nobody seemed to have been there in years. Maybe it had been used as shelter while traveling. After the Roman roads were constructed; the path across the mountain was less used. Mariam liked what she saw.

"Joses, please understand. Most of the things we did in the temples were done inside thick layers of stone. The lines of connection work differently through stone than anywhere else. I need a space like this to work in."

Joses understood. He had seen what she did among his brother's followers. Having been very young at the time, he had applied the limited understanding of a child. Now he was ready for more.

"Priestess Mariam, will you teach me?"

Mariam was surprised. She had only seen this kind of devotion towards her husband, and she didn't expect it from Joses. She knew he had gone to the temple school in Jerusalem. Her days in Judea had turned her away from the temple, and she wasn't quite sure what he had been taught. The old Temple of Jerusalem held much old wisdom and knowledge. How much were they willing to share with their students? How much did the priests know themselves?

Mariam had seen the effect of the Roman Empire on the practices of the temples. The importance of the rituals was watered down. The knowledge of how to reach the Gods and travel between the worlds was only kept alive in secret and hidden places.

Were she and Herodias the only priestesses left? Maybe they were the last with their depth of knowledge. Sibyl had spent as much time as Mariam at the temple, but her studies had made her a master in herb cultivation.

Mariam missed the astrologers who kept track of time. She missed the big assemblies and the tableaus at the rituals. She missed the reenactments of the legends. She missed the wiser older priests for consultations. And she missed Yeshua. She realized how much she had avoided allowing herself to think about him. Not wanting to show her emotions, she slumped down on a stone.

"Yes, I'm willing to teach you, Joses. I am honored by your request. I understand you went to the temple school in Jerusalem, and I know you learned from your brother. I have a different background."

"I understand. I am open to what you want to teach."

Mariam wasn't quite sure if this was a relief or an added responsibility. She realized she needed his help, and if he wanted to learn, so much the better. Teaching felt like an inevitable effect of everything that brought her here.

She thanked God one more time. She had a sturdy house to live in. There was food on the table everyday of items they had grown or caught. She was surrounded with loving hardworking people, and a potential herb farm had been placed in her hands. The groundwork had been immense, but now she had a safe base situated on a hilltop next to a beautiful mountain in the most pastoral part of Gaul. Her child was safe here. She and her followers were safe. The thought shocked her. Were they her followers? She hadn't thought about it like that, but they all seemed to defer to her.

Mariam decided to accept her new position. If students started coming to her, she would teach.

"Let's start with cleaning up the cave and doing a ritual that will claim it as ours."

They swept the cave and ate the meal they had brought. The ritual that evening was the first in the cave, now claimed by a priestess from Ephesus. Mariam taught Joses to honor the four directions and the four elements. She taught him how to sing the tones and introduced the vibration she wanted to establish. They felt the surrounding stone respond as they dedicated the cave to Venus.

On the way home the following morning, she taught him how to communicate telepathically. *So useful over distances,* she sent him. Joses laughed back at her.

Walking through the forest, she had her own thoughts and wondered how Yeshua was doing. His answer came to her, which said he was safe and fine. He sent his love to her and his daughter. She had hoped for something more personal, more details from his everyday life, but sensed that there were several cultural filters between them. She tried to explain this to Joses as they walked, and found that he was a willing listener and a quick learner.

So much like his brother, she thought with a sting of pain in her chest.

CHAPTER 6

THE GROTTO

MARIAM FOUND HER WAY TO THE CAVE quite often. The others understood. Sibyl came with her some times, Joses was often her companion. He liked taking the hike with her. She always had something to explain as they walked.

The cave started to take on the qualities of a small temple. Mariam knew it would take her some time to season the space, before it could hold the energy of the more involved rituals she felt the need to do. So far they had worked with honoring the seasons, finding where the stars were positioned in relation to the place, and how the other mountains could be used to strengthen the field she was working from. She had found a water trickle inside the cave, and she and Joses had made a basin for it to collect in. Honoring the water was important. Water is essential to human life. Mariam knew how important it was to the balance of nature that humans everywhere honored their water source. The first rituals for the water in the cave became very emotional. Joses asked afterwards if they should give the same blessing for the water they used at the farm. Mariam thought that would be a good idea.

It felt good to be back as a priestess. This last year had been filled with a search for a safe home for herself and her child. As a group of supporters and followers grew around her, she had to become their leader and had to look after their comfort and engagement. Her work hadn't had any place, and she hadn't felt compelled to do any of it, other than offer healing when needed. Now the place and time had presented itself to her, and she could practice the ancient knowledge again. The priestess was back at her work.

Mariam was taking in the landscape she finally felt she belonged to. She took note of the positions of geographical landmarks and made a mental map of mountains, creeks meadows and valleys. Together with Joses, she identified the metals present in the ground, the position of underground water ways, and the roads and pathways made by people through the ages. She needed to find the breathing points of the land, the pulse of the earth she was standing on.

She used the astrology she had learned at the Serapium, and found again that young Joses knew more than she expected. She knew they taught this knowledge at the temple of Jerusalem, and apparently they taught it well. Together they identified the star patterns working above them and found the time for the solstices and equinoxes. Venus was an evening star this year, and Mariam thought for sure she would be that next year too, according to her erratic pattern. She would have to ask next time they came to a bigger temple, to make sure they had it right. But what they had figured out so far was a good start in their desire to establish a relationship with the cycle of the year, the movements in the cosmos and the land itself. Mariam felt she had planted her foot in the ground and stretched an arm up towards the stars. Now people and plants could grow.

The first product they decided to make from their herb farm, before they sold anything on the market, was the holy balm for her jar. Sibyl knew all the ingredients and Mariam knew the ritual that gave it energy. They took it all up to the cave to give it the right potency.

"Remember how Suri taught us?" Mariam was reminiscing.

"Remember how strict she was?" Sibyl had her own thoughts.

"Yes, but we learned it well, didn't we?"

Together they dedicated the space. They created a sacred square within the cave for their work. The four corners got oil lamps and the four sides were protected by guardians. Since Sibyl hadn't been to Ephesus, Mariam didn't see any reason to overwhelm her. Yochanan and his story remained her own secret. She placed four special stones there, and invoked protective spirits for them. The brassier got placed in the middle, and the fire inside it was started. They needed the smoke from the origen, the plant of Osiris, to fill the place.

"Not too much, remember we want the smell of this one to be dominant," said Sibyl proudly as she showed Mariam another plant.

Sibyl was particularly proud of the flower she had found. The tuberose was hard to come by, and as soon as she saw it she had dug it up to replant it at the farm. When it bloomed, she had distilled the flower into oil which was going to be the base for the holy balm. The fragrance was like a fine perfume, even without any extra preparation. They also had fresh lavender ready to be cut up and myrtle leaves, the plant of Venus, together with other plants Sibyl had prepared.

Mariam started invoking Venus. The song accentuated the tones from the planet, and she kept a beat with her foot to ground the sound. Sibyl's lovely soprano took the overtones and soon they had the whole cave resonating with the vibration they wanted.

We could never establish this in a building made of wood, thought Mariam to herself. *Surrounded by stone that remembers what you've invoked, that's the only way to do this work. This stone might not have thousands of years of memory built up, but it's a beginning, and stone, like water, is also connected to everything.*

She knew where her star would be situated in the night sky. She knew where to place her request and she knew how to anchor it when the answer came.

321

The ingredients were all mixed together and the jar was put in the center of their square. Mariam and Sibyl were sitting on the floor across from each other with the jar between them. Their song changed to include words. Together they were asking the help of Isis and Osiris, of the spirits of the vegetation of the region and the special consciousness of the mountain surrounding them. They needed to be in line with all these beings and to saturate the balm with blessings.

The song invoked Venus and her powers. As Mariam felt the energy as a clear line coming through her body, she straightened her back, lifted her head and exhaled. She held it in her body for a while, allowing it to gather strength from her to become more manifest. A beam of light came through the roof of the cave and settled in the alabaster jar. They saw a star of light form on the bottom, giving the substance luminescence as if the star above duplicated itself inside the balm they had created. The herbs they used held the right frequency to call the star forth. Together they created the rhythm that would keep the vibration. The star in the container exploded in a flash illuminating the whole cave. Then the light disappeared, and Mariam fainted on the floor.

Sibyl knew what to do. She straightened out Mariam's body and made sure that she breathed properly, being careful that she didn't step out of the prescribed square of protection. She thanked all the guardians for being there with them, and extinguished the oil lamps. The brassier she left on for warmth. Quietly she sat down next to her friend and took her head in her lap. Mariam smiled in recognition, but did not become conscious. Her breathing pattern told Sibyl that Mariam was sleeping normally and soundly. She put a pillow under her head and found a blanket to cover her with. Sibyl put all the things they'd used in order and lay down next to Mariam to sleep.

The next morning they decided that the herb farm should be called Tuberose after the holy balm which would be the most important product they made. They also decided that Mariam was not going to go to the cave alone from now on.

Mariam was pleased with the development. The cave had proven that it could be used. It wasn't a temple carrying thousands of years of tradition, but it was taking on its own field, resonating with the nature it was part of and the sounds they made vibrate inside. The cave was taking on her frequency and did respond to her intentions. She knew it would take years to build true power there, but felt she was off to a good start.

Mariam immersed herself in physical work. There was an endlessness of tasks at the farm. She was grateful for all the good people that had become her community. She helped Sibyl and Trym in the field. She helped Joses overseeing buildings and land. She helped Johanna with supplies and household concerns and she helped Sarah with Tamera and her care. Mariam became the shuttle running in between everyone, weaving a fabric of connections, of appreciation, of care and love between them all.

They gathered for the meals twice a day, for the midday meal they were each on their own, often packing something with them from the breakfast. The early meals became the meeting time where plans for the day were discussed. The evening meal became the time to share what had been accomplished during the day. Suggestions were heard and discussed. Everybody had a voice. Mariam taught them the songs for morning and evening. The teachings from Therapautae were honored.

Mariam also used this time to teach. She realized that they all came from different levels of training. Joses and Johanna hadn't received the same education as Yeshua or Yochanan. It took her a while to study everybody's behavior pattern to grasp where they were at in their understanding. As soon as she felt she had an overview, she started introducing concepts to them that she felt were appropriate for the moment.

"Communication is all about intention," she said to them one morning. "If you want to get your point across, first of all check yourself. What is your intent? What vibration are you sending with your message? What frequency is carrying your words? It usually is not a matter of people not understanding your language. It is a matter of whether the vibration you sent your message with resonate with the people it's intended for."

"Like with Tamera. When she was still an infant, she would respond to soothing sounds regardless of what the words meant," said Sarah.

"And now, she'll respond to a sharper sound if you want to alert her of danger," Johanna had observed.

"And we're supposed to think of all this all the time?" Trym wondered.

"As long as you remember that love is the driving force between everything, your heart will be in the right place," Mariam reassured him.

After some days of letting them take in this message, Mariam told them why this concept was so important.

"I've wanted to teach you to communicate telepathically with each other. It makes a lot of things much easier. But when doing that, there is no room for deception. I needed you to be comfortable checking your motivation behind communication before I could teach you this. A telepathically sent message holds a lot of your own frequency, and the more love you can have in your field, the more comfortable that message is to receive. Any irritation, any negative thought, any blame, any concern you might have with the other person will present itself and clutter up your message. It will disturb the other person's field. So before we can learn this, we have to become totally honest with each other. For the next week, I want us all to come clear with everybody. If you have an issue with someone, bring it up or clear it within yourself. Discuss it with Joses or me if you feel it needs more insight, or take it up with the whole group. This is all done in preparation for safe telepathic communication."

Mariam felt that she had good students. Once she had them tuned with each other this way, their group would function even better. She expected some confrontations. She had seen who went on each others nerves, and could see good reasons for why.

This had to be cleared up for the collective health of all of them. She hoped that they would solve it within themselves, but was also prepared to assist if necessary.

The one that amazed her most was Trym. He had no experience with any of these concepts, but took to it like a fish to water. His devotion to Sibyl helped a lot, but Mariam was watching that development too. She didn't want anything unhealthy to develop between them. Sibyl's family history was known to most of them, and her scars were deep. Mariam saw that Trym could be a healing factor in Sibyl's life, but also that she could reject him and cause new scars to be formed. Sibyl had her own healing to do here, and Mariam hoped that their shared care of the plants would further that.

As soon as Mariam took on a more active role in teaching them and introduced the concepts of Therapautae gradually, the productivity of the group improved. There had been some rocky weeks, accelerated evolution isn't comfortable, but she'd had no choice. If there was something bothering one of them, they all felt it. Mariam wanted everybody to take responsibility for what they brought to the group every day, and she meant their inner life, not the work ethic and devotion they all showed in abundance. As they learned telepathic communication, they felt the unseen energy lines created between them. As they tuned to each other, they felt each others emotions and underlying, sometimes unconscious, motivations.

"This is what we're working with and helping each other with. Just like the undertows in the ocean, which can pull somebody under with no warning, we have to identify our own undertows of negative emotions. The deeper we go, the tougher they are to deal with, but even more important to come to terms with," she explained to Sarah one day as she was struggling with the concept.

Mariam was strict. This was a tough phase for all of them. Being confronted with your own worst sides can be like meeting scary monsters with faces you'd rather not see in your nightmares. She took them through this under the stars of Cancer, the water sign, so they could zigzag through their own underwater terrain. She knew Leo was coming next when they would find their fire and know their own majestic selves. *Nothing like Leo to build self confidence,* thought Mariam.

She observed them all keenly. Who needed more encouragement? Who needed to get clarity? Who was in their own downward spiral? Who thought they had figured it all out and had a big smile plastered on their face? Mariam found she had all these things displayed among them, and worked with them as they did manual labor according to their responsibilities. *Nothing like physical work to anchor spiritual teachings,* thought Mariam and blessed her years at the Serapium.

After a couple of months of intense work, she could feel that something had lifted. People's issues had a lighter tone, the deep undertows had gone out to follow bigger streams and find their way to the ocean. There was a new respect for the health of the group as an organism. Mariam felt they had achieved a breakthrough.

At the evening meal she told them how proud she was of the group as a whole.

She continued in her teachings of silent communication, but now she also introduced something else.

"I want you to know how much I miss him. I'm teaching these things, because he lived them. We lived these concepts in the colony in Bethany. We learned them from the Nazareeans, from the Essenes, from the beautiful people at Therapautae.

"I'd like to write down what we remember," she continued. "I know only Johanna and Joses actually lived with him, but all of you have lived with other members of the flock and learned things too. Please help me create a memoir, a script honoring him and all he taught us."

She suggested that they started when they were resting around the fire at night. "We are used to sharing stories together. Let it now have an even more dedicated purpose. Let's commemorate him. Let's put it in writing for next generations to come."

Her script grew. It became a book she treasured and kept with her always.

CHAPTER 7

THE WISH

MARIAM GREW RESTLESS. SHE HAD HELPED HER group grow into a beehive of activity. With her help they had also achieved the harmonized life of bees. Was she the queen bee? If she had asked the others they would laugh and say a definite yes.

She had hidden her own emotional life and kept herself stable to support the others through their growth. Now she could let them work on their own, and concentrate on her own inner balance.

She had to admit it. It wasn't good for the group at large. She couldn't deny it anymore; she had problems of her own. Just as she had taught them, she would now have to put the same standards to herself. Mariam hoped she'd been able to hide it well enough while she taught the others these last months.

The nights were the worst. Little Tamera provided warmth and comfort, but she would sleep just as happily with aunt Sarah or aunt Johanna.

Or maybe it was worse during the day, walking alone among their fields. Time alone, left to her own thoughts, often brought tears she didn't want the others to see.

She tried to be sensible. Most of her life she'd lived without him. He'd been the man she was going to marry, the man she was connected with through an old agreement. The time in Judea had been intense. She had fused with his powerful essence. Her body had learned to vibrate with him, and it still sang their melody.

Where was he now? Where was he traveling? She sensed that he was alive and healthy. Was he going to stay in foreign countries for many more years? Why didn't anybody have word from him? And why couldn't she reach him the way she was now teaching the others? How could she teach when she couldn't even stay in touch with the man she loved?

Her heart ached for the man she had cleaved with. She didn't even have words to express her pain. Since she left Jerusalem, her life had been in constant motion. As she settled into a new stability, she could hear how loudly her body cried.

The answer came to her when she felt most abandoned. Had he broken the line between them? That would be totally out of character for him, but he was a man after all. He couldn't possibly have done that. He knew how important it was to keep the royal lines in order. He knew how to keep the frequency of his body tuned to her. If he disturbed it, it would reverberate to all the people he was related to. He couldn't have. She would have felt it in little Tamera, and she hadn't sensed that. The line between them had to be intact, she tried to reassure herself. But why couldn't she reach him?

Remember Arcadia, resonated in her head. Yes, she had remembered that. But to establish that connection required a much bigger ritual than what she had capacity to accomplish on her own. She needed another priestess.

She sent a letter with Trym to give to Thaddeus which then could go to Arelate next time someone went that way from Villa Lata. It was the best she could do.

The following day a gilded carriage came to Villa Lata and a single fine horse found its way to Tuberose Herb Farm.

"Letter? I didn't receive any letter. You were broadcasting on high frequency all over the place! Woman, you know how to contact me directly. Didn't you learn anything in all your temples? Have you forgotten Ephesus?"

Herodias was almost angry with Mariam for not having contacted her earlier. The telepathic line between them had been established years ago. Had Mariam forgotten that? She would prefer a polite "Hello, how are you, Herodias, I need your help," instead of receiving desperate whimpering at high volume giving her a headache.

"It couldn't possibly have been any good for the other people here either, to have you moping about by yourself. Do you know how strong your sound is?"

Mariam listened to everything Herodias said, and knew that she was right. She collapsed in her arms and made her elegant silk dress wet with snot and tears. Herodias continued scolding her, but her tone was soothing and her hand was stroking Mariam's back.

Herodias spent some days admiring the farm and calming her dear friend. She was impressed with how much they had accomplished. Sibyl had defined her fields and transplanted starter plants, both from the surrounding wildlife and from plants she purchased on the markets in Massilia, in Aquae Sextiae and from the local farmers. Trym had dug for her, watered for her, weeded, carried and built for her. Sibyl appreciated him just as much as he admired her. *The man was worth his weight... – in myrtle,* Herodias finished Mariam's thought, knowing that it was the herb that gave the best price.

Joses had hired local craftsmen and gotten the stone houses to be quite comfortable. "He is talking about putting tiles on the floor," said Johanna proudly. The terra cotta tiles were well known in the area and made by the same people who made the roof tiles. It would be a tremendous improvement in the kitchen.

"You'll need more buildings," said Herodias practically. "You know more people will come."

Mariam hadn't thought about that. This was just a humble herb farm on a pretty hill. They paid their dues to Suzanna in services, but otherwise they didn't have that much to do with the Roman mansion. Why would this place be attractive?

"Don't you know? Your numbers are growing. Your brother's flock in Aquae Sextiae has doubled. I hear of groups getting stronger in Rome, in Athens, in Alexandria."

Alexandria. Mariam thought of her parents and Ezra's promise to bring them to Gallia. She needed to write to him. How would they take seeing the farm and how simply she lived? She was raised with servants and an atrium with a fish pond. Mariam didn't exactly miss it, but she thought of her earlier life with fondness. She wondered about Sarah, though. Her sister never complained, but she could see that nature didn't give her the same stimulation as culture did, whereas Sibyl wouldn't have it any other way.

"And now you're teaching here. Of course they'll come," Herodias continued. "You didn't think you could sit undetected on your hilltop forever, did you? Mariam, a priestess at work in a cave will attract people with the song of the mountain," she finished with a knowing smile.

More students? More people? Mariam wasn't quite sure how to handle that. She had just gotten this group to function well together. New people meant new challenges.

Yes, we're the core, said Sibyl silently. *But we could use some more hands. I would welcome them, as long as they were willing to put in a days work.*

She received nods from the others, who each hoped that a new person among them would love to be their own special assistant. Mariam realized that they were all overworked.

The two old friends were sitting on good rocks in the hillside above the farm admiring the view.

"You have a good group her, Mariam. There is love between you. It is evident in how everybody is thriving. The child is healthy and happy. I haven't seen you in a while, and it is'nt just the fresh air, meaningful work and Johanna's good cooking that keeps you all well. These people love working for you. You take good care of them. You're a good queen bee, Mariam."

"Thank you, Herodias, that's very good to hear. We're thinking of getting bees. It would be good for the fields." Mariam couldn't get out of her practical thinking.

"You've been teaching them, haven't you?"

"They asked me, and it felt right since we're living together and are all so dependent on each other."

"I admire your farm. This is a very peaceful place for you, Mariam."

"I love this land. The beauty of the landscape is soothing. It has the sound of a love song," said Mariam with dreamy eyes.

"No wonder you're love sick," said Herodias. She finally got the picture. "Let's get this man of yours back. Where is this cave you've been working in?"

Mariam loved her friend's practical approach to everything. She made it sound so simple. Mariam realized that she had allowed the beauty of the land to hypnotize her. For a while now, all she'd wanted to do was to sit on a rock and admire the undulating fields, adore her daughter and take in the aroma of roses and lavender. When tears rolled down her mother's cheeks, little Tamera had stood there and looked at her with her fathers dark, gentle, loving eyes. Herodias was right. She was love sick.

Sibyl supplied the herbs they needed and Joses offered to help them carry. He understood their need to be alone, and promised to stay by the beginning of the trail and wait until they called for him. He had learned the silent calls now, he explained proudly to Herodias.

On the walk to the cave, Herodias understood their love of the landscape. There was indeed an enchanting quality here. Was it just that it was all so aesthetically pleasing? Was it the harmonious way the trees grew complementing each other? Herodias didn't have an answer, but could feel the charm of the country side softening her, as well.

They had more things with them this time, and Joses had insisted on loading one of the horses. He knew that these ladies would rather talk about the beauty of everything than carry heavy loads, and he saw no reason to wear himself out. He needed a couple of things himself to be comfortable for the night, and the horse would be a good companion.

Mariam led the way and she and Herodias were chirping like birds. It was fun to feel like young girls on a path through the fields and forests, and wonderful to be together with someone who was not also her student. Mariam went into a lighthearted state and skipped between sage and ivy humming to her self. Somehow she felt as if she was on her way to meet her love. Herodias thought Mariam was edging on silly, but allowed her friend some moments of giddy happiness. She certainly had worked hard enough this last year. Joses smiled to himself and felt like an old man, even though he was more than a decade younger than them.

At the foot of Mount Aurelia they rested and ate some food Johanna had sent with them. Joses made up a camp for himself before he led the horse up the narrow path to the cave higher up. They unloaded on the platform outside the cave, and with some coaxing they turned the horse around and Joses went back down to his camp site.

"So this is your temple," said Herodias as they walked further into the grotto.

"Yes," said Mariam. "It isn't exactly Ephesus, but we've had many good sessions of work here. The stone of the mountain seems to respond to the sound we're sending out, and I can work undisturbed here. Sibyl has been great and sometimes Joses has joined us."

"Maybe you should do a session with all of you, just to strengthen the bonds."

"That would be good too. We haven't felt ready for that yet."

"Any initiations? You know that would change the whole field."

"Not yet, but I know that Joses will ask soon. He's been so eager to learn."

"He looks so much like him," said Herodias.

"A younger version of him. Like the one I met in Leontopolis. The one I went to Therapautae with. He also reminds me of Father Joseph. Joses has his father's soft humor and gentle wisdom. Yeshua is more like Mary, gentle eyes and a soft smile and a way to make you feel that the world is a better place because you're in it."

"You miss them all, don't you."

"I love them, Herodias. I have loved them all my life. And I don't know if I'll ever see any of them again. They're all spread out. Mary went to Ephesus, I left Joseph at Serabit and Yeshua is beyond the Roman Empire. I don't even know if they're alive. What am I going to tell Tamera when she gets older? Yes, my dear, you're a princess. But we live in hiding on an herb farm in another country. Your father has only seen you when he materialized in a red flame. And your lovely grandmother hardly knows that you exist, whereas you can thank your foreseeing grandfather that we are both alive."

"Oh, don't paint such a bleak picture. You all had to disperse. It happened quickly. You might all reunite in equally surprising ways. Patience, dear. Patience."

Mariam wished she could be equally optimistic. The quick turns of fortune of her friend over the last years escaped her entirely. Herodias didn't say anything. She knew what happened. No need to rehash her own prickly adventures. Mariam needed her now. If she could give her some of her own strength and build her trust in her own league of otherworldly guardians, she was glad to be of help. The guardians around her all agreed that watching over Herodias was a full time job. They shook hands with Mariam's own league, they had met before, and they all agreed to assist this evening in what their ladies were planning to do.

"So where do we start. I see the mountain itself has furnished you with handy shelves." Herodias was pointing at oil lamps, some shawls, a brassier and some odds and ends of herbs which were kept in the walls of the grotto.

Mariam started to set up. The square blanket she put on the floor was Egyptian cotton with a thick wooly camel blanket attached underneath. Eurochia had sent her both items intending them for the floor of the baby's room. Mariam had sighed, wondering how her mother would have approved of their living arrangement. Tamera didn't really have a room. She slept in the space shared by all the women. They were actually quite comfortable. Little Tamera loved the closeness of all her mothers.

Mariam looked at the colorful pattern on the top and noticed the red elephant woven into a blue square in the middle. Somehow that seemed just right for what they were about to do.

Herodias was ready with the oil lamps for the corners and found a brass tray to put the brassier on. She even found a trivet of bamboo to place under the tray for proper protection. The space started to get definition.

Mariam had intended to include Yochanan tonight. She wanted Herodias to meet him again. The others didn't seem ready for that yet, so he had been wrapped up since they had been together in Arelate last winter. She fetched the round bag out of the things Joses had brought on the horse.

"Wait a little until we have created a protective space for him. This place is still new. We can't count on thousands of years of established energy for protection."

The guardians were almost insulted. They had followed them through thick and thin, lifting a twig here, arranging a meeting there, turning someone's head another way so these secretive ladies could go about their business undisturbed. They had blindfolded Romans with momentary fog, made sure the dungeon they were sent to at least had some sand to lie down on, and made sure the plant they needed had grown in the right place. They followed their people everywhere. Had their people forgotten?

There was another sound heard too. The spirits of the mountain also wanted to say how strongly they had protected this space since this good work had been started. The angels greeted the nature devas, and together they formed a force field creating a humming light emanating from Mount Aurelia.

Joses was sitting at his campfire warming some soup thinking his own thoughts about what the two priestesses were doing up there. He understood more about rituals, and their power and purpose after working with Mariam. His respect had grown for the priestesses' knowledge and what they could accomplish with what they knew.

He raised his head and looked at the stars above. The constellations were familiar to him. It had been an important subject at the temple. He had learned to read the skies, and had helped Mariam define Venus and figure out her movements.

As he gazed upwards, he noticed another light. The mountaintop had layers of light making round silhouettes of its contours. A light yellow shade was closest to the mountain, then a light green layer, before a turquoise halo gradually blended with the night sky.

Joses put down his bowl and spoon. He turned his head to see the opening of the cave. The light inside was orange.

Joses jumped to his feet. The horse was tethered by a tree, and his few things were making a comfortable place around the fire. He checked his inner sense of the safety of Mariam, and the answer he felt was peaceful. Still, his logical mind was alert. Was there a fire in the grotto? If so, they had water to put it out with. He knew the basin in the back was full. Joses felt uncertain what to do. He didn't want to disturb them, at the same time, he would never forgive himself if they needed his help and he wasn't there.

"Joses, come. Come now," he heard loud and clear in his head.

Joses quickly put out the fire and made sure the horse was tethered. He abandoned his things except for his knife, and headed for the path that led up the mountain side.

As he took the path in a wide legged stride, he started thinking again. The voice he had heard was not Mariam's, and it certainly wasn't Herodias'. It had been a male voice talking to him. Was there somebody there with them? He didn't know of any other way to get there, than this path upwards. To access the top of Mount Aurelia on the other side was physically impossible.

He kept getting a feeling of peaceful, but focused intention, from Mariam. If they were in danger he would have felt it as a stinging pain in his chest. He hesitated calling her directly, being more afraid that he would disturb something that needed her full concentration. His profound respect, and tinge of fear, of the power they possessed, kept him to himself.

If some male being was threatening them, he most certainly would not have prompted Joses to come. This realization almost made him turn around, there was probably no danger. But he had been called. His curiosity was also triggering his speed, and the closer he got, the more he could feel a magnetic attraction pulling him towards the opening of the cave.

The sacred space was in function. The brassier was burning, the incense was filling the room and the oil lamps were glowing. A protective symbol was drawn on the floor. Mariam had used white sand this time to mark the sign of Venus. The five pointed star honoring her path in the sky gleamed against the dark stone. The pieces of crystal in the sand blinked in the darkness.

Yochanan had been unwrapped. He was placed on one side of the square and they sang the tones to wake him up. His eyes opened and he blinked at them in greeting. The skin around his skull had become hardened with time. It wasn't supple and pliable as it had been when he was alive. His long hair was still attached and flowed down on the blanket underneath him. Every time they brought him in, though, his face became animated and he could move both his mouth and his eyes. Mariam didn't really know how it all worked. She knew she would be exhausted after the ritual and need loads of food to replenish her self. Did he borrow some energy from her to enliven himself? If so, she was willing to share with him. They were both aware of each other's intentions, and the bond between them was old and deep.

Herodias greeted him formally. He answered in the proper formal phrase. Then he closed his eyes and took in the setting and everything in it. The women didn't know that he also took in the mountain and the young man hurrying up the hillside to join them.

"Mariam, is this enough?" Herodias counted up all the factors they were working with. "Last time we had Tamera with us, and her birth water. We don't have any genetic material for him to identify with."

"I thought Yochanan would be enough. They were first cousins."

"That's good, but too weak of a link. Tamera was a better anchor for him. We need something stronger. I know you love him, Mariam, and that's good. But you don't carry any of his seeds with you right now. It's been too long since you guys were together, and your body was cleared out with the birth of your daughter."

"It's all I have, Herodias. What do you want me to do? I thought we could use Bashra."

"Bashra is good at strengthening the bonds, but she's only related to you. The tie back through the tribes is more than a thousand years old and of no use."

Mariam was getting desperate. She had counted on this to work. And she had looked forward to see him. She had longed and worried for too long. She needed some reassurance.

"What can we do?"

"I don't know. Who's closer related to him?"

"Your request will soon be answered," Yochanan announced.

Both the women turned and stared at him. What was he saying? What did he mean? He had never taken an active part in their rituals before, but been a powerful supporter. They were both about to say something in protest, but caught themselves just as they heard a soft step at the opening of the cave. Three sets of eyes were directed at the person appearing in the light of the star.

Joses stood there, clearing his throat and not quite sure what to say. He had tried to take in the scene in front of him as it gradually revealed itself when he came closer. He saw some things that were familiar. Oil lamps and incense were common. The thick blanket for the floor for the women to sit on didn't surprise him. The protective star gave him pause, but what really opened his eyes wide was the round object on the edge of the square facing him.

"Welcome Joses," it said. "I'm glad you came."

The look on the women's faces was almost comical. They were shocked and surprised, and looked at him as if they'd been caught by a parent doing something they shouldn't. He managed to stay standing, and not faint, and by all means not laugh.

"Mariam, if you open the line of the star, Joses can step over and then you can close it again," said Yochanan after a moment of frozen silence.

Mariam closed her mouth and got to her senses. She stretched out a hand and scratched a dent in the white sand near his feet. Joses took a big step across it, and she rearranged the sand closing the line behind him.

"Please sit down across from me. We need your help." Yochanan was in command.

Joses dropped down on the open fourth side of the square, grateful for being allowed to sit down. He couldn't help a triumphant smile. It was quite an honor for his presence to be requested by... by his cousin?

"I am Yochanan, son of Elizabeth and Zachary. Anya was my wife, and Yahya is my son. Yes, I am your cousin. Your oldest brother and I were very close friends. I am first cousin with you and your siblings. I have now taken my place among my ancestors."

"I recognize you, Yochanan. I thought you were dead."

"I am counted among the dead. But with the help of the two priestesses in front of you, my wisdom is preserved in this form and can be accessed by future generations. Our precious lives are but short and flighty. What some people collect during their lifetime is sometimes valuable enough that their future people want to reach it. This is a way of ensuring that what I know stays in one place, and doesn't dissipate in the ethers of human thought."

Joses thought that explanation sounded reasonable enough.

"You called for me. How can I be of help?" Joses recognized the voice he'd heard inside his head.

"We are going to call in the spirit of your brother Yeshua. You have the same parents. He will resonate with you. We need you r help to anchor him here. Please follow and copy my tone. The priestesses will do the rest."

Yochanan proceeded with starting the chant. His powerful bass made the stones vibrate with a deeper tone, anchoring their purpose further. Joses started carefully, but soon revealed that his young body held a similar bass voice. Together, they made the mountain vibrate underneath them.

Mariam and Herodias collected themselves, and looked at each other across the square. They felt the power of the combination of the people present, and found the part of the chant intended for an alto and a high soprano. Soon the part of the mountain above them was also pulsating in the frequency they established.

The guardians and devas were pleased. They knew that this would reverberate for miles in any direction. It would create peace wherever it went. It would make anything disharmonic fall in line. Balance would be restored between the people and the land. Small children would fall asleep happy, old people would feel their pains lighten. Tired couples would find their love again. Young people would feel their enthusiasm ignited, because a star had been lit in their personal sky.

Herodias fed the brazier with myrtle and origen. Mariam invoked Isis and Osiris. Ripples formed in the water in the seashell. Right in front of them the seashell grew to a much bigger size.

She continued invoking his name. She called out all the different ways she could say husband, lover, friend, the owner of my heart. "Come to me, come to me now!"

Herodias stared at the water container. The water was from the basin in the back of the cave. The shell was from the seashore near the temple of Ra. Was it blessed by the Celtic water goddesses? Did they make it magically grow larger? She kept her concentration on her tone, and kept monitoring Mariam to make sure she was safe.

Mariam had surrendered to the process. Nothing surprised her anymore. She was a singing instrument resonating in all the ways she could name him. She wanted her entire body to vibrate with him. She wanted to experience that closeness with him one more time. A current started to form at the bottom of her spine.

His eyes were locked on the enormous seashell. Did they do that? Who controlled this event? Joses was starting to wonder whose hallucination they were part of. Still, he felt somewhat locked in position by his cousin across from him. He also had a strong sense that if he disturbed anything now, it could have dire consequences. Joses decided to suspend his questions for now, in the hope that at some time it would all be revealed. He continued to focus on the chant.

It was time. Mariam called out the cry for the mists and the water in the seashell started to froth. Mists formed from the water and solidified into a shadow. She called his name one more time, and he became more solid. A moment later Joses watched his brother Yeshua stand in the seashell. He observed a long white shirt and a colorful shawl draped around him as he materialized. A line of smoke went from his brother to his own body.

Herodias helped Yochanan hold Joses in place energetically when she saw the young man faltering. She knew this was way over his head to experience at his level, but it couldn't have happened without him, and he had volunteered. They held the high tension, until Yeshua had materialized completely.

Yeshua helped, by behaving as if he had just stopped in for tea. He looked tanned and healthy, and flashed a big smile to them all as he stepped out on the elephant in the middle of the square. He sat down as the seashell reduced itself to its normal size.

"Joses, brother, good to see you in such esteemed company. Herodias, I am eternally grateful for your generous support for my people. Yochanan, Namaste. Mariam, wife, my Mariam."

Mariam collapsed in his arms. She curled up against his body and stayed there. It had been so long. So terribly long.

Yeshua ruffled his brother's hair, and Joses laughed. This was his brother, his loving, wonderful, big brother. Yeshua was with them. Was he real? He seemed so, but for how long? The questions were silenced and shuffled to the back of his mind. Right now all he wanted was to touch him.

Herodias needed to touch him too. She stroked his ankle, and took hold of a foot. Yeshua knew he had to physically unite with them all and he put a hand on top of Yochanan's head. He couldn't do it without tears. His love for his cousin carried too many emotions.

As they sat there, allowing the love they all felt for each other to fill the space, absorbing the love into themselves as part of their own body, a new commotion happened in the back of the cave.

They all straightened up slowly, feeling a need to see what was happening, but a reluctance to change out of the field they had created.

The water in the basin in the back started to splash about. There was a noise of churning water and people yelling. Soon there were waves in the basin which had grown twice as big, and water splashing up on the wall behind. Water landed on the floor in front and splashed water drops over to the people sitting in the blanket. They all hugged closer up to Yeshua, Herodias grabbed Yochanan, as they stared in disbelief at what was happening.

Four men climbed out of the water basin. They had white shirts and white turbans and were soaking wet. Their skin was golden brown, their hair was black and wavy and they were all complaining in a language Mariam had never heard before.

Yeshua stood up and faced them. He said something in their language and the four men changed their demeanor immediately. Mariam got up and stepped towards them.

"Stay within the star!" shouted Yochanan. "All of you."

They all froze again and a barrier had been defined between the two groups. The men talked a little between themselves. Then they all agreed on something and came closer with smiling faces. Herodias felt all her red alert warnings wave like signal flags streaming out of her body.

"Jesu, we've come for you," said one of them.

"You left so quickly."

"And what a way to travel!"

"Only Hanuman travels with that speed."

"And you don't even have wings!"

"Or do you?

"Jesu, teach us. Teach us how to travel like this."

Yeshua smiled at his friends.

"I'm visiting with my family," he said. "They invited me here. This is my wife Mariam."

The others were getting over the first shock. They stayed dutifully inside the star just like Yochanan had told them. Mariam stood by her husband with an arm around his waist.

"Yeshua, tell me who they are," she said calmly.

"These are my friends from the ashram in India. We're all learning from the same teacher and exchange healing techniques between us. It's been mutually beneficial. We've become very close. In fact, so close that they followed me here. We were sitting in meditation together."

Yeshua asked his Indian friends to sit down carefully in designated places between the spikes of the star. They were asked to not touch the lines and not come any closer. He would explain later.

"So these people are keeping you? Are they holding you back from leaving India? Are there ties between you that hinder you from coming back? Yeshua, your people are here! They are waiting for you." Mariam couldn't hide her rising concern.

Herodias didn't say anything. She'd never thought the situation could have this many sides to it. There were many people here who would like to have him back. But there were apparently another large group of people somewhere else, who also loved him.

Yochanan was taking in the reality of this magical moment. He knew that everybody did not understand the ramifications here. This moment existed by itself, parallel with other people's existence, but not in it. The strings holding this situation together were very fine, and very fragile. If it collapsed by someone mishandling something, he wasn't quite sure where everybody would go. He held the pentagram in his consciousness and hoped that all these people would respect it. The appearance of the men from India had weakened the lines.

Joses watched with a stunned expression as Yeshua turned to Mariam and took her hands.

"I have other people who need me too, Mariam."

"But we're your family!"

"I'm learning things from these people, truths I've never come across before. I want to know this. Soon I'll be at a level where I feel I can leave. Dearest Mariam, please do not feel that I'm doing this because I don't want to be with you. I'm doing this to build my body of knowledge. It is for the good of everyone."

"I can't carry this alone much longer," Mariam said quietly.

Yeshua tuned into her and saw that she held this group, the people in Aquae Sextiae and all the people she loved, wherever they were, in her consciousness. The responsibility weighed heavily on her. She was teaching them, inspiring them, feeding them spiritually and parenting them. She had help with little Tamera, but all her other students were more demanding.

"I will come back, Mariam. Give me six months."

He was starting to fade.

"I'll meet you at the temple of Ra."

Calmly he told his Indian friends to go back to the water basin they had come out of and just stand in the water. They all greeted them Namaste and watched the four men walk further into the cave. They heard water splashes again. Yeshua picked up the seashell and the men from India traveled through the water back to their ashram.

He smiled at each of them as his body faded slowly out of sight. Mariam tried to hold onto the last streams of smoke as he evaporated, before she fell down sobbing on top of the red elephant.

CHAPTER 8

ON HER WAY TO THE
TEMPLE OF RA

ERODIAS STAYED FOR ANOTHER WEEK TO MAKE sure Mariam and Joses were back to normal after the intense ritual in the grotto. They didn't talk much about it, but she observed them slowly come out of their daze. She was especially concerned about Joses. Mariam and Herodias were seasoned in this work. This experience had been thrown upon him without much warning, let alone training and preparation. She wasn't sure if he would turn away from Mariam's teachings or want to know more. His hiking stick was gone from its corner quite often, and they saw his blue cape roam the hills.

"You have to talk to him, Mariam. He can't go on like this on his own. It's simply not healthy for the boy. "

"He's not a boy, and if he wants to talk, he can come to us," Mariam replied with some irritation.

To be quite honest she wasn't quite sure what to tell him if he asked. This experience had been beyond what she had expected or could explain. She hadn't felt in danger, but she had felt that they had contacted things beyond what they had control over. What if something went technically wrong? Would somebody get stuck somewhere in transit? Was it his body she touched, or was he at the same time located in India somewhere? It certainly felt like him. And it had felt good to hang onto his arm for a moment that had been too short.

He had asked for six months. Even though that was a long time, she felt that it was a reasonable request. He wanted to finish his time of learning there, and he needed to hook up with a caravan going in the right direction. To get his entire physical body here, he would have to take the road. To travel through the elements was convenient for a short visit, but, oh, so temporary. She knew he couldn't sustain his physical body in that state.

Her mind started to think in months, weeks and days. She would take Tamera

338

with of course, and probably Sarah. The temple of Ra would welcome them, and she would send word of their coming.

Maybe you can visit with me in Arelate, as well. Tthat would be nice. Herodias had plugged into her thoughts and answered silently in her head.

"Mariam, you send out high powered signals all the time. You're like a bat, always sending out sound, so you know everything by the echoes coming back to you. It's a mothering technique, I'm sure. You're a mother of the world, Mariam."

Mother of the world? Maybe for our extended flock, corrected Mariam. She thought of Joseph in Sinai and Mary at Ephesus. Her inner sense told her that they were alive and well, but would she ever see them again? Did they pick up her concern and good wishes for their well being? She thought of Lazarus and Martha in Aquae Sextiae and the group at the city called the Mouth of the Rose where they had landed in Gaul the first time. These were all growing communities. Lazarus had helped start a new one in Massilia, where he stayed for a while. Maybe this time she would have a chance to go and visit them all. How long could she be away from the herb farm? Would "Tuberose" be taken care of in her absence? She sensed that it would indeed do just fine. There were many able hands among them who loved the place just as much as she did. Their community had grown. Would they keep up the fine relationship they had developed without her monitoring them constantly? She would put Joses in charge of that and trust that they all had learned enough.

Suddenly she felt lighter. This would work out fine. She could be gone for some time, and her work would continue. Her newly established community would continue to grow and prepare the herbs, and they would continue to develop the skills of their heart. The ground work had been done. She had done some powerful teachings with them, but they had been exceptional students as well. One more time she sent her thanks in prayers to the Gods that held this creation together and had protected her so well. She thanked them for the beauty of the people and the landscape she was surrounded with, for their health and for the child that brightened their days.

Herodias noticed a shift in Mariam, and knew it was time for her to go. She offered to take letters to her family in Aquae Sextiae and to the temple of Ra. Inside she was excited like a child. She hoped Yeshua and Mariam would come and visit her in Arelate. Oh, the fun they would have. How often did she have guests like them? How often did she have guests that she could communicate with? Who else knew how to use the soundless language? She told her inner child to stop hopping up and down. Nothing was for sure, and there was a lot of traveling that had to happen safely before any of this would come to fruition.

Mariam put her focus on getting the farm in good shape before she left. Joses seemed to have found his answers in the hills. After some very quiet days, he was back to his warm, cheerful ways. His eyes had a new depth, and they seemed quiet and untroubled. If he was still brooding, he didn't let her know. For the next seasonal ritual she took Sibyl with.

How would Yeshua like the farm? Could he live here? For how long? Would another crowd follow him? There were many questions to be answered, which she wouldn't know until he was here.

Joses surprised her one day starting a conversation about improvements on the farm.

"When he comes, you will need to have your own home," he said. "You'll be a proper family then, and should be more private."

She couldn't believe he thought that far. *She* hadn't thought that far.

"We could start building now and by the time you come back it will be ready for you."

Mariam thought that was very thoughtful of him, and listened to his plans for where the new one room stone house would be situated. He wanted to build it for the return of his brother, for the unification of his family. Mariam felt her heart get warmer and felt his pain as well. He needed his brother. He needed some concrete answers, which she couldn't give. She understood that he wanted to give himself a new large project to focus on. Working with his hands always cleared his mind.

Sibyl told her of the next steps with the fields. The new storage shed was working well for drying. The tools they had were sufficient for their work. She hoped to develop another plot with some specific plants she had seen on her walks. They were soon ready to be transplanted. She wanted to hire local help to handle it all. Mariam knew that her friend had found her place. Sibyl had found her purpose.

Trym had taken to the hills to check the traps he set for small animals. He often came back with rabbits or birds. Johanna appreciated the additional food items, and there was a smile shared between them. But his heart was with Sibyl, Mariam knew that. She also knew that he probably wouldn't get anywhere with her, but they would have to figure all that out themselves. They were adults. Should she talk to Sibyl about it? Mariam decided against it.

After five months, she felt ready to leave the farm and head for the sea. She wanted to spend some time with Martha and Lazarus, and she needed to calm herself down and not get too excited. Yeshua might be delayed, or have any number of problems along the way. She decided to trust that he would arrive whole and sound. After all, he had come back from the dead. He should be able to survive a trip on a camel and a voyage across an ocean. Somehow that seemed more challenging. While he visited the land of the dead she had been watching over him staring at his body right in front of her. The travel he was facing now depended on many variables out of their control.

They left together with Trym and Sibyl who wanted to go to the market in Aquae Sextiae. Little Tamera sat with Sarah, who had stars twinkling in her eyes. Mariam hadn't seen her sister this happy in a long time. Didn't she like the herb farm? Was it too quiet in the hills for her? Mariam got a sense of that the simple life the others cherished might be too simple for her sister. She needed some life experience, thought Mariam. *It has been good for her to care for the child and help Johanna. It has given her an appreciation for the hard work that goes into keeping a household running.*

Sarah had tears in her eyes. The others thought she was sad about leaving them. Sarah tried to hide that she was thrilled to be heading away from the farm on the hill. *I've done more physical work than I ever saw our own servants do. Our servants had slaves who did the work that we've been doing,* she thought. *I don't share their romanticism about living next to nature.*

Mariam heard Sarah's thought, but decided to not say anything. She knew she would say all the wrong things. Silently she admired her sister for quietly working all this time without complaints.

Martha received them in Aquae Sextiae with open arms, a big heart and warm soup. Lazarus was in Massilia, but would return in a couple of days. They met the new members of the group, saw the additional housing they had acquired and admired the crafts they mastered. Mariam tried to read further between what was said. She understood that they had many different levels of training among them. Some came to learn more about the old scriptures, some wanted more esoteric knowledge and asked for spiritual experiences. Some liked the singing which filled their day and some came to show their devotion. What united them all was their desire to live in a loving community. Women and men were respected equally. They shared responsibilities. The same teachings she had worked with in her group, were practiced here. She felt clean fields among people. The air was not cluttered with unexpressed emotions. Communication between them was calm and clear. Did they know how to communicate in silence? She got an immediate answer that several of them did.

Mariam wondered how young Yahya was doing. Having lost both his parents at an early age had been devastating for him, but he was now in a community with many loving aunts and uncles. He lived with Bartholomew and Celia and they all took turns teaching him. The child had a smile on his young face, but it changed when he saw Mariam. His face darkened, and he turned and walked away. When he came of age he would need to know the story about his father. At some point she would have to let him see him. Mariam knew that. She also knew that it was going to be a long time from now. How much had Anya's anger towards her rubbed off on him? She didn't know. Right now all she sensed was a young boy, grateful to feel safe and loved. But his time alone, at the edge of the desert at an extremely young age, had not made him forget his mother's harsh words. How could he forget having heard his mother screaming at her, that she was the one who killed his father? How could he not feel that it was true? And how could she ever tell him the truth?

"Mariam, dear sister," Lazarus towered over her and enclosed her in his long arms before he even sat down after his trip from Massilia. Mariam was glad to see him and got news about the new group forming there. After the meal that evening, he had his sister alone with him.

"We need to help these people. There are so many serious seekers among them. They are all devoted to the gentle teachings of Yeshua and the communities we are establishing. Women are finding new meaning in cultures where their roles have been circumscribed. They are taking on leadership roles everywhere. There are of course older representatives of their families, who think we are taking their women away from them. Nothing could be farter from the truth. We are simply offering a friendlier alternative."

Mariam listened with interest. She was surprised to hear how much their flocks had grown. Of course, it happened in Judea and in Jerusalem, when Yeshua was standing on the steps of the Temple teaching. They would gather around him in hundreds, sometimes thousands, wherever he went. The attraction now was his teachings presented by his closest followers. It had been like that for a while now. And still people were flocking to them.

"Mariam, should we offer initiations to the ones that think they're ready?"

"What do you mean?" Mariam couldn't believe what Lazarus was proposing.

"I have many who are interested. They have learned a lot, and feel ready for their own experiences."

"Lazarus, that's too risky. The only reason you came back was because Yeshua came and called for you. I can't do that kind of work on my own. We can offer them simpler rituals."

"But I'm here, I can help. These men have worked hard, reading scriptures, preparing their bodies."

"Dear brother, you've had one experience with a powerful ritual. And you were rescued by the most powerful healer I know of."

"Yes, Yeshua helped you. But you're just as powerful as he."

"Reading some books and fasting, is not going to prepare you to unite with the stones of the earth so you can shoot out and join with the stars. You think I'd risk the life of young people just because they feel adventurous?"

"We would do everything we could to make it safe for them."

"Brother, you don't understand. Many of these people come from cultures where there is no work done in the temples. They hardly know that there are forces they cannot see. Their bodies don't know what you and I are talking about."

"We accept people here of all cultures, Mariam, don't be prejudiced."

"I'm not! I'm being practical. How are their bodies going to respond to being put in a cold stone box, show all the signs of death, and then be asked to wake up again and come back to life, when in their own culture the signs of death mean nothing else but that they're dead?!"

"But we know that it works! Yochanan, Yeshua and I, we all came back."

Mariam was getting irritated. She had to make him understand. How could he be so stubborn?

"You had all visited the temples. You know what is written on the walls. You have a whole culture behind you that says that it's possible. The pharaohs went to visit Isis and Osiris and came back. Your mythological heroes did it. Tammuz came back after his journey in the world of the dead. Who came back among the Romans? All the heroes they worship are dead! They died in the battle field or by a sword at the arena. They died heroic noble deaths and disappeared. And they certainly didn't come back to their families."

"But they do believe in life after death," Lazarus protested.

"Yes, I've heard what they believe. Their stories tell them that they will go to a place which looks like the palace of Herod the Great. They will be entertained by Princess Salome and her attendants to the sound of sweet music, and then enjoy the fresh bodies of virgins. That is the reward of the hero. To them life after death is a sensuous experience, where they can surrender to luxury and pleasure. This is not a mythology I can work with. I don't know where their journey would take them and their story doesn't contain a plan of return."

"You're being mean, Mariam. You don't even know them." Was his sister getting narrow minded? Lazarus did not like the tone this had taken.

"If that's the belief of their grandfathers, if that's what their culture collectively thinks, then there is no way I can convince their body that they can return to life. Their lungs, their brains and their hearts wouldn't believe me. They would register the signs of death as death, and stay dead."

Mariam was starting to feel a fire burning deep down in her body. It burned to protect the old knowledge, but she also had to protect the people too ignorant to understand.

"But Mariam…"

"I will not be accused of murder again!" She shrieked, shocked at her own voice.

Mariam felt as if her body had grown spikes. Her insides felt like churning water. She got up and left the room. Lazarus sank down in the pillows with a taste of mud in his mouth.

They avoided each other for a couple of days, but when Mariam was packing up to go to Arelate, her brother came to her and mumbled something before putting his arms around her. Mariam still felt prickly. She wanted to have a decent discussion about this, without the emotional engagement.

Gently, she separated from him and took his hands. He was looking down at the ground between them, feeling the authority of the small figure in front of him. His sister spoke very softly to him. She loved her brother, and did not want there to be any rift between them. But on this issue she could not be moved.

"Lazarus, I understand you want your people to be able to have deeper experiences.

We all have a desire to feel the presence of the Gods. We all want to know we're being protected by unseen forces. There are many ways to achieve that. Maybe you could introduce some easier steps for them. Something that isn't so grounded in thousands of years of a culture infused in stone, in a culture they have no connection to. Teach them the beginnings of healing. Show them silent communication and teach them how to keep a clean emotional field. There will always be people needing help. Write down everything Yeshua said, and then translate it into all their languages."

Mariam was throwing ideas in the air, hoping her brother would grasp onto something. He still had an abandoned look. He had hoped so strongly that she would say yes, and they could eventually build a group of enlightened priests among them. His vision felt prophetic. Now he knew it would never be.

"You can always give them treated water. That at least is not life threatening. The water and the blessed bread will bring enlightenment from within and will work on anybody."

"I'll just need a source for the ingredients." Lazarus wanted to agree with her on something. He looked up with tired eyes and met hers.

"And someone who knows how to make it. There must be mines around here. Didn't Martha learn from the Nazareeans?"

"She assisted on some occasions. I think she learned more at Therapautae. I'll ask her."

A new hope was lit. Mariam saw a new focus take form in her brother, and she hoped he had found a new direction for his considerable energy. She knew he only wanted the best for his people. But sometimes the very best can be too much.

Traveling to Arelate was pleasant, but quiet. They got a ride with some herb growers Sibyl knew, who were returning from the market in Aquae Sextiae. It was only Sarah, little Tamera and herself. They blended in with other farmers on the road sitting on the back of the cart with their bundles around them. Sarah would have preferred to be picked up by a carriage sent by young Agrippa. Mariam was grateful for the anonymity. She had enough on her mind.

Maybe Lazarus had a point, she told herself. Maybe they needed some more structure behind their teachings. Maybe there should be levels of instruction, and maybe some acknowledgment for the students who reached a certain level. Another issue she had noticed was that with the growing numbers, there seemed to be a need for a line of authority. Should it follow the more spiritually advanced, or the one who had leadership qualities? She knew that they didn't necessarily belong to the same individual. She was afraid of anything that started to look like a hierarchy. The system they had at the herb farm was so simple. She realized that it worked with a small group, but as soon as you had more people sharing space and resources there had to be some more structure in place.

Was that what Lazarus started to realize the need for, some structure of leadership and instruction? Was there a danger if they put something like that in place? Mariam felt that she had more questions than answers. She would have to write him a letter from Arelate concerning this.

What would Yeshua think of all this? Was this what he had visualized? Soon she could ask him herself. Thinking of him made all the problems dissipate. She felt as if a ray of sunshine lightened her up on the inside. *He has the same effect as the blessed bread*, she thought to herself. *Remembering him is like having shimmering gold inside.*

They left the cart and the herb growers at the market in Arelate, and started walking towards the Herod mansion. Mariam thought it would have been nice to run into Aiu and his ox cart right now.

You're in town? What didn't you say so? She heard Herodias voice in her head. Had she heard her again? Mariam knew she would get a scolding when they arrived.

Shortly after, Aiu was seen on the road with a cart. It had horses in front, but Mariam still thought it was a pleasant surprise. Sarah dumped all their things into the cart and scrambled on with no comment. Little Tamera was tired and cranky. Mariam was tired herself, but smiled gratefully to Aiu who nodded to her in acknowledgement. If these fine ladies wanted simpler transportation, he was happy to provide it.

"Mariam, are you out of your mind? There are soldiers everywhere!" Herodias couldn't believe her friend. "You could have had a Roman escort! Instead you chose to travel like a beggar. Tamera, beautiful, let me wash your face. Go with Mica to the kitchen and get something warm in your body. Sarah, you know where your room was. Gia, fill Lady Sarah's bathtub for her."

Sarah floated out of the room with Gia, Tamera disappeared happily with Mica and Mariam was left with a furious Herodias.

"Doesn't any news ever reach your ears?"

Mariam had to admit that between her ears there had been a long discussion of great importance and not room for much else. Herodias pulled her into her private parlor and ordered refreshments for them.

"I heard it from Juliana who just returned from Rome. She had it from reliable sources in Jerusalem."

"What is it?" said Mariam, she was tired of being led along. This better be worth it, she was more in the mood for joining Sarah's activities and take a bath.

"The board of trustees at the Temple in Jerusalem has made a big decision. They have abdicated Joseph of Aramathea. He is no longer a member of the council, and not welcome in Jerusalem anymore."

Herodias had Mariam's full attention.

"I thought those positions were for life."

"They were. Unless the whole council agrees that somebody is undesirable. They have decided that one of them doesn't have the trust of the others."

"How did this come about? What caused their decision?"

"It became known, that Joseph had been supporting Yeshua much stronger than they had been aware of, to the point of making use of the temple foundations without their permission."

"That's true. You were part of that ritual as well."

"Yes, *we* know it's true. Who else did?"

"Only us taking part in the ritual. And none of us are in Jerusalem anymore."

"You're forgetting someone."

"The sicarii. I did forget. The guards."

"Apparently they were pressured. It was barely mentioned as a service they had performed for their master, that being Yeshua."

"This is preposterous! That ritual was instrumental for his work."

"Yes, but it was not condoned by the council. They don't like people roaming around underneath the temple tempering with items they don't know the use of themselves."

"And if we had explained the purpose of the ritual they wouldn't have understood either."

"Wrong! They understood perfectly well, but they didn't want you to go through with it. It was the most powerful ritual you could do, Mariam. Don't you get it? With this decision they are actually saying that they understand how much power you two were able to generate. In doing this they are acknowledging who you are, and rejecting you."

"...and saying that they do not want to honor their own old traditions. Oh, Herodias, I never thought it would go this far."

"You are officially declared enemies of the Temple in Jerusalem!"

"They don't understand that we *are* the Temple of Jerusalem."

"You are forever anchored in the stone it stands on."

"We anchored the star of Venus in the foundation it stands on, which is the main purpose of the King and Queen."

They were silent for a moment.

"Where is Uncle Joseph now?"

"On his way here, as far as I understand. Lazarus and his colony is a safe place to stay, but not for long. He can come to me if he wants, but all I can do is hide him. He can't go to Rome or Athens, or Alexandria. The best would be if he returned to Hibernia or England, where he has contacts."

"But you said there are soldiers everywhere. Why would this be safe? Do they want to arrest him? This is a matter between him and the Temple. Why would the Romans care?"

"I don't know. But I heard he's heading here. Besides, you and Yeshua are on the black list too, don't forget that. You're the ones who started all the trouble. It didn't get any better after his followers are proclaiming loud and clear that he didn't die. Or as they say, he didn't *stay* dead."

"But we're peaceful. We didn't want to cause any trouble."

"Mariam, don't be naïve. If you arrive in an occupied country and announce that you're the King and Queen, you don't think somebody would object?"

"But we didn't announce it! We kept it all very silent waiting for things to change."

"Well, the Romans knew. They put it on his cross for the crucifixion so everybody would know what he was accused of. Judea was troubled enough as it was. They certainly didn't want a rebel who would upset the thin relationship they had with the Temple."

"So what does this mean? Are they looking for us?"

"Maybe not openly, but they certainly would like you out of the way. Actually, they're more concerned with his followers. Even Roman high officials are converting left and right."

"Converting? As if we started a new religion? Herodias, that's ridiculous."

"You mean, you didn't start a new religion? You just took the old traditions, added some new ideas, told people the path to enlightenment outside of the temples, told them they didn't *need* the temples to get there, and established colonies where people lived in blissful harmony between men and women. Mariam, don't you see what you've done!"

"I didn't mean to cause all this! I just studied, and applied what I learned. My heritage expected me to marry a certain man and live up to the expectations inherent in my position."

"And now the Roman Empire and the Temple in Jerusalem are after you."

"You might as well throw in the temple in Alexandria too, after what Sibyl did."

"And Ephesus. I'm sure they were questioned after the drama around Antipas and your cousin's famous head."

Herodias was getting a sarcastic enjoyment out of the situation. Marvelous entertainment. Let's watch the scandals blow out of proportion. Let's watch the Romans make fools of them selves one more time.

"Mariam, you know the Romans don't like to feel stupid. It goes against their hero worshipping ideals."

"Do you think they want to kill Yeshua again?"

"That would be to admit that they didn't do it right the first time. I think they would rather silence the people who claim that he lives."

"But he's planning to come here. Is he in danger?"

"Not as long as he lies low and doesn't step up on a tall rock and opens his mouth."

"We've got to warn him."

"How do you expect to keep him silent? As soon as people know he's in town there'll be hordes around him. Mariam, he's already more famous than the emperor."

"As long as the council at the Temple were calm, we were fine."

"Well, you can't blame them for being upset. Everything you did was under their noses and against their judgment."

"Are you on their side?"

"Don't be silly, I'm just trying to be in their sandals for a moment. You weren't exactly following orders or proper traditions. Yeshua spoke against them many times. And he had friends among their enemies."

"Why does religion get confused with politics?"

"Knowledge? Power? Men? Wealth? Take your pick."

"But Yochanan only wanted to bring blessings to people."

"And he spoke up against Antipas' despicable behavior. That's putting his religious nose in a political hornet's nest he should have stayed out of."

"We warned him to not be so outspoken. Anya was so afraid. I guess she was right all along."

"When are you expecting Yeshua to be at the temple of Ra?"

"In two weeks it will have been six months. That's all I have to go on."

"At least you're here for now. Get some rest, Mariam. Tomorrow we'll look into this again and see what we can do."

Even an herbal bath wasn't going to calm Mariam down. Herodias ordered tea with strong wine to be brought to her room. The following morning her friend seemed even smaller than before. For once Herodias didn't have any easy solutions to offer.

CHAPTER 9

THE TEMPLE OF RA

MARIAM DIDN'T KNOW WHAT TO DO. HERODIAS didn't either, which was quite shocking to both of them. Sarah knew exactly what to do. She luxuriated in the big mansion and felt totally at home. Little Tamera found new aunts and enjoyed baths in fancy tubs with aromatic bubbles.

Herodias watched her friend walk like a shadow between the columns of her atrium. She was still trying to analyze the situation, and had sat down between pillows in a comfortable seat with a cup of warm tea. Watching Mariam, usually so strong and on top of the situation, shuffle aimlessly about, trying to get answers from the fish in the pond, was worrying her.

"Stop being pathetic, I can't stand it," she said as Mariam rounded the fishpond for the fourth time.

Mariam turned slowly and looked at her with vacant eyes.

"I understand the situation is bleak, but any action is better than you moping about like that. Come here and sit down. I made tea for you," said Herodias as she patted the seat across from her.

Dutifully, Mariam came and sit down. She accepted the tea cup and prepared herself for a lecture.

Herodias was not planning to lecture her. She wanted to plan to do something instead of staying in this cloudy inactivity, which was going on her nerves.

"We know you need to get to the Temple of Ra. Beyond that we don't know much."

"I don't know if he'll even come."

"We have to count on that. He hasn't told you anything else."

"I sense that he's on his way, but has been delayed by an accident involving a camel."

"Well, they have a powerful healer in their midst, he would fix that quickly."

"If he dares to do any healing work in front of people. He doesn't want to draw any attention to himself."

"I hope he stays clear of Jerusalem."

"Do you think he is going over Greece?"

"Maybe. There are other routes he could take. The route over Greece would bring him close to Rome, and that's the last thing he wants."

Mariam closed her eyes. She tried to find him, find the connection between them. The pain of the long separation had overshadowed her abilities to tune in. He had only appeared to her inner fields in vague images, confusing her more than helping. Her heart had ached searching for him, but she felt as if he had blocked her. The meeting in the cave had been a moment of painful desperation. There was so much unsaid, so many things unclear between them. The joy of seeing him carried the knowledge of the etheric nature of the human body and its fleeting reality. Yes, she held around him for a moment, but every fiber in her body knew that he was just as present in India. Where was he now? Could she find him through her own inner fog and the distance that had been established between them?

"What do you see?"

Her inner sight was still unclear. She had to allow her pain to exist and bypass it, to reconnect. It felt like circling around a field of fog, and finding some clearer view on the other side. She saw a boat, a big ship on an ocean. Sweeping along its side, she felt pulled towards something familiar. The blue water reflected the blue sky, and she saw another reflection in blue eyes. Her whole being was pulled towards the man standing at the railing, and to her surprise she also took in his two companions.

"There are two other men with him. They are close to him, and they all appreciate being together. The air is fresh and the wind is blowing his hair back. I can see his face smiling in the salty wind."

"Mariam, you have no time to lose! He's on a boat somewhere in the Mediterranean! Let's pack you off. And this time I insist on providing your transportation."

"No fancy carriages. I do not want that kind of attention. Something plain. Aiu can take us."

"Sarah will be disappointed."

"I know. Who do you think the other men are?"

Thrilled to have agreed on some movement, Herodias was back to administrating everybody. The following morning they were off. Aiu's wagon had horses, and Herodias sent another man with them as a bodyguard.

"It will look more complete too. You can pass as being a family." Herodias would have loved to come with, but knew her presence would attract attention which nobody wanted.

Mariam packed together her things, and felt she had entered another cloud. This one did not carry pain, but eager anticipation, and a lot of uncertainty. It didn't erase the pain she felt, but it gave it a new quality. It was still unsettling, and she wondered if she would ever feel stable and whole again. How come she hadn't been able to connect with him before? How come he hadn't contacted her?

Sarah looked sullen. She didn't like leaving the mansion, and she couldn't be told all the details of why they were on the road on a wagon again. As a small comfort, Herodias had secretly put an extra pillow underneath the blanket she was sitting on. It was covered in peach silk fabric and had multicolored tassels along the side. Sarah's fingers stroked the side of the pillow underneath her, as she endured sitting on a rough camel blanket. On her plain dress she had put her woven belt of atlas silk from her father. Mariam noticed, but didn't say anything. Little Tamera had made a little nest for herself out of colorful blankets among their bundles. Mariam sat quietly and tried to not show how jittery she felt. *I'm a priestess,* she chided herself. *I know how to handle my inner balance.* She breathed deeply and took in the aroma of the cypress trees.

It took them a whole day along a busy Roman road. They didn't stop in any of the cities, but paused briefly to rest the horses and eat the food Herodias had sent with them, before setting off again.

They arrived at the city called The Mouth of the Rose and looked for the home of Mary and Jacob. Their group had grown too, and they had been given a stately home as a donation from an older widow.

"The agreement is that we'll take care of Lydia for the rest of her life, and believe me, we are happy to do so. Without family, but with means, she now feels she has adopted a clan," Mary informed them. "This is so fortunate for our work. Many people have been rescued here from the awful prosecutions in Rome."

Mariam listened to their stories with controlled patience. The stories from Rome were alarming. It seemed like a new movement had started, against their group in particular. She knew the Romans weren't forgiving of people who had opposed their ruling, but this seemed a little excessive, even for them.

"Oh, they are supported by plenty," said Mary. "My brother defied them openly, but he also angered the Temple in Jerusalem and the Sanhedrin is a powerful group."

"We are people without the distinction of a nation. We don't have a country that will defend us. We don't even have an old religious tradition behind us any more. We're easy prey," Jacob added.

"Let's hope as many as possible make it over here before it gets any worse," Mary said with worried eyes.

Mariam told them of her sister Johanna and younger brother Joses, and how they were doing at the herb farm. There were letters from them, in their own hand writing. They were treated like precious documents and shared with all their members.

Mariam didn't say why she was going to the temple of Ra. What if he didn't come? What if the word got out that he was expected? People would flock to the place and cause more havoc and confusion. They would attract the attention from Roman officials. However much she wanted to scream the news from the roof tops, she had to keep it to herself.

Sarah walked around the spacious home and admired the beauty of the architecture. Even though this was much smaller and less ostentatious than Herodias' place, it had dignity in its simplicity. It was situated nicely in the landscape and had stables for the white horses and black bulls which were raised in this area. Sarah found curtains of Egyptian cotton around windows framed by large wooden beams. There were sturdy wooden tables with colorful linens on. There might not be gold and silk, but the colors and the space suited her. The air was fresh so close to the ocean, and the mouth of the river was near by. The scents reminded her of Alexandria. She took Tamera's hand and showed her the lovely textiles, teaching her about colors and weaving techniques.

The following morning they thanked Aiu for his services and sent him and the body guard back to Arelate. Then they booked a boat ride to the island of the temple.

"We're taking a small boat to the temple that is also called raft in the local language. How is that?" Sarah wanted to know more about the customs in the area.

"I honestly don't know. It must have something to do with the pronunciation of the Egyptian word for temple which sounds the same as their word for raft," Mariam tried to explain.

Tamera was used to traveling now. She was standing on a piece of cargo near the railing so she could see over it. Her small hands held onto the rope along its top and she allowed Sarah to have a protective arm around her belly. The wind tousled her hair and she sniffed the salty air. The adventures of little Tamera would never end. She knew that, and she loved it. Mariam looked at her young daughter and felt that the child's destiny was totally different than her own. What education did Tamera need, to be prepared for the tasks awaiting her?

At the temple they had received her letter, and welcomed her back. They explained that they hadn't had any ships coming in with visitors expecting her yet, but they knew some new ones were due to arrive soon. Would they be comfortable in their rooms? Mariam assured them that they would, and thanked them again for their hospitality. They settled in for a time of waiting.

"Look, Tamera, see the seagulls!"

"Seagulls," said Tamera firmly and pointed towards the birds.

Sarah and Tamera were exploring the temple grounds. This was an Egyptian temple, and an ancient shrine to the Celtic water goddesses, but its location necessitated that it was also a fortification to protect the land. Since the Roman Empire had been established, there hadn't been any attacks here, so the fort was somewhat dormant. The lookout waived at them, having done his job of raising the flag for the day.

One of the temple priests came over to Sarah.

"Would you like to see the temple to the Celtic water goddesses?" He asked politely. He knew they were waiting for a big ship to come in. But this was the second week of waiting, and he could tell that his young guests had run out of ideas to entertain themselves.

Sarah thought that would be interesting, and took Tamera's hand again. The toddler followed her aunt happily in search for new places to explore.

There was another staircase inside one of the towers, which they descended together. The priest explained about the age of the temple, and how the Celts had left it, and were glad when the Egyptian priests revived the honoring of the water along with their other practices.

The temperature dropped, as they came further down along the massive stone walls. The humidity felt cold against their skin. Some of the steps were wet and Sarah held the little girls hand closer. The priest picked a piece of wood out of a holder on the wall, and lit it from a small flame on an oil lamp in a niche. The flame took hold in the tar on the wood and gave them light for continuing into the temple.

Sarah wondered what she had agreed upon. Most of the temples she was familiar with were on hills and had air flowing between massive columns. This was a different experience. She felt they were going into the earth to be near the private water ways of the goddess of the earth itself. Tamera looked around with big open eyes in the semidarkness.

The steps ended at a pool with water flowing through it. The water was led there from the ocean and would ebb and flow with the tide. She could tell that the steps continued beneath the water level and would be slippery, but accessible at low tide.

The priest lit more torches already hanging on the wall ready for use. Sarah watched as he put fire to two on the back wall and one on either side. They provided enough light to see the space. The wall across the basin was built with large uncut stones. Between the bigger stones were smaller ones, some of them were clear, letting the sun shine through from the outside. The torches lit the staircase, but did not disturb the effect on the water.

Tamera was totally quiet. She had set her eyes on something in the water. Sarah had to bend forward to see what caught her attention. Soon she saw what intrigued the child, and after getting used to the strange lighting arrangement she was mesmerized herself.

In the wall was a larger green clear stone. The light came through it, and went down in the water creating a green orb of light, playing a foot beneath the surface. The sphere of light was the size of one of Tamera's balls, small enough to grasp between her hands and big enough to throw between them. But this one had no substance. It existed as a free floating image of light, playing with the texture of the water. The water from the ocean was dark blue, or was it green? The sphere of light had the color of green glass.

"They called her Bridget," said the priest quietly. "She's always here."

Sarah could hear that he felt reassured by the presence of the image. He liked having a goddess present on this island dedicated to Ra who was considered a male god.

"The fire in the sky can play with the water. They are constantly flirting with each other," he said poetically, making Sarah smile.

"He is fire, she is water. This is the way they can meet," he continued with sympathy admiring the orb of light.

The light flickered underneath the water. Another color joined them. The sun had shifted slightly and a smaller red stone became the next crystal to catch the light. It bounced on the surface of the water, but didn't penetrate further down.

"Only she can do that," he said finishing Sarah's thought.

They stood there for a while admiring the movement of the green light. Sarah felt herself shifting out of focused thought, and taking in her surroundings with her peripheral vision. Her attention was not going out through her front anymore. Instead she felt a flow coming into her sides making her notice her surroundings with different senses. It felt as if her skin could see the cold wet walls, and her nose could feel the texture of moisture on stone. The water flowed underneath the basin in front of them. She could sense the constant intake and outpour of the current. This unending renewal of water, changed the quality of the air in the room. Sarah felt surrounded with moist air, always ready for new life, ready to receive the green light again and again as it twinkled in and out of ripples in the water.

"Bridget," she said quietly to herself.

"Bridget," repeated the child next to her.

A commotion was heard above them. From beyond the staircase someone was calling their names.

"It is time to leave," said the priest. "They're looking for you."

He extinguished the torches and led them upstairs. The green light in the water was even more intense behind them in the dark.

Sarah's eyes had to get used to the strong light of the day. She was affronted with sunrays. The God Ra was greeting them head on. The gentle approach shown at the temple of Bridget became a soft, green memory of motion.

On the terrace in front of the temple there were people milling back and forth. Tamera stopped stubbornly and didn't want to move. Sarah gave her a little time to shift out of what they had experienced in the Celtic temple, but then she told her that they had to go and find her mother. *Maybe also her father,* she thought silently.

Many people had arrived with the big ship Sarah saw anchored a little further out. Most of them just wanted immediate transportation into town. The ship let the passengers off here before heading for Massilia with their cargo. The temple enjoyed the traffic. It didn't happen very often, most ships did go to Massilia without stopping, or continued to Ruscino so their passengers could catch Via Aquitania and head for the Atlantic coast on land. But for some, this was a perfect stopping point. The road to Arelate went directly from the Mouth of the Rose, and the boat connection between the temple and the small town was constant. No wonder the locals started to call the temple the local word for raft.

Sarah saw Mariam standing by the stone fence, watching the smaller boats come in with passengers and their bags. She held her shawl tighter around her chest against the wind and allowed her dark hair to flow freely behind her. Sarah saw her sister's beauty, but also that she was getting older. Her fingers were grasping around the fringes of the end of her shawl. This was the third ship that had come in while they were there. Sarah knew that Mariam needed her husband. The separation had been long. Their daughter was almost three years old now.

One dinghy came in with merchants eager to come home to their families in Arelate. Other people would handle their shipments in Massilia. They chattered eagerly as they asked for the next boat into town. Mariam smiled at them with friendly but tired eyes.

The next boat had three men and some simple bundles. Could he be one of them?

They came closer and she recognized their faces. She turned quickly to Sarah with a beaming smile. Sarah felt warmth on her face and thought her sister was shining brighter than the sun itself. She picked up her niece and carried her to the fence where Mariam was standing.

"Your father is coming," she said to the child.

"Father is coming," said Tamera mimicking her aunt.

They disappeared into each others arms as soon as he was safely out of the boat. The other two men waited politely until Mariam could give them her attention.

"I've brought my father. And my uncle," said Yeshua as soon as he could catch his breath.

"Father Joseph," said Mariam, "how wonderful to see you again. I want to hear your story soon. Uncle Joseph, I've heard the news. I'm glad to see you here."

"Mariam." The two men were obviously relieved to find her, and find her well. They admired the child, and greeted Sarah who was praised as the best caregiver Tamera could ever have wished for.

Mariam was overwhelmed. She didn't just get Yeshua back. She got the other two men she respected and loved. After leaving Joseph at Serabit, she didn't think she'd ever see him again. And Uncle Joseph, who was now unwanted in Jerusalem, she wasn't sure if he would make it here either. How did they happen to all come on the same boat?

The conversations in the dining hall at the temple that night went in all directions. They all wanted to hear how Father Joseph came through the desert. And they all wanted to know how Uncle Joseph got out of Jerusalem. But the story of how Yeshua found his way back from the Far East intrigued them the most.

"I knew he was there," Yeshua said, "so I had to go to Serabit. I was coming through the desert from Persia anyway, and I couldn't go anywhere near Judea. I got a ride with a caravan, and found him at the temple."

"You can say I was surprised," said Joseph laughing at them all.

Uncle Joseph was remarkably quiet. The ocean air had been good for him, but there was a lot on his mind. After recounting how they had all found each other in Alexandria looking for suitable passage to Gaul, he retired to the room provided for him.

Mariam felt her body sink into the chair she was sitting on. Her heart had settled into calmer rhythms and her inner organs seemed to have lowered their position. She listened to their stories without taking in the words being said, but seeing in her inner vision what they had seen on their journey. In front of her was her husband, her Yeshua, her king, with Princess Sarah Tamera in his arms. As his father filled them in on his time on the caravan, Yeshua looked at her quietly across the table. She saw that she had been right. His eyes did reflect both the sea and the sky.

While they were eating, another boat came to the temple. This one came from the Mouth of the Rose. It had a single passenger who had paid extra to be taken to the temple at this hour. He hurried up from the pier and was looking for the visiting priestess and her lady in waiting. One of the temple attendants came to Mariam with the message. She left the warm dining room and greeted him in the courtyard.

"Jacob, what brings you here? You came just in time. Your brother…"

"Yes. Indeed I came just in time," Jacob interrupted her looking nervously around him. "Mariam, why didn't you tell me he was coming?"

"What is it? What's bothering you?" Mariam changed her expression.

"Take me to him, sister."

On the way to the dining hall, Jacob told her to keep everything very quiet. He would explain. They arrived seeing Yeshua holding Tamera, and Joseph talking to her. Sarah looked golden, as she took in the reunion of the family. Mariam sent a silent message to all of them, about not making too big of a happy outburst. She could feel Jacob's inner turmoil, and realized she had made a mistake. The others looked up when they saw them, nodded to Jacob, and their eyes were questioning.

"Are you out of your mind?" Wheezed Jacob to his brother.

"What a greeting, brother, what news do you bring?" Yeshua tried to keep a light tone in spite of Jacob's insistence on that things were quite serious.

Jacob calmed down and hugged his father, with tears in his eyes.

"Traveling all three of you together? Don't you know? And now coming here to the mother and child?"

"But Jacob, I promised to be here. And I wanted to see my daughter. Isn't she something else?" Tamera giggled to her father in agreement.

Mariam suddenly understood what Jacob meant. She counted how many they were, and realized they were all related. Not just related to each other, they were all the very next of kin to Yeshua and Joseph of Aramathea. She looked across the table at Sarah, who gasped and put her hand to her mouth. This time the telepathic contact between them was instant.

Jacob had heard soldiers talk. They knew that two men were on their way to Aquae Sextiae together with Joseph of Aramathea. The soldiers had joked that the King of the Jews couldn't be stupid enough to travel with his uncle. Then they could catch both of them. Jacob had felt the blood drain from his face. His brother could indeed have done that without knowing the danger he put them in. Wondering who the third man could be, Jacob had seen his father smiling at him. He knew that since Uncle Joseph was unwanted in Jerusalem, he wasn't welcome anywhere else in the Roman Empire. After all the rumors about Yeshua not dying, there were enough followers to worry the emperor, to the point were he was starting to hunt them down.

Jacob was crying. He would love to have his brother in Gaul. He had hoped for a time when Yeshua could come and teach at all their colonies. His followers were strong here. Mariam had been teaching. Lazarus had been administrating the beginning colonies. They were growing in Massilia too now, thanks to his work. They would love to see Yeshua. It would be an incredible event for them all. But that was exactly the problem. If he arrived in Gaul, they wouldn't be able to keep it quiet. How many people here at the temple knew who he was? Jacob couldn't be too careful.

"They want to get rid your kin!" Jacob was adamant. "Rome has started a hidden campaign against this family. And how many of us have you assembled right here? What were you thinking?"

Yeshua looked around at all the people he loved. How could this be wrong?

"Gaul has welcomed us," Jacob continued. "And it would welcome you loudly and with great enthusiasm. But we can't afford that. You are still wanted under Roman law. If they didn't kill you the first time, they'll do a better job when they catch you again. Brother, you have to go far away from here, where the Roman arm cannot reach you."

"That was exactly my thought as well," they heard an authoritative voice say. Uncle Joseph had returned to them. His presence had been needed.

"Uncle…," Jacob caught himself before he said his name.

"Nephew," said Uncle Joseph in greeting and sat down.

Mariam was crying by now. Little Tamera had returned to her mother to comfort her. Silent tears rolled down Mariam's cheeks making Tamera's hair wet. Sarah wasn't sure what to think. She felt more bewildered than anything else. What did all this mean?

CHAPTER 10

THE CELTIC WATER GODDESS

SARAH COULDN'T SLEEP. THERE WERE TOO MANY thoughts tumbling in her head. She had listened for as long as she could, to the talk between the men about the good things building around them in Gaul, and all the destruction happening in other places. Then they had to discuss what to do next. They had tried to keep the discussion low and short. They were still in the dining room at the temple. There were other people present who could hear them. Sarah noticed that they tried to not say names of people and places, but give code phrases instead. They also tried to keep it all in a lighter tone than what they felt. But with Jacob looking like a funeral, and Mariam not able to keep her eyes dry, anyone could see that they were discussing serious matters. Father Joseph had just stared at all the people he loved so much, including his grandchild whom he had only known as a hovering spirit before she was born. As little Tamera fell asleep on her grandfathers lap, they had sent her to bed with Sarah.

She tried to rest as she held around the small body in front of her. Pulling the warm child closer to her, she clung to the hope that they had found a solution. Dreamily she made her own wishes. She didn't want her sister to leave her, and she didn't want Mariam to be alone again. She wanted father Joseph to be able to spend time with all his children. She wanted Yeshua and Uncle Joseph to be safe, and for Yeshua to be able to teach again. But beyond all, she did not want to be separated from the child. Tamera whimpered as Sarah squeezed her too hard.

Finding the last thought as the only clear one she could recognize, she felt wide awake. Leaving Tamera tucked in the blankets on the bed, she left the room for some fresh air. She grabbed a cape against the cold night and closed the door to their room behind her. At the end of the corridor she pulled the door to the outside and felt the air on her face. She let it brush away the troubles that didn't concern her directly, and found strength in her own strongest desire; to continue the loving care of her niece.

The dark night sky was clear, and she saw her familiar constellations. The bright star low in the horizon was unmistakable. She smiled at it, and prayed to her favorite star friend for a resolution. Standing at the railing at the court in front of the temple, she watched the waves on the ocean for a while. Her feet wanted to move, so she walked along the stones and let the night sky have her thoughts. Watching the pattern of the stones, allowing her eyes to rest on something predictable, she let her feet wander for a bit. She soon found herself at the steps to the Celtic Temple.

Did she want to go down? She wasn't quite sure. It was dark and she was alone. Remembering the beauty of the green light, her curiosity got the best of her. How did it look at night?

Grabbing her dark cape closer around her she ascended the stairs. A faint glow came from further down. Did it really shine that bright in the night? Keeping her hand along the wall and stepping down carefully with her soft leather sandals, she was entering the temple with a new reverence. The beauty of the light from the water was shimmering along the walls, giving her face a green tint with a pattern of moving water across. Coming closer she saw a shape in the temple. As she realized what it was, she made herself be quiet, even though her immediate reaction was to gasp and run away. She sunk down on the steps to an unrecognizable clump and disappeared among the stones, as she pulled her knees and feet inside the dark cape. Her brown eyes were clear, as witnesses in the dark.

They had taken a blanket with them for the floor, one of those with camel hair on the outside and fine wool on the inside. Thinking they were alone, their clothing was on the edge of the blanket that marked their territory. A single small oil lamp was on the floor giving a dim glow around them creating a golden sphere around their bodies.

He was sitting with his back to her. Sarah recognized his long light hair. Her sister's darker skinned arms were around his neck and her dark hair mixed with his on his left shoulder. She lifted her face to him and they kissed while he lifted her up and positioned her above his crossed legs. Her ankles locked behind him around his hips as she lifted her head and took in air. As she exhaled she sunk down, uniting with him allowing the longing of many empty years its expression.

Sarah watched their breath become fog in the cold chamber. The tide came in and flooded the basin next to them. The fire inside her own body united with her own holy water, as she watched the light of Bridget glitter with the sparks of a thousand stars through millennia of time.

CHAPTER 11

LEAVING GAUL

SARAH WAIVED AT HER SISTER AS THE boat left the shore. It was barely dawn and the wind was bitter. Tears were streaming down her face, at the same time she was smiling. Little Tamera was crying for her mother and pointing at the boat. Sarah used both her arms to steady to the child, and was happy and sad at the same time. Jacob stood next to her. They were scheduled to take the next boat in the opposite direction.

Mariam was sitting next to Yeshua in the rocky small boat that would take her to the big ship heading for Ruscino. The captain was waiting for Uncle Joseph anyway, but he thought he would have only the noble man back from the flock of people who had left them the night before. Father Joseph was very quiet. He left four children in Gallia, whom he wasn't sure he would ever see again. Joses and Johanna were on an herb farm in a landscape he was unfamiliar with, and Jacob and Mary were in a small town taking care of en elderly widow and a growing community. And with them, a beautiful grandchild he had only enjoyed for a few hours.

Yeshua was also thoughtful. He had looked forward to see what his brother and brother-in-law had accomplished in Gaul. Their stories hadn't reached him until he came to Alexandria. He still felt the sweet flavor of the beginning of important things. Mariam would fill him in, he knew that, but to see Lazarus again, his sisters and brothers, the three different colonies and the herb farm. He was almost sick with the thought that he hadn't been allowed to visit his people. Was Jacob too cautious? Maybe, but Yeshua knew he had no right to put the colonies and his family in danger to satisfy himself.

"It's better if they never knew you were this close," said Jacob with pain in his eyes.

He had to agree. He bit his lips and hugged Mariam closer. Would he ever see his daughter again? Mariam felt his pain, but had too much pain of her own to be of much comfort. Nobody should have to choose between a husband and a child. She lifted her hand and waived again as the heads of Sarah and Tamera blended into one in the distance.

Uncle Joseph held his head high. He had a precious cargo to bring safely to his other homeland. A chapter of his life was over. He knew he would never travel further east in the Mediterranean Sea than Gaul. It was more than a country he left behind. It was a heritage. The salty drops of water refreshing his cheeks were coming from the north.

CHAPTER 12

ARRIVING IN AQUATAINE

THE CAPTAIN WAS GLAD TO HAVE JOSEPH of Aramathea back on board. He had carried cargo for the wealthy man many times, and was proud to do so again. The people he took with him this time all seemed sad, not like previous times when his visitors had been excited about the voyage. Give them some time. The brisk sea air could clear the most miserable dispositions.

The captain was right. Another day of sea travel and they all started talking again, mostly about details of the ship and the ocean. The captain understood there were many unsaid things among them, but that didn't surprise him if they were traveling with Joseph. He liked watching the younger man and his wife. They were obviously delighted to be together. Were they just married? They seemed a little old for that. Their gentle movements towards each other told of a longer relationship. And their obvious enjoyment of being together, gave him the impression that their relationship was alive and well. In fact, there was something different about them. Everybody else was on their best behavior when they were around. The captain had no explanation for this. Was it the beautiful woman who surrounded herself with civilization?

The port of Ruscino was calm and quiet. They approached it in the morning sunlight, and the pillars of the forum further inland turned orange against their own sharp shadows. Joseph explained that he preferred this port to the one in Narbonne, which was more used and sported an incredible volume of traffic. Via Domitia went through both ports and they could easily hook up with Via Aquitania from Narbonne as well as Ruscino.

"We could also choose the inland roads. There is a network of local roads here, parallel, but at a good distance from Via Aquitania. I have traveled them before. There are interesting places along the way, and we'll be out of earshot of the Romans. They prefer their own roads."

The others thought that was a good idea. Mariam stood at the railing and looked at the landscape in front of her. Even though this was also Gaul, it looked very different than where she had lived for three years. Massilia and Arelate belonged to one of the first Roman provinces and had lovingly been called Provence. The peaceful harmonious landscape had appealed to her, and put her nerves at rest at a time when she needed it. The land meeting her here was rougher. She could see high mountains in the distance and cragged mounts told her of a more challenging climb, than the rolling hills she had grown to love. Whereas Provence put her at ease, this made her excited. Mariam was looking forward to explore a new territory.

Father Joseph looked at the landscape as well. He had been told that there were several Celtic settlements in this area, and many Celtic holy places. Would they see any on this journey? He knew they had a lot of land to cover before they could catch up with the next boat in Bituriges, or Bordeaux as the locals said it.

Uncle Joseph had a contact in Ruscino that handled the tin and other metals which he mined in Cornwall and Somerset in Britain. The trade routes for these metals had been established over centuries and had gotten stronger with the growth of the Roman Empire. The roads and sea ports had been built for this purpose, and the Romans had encouraged trading between their colonies. The generals in Rome watched the healthy exchange of goods produced in different places, with as much care as they gave their military campaigns. Rome wanted power and dominance over land, but they were equally interested in resources, and how it could be distributed over their vast territories. The colonies and cities along the Mediterranean all enjoyed the wealth of grain harvested in northern Africa, the linen grown along the Nile, the fine olive oil from the Greeks, along with the wines from Gaul. Goods were brought in from other strong empires as well. With the support for commerce over land and sea the people were familiar with the silks and spices from India and pearls from Ceylon. The horses bred along the silk route stretching all the way to China, were legendary.

Along with commerce came an exchange of ideas and written material. The Library in Alexandria held the largest collection of documents originating from the entire known world. It was open to anyone who wanted to study and find their way through their extensive organized files. People traveled to follow their tradable goods to their destination, to visit relatives who had settled in other countries, and to explore the vast world so readily available to them. Different religious traditions existed side by side with due respect for each others practices. The Romans had a tendency to pick up local deities and give them new Roman names creating hybrid gods. In some places such practices were welcomed. Serapis was a composite god from the Apis bull of old Egyptian origin, Zeus from the Greeks and a local water deity. The wisdom of Isis and Sophia was also represented in this image, and his statue in the columned temple at the Serapium was immense. The material of the statue had ground semi precious stones mixed in and glowed in blues and greens. During the Triumvirate ruling of Egypt, people liked the new temple where all the different populations of Alexandria could honor a version of a deity they recognized.

A lot could be said about the Romans and their conquering of other nations, but in the wake of their colonization, a new hybrid of culture materialized. It had a level of democracy, a level of law and order, sanitation had been introduced cleaning up filthy cities, and people were introduced to the theatre, the arts and the sports displayed on the arenas. Civilization had arrived, and if the people accepted the powerful version of Rome, a new form of wealth and culture seemed to follow. It was the more subtle values that seemed to be swept aside by the strong arm holding up the Eagle. The ancient Egyptians became known for worshipping the dead, Venus was reduced to a star, and nobody knew how to work with unseen forces anymore.

"How about a good meal?" suggested Uncle Joseph. "I know a place that makes the best breakfast. You can hear the clucking from the chickens in the back yard, who just laid the eggs you're eating."

The faces around him turned from weary to welcoming smiles. Laughter is always the best medicine for gloom, and they left their bundles with Habib, the tin man who promised to have horses for them when they returned, and went in search for Uncle Joseph's favorite place.

The food was indeed good, and they felt freer to talk again here, far away from Eagle standards.

"We still have to be careful," Uncle Joseph warned them. "The ears of Rome reach far and wide."

"What's beyond here, Joseph, what's awaiting us?" Yeshua was curious, holding onto Mariam's hand.

"Evergreen trees, rugged stony hills and mountainsides, good rivers and small towns and settlements."

"You mentioned interesting places," Mariam wanted more details.

"You'll see," said Joseph with a smile full of secrets.

CHAPTER 13

THE LETTERS

MARIAM'S FIRST LETTER TO SARAH

Dearest Sister,

I hope this finds you and Tamera well. Please kiss her every night, telling her that her mother loves her and will return.

We arrived safely in Ruscino, and Uncle Joseph arranged for horses to be readied for us for our further journey. The town of Ruscino is small and charming. There is a Roman Forum there which holds some officials, but other than that, there is not much to find of the Roman presence so prevalent other places. Aquitania has been an independent sovereign country for a long time, and has a somewhat different culture than the section of Gaul we call Provence. We meet Celts here, and people from many of the northern countries of Africa. There is a whole colony of people of Judaic descent and many from places farther north.

The horses are friendly. I'm riding with ease. The roads call for horses, wagons would have a harder time on the journey Joseph has laid out for us. We left the coast with two extra men and provisions, and started inland along local small roads to avoid the more populated Via Aquitania. The local people here speak a colloquial Latin which Joseph understands. I can pick up a word in between, and I can make them understand me. We stayed overnight the first night in a small town at an inn Joseph knew from before. The next day we followed a river called Agly inland, heading almost straight west.

Joseph promised that we would see interesting places, and he is not disappointing. He led us to a hidden gorge between two mountains. The locals call it Gorges de Galamus. We had to make the horses climb the steep hillside, following a trail he found with some difficulty. It led us to a shelf, following the mountain wall where we could observe the 300 feet deep gorge

364

as we climbed along it. The men insisted on a rope between us to keep us together. Sarah, it was scary. The mountain side is almost perpendicular, and there is a river far below. Between, there are countless juts and rocks that most certainly would kill you if you fell. The vista is breath taking. I've never seen such scenery. But what amazed me the most was the people who live here.

A side trail took us to a hidden grotto in the mountain side where some people lived, keeping perpetual watch. They considered it holy according to old Celtic traditions, and stayed there to honor the water inside the mountain. Remember the temple to the water goddess at Ra? There is a beautiful side to the Celts; they always honor water. It is so essential to our well being and for the balance in nature. We seem to take it for granted.

I stayed in the grotto for a long time. There was water dripping from the ceiling, and a water basin had been built at the back wall. Sarah, this inner space was as big as a temple. It resonated with the sound of the mountain, and our own voices. You know the great voices of Yeshua and his father. Now add Uncle Joseph's, which we rarely hear, and my high alto and you have an amazing effect. I assembled our choir and led them through the evening songs from Therapautae. The humble people who live there sat down and listened. They liked that we established a vibration in the stone that could resonate better with humans.

Remember we talked about the stones near the mountain farm having faces? They seem to have personalities. You used to show Tamera, making her laugh. Well, here it seems even stronger. This mountain has such a strong peaceful presence. I feel at ease here. The inner voices between us are easily heard. The flow of essence between husband and wife is effortless. Does it have something to do with the honoring of water, since it is such an old and established tradition here? Water flows, water runs, water nourishes. Water has the ability to crawl under obstacles, and finds its way through the smallest of openings. It brings things, it is the carrier of other substances. It brings life. Water flows through our bodies, through the rivers and makes waves on the ocean. It travels over long distances as raindrops and finds other groups of people to nourish.

Dear sister. So far this journey finds me well. It is good to be with Yeshua again, although I miss you and Tamera. You know I will return. Please share my letters with the others. Father Joseph sends his greetings to all his children. Uncle waves at me as he is arranging for this letter to go with a lone traveler heading for Ruscino. Habib will send it on a ship in your direction. And thank you, Sarah, for being a mother to my child. I couldn't have left her with anybody else.

Your loving sister,
Mariam.

MARIAM'S LETTER TO HERODIAS

My dearest friend, dear Herodias,

I'm writing from my journey through Aquitania, and I trust that before you get this letter, I will be further on my way towards my goal. I hope this finds you well, and that you can keep some contact with people that inspire you.

We have traveled along hidden roads and paths, meeting welcoming local people. Uncle wanted to show us certain places along the road, which we wouldn't have found any other way, and I'm grateful for his local knowledge. Having traveled the route several times a year for decades, obviously made him explore the territory thoroughly.

Herodias, you won't believe what he knows, and where he's leading us. After a harrowing route through a mountain gorge where we visited a grotto, much bigger than the one you worked at with me, we have arrived at a hidden community I would never have believed existed. They live the way we have tried to establish healthy communities; with equality for all and honesty between everybody. This is nestled between five mountain tops. One of them is called Bezu. It is one of the places of the earth, where Venus makes a footprint of her pentagonal path.

In the center of the pentagram there is a temple dedicated to her. It is not Roman, Egyptian or Greek. This is established by older people, Celts, who settled here hundreds of years ago. They say they come from the ocean, long before anyone can remember. Their rough stone dwellings are at the foot of this narrow ridge, but the holy place is on the top. There is a ceremonial path to walk up there, and they honor the star at the seasonal events taking place.

We walked with them up there. They invited us to join them, especially father Joseph with his background. At his age he was a bit slower, but arrived on the top with everybody else. We stood in a circle on the narrow space, people are not scared of heights in this area, and they did a ceremony between their standing stones to honor the shifting of Venus, from a morning star to an evening star at this time. Joining voices with them, we sang her in, as the daylight faded and she was again visible in the night sky. The connection between the earth underneath us and the star above was again established. Later that night, Yeshua and I went up alone, and did the Hieros Gamos on the central stone in her honor. I couldn't have wished for a more powerful bridal chamber.

Herodias, these people know so much. They work with the blessed fields, the way we learned at Serabit in Sinai. The knowledge of Joseph is again welcomed. He knows how to refine the gold. Yeshua knows how to use it, and how to prepare people for its effect. We've been learning new things from these people. They know how to connect with Venus, through developing further the same techniques we have learned. Yeshua is intrigued. He wants to learn more from them. We'll see how much time we can spend here. There is so much light inside these people. They seem to illuminate the spaces they occupy. As if they have become children of the star they are devoted to.

I had to share this with you, dear friend. I knew you would find it interesting I hope this beautiful place can stay untouched by other influences for a long time. Maybe we can visit it together some time.

With the blessings of Venus,
Mariam.

Mariam's Letter To Lazarus

Dear brother, dear Lazarus,

with greetings to Martha and the people of your growing colonies.

I've thought so much about you. Dear caring brother, I hope this finds you and your people well. I send my blessings to you all, and to you as a teacher.

The journey through Aquitania continues to be an adventure. We are all faring well, and are grateful for this becoming a journey of learning, as well as an adventure. Having just left the temple of Venus, we stopped at the town near the river which tastes salty, even though it has no connection to the ocean. There are so many springs leading into this river, and one of them apparently goes through a field of salt before reaching the surface. The locals call it river Sals, for good reason. We found a spring coming right out of the earth emptying into the small tributary called The Lovers, before it found the bigger river. Then we followed it until it widened out. There were many flat stones in the middle of the water, so we were bathing in the refreshing mountain water. It smelled different than water in other places. Not just from the salt, but from the many minerals in the streams of water coming down the mountain. It is as if the water shares the life force of the lush green landscape we see along the hills. Father Joseph said his joints felt better, after allowing the water to cover his body. We noticed a change to the better on Yeshua's scars, after he had been floating in the river for an hour. I didn't know he loved water so much. I guess all his years in the desert make him appreciate it more. The people here are friendly. They look extraordinarily healthy for their ages, and attribute it all to the healing effects of the water. Again, I'm finding people honoring the water, respecting the water.

But what I really wanted to share with you, brother, appointed voice master of our people, is something that will stretch your imagination.

We continued traveling along the salty river until it reached a bigger river they call Aude. We followed it a little north and came to a town where the people called Velleta lived. They were also called Attax by another tribe. These people had developed a way to speak, using the sounds of birds! They could communicate over large distances, talking in codes using the song and sounds of birds. This could make them invisible in the landscape, but with a high level of detailed communication possible. In fact, they identified so much with birds that their burial ground looked like the holes birds make in trees for their homes. The bird people had cut holes in the mountain and placed the bones of their dead in there, the way some of our people do with ossuaries.

But this is not all. These people have developed their techniques over centuries. They have even figured out how to make notification on stone that signifies the different bird calls. A man showed me a cut stone which had different lines and scratches on each side. He whistled each of the tones for me to understand which ones were depicted. Than he called five of his friends over, and had them each whistle a phrase as it appeared on one side, while he took the sixth. Together they formed a lovely choir of high and low birdsong. Then he pointed at his stone. I looked at it. He put his ear to it and told me to do it on the other side. Lazarus, the stone was singing their song! These people have figured out a way to tune cut stones to sing. The man took me to where they were building a new temple. He showed me that each stone had been tuned differently. I stood for a while in an alcove which they were planning to build a curved ceiling above. Around me the stones were humming a complicated musical piece, with the voices of hundreds of beautiful birds. My body resonated with them, and I stood there sensing how we all belong to the same substance, how my body and the air around me are made of the same material. It is all just different collections of sound. As I left, I felt that my body took in what had been air in front of me, and the air behind me took over the body I left behind. I was a piece of sound manifesting myself as I moved. The birds around me chirped. Did they read the stones they were sitting on?

From there Uncle Joseph led us up a narrow, rocky path to the nearby mountain top. He wanted to show Father Joseph the standing stone marking the top of the mountain. This was the work of the Druids and Celts from a long time ago. We sat on our horses next to the menhir and looked at the landscape as it appeared in front of us. Brother, the snow dotted blue mountains circling us in the distance, met the sky and played with the clouds. Below were fertile green valleys and forests with small farms and villages. Along the river Aude we could see a herd of cows grazing in the meadow. There were poppies blooming, creating a touch of red next to the yellow orchid like flower on the broom plant giving a scent of honey along our path.

Lazarus, I have fallen in love with another beautiful landscape. I would love to come back here, and learn more so I could share it with you. May you and Martha do well in your work, continuing the beautiful traditions we learned at Therapautae. Keep singing.

Your loving sister,
Mariam.

MARIAM'S LETTER TO SIBYL

Dear Sibyl,

May this letter find you in good health. My greetings go out to Johanna, Joses and Trym. I can smell the aroma of the herbs fields, as I think about you. A small vial of your perfume is always with me.

The journey through Aquitania has given me much inspiration. I've learned so much from the diverse populations here. They are older than the nations we find in Alexandria, and they keep to their old ways. The Celts have many traditions of honoring the water and the earth, which remind me of the way we honored Isis and Osiris. Did we learn from them?

Uncle Joseph has taken us to a dolmen, a Celtic holy place. He knew the druids who live there. It is in Gayda, not far from Julia Carcas, the Roman garrison, which we obviously avoided. They welcomed us all at their simple dwellings, and were especially interested in Father Joseph and what travels brought him their way. Joseph had a long story to tell, which he would have loved to tell among his children. He speaks fondly of them every day.

We were invited to partake in their ceremony at the summer solstice. After several days in their settlement we were told to be ready at midnight. The druids led us in a procession along the periphery of a hill. I had been admiring the stone formation visible on the top. To visit their ancient temple was an honor. We sang songs to the Earth Mother and the balancing points of the year as we walked along the path.

There are several large flat stones lying on top of standing stones creating a building that is partly submersed in the landscape. The stones are remarkably smooth. The standing ones forming the walls of the entrance corridor have been arranged in a pattern, alternating with of groups of smaller stones in between. The low tunnel entrance leads into a larger chamber with a taller ceiling. From there you find a small round opening forming the entrance into the last chamber. The opening is formed by two flat finer stones standing next to each other, meeting in a fine line with a slit of open space between them. Each stone has had a half circle chiseled out of it, and together they form the round opening in the middle to enter the inner space. The druids explained the magnetic field there, created by the metal content in the chosen stones.

We bent our backs and walked through the first entrance tunnel. It was dark and damp, and I sensed the closeness of the large stones. The sections of smaller stones in between gave a different sensation, creating a rhythm on your skin as you passed through. In the taller chamber we stood up and stretched. I noticed water flowing along the sides of the walls. The room felt cool and moist. Yeshua took my hand and we continued singing to the Great Mother, asking her to water the land and grow good crops for this year. The druids let us go through the circular opening, one at the time. They showed us to carefully put our head in first, and then lift our feet high over the tall part of the thin stone by the floor beneath the circle. I made myself small and bent my head down, arching my back as I passed through the stone membrane. Inside the next chamber, the feeling of the stone walls changed. It felt warmer and I could smell iron ore. In the dark room I entered, I could make out the back wall made with two triangular stones standing back to back to each other. One had a taller tip than the other. We stood along the sides of the room singing to the earth and the sun as we waited for the morning light to arrive. I leaned against Yeshua's arm and rested my head against his shoulder.

The Solstice morning came in as a thin beam of light, starting at the upper part of the back wall. We all held our breath as we watched its movement. In the dim light, I noticed that the water trickling across the stones had collected in the furrow between the two triangles. As the light came in, it moved slowly down along the same line, creating sparkles as it played with the water. Then it exploded in a large circular shape on the wall, as the sunlight found the round opening we had crawled through. A collective gasp went through room, as the bright light blinded our eyes. Ra had come inside Mother Earth. It lasted only a moment. Then it became a thin line again following the furrow on the wall and crawling across the floor before it pulled back and disappeared as the sun rose above the entrance.

Sibyl, it was beautiful, and reminded me of the work we did at the Serapium. I think of our time as temple novices with fondness. We learned so much as we partook in the big ceremonies. I haven't seen any other temples, besides Ephesus, doing it on the scale we did. Have people forgotten how important this is? We must work to bring back the honoring of the earth, the sun and the water. We need to work with the Great Mother to help the growth of the land. We need to honor the water, so it will continue to nourish us and the plants we work with. We need to honor the sun for its warmth and life giving light. And we need to honor the stars that keep us connected to everything. Sibyl, on my return I will need your help with this. Keep this in your thoughts.

> With the blessings of the Great Mother Isis,
> Your Mariam.

Mariam's Letter To Mary And Jacob

Dear Mary and Jacob,

sister- and brother-in-law and friends in spirit.

May this letter find you well. I hope your colonies thrive and grow in knowledge and health. My eternal gratitude goes out to your for the care of my sister and my child. My companions send their greetings to you all. I hope my other letters have arrived and been shared with everybody.

We are now traveling along Via Aquitania from Tolosa to Burdigate where another ship is expecting our arrival. We avoided the section of the road between Narbonne and Tolosa, and opted to travel the paths among the local people. I will never forget the welcome we received in Languedoc nor the profound understanding these people have of the relationship between human beings, the landscape around them, mother earth and the spirits of the stars. I have learned much, which I look forward to share upon my return.

We can say much about the Romans and their presence in countries that are not their own, but we also have to admire their skills in building roads and cities. Tolosa has turned into a Roman city with a Forum, a theatre and an arena. We had to go into the city and get new horses and a wagon. Habib's men were paid and sent back to Ruscino. Uncle Joseph knew who to trust, and we are again traveling comfortably and anonymously. With a wagon and horses this time, since the roads are better. Tolosa is less than half way to the Atlantic, but the road is straight and built for faster travel. We haven't seen a single soldier yet, and Joseph thinks we'll be there within a few days.

Father Joseph is telling us about Hibernia. He hasn't been there since he and Yeshua took their second trip there together. They both look forward to see their relatives again. In the mean time he is telling us about the green rolling hills and the clean swept rocky crags overlooking the ocean. I understand their stone houses have stood there for centuries, some of them since Princess Scota arrived there from Egypt more than a thousand years ago. The people are proud of their heritage, and go to great lengths to teach their children. The seats of learning in Hibernia are well known and sought out by students and scholars from the rest of the known world. Their collections of documents have been built over hundreds of years. Some of them are very old.

The weather is getting colder even though it's still summer, as we are getting further north and traveling through thick forests. I'm wearing more layers and had to buy another blanket for the nights. Father Joseph made sure it was made of good wool from his home country, and explained about the natural colors of the sheep.

Uncle Joseph is getting more thoughtful. We're hearing rumors among the people we pass, about the battles still going on in Britain. The Romans insists on conquering this country which so far has proven itself invincible. He says we will enter the country from the west side, and be safe behind British lines. Apparently the Romans are sending their best generals and legions to fight from the east, where the passage across from the Roman Empire is shorter. I admire this steadfast people, who will not give up their island under much persecution. Take heart, and send your prayers to the British in this time of hardship. I will write more about their situation when I have more information.

Give my best hugs to my sister and child. I think about them often and I sense they are being given the best of care. I can never thank you enough for what you are doing for me.

> Written within the limitations of what is safe to share,
> Your sister Mariam,
> who sends you all her love.

THE LETTER FROM FATHER JOSEPH

Dearest wife, my beloved Mary.

This is written from the shores of the country of our origin, blessed green Hibernia. May it find you well, in body and spirit.

How long has it been since we took the first journey away from here? How long since we visited with our children? How long has it been since I saw you in front of me, and could hold you in my arms?

I bring you good news you will treasure. There is a new grandchild among us. Little Yesu was born on our holy isle this winter. He is destined to follow in his fathers footsteps and will be properly trained as he grows of age. He will join his sister when his parents return to Gaul. Our beloved daughter-in -law is continuing in her wise and graceful ways, and our son is teaching the blessed word to our people.

From Gaul we traveled over Ruscino, through Tolosa and to Brigante in Gallia. Your brother found us comfortable transportation along the way, and had a ship waiting to take us to the shores of Cornwall when we reached the Atlantic. We arrived in England and received a warm welcome by his people. Mary, you won't believe how well known and respected he is. The king's brother, Arviragus, of the royal Silures of Britain, held a reception for us, in the presence of nobles. They recognized Yeshua and Mariam as the king and queen of Judea according to their heritage. They feel they share common ancestry with us. Joseph and I were acknowledged as patriarchs, and received a gift of twelve hides of land, each of 160 acres. Your brother will come back to Gaul, and bring people to establish ownership of the land, and build a church there. Arviragus has promised his protection.

We stayed with the druids. They reside on an island overgrown with apple orchards. There is a mountain top on the island where they do their work, and we were invited to attend a ceremony with them. Mariam was so taken by the priestesses of Avalon, she wants to return and stay with them for while. Yeshua built an altar on the land we were given, which we honored with several masses before we left. Joseph wanted to stay, to plan the further building projects of the church, and find out whom he could invite to start a colony there. Yeshua and Mariam went with me to Hibernia for their child to be born among our family.

Mary, I trust you are being well cared for at Ephesus. Yahya is a reliable young man. I would like to ask you, if you would consider joining your brother on his project in England. The land is beautiful, the people more than friendly. You will have the protection of the king and his brother, Caractacus. As long as the Romans can be kept off shore, this is a safe place to be. I feel your loneliness in a foreign country. I feel my loneliness on the island of my origin. I would join you there. There is much building to be done.

If you could get a ship to take you to Alexandria, our in-laws would handle it from there. Or go directly to Gaul, to Provence. There are many of our people there already. You'll find them in Massilia, in Arelate, in the Mouth of the Rose and in Aquae Sextiae. Please come. I believe we could do good work in Britannia. Your presence is needed.

Your loving husband,
Joseph.

Mariam's Second Letter To Sarah

Dearest sister,

I trust your colony is growing steadily and that you keep in contact with the ones in Aquae Sextiae and Massilia. I sense my child is doing well, and I hope you are too.

Please tell my daughter that she has a little brother. Baby Yesu, we call him Geiss to separate him from his father, was born on the island of her grandparents, beautiful Hibernia. He was welcomed by his closest relatives and smiled immediately to his doting grandfather. During the winter, which we spent there, he grew to a happy baby, delighting his parents, who know that they also have a daughter whom they love, in the care of her incredibly devoted aunt.

We left Hibernia in the spring, and went to visit England to see how Uncle Joseph was doing with his plans. The cragged lines of the shore of Cornwall received us one more time, and we found our way to the island of apples, Avalon. The priestesses there were happy to see us, and again we were invited to take part in their festivals. They honor the sky, the stars and the moon, and have developed a sophisticated level of intuitive communication. The hill, which they walk around in an intricate pattern to get to the top, is their observatory to study the movements of the star. The druids are greatly respected for their expertise in these matters.

I stayed with the women on Avalon for a while, and took part in the many workshops they have to prepare wool and linen to be cut, carded, spun and woven into amazing textiles which they wear or use in their household. The yarns are died with various parts of suitable plants, so their clothing and table wear is colorful and lively.

I admire how self sufficient their settlement is, and how protected they live behind the British army. Arviragus is king now, and he has promised protection to the island of the priestesses, the druid settlement and to us, who own the land further in. The king gifted it to us when we arrived here the first time. The Romans are still pushing for control of Britain, but in every battle they engage in, they're defeated. The British soldiers are fearless of death, and their brave leader, Caractacus, have outsmarted the Romans many a time. Uncle Joseph was invited to the king, and we were introduced to Caractacus and his family. He is an impressive man, both of stature and wisdom. His wife and children also displayed a high level of education and culture. His daughter Gladys was a pleasure to meet, even at her young age of nine. They listened to us intently, and wanted to learn more. When Uncle Joseph has finished his church here, we can continue teaching.

Sister Sarah, Uncle Joseph needs people. Upon our return to Provence we will assemble a group of people who want to become the first settlers in his new colony in Britain. This is an opportunity to establish a full colony including a church, in a country that is already welcoming our work. I trust you will discuss this with our people.

Yeshua and I, with baby Geiss, are leaving the beautiful shores of England shortly. We will take the same route back to Provence. Father Joseph stayed in Hibernia and Uncle Joseph wants to continue his work in England. Uncle has arranged for a boat to take us to Burdigate, and we will go with some merchants all the way to Julia Carcas. As a small family we will attract little attention. From there we will find our way through the Languedoc area again, before we reach Ruscino. There are so many places we want to revisit there. Yeshua wants to go back to the temple of Venus between five mountain tops in the area called Razes. We will be with you before the end of summer. Then we'll spend the winter planning the journey to England in the spring.

Sarah, this is all so exciting. I'm looking forward to share it all with you. I'll have stories to tell for many winter nights by the fire. Yeshua feels that it will be safe for him to come to Provence now. He will finally see all his people and what they have built, all because of what he taught and the wisdom he shared so freely around him. I look forward to show him the herb farm, and see how much Sibyl and Trym have expanded it by then. Give my greetings to all our groups of people, and tell them how much we look forward to see them all.

Kiss my dear daughter, and tell her about her beautiful new brother. He is sleeping next to me as I write these greetings to you, and if Tamera has the features of her handsome father, then this beautiful boy looks like his mother's family. In fact, dear sister, he looks exactly like you.

Your loving sister,
Mariam.

CHAPTER 14

THE TEMPLE OF VENUS

1

THEY LEFT THE FRIENDLY MERCHANTS, WHO HAD been their traveling companions all the way from England, at the market in Julia Carcas. At the same place they had been with Uncle Joseph, they got new horses and an armed guide who would stay with them all the way to Ruscino where Habib was expecting their return. Remi was a friendly man, who had followed Uncle Joseph before. Mariam could also sense that he would be a dangerous opponent, if provoked. She felt safe in his presence.

Baby Geiss slept peacefully in the long, colorful fabric the priestesses of Avalon had given her to carry him in. They had shown her how to tie it across her shoulder and under her arm. She could even nurse him while he was in it. She could also tie it twice across her back, and he would sit up along her front. Mariam couldn't believe how practical those women were. She felt a strong kinship with her sister priestesses in Britain.

The road was narrowing the further they came away from the Roman city. It felt relaxing to be on their own again, and be in a territory where they didn't have to watch what they were saying or be careful not to use each others names. They hadn't heard anything to cause worry among the Romans along the road, but they were still cautious.

They followed the river Aude, and rode between the many rows of tall cypresses and sycamores that had been planted to mark the road. Mariam admired the tree canopies creating arched rooftops above them. The birdsong around her made her wonder if it was birds making the sounds, or if they had entered the territory of the tribe of Attax, the Velleta, the bird people famous for imitating bird sounds creating their own indecipherable language. The worlds of animals and humans seemed to overlap here.

The veils between many worlds seem thin in this area, Yeshua finished her thought.

Doesn't it? said Mariam dreamily, checking the baby in his sling.

They had decided to go directly to the temple of Venus. Remi knew to turn where the river Sals ran into the river Aude, and was familiar with the location of the safest crossing points. Mariam would like to bathe in the healing waters one more time. Yeshua was eager to come to the observatory in the mountains.

"There is a small settlement here along the river," Remi explained. "They probably have a meal we can buy."

They followed the river Sals on the north side, until they came to some stone buildings and enclosures for animals. Some friendly people recognized Remi, and offered food for the horses and a hearty soup that was cooking for their evening meal.

"Are you here to use the stone huts?" An older man asked. "They're warming up now in the afternoon sun."

Yeshua asked him to explain. The man told them that small stone enclosures had been built here for centuries by young novices from the big temple up on the hill. They were just big enough for one person to sit in quiet meditation inside. Long ago it was only the initiated ones, who were allowed to use the huts. After a while, that tradition changed, and now anybody could have their time there as they wished. They were intended for spiritual purposes. Besides, they were hardly even big enough to lie down in, so they weren't suitable for anything else.

"People fast as they enter these sacred spaces for their quiet time. The animals avoid the huts. They look like they would make perfect nests for small animals, perfect shelter for bad weather for goats and sheep, but we find no trace of them. The animals seem to respect their purpose."

Mariam was intrigued. The small structures were visible like small stone piles scattered along the hillside. They were all facing south. She couldn't see the Venus temple from here, but she knew it wasn't far away. She nodded to Yeshua, and hand in hand, they followed the road along a stone fence to where the paths to each individual hut started. They separated as they picked one stone structure each, and walked up the hill to their own private place for reflection and meditation. The baby was remarkably calm, as she hiked between fragrant bushes and plants. Honeysuckle, verbena and eucalyptus, gave a refreshing green scent, softened with the sweetness of the pink flowers and their scent of honey.

She followed her path towards the hut, which indeed looked like a pile of stones from a distance. As she got closer she lost sight of it, but continued on the path knowing it would take her there. It didn't reappear until she was right next to it, and it still seemed hidden under vegetation. The ingenious placement of it made her admire the engineering of the construction. She found her way around to the opening and saw how it was built around its doorframe. The flat stones were carefully laid on top of each other to form the rounded shape.

Looks like a beehive, she thought to herself.

She bent her head and peeked inside. The old man had been right. There was no trace of animal use, nor any sign of fire or human habitation. She patted the dirt floor, and found it dry and clean of anything but soil, so she sat down and looked out the door. The view of the valley was peaceful and soothing. Evergreen trees and bushes formed a backdrop for the flowering plants she had noticed along the path. The hills in the distance were framed by taller mountains further away. She breathed in deeply to calm herself and settled in to nurse the baby.

As baby Geiss was nourished, she looked at the stone walls surrounding her, only a couple of feet from her body. The layers of flat stones were balanced perfectly, as they formed the rounded roof above her. The simplicity of the design, made the structure ageless. No tools had been used, only human hands and ingenuity. She breathed deeply again, as she admired its beauty, while remembering more grand designs she had seen in Ephesus and in Jerusalem. This was built for a single person to let the quiet landscape surround ones own thoughts.

She closed her eyes, and was overwhelmed with the scent of honey. It must have been the plants outside, she though, but she didn't see any honeysuckle close by. A fly came in, but quickly left again. She tried to quiet her mind, as the baby fell asleep in her lap.

A buzzing sound entered her awareness. She recognized a yellow and black bumble bee having entered to join her in her space. Smiling at the insect, she didn't want to disturb it. She closed her eyes again, and was aware of how the buzzing changed. The bee seemed to have picked up an overtone. A loud high pitched sound, clearer than a buzz, was also coming from the bee. She had only heard throat singers from Persia do this. Was it the space she was sitting in that doubled its sound? Listening to the two simultaneous sounds, she realized they were pitched at a specific frequency. As soon as the thought occurred to her, the bee left out in free air. She was now aware of another sound. A very high single note was humming inside the stone chamber. Did the bee start it out? Or did the bee make her aware of something that was there all the time? She closed her eyes again and listened intently. The sound was the tone of the landscape itself. The earth underneath her vibrated with it, so did the mountains in the distance. The iron and copper content in the stone picked up the tone from the earth, and amplified it for her to feel. She was sitting inside a tuning fork.

Smiling to herself, she allowed the tone to influence her body. Soon she had the sound humming in her head, and vibrating her skin. The child in her arms seemed to find it soothing, and slept peacefully in his sling as she shifted him around for comfort. She rested for a while more, before she stood up and bent underneath the low doorway again.

She almost expected to hear the sound continue, as she found herself outside, but only heard the silence of trees and stones, and the soothing wind blowing over her cheek. The two tones from the hut reverberated inside her while she walked slowly through the enchanting landscape, back to the camp and a bowl of hot soup.

2

The following morning they rode across the river Sals, and headed up the hills for the top where the Venus temple was located. As they passed through a valley between two lower hills, Mariam became more aware of the taller mountain tops surrounding her. They were entering into a plateau, protected by five giants with a sharp edged smaller hill in the middle, where the Venus temple had been built. Its standing stones were visible from a distance against the clear blue sky, even though they were several hours of riding time away.

They were both quiet, and hadn't shared much about their experiences in the stone huts. Maybe it was because Remi was with them, maybe because they had felt very different things, and didn't need to share. Mariam was content either way. She felt tuned to the landscape, and the interesting plants around her. As they came closer to the temple, she saw more rare plants, things that didn't grow indigenously here, but had to have been planted with care. She guessed the temple had established the herbs, trees and shrubs they needed for their work. This temple had been here for centuries. They'd had plenty of time to develop their own pharmacopoeia. The typical household herbs of thyme, lavender and soapwort were easy to spot. They also passed an orchard with healthy trees growing fruits of apple, apricot, cherries, pear and plum. A patch of strawberry leaves told her of an early harvest of the prized berries, and an unruly hedge of raspberries was close by.

As they came closer to the temple, she noticed more unusual plants. Tansy, with its yellow buttons and strong smell, lifted their stiff stems. The scent of elder, the plant all mothers warned their children about because of its poison, took over her nose and made her lightheaded, but the trees lining the entrance to the temple made the strongest impression. They were called Angel Trumpets, and the huge trumpet shaped flowers gave off an intoxicating scent at night. She recognized the large sphinx moths flying in and out of the flowers helping the pollination. Their fuzzy wings did an excellent job, and she wondered if the moths had been imported together with the trees. They seemed to thrive where they were planted, and Mariam knew they were chosen for a reason. Their level of poison was not to be trifled with, but used in the right proportions the essence could induce visions and lucid dreams.

The choice of herb material close to the temple taught her about what kind of work they were doing here. This was not your usual collection intended for remedies of various sorts, nor for producing refined perfumes. These were herbs needed for divination and in preparation for visiting the gods. Mariam was familiar with this work. She had learned at the Serapium how to prepare and use the seeds and essence of these plants and was surprised to see such a sophisticated collection hidden away in the Languedoc.

This temple has to be hidden away. That's the only way they can do their important work, said Yeshua silently answering her thoughts. *If you want to hide something, hide it in the middle of your opponent's territory.*

Mariam followed his thought. This place was indeed tucked away between major Roman roads, but in an inaccessible area the Romans didn't find interesting. She thought the temple was older than the Roman Empire, and that the location had been chosen because of the pattern of Venus, so visible in the landscape.

Remi took them through the gate at the foot of the ridge, to the dwellings of the priests and priestesses in attendance. Then he guided their tired horses to well stocked stables, where he also found a room for himself. The priests welcomed them back, knowing that Yeshua and Mariam were trained initiates. They were shown comfortable lodgings and invited to share the evening meal with them.

"Be welcomed among us. We're glad to have you back. We don't get such distinguished guests often. I'm sure we'll have lots to share throughout the time you chose to stay with us."

The evening meal was a nourishing stew, served in front of the fire, in their main hall. The flock of nine priestesses and seven priests told them of the various work they did at the temple, and how they had people from the nearby villages help them with the orchards and herb gardens.

"And then of course there are some materials we prefer to tend and harvest ourselves." Mariam could believe that. You could get killed, if you didn't handle some of these plants correctly.

They shared more pleasant conversation, and before going to bed, she had learned that most of them had been trained in temples far away from here. Only two priestesses were from the local communities and trained at this temple. All the others had chosen to come here after years in Hibernia, from Ephesus and even one from the Serapium. She remembered she had heard about this temple before, but not paid enough attention to know where it was, believing she would never get as far away as Gaul.

Together they created a nest for the baby as he fell asleep for the night. They were given the same guest room as last time they visited, and found the simple bed quite comfortable. Mariam noticed again the sheets and blankets they were given. Such fine handiwork deserved to be admired. Yeshua urged her to crawl in with him. It had been a long day with many impressions.

"Mariam, the work they are doing here is important," he started.

"I can see that from the herbs they grow. These people are familiar with the journey of Osiris."

"I know. I haven't seen such a well developed facility, well, ever."

"But you've studied at Heliopolis. I'm sure they had well trained priests there."

"Of course. But here they have a complete observatory to follow her path."

"They focused on that at the Serapium too. At Ephesus, there was more interest in the moon."

"That's what's so fascinating here. Not only do they know how she moves, they live in the middle of her footprint," said Yeshua in awe of the presence Venus had in this landscape. The land itself had risen to mirror the pentagonal path of the star.

"This time I noticed the five surrounding mountains as we were riding across the plateau. I didn't totally understand when they told us about it last time we were here."

"They draw the lines of the pentagram. I've never seen it so present, so laid out in the landscape. It's like the geography is humming her song, Mariam."

Mariam thought about the experience with the bee the day before, and could only agree with him.

"The mountains in the periphery sing, but the line of her path starts with this spot. This very point of the earth is the beginning, and then it goes in widening lines forming an ever growing spiral of pentagrams. It continues all the way out to Venus herself."

"You mean like a cone shape?"

"Yes, you can call it that. Standing with its tip on the top of this ridge, and created by her ever circling, spinning spiral lines. Pentagrams, yes, but more the five petal blossom we remember her by."

"Yeshua, that's beautiful."

"I think so, too. And powerful. Like you," he said as he turned his attention entirely to her.

3

They had spent a couple of days at the temple, and been introduced to the preparation halls for the herbs, the rooms with looms and spindles for winter work, and the halls they used for their daily meetings. They had gone on their own hike to the top of the ridge, and walked between the standing stones. Albion, the head priest, had gone with them and had explained how they kept track of the movements of the star through out the year.

"Her light falls between different stones at different times of her journey. That's how we can also know when she'll be an evening or morning star."

He continued saying that they also followed the star Sirius, and kept a close eye to some other stars that were less known. Mariam listened with interest, but she noticed that Yeshua wanted to go deeper. He asked many good questions. There was nothing Albion didn't want to answer, and he seemed to like his new student. Yeshua absorbed everything he said.

"Albion, I've been wondering, how come you keep so many dangerous plants growing here?" asked Mariam when there was a pause in the conversation.

"We need their potency from time to time. Our people are taught how to harvest them, and children are watched carefully if they stay with us. I understand your concern as a mother," Albion had read her better than she had intended.

"Any one of several I have observed, could kill."

"But they could also bring you to everlasting life."

At the evening meal that night they were discussing the approaching summer solstice. A committee was selected to plan the ritual. Yeshua volunteered to partake, and was welcomed among them.

Mariam sat on the seats along the wall nursing her son, and watched her husband's enthusiasm. She observed how easily he communicated with these people. How he had talked more here, than among any other group on this entire journey. His face became animated and exuded warmth and light. She had never seen him this handsome. He wasn't flirting with the priestesses. She would have noticed that. Here he could share ideas freely. He had found people who were his equal in learning.

Between five mountains hidden in an unexplored section of Languedoc, said Mariam to herself. *After having visited almost every temple in the known world, and some in a world far east I'll never see, this is where he finds his peers, on a point called La Pique.*

She was glad on his behalf, and it was interesting for her to see this side of him. How much he loved learning. How much respect he had for the knowledge he carried. How important he felt it was to share this, to make sure that this body of knowledge would never be lost.

Mariam thought further about the news they had overheard while they were traveling. The situation in Jerusalem was getting more intense. All the groups they had been in communication with were getting stronger. They used the story of Yeshua to promote their own cause. Instead of uniting behind it, they used different interpretations against each other. None of their closest disciples had remained in Judea. It was far too dangerous for them, so they had spread out and were teaching in many different countries. She admired their courage, but she also worried about the safety of the Temple. There was knowledge from ancient times that should be protected. She wasn't sure if the priests understood how important it was, or if they even knew how much their temple contained. A whole generation of priests had been killed by a zealous Persian ruler, Nebucadnezzar, centuries ago. The temple had never been able to replace them with equally adept scholars.

Those priests were descendents of Aaron and Melchizidek, Mariam said to herself. *Their bodies knew the knowledge taught through generations. By destroying the people who carry the blood, the wisdom only reachable through intuition, will be lost. It cannot be written down or taught. It can only exist as a hovering entity of knowledge attached to the memory in the body.*

Again she watched Yeshua, and thought about the wisdom he carried. He was of the House of David. His mother was descended from Scota, an Egyptian princess, who was again descended from Joseph, the pharaoh's adviser and the favorite son of the twelve brothers. Yeshua's father, Joseph, was a respected druid like his father before him. In Yeshua's body was wisdom built through numerous generations.

Mariam looked down to the beautiful face of her baby, and thought of how he was a child of both of them. She carried her own impressive pedigree, and this little one embodied both. Suddenly she realized how precious this was, and how much her children needed protection. She wanted to hide them both in a forest somewhere and not even let them know themselves who they were. It dawned on her that she had an enormous responsibility.

Mariam, we need your help, she heard her husband's voice inside her head. She looked up, and saw him smile at her. Shifting the baby in his sling around her, she moved over to the people gathered around him.

They were discussing how to prepare the herbs to travel in the lands behind the veils, and wanted her input on dosage and preparation.

They're preparing for the journey of Osiris, she said to herself in astonishment. *They just have other words for it.*

They had all the herbs prepared and stored for usage throughout the year. There were only a couple of fresh ones they needed, which were in season before the summer solstice. Mariam mentioned them and the priestesses agreed. They were not difficult to obtain. Teresa had worked at the Serapium and understood Mariam the best. She was older, and had been there before Mariam had started as a novice. Mariam appreciated her expertise and willingness to explain.

"The journey goes through the veils of the world. Then the traveler has to prove his knowledge of the worlds beyond. Most importantly, he has to be able to prove that he is prepared for the journey, or the guardians on the other side will not let him through."

"For his own protection," continued Mariam.

"Yes. He'll need to have his djed pillar developed to be able to return from the stars." Mariam understood about developing the spine of your body to hold enough spiritual energy to sustain both your body and the journey. But all the way to…

"The stars?"

"With our techniques we've had people visiting Venus herself."

Mariam had heard about this kind of travel. It was only done among the female black panthers at the Serapium because of the endurance needed upon their return. She retreated into thoughts about the powerful techniques she knew, and had been exposed to. She hadn't been able to partake in anything like this since Ephesus.

She understood the figure of the cone shaped field the star created in the landscape. She realized that the point of the tip of the cone must be located below the temple, somewhere in the ground underneath the ridge. She sensed that it was firmly grounded in the earth, and took in information from the cosmos constantly.

"Specifically from Venus and the heavenly bodies she is traveling by. And right now we have a very special situation. She's not close to it, but right behind her, in a straight line from earth, is the galactic core," Teresa explained.

Mariam's eyes widened. She had only heard about the galactic core in her astronomical studies at the library of Alexandria, when she was very young. The next time she heard it mentioned and had it explained better, was in Hibernia. This strange phenomenon was such an enigma. It seemed to suck things into it and to spit things out again. In other words, it was a gateway out of this universe.

"And an entrance for new entities who wants to join us. It is where new information comes from," said Teresa with ease.

"How do we know all this? It isn't even visible in the sky," Mariam protested.

"From the precise observatories in Persia. Their astronomers are legendary, and we've had priests here that were trained there. And from people visiting the gateway and telling us what they saw."

"The journey of Osiris?" asked Mariam wide eyed.

"The journey of Osiris," Answered Teresa as if she was talking about brewing tea.

4

Mariam needed a walk in the hills to digest all this. Putting the baby in his sling after changing his wrappings and feeding him, she walked out into the sunshine and the warm afternoon. She was glad the child gave her practical concerns to think about. It was easier to solve problems of how to clean a baby, than to fathom what had just been proposed to her.

The journey of Osiris was not unfamiliar. On the contrary, this was something she had been taught in detail. The initiations she had partaken in were shorter versions of the same idea, shorter journeys that were safe travels for novices and beginners. She knew about how to stay with them through the process, and bring them back at the appropriate time. What they were planning here was a more dangerous process, allowed only for the most advanced adepts. They had to have a developed djed pillar.

Mariam knew what that meant. Like Moses in the desert, you have to learn how to straighten your serpent into a rod. It is a matter of self discipline and awareness, of working with yourself until every part of your body vibrates at the same frequency. The serpent has to be identified in the big nest at the bottom of your spine. This is the river Nile and the two tributaries, Isis and Osiris, which Gyasi had taught her about many years ago. This river, or serpent as they called it here, has to be lengthened through every painstaking vertebra until it meets the other nest inside your head. It has to find the very fine little knob, in the shape of a nut, the hidden glands in the middle of the brain. As the serpent turns into a dove, on the last section up your neck, it gets colored blue. When the beak of the dove finds the nut it is seeking, the nut will make an excretion of a divine substance. If your body gets to taste this holy libation, it will know it is divine. The substance will awaken the nut, and with the sand already waiting at its base, it will create a crystal layer surrounding it. This will both be its armor, and the proof that this body is ready for the journey. The white diamond, the stone of wisdom, will have formed, and the djed pillar, the river up the spine, will be considered activated.

This whole process was arduous, but beautiful. She knew of few people who had completed it, besides Yeshua and herself. It was hard to explain to people. If they weren't familiar with the mythology, it wouldn't make sense. Few people were willing to see what their bodies were capable of. Few people wanted to develop themselves to that level. Their daily meals seemed to be more important. Mariam sighed.

Did she want to teach about the djed pillar? Did she want to learn more herself? She knew this was hidden knowledge, given only to individuals the priests felt were ready. She realized that being here, might be a once in a lifetime opportunity.

Yeshua had taught the beginning steps of how to grow light inside your body. For the ones who mastered the first steps and asked for more information, he was ready with further teaching. He was also a master at making everything seem so simple. Yeshua was a storyteller, and a poet, creating beautiful metaphors understood by the initiates, but somewhat cryptic to others.

She sat down on a suitable rock, with a view of the plateau in front of her. The cedars and pines around her gave off a scent of clean green. The wild flowers added sweetness to the landscape, and in the meadows further down she saw a herd of cows grazing peacefully in their own version of heaven.

Analyzing the information she had been given, and Yeshua's enthusiasm for the preparation for the summer solstice, she found enough pieces to understand where this was heading. One thing still puzzled her. Where were they going to do the ritual? So far she had only seen their charming dwellings, and the open air temple on the top of the ridge. This ritual had to be done inside stone. They needed the resonance of dense matter, even though the purpose of it was to become immaterial. A natural grotto wouldn't do, unless it could be sealed from the outside. Besides, the rules for purification would make it unsuitable.

Baby Geiss whimpered. She turned his sling around and looked into his face. So like his father. He smiled at her when he got her attention, and made spit bubbles at his mouth as he tried talking. She noticed that he had Mary, his grandmother's eyes, thoughtful, friendly and peaceful. "Where will we send you for your education?" She cooed to the child. "You need to know all this, too, if your destiny is to continue your father's work."

She put him to her breast, and felt the milk flow through her in a nourishing stream. He was eager to nurse, and locked onto her nipple strongly. Mariam admired the connection that continues between a mother and her child for so long after they have been separated by the birth.

She started to see similarities between the birthing process and the journey of Osiris. Both Osiris and the baby had to develop a spine strong enough to exist outside of something soft and familiar, into the new environment that would seem harsh and demanding. Both had to leave the darkness of comfort, go through a tight canal where they would be squeezed and probed, before arriving in a new world of bright light. It was just as futile for Osiris to try to explain it to the uninitiated, as for an older child to try to explain the process to an infant inside his mother's womb. The modes of communication would be different, and the membranes and skin containing the unborn child would prevent anything, but the most muffled sounds. She knew that the few people, who had gone through the journey of Osiris, felt equally unable to communicate their experiences. And like the babe, there was no going back. The space they had occupied didn't exist for them anymore once they had left, and the tunnel they had come through only went one way. After their return, they were new people. Their lives and their lives purpose had changed.

Putting it all in this perspective, she saw a new beauty to both processes. But who was going to nurse Osiris when he arrived on the other side? When he came back as a light body, who would take care of him the way a mother naturally cares for her child? She knew the answer in mythology. Isis was always at his side. She was his sister, his wife, his queen, his companion. She was also the one who had already taken the journey, and explored the new territory for a while. She already was a body of light. Isis was the star Venus.

Mariam looked down at the nursing child. The golden skin of her breast had a glow to it, and her son's cheek did as well, while the nourishing milk flowed from her to him. *I'm Isis,* she thought, *and you are my little Horus.*

5

Mariam put baby Giess to sleep in the little nest they had made for him close to their bed. He had fallen asleep while nursing, and a little drop of milk was on his cheek. Yeshua was standing next to her with an arm around her shoulder, admiring the child.

"He's so peaceful."

"He takes after his father."

"Do you really think so? I think he looks like you."

Mariam laughed at him. "Don't you see yourself that way? When you're asleep the village around is at peace as well. Your inner light pulsates around you with your breath, just like him."

Yeshua looked more closely at his son. There was indeed a glow around the child. And as he breathed evenly in and out, the light around him seemed to undulate. He had never noticed this before, and certainly didn't know he did so himself.

"Mariam. That will become even stronger, after this journey."

"Yes, you will illuminate the night. We won't need torches anymore," Mariam joked, hiding her fear.

Yeshua laughed with her, concealing his own concerns. Then he turned his attention to her.

"Your glow has illuminated my life for a long time. Let's make some light together."

They undressed and crawled under the blankets the temple had provided for them. Mariam noticed how lovely Egyptian cotton felt towards her skin, especially cotton that had been washed repeatedly and achieved a softer texture. She felt Yeshua's skin against her back and the softness of the blanket over her shoulder. On top of the cotton they had a heavier woolen blanket with a pattern of diamonds in muted earth tones. She recognized the hues achieved with plants, from when she had helped with the vats of liquid dye baths on Avalon.

His hand kept stroking her body along her side. He loved feeling her skin against his own sensitive fingertips. Her body spoke to him through her skin. It told him how she was feeling, the concerns and joys she had let color her day. He closed his eyes and followed her rounded curves along her hips and down her thigh. Then his hand changed direction and found the curves across her belly, blessing the marks of childbearing as he continued across her navel and further up along her abdomen. The same gentle hand closed around her breast and felt its full roundness. She snuggled closer to him and let his chest hair tickle her back.

His chin rested against the back of her head, and she turned to kiss his lips. Did he illuminate the night? As she closed her eyes, she could sense him as a glow of warmth and comfort, and as their arms closed around each other, there was a sphere of blue light visible above his shoulder.

It's the color of "we", he said silently.

""We" have a color?" She asked.

"With love as strong as ours, the entity of "we" definitely has a color," he voiced, and smiled at her as he took in her beauty, her wisdom and the light beaming in streams from her body.

"It's the color of the sky on a late afternoon," she said.

"That's beautiful," he answered as he kissed her forehead.

Carefully he put his mouth at the tip of her breast and licked the nipple. He didn't want to cause the milk to flow too strongly, at the same time he liked the flavor and loved to relate to her as the mother of his children. Nothing proved her motherhood as strongly as mother's milk. The breast was generous. It squirted some in his mouth and she sighed with pleasure as she felt the stream of liquid from her to him.

His hand continued to caress her body. He loved to touch her. The line between them was always there. They could reach each other silently through so many ways throughout the day. Relating physically, skin to skin, was the manifestation of all the unseen ways they were united. He wondered if the angels could have any way to relate more holy than this.

She stroked along his chest letting her fingers find the curls of his hair. Knowing how sensitive his nipples were, she just allowed a light touch across it as she came across, before she followed his abdomen and found another group of curly hair. She closed her hand around his erect member, and he gasped for air. Finding the outline of its helmet, she let her fingers follow the slit leading up to its fountain opening. He murmured and caressed her shoulder.

Pushing him gently, she made him lie on his back as she kissed his mouth and continued her kisses down his neck. She closed her lips around his other nipple, and pulled gently, as he made a laudable sigh. Burying her nose in his hair, she followed it down his torso, across his navel, to where a thin line was pointing towards the darker hair surrounding his life giving parts. She placed herself between his legs, and leaned her head against his hip, while her hand found the base of his member to direct it towards her mouth. It made its first libation to her, and she licked its salty flavor. Her tongue followed the edge of its helmet, before she let her mouth close around it.

Yeshua surrendered to his body, to sensation, to intense pleasure and to her. Wave after exquisite wave, flowed up his body, from this point capable of receiving such heightened sensational impulse.

She crawled up along his body and lay down on top of him smiling. He laughed back at her as he admired the beauty of her dark, brown eyes and embraced her. With strong arms around her back he rolled them over on their sides as he noticed the blue light between their bodies.

Kneeling between her legs he kissed her lips and got a taste of his own salty flavor. He rested his hands on either side of her, and his lips again found her nipples. She murmured to him letting him know how much she liked it. Her golden olive skin had a trail from his tongue, as he aimed for her dark triangle of curls. She lifted her legs to the side, to invite him to taste the dew of her rose petals. His expert tongue found her rosebud above and she gasped as he massaged it. His hands came up along her side and found a breast each to fondle. The three rose buds on her body all got attention, and she yelped as the waves of pleasure took over. She surrendered into the blankets behind her, and to his caresses, until her body flowed with sacred water, and his mouth was eager to drink it.

He emerged from between her knees, laughing at her, with his face wet. She blushed, smiling, as she pulled him up towards her. Her rose was so ready for him, she wanted him, she needed him. Now. He couldn't have been happier to oblige to the invitation.

He entered her, and they both made a gasping sound. She closed around him as he pulled out and entered again. Her legs held around his back and the back of her thighs held him at the right distance. Together they established a rhythmic motion, as their bodies assumed a spherical shape. The wave of pleasure she felt from their joined bodies, flushed up along her entire body. She curved her back and neck to fit better with him, as she sent an energy line towards him, the same way he did to her. He felt it go up along his spine, and flow out of his head towards her, just as the wave he created followed her body and through her head. They were doubly joined now. There were two circles of loving intentions flowing through their bodies. Everything existed in undulating lights. Their embracing arms made another double circle of love and they lost themselves in each other. The angels observed the creation of a perfect gyroscope glowing in blues and greens. The whole angelic realm applauded, and a new sparkling star was lit at the center of blue.

6

The preparation for the Summer Solstice had been going on for weeks, even before they arrived. There was going to be a procession walking to the standing stones on top of the hill, and there was going to be a ceremony inside a stone chamber underneath.

Mariam had wondered where they would do the ritual of Osiris' journey. As far as she knew, it had to be done surrounded by stone. The safest place she could think of was her own experience inside the big pyramid of Giza. She would never forget the power of the black room, the perfect cube surrounded by perfect stones. Each stone had gold powder inside it, both to be able to move it with ease when it was built, but also to anchor spiritual power in the place. You needed metal and stone to be able to accomplish that. The materials of the stars were needed to be present, to resonate with each other.

Mariam had walked the country side, and admired the beauty of the landscape. She had walked in a smaller procession up the hillside to honor the recent full moon. The priestesses had taken her around, to show her the activities they were engaged in involving the preparations of herbs, wool and linen. She had seen the dyeing vats by the creek, the weaving hall with the looms and the sewing spaces with good light were new garments were made. The priests had shown her the fields, the orchards and the simple stables where they kept their animals. Mariam had admired all the activities that made this a self sustained community, which had been in function for hundreds of years.

True to her training at the Serapium and at Ephesus, she had also been looking for something else. Finally she asked Teresa, who had been friendly and open to other questions.

"We don't show that to people unless they're taking part in the ritual," she explained. "And we rarely have visitors with enough training to join us. You two fall in a different category."

Mariam understood. She knew she had been included in the preparations for the celebration due to her own experience.

"There is a space inside the mountain, which we use when we need the power of the stone to enhance the ritual. We will use it for the journey of Osiris. It is situated in the center of the hill, right below the standing stones."

Which take in the power of the star, Mariam thought.

"Yes," continued Teresa, having heard her. "It functions quite well, and this year we're especially excited, since the galactic core is right behind the star, and will become an added force beaming down to us on the solstice."

Mariam needed time to think again, and was once more wandering the hills. She sat down on a stone in the valley, and looked towards the ridge. As she allowed it to speak to her, she got a familiar sense. There was another hill she had studied at some point, which had a similar impression on her. As she realized which memory had been triggered, she hugged the baby closer to her. This hill did indeed have a hollow room inside. Just like the hill of Golgatha, the hill of the skull.

She calmed her body, and reminded herself that Yeshua's initiation had gone very well, everything taken into consideration. The hollow hill had taken in the love of his followers and transferred that to him. The hill itself had saved him, in its function as collector of loving intention. She knew she couldn't have done the work she'd done, bringing him back, without this backup of strength from all the people who loved him.

She thought of other meanings of the word skull, and Yochanan came into view. Lovingly, he smiled at her, thanking her for making his wisdom immortal. If he simply had died as an old man, it would have been lost. Tears ran down her cheeks, as she bowed her head to him in acknowledgement.

The metaphors teaching about the snake in the spine came to mind, and she thought of the small glands in the middle of the brain, which seem so insignificant for daily life, but are so crucial for deeper spiritual development. Yeshua had said that in India they called the substance these glands made, Soma. He had recited poetry for her, rejoicing in the flow of Soma in the human body, bringing bliss and happiness to the person who had achieved this level of understanding. This small organ was called the black pearl in some traditions, the white diamond in others. Some would refer to it as a blue bead of light visible around people emanating enough inner light.

Mariam sat still allowing her thoughts to roam around the subject. She had learned so much from different places, so much had been shared with her from traditions far away. And so much had been experienced, inside sacred stone enclosures. She looked at the hill she was starting to love and respect, and could see that inside the middle of the stone there would be a perfect place to have the ritual. The reflections of everything made her feel that she was part of a world of symbols, all reflecting each other, all telling the same story, all trying to teach human souls how to find their way between matter and light.

She turned her head, and sang a lullaby for her child, wondering what message he would bring, having just arrived in this miraculous world.

7

Mariam was sitting on her stone, deep in thought, as Yeshua came up to her. She'd seen him coming along the path, and been glad that he'd found her. He sat down quietly next to her, placed a warm hand on his son's body and gave a reassuring stroke to her shoulder.

"You've spent a lot of time alone in the hills," he said after a while.

"I needed to collect my thoughts," she answered. "And you were talking to the priests. You've spent a lot of time with them these days."

"Yes, I have."

There was another silence between them. This time the silent language didn't seem appropriate. There was something between them that had to be said aloud.

Mariam sighed. Usually communication between them was easy. But this time the topic held too much weight. It needed to be respected, for the ancient knowledge it represented and the impact it would have, if acted out. They both knew they had been avoiding this conversation, even as silent communication, which was unusual for them. Maybe it was because words were hard to come by? How do you express something of this magnitude with the limiting means of language? Mariam felt she was swimming inside a sphere with many symbols floating freely about, each containing huge concepts of understanding that could be grasped intuitively in an intake of breath, but needed a thousand words to explain. Which one should they start talking about? She sighed again.

He felt how difficult this was for her. It wasn't any easier for him. He knew the dangers, just as well as she did. But he also knew that this was an incredible opportunity to complete the work he was sent out to do. He knew the only ones who could do this were the two of them, with the help of the priests of the Temple of Venus, and the landscape surrounding this incredible setting.

"Mariam, this is the most romantic place I've ever been to. I've never felt the love between us stronger than here, among these hills."

"How about Leontopolis? Or Baia?" she answered him back. "That was intense as well."

"It was intense with the passion of youth, and the exhilaration of an adventure, yes. But this is different. Here, I feel our mature love, love as adults, love that has developed over time, gone through its hardships and grown into a protective field around the two of us. It is so strong, Mariam. It will protect us."

"Yes," she said quietly and looked down on her feet.

"The priests have invited me to do the journey of Osiris of this solstice," he said.

"I have gathered that," she said studying the clouds.

"They do it every year at this time. They have all traveled to the stars, and felt that I have enough training to do it."

"Yeshua, you have too much training. You have so much light in your body you're luminescent wherever you go. Of course they want to honor you offering for you to do the ritual. The place will be honored having had someone of your stature go through it here. You will make the mountain undulate in light. In fact, you'll bring the whole star back with you."

Yeshua just sat still on the ground listening to her. He knew she was right. And he understood what she was building up to. He looked at his normally calm wife. Right now she looked ridden with concern that had built up for a while.

"They'll all be there to make sure everything goes well."

"Yes, but this is not the tradition you were trained in. This is not the pyramid of Giza. Your body vibrates with a slightly different version of the same teachings. This procedure needs to be fine tuned, so you can travel safely and come safely back."

"I'd like to tell you what I showed the disciples in Jerusalem before I left for the East."

Mariam turned and looked at him. Was there something he hadn't shared with her in all their travels?

"After you left, Nicodemus took care of me until I was well enough to meet them again. I found out where they had their evening meals and showed up. I guess my appearance was somewhat altered. They didn't believe it was me at first. I had to show them the marks in my hands and feet to prove that I had indeed survived the whole ordeal. They insisted that I had died and come back from the dead. I thought that fitted better in the mythology of most of them, and left it at that.

"But some of them understood more. You know I had an inner circle of disciples that had gone through some initiations, some that understood the underlying meanings of what I taught."

Mariam knew. They were so much easier to communicate with, and accepted her on a deeper level. Her brother belonged to that group, so did his brother James.

"One night I had most of them around me. I knew that the effect of the holy bread would soon be upon them. I could see the light forming and developing inside them. Soon the light shaft would shoot through their heads and be visible from the outside. I hoped they all would be able to sustain the effect. It can be somewhat harsh on your body."

Mariam knew. She'd seen it. Unprepared people could get seriously ill if they weren't ready for the experience.

"I explained about the initiation I had gone through, and about the level of light I was now carrying. They looked at me, struggling to take it all in. I told them that I could open up gateways in the structure of the universe."

Mariam was listening with her entire body. What had he done?

"Mariam, during the initiation, the prophets of old came to me and told me that I was bringing in the new light for this new time. The stars have shifted. The earth have left the sign of Aries and entered Pisces. A new way of thinking is on its way. People will vibrate differently. There is a new wave that needs to find its way into matter.

"They told me that my soul has been prepared for a long time to be the bringer of light. Mariam, I'm not just your husband or the King of Jerusalem. There is another side of me that has an important job to do. All my different roles support each other and only someone as strong as you could comprehend it all. That's why you're my wife, my Queen, my partner in light."

She felt honored with the acknowledgement, but it didn't make it any easier.

"What did you show the heart core of the disciples?" she asked after a while.

"We went to Galilee, to the mountain top we had been to so many times. I knew the time was right, that they were ready for me on the other side. The message had come that the disciples needed to see this, so they could write about it and prepare for what would happen later. I told them to sit down, and watch what would unfold. I needed their support, their attention, their strength and belief in me, to make this happen.

"I invoked the prophets, Mariam, telling them I was ready. And as we watched, an eye opened in the sky. An opening in the shape of an upright eye was apparent, and light flowed out of it. I turned to the men and told them to spread the word, and take care of the flocks emerging in other countries, but to stay in Jerusalem until the light would be visible on them. I knew the process was almost completed.

"Two prophets were standing on either side of the eye, welcoming me to join them. Leaving the disciples sitting on the ground, I joined the prophets, and stood in the doorway, ready to leave. The light was flooding the mountain and the men on the ground were almost blinded.

"Then the prophets turned to me and said; *Now you know how the doorway works. Now they know how to describe it. You still have work to do. There is more light that needs to be anchored. We need you to stay on earth for a while more, before you can complete your assignment.*

"So they sent me back. I told the disciples to keep this to themselves for a while, before they could share it with the others. I wanted them to have achieved the effect of the internal process, before they could speak about it with some understanding.

"Then I left them and went east. I couldn't explain anymore to them. It was a mystery to me as well. But now I understand.

"Mariam, the time is now."

She looked at him, not comprehending completely what he had just told her. What was the purpose of showing the disciples the gateway? What knowledge was imparted to them? What had it done to Yeshua to again touch the other side? Could he truly walk between the worlds? She felt herself as a gatekeeper. She could lead people to the gate and call them back when their time was up. She had taken the journey, in the safety of the ancient pyramid surrounded with priests with no age. But she couldn't walk between at will. Could he?

"Mariam, my body holds so much light, it has a hard time staying solid. I have to complete the responsibility that was laid upon me. My spirit controls my body, and however much my body wants to be your husband, to stay here in this beautiful piece of land and watch our children grow up, my spirit has another agenda."

Streams of tears were rolling down his cheeks. He'd let down his guard a bit, and his light around him was pulsating in blues and greens. She felt enveloped in his loving, life giving field, and could only open her arms to hold around him.

To her he felt solid, but she could also feel how their two fields melted together, how her arms merged with his skin and vibrated green and blue together with him with the glow of the child between them.

"What do you think will happen?" she asked after a while.

"I only know this. Through me, the new light will be established on earth. The time is now, and the place is here, at the Temple of Venus, next to the woman I love."

8

Mariam took part in the preparation for the ritual, but her head was filled with thoughts. There were too many for her to get into any form of organization, so she decided to congeal her inner thought world into one purpose. She would protect Yeshua in the journey of Osiris, the way she had done before, and the same way she'd been protected herself. That was the safest approach for his journey and for his return.

The priests of the Temple of Venus in Razes were thrilled to have such a prestigious teacher with them to do the journey. They knew this would anchor new knowledge at their temple and they all looked forward to hear what he would tell them upon his return. This would also anchor more power inside their mountain and they would be able to take in new messages easier in the open air temple on the top. This mountain would again beam with light, as if the stone itself had eaten of the holy bread. The priests and priestesses were all beaming with delight as the physical work was done for the festival and the upcoming events.

Teresa took Mariam aside and wanted to prepare her for what would happen. She told her that baby Geiss could go with the group that would be among the standing stones on top of the mountain, while she would be inside the chamber with Yeshua and the highest adepts among them. Mariam agreed that was a practical approach.

"Would you come with me today to mix the herbs for the potions and unguents we need? They will all be more potent with your attention."

Mariam was happy to be given something to do.

Yeshua was spending his days in preparation of his body. There were prescribed foods for him to eat, hours spent in silence on the center stone on top of the mountain, all activities intended to tune him to the process ahead.

Mariam knew that this was all done for his protection. The purer his field could be, the safer he would be on the journey. If there were areas of negativity in his body, from thoughts, emotions, foods or poison, even from misguided beliefs, the light energy invited to travel through his body would clear them. It did not function like a plow in the field that pushes things aside. This high powered light force would explode impurities and make the pieces ricochet like bricks between walls. An unprepared body would be in severe danger and could become deadly ill or turn insane.

She wasn't worried about whether he was prepared or not. She knew Yeshua was purer and carried more love than any other body she'd ever known. She was more worried that his body held so much light that it would all go with him when he traveled. Then there would be no life force left behind in the body to keep it alive or to call his spirit back. What did the prophets mean when they said he would anchor more light? He was already a walking light house!

But you're the tower, Mariam. You're the tower of strength. You're the Magdala. She heard him inside her head. She wasn't quite sure where he was, but he could reach her, and had wanted to calm her. Then she remembered. He was on the top of the mountain, between the standing stones.

She remembered her time at Avalon, doing rituals among their circle of stones. They had also taken a trip to a larger group of stones, not far away. These huge stones were so old the druids didn't know how far back the circle was constructed.

She thought of her time in Hibernia, among his lovely relatives, among the wise druids there. Mariam had been invited to visit their university, and found many similarities to the Serapium and Library complex of Alexandria. She realized that this was his heritage too. As much as Jerusalem was their anchor from the tribes they both sprang from, there were many other cultures represented in their lines of ancestry. His strong heritage from the north, her strong heritage from further south, she could feel Bashra murmuring in her herb bag, all made a powerful force of wisdom. She looked at the baby next to her, and felt how all these lines crossed in him.

Then she tuned into the man she loved, in his quiet moment sitting on top of the stone in the center of the circle of stones. She realized that this place held the lines to all their ancestral knowledge. Venus, the star of Jerusalem, was honored here. The standing stones of the druids were present, as well as the initiation chamber of the great pyramid. Furthermore, *he* was honored here. In this place, Yeshua was recognized as a great spirit.

Could he have done this in Jerusalem? She remembered the danger they faced as they did the Hieros Gamos ritual underneath the temple. Could he have done this in Egypt? In Egypt, Yeshua was a dusty rabbi from the desert causing trouble with the Romans. His druidic learning, or the teachings from the far East would not be understood. He couldn't even have done this with his loving followers. In their naïve simplicity they wouldn't have understood. They could surround him with love and gratitude, and continue teaching what they had learned of living in deep respect for each other and the Gods above. Several understood the spark of God within, and could teach people how to find that.

In this place, Yeshua was among peers of a different caliber. The wisdom honored here was collected from many traditions for hundreds of years. She'd heard Albion say that some of what they taught had come from the ocean people who arrived mysteriously from a land that had disappeared. These people held so much light themselves, they could recognize his. Yeshua had been honored to be asked to take part in this ritual with them.

Mariam had reached a new understanding. He couldn't be anywhere safer than here to fulfill his assignment. If the Gods and prophets wanted him to anchor more light on the earth, this was the perfect place to do so.

She tuned in again to her husband on his rock. She could feel the lines of connection going from his body to the standing stones around him, and to each of the five mountaintops surrounding him in the distance. Suddenly they didn't seem that far away, but were the anchor points for the star herself in her journey through her five petal rose pattern. From where he was sitting, she could sense other lines going to important places. The standing stones resonated with the large stone circle in England. And if you made a line, following the gentle curve of the earth itself, from Avalon, through Yeshua on his rock, you would find the pyramids of Giza.

"Do you get it now?" asked Bashra by her waist. Mariam could only nod.

9

Before dawn on the summer solstice, the procession was gathered on the bottom of the mountain to walk the winding path up the hillside to the standing stones on the top. The priests and priestesses were wearing ceremonial robes in darker colors and baby Geiss was carried by his favorite priestess. At a signal from the high priestess, they started their walk in silence, circling the hilltop many times before they reached the top.

Yeshua and Mariam had been led through staircases and corridors, through tunnels cut in the stone of the core of the mountain, to reach the inner chamber only used for this purpose. Albion led the group, Teresa was with them and another priest and priestess carrying torches were also present. Albion and Teresa were wearing ceremonial robes. The other priest and priestess had hoods resembling black panthers. *Where had they learned that?* wondered Mariam. *And where did they get the skins? Were there panthers around here?* They had been arranged in three couples with Yeshua and Mariam in the middle.

Mariam held her husband's hand. She felt like the young girl she had been in Leontopolis, looking for a place to sit down to watch the enactment of an ancient mythological story. They had found a small sphinx to sit on, she remembered. The lights and sounds of the tableau created on the temple steps came back to her in a vision of impressive theatrical techniques. The story of Tammuz and Inanna was shown that night, and earlier she had stood on the steps herself, singing for the other show, the story of Isis and Osiris.

Walking through these corridors, the songs kept singing inside her. She heard the beautiful melody sending Tammuz off with Enki and the rejoicing upon his return. She heard the song of Isis as she travels the world to find the pieces of her husband. She heard the wake up call for Tammuz sung by Sibyl, sounding like morning birds. She heard the Song of Salomon sung at the bridal chamber of the King and Queen as they celebrated their union. She heard the song sung by two young bodies betrothed for time immemorial, as they celebrated eachother among the fine silks of a royal bed.

She had lived the mythology the music described. She felt the stories reverberating with the stone of the mountain. Yeshua squeezed her hand, as he walked silently next to her, enveloping her in the soft glow emanating from his body.

They passed through many doors on their way, each guarded by a sentient priest. At the last large entrance, there were two priests with spears held across the sturdy oak door. Albion said the right words, and the door was opened for them. The six of them marched in, and the doors were locked behind them.

Mariam looked around. The space was about the same size as the chamber inside the pyramid. She was again inside a perfect black cube. The air was surprisingly fresh and she marveled at the ingenious engineering at work. She felt that they were situated immediately underneath the standing stones above, and felt that the procession had started their way up the hill.

Yeshua took in the situatio,n as well. The position of the chamber and the stone surrounding them, together with the copper content in the mountain itself, made it easy to form connections to the star above, copper being the metal of Venus. She was arriving soon as a morning star, and would connect to the center of the earth. *And to the galactic core directly behind the star,* completed Albion in his head.

Yeshua also noticed the connection to other important sites. *There will be other people doing important rituals in many places this morning,* he heard from Teresa. *Remember the network we are part of. All the mystery schools participate in the same annual celebrations simultaneously.*

Torches were lit in the four corners of the room. Brassieres were lit on the floor. Herbs were burned, creating a soothing scent. An alabaster jar smelled strongly of the balm that had been made for this purpose.

Yeshua's outer robe was removed and he was wearing a thin, white linen shirt. In the middle of the room there was a stone bench. White linens were made ready to wrap him in. They were being warmed by the brassier standing nearby, and scented with herbs.

Mariam and Yeshua stood by the foot end of the stone facing each other. Nothing was said. It was enough to look into each others eyes and share their life together. They sent their silent greetings to each other, but did not touch. There was no need for physical contact. Right now that would disturb him out of the focus he had, and the merging they experienced through their shared fields was complete.

Albion took position at the head of the bench and motioned for Yeshua to sit down on the stone. His shirt was removed, and the two priestesses helped him lie down with the linen underneath his body. Albion started the incantations with his deep baritone. Teresa followed with her alto, and Mariam joined in alternating with Teresa.

Yeshua had already had his first drink of potent herb tea. It was time for his second. Water was heated and the herbs were sung over. A carefully measured portion of the golden bells from the blooming trees were given. It had been harvested under the recent full moon, when the blooms were giving their strongest fragrance.

Mariam was instructed to start massaging the unguent into his body. She was familiar with the procedure and enjoyed working with the strong fragrance. This one she had helped mix the day before. Among their stock she'd found some oil from tuberose, and she was happy to be able to include it among the ingredients. The other priestesses worked next to her, enclosing the skin covered in salve, in linen strips from rolls that fitted in their hands.

Holding his feet she thought of how many miles he had covered in his travels. She remembered marks from his sandals after days of walking in Galilee. In Hibernia they had been given sturdy boots for the winter. When he came back from Kashmir, he had some interesting shoes with fur and colorful beads on them. She counted his toes the way she'd done with both her children when they were born, and found that his now had veins and angles from the way they had gotten used to molding with each other through uncountable hours of walking.

She continued up his legs and found his muscles proving that he was a strong man in his best age. And she knew, like his father, he would keep this appearance for many years to come. The marks above his ankles showed his history.

The middle of his palms still had the marks from the nails. *They're marking the most powerful healing spots,* she thought to herself. *This is where his power goes out when he works with people.*

He had to sit up so she could cover his back. *How much have you carried?* she thought. *How much of the world's misery have you seen?* She thought of how much she'd observed him willingly give of himself, how openly he allowed people access to his immense energy source. It seemed like the more he gave, the more was given to him. His little device with the ruby was left in their room. There was no need for its work today. All it did was amplify what he already was, so he could reach farther, and today this process was going to be reversed. He was going to stop beaming outwards, and aim it all to his inner worlds, where a gateway would take him to a much larger universe.

She shifted position with Albion and continued working from the head of the table. The priest and priestess attending them continued wrapping Yeshua's body in linen as she went up his body. He was lying down again, and before he would cross his hands over his chest, she covered him with the strong smelling herb salve.

She had done this before many times, to heal and sooth him after a long day. She had done it many times to bring them to intimate closeness and pleasure. Once she did it to cover in him in a potent cream to reduce his pain level and possible infections. Once she did it to honor him anointing him as the King. This time she also felt like his Queen, preparing him for a process the way only she could do as his wife. As she swept across his heart she felt it beating with her. She lingered her hand above, and found the line of connection going straight through the stone above, to the people watching the sunrise among the standing stones. Little baby Geiss resonated with them, as the combination of his parents. Like a light beam from the sun itself, he sent a blessing to them, and to her surprise, united with another little star inside her. Yeshua shifted a little underneath her hands and smiled ever so slightly. *Is it true?* She asked. *I was hoping,* he answered. *Geiss is telling us it is.*

Mariam felt elated, and the connection to her husband became even stronger. The priests and priestesses in the room continued their singing without interruptions. She looked up and met the eyes of Albion, who nodded to her in acknowledgement and smiled in delight. He'd heard it all, and he already knew. Mariam could only smile back, and share the blessing with everybody around her.

She continued massaging Yeshua's face with the gentlest of fingers, and when he opened his eyes and laughed at her, she bent down and kissed him. Albion didn't say anything, even though he didn't want Yeshua's body engaged right now. It was time to put his body in a trance, not excite it. Mariam knew that, collected herself, and continued her work.

His scalp had gone through so much. Many unseen energies had entered his body through this powerful center on the top of his head. The Romans tried to keep this area of his body in severe pain. They had tried to limit his powers, which meant that against their own belief system, they knew he had some. Mariam thought of how the Roman's didn't like to appear foolish, and how Yeshua one more time had shown them from their weakest side.

She found the holes from the thorns. The scars had formed little indentations underneath his hair. She also found the area on top where the skin seemed to have a different quality. Again she was reminded of her newborn children, and the soft spot they all show on the top of their heads. *Were they still receiving messages from the cosmos at that age?* she wondered. *As we grow up we become hardened to this influence and learn to focus on the needs of our earthly lives.* Why had Yeshua kept his head open?

Was it something he had decided to do at some point? Had his beautiful mother and wise father advised him on this? Mariam thought of his other siblings. They were all lovely people, but none of them had the same level of sensitivity. What angelic being had connected with him at an early age? She sensed a feather stroke her cheek with the lightest of touch, and she knew they were nearby.

As she did the last strokes on his head, she saw that he had fallen into deep trance. The last pieces of linen covered his body and a special wrapping had been prepared for his head, keeping his face free. He now had the protection of Isis.

Albion changed the incantation. He took on the role of the hosts meeting Yeshua on the other side. The questions were sung that would indicate weather this candidate was ready. First there was a request for the waters of Osiris to be poured over him. Mariam thought of the Soma described so beautifully in the holy poetic songs from the east. Each song held a request for this divine libation to be poured generously over mankind. She visualized liquid honey to cover Yeshua and be his protective field.

The questions asked him to identify all the parts of the magic net that he had escaped to find them. The others answered for him, and described all the pitfalls of matter, that could keep him back from the journey he was preparing for. As the last verse was sung, Yeshua was becoming luminous at a new level.

His light body hovered above his physical body, like twin images in light and dark. Albion had joined the priestess with the panther head on Yeshua's left side, and Teresa and the panther headed priest were on his right. Mariam remained at the head, but they'd all taken a couple of steps back to allow space for the process.

Yeshua's light body sat up as a boat formed underneath him. Was it a simple small rowboat, or a raft of reeds with curved edges and pointed ends? Mariam wasn't sure. They watched as the stone wall facing him formed an opening in the shape of an eye. A vessica piscas created of light in bright white, green and blue was visible. The boat started to move, and slowly it floated towards the opening. It crossed the barrier, picked up lightening speed and disappeared in a flash of green. The upright eye closed and became a stone wall again.

They assembled around Yeshua's physical body on the stone table. The normal glow around him had left his body. Albion led them in blessings, and the body was covered in another white linen sheet. Mariam had to control herself to not touch him, but she knew that would disturb his level of disassociation with his material body right now, so she let it be.

They continued singing while they collected the items they had brought into the chamber. Only one brazier would be left with another collection of carefully selected herbs. When it burned out, he would be left in total darkness. Ceremonially they left the chamber, and continued out through the corridors inside the mountain. The sentient priests would keep the door guarded for three days.

10

Mariam was invited to come with them to Albion's rooms where a hefty stew was served. She realized that she was hungry and ate happily. Young Priscilla came with little Geiss who had been calm with them during the ritual on the mountain, but was starting to miss his mother. She nursed him to sleep, and made herself comfortable on a bed among colorful blankets and pillows. Soon she was fast asleep herself. Albion covered her with a blanket, and they all went to do their daily activities.

She woke up when the baby whimpered, and realized that they had slept for some time. She changed his wrappings, and arranged him in his sling around her body, before heading for the path up the mountainside. The sun was already getting lower in the horizon and the ceremony on the top was long over. The temple was preparing for a festive evening meal with musicians. She could be alone among the stones for a little while.

Finding the round flat stone in the center, she sat down upon it and noticed the flower wreaths that had been used to decorate the space for the solstice. They were leaning against the standing stones and had been carried around during the ceremony. She would have loved to take part in it, but there had been other duties calling her this morning.

The beauty of the hours she had spent inside the mountain stayed with her. Everything seemed to have existed outside of time, just like Yeshua was now somewhere outside of space. Dreamily she looked out over the landscape surrounding her. She saw the little beehive stone structures in the distance, and the lovely mountain tops forming the points of the pentagram. Languedoc was different than Provence, and Razes was especially picturesque. She thought of the views from her beloved herb farm, and remembered the charm of the gentle hills and meadows. Here there were taller pines along with deciduous trees, blooming bushes of many sorts and lovely wild flowers. The mountainsides were sharper and the air had a crisper quality. She loved this just as much as her beloved Provence, and knew she would come back here.

The sun was making long shadows of the menhir, creating new effects on the ground around her. She looked around the circle, counting up the thirteen stones surrounding her. The temples in Egypt seemed formal. This place had an earthy tone. Knowing the level of knowledge the place contained, she appreciated the honoring of nature. The civilization of Egypt was further removed from this direct interaction with nature in every activity of their lives. The Romans might think they had the epiphany of culture, and in some respects that was true, but they were so far removed from what this place represented, they wouldn't understand its significance. In their ignorance, they would fear the invisible power these people were working with. *Fear and ignorance is a dangerous combination*, thought Mariam and shuttered.

Geiss warmed her body, and she thought of the new little star she carried inside.

It could only just have been started, since she hadn't even missed any days yet. She sent the new little light her blessings, welcomed it into their lives, and hugged Geiss closer.

Sitting on the stone, she realized she was right above Yeshua's body alone in the chamber in the center of the mountain. She did not try to make contact with it. That would call his spirit back to his body, and it was not time for that yet. She trusted that his physical body had been well prepared, and would welcome his wiser spirit back upon his return.

Instead, she tuned to the guides that were working with him in the universe he existed in right now. They echoed in her mind, seeming both extremely close and extremely far away. She had a sense that they spoke through the vibration of her body, and that they existed far out in the edge of the galaxy. Albion had said that right now the planet Venus was right above the galactic core, in a straight line from the earth. She tried to visualize what that would look like, remembering her astronomy classes at the Library when she was young. Her teachers had made it all come alive, with models of the planets, showing their movements. Venus was always the most fascinating, because of the pattern she made when viewed from earth. Mariam considered her the artist among the planets, the one who makes her life into beautiful artwork as she transverses the cosmos.

What was the galactic core? Some said poetically that was where new souls came from. She looked down at her son and wondered if he had the answers. She knew Tamera would have answered her and come up with an explanation. Sarah had taught her to speak very early, and the girl was quite adept at expressing herself. She sensed that her daughter was doing well, and that Sarah was enjoying her assignment tremendously. Mariam thought fondly of them both, and looked forward to see them soon, wondering how much the girl had grown.

The sun was warming her rock, and she enjoyed feeling one with the landscape around her, her family in many places, and the beloved star above her, whose footprint she was sitting in the middle of.

11

Mariam spent another day wandering around admiring the beautiful landscape. She had to allow this all to sink in, to fuse with the landscape surrounding her and let it expand her awareness to where she took in all the rivers, valleys and mountain tops and let the air breeze through her body.

The baby usually came with her, and with the added life force of the child in his sling, and the new life started inside her, she felt their combined strength, and their wordless communication with nature. Thinking back later, she saw herself as a walking landscape painting, a mirror of everything she saw.

Albion watched Mariam's movements. He kept knowledge of where she was, and followed her in his thoughts, if not on the path. Nothing could happen to this wonderful woman. They needed her strength upon her husbands return, and he looked forward to have her visit his Temple many times in the future.

Teresa watched Mariam as well. She made sure that her physical needs were taken care of. There was always food cooking, hearty small meals for her were kept ready at hand, and she made sure Priscilla was ready with new wrappings for Geiss, or to take him off his mothers hands for a couple of hours.

Mariam realized she had very physical guardians who took good care of her, and found ways to show her gratitude.

On the third day Albion assembled the same group that had sent Yeshua on his journey. It was time to bring him back.

They started at the bottom of the mountain, again attended by a man and a woman wearing headgear resembling panthers. Priscilla came with today too, both to assist with Geiss, and to be the sixth person to complete their number. Albion started them walking in procession to the top of the mountain, to do a ceremony among the standing stones. Mariam felt the menhir nod at her in recognition, and blinked.

They gathered around the center stone. This time little Geiss came with them. Albion felt that his son's presence would strengthen the anchor for Yeshua's return to physical life.

They sang an incantation, and started the reverberation among the stones. The circle of stones lying on top of the standing ones, created a conduit for the spiraling motion of the sound. Mariam realized how expertly Albion conducted the forces he worked with. His knowledge of the unseen physical properties and connection lines you could establish was impressive. To untrained eyes, he would look like a magician. *Or a wizard druid from Hibernia,* she heard Bashra complete her own thought.

Albion asked Mariam to step up on the stone and sit down in the middle. Then he positioned the others and himself in the points of the pentagram of the star. Mariam sat down with her legs crossed in front of her, and placed the baby across her lap. She closed her eyes, and could see the pattern of Venus being painted on the ground between them. The five petal rose pattern was visible to her in pink light between their feet. As she listened to the tones of the others, she realized that they were creating the musical structure and rhythm of the pattern. The song was waiting for its melody. Mariam thought of Sybil and how she would have interpreted the music with her beautiful soprano. She thought of her brother Lazarus and how he was able to interpret songs out of the task at hand and the time of the day. She started a melody line, and found that her lower voice also had a nice range, and created a melody reflecting the mountain lines surrounding them. Her song undulated in the petal pattern of Venus, while the other participants held the hum of the Earth.

Albion started invoking Yeshua and call for his return. He knew he was far away, and needed to hear this call from his people standing above his own body safely kept in the chamber inside the mountain. The song got stronger. Albion wanted to send a powerful signal and used his people, the stone circle and the surrounding mountains as amplifiers.

Mariam called her husband from her heart. She could feel his answer as a flash of light. First it was a passing flicker, then, as she joined strength with their son and the small star inside her, she felt it come stronger towards her. The light became a bright white light illuminating her inside, and she smiled in recognition.

Albion saw the light coming to her as a beam the thickness of a spear, landing on her head, going through her body and down into the mountain. He marveled at the strong connection between this husband and wife, apparently partners in so much more than marriage.

The visible light only lasted a moment. But it changed the vibration of the mountain. The stones changed their tone, and the singers also shifted. Mariam's song had changed into a lullaby for the child. Albion brought the song to a quiet hum and signaled them all to follow him down the hill. It was time to assemble again in the secret chamber inside the stone.

Teresa helped Mariam off the stone, and assisted her as they started down the path. The others fell in, and they continued a soft hum as they descended in wide ceremonial circles around the mountain top.

12

At the end of the path they found the entrance to the insides of the mountain. Albion opened the gate and they walked through the first entrance. Mariam hugged Geiss closer against the colder temperatures. The dampness inside the stones where water was running between the cracks created moisture on her hot skin. She shuddered in the cold humidity, and thought about water finding its way in the smallest of spaces, always desiring to unite with a larger body. This water had come from the top of the mountain, found its way through plants and vegetation and arrived here, looking for the ground water level beneath.

They continued the hum as they descended further into the mountain, passing through more doors and gates. At the last gate, Mariam recognized the two sentient guards, who had stood there since they left three days ago. They looked unchanged, and Mariam wondered if they even were human with their animal hoods over their faces. They removed their crossed lances to let Albion and his crew through. Inside the chamber, she heard the guards close the heavy stone door behind them, and they were again alone inside a black cube.

Yeshua's body was outlined in the linen covering him. Underneath, he was covered in the linen straps they had used. Mariam sensed the presence of the light they had called for on the top of the mountain, but wondered if it had anchored in his body yet. They were here and ready to help him.

Braziers were lit, herbs were burned, oil was heated, and the unguent in the alabaster jar was brought to the stone table.

Albion gathered them around the stone byre. Mariam was again standing at Yeshua's head. There was no life signal in his body. She recognized the appearance. She had seen it before in other bodies she had helped back from initiations. In this powerful chamber, she felt safe about doing this ritual. This place had witnessed this before. The stones here remembered how to send people off, and how to call them back. The whole mountain had functioned as an anchor for these activities for hundreds, if not thousands, of years. She trusted Albion and his priests and priestesses without hesitation. All of them had taken this journey at some point. Yeshua had been invited as a teacher in high standing, and had wanted to do this ritual for his own reasons as well. Mariam could only stand in awe at what she was witnessing.

Albion signaled to her. It was time to sing again the lovely tone she had found between the standing stones. Mariam found her notes, found the way to express the form of the five petal rose one more time, and watched the light hovering along the ceiling of the chamber collect itself into a cloud above Yeshua's body. The assistants lifted off the linen covering him.

Mariam started to uncover his head. She rolled up the linen as she went, and found that his skin had kept its tone very well. Of course, with no circulation, he was taking on a grayer tone, but compared to the condition of Lazarus, Yeshua's color was quite good.

She continued unwrapping around his neck, but found that she needed to move his body to get access to more. She stroked his beautiful hair, and looked up at Albion for further instructions. He signaled to his assistant to bring something, and he returned with small wooden table the same height as the stone bench. It was placed on the floor behind Yeshua's head. The two assistants gently held Yeshua's head and shoulders, while Albion and Teresa lifted his body on the sheet he was lying on and moved the body off the stone fir his head and shoulders to rest on the extra table. His body was strong enough to hold the short section of his back suspended, and they quickly removed the linen down to his waist. The body was lifted in its linen sling back on the table. Establishing a rolling motion between them, they removed the linen around his hips. Then the wooden support was moved to the other end of the table to rest his feet. His body was positioned further down on the stone and the linens covering his legs were removed. Then Yeshua was placed back in the middle of the byre, and the wooden support was put back in storage.

Mariam marveled at their efficiency, and again realized that this was all very familiar to them. Did they do it at both equinoxes and solstices? She would have to ask Teresa later.

Standing behind his head, Mariam looked down the body of her beloved husband. His scars had healed, but the work of the Roman whips still showed their marks. His wrists and ankles would always have the large mark from nails going through them, but the holes had been closed for a long time, and all the scars were starting to fade. Mariam thought of the healing water nearby which Yeshua had insisted on swimming in. She had watched its effect on him. She noticed how strong he was, with well built muscle structure, even though he was not a young man anymore.

Teresa stood next to her with the alabaster jar. They wanted her to start the application on his head. She opened the lid, and included a blessing of the herbs in her song, while she scooped out the needed amount and placed it on his forehead. Teresa continued around the table and gave the two assistants some salve to work with as well. They started with a leg each.

Mariam had given Geiss over to Priscilla to have her hands free. He was sitting on Priscilla's arm staring at what was unfolding. They all knew it would be easier for Yeshua to return to something familiar. His son, holding his fathers essence, would be a powerful magnet.

Starting applying the pungent unguent in his hair, Mariam thought of Yochanan and the first time she and Sibyl had worked together in a waking ritual. How they had marveled at the combination of herbs for the salve they were making. It all contained heart stimulants, including Bella Donna, which would be deadly if the dosage was too strong. She had overseen the making of this salve herself together with Teresa. The ingredients were almost the same, with some added sweet smelling herbs grown locally around here. She had learned something over her years of priestess work. If anything, her work had become more refined. She had learned to discern better. There was no need to shock his system, if you could get the same effect in a more gentle way.

As her fingers worked, she breathed in the scent of the herbs. The fragrance was pungent with overtones of sweet flowers. Lavender was in such abundance here, and an expression of the hills surrounding them. To call him back to this beloved ridge, she had needed to use this wonderful flower. Rose was obvious, resembling Venus. She had even found a green herb to represent Hibernia, something familiar to him.

She watched as his body systematically got covered in fragrance and thick oil, while surrounded with the sounds of the landscape, as they all sang the intonation out in the room.

The light above them was starting to change shape. Albion had monitored the development of the situation, and found that it was time to call for him even stronger. He motioned to Mariam to call her husbands name.

"Yeshua", called Mariam, whispering his name gently out in the open room. The others included his name among the notes of their song. Like an echo, he was called from wherever he was. Mariam felt his presence from somewhere far away, right next to her, and inside her body.

The light above them responded to their call. Mariam saw it become more concentrated in a large sphere. Slowly it formed a star inside. Did Venus blink at her? Was there a thank-you-note in that blink, in gratitude for the visit of her husband? Mariam smiled to herself and her own sweet interpretations. Did the planet Venus have that much personality? From her herb bag she heard a snort from Bashra. *What a dumb question. Of course she does!*

The star inside the light sphere grew bigger. Now the others could see it as well. They directed their attention and their song towards it, encouraging it to find its body and choose to return to them.

Mariam shifted her attention to the body in front of her. She appealed to Yeshua's heart. Like she had done in the burial grotto near Golgotha, she had to find the hidden spark inside him, to appeal to his body to want its spirit back. The body in front of her had to give out its signal, saying it was ready to receive its resident soul after its long journey.

She remembered last time, how she'd had a hard time finding him. The whole ordeal he had gone through prior to being put in the trance, had scared his flesh. She was dealing with a body that didn't know if it wanted to be brought back to life. It would have to go through weeks of pain to recover, and wasn't quite sure if it wanted to endure that.

This body was quite different. The body was healthy and there was no pain to return to. On the contrary, this body was going to return to a delightful child and a growing family, a loving wife and a daughter they would unite with soon. There was happiness in his future. There was so much to live for. Mariam felt the excitement grow in her own body as she was thinking about it. She was looking forward to share all this with him. And she could see it all unfold on the herb farm near beautiful mount Aurelia in Provence. If they lived quietly, it would be safe for him.

She searched his heart and heart region. She was familiar with this section of his body. Many times she had put her attention inside him, to monitor his state of health and what he could need at the moment. The whole area of his body had a green sheen around it. *For balance*, she thought to herself, *for being the connection point between his upper and lower body, and his inward and outward life.* She knew how this green light would form a line going up and down through his body. It would also go between his two hands, creating a strong cross section when he stood with his arms outstretched. This was the power spot of his body.

But she didn't find him in the obvious crossing point. The green sheen was hardly visible in his cells. She sent her own search light like a laser beam inside him to find the familiar spark. Silently she called to her son, *Geiss, where is your father?*

Little Geiss didn't like the situation. He whimpered slightly on Priscilla's arm. His whole attention was on the light cloud above his father's body. Suddenly he laughed out loud. Geiss had found his father. The light cloud made a sound, and seemed to try to amuse the child. The others noticed as well, and the display brought smiles to their serious faces. They weren't expecting to laugh at this hour.

Geiss stretched out his hand to touch the light, and the light cloud seemed to elongate itself to meet the child. His little hand disappeared inside the light, and the child laughed louder. A new light was formed around the baby, and light seemed to be streaming through his body, from his head to his toes. Priscilla disappeared behind a new sphere of light.

Mariam observed it all, recognizing her husband's sense of humor and delight in their little son. She watched the light again take on the shape of a spear, and shoot downwards, towards the body below it.

Yeshua's body convulsed and lay still. Mariam was thrilled. Now it would start functioning. Little Geiss was gurgling spit balls in delight. The body on the table took a deep breath. Albion and the others exhaled in relief.

13

Albion was smiling with the others. He finally understood why he had decided to take the child with. This was indeed good news. This part of the ritual always had tension, because some souls would simply decide not to return. They had good reasons to make that decision. They had experienced a richer form of life where they went. It was a place they could learn so much more and most initiates had wonderful teachings for the Temple upon their return. He was looking forward to hear what this well educated man would say.

They all continued massaging Yeshua's body to bring the blood flow back. Soon he was glowing with a healthy pink sheen. The priests and priestesses were proud of their work. They knew how to do this. Albion thanked the Gods that had guided Yeshua on his journey, the ones that had taught him in the other world, and the ones that had sent him gracefully back to the temple and his family. Then he thanked Venus for sharing her light with them one more time, and for using this particular traveler to send such powerful light beams to their temple and the neighboring mountains. The sun was honored on his journey across the sky, and thanked for sending extra light on the summer solstice. Then he said some mysterious words Mariam did not understand, but she had a sense that he was talking to the Galactic Core. They all intoned the echo answer for each part of his blessings, while they continued working on Yeshua's body.

Mariam was feeling her heart beat in a different rhythm. She wasn't quite sure if she ever wanted to go through this again. The tension was so intense, and the risks enormous, even here among well trained people. She put her hands on her husband's chest above his heart to feel the familiar rhythm. It was there. The heart was working normally under her hands, and once again, she felt tears run down her cheeks.

Albion took in the situation. He was able to tune in to the heart region as well. The heart functioned normally. That was good. The blood was flowing to the body, giving life to dormant muscles. But the light was still hovering above his body. Part of it had gone into the flesh on the table, but part of it was still hovering above it. Little Geiss seemed to have a small sphere of light he could play with like a physical ball, and Albion wondered how this advanced spirit had managed that. Had he fragmented himself? If so, that was not good.

Teresa noticed that something was unusual as well. The body on the table was breathing, but was there anybody inside? The light in front of their eyes had more life to it than the flesh they'd been working on. The child was delighted, but what was it he was playing with? As she looked around puzzled, she saw Mariam having sunk down next to her husband. She had kissed his lips, and was holding her cheek next to his, continuing to whisper his name. Usually, he would have opened his eyes by now.

The priest and priestess with the panther heads had taken a step back. They saw something they were not familiar with. The light seemed to be everywhere at once. It was a light cloud above the body. It was inside the body, glowing from the heart. It was around the child and appeared as a toy for him. It was glowing around his wife, swimming through her body, and it was appearing behind them all illuminating the walls. The floor took on an appearance of glowing snakes, swirling, squirming underneath their feet. Everybody stopped what they were doing and just stared.

The light in the ceiling became a big star above his body, which exploded into streams of light from one point right above him, spreading out across the ceiling to the corner of the wall and streaming down the walls like melted gold flowing like water.

Mariam had held her face buried in his neck. Now she lifted her head and saw the lights illuminating the chamber. Without thinking, she shouted "Yeshua!" and wasn't quite sure if she was fearful or amazed.

The golden light floating like a liquid in the room condensed and took on form above the body. Mariam held her place by the head of the table and watched as her husband materialized him self as figure of pure light. It hovered for a moment, then sat down where Yeshua's body would have sat, if it had risen up and swung its legs over the side of the table.

"There you are," said Mariam. "We've been waiting for you."

14

Yeshua sat there and smiled in gratitude to all the people who had been working on his body to bring him back. The smile made him beam even stronger, even though he was already shining like the midday sun from a bright blue sky.

Mariam tried to touch him. Did he have substance? Her hand disappeared in the light and found nothing to hold onto. He smiled apologetically. He opened his mouth and spoke, and they could hear his voice, but it didn't come from the light body in front of them. The voice came from the walls around them, reflecting in the stone so they could hear.

"Mariam, my Mariam," they heard. "I'm all light now. My work in a human body is finished. From this state I can work on bringing light to the people of the earth. I'm free to move through time and space. I'm free to teach people how to bring more light into their bodies and to infuse light where there is darkness.

Mariam, this is my work. This is what I was destined for. This is what you were destined to witness, support and teach. And to bring forth children who will bring this knowledge further.

I will always be with you. You will always be able to call for me and call me forth in this form. But my body cannot hold this level of light. It is alive, but it cannot hold me. It holds my wisdom, but it cannot hold the light that I've become.

Mariam, I want to join my ancestors and allow my wisdom to be accessed by the people who know how. I want to join Yochanan as the next in line of good people holding the knowledge."

Mariam understood every word he said. She knew exactly what he meant and she hated him for it. A scream cut through the room. It was her scream of agony, disbelief, grief, anger, and love. If he had been a child, she would have grabbed his shoulder and shaken this horrible idea out of his head.

But he was not a child. He was not even a real person anymore. He might as well be dead. She had brought him back to life one more time, brought him back to the happiness of a growing family, only to hear him say he had chosen something else. She felt like a jilted wife. She felt rejected. But there was no other woman. How could she compete with pure light? Her face exploded in fury and tears.

She felt him stroke her cheeks. Trying to touch his hand, she felt nothing. If she closed her eyes, she could feel his skin gently next to hers, his fine fingertips, so used to healing any ailment, so used to giving generously from his unending love for her. She let her tears flow in silent streams from her closed eyelids, while she allowed him to touch her cheek undisturbed. She still wanted to strike him for putting her through this. How could he ask her to do what he was proposing?

Her love for him and respect for his teaching, her understanding of their shared destiny and purpose in life, became entangled in a big knot, mixed with feelings of contempt towards the universe for using people in this way to get their own agenda across. She felt like a powerless pawn in the chess game of the Gods. How come he took his new role so easily?

A new sensation was felt on her cheek. It was his tears. His tears were streaming down on her, tears manifested out of love for her. Tears of empathy knowing what he had asked her to do. Tears of sadness for leaving her like this. Tears of love that would never again be expressed in the touch shared between husband and wife. Tears for the misery of humanity he now faced, and the new monumental task ahead of him; to lift them out of it.

She understood. She understood his new sacrifice. Was this man never going to be left alone? She railed against the Gods. They'd had a blessed year in Hibernia. After all his learning, all his devotion, all the people he had helped, the sacrifice he made in Jerusalem, was this his reward?

Maybe there was no reward, only more work. Maybe the reward *was* more work, but in a more advanced form, given to you according to your new level of understanding. Oh, that sounded lofty and lovely. She couldn't hide her rage, which was turning over to despair over the inevitability of the situation. Quietly, Mariam sank down on the floor.

The others saw what was happening. They had also heard his words, they had seen her response. Now they watched her sit on the floor with a vacant look in her face, while the light of her husband enveloped her completely. She disappeared inside the light he surrounded her with, and all they could see was a sphere of bright white light hovering above the floor containing both of them.

Baby Geiss had watched it all, as well, and Priscilla wondered if she had an orphan on her arm. Now he called for his mother, since she had disappeared from sight.

Mariam fell out of the light sphere, and was left lying unconscious on the floor. The light in the room collected itself above the stone table. Then it became a spear of light, which pierced the heart of the body on the table and shot into the ground underneath. They could feel a reverberation in the floor they were standing on, a shift in vibration, and saw the light reappear in all the sparkles of gold in the black stone they were surrounded with. Then the chamber was again the inside of a black cube.

15

Teresa attended to Mariam, the others lit the braziers that had blown out and checked on the body on the table. Albion looked frozen in a daze. His eyes were wide open and there was a new light shining from his face. One of the attendants found a seat for him to sit down.

Priscilla had been wise enough to bring a piece of bread for Geiss to divert his attention, and the child was content for now.

The priest and priestess with panther heads were standing by the stone table. They found nothing wrong with the body in front of them. The heart was beating, it was breathing softly and the blood was giving a healthy color to the skin.

Mariam was the one looking like a ghost. Teresa had laid her out on the floor.

She was breathing and her heart was beating normally, but her color was ghastly, and Teresa couldn't wake her up.

Albion understood that his attention was needed. As soon as he had stated his intention in his mind, he felt a connection to the woman on the floor. He sensed that she didn't want to come back to the reality that faced her, and had opted for complete denial. Albion was worried that she had followed her husband where he was going, and they would have two comatose bodies to deal with.

Quickly he found that was not the case. He could sense that there was no spirit in the body on the table, although it appeared alive. But the woman on the floor had her spirit intact, she had just fainted.

"Mama," said little Geiss, and Mariam slowly opened her eyes. Again, Albion blessed the presence of the child. Priscilla had heard him say a few words, and thought the boy was quite advanced for his age. Right now he was exactly what they needed.

"My child," said Mariam and reached for him. Priscilla placed the warm boy in his mother's arms, while Teresa helped her sit up. Mariam hugged her child to her body so hard that Geiss started to squirm. She loosened her grip, and let him sit on her lap with her arms around him.

Slowly Mariam tried to take in the situation around her. *So it had been real*, she thought.

She needed some time to sit still and breathe before she could speak. The others were waiting. Depending on Mariam's words, they would respond in different ways. If she showed distress, they would care for her. If she had an overview of the situation, they were ready to take orders.

Mariam sensed that. She also sensed their deep love and concern for her, their sympathy with her and empathy for her emotions. She recognized the overflow of good will coming her way. It was what Yeshua had received from the thousands who followed him to Golgotha. Here she received it from five well trained empaths in a chamber that had just been bathed in universal love. She allowed it to flow over her, to nourish her, to help her define the many feelings flowing in her body. With the shared strength from the others, she could differentiate between the emotions she needed to work with now, and the ones she would have to wash away later in the deep blue sea.

She hugged her child softly one more time and handed him back to Priscilla. Looking at the others, she saw the shocked look on Albion and could feel him trying to make sense of it all. Teresa looked grief stricken and worried about Mariam's well being. Priscilla figured as long as she took care of the child, someone would sooner or later explain what had happened. The two other attendants had taken their panther hoods off and were standing there waiting for her response. She recognized them from the temple as other adepts, and thanked them for their work with her eyes.

Mariam gave the strong priest her hand and let him pull her up. She took a few steps over to the stone table to be at her husband's side. Again admiring his strength and beauty, she couldn't believe that this body would never be able to wake up. Part of her wanted to keep trying, but she knew it would be fruitless.

Then she remembered his wish, and she almost fainted again.

Albion was so tuned with Mariam that he had seen the vision in her mind. He raised his eyebrows even higher, and as soon as he came out of his shock, he realized there was work to be done. He also realized that this work was not suitable for all of them to attend.

Quietly he thanked the attendants for their services and told them to go with Priscilla and the child and get a good meal. Mariam thanked them all and promised to join them later.

"Mariam, what do you need?" Albion asked. "I will send Teresa to go and get it for you".

Mariam took a deep breath. She already had her herb bag on her, it never left her side. But there were other things she would need, specific for the task at hand.

"I'll need my tool bag, and the two bags with red tassels on them," she announced. She realized she was starving, but couldn't see how eating anything would make her feel any better. "And some water to drink?"

Teresa understood. Tears were streaming down her face as she stood by the door and looked at her new friend. There was nothing to say. She bent her head in a soft nod, and left to find Mariam's things.

Mariam sat down on the seat the attendants had put out for Albion and tried to breathe normally.

"Albion, we will need to bury him," she said matter-of-factly, looking straight at him. Albion just nodded, and knew he would have to send Teresa on more errands.

16

Mariam instructed Albion in what she had to do. She needed his help, both with the surgical preparation, and with the ritual around it. Her concern for the burial was eased when Albion described the many caves in the mountains surrounding them. She felt they needed a casket for him, and Albion assured her there were some in storage close by. Simple ones used for their own people. She told him that would be fine.

When Teresa returned with her bags, she also included a skin for her with water. She was a little disappointed when she was sent off again to look for other things, but understood that whatever was going to happen next, Mariam wanted to be alone with Albion. She went to the kitchen garden to look for a gourd, wondering what they needed it for, and to ask the carpentry shop about a suitable casket. It was needed for a rather tall man.

They counted on Teresa to be gone for long enough, and started setting up the room. Albion, who usually gave orders, was accepting directions from Mariam. He was curious about what would unfold and was holding back his tears.

Mariam needed to set up the room for ritual again. The braziers and incense were all ready to be used, that was a relief. She tied her work apron over her dress, while she looked over her tools and laid them down next to Yeshua on the stone bench. She decided to remove the linen he was lying on to keep it clean so they could wrap him with it for the casket. She hoped they could get enough water to scrub the table clean afterwards, and promised herself to do everything she could to keep the blood spill low. *Oh, Herodias, where are you when I need you?*

"By all the Gods, Mariam, what are you up to?" sounded a loud and clear voice in her head. Mariam tried to convey back in images the situation she found herself in. Herodias was horrified as it became clear to her what Mariam was about to do. Memories from a dungeon in Jerusalem were vivid for both of them. Herodias saw Mariam's vacant face as she lifted her red tearstained eyes in quiet resignation. She was done fighting against the inevitable. Yeshua would never come back to his body. All she could ask from Herodias was if she could help guide Albion as her assistant. Herodias wanted to scream in protest, but was silenced by a look from Mariam. After curbing her reaction, Herodias promised to do what she could. She tuned into Albion and found him quite capable. The she took in the magnitude of what was going on and was heart struck. *Was there no end to what this woman was asked to do?*

Mariam breathed in Herodias' strength. She wiped her face dry and cleared her emotions before she started the incantations asking Yeshua to pull his essence up in his head. She wasn't quite sure how this was all going to work since he technically wasn't in his body at all, but trusted that since he'd asked for it, that would have to count as permission and a wish for it all to work correctly. She taught Albion to sing the counterparts, and was surprised how easily he took to it. She guessed Herodias was doing her job, and that Albion must be particularly open for her influence after the shocked state he had been in. She was grateful to them both.

Mariam unwrapped Yochanan. He hadn't been out of his bags for months. There hadn't been any ritual he was needed for in quite some time.

Albion's eyes grew wide again as he took in what she held in her hand. He realized that she was just as learned as her husband. Yochanan was placed on Yeshua's left side. "A prophet," Mariam explained. Then Mariam opened her herb bag and unfolded Bashra. Albion understood that this one had been with them through everything that had happened.

"About time," announced Bashra as she was placed on Yeshua's right side. "I've been waiting for you to ask for help. How are you, child?"

Mariam wished she hadn't said that, and was about to lose her grip on the situation. But the first lesson for the temple trained is self control. It would take more to tip her over this time. Mariam had found her strength, and had locked her own raging emotions in a safe place to be dealt with later.

Albion's eyes grew even bigger. He'd heard about shrunken heads, but never seen one. "It's my ancestor from Ethiopia," Mariam explained.

It was time to turn her attention to the other bag with the red tassels on. Since she left Jerusalem, this one had been at her side through all her travels. If something should happen to him by accident, she wanted to be prepared and follow the prophecy of the magi. She never thought she would need it in this way.

The carved stone jar was of such fine quality, Albion thought only kings would see such craftsmanship. "It's from Persia," Mariam said and left it at that. She'd known its purpose since she first saw the jar in the niche in Uncle Joseph's house in Jerusalem. This was the last of the three gifts from the astrologers, the gifts that had been waiting for a priestess of the highest rank to know their use and purpose. This unguent was intended for the embalmment of his head.

Mariam knew she held the title of the Panther of the Serapium. She hadn't been there for years. Was she still a panther? She looked up at Albion. He understood. He picked up the hood the other priest had been wearing. Who was this woman? Who was the man they were working with? Albion bowed his head in the sign of respect. He stood and faced Mariam, and tied the hood correctly on her head. When she opened her eyes, the old man saw that her pupils had elongated and taken on the colors of tiger eye gemstones. Albion understood that there was nothing ordinary in this situation.

They returned to their positions at either end of the table. Her surgical tools were laid out next to her, and some herbs and oils were at her side. The elaborately decorated jar had been opened and was giving out its remarkable fragrance. Myrrh, Albion knew the perfume, and he knew what it was intended for. This man was a King, he understood that now.

Again Mariam started the incantations. The words this time were to prepare Yeshua's body for what would happen, and again ask his spirit to confirm that this was his wish. She sang the incantations inviting Yochanan to join them, and the eyes that looked like he was just sleeping opened up. He responded to Mariam's song and expressed his delight at being called forth. Then he looked at what was in front of him.

"Please don't cry," Mariam voiced to him silently. "I can't handle you crying."

Yochanan simply acknowledged the situation, and sang the bass notes. Bashra knew what to sing as well. Albion was too curious to do anything else, and followed Yochanan's lead.

Mariam looked at the body in front of her. His beautiful serene face and his lovely light hair surrounded his head like another halo. There was light coming from his body, but not at the level they had seen earlier. She watched his chest move up and down in quiet breathing. His skin looked healthy and was warm to her fingers.

She looked at the scars on his body she had nursed back to health, the signs of holes on his wrists and ankles. Why wouldn't this strong body sustain his spirit? Why wouldn't his tall handsome frame be able to hold the beautiful spirit she loved? She had to pull herself away from the way she was thinking. She knew she would break down if she went on. She was glad there was a small cloth around his hips, or she would have gone into another line of thought which would not have helped her at all. She sighed and collected herself. There was work to do. This was what Yeshua had requested, and she had to honor that.

She knew what would have to happen first. She had to kill the body. Looking for her large, pointed knife, she knew she needed to stick it in just right, through his heart, to make it swift and painless. She wasn't sure how much pain this body could experience, but that was irrelevant. She also needed to do it right to minimize the blood flow. Her sutures were ready to quickly stitch up his aorta and his veins. Albion was ready to assist her in every way.

Inside she called for Herodias again, and got an immediate reply. *I'm here, girl, I'm right beside you.*

That was the reassurance she needed. She felt another strength join with her, and thought it was the newly conceived child who wanted to prepare his father so he could meet him some day. The child had already understood that otherwise his powerful father would be gone from history forever.

Mariam understood her responsibility. This was done for prosperity. How old was Bashra? *Don't even try to count!* she heard in her head. She knew she had to be several hundred years. Yochanan would be accessible for centuries. It was only natural to prepare Yeshua the same way. Maybe he could even explain what had happened here today. Maybe he could continue his teaching in a new format. Mariam hoped so.

She found the large knife. She found the spot on his chest where she had to send it in between his ribs. She took one last look at her husbands body, one last look at his head when it was still attached at his neck, said a prayer for his soul in between the other notes she was singing, before putting her weight on the knife and sending it straight into his heart.

The body convulsed a time or two. Blood started coming out through the opening she'd made. He made a rattling sound in his throat, and stopped breathing. Quickly Mariam made the correct incisions. She needed a longer cut down on his front and back to be able to wrap it back around the base of the head. After having loosened the skin and pulled it over his face, she started making cuts in his throat. The break had to be at the fifth vertebrae, and there were many small organs around the neck she wanted to include. Glands were small message centers. They needed to accompany him in his next mission. Albion handed her the sutures and she quickly stitched up the main blood veins to stop the bleeding. Yeshua seemed to have done a fine job preparing his body for this. It seemed to accept what she was doing as if it was cooperating on its own.

Before she cut the bone, they turned him over and made a similar large piece of skin below the cut so they could make a nice cover around the neck. Then she used a bigger knife to cut through the spine. It needed all her weight, but she managed, and hoped to preserve as much bone marrow as possible within the head.

She looked over the cuts, both on the body side and the head to see if any more needed to be stitched. Then she pushed to body aside, and focused on the head. The skin was folded nicely around his neck and quickly stitched up along the seams. Albion could only marvel at her speed and accuracy. He handed her tools as needed, wiped off the ones that were handed back to him, and listened to Yochanan and Bashra welcome Yeshua among them.

When the head was finished, she applied the embalmment myrrh generously on it. His skin took on a golden tone. She let her able fingers find every crevice of his familiar face, around his nose, around his eyes, covering his ears. She massaged it into his forehead and cheeks, his chin and neck. The seams of skin got an extra application to stay supple. She handled the head expertly between her fingers, Albion could only think of people working with jewelry with such refined movements.

Mariam used the entire jar. The whole chamber smelled of the powerful oily substance. When she felt she was done, she laid the head down and blessed it one more time. Then she wrapped it up in the wrappings the jar had been in and placed it in the bag with red tassels. The beautiful jar from Persia was donated to the Temple. Albion felt honored to receive such a fine gift. Together they thanked Yochanan and Bashra for their help, closed their eyes and placed them back in their wrappings as well. Mariam saw no reason to alarm the whole temple that she knew more than she'd let out. It could so easily be misunderstood and misconstrued. Albion understood, and was not going to tell anyone what he had just witnessed.

They wiped off her tools and replaced them in her tool bag. She could clean them better when she had more time. They had some water to clean the stone table as well, and got it pretty well wiped up before Teresa returned. She knocked on the door and said she had the gourd they requested, but the casket would be carried over by the carpenters. They were on their way. They received the item and thanked her, while blocking her view.

Mariam felt really silly doing this, but she felt she had Herodias' instructions, and given the strangeness of everything, this felt practically normal.

Albion understood what she intended. They focused on the body again. The end of the gourd was attached with more sutures at his neck. It functioned as a substitute head. Mariam was sure it was Herodias' idea, and could only admit it was genius. However evolved the temple was, the last thing she needed was gossip which could follow her all the way back to Provence, and even reach Roman ears.

They wrapped up the body in the same linens which had held his body for the journey of Osiris. With some creative turns of the bandage, Mariam made the gourd look like part of him. She and Albion covered the rest of him in the linen strips used earlier. When the priest and priestess who had been in attendance before arrived with the casket, they were ready with a corpse properly wrapped in linen strips with a linen sheet as an outer cover making it easy to transport.

He was placed ceremoniously in his casket where some straw had been put to cushion him. The carriers showed sympathy for the grief stricken wife with respectful bows. They had also known the handsome, gentle man who had been so eager to learn from the temple. They grieved themselves over his fate at a ceremony the temple did successfully several times a year. Then they carried him silently through the many corridors. Mariam walked right behind them, finally allowing her tears to flow. Albion and Teresa made the rear carrying her important bags, crying their own tears.

17

Coming out in the sunlight was shocking for everyone. They carried the casket to the open courtyard between the main buildings and placed it on some stones on the ground. A new procession of people had gathered. Everybody had liked the friendly rabbi who spoke Latin with an accent. It was so sad to hear about his unexpected death. The poor widow. What would she do? She had a child with her, and they'd heard of another one in Provence. Hopefully she had family there to return to. The whole temple complex was concerned for her well being.

Albion announced that they were going to place the casket in one of the caves they used for burial. He would appreciate that they came with as far as the river, but then, please, let it be only the widow, Teresa and himself for the last part. She needed this time to be alone. People understood, and were glad they were given an opportunity to show their respects, both to the learned man and his sweet wife.

The procession was long, and they followed the wider road along the valley towards the river. People sang funeral songs from their local traditions and Mariam was glad she didn't know them so she could let the people take care of the music. Someone had handed her a bouquet of white lilies which smelled intoxicating in her hand. Many people had brought flowers and placed it on top of the casket. Mariam could hardly see the beauty through her tears. She managed to walk, but couldn't hold her grief in check anymore.

It was a lovely summer day, fragrant with the flowers of the season. On another day she would have skipped down the road thinking about her sister Sarah, and picking flowers to delight her child. It was a somber crowd coming down the road. The local people, who were not connected to the temple, observed the procession and understood that the temple had lost someone today. The tradition was to bury immediately, so this person had died just hours ago. The farmers in the field took their hats off and stopped their work, as the procession walked by to the mournful hum of soft singing. Mariam appreciated their attention.

When they reached the river, people stayed in a group as the smaller procession continued on the other side of the bridge. The people watched the funeral attendants follow the narrow path up the mountainside.

Mariam followed the casket carried by four strong priests, who walked dutifully after Albion up the smaller path that had taken off to their left. Teresa came up next to her and took her hand. Mariam appreciated the added strength, and leaned on the caring woman as they found their way up some rather steep terrain. Where was Albion taking them?

The well worn path straightened out, and she could view the valley in front of them. They passed some caves that already had caskets in them, but Albion went on. He apparently had something else in mind.

They rounded the mountain and came to the other side with more trees. After meandering between evergreens and sturdy oaks, Albion made a sharp turn and stopped. He signaled to the pall bearers to put the casket down and help him clear some brush. He knew there was an opening here. After some work they found the cave. It was large enough to hold the casket and Albion, Teresa and Mariam standing upright. The casket was carried in as far as possible. Mariam counted twelve steps from the entrance. *This was very well hidden, both from man and beast,* she thought. She looked at Albion in gratitude. The bearers were sent outside, and the others stood around the casket to say their goodbyes. Mariam looked at the wooden casket with the lovely flowers piled on top. She knew Yeshua wasn't there. She knew she could find him anytime, anywhere, maybe even easier, now that he didn't have a body to deal with. She stood there, staring at the lilies she was holding and felt him so near. Even though her tears were still running, she felt an inner smile, an inner acceptance of that this was the way it had to be. This was the way it was supposed to end. Or start?

Albion looked at the beautiful woman in front of him. He had a new deep admiration for her. He knew he would think of her every day, from this day forward, sending her well wishes, hoping for her well being.

Teresa had been crying for hours. Her head was dry and in pain. She stood there looking at her new friend whith such remarkable strength. Mariam's grief showed in her entire body, but was carried with such dignity, it made everybody else straighten up and find their own inherent strength.

As they watched Mariam, she closed her eyes, and a new light seemed to form next to her. The bright light from earlier in the day was again present, and they recognized her husbands beautiful face, his height and strong body as he put an arm around her shoulder and turned his head to kiss her forehead.

CHAPTER 15

THE VOYAGE

MARIAM WAS HANGING AT THE RAILING HOLDING onto her child. The captain thought she looked like death. He wondered what the beautiful woman had experienced to give her the appearance of utter despair. Seeing her traveling alone with a child gave him some idea.

Mariam wanted to bury her grief in the waves, and found that if she hadn't had baby Geiss next to her and his needs to take care of, she would have followed her tears into the water.

She had tried to leave her grief behind on the path through the landscape of Languedoc hoping that it would stream out of her, leaving a trail behind her horse, which the forest would absorb and transform into something life giving. She had ridden silently, like a statue, behind Remi all the way back to Ruscino. They had a third horse to take back with them. It needed to be returned to Habib's stables. Remi would probably lead another party back to Julia Carcass. He hoped they would stay on the roads, and go directly to the city. Remi had had enough adventure for some time.

To make the horse look like a pack horse, not a horse missing a rider, Remi had packed all of Mariam's bags on its top. The horse didn't seem to mind, and Mariam was grateful for his thoughtfulness. Little Geiss was with her, and gave her comfort. He seemed to understand that his mother needed silence, and slept happily to the movements of the horse.

How many bags does a woman need? wondered Remi. Not being married himself, he had no understanding of the needs of a small child, or of a woman's habits when she travels. Mariam looked at the horse in front of her, tied behind Remi's own sturdy mount.

She noticed the bags with Geiss' wrappings, blankets and clean clothes. Priscilla had, through tears, made sure everything was pristine before they left. Mariam's own bags contained some shifts of clothing and her hairbrush, a gift from her father for her fifteenth birthday. Her herb bag was always attached to her and her bag of tools never left her. Neither did two bags made of tapestry fabric and leather with red tassels on the bottom. She'd had them made in Jerusalem, for very specific purposes. Now they were tied on the top of the horse in front of her, reminding her of their content with every sway of the horse.

Mariam was exhausted. She'd hoped the ride through the forest would quicken her, but it really was quite tiring in a different way. Remi knew he had to make frequent stops, and hoped the inn along the way had their best room available for her.

It had been ready, and been very comfortable. She wished they could have stayed another day there, but knew that they had already passed the time Remi had allotted to this excursion. He also counted on a ship in route to Massilia from Ruscino to take her back to her family, and he knew the captain couldn't wait.

They had made it to the ship, Remi had been generously paid and the horses were returned to Habib. He was stricken with the news of Yeshua's death. He had also liked the learned man, and had known him since the first times he came this way to visit Hibernia with his uncle. Mariam could only stand still and receive his sincerest condolences, before she was rushed on board the ship, which had been waiting for them.

All her things were carried on board. She remembered walking the plank from land to ship, holding onto the rope along its side, becoming seasick before she was even on board.

She'd hardly eaten anything for several days while on horseback. Now she had to eat some to be able to nurse Geiss, and to be able to hold anything down while at sea.

The fresh air was good for her. She let it flow through her hair and cool down her head. Hugging Geiss closer, he was almost too big for the sling now, she spent her time showing the boy the intricacies of a ship. "Sail", she heard him say, "Mast", another time, as she gave her mind something else to be occupied with.

The captain was glad she was only going to be with them for two days. Depressed people, however justified, make the whole boat go into a gloom. He had to admire the woman, though. She had lost her husband recently, and here she was, teaching her child.

Mariam thought of the voyage from Ephesus back to Alexandria and remembered ow strong she had felt. She had just graduated from the temple schools, and returned to the Serapium a fully trained Panther. Now she was returning to her people in Provence, and she felt more like a drowned black cat.

She knew her training was impressive. Her level of education was almost impossible to duplicate. But what had it gotten her? Three bags with mysterious contents she couldn't share with anyone. She couldn't return to the Serapium, or to Ephesus. Starting her own traditions in Provence was going to be primitive at best. She longed for the familiar voice of Sibyl, Johanna's warm caring and Sarah's unbeatable good mood. How was Lazarus doing? How was Martha? She felt she'd been gone for a long time, and the length of time became palpable as she got closer.

Geiss was pointing at other ships sailing in the distance. She leaned her head against the child's soft light hair, so like his father. The boy was calm and attentive, the way she could visualize Yeshua as a child. Would the new child inside her possibly be like her?

Again she watched the movements of the waves, allowing them to take the emotions swimming through her and lull them about. There were no answers. She had absolutely no answers to calm herself with. She was heading for Provence to tell his siblings of Yeshua's second unnecessary death. She would have to write his mother that he finally had left his earthly body behind. He had left by choice to become a beam of light from the star of Venus. Mariam would have to write to her beloved father-in-law that his son had joined forces with his cousin, and had become one of the ancestors she carried in a bag.

She couldn't think that far. She couldn't say it out loud. She didn't think she could ever tell his brothers and sisters where their older brother was. She remembered Sarah's response to her when she had discovered what had become of Yochanan. How could she expect the others to think any different? She would have to send those two bags to a temple somewhere where they could store them properly.

No, she couldn't do that. Yeshua and Yochanan, she gasped even thinking their names, needed to be honored by their own people. She would have to teach someone how to wake them up and continue the rituals. She thought of her own young daughter. When Tamera came of age, maybe she could teach her. But the girl was only a small child; it would take years before she was ready to start even the most rudimentary training.

Could she teach Sarah? Probably not. Herodias was of course her partner, but they weren't getting younger either of them. Young Salome, Herodias' daughter, had been married off to a Roman official, and had long refused to have anything to do with her mother's knowledge.

Again she stared at the waves. As one top came up and the water made a steep valley before the next wave presented itself, Mariam understood that right now she was in a deep valley. The waves of her life would eventually lift and bring another peak.

But right now, the valley of her life was wet, cold and dark.

Her lips tasted salty as she left the railing and carried Geiss into the dining hall to find a piece of bread for him. The sailors tending ropes and sails on the deck looked after her as she passed them. Everything about her looked gray. There was something transparent about the woman they could all see was beautiful. Her inner pain became a sheet of ice around her. The sailors hoped she would find her family soon. That woman needed some reassuring hugs from people she loved.

Yes, she thought having heard their thoughts. *But can I tell them what I'm carrying?*

CHAPTER 16

THE MOUTH OF THE ROSE

THE SHIP ARRIVED AT OPPIDUM PRISCUM RA, and Mariam was put in a dinghy rowed by strong men heading towards the island. The priests at the temple welcomed her back. They had hoped to see her again. They had only met her husband once, but were sad to hear of his death. There were no questions about the contents of her bags.

She planned to stay overnight there and rest, before heading for the mainland the following day. Should she send a message to Sarah that she was coming? Were they still at the colony in Lydia's house? She felt sure she would be welcomed, whoever was there at the time, but she'd be disappointed herself if she didn't find Sarah and Tamera. And there could be any number of reasons for them to be traveling elsewhere.

The last boat had left for the mainland before she could make up her mind, so she would have to arrive unannounced. She asked the priests if they could arrange for transportation for her from the mainland port to Lydia's house, she knew they had reliable connections.

The journey from the temple of Venus in Razes had been through Aquitania. The Roman presence was lighter there. She hadn't needed to be too cautious. Now she was starting to see the togas and helmets, and the standards with the eagle on top. It was time to be more careful about how she presented herself. She had been married to a condemned man, and been one of the leaders of a group of rebels who caused no end of trouble in Judea. From the Roman perspective, she was a persona non grata in the entire Roman Empire. Mariam longed for the anonymity of her secluded herb farm. Could she carry all in silence until she got there without exploding into a scream?

The beds were comfortable, and she tried to sleep in the calming atmosphere of the temple. Her thoughts kept churning around the events of the last weeks. She knew she needed sleep, and hugged her child closer to join him in his sweet slumber. Her body was exhausted, and it finally succumbed to a form of sleep, filled with images she would rather forget.

She woke up with a start in the middle of the night. The room was bathed in a golden glow. Geiss continued to sleep with a content smile even though the room was filled with light. Mariam recognized the bright white light, and felt the warmth and love it sent her.

I can find you here, love, it said to her. *This temple is an easy place for me to find you. Please come here often.*

But Yeshua, you have to find me at Tuberose too. That's where I'll be most of the time.

Do the rituals, Mariam. Purify the place. I will always try to find you and the children, but I can't always reach you through the filters.

I will. Please stay with me. I'm frightened.

Come. The child will sleep, you can leave him behind.

Mariam secured him so he couldn't roll out of his blanket, and watched a small sphere of light hover above him. Geiss would be safe. Then she turned, to follow the light waiting for her at the door.

It turned down it's intensity outside her door, to not attract unneeded attention. She followed a ball of light through the corridors of the guestrooms and out to the courtyard. The new moon gave a faint light in the night, and her light guide became a small dot shooting across the stones, and disappearing down the stairs to the Celtic temple of the water goddess. She hurried across the stones of the courtyard to follow.

The stairs were again cold and damp, but she knew the beauty she would see in this underground chamber, and wanted to go down. The light sphere became bigger, and it lit up the torch in the wall at the bottom of the stairs.

The temple glowed in green, from the moon shining through the round green glass above. Again, she saw the light playing in the water, creating red and blue light shining through the gemstones embedded in the wall. She thought of the constellations at night, where some stars also displayed gemstone colors to complement the familiar pictures.

The water from the sea came flushing in through the channel created for it. She watched the green Mediterranean water play with all the lights beaming through it. Quietly she sat down on the bench at the back wall to watch. *Bridget,* she thought, *how beautiful you are.* She was so glad she had been to Hibernia and understood more of the culture this tradition came from. Green was the color of the heart and the color of everything growing from the earth.

The guiding light hovered over the water, admiring its beauty with her and flew like a streak of lightening through the water, making her laugh. *Yes, I know you like to play,* she thought. *You deserve it. Do play. I like to watch you. It's been a while since I've seen you.*

She heard him laugh at her, and saw the light sphere make one more swoop through the water, before flying over the stone wall separating the channel from the temple. The light sphere expanded in front of her, became elongated and took on form. As it approached her, she could make out the features of her husband and his feet walking towards her. His body was covered in white garments shining brighter than the sun.

He sat down next to her. Could she touch him? Was he solid? What would the light intensity do to her? He wanted to hug her too, but wasn't quite sure if that would be wise. They sat there looking at each other for a while admiring each others beauty, while knowing painfully that they were as different as air and stone. He could pass by her in a breath. She could only be found.

He looked happy, very happy, but in anguish over what he had sent her through. She sensed that he felt he had fulfilled his mission and was onto the next step. What did that entail? She felt the answer was beyond her comprehension, and however much she hungered to understand, she had to admit her limitation. But if her brain could not take in what he was experiencing, or the reasons why he had transformed into a new being, her whole body could feel his presence. She felt encircled with warm compassion and understanding for her own difficult situation. His love for her, felt burning hot on her skin, as he took in her physical pain. She felt him send a gentle wave to the light inside her, and she hoped the little one didn't get harmed by her grief.

Last time they were in this temple together, they had shared a tender beautiful time, in the green light of Bridget. She longed to merge with him again. He smiled at her, as he sensed her feelings and stretched out a hand. Carefully he pointed a finger at her forehead, and she watched, as golden light streamed out of him and joined with the natural light she had around herself. She saw herself grow a larger golden aura, and felt the unification with him stronger than she'd ever felt when their bodies were united in love and passion. This was a true merge, to the degree that their different bodies could come together. Mariam felt honey pouring into her body as a gift of nectar from the Gods. It held the sublime truth that love is the strongest force in the universe.

She sat there for a while, enjoying the sensation in her body, allowing it to soften the grief that had been filling her insides. The beauty of the moment gave her reassurance that all would eventually be well.

Yeshua turned back into a sphere of light and guided her back to her bed. She slept, feeling his presence like an extra blanket around her, as she clutched Geiss closer and thought of the three children she would have to rare without a father.

The following morning she felt better, and prepared to take the next boat into town. She packed together her things, and even though the previous night had been profound and beautiful, she couldn't handle her red tasseled bags without pain. The priests watched her have better color than the previous day, but still look forlorn between her things, as she waited for the boat to come in.

The short boat ride was refreshing, and again she let the salty wind brush through her hair, sweeping her heaviest thoughts away. Little Geiss was in a splendid mood, and pointed at all he could see and identify.

There was a wagon waiting for her, to take her to Lydia's house, and the driver helped her load up her bags. She had to count them to make sure she didn't forget anything, and tried to think of her things as extra jewelry, dresses, shoes, oils and perfumes. That was what she wanted the driver to believe, and she could never be too careful.

Lydia's home was stately situated in a garden with a short alley of trees they passed through to get to the entrance. Mariam saw people working in the fields and gardens, and knew the place had prospered since she was there last. Someone ran ahead and announced that she was there, and by the time she reached the front steps, Lydia was standing in the door way, together with Mary. Lydia had aged, but was happy and content with her created family. Mary was glad to have her sister-in-law back, but why was it only her? Mary was alarmed.

As Mariam climbed off the wagon and watched other good people be ready to carry her bags and pay the driver, she heard Sarah's voice screeching through the house as she was galloping to meet her, little Tamera in tow.

Mariam smiled bravely at the people on the steps, straightened her back, and walked up towards them. She couldn't hide her harrowed face, her heavy walk and the overall gray sadness around her. She was glad she had the child to present, to divert the attention from herself.

Lydia and Mary calmed their enthusiasm to match their guest. It was easy to see that Mariam brought sad news.

Sarah came running through the door, but stopped in her tracks like a halted horse.

"Mariam, what happened?" she asked as she saw her sisters stricken face.

Mariam had already greeted Lydia and Mary. Mary had turned and went crying into the house. Lydia was full of grief, but wanted to take care of her guest. Mariam let Sarah see her grief and simply said, "He's gone, Sarah, for good." Now she could hang onto her sister and let her own tears fall. She let Sarah hold Geiss while she bent down to her daughter.

Tamera recognized her mother, but the sadness so apparent in her face, scared her. She had barely met her father, so his death didn't have any impact on her. But her mother's grief shocked her, and she hung onto her aunt's skirt.

Sarah took Mariam to her own rooms and put her to bed, upon Lydia's insistence. She reappeared with tea and soup from the kitchen, finding Mariam surrounded with her children. Mariam looked up at her sister with tears of gratitude streaming down her cheeks. Her daughter couldn't have been better cared for. Tamera looked at her brother with curiosity, and Sarah marveled over the difference between the brother and sister. You could hardly believe they were from the same family. Tamera had olive skin and dark hair with lovely curls. Little Geiss was pale and pink, with a touch of strawberry in his golden hair, but his features were the spitting image of aunt Sarah.

"Tell me about it," said Sarah as she sat down on the bed. "I want to know."

Mariam started describing their journey. She mentioned the beauty of Hibernia, the land near Glastonbury, England, waiting for them to start a colony there. She described the lovely days she and Yeshua had shared and the simple church he had built together with his uncle. There was a lot to tell about Languedoc and Aquitania, before she had to get into the temple of Venus.

She chose her words carefully. Sarah was not temple trained, and wouldn't understand everything. She described the preparations for the annual journey of Osiris done by the temple, and that this time, Yeshua had asked to be the one traveling.

"He never came back to his body, Sarah. I believe he exists as an entity of light somewhere. We buried his body in a cave in the mountain."

"Oh, Mariam," said Sarah. Gently she took her sisters hand, knowing that there was no way she could reach the depth of her grief. Silent tears kept running down their cheeks as they watched the children get to know one another.

CHAPTER 17

AQUA SEXTIAE

MARIAM STAYED IN LYDIA'S HOUSE FOR SEVERAL days. The women took turns staying with her, and Lydia made personally sure that she got the most nourishing food. Jacob was traveling with Lazarus, and hadn't returned yet.

Mariam stayed in the bed next to Sarah's. She slept most of the time, when she wasn't offered a warm bowl of food that smelled heavenly. Sarah took care of both the children, and since his mother was out of reach most of the time, little Geiss was weaned and accepted hearty goat milk instead.

Lydia sent a message to Martha in Aqua Sextiae and asked her to come. Two days later Martha was on their doorstep, having left immediately.

The three sisters fell upon each other and blessed Lydia for her thoughtfulness. Martha joined them in their grief, but also in practical matters. After a couple of days of caring for Mariam and her children, she felt she had to ask.

"Mariam, dear sister, are you expecting again? I see the signs. How are you feeling?"

Mariam had tried to forget about the third life she was carrying. But she hadn't eaten as much as they expected, and requested warm herb teas in the morning that would settle her stomach. Also, in addition to her grief, her body seemed to delegate her life force elsewhere. Martha had seen it all before.

Mariam had to admit that she felt miserable. She should be glad for the next child, but she felt only confusion, and although she was grateful for all the help she was receiving, she longed for the solitude at the herb farm. Martha understood.

When Jacob and Lazarus returned, the next step was already decided. The men joined in their grief, but were given practical things to consider.

"Mariam, I know you would love to have Tamera with you, now that you're finally back. But maybe you should consider giving yourself some months to recover. Your daughter is happy here with Sarah. Let her stay for a little longer, then Sarah can bring her to the herb farm in a little while."

The mother part of her was screaming, but another side of her sighed in relief. She knew that, in her condition, she would not be a good mother for the child. Sarah was glad to not be separated from Tamera, which had been her worry, and promised to bring the girl, when Mariam was ready.

Mariam left the house of Lydia with Lazarus and Martha the following day. A sturdy wagon was going to take them to the inn where they usually stayed in Glanum before heading south again to Aqua Sextiae. The thought of visiting Herodias in Arelate ran through Mariam's mind, but she felt taken well care of, and didn't want to bother her friend. The effort of traveling a little extra out of their way was too much for her right then. When she checked inside, something told her that Herodias was in Rome.

Mariam made herself comfortable in the wagon, and created a little nest for Geiss to sleep in. Lazarus and Martha sat in quiet conversation in the front, while Mariam let the soothing landscape calm her nerves.

The stay at the inn was pleasant and the food was wholesome. The next morning they continued along the sturdy Roman road. The pleasant weather and the sweet scents from the plants along the road did their best to lighten people's moods. Martha noticed that a smile started to appear on her sister's face, and the sunshine gave her back her golden color. The grief wasn't far behind, she knew that, but at least the fresh air gave some respite.

They tried to arrive quietly, but there were always people in their home. The extended colony had grown around them, and everyone was considered family. All Mariam wanted was to be alone. Martha guided her into a guestroom she had given instructions to be prepared, put Mariam to bed with another cup of tea, and promised to return with a bowl of stew shortly. She had to talk to her people.

Lazarus had called them all into the hall they used for inspirational meetings, and announced he had something to share with them all.

He looked over his people. They were all dedicated to the teachings of Yeshua. They wanted to perpetuate what he had taught them. Among them were different understandings of what happened on a hollow hill in Jerusalem, but they all were hoping that their teacher would come and visit them soon. Lazarus had to tell them that their teacher was buried somewhere in the Languedoc.

He started by telling them another story from his life. Lazarus shared the story about the never-ending fish and bread feeding people on a mountain top in Galilee. Then he reminded them of the last meal Yeshua shared with his followers before he was crucified, and invited people to share the bread and wine with him, the way their master had done that night.

As he broke the bread and passed the wine around, he told them that this was the closest they would experience Yeshua's presence. He had left the earth to join his Father in Heaven. People had seen him leave in a bright light.

He blessed the food they received, blessed their presence, and several people thought that Lazarus shone with a special light that evening. Martha admired his beautiful way of gently sharing the news about their teacher's departure.

431

Mariam heard about her brother's speech later and thought he had made it a little too mythological, but then again, how do you explain what happened? She couldn't explain it completely to herself, and she was considered an adept. She was grateful Lazarus had found a way to speak to their people in a way they could accept.

Exhausted, she lay in her bed, thinking of fields of lavender. She remembered the fresh air of Mount Aurelia, Sibyl's quiet practical approach to everything, Joses' appreciation for the nature around them and Johanna's nurturing care. Trym, how was he doing, among gardening tools, rows of plants and his love for Sibyl? Absentmindedly, she patted her son on his head, and looked out the window and felt the busy life of the colony and the city.

Martha came into the room the following day and said she would send her to Tuberose as soon as possible. Trym was going to be in town for the market on his weekly errands, and she could leave with him.

Mariam looked at her sister. She had vacant eyes and mumbled that it sounded like a good idea. Martha was even more concerned. She left her sisters room, taking Geiss with her to find some food in the kitchen. The little boy liked his friendly aunt, who always seemed to know what he needed. Martha had borrowed clothes and wrappings for him from other parents in the colony. She had looked over the few things Mariam brought with for him, and been appalled at their condition. How long had she been traveling like that? The child seemed healthy though, and he showed a lively mind interested in his new surroundings. He was almost walking, and would soon require a lot more attention. Lazarus had also taken to the boy, who looked so much like himself.

Martha started to come to some conclusions, and knew she had to talk to her sister soon.

"Mariam, how are you feeling?" Mariam had been staring out of the window for hours, and hardly even noticed that the child had left with Martha. She looked like she had retreated deep into her body, and only allowed the smallest amount of herself to interact with the outside world. Martha made up her mind right then, and knew she had to broach this issue with her brother, before bringing it to her sister ever so gently.

Lazarus was concerned, but also delighted at Martha's suggestion. "For how long do you think?" he asked hopefully. "At least until her next baby is born," Martha answered.

Trym got the short version when he stopped by, which he usually did once a week when he was in town. He was happy to take Mariam with him back. "Make her walk outside a lot," advised Martha, and Trym agreed, that would help her heal.

Mariam was packed up with all her bags, except for the ones belonging to the child. Sitting next to Trym, with empty hands and new tears, she waved goodbye to her sister, who was holding baby Geiss. The strong arm of Lazarus held around Martha's shoulders, protecting his nephew.

CHAPTER 18

TUBEROSE HERB FARM

MARIAM BREATHED. SHE BREATHED IN LONG, NOURISHING breaths as she sat on the wagon next to Trym, while the lovely landscape unfolded around her. They had left the city. They were still on Via Domitia, but would soon turn right on Via Aurelia.

Trym was a man of few words and hadn't said much on their entire trip. They stopped and ate the food Martha sent with them, and sat next to each other in silence, each with their own thoughts. His silence suited Mariam well. She had enough on her mind that was difficult to share with anyone.

Leaving Geiss with Martha and Lazarus? What kind of mother was she? She was returning to her herb farm without her children, and with three bags she couldn't let anybody unpack. If she was unfit as a mother, how come she was now bringing a third one into the world? Mariam allowed the scent of the thyme and myrtle next to her, to keep her sane.

Sibyl was expecting Trym back from his weekly trip to the market. She did not expect him to bring anyone with him. Having observed the wagon make it all the way up from Villa Lata, she had hoped, but couldn't be certain. Seeing Mariam sitting next to him, made her heart leap. She called for the others to come to welcome her, as the wagon made it up the last feet of the path. Their joy turned to concern, as they saw the condition of the woman returning to them.

Mariam needed help to get off the wagon. Johanna and Sibyl supported her as they walked her in, and sat her down in the kitchen. Trym whispered that her husband had died and her children were left with her sisters. They all wanted more information, and as they put a cup of tea in her hand, they all stood around, waiting to hear her speak. Joses came in the door, having seen them all gather from a field farther away. He looked at everyone, and understood quickly this was not the time to ask questions.

Mariam held her warm cup of tea and looked around at all the loving faces showing their deep felt concern for her, while also showing they were glad to see her back among them. Mariam cried again. Finally she felt at home. She wanted to hug them all at the same time, before she could say anything.

Sibyl sat down next to her and took her hand. Johanna stood on the other side with a hand on her shoulder. Joses sat down on the floor next to her, leaning against her knee. Trym wasn't quite sure what to do, but wiped his nose with the back of his hand making a loud sniffle. It was so good to have her back. They would learn the stories soon enough. Through tears and smiles, Mariam told them as much as she could. They knew more would come later.

Johanna had a pot of soup cooking. They all gathered around the kitchen table. The kitchen floor had been tiled while she was gone, and she admired the good work. The smiles were sweet and tender, expressing the relief of having her back, and their deep sympathy with her sorrow. The news of the child that would be born among them was met with delighted anticipation. After they had eaten, Sibyl asked if she wanted to go for a little walk. Johanna wanted to get a bed ready for her. Joses took to the hills on his own, and Trym had to take care of things from his wagon.

They walked silently and slowly among flowerbeds and herb gardens. Sibyl told her of the improvements they had made, the new plants they had acquired, and the ones they had thought would thrive on the mountain side. She mentioned that they had extra help. A whole new field was planned, next to other established plants. Sibyl went on about things that felt safe to talk about. Finally, she sat Mariam down on a stone bench, where she had a view of the whole farm and the valley in front of them.

"I've been to the grotto," she said. "Joses and I have tried to keep up with the solstices and equinoxes. We might not have gotten every date right, but at least the rituals were done there." Mariam was grateful they had continued to season the cave. Later she would have to visit it herself.

She leaned back and looked out over the horizon. The gentle rolling hills, the greens that ran into eachother across fields and meadows and her devoted friend next to her; Mariam took it all in and breathed. She was finally home.

As the sun was setting, they walked slowly back to the stone buildings which now were bathed in the orange light of the sunset.

"There is a new house there," said Mariam surprised.

"Yes, Joses completed the home intended for you and Yeshua, and your children."

Mariam turned towards her life long friend. Her face contorted in pain, as Sibyl's words made it clear for her what would never be. Her pent up grief found expression in a piercing shriek as her body twisted and she fell to her knees on the ground. She dissolved into uncontrolled loud sobbing, as Sibyl sat down and held around her shaking shoulders, crying with her.

Johanna came running and fell down crying with them. She had her own grief over her brother. Trym came and stood silently wiping his nose on his sleeve, until

Joses came down from the hills. With wet cheeks, Joses lifted her gently up, and carried her inside. A bed had been made ready in Johanna and Sibyl's room. Mariam curled up with her face to the wall, and continued sobbing and shaking for hours, while Sibyl stayed at her side.

How can you console a woman who has lost her husband and left her children behind? How can she tell anyone, that in her bags she has the severed heads of her husband and his cousin? They should have been stored honorably in ossuaries in the foundations of the temple of Jerusalem together with their ancestors, but instead, they had been dragged endlessly around, in hiding. How could she ever put her mind at rest, when the responsibility of the perpetuation of the wisdom of the tribes rested on her shoulders?

Some days later a gilded carriage found its way to Villa Lata, and a lone horse with golden tassels followed the path to Tuberose Herb Farm. The Roman woman was crying all the way up, and arrived in Johanna's kitchen with her silk dress soiled.

"Where is she?" was all she said, wiping her face, and Johanna led her into the bedroom.

Mariam was still in bed. She was now a round ball in a disarray of blankets. Two wild eyes looked up when Herodias addressed her. Nothing was said. Herodias sat down on the bed and took Mariam in her arms. She sat there and rocked her softly, sobbing with her for a long time.

Herodias stayed for weeks. She never left Mariam's side. The others went on with their daily tasks and left the two priestesses to themselves. They accepted the need for privacy among the temple trained, and hoped by all the Gods that Herodias could bring some health back to their dear herb farm founder.

Sibyl suggested the best she knew of healing herbs. Johanna made the most nutritious meals. Joses looked over the house he had intended for his now deceased brother, cleaned it one more time, and hoped his sister-in-law would be well enough to move in there some day. It was meant for her, and he started making another bed for the room. Maybe the children would come back, and there would be little feet running about, blessing their fields. Trym wiped his nose with a loud snort, and kept chopping wood, trimming plants, digging roots, and admiring Sibyl in the distance.

Herodias managed to get Mariam out of bed and on her feet. She looked thin and bony, and Herodias insisted that she would sit at the table and eat food in the kitchen. Soon she started taking her for short walks. Eventually they went inside the new home, all made ready for her by Johanna and Sibyl. It was now a cozy place, with the window valances she had received for her wedding. Even the fine alpaca wool blanket had found its way to the herb farm. Martha had found it among the things they packed up from the colony, and had sent it to them. It looked inviting on the bed in the one room cottage. With the help of Johanna, Herodias made the place ready for two, and took Mariam out of the crowded room where Sibyl and Johanna slept. The two priestesses stayed together in the new stone cottage, and after a while Mariam started to understand that this would be her new home.

Herodias had no intention of taking Mariam with her to her mansion in Arelate. Luxury had never impressed Mariam, and the fresh air of the mountains was best for her. She wanted to make sure Mariam was settled into her new home, with the privacy fit for a priestess. She knew Mariam would need that, just as much as she needed the companionship of the others. The new cottage was a perfect solution for her. All she needed was some help to get herself organized.

Mariam started smiling again. Her pregnancy started to show, and they heard her speak to the unborn child as she walked among her favorite plants. Herodias and Johanna agreed that was a good sign. Letters were written to Martha and Sarah, describing their sister's recovery. Everyone breathed easier.

Herodias looked over the cabin, talked to Johanna and Sibyl about further care of Mariam, and felt that it was time to leave the mountain farm. Truth to be told, she missed her mansion, even though the simple life on Tuberose had been good for her, as well. Still, there was one thing she needed to do before she left.

"Mariam, I think we should go to the cave. I haven't seen it since I came here, and I believe we need to do a ritual of purification for you after your travels in your dark valley. It is time to honor the seasons."

"It isn't winter solstice yet, is it?"

"We're not that far along, but we're getting close. I have to be back in Arelate by then. Salome is coming to visit with her husband and daughter. I think we need to bless your child before I leave."

"Oh, he's so protected, but he misses his brother and sister. He has such a sweet personality, Herodias. I think I'll name him Joseph, after his grandfather."

Herodias thought that sounded like a good name for the child, and hoped that Sarah and Martha would arrive soon. They had sent letters asking them to come. It was time to reunite the children with their mother.

Herodias knew they needed to go to the cave. The bags that had come with Mariam from her trip had not been opened. She knew she was the only one who would be able to handle that situation. Herodias felt that if they didn't open them together, Mariam would never do it on her own. She had to come to terms with her husband's fate at some point.

With the help of Joses, they loaded up one of the horses with the two bags with red tassels, food for the day, blankets and pillows, and some other small things Herodias thought might be helpful. Joses insisted on accompanying them on the way.

Mariam was so glad to be walking the hills again. The walk to the cave was a good distance, and she relished being out in fresh air and free to admire the landscape. She was in the middle trimester of her pregnancy, where her body felt wonderful and strong, and she just knew she had a beautiful secret inside. She skipped down the path, like a happy child, bringing smiles to everybody's faces.

Joses saw this opportunity to talk to Herodias alone. There was something he needed to ask her.

"I wanted to thank you for coming and staying with us for this long. You brought her back to life. We are all grateful to you."

"I heard her anguish all the way to Rome. It wouldn't let me sleep. I had to come, to get some peace myself," said Herodias minimizing her own role in Mariam's recovery.

"Well, thank you. I hope you've been relatively comfortable. I know we live a simpler life up here, but what we lack in luxury, we have in abundance of vistas," he said, pointing out the valley and mountains he had grown to love.

"It is really beautiful," said Herodias thoughtfully. "It restores your soul".

"I've wanted to ask you, I don't think I can bring myself to ask Mariam, it would be too emotional. It's emotional for me as well."

There was a silence between them, while Joses tried to find the right words. Herodias felt what was bothering him, but wanted him to formulate it himself.

"When my brother died, what happened? What really happened? The information I've gathered is too vague for me."

"Joses, you're wise beyond your years. You have the gentle wisdom of your mother, and the sweet humor and dignity of your father. And you're brave. You came to the cave when we were in the middle of a ritual, because Yochanan called for you. We needed your help at that time, and you stepped right in, without any preparation for what you were taking part in. I hope it didn't frighten you."

"It did. But curiosity kept me there, and Yochanan gave me strict orders to stay and observe, and not let whatever I saw affect me."

"You know your brother had been refining his body for years. You saw what he was capable of."

"Yes, the miracles are already legendary."

"Those are the outward signs. To be able to do those, he worked on refining his body from the inside. Yeshua had eaten the blessed bread and drank of Yochanan's holy water for years. He also knew how to never keep any negativity in his body. Constantly monitoring his own balance, he made sure his system functioned at optional efficiency. Yeshua was a super conductor of the energies between the Gods and mankind.

"Joses, all the things your brother did, which seemed so miraculous, happened because he knew how to work with the physical laws of the world of spirit. It seemed like magicians work, but was in reality advanced techniques he had learned during his years of study. Yeshua was always ready to learn something new, and never afraid of experimenting on himself to understand the effects."

"Did he die because something went wrong? I know Mariam administrated initiations for Lazarus and Yochanan. I understand that what happened at Golgotha had some elements of that. She seemed so confident in all this. Did she make a mistake?"

Joses said this without blame, but with a need to know the truth.

"I don't think so. What I've understood is that this was the journey of Osiris, which apparently the temple of Venus in Razes does every year with a chosen adept at the summer solstice. Your brother left his body, following the normal steps they were all familiar with, went through the porthole and joined with the Gods. Upon his expected return, the body came back to life, but his spirit couldn't come back into it."

"I didn't know a body could live without a spirit."

"A body can have life force, making it breathe and pump blood, but if the spirit doesn't come back, it's like an empty house where the fires are still going."

"Couldn't they have called him back?"

"They did. And he was right there. He chose to not inhabit his body again. Joses, he had transformed into pure light. His body couldn't hold that intensity. Your brother is onto other assignments from the Gods. He fulfilled his mission here admirably. Now he can continue his work on bringing light into the world."

"...which was all he ever wanted to do, anyway."

"Yes, that's true, but there are many ways to interpret that assignment. You can educate people and bring light to their minds. You can enlighten them from within with holy bread, and make them physically able to hold more light. You can send more light into their bodies to cure an illness, dispersing the darkness. Yeshua was an expert in all of this. He was an adept. I admired the man tremendously. Now he can work behind the scenes in a very powerful way."

"But you said his body was still alive. What happened to it after he left them? Did Mariam...?" Joses couldn't finish the sentence.

Herodias knew what he meant.

"Joses, this is priestess work. I can't expect you to understand."

"I want to know. He was my brother. I recognize the bag on the horse. It holds Yochanan...in his present form. There is a similar bag which came back with Mariam, which is now on the horse as well. Does that one contain...?"

"If you can bear to hear the truth, Joses, I'll tell you. You know more than you should. I know this can frighten people. The Roman's kill the people with this knowledge, it scares them too much. I have to protect what I know. The content of those two bags is irreplaceable in history. They contain wisdom accessible for people who know how, and understand how to use it wisely and for good purposes. It can be used for evil, with disastrous results. Antipas tried. It built power for a while, until the wisdom itself took revenge on him."

Herodias couldn't hide a satisfied grin, and Joses had to smile with her. Sometimes revenge is indeed sweet.

"I heard that story. You were heroic. Why did you risk yourself for my family?"

"I didn't necessarily do it for your family. I did it to stop Antipas in his hunger for power, and to preserve the knowledge I'm privileged to be part of. There aren't that many of us left. The Romans are changing the temples. The priestesses are turning into nymphs in light clothing. Very few own the deepest secrets anymore, and even fewer volunteer to live the lifestyle that is required to be able to hold the wisdom. Yochanan will be able to share his knowledge for as long as someone knows how to wake him up. There is a reason for creating oracles."

"So my brother has joined Yochanan, in his form?" Joses changed color at the thought.

"Can you carry that truth, young Joses? Can you hold onto that it was the right thing for Mariam to do? Can you hear that your brother requested that treatment, to join his ancestors? Do you understand the powerful traditions you're part of? And do you understand that your people have been displaced many times from your land of origin, and had to preserve this knowledge, through even harsher times than what you or I have experienced? "

"I do understand, Herodias. I do."

"If you can stand by all that, then you're the one who'll protect this knowledge further. You're the one who'll have to preserve and protect the contents of those two bags for the next generations to come.

"You have a niece and a nephew, and a new one soon to be born. These children carry two powerful lines of heritage. They need to be taught the traditions they come from, or they'll never understand the powers that are latent in their bodies. In fact, if they're not taught about it, that same power can do harm, if not handled correctly. There is a fourth child that needs protection, and that's Yochanan's son Yahya."

"He's a bright young boy. He's being educated by Lazarus and Bartholomew, as far as I know."

"That's all well and good. But sooner or later he'll need to know the truth about his father. He still only has his mother's interpretation of the story, and holds a hatred for Mariam she doesn't deserve. When he comes of age, that story needs to be set straight."

"How come you know so much about us? We're not related, as far as I know."

"Mariam and I were partners in Ephesus. We learned to tune with each other, to the point where we could share images and emotions. I can pick up her thoughts over a long distance. She can pick up mine too, but I'm better at shielding mine if I want to. We share a bond deeper than sisters. So, you're all my family. And if you didn't already know it, you're a fascinating bunch," Herodias said with a flashing smile.

Joses smiled shyly back. He had to agree. They were an interesting family.

CHAPTER 19

RETURN TO THE GROTTO

They continued walking in silence. Joses had a new set of thoughts to consider. Herodias knew she had given him a whole collection of new responsibilities. She was glad he had started the conversation. He had practically volunteered to take on the protection of his family tree, backwards and forwards. Herodias could only marvel at the bravery of this young man. He was the youngest in the family, and had taken on so much. She admired the parents of these strong children. She had only had the pleasure of meeting them once, in Jerusalem, and that was not a time for socializing.

Mariam returned to them, after behaving like a butterfly for a while. Joses had admired her beauty, and after having observed her profound depression, it was a delight to watch her dancing in the hills.

"Is it always this lovely, Joses? You walk the hills at any time of the year."

"It changes with the seasons, but it just shows a different beauty," he answered poetically. He had just been floating in history himself, and felt loosened from time for a moment.

Mariam laughed, swung her skirt around, and continued dancing down the path. Herodias thought of the serious discussion she had just had with Mariam's brother-in-law, and wondered if a ritual in the grotto would be too much for her friend. *Maybe I have misjudged the situation,* she thought. Should she have let Mariam be a nymph a little longer? Herodias had to remind herself that it wasn't like Mariam to be a butterfly. However much it was wonderful to see her come out of her grief, it wasn't good for her to float about like that. The knowledge of a priestess, be it ever so esoteric, was rooted in practicalities. She knew she had to bring Mariam's feet back to earth, but not yet.

They had entered the forest at the foot of the mountain. The path had grown in a little, due to lack of use. Herodias understood that Sibyl and Joses had been here, but not frequently enough to prevent the trees from spreading.

Mariam calmed a little in the cool air of the trees. She was looking for the path that went up the mountainside, the thin line in the rocks along the steep mountain wall.

She found it and called triumphantly to the others. Joses talked to the horse, to prepare it for the ascent. The horse had done it before, but still looked apprehensive about the conditions. Joses calmed the mare, and gave her confidence.

They started on the path. Herodias knew that Mariam would have to watch her feet here, otherwise she would fall. There could be no dancing on the mountain path. Mariam watched the horse, and understood that she had to be careful. Still, she went ahead of them all with the enthusiasm of a child.

After following the switchbacks up the hill, they saw the opening of the cave, a dark mouth in the side of the mountain. Joses hoped no animal had moved in. It would have been a great place to raise their young born in the winter months.

Mariam became more thoughtful as they came closer to the entrance. She remembered powerful meetings at this place, surprising meetings with unexpected outcomes

She turned, and saw Herodias arrive, and Joses lead the tentative horse up the last steps. The red tasseled bags were showing against the blue sky, hanging on the side of the horse.

Mariam cocked her head a bit, but showed no comprehension. Herodias wondered if Mariam truly had lost her mind during her months wandering in the dark dungeons of her grief. She had to do this, even though it pained her to have to brutally bring Mariam back to the reality of her situation. Herodias was truly grateful that Joses showed so much understanding. *What a remarkable young man,* she thought with profound admiration.

Herodias decided to go about setting up for the ritual and just let Mariam join her as she naturally felt inclined to do so. She went inside the cave to look at its condition, and found that it was reasonably clean, relatively dry and had some supplies waiting for use on the natural shelves in its walls. She motioned to Joses to unload the horse.

The thick blanket with the rough camel hair was placed on the floor, and a finer wool blanket was placed on top. Herodias unpacked the brazier and started the fire in it. The bags were placed on the floor, and Joses tethered the horse to a tree where she could feed on thick mountain grass.

Joses returned and stood at the entrance, waiting for further instructions. Herodias asked him to fill a container with water, and watched him walk to the back of the cave to find water in the basin. When he returned, he saw that the ritual space was being prepared like last time, a star was drawn and fragrant incense was burning. He gave Herodias the water container, which was placed opposite the fire.

Mariam was opening one of the bags, humming to herself. Herodias motioned to Joses to sit down and just watch. They observed, as the head of Yochanan emerged and she said some welcoming words to it, before placing it in one of the points of the star. Herodias gave her the other bag. She knew the final ritual at the temple of Venus had happened quickly, having seen it through Mariam's eyes from her ritual space in Rome. Herodias had indeed been there, assisting Albion and Mariam herself.

During the ritual at the Temple of Venus, Mariam had managed to put her emotions aside. She engaged her mind in the technical aspect of the work and was proud of her surgical skills. Self control was an early prerequisite for Temple work.

Here in the grotto, she wasn't hiding her emotions as a conscious choice. She didn't seem to have any feelings at all and was humming absentmindedly to herself, not totally aware of what she was doing. Herodias was becoming increasingly alarmed and kept herself ready to handle any situation that might develop. Joses watched the unfolding of a round object in Mariam's hands, and could only guess what it would look like. He hadn't learned any technique to control his feelings, but he certainly showed that he came from a capable family. The only thing giving him away was his rising eyebrows as his eyes got bigger.

Mariam was unrolling the linen covering Yeshua's head. Her mind was in denial and told her that she was unwrapping Yochanan for the second time. As the hair started to emerge in her hand, she saw that it was much lighter than her dear familiar friend. It had a golden streak to it, and had waves. The neck had been stitched differently. She recognized it as her own work, but couldn't remember when she had done it. Her face had changed now. Through the cloth, she recognized the beautiful profile of the man she loved. Mariam had stopped breathing. She didn't feel pain. She felt as if her life had stopped.

Herodias couldn't ease this in any way. She was the one in pain at this point. An angry prayer went up to the Gods. *Was all this necessary?*

Mariam studied the napkin covering his face. There had been a beautifully embroidered piece of cloth wrapping the container of myrrh. She remembered being glad the Persian astrologers had included it. It gave her a dignified piece to use.

All three them of them were holding their breath, as Mariam lifted the cloth. A golden glow came from his beautiful countenance. Mariam held his head in her two hands in front of her and silently admired her husband's beauty.

Joses recognized his beloved brother, and thought he looked remarkably good for the age he must have been at the time. *In his prime, with a beautiful wife and a third child on the way, why did he choose to leave?* he thought. Joses felt a pang of anger towards Yeshua. *What was the reason for his choice?*

Herodias had worked with him at the Hieros Gamos ritual in the vaults of Salomon, and met him briefly at the initiation of Lazarus. She remembered him as remarkably calm in the midst of the chaos of followers and endless requests for help from people. He had addressed everybody with the same serene attention. They were all important to him, even late at night when he'd been doing it all day. She saw the same peace on his face now.

Yeshua's tranquil appearance calmed the others. There was a sweet glow from him, as Mariam held him tenderly. The light spread around him, like a soothing breath. Mariam inhaled, and allowed the weight of her body to sink into the thick blankets she was sitting on until she could feel the stone floor underneath her. She smiled at him, breathed normally, and looked up at the others.

"Isn't he beautiful?" she said, presenting him like a proud mother. Herodias turned pale. This was not what she expected. Hysteria, fury, accusations, anything like that, she'd been prepared for. She wasn't sure if Mariam had totally lost her grip on reality, or created a new world for herself, where his head had become her child.

Joses got up and joined Mariam in her admiration. He agreed with her. His brother had indeed been a handsome man. He sat next to her studying the head for a while, making comments about how well it was preserved, the lovely scent of myrrh, how honorable of him to volunteer to become an oracle.

"I think he should be placed here, opposite of Yochanan. Do we have a stand for him?" he asked in a light tone. Joses, in his young wisdom, had met Mariam where she was in her process and brought her back with him.

Herodias, astonished, found a dish from Johanna's kitchen, and Yeshua's head was placed in another point of the star of Venus.

The three people found their positions in the remaining three points of the star, and Herodias sang the first tones. Mariam fell naturally in, and Joses found his deeper bass notes. The brazier made the incense fill the space with Sibyl's best fragrances. The water showed a little ripple in its container in response as they established a new vibration in the cave. It reverberated out in larger circles to include the entire mount of Aurelia.

Herodias led the singing for a while. When she felt she had the other two in full support, she introduced the incantations to wake up the oracles.

Yochanan opened his eyes and greeted them, as his name was called. He joined them with his deep bass tone. Looking across the space, he stared at his cousin and best friend. Herodias intoned the notes again, and asked Yeshua to join them. Mariam looked at her husband and sang the tones together with Herodias and Joses, with calm and dignity.

He opened his eyes, greeted them formally and cleared his throat before singing the notes with them. After all, he knew them from before. He had sung them as one of the celebrants in the foundations of the temple of Salomon. At that time they had woken up heads that were hundreds of years old, remarkable people from different parts of history, all his ancestors of old that had been preserved in this way. He was in a whole body ready to join in Hieros Gamos with his wife. Yochanan had been the most recent member of the oracles. Now he was one of them himself.

Herodias couldn't sense what he felt. *Should they have been left with their historic ancestors in ossuaries in the foundations of the temple? Should these two have been given a dignified storage space in a place honored through time and built by the most revered of Kings? What were they doing here in a cave in another country?*

Mariam gave the answer. She showed them the future of Jerusalem. A new riot would arise against the Romans, and their people would be crushed with the hard hand of Rome. Herodias received images of fire and blood, falling buildings, and people screaming through the streets. She saw the destruction of the temple. The insides were burning while soldiers with tools were cutting lose the gold ornamentation and carved stone epitaphs. That's why they couldn't have been left in the Temple. Jerusalem as they knew it would soon seize to exist.

What would happen to the ossuaries of your ancestors? What about the Ark of the Covenant? Herodias was sick with concern.

Mariam closed her eyes and tuned into the future. She saw the thick slabs forming the top of the foundation staying intact during the destruction. It was made of three layers of stone, held together with gold technology. It would stay. The entrances were covered in debris and became inaccessible. Their people scattered, and showed up in other countries. The vaults of Salomon would be forgotten, well protected under stone and sand.

Mariam saw another building being built on the temple mount in a different architectural style. People dressed differently would go and worship there. She saw other battles over the land, more bloodshed and more destruction. New people arrived from places across the ocean and further north. They had talked to people of the tribes with memories from their ancestors of the old city of Jerusalem. It was whispered to strong men, clothed in metal and riding big horses. They were told that if they dug underneath the foundations of the old temple, they would find mysterious, wondrous things.

Mariam saw them spend years digging through debris, digging through dirt and sand and history. They were digging through skulls and dried blood, until they found a staircase that could be cleared. The men clothed in metal carried out large objects draped in cloth. Secretly, they were loaded on camels, then on ships which sailed on blue waters. She saw the men return to their country in triumph, carrying the large menorah of the temple of Jerusalem between cheering people through the streets of a city that didn't exist yet. She also saw that the ossuaries and other things were being taken secretly to big forts and castles in the countryside, where men of their own tribes were anticipating the return of their ancestral secrets.

Who were they? Herodias wondered. *When would they live? What country did they bring these treasures to?*

Mariam knew. She recognized the scenery. They were riding through the landscape of Languedoc. But trees were trees. She couldn't tell if it was ten years into the future, or a hundred. It might even be several hundred years before that rescue mission would be accomplished.

We'll be there. We'll meet them, thought Mariam. *Whenever this will happen, our future generations will be present. Other priestesses will be trained, under different names and different traditions, but the mother will be honored. Like a lantern in the dark, light will reappear in the bodies of people with the golden blood. The ancient knowledge will again be ignited.*

Herodias shook the imagery out of her head. The vision had only taken moments. It was time to get back to their ritual and their own time.

So it will return after all is lost, Joses thought. *The old wisdom carries its own protection. Who were the men in metal clothing?* he wondered. *That seemed extraordinarily cumbersome.*

Herodias had held her tone throughout the vision, together with Yochanan and Yeshua. She realized that they had helped create the vision they'd shared. Their traditional world was falling apart, disintegrating in the countries they all had left. If they were the last adepts, they were also the teachers of the new.

Herodias bowed her head in acknowledgement, and counted herself as one of the last priestesses of the old tradition. Mariam bowed her head to the power of this body of knowledge, and saw herself as the mother of the children who would carry light in their blood. Joses bowed his head with them and understood that he was the protector of a new generation and the knowledge in their bodies.

Yeshua and Yochanan knew they had done their job, and closed their eyes.

CHAPTER 20

REUNION

They returned from the grotto, each absorbed in their own thoughts. The horse trudged ahead of the women, led by Joses, loaded with their most precious possessions.

They all knew their responsibilities from this point forward. Even if their purpose seemed beyond human proportions, there was always another practical task right in front of them pulling them out of cosmic flights, to where their feet were touching the ground.

As they approached the farm buildings, they noticed that new people had arrived. There seemed to be several guests at the farm, and some in smaller sizes. Mariam started to run.

They were all there. Sarah had arrived with Tamera. Martha was there with Geiss, who was walking now. Lazarus was there, together with two people they hadn't seen for a very long time. The disciple John had traveled all the way from Ephesus together with Mary, her mother-in-law, the mother of so many of Mariam's best supporters, and the grandmother of her children.

Herodias stood back a little, giving the family reunion in front of her some space. Her parents had died many years ago, shortly after she'd been reluctantly given in marriage to Philip. They saw Salome as a newborn. They never knew that their marriage grew into a caring union which she remembered with fondness. His untimely death, and her subsequent marriage to Antipas, had been a sparring match of strong wills, a silent war between two powerful individuals. She won in the end, she knew that. But even though revenge is sweet, it doesn't bring love and companionship. She looked at these people, who across family ties and devotion had developed a network of support for each other. A network that had survived harrowing escapes across long distances. They always managed to find each other. Herodias thought of her estranged daughter and young Agrippa who was becoming a powerful Roman politician. *Were they really her family?*

Before she could think any further, she was surrounded with strong arms, hugging her tight, shaking her hand, expressing their thanks that she had come and

446

brought Mariam back to life. Herodias let herself be hugged and shaken, and tried to stay open for the appreciation that was pouring towards her. She had to let down her substantial levels of guarding mechanisms to take in these people who functioned with very few. They all could communicate silently with each other, which left little room for mind games. Herodias had lived most of her life in situations where your dexterity with manipulating others determined your survival, and she'd become an expert at it. It was unusual to be in a place where that skill was not needed.

Mariam was sitting on a bench next to her mother-in-law surrounded by her children. Tamera had grown to a tall beautiful girl with deep brown thoughtful eyes. She held her mothers hands tentatively, wanting to get to know her again after their long separation. Little Geiss had his grandfather's delightful optimistic smile. He was so proud of the words he could say, and sat on his grandmother's lap laughing with her. Tamera patted her mother's belly and was told she would soon be a big sister one more time.

The others stood and watched them for a while until Johanna called for kitchen help, and Martha and Sarah went with her. Joses wanted to show Lazarus and John the farm and asked Trym to come with them. Sibyl went to make bedding places for the night for everybody. Herodias was grateful for all the practical concerns, and joined with Sibyl offering to help. The new cottage needed to accommodate Mary and the children, in addition to Mariam and herself.

Mary and Mariam sat with a child each on their laps. The grandmother had never seen her grandchildren, and marveled over the new generation growing up right in front of her. Her blessings went out to the new child, only a couple of months away from arriving.

She had received news from Mary and Jacob. Her daughter had been writing her at Ephesus and had told her of the children and of Yeshua's departure. She understood it wasn't an ordinary death, nothing about her son was ordinary, but she was patiently waiting for Mariam to explain, and knew this would take time.

"He transformed into light," said Mariam. "We buried him in a cave in the mountains near the temple of Venus."

"Did you preserve his knowledge?" Mary asked, using inconspicuous words, knowing Mariam would understand.

"He has joined the ancestors, together with beloved Yochanan," said Mariam.

Mary nodded in approval, sending her sincerest admiration for her daughter-in- laws strength.

"So when can we expect the new baby? I think it is a boy," said Mary with a smile.

"He was conceived around the summer solstice, so he should be born at the spring equinox," answered Mariam. "And I think it is a boy too. His name will be Joseph, after your beloved husband."

This brought tears to Mary's eyes. She had received her husband's letter, inviting her to come to England. She knew she would see him again.

Tamera took her brothers hands and helped him walk across the courtyard. Soon they had found something to occupy them with, and were busy with sticks and rocks.

Johanna called for help to bring the kitchen table outside. They found all the chairs they had so everyone would have a seat. Smells of fresh bread told of busy kitchen hands, and soon a big pot of stew and a stack of bowls and spoons found their way outside. The men returned from the field, and they all gathered in the courtyard to enjoy a simple meal celebrated like a feast fit for kings. Wine was shared, and Lazarus said the blessings of the food.

"Gathered here, are my best friends and my most beloved family. We give thanks for our health, for the incredible feat that we're all here and for special guests that arrived from far away. We give thanks to Ephesus for caring for our mother for many years, to the three places here in Gaul that sustains us, and the new place England which is welcoming us. The colony in England is waiting to be started, and we'll spend this winter planning our journey there in the spring.

But for now, let's enjoy this time, where we can all be together on Tuberose Farm. I have admired your accomplishments. You have all done a remarkable job.

Special thanks goes to Herodias, for bringing Mariam back to health. You're also a strong part of our family, and we appreciate all your help over the years. A special blessing goes out for the children growing up among us. I'm the proud uncle of these two, and look forward to meet the next little one who will soon be with us.

I break this bread and share this wine, in memory of the man who is no longer with us. I trust that he's here in spirit, right here present among us, inspiring us as always. He will always be the bringer of light."

"Hear, hear," was said in response.

"The food smells delicious, let's all join in and eat."

CHAPTER 21

PLANNING A COLONY

They stayed together, enjoying the farm life, for several days. A bigger table and benches were built so they could accommodate everybody, and Trym and John went to the local market to pick up more supplies. Joses set traps in the hills, and came back with a ptarmigans and rabbits for Johanna's pots. Herodias went to visit with her friend Suzanna. She came back reporting that Suzanna loved their oils and fragrances, and had new orders for her friends. They were also invited for dinner at Villa Lata. Herodias wasn't going to hear that anybody weren't going, and invited Sarah to come and look through her own bags to find additional pieces of linens and silks.

It was a fine dinner, served on the patio in the inner courtyard of the lovely villa. Suzanna was a wonderful host, and they found that she also served stew and bread, along with cheeses and green herbs, like they ate at the farm.

Herodias realized her time on Tuberose was coming to an end. Her duties called her back to Arelate. She helped young Agrippa in his business, and as a hostess she was irreplaceable. In all honesty, she realized that she missed her mansion. A warm scented bath in a tiled bathroom sounded heavenly. She talked to the stable boys to look over her carriage and horses and have them ready the following day.

"Please come to Arelate before you head for England," she announced to the flock at large. "I have to see the new little one before you leave."

Mariam couldn't thank her friend enough. She hoped she could do something in return one day. *You already have,* came in reply. *I couldn't have ruined Antipas without your help. I still owe you.* Mariam saw a sly smile, and knew Herodias still enjoyed the story of the birthday party. She was famous for her shrewd achievement of ruining Herod Antipas' career, in one great celebratory evening. The accompanying memory of being imprisoned in Rome for a year after the events in Jerusalem was shielded from her friend.

Lazarus and Martha left with Herodias. She had to go through Aquae Sextiae anyway, and they cherished having fine transportation. John decided to go with them, as well. He wanted to know more about their colony there, and felt that Mary was well taken care of on the mountain farm. He would come back with Trym and Sibyl next time they came to market.

Sarah wanted to stay for a while. She hadn't seen her sister in a long time, and she hadn't seen her this happy in years. Mariam had accepted her husband's destiny, and could finally settle down to enjoy her children. Sarah watched an additional glow appear around her. They kept talking about Yeshua being light. Did he encircle her wherever she went? It certainly looked like it.

Mary seemed to have the same quiet light around her. Sarah guessed that they were the two women closest to him. It would be natural for him to stay around his mother and wife.

The children brought a new liveliness to the farm. Sarah continued her care for Tamera and included Geiss as a natural extension. Why did the boy have a Greek name? She'd have to ask Mariam someday.

"It is his father's name. He is Yeshua the second. Geiss is another form of the same. Jesu is a form as well. We needed to separate him from his father when we spoke of him, and we wanted to protect him from being associated with Yeshua too directly."

Sarah understood the reasoning. She knew Yeshua had both devotees and enemies. Either group would put undue pressure on the child. She realized that having them here on a secluded mountain farm, was probably best for the children's safety.

Mariam was feeling heavier. It was harder to move about and harder to find a relatively comfortable way to sleep. She occupied her day with small tasks Johanna gave her. Sarah found her often outside, in conversation with Mary, at the new table shelling peas or pealing vegetables.

They started making things ready for the imminent birth. Clean linens were collected and the right herbs were made ready. Trym collected firewood enough for a whole year, thinking that a new child needs to be kept warm.

Mary watched the signs. She kept Mariam's hands busy, and the conversations light. Asking her to describe Hibernia and England, would keep her talking for hours. Mary found it interesting to hear her daughter-in-law describe her own homeland. She also wanted to know more about the political situation in England. What was the relationship between her brother Joseph and the king, Arviragus? And who was Caractacus? His famous name had reached Ephesus.

Mariam told her in detail. She'd been impressed with the country, with the friendly people, the druids she'd met and the sister priestesses of the island of glass.

She looked forward to claim the land that was given to them, and start the colony there. She would walk the circular pattern around the Tor every day, Mariam told her. "But you know I'll have to return here. This is my home."

Mary listened. She looked forward to see the land that had been so generously gifted to them, as well. How was her brother doing, having been exiled out of the

Roman Empire after he became ousted from Jerusalem? How was her dear husband, who must be getting up in age at this time? Mary sighed. She was aware of her own age as well. She knew she would live out her life in the new colony, and hopefully have many years at his side in the beautiful country of England.

Knowing that this was her only visit to the herb farm in Provence, she tried to take in as much as possible. The serene peace she always surrounded herself with, spread to the others as well. The days went by in quiet appreciation for the beauty that surrounded them, and in gratitude that they had gotten this far.

Little Joseph was born near the spring equinox. He picked a lovely spring day filled with colorful flowers in the hills. Mary said she heard the child laugh as he arrived. They all recognized his grandfather's lively eyes, and thought the child had chosen his own name before he was born.

Mariam was sitting up in the bed holding her newborn son wrapped in a blanket. He'd been washed and cleaned by his grandmother and aunt, and Mariam had been taken care of by Johanna. She felt a little sweaty, tired, but intensely happy.

Joses came in. He needed to see his nephew. He had been remarkably quiet for several days. This newborn child was the last greeting from his brother. Would the child have his eyes? Mariam smiled at him. He looked past her and stared at the child.

"His name is Joseph after your father," she said.

Joses found a chair and sat down next to her. He studied the woman he admired so much, the sister-in-law who had accompanied his brother the last of his days. The child was beaming with a golden light. His eyes were closed, but from the little body came a wave of peace. Joses stared at his new nephew. The mother and child image in front of him bathed him in golden light, the way Yeshua so often did, just the way he remembered him. Tears rolled down his cheeks, and Joses could finally cry his grief over his lost brother. He collapsed across her lap, and Mariam stroked his shoulders with her free hand. The light around them all grew stronger, and they all felt Yeshua's presence, surrounding them with peace and love. Mary felt her oldest son's peaceful light encircling his family, welcoming her in as well.

Little Joseph took after his grandfather, becoming an easy child to care for. Soon Mariam could take part in the lighter work in their household again, with a laughing child in a sling around her body.

With the arrival of Joseph, it was time to go to Lazarus in Aquae Sextiae and solidify the plans for traveling.

There were many concerns. With the protection of Arviragus, they would be safe behind the British lines in England. But Rome was at war with England, albeit losing pathetically to Caractacus and his men. Gaul was in Roman hands. They had to be quiet about their plans.

"True," said Lazarus. "But as long as they feel they've won the country, established some cities with their arenas and their theatres, seen that commerce is strong, the

Romans generally leave people to themselves. Gaul doesn't show signs of rebellion. The people have accepted the occupation and see good developments in its wake. There are good roads connecting the country. There is sanitation in the cities. The aqueducts deliver water to their households. Business is thriving. Ships are sailing the sea safely with merchandize from interesting cultures. There is no need for the Romans to fear Gaul. So as long as we don't register ourselves as rebels, we'll be left alone."

"That's all well and good, Lazarus, but by announcing that we're traveling in a large group to England, which is considered a problem and an embarrassment, we are associating ourselves with Roman enemies."

"Do we have to say we're going all the way to England? We only have to admit we're going the piece of the journey we're on at the time."

"Still, if fifteen people are going, we'll be a noticeable crowd."

"We can leave in smaller groups. Boats go to Ruscino all the time. Joseph has established contacts along the way. As long as we all arrive within a month or so, we'll be fine."

"Twelve hides of land are offered. We should be twelve companions that claim them."

The discussions had been going on all winter. They were all waiting for little Joseph's safe arrival before deciding on the details, since Mariam was a natural leader of the expedition.

How many children could she take with her traveling? Three, including a newborn, was quite an entourage. "Of course they're all coming with. Grandfather Joseph has to meet his grandchildren." Mary wouldn't hear of anything else. Mariam took a deep breath, and agreed. "As long as Sarah comes with."

CHAPTER 22

Before They Leave

"Mariam?" her mother-in-law approached her. "Come with me."

They were back at Tuberose and Mary invited Mariam to come for a walk a little up the hills to a rock you could sit on and get a good view. Mariam followed, feeling her gentle movements lulling the baby to sleep in his sling.

They sat down next to each other on the rock and looked out. The herb farm was laid out in front of them, and further down to the side, they could see Villa Lata in the distance.

"You've done some impressive work in the years you've lived here," Mary started.

"Oh, the credit goes to Trym, Sibyl and Joses and all the good workers they've hired over the years. I've had other things on my mind."

"They wouldn't have been here without you," Mary replied. "They're all devoted to you and the safety of the children."

"I know," said Mariam, "How could I ever thank them enough? Johanna and Sarah?"

"You don't have to. You've given purpose to their lives, and you've taught them. They live a richer life here then they ever could anywhere else."

"Thank you for saying that. I've wondered if I've kept them separated from the others, and that they've missed life in the city. I know Sarah needs to go back soon."

"They're not city people like her. Tamera seems to enjoy herself. Sibyl is teaching her about flowers and herbs. She's got your sense, but she looks like Sarah."

"She's lucky. And it might be safer for her that way. Little Geiss looks so much like him, he'll be recognized."

"Yes. I've seen that as well."

There was silence between them for a moment, and his peace spread around them one more time.

"Mariam, you mentioned Yeshua has joined his cousin and his ancestors. I'd like to see him before we leave."

453

Mariam had thought about it, and wondered how Mary felt regarding her son and what had been done to him. She didn't want to bring it up, unless Mary herself initiated the conversation. And frankly, Mariam had been so focused on her newborn son, and the imminent travel to England that she hadn't thought about her priestess work for a while. She took a deep breath before she answered.

"We would have to go to the grotto. It would be good to do a ritual there to bless the journey, anyway."

"Will you take your priestess tools with you to England? After all, you're planning to take the children."

"Oh Mary, what should I do? I never travel without them. I don't really want to leave them behind, and the priestesses of Avalon would understand."

"There will be a lot of luggage anyway. Three extra bags won't be noticed. I'll help you."

"Yes, Mary, but you're going to stay there. I have to get back here. Sarah will help, but she doesn't understand the way you do. Mary, the last time I traveled, carrying it all as my luggage, was a very difficult time for me."

"Your strength is admirable, Mariam. I can hardly believe that you managed." Mary took her hand and squeezed it gently.

"His light surrounded me, but that made it almost more unbearable." Mariam turned her head away. "But he should meet his son. You're right. We should do it before we leave. Joses can help us. He's joined me before."

Mariam was glad to show Mary the grotto. They set out the following day. Johanna sent some food with them, and Sarah was watching Geiss, while Tamera was at her herb lessons with Sibyl. Joses got the horse ready, and found a blanket for it so his mother could ride.

The horse got several bags tied to its harness, and Mary enjoyed the view from horseback as they followed the path down the hillside. The beauty of the landscape enchanted her. It was so different than the dry desert land she had lived in for so long. This was lush and fertile and there were wild flowers along with ever green bushes and trees. The air had a fresher scent, and she could see how easy it was for Sibyl and Trym to find wild herbs to transplant, and how willingly they would grow once established. She was impressed with the pharmacopoeia established at Tuberose.

"Why Tuberose, Mariam?" Mary asked.

"It's our main perfume ingredient, for one thing. Sibyl chose the name since the word for the Tuberose bulb around here is *maryam*."

Mary understood some of the underlying devotion to Mariam. They did indeed consider her their founder, and the whole farm was dedicated to her name.

Joses understood why they were going. He was not going to England, but the blessing of the journey was important, and he also wanted his mother to see what he'd seen himself not long ago. How would she take it? How would Yeshua take it? Joses wondered if he again had to be the stable one in an emotional family gathering.

Mariam walked ahead with baby Joseph tied around her. One more time, she was overwhelmed with emotions, however much she'd been trained to ignore them and let practical matters take precedence. She knew she would never see the temples of Alexandria again. The temple of Jerusalem would soon be once more erased from history. Mary would never return to Ephesus. The temple she had to work with right now was this grotto. A new building would be built in England, she knew that. A new form of temple that would be dedicated to their ways. She knew she would see it before she'd leave.

The grotto was set up the way they'd gotten used to. Mariam wished Herodias was there. She would have to lead this ceremony herself, and she hadn't done it in a while. Joses was getting used to how this was done. She was still marveling at her young brother-in-law who had taken in so much. In his quiet ways, on his strong young shoulders, he carried a lot. Mariam stopped for a moment and looked at him. She knew she could entrust her children's safety to him. Suddenly she also knew that he would make sure they'd receive proper education according to their responsibilities. Joses had taken on the responsibility for his brother's family. Mariam's heart warmed towards him, and she felt Yeshua's gratitude as well.

They were sitting in the points of the star. Mariam had unfolded Yochanan and placed him in another point. She handed the other bundle to Mary. Honored, she accepted, and started to unroll the covering linens. Joses watched his mother, watched her fine finger movements, and wondered what she was thinking. She seemed calm and composed, at the same time conscious of what was unfolding.

As she lifted of the fine embroidered piece covering his face, she held her breath. The silence in the space took on a tangible tone, as they all looked at his beautiful features, his golden hair and felt his presence unfold around them.

Mariam started the intonation, Joses fell in, and as soon as she called for Yochanan, he was awake and present among them. Mary understood, and placed Yeshua in the last point of the star. He was called for, and they watched him again open his beautiful blue eyes, and stare at them in greeting. He smiled at his mother, who smiled back through tears, but kept her calm, and continued her tone. Mariam placed baby Joseph in the center of the star. He was awake and apparently liked the incantation.

As they continued singing, the light around them intensified. The golden glow they had established became a white bright light, and soon Mariam recognized Yeshua's outline near the child. Little Joseph was bathed in strong white light, and they could see the contour of a hand stroking the cheek of the baby. He moved closer to his mother, and the same hand blessed her head briefly, before turning to his brother and repeating the gesture. He then turned to his wife, and Mariam received the same gentle reassurance. She closed her eyes and allowed the light to fill her.

They couldn't make out the form of a body. It was simply a cloud of light, which blessed them with the faint outline of a hand, but they all knew it was him. They all knew he gave them strength from his side, strength to take on the journey, strength to start the beginning of a new colony, a new group of people who would teach The Way he'd been teaching them all. Joses knew he had to come with to England. His brother told him it was important. All this had to come with as well. Across the light they all nodded to each other. Yes, it all had to come with.

This blessing had to be repeated in England. This blessing was intended for the first building above ground dedicated in His name. And it would be in Glastonbury, near the island of glass, on the twelve hides of land given to them by the Silurian Prince Arviragus.

CHAPTER 23

ENGLAND

MARIAM WAS WALKING UP THE HILL, FOLLOWING the meandering circles around the Glastonbury Tor. At her hand was Princess Tamera, her brave daughter who had traveled without complaint, all the way from Provence. Attached to her back was her young son Prince Joseph, asleep in the fresh air and rocked by the movements of his mother. Next to her was Sarah, carrying Prince Geiss, who was also invited to join the festivities on top of the hill.

They were following Uncle Joseph, who was led by the head druid, and right behind him was his sister and brother-in-law, Mary and Joseph. The proud grandparents were now also proud colony founders. They walked hand in hand, happily together like newlyweds, after years of separation. After Mariam came Joses followed by the rest of their flock who had eventually found their way to Cornwall, and been led to the holy isle of Avalon.

This was a day of celebration. The church had been completed. The simple wattle church had been erected around the first altar Yeshua had built, when he was visiting here with his uncle many years ago. The first temple above ground, the first place where The Way could be taught in peace, was a reality.

This is a triumphal march, thought Father Joseph. He knew he would stay here and assist his brother-in-law in the teaching work. There were also mines nearby, where his knowledge of metallurgy could be of use. And his beloved wife was here with him. Father Joseph looked forward to many good years, living here in this beautiful land promoting the work of their son and their people.

Sarah thought about the beautiful ceremony they had been invited to at the court of King Arviragus. His brother Caradoc and his family had been there as well, well known and well feared as Caractacus among the Romans. Sarah had admired the tall, imposing figure of the famous warrior, and been surprised at his apparent culture and education. He could converse with them in Latin or Greek, and he had news for them from Jerusalem and Rome. Sarah had gotten to know his daughter Gladys, and made a friend in the Silurian court.

Little Geiss was getting heavy. He was a bigger boy now, but still too little to walk at their pace up the hill. Sarah turned, and handed him over to Joses, who happily accepted his nephew. He was still grateful that the travels had been uneventful, besides an unending care taking of children and luggage. Here, he found plenty of help for it all, and was aware of that he would return to Provence with Mariam, Sarah and the children, repeating the whole procedure. Joses smiled to himself. For the experience of being here, for the privilege of building the church together with his father and uncle, he was happy to be the appointed travel companion.

Martha and Lazarus walked right behind him. Lazarus had been given a title by now. He was bishop of Massilia, besides being the leader of the colony in Aquae Sextiae. Martha was held in high esteem, as one of the founding members of their group. She looked at the family ahead of her, and the three children, so well protected, and so incredibly important. They were His children. And Martha was the proud aunt. Teaching The Way, His Way, had been an adventure, had been a privilege and an honor. And now it was culminating in this celebration.

Lazarus knew they were doing this to honor the work of the druids. These wise men seemed to have known about the life of Yeshua, long before his own people had come to know him. They knew of his education, his work and his sacrifice, they even knew his name. He had been called Yesu among the druids for decades already. How come they knew all this?

Behind Lazarus were Mary Jacob, Mary Salome and their husbands. Lazarus thought of their steadfast work over the years, the unending support these good people had shown. Some of them would stay here and establish the new colony together with Mary and Joseph. Lazarus could only send them blessings, and hope that strong King Arviragus would continue to keep the Romans at bay.

They reached the top, where the standing stones had been for centuries, marking the changing seasons, marking the outline of the ancient circle. The flock spread out between the stones, squinting in the bright sunlight of the late summer morning. The head druid took his place by the central stone, and the other druids blended in between the holy family.

"Welcome, friends. We are honored to have you here, the family of Yesu, the founder of the teaching of The Way, the way of God teaching us a new way of living in his name. According to his tradition, I will share wine and bread with you. Please come up and enjoy this with me." He showed them that he had brought newly baked bread on a wooden board and a bottle of wine.

People formed a line and came up to the druid who broke a piece of the bread and gave them of the wine chalice to drink. For each person he gave a blessing, and people received it, nodding back at him in acknowledgement. The light around the druid was growing, and soon the top of the Tor had its own glow, which the people in the nearby village noticed, and talked about for years.

Mariam took in the blessing, and thought of other hills that had glowing lights in them at auspicious times. She knew Yeshua would want to be here among them on this day, and could feel his presence as a profound peace descending among them. There was much unrest among his followers in other countries, but here, far north and far west from the shores of Galilee where most of his work and teaching took place, the first building in his honor was completed, and the first land dedicated to the cause, was owned by his family. Mariam could only marvel at the turn of events, hugging his son closer to her body.

Later on that night there was a full moon, and Mariam found her way up the Tor one more time. Mary and Joseph walked silently with her. Uncle Joseph led their procession and Joses made the rear behind her. Her brother Lazarus held her hand. She knew she had to do this, and she was grateful for the other family members who understood.

They reached the top, and gathered around the central stone. Joses and Mariam had carried some supplies, and quickly they put together what they needed. The brassier was lit, the incense was started, a cup of water was prepared and a stone was brought forth having found its way all the way from Jerusalem. Two bags with red tassels were opened. Mary was asked to unwrap one round object, while Mariam took care of the other. Soon, two family members representing their ancient and immortal history, found their places among them.

They formed a larger circle on top of the rounded hill. This mound was made of dirt, piled up by long gone ancestors, who knew its purpose. There was more volume here than in the pyramids, and it was also compiled by people longer back in time than anybody could remember. The ancient pattern around it, the meandering circles with the mysterious order, was still the path to reach the top and the menhir surrounding them continued to tell the stories of the stars.

Mariam looked at the bags with red tassels as she put them aside. One of them came from the astrologers of Persia who had visited Yeshua as an infant. They also knew who he was from reading the stars. They knew his destiny, his gentle intelligence and his incredible potential. Did the druids find the same information, and had been waiting for the man they called Yesu?

She looked at the circle she had assembled, and wondered what the stars told of them, and the work they had done, anchoring these profound teachings in stone. Gently she started the tone, and heard her musically gifted brother take over, carrying the sound. The others fell in, and with the silent directives of Lazarus, they created a choir of pleasing sounds, honoring the moon above and the earth below, starting a blessing for this new building, this new colony and the teaching work that was just begun.

Mariam sang the incantations, inviting Yeshua and Yochanan among them. She saw their eyes open in the dark, and heard two new voices join them. The light multiplied manifold, and soon Mariam could feel the hill they were standing on reverberating with them. She thought of the hollow hill in the middle of Jerusalem. The hill called the skull had filled with the love of his followers, giving him strength to complete his sacrifice. She thought of the hill in Razes, where he had completed his human life, and become the body of light he existed as now. His ancestral head held the wisdom he had collected on earth, but the incredible life force he had established, existed as an independent unit, working in a different capacity, beyond her immediate comprehension.

The moon above was illuminating the landscape. She noticed the star of Venus greeting them as an evening star, blinking down to them on their large stone. A shaft of light was forming on the central stone. It grew in width and height, until it took on the circumference of the inner circle of standing stones. As the sounds they created reached a crescendo, the light became a powerful tunnel reaching up into the night sky, and down through the hill to the earth itself. Mariam felt its power, like a wind blowing across her face. She saw the other faces lit up by the bright bluish light, and their hair blowing behind them, while they continued the powerful chant.

Yes, she thought. *Yes. The new agreement with God is being established.* The new love for mankind, the new light illuminating from within, the potential for human enlightenment, all the teaching she and her husband had labored so endlessly to anchor in human minds, was finally being encoded by light into the earth.

Lazarus led them in a melodious interpretation, before bringing all the sounds back to one note, the first sound of creation.

CHAPTER 24

WHAT DOES THE FUTURE HOLD?

"**B**UT HERODIAS, THIS HAS TO BE THOUGHT OUT carefully," Mariam continued over her tea cup. They'd been discussing this for a while, and she didn't feel that all the details had been laid out yet. She turned her head, and stared at the fish swimming in the pond in the middle of Herodias' patio.

Her children were older. Tamera had grown into a beautiful young maiden, wise beyond her years, and quite learned already. The colony had taken their education seriously, and the children had been taught by their own scholars. Young Yahya, Yochanan's son, had been included among them. It was time to send them off to higher education.

"It seems pretty straight forward to me. They have all stated where they would like to go, and it makes perfect sense according to their personalities." Herodias had listened to this for a while, in fact the discussion had been going on for some years, and she had to admit there were some complicating factors. For one thing, who would take them to the appointed seats of learning? Which temples were still teaching? Mariam and Herodias couldn't travel far within the Roman Empire without danger. How far could the young ones go? Would they ever be able to say who they were?

"Did you hear what happened to Caractacus and his family?" Herodias had news from Rome. "We all know how the Christians have been persecuted left and right. There have been more awful stories than I can recount," she said shuttering.

"I dread the stories from Rome. Saul has led a whole campaign wanting to extinguish anybody mentioning his name." Mariam had heard enough over the years.

"But listen to this. Your friend Caractacus, the fearless British warrior who has defied Rome for almost ten years, has been captured."

"Really? That's terrible!"

"Well, hear me out. He was taken to Rome in chains, together with his entire family. And for some reason, the Roman soldiers feared him so much that they didn't mistreat them. As Caractacus was paraded as a prisoner through town, citizens of Rome came out in respect, standing quietly along the roads, honoring him. He walked with dignity, tall and imposing, spreading awe wherever he went. At the senate he gave a speech, which so moved Caesar Claudius, his wife and the senators, that they let him live!"

"So he went back to England?"

"No, he has to stay in Rome for seven years. But he's been given a palace and access to his income, so he can live in style. His daughter Gladys stood next to him at the senate, another anomaly, and now the young girl is being courted by high Roman officials!"

"This is incredible!"

"Yes, and guess what, the British Palace in Rome is becoming a free space for Christians. Since Caractacus is stating his religion, and flying his flag with the cross on it, Rome can't touch them. His household is a center for teaching The Way, and a safe haven for the persecuted. Something good is happening."

"Thank the Gods above. We've lost so many. I feel we're sitting here on a safe hillside, not engaged in what our people are going through."

"You were engaged enough for the time you were in Jerusalem. Don't tell me you weren't in danger yourself, Mariam. You hardly escaped with your life, thanks to some quick thinking by your father-in-law."

"Yes. That was close," Mariam said thinking back.

"Herodias, can we send the young ones out? Is there any sense in that? There is danger everywhere. I know they need their education, but I want to keep them safe. The temples are not the same anymore."

"It was easier when you were young, and unknown. There is a danger in having well known parents," said Herodias with a sly smile.

"I wish I wasn't," said Mariam.

Joses came into the room. He'd wanted to be part of this discussion for a while, and had finally found his opportunity to talk to the women.

"I'll take them there. I'm not well known. And we're not talking about going to Rome or Jerusalem. I know where Yahya wants to go. He's definitely old enough, and Geiss has shown interest in going to the same place."

"But he's too young. Definitely too young." Mariam's mother's heart couldn't part with any of them.

"The temple school in the desert north of Heliopolis is so well hidden. Once we get there, we'll be lost in obscurity," Joses said wisely. "And Sarah wants to accompany Tamera to the Serapium. The Romans don't know who she is, and she has practically raised the girl, she can pass as her mother."

"You've figured it all out, haven't you? What about young Joseph?"

"All he wants is to join his grandfather in Glastonbury, and learn from the druids."

"That's at least safe, "said Mariam. "Why don't we send them all there?"

"They've all made up their minds, Mariam, I don't think you can persuade them otherwise."

Mariam sighed, like all parents watching their children come of age. She knew she had to give in. Lazarus had already recommended that they were sent to further their education. He felt they had a good foundation from the resources in the colony, but were ready for a new commitment.

So it was decided. Joses would go with Yahya and Geiss to Heliopolis. Sarah and Tamera would go to Alexandria and enroll Tamera at the Serapium. And later young Joseph would be sent with a merchant ship to England to go to the University of the Druids. Mariam could only bite her lips, and hug them all as much as she could. She knew it was the right decision, however much she hated to part with them.

Before Tamera left, she took her aside, and repeated the ceremony her own mother had done with her before she started at the Serapium. Tamera was given a shrunken head from Ethiopia, and Bashra was given a new family member to protect.

Their colony had grown substantially over the years. They still met in their homes for their teaching and gatherings, although plans for buildings were being made. Lazarus had established a system for learning and a structure of organization among their followers. He engaged his sisters in his teaching, and Mariam was becoming known for her gentle, wise approach. She was requested to speak in Massilia, Aqua Sextiae and Arelate, and welcomed into stately homes. Still, her home was Tuberose Herb Farm, where she could create the perfumed oils and medicinal products she was famous for.

Mariam continued her seasonal work in her grotto. When her daughter Tamera was home from Alexandria, they would do a ritual together, and when Herodias was visiting they would find their way up the hills. Sibyl would come with from time to time, but there were fewer people she could do her priestess work with.

The people who followed The Way learned what Yeshua had taught. It was all beautiful wisdom, teaching them to find their own empowerment within. But it did not make them temple trained. Mariam made that distinction very clear. She hoped young Yahya and Geiss would get to experience the great initiation. She hoped Tamera would learn to administrate it. She hoped young Joseph would learn similar things among the druids. But she would not take on that responsibility again herself. She felt she was getting up in age, and she didn't have the right helpers available or the right setting.

"I'm turning into a hermit," she thought to herself. "I'm sitting here among my herbs and plants..." "...growing flowers out of your ears" she heard Herodias' familiar voice in her head. "Come and visit me. I miss you."

Mariam went with Trym into town and found transportation to Arelate.

463

Herodias was delighted to see her. She dressed her up in her own latest gowns, served a splendid dinner, and took Mariam to the theatre. The Roman Theatre in Arelate was quite popular, and famous for their productions. Particularly, their music performances were considered excellent, and compared with quality elsewhere. They sat in Herodias' stately carriage on their way home and passed by the arena, just as big as the Coliseum in Rome.

"The building is impressive, but I don't care for gladiators or animal fights. The arts are my entertainment," said Herodias fanning herself.

"And what a splendid performance," concluded Mariam listening to the sound of her silk dress as she moved. "Thanks for calling for me."

"I'm glad you enjoyed it. I knew the music would be to your liking."

They enjoyed driving through the pretty town at night, and were glad to be taken back to the Herod estate.

"Tea? Ruby will serve it by the fish pond."

Mariam thought of how lovely Herodias lived, and relaxed into a different kind of life than her own for a while. The years had been kind to her, but she realized that her body wasn't as flexible as it had been, and the bathtub of her guest room was a delightful convention. She sat down in the exquisite patio room where small lamps had been lit among the large plants. The colorful fish added another exotic touch.

Ruby brought in a tray and placed it on the table between them. Mariam accepted a cup of red liquid and leaned back in her cushions and pillows.

"Herodias, I see him more often now. His light stays with me longer."

"Your husband? Maybe he misses you. You guys were quite a team."

"Maybe. It's nice to feel him close."

Herodias looked at her friend. Did Mariam glow stronger than usual? She had attributed it to the enjoyment of the evening and Mariam's natural beaming personality, but now she noticed that there was indeed more light shining from her. This was not just a pretty golden warmth, this had more of the bluish white light she had seen before. It accentuated the white hair that started to creep in among her dark strands. Mariam stared at a green palm leaf, and Herodias thought the green colors looked brighter around her. Was this a good thing?

Mariam smiled to herself, like a woman with a secret love life.

CHAPTER 25

HERODIAS

SOME TIME HAD PASSED SINCE MARIAM HAD spent another lovely month in Arelate, an annual retreat she was invited to for years. The summer of the year had passed into fall, and the days were getting colder. Herodias thanked her sturdy constitution for keeping her healthy, even though her hairdresser kept coloring her white strands, and her health advisor kept pushing stretching exercises. She did her morning ritual, dedicating her day to live in close connection to the powers that be, and was grateful for the comforts life had presented to her.

Her concern for her friend's well being had grown. She had tuned in and heard her several times, had seen her busy with daily activities involving harvesting, preparing and storing plant material. The farm had become a larger endeavor, and their houses had been improved several times. There were other people living in the first stone houses they had moved into. A larger whitewashed home with a lovely view of the mountainside, housed the original founders of the herb farm now. Rocking chairs were on the front patio, waiting for them to sit down and rest. A quiet sweet gratitude had settled upon them.

Herodias arranged for her carriage to take her on a journey. She felt her presence was needed. The day trip to Aquae Sextiae was pleasant enough, and she stayed overnight with Martha, before heading up Via Aurelia the following day. Their colony had also enlarged and improved. There were schools for children, regular meetings and instruction in The Way for the adults. A new building was planned, a larger house of worship. Herodias was impressed.

Her carriage continued along the Roman road between cypresses and sycamores. Her driver knew where to turn towards Villa Lata. Herodias looked out the window, and admired the graceful curves of the landscape.

Suzanna was glad to see her. There weren't many visitors along Via Aurelia anymore. They shared a light luncheon, while the carriage was cared for and a riding horse was being prepared. "They still deliver their high quality herbal products. My skin hasn't had anything else, for close to thirty years now." Herodias admired another golden glow on a serene woman's face, and wondered if the light surrounding the farm followed the oils and fragrances.

Her horse was calm, as she found her way along the narrower road, up the hills towards Tuberose. She had changed into a simpler linen outfit, more suitable for her ride than her usual silks. The road had been improved several times since the first stony foot path. A smaller wagon could definitely be used here now. Her horse took her safely along sage bushes and broom. A creek followed the road and sang its song among stones, as she rode in the afternoon sunshine.

Sibyl's rocking chair was occupied on the patio when she arrived. Another woman was sitting there. Trym had buried Sibyl among her beloved herbs some years earlier. Later, Mariam had asked their younger workers to help her bury him next to her. When Johanna became ill, she had been taken to Martha in Aquae Sextiae. She'd been buried there, at their burial ground for their community. There was nobody left of the original founders, except Mariam. A young man stepped up to take care of the horse. Herodias was invited in for tea, by the woman on the porch.

"Mariam has gone to the grotto. She goes there often by herself now. We usually don't see her until the next morning."

Herodias finished her tea, and continued down the hillside with her horse. The path was well worn. It was not hard to follow, even though she had usually gone it together with Joses. He was in Egypt with Yahya and Geiss. They had traveled for several years, as far as she knew. They wanted to follow the silk roads and find where Yeshua had gone. They had already spent time at Ephesus. But Jerusalem had been avoided. After the fall of the Temple and the brutal massacre of their people, just the way Mariam had predicted, there was no sense visiting there. Herodias knew they were creating their own adventures. Their education merited that. Joses deserved this time as well. He certainly had put in his time at the herb farm.

She knew that Mariam heard from Tamera at the Serapium. Her studies were focused on the healing arts. Sarah had been with her, studying next to her, but was now with her brothers in Alexandria. Tamera was considered a priestess by now. Young Joseph had passed another level of druidic learning. Both his grandparents had died, and were buried next to Uncle Joseph near the thorn bush he had planted.

Herodias thought of how the three children were continuing their family's legacy of scholarship. She knew it must please Mariam tremendously to see them grow in wisdom, similar to the way she collected her own body of knowledge. Now they were all way into adulthood and respected for their knowledge.

How was her friend doing? Herodias was a little alarmed about her going to the grotto alone. Since they were getting up in age, she didn't have anybody to go with. Maybe she preferred being by herself. Herodias could recognize how they all turned into hermits as they aged. She smiled to herself, admitting that it crept up on her, however much people claimed that she used her priestess magic to keep it at bay.

No, no magic, she said to herself, *just common sense. Good food and fresh air goes a long way.*

The path along the herb fields was lovely. Had Sibyl planted the herbs to color coordinate them? They certainly created a pretty pattern in the landscape, especially now that they all were turning colors with the season.

She entered the forest, and admired the old trees. This old oak she remembered from earlier. It was an old tree when they had started working in the grotto. Now the limbs were drooping towards the ground, and the clusters of green leaves seemed heavy on it. She passed some sprightly evergreens, and remembered when they were smaller bushes. Yes, time passes.

At the foot of Mount Aurelia, she found the path along the mountain side. She had to get off her horse, but decided to take it with her up along the narrow path. There was light shining from the opening of the cave. Mariam was sure to be there.

As she came closer, she became more alarmed. There was something unnatural about the light. This was not the glow from a brazier or small oil lamps. The light was white and bright and had a bluish sheen to it. What was Mariam doing?

She soon had her answers. There was indeed a brazier burning. But the light it gave out was puny, compared to the brightness inside of the familiar grotto. Herodias made haste. Mariam needed her help. Now.

She ran into the cave, facing the brightness, having to shield her face with her arm to be able to take in the situation. Mariam was spread out on the layers of blankets. The lights were pulsating through her body. Herodias fell down next to her and took her head in her lap. *Dear friend, what's happening?*

Mariam's skin tone was gray. Her hair had turned totally white by now, and was laid out like a halo around her head. She was sweating, and the light emanating from her body pulsed with her heartbeat. She looked up, and registered her life long friend. A weak smile spread over her face.

"Herodias, my dear," she breathed.

Herodias could only hold her closer, as tears wet her cheeks.

"He comes closer every time, now," said Mariam. "Soon I have to go with him."

Herodias looked up, looked into the light. She couldn't make out any familiar face or figure, but she could recognize the peace and serenity he was known for. He had left the familiar form now. His work had taken him deeper into the mysteries of light. He could work easier this way. And apparently, he wanted her to come and help him. They would be a team again, like they had been in Jerusalem. *No, not yet. Please,* Herodias pleaded. She couldn't bear being without her temple sister and life long friend.

"Herodias, you have to help me," Mariam whispered.

"No, I can't, please, Mariam, don't ask me."

"You said you would like to repay me for helping you bring revenge on Herod Antipas. I need your help now."

"No, Mariam, I can't."

"Herodias, you're the only one who can."

Herodias knew she was right.

"Don't let my knowledge disappear, dear friend," Mariam pleaded.

"But who will know how to retrieve it? Who knows the incantations anymore?"

"New people will come. They will know. But if the knowledge is lost, they won't even have the possibility. Please, Herodias. Let me join my ancestors so my children can speak to me. Let me join my husband, so we can continue our work."

Herodias bent over Mariam and cried. She was not ready for this.

Mariam let her friend grieve. Her breathing was getting raspier. It was time.

Herodias carefully laid Mariam down on the blankets again. She stood up, wiped her nose with her arm, and looked at her dying friend. The signs were obvious. She took a deep breath. There was work to be done.

Quickly, she looked around for Mariam's herb bag. She found it next to the brazier, and inside it her tools, all cleaned and oiled and wrapped up. Herodias redrew the star on the floor around them, refilled the brazier and started more incense burning all the while monitoring Mariam's deteriorating condition.

"I'm here, Mariam," she said, as she again took her head in her lap.

"I hereby relinquish my life to the preservation of the old wisdom," Mariam started. "I will pull my life force to my head, and allow my body to die."

Herodias let out a cry. This was not what she wanted to do. She grasped the light body in her arms, and hugged her closer. Then she started the incantation encouraging the life of the body to concentrate itself inside the skull.

Her hands fumbled among the tools. Herodias needed the long, sharp knife with the slim blade. Mariam looked up at her, and pulled her dress aside to expose her chest where her heart was still beating feebly.

"Thank you, Herodias, you're a true friend," said Mariam. "My love will always be with you," was her last words, as she locked eyes with Herodias one last time. "And mine with you," Herodias whispered and hugged her close, before she cried loudly and pushed the knife into the chest of her friend, knowing that it would find its true aim. Mariam's dark eyes rolled back into her head, and as blood was bubbling out of her wound, she collapsed into Herodias' arms.

As Herodias cried loudly, she noticed that it wasn't just blood coming out of the hole in Mariam's chest. The opening had widened and out of the hole came more light, as if Mariam had a powerful lightsource inside. Herodias stopped crying and watched the effect, as the light escaped out of her body and joined with the bright light already present in the room. Herodias sat mesmerized watching the light merge into a bluish white bright sphere in the middle of the space. Fragments were moving inside it and turned into small symbols flying with lightening speed in curving motions inside the orb. In a flash, the orb became a shaft which anchored in the ground and connected somewhere in cosmos before it disappeared. Herodias was left in the cave with the feeble light from the brazier.

She knew she had to work quickly to preserve the head. Finding the familiar tools, she made the cut further down on the chest and on the back. She found the larger knife to cut between the fifth and sixth vertebrae, and put the body aside. She remembered to sing, to make sure as much life force was preserved in the head as possible, all the while aware of that Mariam's spirit had joined with Yeshua.

The needles were there to be used to stitch the skin together, and Herodias tried to make a pretty seam after she folded the skin flaps together to give the head a neat finish. She found water and a piece of cloth to clean the head, sang a blessing for it and put it next to the brassier. In the herb bag she found an unguent she could use as a base, and in her own bag she found some myrrh to mix with it. The skin was rubbed in the powerful mixture and took on a glow, as if it were alive.

What could she do with the body? It would need to be buried, and she didn't think the people on the farm would understand its present condition. She would have to disguise it. But how?

Herodias suddenly felt very old. She sat down and looked for some water to drink. There was still some left in Mariam's own water skin.

She looked at the peaceful head of her friend. It looked like it was sleeping. Herodias tried to smile at it through her tear streaked face. Mariam's refined beauty was even more apparent in the preserved head. She knew she had done the right thing.

Herodias took the body and placed it in the middle of the blanket on the floor. She put the ocean shell they used for the ritual water in place of the head and wrapped up the whole body in the blanket. A rope was used to hold the blanket in place.

Herodias needed to rest again. She drank some more water and looked around the grotto. Realizing that nobody would come here anymore, she decided to pack up the things that had been left there, and take it all with her back to the farm.

Taking a look at Mariam's old herb bag, she thought it should be honored with a new purpose. She took all the herbs and transferred them to her own herb bag. Then she carefully placed Mariam's head inside it, after covering her face with a towel she found in the bag. The now rounded herb bag was placed next to the two leather bags with red tassels. Herodias cried again, as she looked at the group. What could she do with them all? The answer would have to come to her later.

Her horse was heavily laden as it walked slowly down the mountain path. The camel haired blanket was draped across its back, and Mariam's blanket wrapped body was hanging across. Several bags were tied to its harness, as Herodias started the heavy walk back to Tuberose Herb Farm in the early light of dawn.

The farm help dug a grave for her next to Sibyl and Trym. A lavender plant was transplanted on top, just like they had done on theirs earlier. Herodias asked them to find a tuberose bulb to put there too, and the young people happily obliged. The *maryam* plant would be her epitaph. Herodias thought her friend would have liked that.

She explained that she wanted to take the items belonging to a priestess with her, since she would know how to dispose of them. The people at the farm had no objections. Herodias rode her horse down the hill to Villa Lata, with three bags hanging from its harness in addition to her own herb bag. The grotto inside Mount Aurelia was empty.

Herodias rested for a day with Suzanna, who was sad to hear of Mariam's death. They sang a song in her honor and knew she would be warmly remembered.

The gilded carriage found its way to Aquae Sextiae, and found Martha's familiar house in the side street where by now her people owned all the other houses as well. Herodias cried in Martha's kitchen as she shared the news, and asked for Lazarus.

"He's in Massilia, but I'm expecting him back tomorrow," said Martha sadly. Herodias admired Martha's strength and quiet beauty, so much like her sister in so many ways. She asked if she could stay and wait for his return.

Lazarus arrived before dinner the following day. Herodias took him aside, after he had been given some time to absorb the news about his beloved sister's death.

"Lazarus, you remember the ritual underneath the temple of Jerusalem."

"How could we ever forget?"

"Do you remember that many of Yeshua's ancestors were present? We needed their help to complete the ritual."

"They sang with us in their old, historic voices."

"Yes. Did you know that your brother-in-law is also among them?"

Lazarus turned towards her. "Yes, he was with us in England, bringing the blessing to the new colony there together with Yochanan. Did Mariam bring it with from the temple of Venus when we visited there on our way? I thought he was buried in the Razes."

"She prepared him before she left there the first time. He's been with her ever since. His light has been hovering around her since he left us."

Lazarus looked down. Why hadn't Mariam shared this with him?

"She kept it all very quiet. Very few people knew. It's not easy knowledge to carry."

"She must have had both of them with her together with little Geiss when she returned to us after her time in England."

"All the while carrying the beginning of a new child," Herodias completed the thought.

It was silent between them. They both realized Mariam's incredible strength.

"And now Lazarus, I have to ask you to be the keeper of the ancestral wisdom."

Lazarus looked at her with tired eyes.

"I understand you are planning a new house of worship. Maybe you can plan a place of honor for all three of them."

"Three?"

"Lazarus, please understand that we've done our duty to keep this ancestral line intact. Mariam and I were trained in Ephesus for this purpose. I have now done my last work as a priestess. And my knowledge dies with me. Please preserve your sister's."

Lazarus needed a moment of silence to take in what she meant.

"Herodias, can I call upon you when the building is completed, and we can have them bless the cathedral?"

"If I'm alive then, Lazarus, I'd be honored."

Lazarus had an ossuary built to hold the three heads, and had it properly sealed. Herodias died, and was buried on the Herod estate in Arelate before the new house of worship was completed. The ossuary was never opened in his lifetime. The small marble sarcophagus was given a place of honor inside the dignified stone building, and revered for centuries.

EPITAPH

EPITAPH

In Southern France, in the region of Provence, there are local legends of Mary Magdalene and her work. Many of the churches there carry her name. The basilica in St.-Maximin-la-Ste.- Baume, near the foot of Mount Aurelia, is dedicated to the Holy Balm. Along the interior side of the basilica there is a chapel to John the Baptist. In the altar there is an opening with a sealed octagonal lid which would accommodate an honored head. Beneath the basilica there is a crypt, where the skull of Mary Magdalene is displayed. A thousand years after the crucifixion, the head of Christ was revered by the Knights Templar, and the Cathars in the Languedoc region claimed to own the secret wisdom taught by Jesus and his wife, Mary Magdalene.

CPSIA information can be obtained at www.ICGtesting.com
Printed in the USA
LVOW13s1538050114

368168LV00002B/85/P